Faces in the Mirror

By

J. A. Smith

This book is a work of fiction. Places, events, and situations in this story are purely fictional. Any resemblance to actual persons, living or dead, is coincidental.

ISBN: 1-4033-8922-5 (e-book)
ISBN: 1-4033-8923-3 (Paperback)
ISBN: 1-4107-0334-7 (Dust Jacket)

Library of Congress Control Number: 2002095414

This book is printed on acid free paper.

Printed in the United States of America
Bloomington, IN

1stBooks - rev. 06/03/03

Dedication

I would like to dedicate this book to the memory of the late

Martin D. Roth

Head of MDR Productions
Hollywood California

Whose continuing support and encouragement
made this book possible

Table of Contents

Chapter One

The Fog

The heavy fog engulfed the stately mansions of old Charleston. It was a strange night. The air was charged with an unseen aura of electricity. Faint traces of St. Elmos Fire moved it's glowing fingers over trees, shrubs and old charter oaks that dotted the landscape. These fingers intermingled with the mist, appearing, disappearing, then reappearing, as if by magic. A soft breeze gave an unnerving voice to the fog, amplifying the slightest sound as shadows continued to create images of dark things born in our imagination.

The old brownstone had stood proud, majestic and tall since the Civil War. Originally, it had been built to house Confederate troops. The property had changed hands until it was made into town homes in the late fifties. The inside was warm, decorated in antiques and bric-a-brac reflecting the traditions of the old south. Classic furniture, tapestry, and old paintings adorned the living room and foyer. The hallway still had the original gas lamps dating back to the turn of the century. Embers of a dying fire threw flickering shadows against the faded wallpaper.

The silence was broken by the screaming hiss of a hot tea kettle as the hands of a young man set the tea tray with cookies, fine china, and silver. The busy hands moved to the cupboard, opened it and searched for the sugar. Softly, a voice began to hum, "Tea For Two". The voice had a southern accent with a slight touch of madness to it and yet seemed at ease with his tasks.

"Agnes? Agnes? How many cookies? Three, four? I think maybe three, we have to watch our figure."

The young man, no more than thirty, wearing a black suit with a white preachers collar, picked up the tray and moved down the hall and into the small parlor. To one side of the room an elderly lady sat at a small coffee table. Placing the tray on the table, he began the ritual of serving high tea.

"Here we go. Done to perfection. Imported orange pekoe with a touch of cinnamon." No answer came from the old lady. Making small talk, the preacher, continued.

"One lump or two?" He paused, then continued without waiting for an answer. "I'll give you two, no more."

The experienced hands darted over the tea service quickly, adding sugar and cream, then stirring the tea gently. Setting the tea in front of her, he asked, "Are you all right?"

The old lady remained silent. The preacher answered as though she had spoken, "I'm sorry about the Beastie... He didn't hurt you did he?" The preacher's face reflected relief as he heard the silent answer. He sipped his tea, then replied, "Don't worry, I'll never let the Beastie hurt you. 'Sides, you're happy and I know it. I did everything you taught me and then some, didn't I." He paused, thinking back, "Remember a long, long time ago, when I gave myself to you? You said you'd never leave me and you promised I'd always be yours and you'd be mine. I've given myself to God now but deep down, I'll always be yours, you know that." The preacher paused in his conversation, "You ran away and that wasn't very nice. Why did you run away?" The preacher became teary-eyed as he went on. "You hurt me! I did everything you wanted and more and you still hurt me." The sadness turned to sinister glee. "It took me a long time but I found you didn't I? You can run away as many times as you want but I'll always find you." He smirked as he sipped some more tea. "You know how I found you? The Beastie, he knows where you are, he knows where you go, he knows how you think, and he can smell you, so I just call the Beastie. Here Beastie, here Beastie." The preacher laughed mockingly then spoke again, "You were good tonight, I mean really good, I've never seen you so passionate. I liked the way you screamed. That was very good. Just like the last time." Putting his cup down he poured a fresh cup of tea from the silver pot. "I know you're going to run away again but it won't do you any good." He raised his tea cup in one final toast, "To you Agnes, my love, until we meet again."

After a moment of silence, the man finished his tea, picked a forget-me-not from the bouquet sitting on the table and placed it in the old lady's lap. The old woman slumped over to one side of her chair revealing a grotesque death face distorting her features. Bluish silver hair cascaded down her forehead framing an expression seen only at the moment of death. The face was muddy white. Her purple lips were parted as if her life was taken in mid-sentence. A pair of pantyhose had been knotted tightly around her throat. Blood was caked and dried around her nose and mouth. One eye had bulged out as the corpse stared at infinity.

This area of Charleston was the home to the old aristocracy of the south. Great estates with iron gates and walled gardens gave one the impression they were in the countryside when, in fact, they were in a chic residential area. The homes had been in the families for generations and were maintained in pristine condition. The night breeze had stopped and the white mist laid heavily on the ground. The old lady had trouble seeing from one lamp post to the other as she inched her way along the red brick sidewalk.

Mildred Potts was in her late fifties and as she did every Wednesday night, was on her way to see her friend Molly Philburn. Mildred and Molly were both widows and if it weren't for their friendship, they'd be all alone. Their kids had all grown and moved to the four winds, as Molly used to say.

Mildred stopped to get her bearings. At some distance down the street she heard footsteps. She cocked her head and gripped her purse a little tighter as she listened. Yes, there were footsteps coming her way. Her eyes tried in vain to penetrate the white fog. Then, a low, haunting whistle came from the white mist. She had never heard a tune quite like that before. It sent shivers up her back and set a trembling in her shoulders. She thought to herself, it must be an old Gregorian chant, forgotten long ago by the church because it had such a soulful sound. Faintly at first, then with more distinction, a figure appeared in the cloud. Mildred was too old to run and too confused to know which way to run. Every fiber in her body told her that was exactly what she should do. It was too late, the man was upon her as quickly as he had appeared. "Good evening, Ma'am," came a refined, educated, yet strangely English accent.

"Good evening, Sir," Mildred replied and then scurried faster, looking over her shoulder, to gain distance between her and the stranger. She stopped, turned and looked back down the street. The man had mysteriously disappeared as if the fog had swallowed him in an instant.

Mildred dismissed her curiosity as she opened the iron gate to the old brownstone. Molly would be waiting with the hot chocolate. They would play Scrabble and read to each other until morning. As she approached the door Mildred had a bad feeling nagging at the back of her mind. Then she saw it. The door was unlocked and slightly ajar. Molly would never let that happen. Mildred recognized the aroma of freshly brewed tea as she passed through the foyer, rounded the corner to the parlor and came face to face with death.

The Charleston Police Department (CPD) is the largest department in the state of South Carolina, consisting of 238 sworn officers and 95 civilians that are responsible for the safety, crime prevention, investigation, and policing of approximately 80,000 people over a land area of 40.4 square miles, 14.5 square miles of water area, 275 miles of roadways and 500 acres of parklands. CPD's Special Operations Branch includes a horse patrol, a foot patrol, a canine unit, harbor patrol, underwater recovery team, a tactical squad, flying squad, aviation unit, an intelligence operation, SWAT team, and a forensic laboratory that is located in the Children's Hospital of the Medical University of South Carolina. The CPD's Operations Branch includes Vice, Narcotics, Internal Affairs, and Homicide all are part of the Central Investigation Crime Scene Unit based in CPD's Headquarters sometimes referred to as 7-5. In place of precincts, station houses, or divisions, the CPD is broken down geographically into four teams commanded by a Captain and an Operations Officer with the rank of Lieutenant. Team One services the northern half of the peninsula which is predominantly residential. Team Two services the lower peninsula area within the boundaries that include the Medical Complex, the College of Charleston and numerous tourist attractions. Team Three serves the incorporated areas of James and Johns Islands, while Team Four services the area west of the Ashley River serving a population of approximately 45,000 residents, more than fifty percent of Charleston's entire population.

Emily Fitch, a large black woman, has been a police radio dispatcher for CPD for close to fifteen years. In other words, she didn't come to work yesterday. The moment the red light flashed on the control console in the communications room, Emily had answered, "Police Emergency." She knew by the timbre of Mildred Pott's voice that it didn't belong to some crackpot who got their jollies dialing 911 and sending patrol cars on a wild goose chase to liven up an otherwise dull night. What Emily did have was a problem, calming Mildred down long enough to find out what had happened and to get an address from her so that she could immediately dispatch the right personnel to the location. It took her exactly one minute seven seconds before she was able to extract the information she needed. Apparently, a murder had been committed and it was Emily's job to dispatch the black and white patrol car nearest to the victim's address and then let the first officer on the scene call in and request Homicide which was standard operating procedure.

The time was approximately 8:20 PM, which was midway between their 4 to midnight watch. Unit Five, of Team One, Corporal Jerry Caughlin, 31, five ten, dark hair and 158 pounds and Private Tim Walsh, the rookie, 27, six one, blonde, blue-eyed and weighing 160 pounds decided to take a Code-7. The decision to stop at Big John's Coffee Shop was made by Walsh of the Perpetual Hard-on Club who enjoyed mind fucking big hooters Ginny, Big John's most voluptuous waitress. Walsh was sure that getting Ginny in the sack wouldn't be too difficult, but with all this stuff about AIDs every time you picked up a paper or turned on a TV, he was kind of reluctant to make a full court press to jump her bones. At least not until he really got to know her a hell of a lot better than he did now. Caughlin couldn't care less where they took their break and as soon as they were settled in a booth, Caughlin placed his Rover, an acronym for "Remote Out-of-Vehicle Emergency Radio," atop the table and buried his nose in the sports pages of the late edition, while, like the saying goes, his partner played "Mr. Cool" with Ginny.

They'd hardly gotten their first sip of coffee from the heavy china mugs, decorated with maps denoting the locations of all the Big John's Diners, when Emily Fitch's voice came through Caughlin's Rover.

"Central to all units in the vicinity of Magnolia and Jefferson. Possible homicide. 8557 Jefferson. See the lady. Code 2... I say again, all units in the vicinity in Magnolia and Jefferson..."

4

By the time Emily had fully repeated the call, Ginny stood holding a grilled cheese sandwich and a BLT on white toast staring after Walsh and Coughlin as they leaped from their booth and headed out the front door for their radio patrol car (RPC). Seconds later the reflections of their car's twirling red and blue lights were dancing crazily through the rolling white mist that engulfed the screaming black and white, dulling it's shrill to a mournful wail.

The TV flickered in black and white as the late night horror show ran "The Bride Of Frankenstein". The monster moved slowly across the tube chasing the screaming woman through the castle. The apartment was a typical bachelor pad with beer cans, popcorn and several half eaten TV dinners decorating the coffee table. The furniture, rugs, paintings and general motif could be loosely described as contemporary slob.

Glued to every movement on the tube, sitting on his haunches, with one ear now and then perking up, was Studs. Studs was a Heinz 57 breed of mutt that had adopted Lt. Beau Gasteneau, Charleston PD, Operations Branch, Homicide, Central Investigations, Crime Scene Unit. That was not quite correct. It was a fifty-fifty proposition. Everyone at the station was not sure if Studs had adopted Beau or Beau had adopted Studs. In any case, they were inseparable. The dog had his own personality and watching TV was one of his quirks. Chasing bitches was another. He came by his name naturally, you just had to look between his legs to see that his name had to be Studs. He cocked his head again and whined as the TV continued to scream. Studs bent down and lapped up some more beer from his bowl, burped, then continued his viewing.

Suddenly, the phone on the coffee table rang, interrupting his TV. Studs went to the phone and gave a short whimper. It rang again. This was his signal. His roommate was wanted at the office. Moving to the bedroom door, Studs stood up and opened it with his paws, as he had done so many times before. The bedroom mirrored the living room. In the dark, one might say it resembled the Black Hole of Calcutta. A king-size bed occupied one side of the room. Women's clothes, underwear, jockey shorts and Levi's were mixed with paper cups and an empty champagne bottle. The phone on the nightstand continued to ring with a consistent buzz.

Beau, in a fit of animal passion, humped away at the beautiful blonde figure spread open beneath him. She met his downward thrust with her hips, screaming with each impact, "More, faster, deeper, Oh God! I'm coming, I'm coming, Oh! Oh! Ahhhh!"

The persistent buzzing of the phone broke Beau's concentration. At the peak of his passion, looking at Studs, he said, panting, "Don't just sit there, get the phone. Oh! Ahh!"

The dog dutifully picked up the phone from the nightstand and laid it on the bed. At that moment, the blonde climaxed and let out a moan of sensual satisfaction as Beau collapsed on top of her. Coming from the phone, the voice of Harry Mackland, Beau's partner, began to shout.

"Beau? You there? You all right?" There was a brief pause, "Studs, put him on the phone." The dog nuzzled and licked his friend's face. Slowly, two bloodshot eyes looked at the dog and spoke in a whiskey voice.

"It was your idea, you take it." The dog nosed the phone towards his master and panted. Beau rolled onto his side, shot Studs a dirty look and put the phone to his ear as the blonde yanked the sheet up around her 'lest Studs get another look at her bare breasts.

"You're a shithead, you know that?"

"I'm a what? Harry responded.

"Not you, my idiot dog."

"You lying down?" Harry asked then quickly corrected himself. "What am I saying? What other position would you be in right now? You get more ass than a toilet seat."

"Harry, I'm in no mood for your old, tired, crummy jokes."

"No joke, pal. Our boy just tagged another one."

"Shit! Doesn't this asshole ever sleep?" Beau growled.

"Pick you up in ten minutes."

Beau glanced at the blonde, "Make it thirty."

"Make it five. I'm mobile and headed your way," Harry said disconnecting them. Heaving a sigh, Harry shook his head and leaned back against the driver's seat headrest. He wondered if Beau's getting piss-assed drunk and screwing everything in sight was ever going to get him over the divorce. How could he blame him, after Beau had found his wife humping another cop in his own bed, a year and two months ago.

"Poor bastard." He muttered to himself and turned his attention back to the fog shrouded street.

Throwing his legs over the side of the bed, Beau looked down, stared at his socks and thought how ridiculous he must have looked humping the blonde at twelve hundred RPM with his socks on. Studs put his paws up on the bed and licked Beau's face.

"Why don't you go out and play in the traffic? Hmmm?" The exhausted blonde mumbled sleepily. Ignoring her, Beau pushed Studs away. "Okay, okay, I'm going. You know the routine." He lifted himself off the bed and fighting a newly acquired hangover, struggled to the bathroom. Studs trotted into the kitchen, opened the 'fridge, grabbing a can of beer between his teeth, trotted back into the bathroom, carefully placing the beer can down in front of the steaming shower door. Almost on cue, Beau's wet hand darted out and snatched up the can which quickly disappeared behind the shower door.

With this part of his job done, Studs then paraded back into the bedroom. Cocking his head, he studied the sleeping blonde and evaluated her on a scale from one to ten. This was definitely a nine-plus. Heaving a sigh, as if a dog could heave a sigh, he took the corner of the blanket in his mouth and pulled it off the sleeping blonde revealing practically all of her firm, busty body. The blonde pulled the cover back. Studs pulled again, this time the blanket came clear off the bed. The blonde sat up quickly, heard the shower running and saw Studs eyeing her with her clothes now in his mouth.

"Okay buster. I get the message."

The unmarked police car sat in front of the apartment building with the motor still running. Harry took a sip of coffee from a half filled container then a bite of his Double King burger as he anxiously eyed the front door. A few minutes passed before a raunchy looking Beau and an equally scroungy looking Studs emerged from the building and slipped into the car. Harry swallowed the last of the burger and almost mechanically handed his partner a capped, luke-warm container of wake-up coffee. Beau silently fumbled with the lid, removed it, took a deep gulp and mumbled, "Drive."

Harry put the car in gear and moved out onto the empty street. A long silence ensued as Harry maneuvered the car down Magnolia Avenue then broke the soundlessness abruptly.

"Jesus! You make the homeless look like models for Gentlemen's Quarterly. A two day stubble on your face, clothes that look like they belong in the 12th Street Mission… and if your hair gets any longer, I'm gonna hafta get you a set of love beads."

"I don't need this."

"Bullshit!, you don't. Studs has better breath than you have. Here,…" Harry reached into his pocket and tossed Beau a candy. "Have a mint."

Beau popped it into his mouth. "I don't suppose you've got any aspirin?"

"What the hell do I look like? A drug store?"

Beau took another sip of his coffee, leaned his head back and closed his eyes as Harry continued his harangue.

"You're not gonna find any answers in the bottom of a bottle or another broad, y'know, so why the hell don't you get your life back in gear?"

"Great," Beau snapped, opening his eyes and glaring at Harry, "Now I've got Mother Teresa for a partner!"

"Fuck off Assbreath."

Had you been able to lift the misty veil, it would have been easy to see that the old antebellum home was surrounded by mature oaks and pine with colorful azaleas tastefully planted throughout the garden. Amanda Hollingsworth had tended this garden, dutifully and lovingly each day for most of her life. It was her pride. It was who she was. Tall, white, majestic columns regally supported the roof of the full front porch laid in herringbone red brick. It was one of the premier homes of Charleston that had been built before the Civil War and, strangely, the ravages of time had only enhanced it's beauty.

At 55, Amanda had only been widowed three months and, although it hadn't been easy, she had taken control of her late husband's bank, the Merchant Bank of Charleston and ruled it with an iron but fair hand. She had always been an avid reader and had been a founding member of the new library. The Hollingsworths had many friends, practically all of whom had extended their sincere hospitality and invitations to dinner following Howard's death. Amanda graciously declined most of them, at least for the time being. Meanwhile, her nightly routine consisted of an early dinner alone, the evening news on the TV followed by a glass of sherry, and reading some poetry before retiring. Robert Frost had been her, and her husband's favorite. Oh, how she missed those evenings when they would just sit and talk at great lengths about poetry, art and music. Sitting there in her favorite chair, opposite the one Howard always sat in, she thought back to those wonderful evenings. The door chimes interrupted her brief reverie. Putting her book down and wondering who could be calling at this time of night, she made her way to the front door and peered through the peephole to find a clean-cut young man in a white preacher's collar standing on her doorstep. Keeping the chain firmly in place, she opened the door and looked out inquiringly. The young man removed his hat, revealing his blonde hair, and with a warm smile, courteously bowed his head.

"Pardon me for disturbing you, Ma'am, but I was in the neighborhood and thought I might finish my business here."

"If you're selling something, I'm not interested," Amanda snapped impatiently. "Especially at this time of night," she added. About to close the door, the young preacher held up a leather bound book, "Ah'm not selling, Ma'am, Ah'm deliverin'. Ah'm with the Christian Brotherhood. Your husband was Howard Hollingsworth?"

"That's right."

The preacher reflected real sorrow in his voice. "Ah was sorry to hear about his passin'. Guess he knew the Lord pretty well and that he was going' to call on him, 'cause he ordered this family bible before he died." The preacher held up the book and opened the cover to the first page. "Look, y'can see he had your name embossed in gold on the front and on the next page is a family tree so all the names can be filled in."

He slipped the book through the opening. Amanda took it and clutched it to her breast. "I had no idea…"

The preacher nodded sympathetically. "I'm just doing' the Lord's work. All the proceeds go to charity. There's just a small outstandin' balance."

"How much?"

"Twenty-nine ninety-five."

"Will a check do?"

"Bless you Ma'am. A check'd do just fine."

Amanda reached out, removed the chain and opened the door wider. "If you'll wait here, I'll get my check book. Who do I make the check out to?"

"Southern Christian Fellowship Ma'am."

As Amanda headed for the stairway and started up the steps, a small smile began to creep across the face of the preacher man.

The smile was interrupted by a twitch. Then another, followed by internal convulsions that made his body seem as though it was possessed by some unseen entity. His head snapped up and looked at the ceiling, then twisted back and forth as he entered the house and struggled to the stairs. Leaning on the banister, the young man looked into the hall mirror. He stared in disbelief as his reflection began a strange dreamlike, metamorphosis. His face took on a grayish tint as his face aged before his eyes, becoming wrinkled and grotesque. His teeth seemed almost canine and his eyebrows grew thick and bushy. He smashed his fist into the mirror, shattering it into small pieces making the reflection even more grotesque. What was happening? Some hellish force was turning his guts inside out, compelling him to reach into his pocket for some object. Looking down, he saw someone's gloved hands, not his. These uncontrollable hands took a pair of pantyhose and twisted them into a rope. His mind cried out, "No! Whoever you are, go away, stop making me do this." The hidden entity moved the preacher's feet, one-by-one, up the stairs. No matter how hard he tried, it was useless to struggle against whatever it was compelling him to respond. He moved up the stairs like a drunk man, fighting, resisting each footstep. This unseen evil inside him forced him down the hall to Amanda's bedroom door. As the door swung open, the courteous, mild mannered preacher was gone. The white collar was gone. The eyes, the hair, the face had changed to one of pure evil. The Beast was loose, controlling every movement of a madman stalking an old lady searching for her checkbook. He slipped the nylon "rope" around her throat and pulled the woman upright. Her eyes bulged out in surprise as her hands clutched at her throat. She struggled for air as the noose was twisted even tighter. The strength of the man-beast was such that it lifted his victim from the floor with a severe jerk. She dangled in mid-air like a rag doll. One slipper fell off as a final

9

sigh was heard. Then, a loud snap as her neck broke. The silence was shattered by a new voice. The voice had hatred behind every syllable.

"How do you like it, Agnes? Does it feel good? You were always into pain."

The lifeless body of the old woman swung freely after the killer hung her by the neck on a coat hook near the bedroom door. Blood oozed from her mouth and nose. The Beast spoke again. "Welcome to hell, Agnes."

Stillness filled the room. He had completed his orgasm. The ritual was fulfilled. The lamb had been sacrificed, feeding the Beast, satisfying the anger of his twisted mind.

Two large loving cups dated 1961 and 1962 sat with pride among the books in the bedroom. The awards were for winning the Charleston Regatta two consecutive years. The antique reading lamp beside the bed, with it's Tiffany red glass shade, cast a strange reflection on the cups, distorting every image in the room, giving them big noses, pointed chins and wavy bodies, like a trick mirror in a carnival fun house. The images were accompanied by different voices, as if they had personalities of their own. The distorted image of the preacher, spoke like a parent admonishing a child. "David, oh David, come out, come out wherever you are? ... We've been a bad boy, haven't we."

The anger in the scolding voice began to grow. "No matter how many times Agnes and I get together, you... you always come along and spoil it for me." With anger turning to rage he continued, "You, you, bring that Beast, from God knows where, and you hurt Agnes. I love Agnes and she loves me, so, you just stay out of my life. Do you hear me? Just get the fuck out of my life!"

There was another silence as shadows played across the face of the other loving cup and a childlike voice spoke.

"I hate Agnes and the Beastie hates her too." The child's voice began to struggle for his words. "She makes me do dirty things. She's not a nice mommy. She's going to hell and burn, forever and ever!"

Light and dark images darted again over the face of the two cups as the other voice retorted. "Oh no! You're just jealous that's all. She's always loved me the best and you can't stand that, can you? You were always the bully and now you've got that Beastie thing to help you... I know you. When you don't get your way, you have to go and hurt someone, don't you... Just go away!"

Singing in a child's voice, the reflection on the cup went on, "Na, ni, na, ni, na, na, I know what you're gonna do... You're gonna touch Agnes, aren't you."

"Go away!"

In a whining tone, the child voice responded, "Okay, you just go ahead and play with Agnes, see if I care. 'Sides, she can't hurt you when she's sleeping... We're going to our secret hiding place, 'way, 'way far away, so don't come looking for me cause you won't find me, that's why."

There was no one else in the room when the preacher lifted the dead woman from the coat hook, brushed her silver gray hair from her face, tenderly took her in his arms and carried her to the bed. Laying her down gently, he explained. "Agnes... please dear, allow me to apologize for David. I tried to explain about us; it's like talking to a brick wall." Tenderly, he began to undress the dead woman.

"Now, don't you worry. He won't come between us, ever... I'm going to do all those special things you like. After we finish, we'll have some tea, you'll see, everything will be all right." There was a long silence which was replaced with the grunts and groans of a madman having rough sex with the corpse. The grunts continued until the madman climaxed and fell silent.

The police had cordoned off the scene with yellow tape. Men, with flashlights, searched the grounds for evidence, giving the impression of lightening bugs lost in the night mist, darting this way and that. The unmarked police car moved into a parking place behind the meat wagon. The detectives, with Studs leading the way, got out, moved to the front door, then into the house. Corporal Caughlin, first officer on scene, met both men inside.

"Lieutenant." Caughlin said, acknowledging the detectives by rank, first Beau, then Harry. "She's in there." He nodded towards the room off the foyer. Following Caughlin's lead, they moved into the sitting room where Molly Philburn's body lay slumped in her chair, the nylon stocking still tightly wrapped around her neck.

You never really get over the sight of death no matter what veneer you manage to wear outwardly. No matter how hardcase you may be, and although Beau had fifteen years with the Department, eight of which were with Homicide, that queasy feeling in the stomach still accompanied the first look at what one human being could do to another. But that queasy feeling came only with the first of the nutcase's victims. After that it had been anger and frustration that Beau had felt and it had increased in intensity with each succeeding corpse that the killer had left in his wake. So far, all they knew was that the psycho who was running around dicing old ladies was AB positive. They had been able to determine that from typing his semen and saliva. They also knew he was right handed and tied one hell of a knot. Outside of that—zilch! No prints, no trace or physical evidence. They had no idea how he was able to gain entry without leaving physical evidence. Nothing that could give them the slightest lead to the serial killer's identity or motive had been uncovered. Was he killing his mother or his girlfriend over and over again? Hell, for all they knew, the killer could be the same age as his victims; however, that wasn't likely, because of the way their necks had been broken. It would take a man with considerable strength to break them so clean, leaving no bruises. One thing was certain. He would continue his reign of terror as long as he was free to do so.

Bending down, Beau picked up the shawl that lay at her feet and gently covered her face.

"You call for the M.E.?" Harry asked Caughlin.

"Right after I called Homicide. Crime Scene Unit, too," Caughlin responded. "They'll get here soon as they can. There was a five car pileup on the Expressway. Been a busy night." Flipping open his notebook anticipating the next question, he began to read from his notes. "Victim's name is Molly Philburn. She was discovered by one, Mildred Potts, age 59, at approximately 1930 hours. My partner and I responded to the scene at 2020 hours. Door was ajar, as described by Mrs. Potts. No outward signs of robbery. No sign of forced entry. Everything else is just as we found it." Caughlin shook his head, "How the hell does he get in?"

"Can't be someone all the victims knew. We've got a list of all the friends and employees of the others and never came up with two names that matched." Harry explained.

"That'd bring it down to someone they'd trust. Someone they wouldn't have any qualms about letting into their homes."

"Like a mailman," Caughlin offered. "Or a UPS delivery? Someone like that, y'mean?"

Beau shrugged, "Someone like that, who knows, maybe even a cop."

Caughlin looked bug-eyed at Beau. "C'mon, you can't be serious. A cop going around dicing old ladies?"

"You know anyone a little old lady'd trust more? Anyway, I didn't say he was a cop. Then again I won't say he's not. We wear badges friend, not angels wings. Right now—anybody and everybody is suspect. Tell me about this Mildred Potts, who found her?"

Caughlin shrugged, "Not much to tell. Nice old lady. Friend of the deceased. My partner is with her in the kitchen." He glanced back at his notebook. "What's this one make? Number five?"

"Six."

"Well the M.O.'s the same. He had tea with her, sexually assaulted her and then strangled her with her own pantyhose."

"Wrong." Beau said. "No tea's ever been found in the stomach of any of the previous victims and I doubt if we'll find any tea inside this one."

"Or any cookies, either," Harry chimed in.

"You saying this guy had tea with her after he killed her?" Caughlin asked.

"Sex too." Beau added.

"That's sick! Screwin' a sixty year old corpse? I don't believe it."

"Believe it," Beau said, glancing towards the M.E. and the crime scene people as they arrived. Within minutes, each of the criminalists and technicians set up shop and began doing their thing while the Medical Examiner removed the shawl and surveyed the victim before beginning his own grisly examination.

"Make sure you dust the kitchen," Harry called out to the print man.

"Why? The body's in here."

"Jeez!" Harry snapped. "You blind or something? You see the tea service? You see a hot plate in here? Where do you think he boiled his water?"

"My what deductive powers you have, Sergeant," the print man said mockingly.

"Elementary, my dear Weisenheimer. Elementary."

"Anybody know what kind of flowers these are?" Beau asked.

"Forget-me-nots," the M.E. responded slipping on a pair of rubber gloves. "Why? You into flowers now Beau?"

"No, but our killer just might be. They're the same kind we've found at every crime scene."

"They're also found in almost every garden in Charleston. Hell, it's Alaska's state flower. Okay for me to remove the pantyhose?" the M.E. asked.

"Oh that's great. Now we've got a fucking Eskimo dicing old ladies in Charleston," Harry interrupted mockingly.

"Soon as we get enough pictures of her," Beau answered the Medical Examiner's question, as he started for the kitchen.

Mildred Potts was still in a state of shock and wasn't much help except for mentioning the man she passed in the fog not far from the house. Unfortunately, as she'd already told the other officer, she couldn't describe the man as he had his coat collar turned up and his hat pulled down over his face. All she could provide them with was that when the man said, "Good Evening," he seemed to have some sort of an accent. What kind, she couldn't be sure. English, or Jamaican maybe.

"Oh shit, you know what that would mean? We've got a black guy doin old ladies in the south? I mean the shits gonna hit the fan pretty damn quick. You think he's our boy?" Harry asked, as they headed back to the victim's body, having sent Mrs. Potts home in a patrol car.

"Who the hell knows? Could've been him or just a guy lost in the fog. Don't you even think its a black guy until we know for sure."

"An Englishman?" Harry grinned. "Makes sense. He'd sure feel right at home in that soup we've got out there. We can call him Jack the Dipper, ha!"

"Been dead for about three hours. I'd say the approximate time of death occurred somewhere between five and six o' clock," the M.E. said, packing up his black satchel, looking up at Beau and Harry as they walked into the living room.

"Strangled her with her pantyhose, did a whim-wham-thank you ma'am on her, dressed her, carried her in here and propped her up in the chair."

"Tell me something I don't know, Sam."

"Got to get her downtown first. Okay to bag her and tag her?"

"Might as well. I don't think she's gonna tell us anything just sitting there like that. Do me a favor though, huh? This time, see if you can come up with something at the post. Something we can work with to nail this guy before he gets number seven."

The M.E. grunted, "I'm a Medical Examiner, not a magician. Keep the faith my friend."

"Faith is for priests and little old ladies. Look what it got this one and the five before her. I need more than faith, Sam. I need something solid."

"I'll do what I can." With that, he turned and nodded at two nearby white uniforms to place the remains in a body bag. Beau and Harry headed for the front door.

Molly Philburn's remains had been found too early for the stench of death to have permeated the house into which madness had entered, yet the damp, foggy night air smelled cleaner and fresher to both men as they positioned themselves on the front porch.

"Quiet as it is, I can hear that son-of-a-bitch out there laughing' at us," Beau said, staring into the night.

"The damn Boy Scouts could probably pick up his tracks faster than we've been able to do."

"We're doing the best we can," Harry said, handing Beau a cigarette from a fresh pack, then holding up a light.

"Tell that to her," Beau muttered as Molly Philburn's body bag was wheeled out of the house and slammed into the Coroner's wagon like so much meat in a butcher's shop.

"Or do you wanna save that little diddy for number seven or eight? Take your pick, because he's gonna keep right on dicing old ladies while we sit around in the fuckin fog playin' with ourselves."

"You said the same thing with number five." Harry retorted.

"Because you said the same thing at number four," Beau shot back at Harry as they both vented their frustration.

"We're missing something."

14

"Like what?" Harry asked.

"The sonofabitch comes and goes like a friggen ghost. Either he's someone the old ladies know or trust or he's a phantom and walks through walls. Wipes everything clean. He doesn't leave anything to be missed."

"C'mon. I'll buy you a cup of coffee," Harry said starting down the front steps.

"Coffee? I need a drink!" Beau yelled, following Harry. The patrol car sat with four other black and whites still engulfed in fog.

Emily's voice broke the short silence with her scratchy message, "Control Central to Charlie 272."

Beau reached through the open window and grabbed the mike. "Charlie 272 to Central, Go!"

"Charlie 272. We have a possible 460 in progress at 5416 Bradbury. Suspect last seen entering an alley between Olive and Oakview."

"Charlie 272 will respond." Beau snapped, replacing the mike.

"The alley is in the next block," Harry announced. "Take the car and try cutting him off at Oakview. I'll go on foot!" Before Beau could argue, Harry was halfway down the block, gun in hand. Beau jumped into the car and seconds later, raced towards Oakview.

The fog hadn't let up. It rolled out of the mouth of the cave-like alley that ran the length of two blocks between Olive and Oakview. The rear of the buildings on either side sealed the heavy mist between them. Harry stopped at the entrance to the alley and quickly injected a shell into the chamber of his gun. Then, cocking his service weapon, he moved into the alley. It swallowed him like Jonah in the mouth of some monstrous dark whale.

Inside the alley, the mist flashed red then gray, then red again as a neon light across the street snapped on and off, advertising Red Bull Snuff. With his back against one wall, Harry continued to move blindly up the alley, his eyes and ears searching for the slightest movement or sound. The noise of a tumbling beer can added to the tension as Harry's foot tried to avoid more trash laying about. He waited and strained his senses for any indication of impending danger. Out of the corner of his eye, he caught a glimpse of a small movement to his left. His flashlight spotlighted the tail end of an alley cat scampering away. The detective froze, then swung his light to the right revealing a pile of trash and an overflowing garbage bin.

Two hands were in the act of washing blood at an outside faucet when they stopped. The preacher quickly shut off the tap and listened. He heard the noise coming from his left. The madness in his face turned to rage. He removed a piece of strong bailing wire from a wooden box and coiled it around two pieces of wood. The psychotic was incensed that a stranger dared to enter his domain to challenge him. He had no right to interfere. It was the night of the Beast, and they would pay for this intrusion into the Beast's world.

Harry continued to shine his flashlight in front of him as he inched his way up the alley. The light could barely penetrate the fog. He moved it from left to right with every footstep. The beam came to rest on a pile of trash overflowing from another trash bin sitting under a fire escape. For a moment, the detective thought he saw a movement behind a larger pile of debris. Moving under the fire escape, his gun ready, Harry directed his beam behind some boxes. Silently, a wire loop slipped over Harry's neck and he was instantly lifted into the air by some hidden force so strong it made the detective seem like a wiggling fish on the end of a hook. Harry dropped his gun and grasped at the wire, biting and cutting into his throat. He fought for air, dangling and squirming beneath the fire escape; his vision beginning to grow dim when the screaming upside down face of the lunatic appeared in front of him. It made no sense, spoke no words, it screamed like an enraged child, as it plunged the butcher knife into Harry's chest. With each scream, the knife was plunged into his chest again and again.

Beau jammed on the brakes, rolled down the window and gazed at the street sign. He'd gone too far. With this damn fog, he couldn't even see the street signs, much less read them. He had to back up and turn at the first corner, not the second. With his adrenaline pumping, he knew he was taking too long. His partner was in that alley alone. Backing up, turning hard right, Beau moved the car to the mouth of the alleyway on Oakview, called for additional backup and jumped out. Studs bounded to his master's side as Beau readied his weapon, turned on his flashlight, and entered the alley. From the other end he could see faint flashes of red mist as though some secret passage to hell had opened and was beckoning him to enter. The fears he had known in his dreams as a boy were coming back. He was afraid and he knew he had better come to grips with it fast. He had to keep it under control. His hand shook slightly as he moved the light in front of him. Studs stopped, then let out a low growl. He had the scent. The dog knew that the prey was somewhere in the alley. Keeping Studs close, he positioned himself behind the trash bin and listened. Silence descended on Beau. He strained to hear the slightest sound. Then he heard it. The faint dripping of water on the pavement, close, on the other side of the trash heap. Someone was there. This was it, the moment of truth. He spun around the bin with his gun ready and yelled, "Hold it right there. Police Officer."

He was confronted with a pair of shoes swinging freely in the air. It took him a second to react, yet it seemed like hours as he stared at the man's feet suspended in air. The water he heard was blood dripping on the toes of the shoes, then falling into a puddle beneath the feet. Raising the light, his worst fears were realized. Harry's body, with a butcher knife protruding from his chest, swung lifelessly from the fire escape. Knotted tightly around his neck was a bailing wire loop tied to a 2 by 4 wedged into the iron grating. In instant panic, Beau jumped on top of the trash bin, lifted Harry's body up with one arm and grappled at the barbed-wire noose with the other hand. The rusted wire cut Beau's hand as he frantically tried to free Harry from this death trap. Finally, using every ounce of energy he freed Harry and both men fell into the trash heap below. Beau shouted at Harry as if he could understand. "Hang in there, you're gonna make it! Don't you quit on me now". Beau carefully removed the knife from Harry's chest. The blood pumped out with each heartbeat. Studs began licking Harry's face sensing something was wrong. His friend wasn't moving. He looked at Beau for some sign of reassurance.

"Studs, go get help." Beau commanded.

Studs knew instantly what to do and took off running. Studs was about as close as to a human as a dog could get and knew that help was only two blocks away. It would take about ten minutes for Studs to attract enough attention to bring help running.

"Oh my God." Beau cried bursting into teary anger. He pressed his hand hard against Harry's chest trying to create enough pressure to stop the bleeding. He scanned the trash to find something to use as a pressure bandage. Time was running out. He hastily wadded some newspaper and placed it over the wound. Then found some twine and tied it as tightly as he could. "You're gonna make it. Do you hear me? This isn't the way you're suppose to go out. You're suppose to go out chasing old ladies in a retirement home, or something like that." Beau cried as he spoke those words. Harry was alive. He moved slightly, then opened his eyes and whispered, "Promise me you'll take care of Lori."

"Knock that shit off. Back up will be here any minute." Harry clutched at Beau's sleeve and, with his last few minutes of breath, spoke. "Could you hold me? Just hold me. I don't want to die alone." Beau crying and trying to laugh at the same time answered, "C'mon, thats' a bunch of bullshit, you're not gonna die, you're too ugly to die." That was his last attempt at humor. He began to cry as he held his partner in his arms and rocked him like a little child.

"Tell Lori I'm sorry I won't get to see the kids grow up." With those last words Beau broke into uncontrollable sobbing. In the mist that carried death and terror to Charleston, Beau could hear the soulful wail of the distant sirens. They were too late. This time the victim was no little old lady.

Chapter Two

Taps

Charleston's homicide squad room would have made any visiting detective from New York, Chicago, or any other city feel right at home. The mildewed walls could have used a fresh paint job and the gun-metal gray steel desks were piled high with file folders, indicating the caseloads were backing up. The aged, wooden chairs were as hard as the day they were manufactured in Toledo, Ohio.

The large electric clock on the squad room wall revealed the time to be ten past midnight. Outside the long, grilled windows, the fog had turned to a light, misty rain while inside the squad room the middle of the night silence was broken only by the pick and peck of Investigator Les Hanlon's battered typewriter, as he laboriously typed Beau's statement. Beau stood at the window. His white shirt and jacket was still soaked red with Harry's blood. He took another long drag on his cigarette. Studs heeled at Beau's right leg, then leaned against his master's side, and looked up for some sign of recognition. Studs knew instinctively that his friend was in pain. He knew that Harry, his other friend, was gone. He wanted Beau to know that he felt the pain too. That's what friends did. They stood by each other when they were needed and he was standing by Beau.

"You through with the fuckin' questions?" Beau asked belligerently.

"You know a reports gotta be filed, Beau," Hanlon answered defensively. "I'm just doin' my job." He studied the form in the typewriter. Right now he didn't feel like making eye contact with Beau. In Beau's case, losing a partner was losing your best friend, no, it was losing family. Hanlon could feel the deep pain Beau was experiencing, knowing how close the two men had been. As Hanlon typed he remembered the story Beau use to tell when he and Harry were caught in the chemical plant explosion back in '91. They were lucky to live through it. It seems, as the story goes, they were recovering in the same room in County General. Beau had hurt his back, and Harry was blinded temporarily. Harry's bed was by the window, while Beau's was on the other side of the room. After a few days, with the curtain drawn between them, in utter frustration, Beau asked Harry to describe what was going on outside. In great detail, Harry described the park, kids playing, old folks sitting on the park bench, the trees in bloom, and paid particular attention to the hot dog stand that sold the biggest damn hot dogs he'd ever seen in his life. They made a promise that when they got out Harry would treat him to one of those friggen hot dogs. Harry didn't stop at that. For Beau's benefit, he described that sexy blonde with the big hooters that came there every day to devour one of those dogs. In vivid detail, he described how she savored that long fat wiener. Beau was in shear panic with his erection raising the bed sheet about 5 inches. In a few days, Beau was able to get up. He got up and walked around the curtain that separated the two beds to find Harry with cotton pads over his eyes. Looking out the window, Beau saw only a brick wall. Beau announced to Harry, "Hey, ooooh! There she is again, oh my God she's actually going down on that dog." Harry laughed and said, "wash your mind prick."

Hanlon smiled to himself, remembering the story, and went on typing.

Beau knew full well that he shouldn't be taking it out on Hanlon but there was no one else around. His inner rage refused to permit him to mourn his loss. Right now his wrath was misdirected, aimed more at Harry than at the madman that had taken Harry's life. Harry had been his rock and now the rock was gone. Mother Teresa, Big Daddy was no more. They had been partners for fifteen years and in that time had come to learn more about each other than perhaps the most intimate members of their own families. They had entrusted their very lives to each other while sharing in each others happiness and despair. Although Beau had been senior in rank, Harry was the elder of the pair by ten years, and had assumed the role of older brother early on. Whereas many men might have been inwardly jealous when Beau was promoted to Lieutenant, Harry watched with pride and admiration as Beau received his gold badge. He stood up as Beau's best man when Beau married Sarah Beth and comforted him when the marriage was shattered by Sarah's infidelity. Harry was always there, there to nurse him through another hangover and cover for him when he was too drunk to report in. He knew when to listen and when to speak his mind. He knew Beau Gasteneau better than anyone and no man had a better friend or partner to back him up.

"Harry, you fuckin' sonofabitch!" Beau cried inwardly, "How dare you leave me like this. No goodbye, nothing. Did you forget that as soon as we'd wrapped up this case we'd planned to take a two week deep sea fishing trip together? Why the hell did you have to go chasing into that alley all by yourself? Why couldn't you have waited?"

"Almost through," Hanlon said, pecking away at the last entry.

Beau watched as Hanlon finished typing the last few lines of the report. Had he told Hanlon about missing the street and having to go back? Was it his fault that Harry was dead? That those few precious minutes Beau had wasted might have meant the difference between Harry's life and death? Studs nudged Beau's leg, seemingly sensing his master's pain and desperately wanting to remind Beau that he, Studs, was still here, that he wasn't really alone in his hour of grief.

It was one o-clock in the morning. The key slid into the Harry's apartment door, snapped, and the door opened with slight squeak. Beau smiled sadly, remembering that Harry said he was going to take care of that one of these days. After Flo's death, and Lori marrying and moving out, Harry had sold his home and moved into this three bedroom flat on the north side of town. Beau had a key to Harry's place and Harry had a key to Beau's pad. Actually, Harry had to put Beau in bed more times than he cared to remember. The only time Beau could remember putting Harry to bed was when they had a two man wake for Flo. They drank their way from one side of town to the other. That was a hard time for Harry and Beau stuck by him and gave him the support he needed to get him through the loss. He was Harry's rock and held Lori in his lap and explained why her mother was now with the angels.

Beau knew his way around the apartment as well as his own. This was also Stud's second home. Studs dutifully trotted into the living room and laid down on a pillow Harry always had waiting for him next to the small fireplace. Beau moved into the office and turned on the desk light, sat down, and put his face in his hands and tried to hold back the tears. Everything in the room had some sort of memory for him. The old photos that sat on the desk of Flo, Harry, Lori and himself brought back the happy times that would never go away. These people for whatever brief time they lived truly touched each other. Beau's grandpa had told him that the measure of a man is not if he were a king, or conquered great enemies, or became a great athlete. His measure is the memories he leaves to others. If that be true, then Harry was one hell of a man. As he looked around the room he knew what grandpa meant by being a great man. Maybe not a famous man, maybe not a rich man, but his greatness was in who he touched, how he touched, and what he gave.

Beau had known he was the executor of Harry's estate and he had better get the paperwork together and give it to the legal staff to process. Everything went to Lori so it was a straight forward deal. Harry's will and legal documents were in the left hand drawer but when he opened it they were gone.

Without notice, the reading lamp on the other side of the room clicked on and there was Lori, sitting in the big red leather overstuffed chair, teary eyed and half drunk. A small box with Harry's private papers sat in her lap.

"Here, have a drink," she slurred holding up a big bottle of scotch. Beau rushed to her side. "Sweetheart, you shouldn't be doing this."

"Bullshit! Isn't this what cops do when they do their thing for one of the fallen? I mean, we must keep a stiff upper lip. Isn't that what they say?" Lori tried to get up but fell back into the chair as she dropped the bottle of scotch. Beau quickly picked up the bottle and set it out of harm's way. Lori in a daze, looked questioningly at Beau, "Or is that what they say at Scotland Yard?"

"I've never seen you drunk before." Beau said with a tone of amusement in his voice.

"There's a lot of things you haven't seen. Look I am all gown up." With that statement Lori stood up, and lifted her skirt to show Beau her beautiful legs. "Nice huh. Now, look at these." Lori began unbuttoning her blouse.

"Lori! Stop it! You don't need this." Lori began to sob uncontrollably and collapsed into Beau's arms. He eased her slowly back into in the chair.

"You know what I wish?" Lori asked, still trying to recapture her composure.

What?

"I wish I could find someone who could love me as much as dad loved mom."

"Tom loves you, you know that."

"I guess so, sometimes I don't know. I just wish people could be more honest about their feelings. Let me show you something." Lori shuffled through the papers and old letters in a shoe box she'd found in the desk. "Read this."

She handed Beau the letter that had turned slightly yellow with age. Beau recognized Harry's handwriting.

> *December 1988*
> *My Darling wife;*
> *This is a letter I should have written a long time ago. I want you and Lori the to know what I've forgotten to say so many times. I love you sweetheart. You used to kid me that I loved my job more than you because I spent more time on the beat than with you. I do love this job because now and then, not always, but now and then I make a difference. I make things a little safer for our kid at least for a little while. You want you to know something? I love you not because you're the most beautiful thing that ever happened to me; but because you've stuck with me through the tough times and some of the rough places too.*
> *Remember when I first started college? You went out and got a job so we could pay the rent and the bills. Every cent I made went into paying for college and books. It was your money that kept us in food and with a roof over our heads. Remember how I complained about school, but I don't remember you ever complaining when you came home tired from work and I asked you for money for more books. If you did complain, I guess I didn't hear you. I was too wrapped up with my problems to think of yours. I*

know its a little late, but I think of all the things you sacrificed for me. The clothes, the holidays, the parties, the friends. You never complained and somehow I never remembered to thank you for being you. If you are looking down on us, please forgive me.

I guess I forgot you were my partner just as much as Beau when I was out pounding a beat or on a stakeout. I was so proud when I made detective sergeant. I was proud of you too but I never told you that. I took it for granted that you knew too. In all the years I pounded a beat, I always knew your prayers were with me.

I know its too late now, you're gone. I want you to know I'm sorry for all the things that were forgotten because I was too concerned about the job or the next case. As I sit home alone tonight I've been thinking about the missed anniversaries, birthdays, and school plays that you went to alone because I was out on some case. I'm sorry for the lonely nights you spent alone, wondering where I was, if I was safe. I'm thinking of all the times I thought of calling you just to say hello and somehow never got around to it. I'm thinking of the warm feeling I had knowing that you and Lori would be waiting for me when I got home.

I've made a lot of mistakes in my life, but if I only ever made one good decision was when I asked you to be my wife. Through the good times and the bad times you were always there for me. I love you sweetheart and I love Lori, too.

I'm really alone now and it scares me. I need you so badly it hurts and I know it's too late. I know you're gone but I feel you're here with me. I can see your face and feel your loving arms around me.

I guess that's about it, honey. My God, but I love you so very much. Wait for me. Watch over Lori and always remember, that I loved you more than anything in this life. I just forgot to tell you.
I love you, Harry.

Beau looked up from Harry's letter and saw that Lori had fallen asleep. He took a knitted throw from the back of the chair and covered her, kissed her on the forehead and turned out the light.

Harry Macklin's funeral had all the pomp and circumstance due a police officer who had died in the line of duty. Hundreds of law enforcement officers came from all over the state came to pay their respects along with a host of politicians and government dignitaries.

Beau, wearing his dress blues for the first time in years, sat alongside Lori. She was veiled in black. Standing in the background Beau noticed the familiar faces of prostitutes, convicted felons, and drug addicts who stood behind the police honor guard. They had all come to honor Harry. He thought to himself, Harry old buddy, that's your greatness.

Harry was eulogized with words of praise, lots of words, most of them fell on Beau's deaf ears. He didn't need to hear those words. He'd lived them, and more. Beau just stared at the flag-draped casket, lost in memories of days, and often longer nights, they had shared on stake outs, in bars, in all-night diners, and on a vacation they took together after the untimely death of Harry's wife. Harry really loved Flo. At least they'd be together now. That final thought made Beau's grief a little easier to bear. Beau's reverie was broken a few moments later when a bugler on the hillside mournfully began to blow Taps. A volley of shots were fired in unison by a thin line of uniformed, white gloved officers, each wearing a black ribbon slashed across their shields in honor of a fallen comrade. Moments later, Chief Paul Wexford stepped up to Harry's daughter, presented her with the folded flag and murmured a few words of condolence.

"Is that it? Is that all you're gonna say?" Beau thought to himself. "Why don't you tell her that when we catch this asshole, we're gonna blow his fucking balls off? He ain't gonna get to a trial so he can plead insanity and some liberal asshole isn't gonna stand in front of the courthouse with signs saying the death penalty was wrong. This animal is never gonna get to trial if he has anything to say about it. I don't give a shit about Miranda, his civil rights, it's gonna end with a 357 to the head as soon as I know for sure." The words were caught in his throat as he watched Lori accept the neatly folded flag.

Beau put his arm around Lori. They walked slowly towards the chauffeured limos and official cars that lined the two lane cemetery road bordering the burial grounds. Lori gave Beau a big hug.

"I'm sorry about last night. I guess you're wondering where Tom is?" Lori paused, "We've separated. We're trying to work things out so don't you worry." She said, turning her head into Beau's shoulder for comfort, "Dad loved you," Lori said, trying to muster a smile.

"I loved him, too," Beau replied, his voice cracking slightly, fighting back the tears that wanted to come pouring out. He opened the door to her limo and leaned over as she kissed him on the cheek.

"Lori, sweetheart, you're the only family I've got. I'm always here for you. You know that... Don't just stay in touch. Remember, I'm your Godfather and I love you very much."

"I know." She looked at Beau tearfully as the door was closed and the limo drove off. Lori looked back as if it would be the last time she'd ever see him.

"Beau!" the Chief's voice called out. Turning, he saw Wexford standing a short distance away motioning him to join him, Captain Peterson and a tall, good looking black man.

"Yes, sir." Beau addressed the Chief respectfully with a nod to Peterson and waited to be introduced to the third man.

"Lieutenant Gasteneau, Sergeant Jack Bellamy, formally of the Philadelphia Police Department. He's a new addition to our department."

Bellamy offered his hand and a small smile. "Hi! Sorry to have to meet you under these circumstances."

"Yeah," Beau said in a rather flat voice, shaking Bellamy's hand then turning inquisitively back to the Chief.

"Bellamy's going to be taking over the Gray Lady Killer case."

"I beg your pardon?" Beau asked, not sure he'd heard right.

"Captain Peterson and I thought it best you took some time off and got away from here for awhile. You could use the time off, maybe if you got away, sorta stepped back for awhile, you'd come back with a fresh outlook."

"With all due respect," Beau said stonily, "I have no intention of taking any time off. Not until I find the bastard who killed Harry."

"Beau, your feelings are understandable, but emotions tend to affect a man's objectivity," Peterson interjected.

"My partner died because of this son-of-a-bitch! You think I can just walk away and go lie on a beach somewhere with my thumb up my ass and forget about it?"

"A personal vendetta's not going to find him any faster."

"The hell it won't. There isn't going to be one hour out of twenty-four I won't be looking for him."

"All right Beau, let me be honest with you. The press is making this whole thing a political football and, with this being an election year, the Mayor has to do something."

"Go to an equal opportunities quota system?" Beau snapped. He was by no means a racist, but it was the only way he could expel his anger.

"Look," Bellamy said, glaring at Beau, "This wasn't my idea but I'm a cop, Lieutenant, no matter what my color is and I'm a damn good one."

"Sorry," Beau muttered, "I didn't mean it the way it came out." With a dead serious stare at Jack, he asked, "Would you walk away if it was your partner?" Jack stood silent. He couldn't argue the point. Beau turned to look

SOUTH JUNIOR HIGH
3.5 HONOR ROLL

is presented to

Amy Casper

for outstanding achievement.

signature _____ date 1/16/04

at the Chief. "I'll tell you this, you can take me off the case. You can take my badge, but I'm going to find this asshole no matter what! And another thing, did you know our perp could be black? You know what would happen if the press got a hold on that little tidbit?"

Peterson and the Chief exchanged a glance as Beau waited for his words to cook and simmer.

"Okay," the Chief sighed. "On one condition. Bellamy's your new partner."

"That's his problem, not mine!" Beau said, saluted and headed for his car.

At precisely eight o'clock the following morning, Jack Bellamy stood in front of the upper-middle class complex and checked it against the address he had in his hand. Assured it was the right one, he searched the call directory for Beau's apartment number. Finding it, he pressed the call button and waited. No response. He leaned heavily on the button for a good fifteen seconds.

"I heard you the first time," Beau's voice shouted through the intercom. "Who is it and what'd ya want?"

"Jack Bellamy. The Mayor wants us down in his office in one hour."

"Shit!" Beau's voice exploded through the intercom. A second later the buzzer sounded and Jack heard the click as the apartment house front door unlocked, permitting Jack to enter. He took the elevator to the third floor and made his way down the corridor to 3C. The door seemed to open by itself magically then Jack heard a growl, and looking down, found himself staring into Stud's unwelcome snarl.

"It's okay," he heard Beau call out from somewhere deep in the apartment. "He won't bite."

"You know that. The question is, does he?" Jack shouted back, eyeing Studs suspiciously.

As if sensing Bellamy's hesitation, Studs took a few steps back and sat on his haunches, still studying the new arrival. Jack shrugged to himself, stepped in, closed the door behind him, and moved into the living room, stopping for a moment to let Studs smell the back of his hand then patted him on the head.

"There's a jar of instant and some hot water in the kitchen. Help yourself. Be with you in a couple minutes. Oh, could you get Studs a beer?"

The sound of the shower terminated any possible future response. Jack looked around and found himself standing in the midst of what the Governor could easily declare a disaster area. The place hadn't been cleaned or dusted in a month of Sundays and on a clear day you could almost see out of the windows.

25

Jack edged his way into the kitchen under the watchful eye of Studs and spent the next few minutes trying to find a clean cup. He finally gave up and removing one from a sink piled high with dirty dishes, washed it out and made himself a cup of instant coffee then popped a cold beer into Stud's dish.

"What's the Mayor want?" Beau asked, standing in the doorway toweling himself. "Are they going to make you Chief Hotshot?"

"I didn't know you were a cheap shot artist," Jack smirked as he gulped the weak coffee. Beau smiled, turned, and walked back into the bedroom, knowing Jack could give it out as well as take it.

"Beats the hell out of me. The Captain said we were to get our asses down there by nine o'clock sharp." Jack raised his voice as he talked from the kitchen.

"You get a chance to read the files?" Beau asked from the bedroom.

"What's to read? From what I saw, we haven't got the square root of fuck all," Jack answered leaning against the doorway, cup in hand. Beau picked up a pair of shorts that were draped over the chair and slipped them on.

"You always live in a mess like this?"

"What are you? Some kind a neat freak?"

Jack chose to ignore any rebuttal. How his newly acquired partner chose to live was none of his business. He was satisfied to know at least Studs liked him.

Charleston's city hall was typical of most southern cities. Large white columns supported a dome with a simulated bell tower perched on top. A large bronze statue of a Confederate general, atop a pedestal, dominated the main lobby. The floor was a large expanse of mosaic marble leading to a wide stairwell bordered by two elevators. One could either take to the stairs or the elevator on the left side of the lobby to get to the east wing that housed the offices of the District Attorney, the City Attorney, courtroom, judges chambers, attorney/client conference rooms, various court clerks, courtroom bailiffs, deputies, a prisoner holding cell, and the press room. The elevator on the right side of the stairwell led to the west wing of the building that housed the offices of the Mayor, members of the city council, and a variety of other city bureaucratic offices necessary to running a city the size of Charleston.

The office of the Mayor was located on the third floor of the west wing. Paintings of former mayors hung on the walls. The room was filled with relics of past administrations. A law library adorned two side walls, and a massive mahogany desk sat at the end of the room exactly in front of two large windows that overlooked the city square. Flanking the desk was the American flag and the flag of the state of South Carolina.

Gil Washington was Charleston's first black Mayor since Reconstruction. He was a hardworking, self made man, a skilled attorney who had served as Charleston's District Attorney, before running for Mayor. Basically an honest and fair man, he listened to both sides before making his decision, but no matter what it was, it was sure to piss somebody off. He was always caught in the crossfire. On one side, the white community would often accuse him of favoritism by hiring too many blacks. On the other hand, the black community would accuse him of being an Uncle Tom and kowtowing to the white supremacists. They were both wrong. Washington believed the minority quota system to be racist and would have no part of it. In fact, he often went to extremes to insure that each and every appointment was made on the individual's ability and personal qualifications.

Although the thermostat situated at the far end of the Mayor's office read a comfortable seventy degrees, the office was by no means cool. With election day only a few short months away, the heat was on. A serial killer was running loose in his fair city, and the press was inflaming the public and blatantly blaming the Mayor and his Chief of Police for not doing enough to catch the maniac who was responsible for the rash of heinous crimes.

His eyes swept the morning headline of the Charleston Ledger for the tenth time, then all six-foot-three, two hundred and eighty pounds of him rose out of his chair. Once a star tackle for the University of South Carolina, he was an imposing figure with intense brown eyes, high cheek bones, a flat nose with flaring nostrils and a full, neatly cut head of hair that was just showing tinges of gray at the temples. Turning his back on the three men who were seated across his desk, he stared absentmindedly out of the window and said, "So what you're saying is that the score's killer, six, the Charleston Police,—zip!"

The only response was that of Chief Wexford clearing his throat. Washington spun around and faced the three men who had been summoned to his office.

"Mind telling me what the hell I'm supposed to tell the press this morning'?"

"We're doing everything we can," Wexford mumbled.

"I told them that crap after the first old lady was killed back in October. I also told them that after the second, and the third. It's God damn July and they're screaming for your head and mine and I'm not about to lose mine." He turned and glared at Beau. "How many men have you got working on this?"

"Six, full time. That's besides Bellamy."

"Of course, the entire force has been alerted as well," Wexford chimed in quickly.

"That won't cut it. I want a special task force set up. I don't care how many men it takes.."

"Manpower is not the answer," Beau volunteered, getting a sharp look from Wexford.

"What is the answer?" the Mayor asked. "Tell me. I'll listen to anything and anybody who can put an end to this."

"The problem is getting a handle on this guy. What kind of man he is; what makes him tick; why does he kill little old ladies? We get the answer to those questions and maybe we can pick up a trail."

"Makes sense. How do we do it?"

"A shrink, maybe."

"What about the FBI?" Bellamy suggested. "They've got a serial killer unit at Quantico. Maybe we could borrow one of their behavioral scientists."

Washington glared at Wexford. "Why the hell didn't you think of that?"

Wexford's face turned beet red. "I did. You bring in the Feds and right away you lose control. They like to run the whole damn show. Not to mention grabbing all the media attention."

"Great! Let 'em have it. You've got a totally fucked up situation. Right now we don't want or need media attention. Whatever it takes, I want this thing wrapped up, and fast. The F.B.I.'s in. See to it!"

A knock at the door and Gladys Poole, Washington's secretary poked her head inside the Mayor's office.

"Sorry to interrupt but there's an urgent call for Lieutenant Gasteneau on line four."

The Mayor shoved his phone towards Beau and gave him the nod to take the call right there.

"Gasteneau... Where?... We're on our way." He hung up the phone and gesturing at the headline on the Mayor's desk said, "The paper's wrong. We just got number seven!"

By the time Beau and Jack arrived, the crime scene unit had partially eliminated the stench of death by pouring DB 45 crystals around Amanda Hollingsworth's hallway entrance and living room. She'd been discovered by her weekly cleaning lady. Even with disinfecting crystals giving off the faint odor of violets, the smell of death couldn't be easily dispelled, especially when a body had started to decompose. Amanda's remains, having been dead for three days, sat in her chair beside the tea service and the vase of wilted forget-me-nots.

"You sure of the time?" Jack asked the M.E. as he finished his grisly job.

"Seventy-two hours, give or take a few. Pretty damn sure of that."

Beau stared at the M.E. "You saying she was killed the same night as the Philburn woman?"

The M.E. shrugged, "just before, or just after."

"Three houses down on the same block?" Jack asked, then looked at Beau. "You think he's the same guy the Potts woman saw the night Molly Philburn became the sixth victim? According to the file, he was walking in this direction."

"Shit! The bastard hit her while Harry and I were in the Philburn house." Beau sighed and shook his head. "If there's any doubt that this guy, the guy in the alley who killed Harry are one and the same, that doubt just flew out the window." Beau turned to Danelli, the first homicide detective to catch the call and arrive on scene.

"Got a log started?"

"Everything the first on scene gave me. Anything forensics finds," Danelli continued, with a nod to the crime scene unit, "I'll add to my report. So far it's just like all the others. No forced entry and so far, everything's been wiped clean or the suspect wears gloves."

"Maybe he's another neat freak." Jack muttered.

"Sooner or later he's going to leave something behind, Beau remarked. "Take this place apart inch by inch. And I don't give a flying fuck who he is, the Chief or the Mayor himself, nobody comes onto the crime scene unless they have a damn good reason for being here!"

Beau picked up the plastic bag where Danelli had put the victim's personal belongings. There was the usual comb, lipstick, wallet, credit cards, keys, hairpins, a small tissue packet and a checkbook. Setting down the bag Beau began to thumb through the checkbook, when he saw it. It was apparent as a fart in church, Harry would have said. A check had been made out to the Southern Christian Fellowship for twenty-nine ninety-five and never torn out of the book. "Bingo!" Beau shouted excitedly. "We've got a check that's signed and never used. Danelli, I want you to check out this Southern Christian Fellowship group. I want a list of everyone from the janitor on up." Beau tossed the checkbook to Danelli who began to examine the check closely.

Jack walked to the large bay window that overlooked Amanda Hollingsworth's garden and stared out at a beautiful day. Too beautiful for death to come visiting. His eyes were drawn to a patch of forget-me-nots. "Lieutenant!"

"If we're gonna work together, the name's Beau. What's up?"

Jack beckoned him towards the window. "Take a look out there."

Beau joined Jack at the window and looked in the direction he was pointing.

"Danelli!"

"Yeah." Danelli answered looking up from the checkbook.

"Have Physical and Trace Evidence check the garden. Especially the area where the forget-me-nots are growing."

"What are we looking for?"

"Footprints, maybe, fibers from a man's clothing. Those forget-me-nots didn't walk in here by themselves!"

Later that day, Beau reviewed the files of the various victims. His office was a small, gray painted cinder block room furnished sparsely with a desk, two chairs, a small bookcase housing a variety of police procedurals, a two drawer filing cabinet and a large wall blackboard on which Jack was listing all pertinent information on the previous six murders. It wasn't very much except for the one additional clue they'd picked up. The light rain that had fallen the night Amanda Hollingsworth was killed had softened the ground in her garden sufficiently to have left at least one clear footprint. Forensics had put the shoe size as 10D. The depth of the print suggested that the height of the suspect was approximately six feet with a probable weight of 160 to 170 pounds, if indeed the print belonged to the killer. And then there was the checkbook. Where that would lead was anyone's guess.

"Not much," Beau said glancing up at the board.

"It's more than we had before." Jack answered.

The telephone on Beau's desk rang. Tapping the blinking plastic button, he put the receiver to his ear and snapped, "Gasteneau."

"Beau", the strained voice of Chief Wexford come over the line, obviously having suffered another verbal assault by the Mayor. "The Fed's put an Agent Thornton on a plane. Flight 231 arriving eight thirty tonight."

"They didn't waste any time. Who's meeting him?"

"You are!" Beau heard the disconnect signaling no argument.

The Stakeout Bar was the watering hole where off duty cops went to unwind and rookies went to hear old war stories, jokes, and cop cynicism. When Beau and Jack entered and elbowed their way up to the "two deep" bar, the blasting juke box made ordering sound like a Marine Drill Sergeant giving a command.

Murph, the bartender and owner didn't have to ask what Beau was drinking, he just started pouring. Jack opted for a beer as he popped a few pretzel sticks in his mouth. Before Jack took his first sip, Murph was already refilling Beau's shot glass.

"It's only six o'clock. Keep that up to eight-thirty and your breath's gonna become a fire hazard." Jack mumbled through a mouthful of pretzels.

"That's the one good thing about being a cop. If I ever get stopped for a balloon test, I'll just melt the damn balloon."

"Yeah, and everything within a ten foot radius," Jack chuckled.

Beau grinned and turned his attention to the six o'clock news blaring on the TV suspended above the bar.

The face of Stan Rush, WXFC's anchor man filled the screen as he began his opening gambit.

"To date, seven, well respected, elderly women of this community have been brutally assaulted, raped and strangled for no apparent reason other than satisfying the lusts and thrill of a serial killer."

Photographs of the murder victims appeared on the screen as Rush continued. "On the night of July 17th, this maniac not only murdered Molly Philburn, but shortly after the police arrived at the Philburn house, the killer entered and murdered Amanda Hollingsworth who lived a mere three houses away and managed to elude the police after stabbing Detective Sergeant Harry Mackland to death. Early this morning, Mayor Washington finally requested the assistance of the Federal Bureau of Investigation after the latest victim was discovered."

Everyone at the bar was stone silent as they listened to the commentator. Occasionally, eyes would look at Beau, then dart back to the screen. The TV camera returned to focus on Rush as he began to introduce his special guest.

"Tonight I have with me a man who's been following this story from the very beginning, the senior reporter with the Charleston Ledger, Danny O'Brien."

The camera angle widened to include O'Brien, a beedy-eyed, weasley faced little man with a self-serving smile and reputation for constantly walking the thin line between sensational reporting and yellow journalism. Beau took one look at O'brien and rolled his eyes at Jack.

"Grab a shovel. You're about to be totally emershed in bullshit."

"Danny," Rush said to his guest, "I understand you've uncovered some recent developments in the Gray Lady Killer case."

Danny sat back and gave the camera a smug know-it-all-look.

"Well, the story's breaking in my paper right now with more details, but earlier today, I had an exclusive interview with Mildred Potts."

"The woman who found the Molly Philburn's body?" Rush asked leading his guest.

"Right, according to the police, she's the only one to see the killer close up and live to tell about it."

"As I understand it, she told the police that the man had an accent."

Danny nodded. "What she didn't tell them, and what she told me, was that it was a Jamaican accent."

"Are you saying the Gray Lady Killer is a black man?" Rush seemed momentarily shocked as were all those glued to the TV at the Stakeout Bar.

Danny shrugged, "I can't say. That's for the police to say, but we do have a black mayor. So, you figure it out. As far as I'm concerned, I think they're covering up something."

The interview continued for a few more minutes with the interviewer trying to extract some facts. His efforts only resulted in more innuendo and speculation. However, it's impact was already felt. The two detectives sat stunned as the TV started advertising the latest hemorrhoid medicine guaranteed to keep you from itching where the sun doesn't shine. Jack thought to himself, "How appropriate, an asshole spouting bullshit followed by a hemorrhoid commercial." He turned to look at Beau tightening his jaws. Beau slammed his glass down on the bar breaking it in his hand. "Sonofabitch!"

Beau leaped from the barstool and plowed his way through the barroom. The men conveniently cleared a path for him because they knew he was pissed, and God help anyone who got in his way. The Lieutenant, with Jack at his side, grabbed the phone at the end of the bar. "Dickerson must be out of his gourd," Beau snapped, angrily punching the buttons on the Stakeout Bar's private line.

"Who's Dickerson?" Jack asked.

"The Ledger's Chief Editor. Damn news people. They don't give jackshit about anything but selling papers and TV commercials. When they end up hurting someone or fuckin' up an investigation they run and hide behind the first amendment. Well they've done it this time. They just declared open season on your people."

"They're not my people," Jack responded bluntly. "They're just people."

"Yeah, well don't take it personally, but they're a few people around here that need an excuse like this to go coon hunting." He turned his attention to the phone as a voice with a low, country twang answered, "City Desk, Filer."

"Billy? Where's Dickerson? What the fuck is going on? Your boss have a mental hernia or what?"

A long hearty laugh came over the line. "Sorry Beau. I tried to get him to sit on it but I don't own the paper. I go along with your hernia theory though. Look, Tricky Dickie saw an exclusive and told Danny to run with it. My idea to confirm with you went over like a lead balloon."

"Well, do those assholes know that they've put a goddamn match to the city? Your hot item can burn down Charleston!"

There was a short silence on the other end before Billy Filer came back with his offer.

"Tell you what. Tell me right now the killer's not black and I'll run a personal disclaimer in bold letters on tomorrow's front page... What d'ya say?"

"Shit!" Beau shouted back. "You know I can't make any disclaimer right now. But O'Brien's has taken advantage of a confused old lady and gone public with half-assed info that's gonna snowball into a hell of a lot of problems."

"Sorry Beau. Best I can do. Paper's already gone out with Danny's story and by tomorrow every paper in the country'll be running it 'les you can tell me different."

Beau uttered a few hundred cuss words under his breath, then hung up the phone after, shouting "Thanks for nothing!"

Turning to his new partner, he let go with a sigh of frustration. They stared at each other, both knowing full well that Charleston was on the verge of going berserk.

"This is all the local Klukkers have to hear to grab the sheet off their beds and get'em over their heads. I give it twenty-four to forty-eight hours and this city's gonna be torn apart." Beau remarked then quickly continued. "Okay, we go on twelve hours shifts starting as of now. Let's go."

"What about the airport?" Jack reminded, "You're supposed to pick up the FBI shrink fink."

"Damn, forgot. All right, get your buns down to headquarters. Tell the Chief I want twelve hour shifts right now. Don't let him blow smoke up your ass about budget. Tell him what's happened. I also want a line on the Grand Kleagle and all the local Klaners and skinheads within a hundred miles of the city. If they so much as fart, I wanna know who gave the orders. Can you handle that? Of course you can. What the hell am I saying? You're a cop. That's what you told me, right?"

"And black?" Jack retorted, not happy that Beau keeps bringing up the color issue.

Beau smiled knowing he'd pulled Jack's chain. "Cops come in only one color. Blue." Halfway out the front door, Beau shouted, "Be back as soon as I pick up the shrink."

Jack watched him go. He was not only beginning to like Gasteneau, he was beginning to respect him. He knew Beau was testing him on the race issue. He realized that he didn't give a rat's ass about the color of a guy's skin only his ability as a cop. He shook his head and muttered to himself, "Can I handle it? Does Dolly Parton have tits?"

Chapter Three

Federal Fuzz

David Delongpre lived quietly in a three story walkup in a seedy neighborhood on the south side of downtown Charleston. Although the building superintendent believed that the tenant occupying apartment 3D lived alone, actually, three people lived in the small, two bedroom apartment on the top floor. He would have been astonished to learn, had he ever gained access to 3D, the excessive difference in decor between the two bedrooms. The one in which David slept was shabby, unkept, with comic books scattered about while the other was kept fastidiously clean for Gaylord Harcourt whenever he emerged from within David. Gaylord was a self-educated man who read the latest books, was well versed in the arts, read the bible continuously. Clean cut, and spoke impeccable English with a pronounced Boston accent. That was quite an achievement, as he was a southern boy, born and bred right here in Charleston. Gaylord was a pious man who attended church every Sunday and as a matter of fact, at one time was almost a Baptist Deacon. Strangely, even though the opportunity had occurred several times, he never married. He could have married well, however, chose to remain a loner. A well liked loner, nevertheless, a loner. Some gay members of the church actually approached Gaylord but were discreetly rebuffed and it was forgotten. He always seemed to have money, but when asked about his job, he would be evasive and politely change the subject. Gaylord was David's other self, the one that would be acceptable in Charleston's high society, and of course, the apple of Agnes's eye. Gaylord's closet was neatly lined with well tailored suits, clean laundered shirts, dignified ties, and highly polished shoes. A bookshelf was conveniently placed at Gaylord's bedside and a Bible lay on the night stand. David, on the other hand, cared little for clean and stylish clothes. He went out of his way to piss off Gaylord by being slovenly, leaving dirty laundry in the bathroom and not doing the dishes. He guarded his bedroom like Fort Knox. It was his private domain. The door was locked and a bold lettered sign, saying "Keep out" was attached to the door.

Not only did Gaylord live inside David, but David, the little scared, abused child also occupied the same body and when he came to the surface, he brought with him the Beastie, an entity filled with uncontrollable rage. When strange animal-like noises came from David's locked room, the neighbors accused Gaylord of having a wild animal in his house, but nothing was ever done about the complaint because Gaylord stayed to himself and always paid his rent on time, which the owner appreciated. David, the man, was strong, well built and not unhandsome, but in many respects, remained childlike in his thinking, finding companionship primarily in television and in reading comic books, especially those committed to horror and unspeakable demons. On his wall David had an array of drawings of dinosaurs eating the flesh of smaller animals. David, the illegitimate son of poor white trash, never knew his father, and thought all women were sluts, like his mother. He had been arrested for pimping and spent eight months in jail before he turned 21. Gaylord, on the other hand, loved the classics, and often visited art museums. Although both men occupied the same body, their minds and ambitions were far apart and they argued with one another constantly, especially over Agnes.

The Beastie, the third being to house himself inside David, was born in anger to punish Agnes who had abused him as a child.

David's main recollection of his mother, Leah Delongpre, was that of a galley maid in the employ of the Gladlows, a wealthy and socially prominent Charleston family who could trace their family tree back to before the Revolutionary War. It was the Gladlows who took pity on the girl and brought her into their household. Having no children of their own, Mr. Gladlow saw to it that young David got at least a public school education. Agnes Gladlow, on the other hand, had different ideas when it came to the duties to be performed by Leah. As a young boy, David remembered playing cowboys in the garden shed and hiding behind the compost pile as he watched his mother and Agnes have sex on the floor. David felt sick to his stomach as he watched his mother perform unspeakable sex acts on Agnes. Strangely, he thought Agnes was beautiful and gentle when she was making love. He wished Agnes was his mother and Mr. Gladlow was his father. As David began to grow into a strong, well built young boy, Agnes was quick to notice. She would give him sponge baths with bubbles filling the tub, then fondle him gently. She enjoyed drying the young boy while looking at him in the mirror. She made him dress and undress in front of her every time she bought him new clothes. When David first entered junior high school, Agnes Gladlow vainly tried to teach him how to become a young southern gentleman. It was then that part of David rebelled, while deep within him another part yearned to be loved by Agnes and it was at that time Gaylord Harcourt was born.

One afternoon when David came home from school, Agnes was waiting with a box of new clothes for the youngster. She insisted that he undress and try on the new suit she'd bought. David obeyed the command and stripped down to his jockey shorts. Agnes couldn't help but notice the bulge in his crotch. She was instantly aroused and began to fondle him as she had done so many times before, but this time it was different. David wanted no part of this act, but Gaylord saw his penis becoming stiff and hard and he knew that pleased Agnes. It made him acceptable to the upper gentry. Gaylord was proud of his sexuality as Agnes began to perform oral sex.

The conflict between Gaylord and David continued to grow with David detesting every time Agnes touched him. But when Gaylord was in charge, he satisfied her most lusty desires. However, Gaylord wasn't always in charge and that led to Agnes's frustration which forced her to brutally demand David to perform. Agnes found that her lust was enhanced after beating David into submission. As her lust grew, she tortured David before sex. When David could take no more, Gaylord would appear and satisfy her twisted sexual desires. David would never forget the weekend alone with Agnes when she put his puppy, Snipper, in the old 'fridge in back of the garden shed. She would not let him come out until she was satisfied. David begged her to let him go. Snipper didn't do anything to her. She didn't have the right to harm that poor innocent puppy for something he didn't want to do. Agnes tied David up and whipped him until Gaylord appeared. Somehow, the more Agnes tortured David, the more passionate Gaylord became. Finally, when the crying young David opened the 'fridge door the puppy was dead. David buried Snipper in a small grassy glen down by Willow Creek and that was precisely, in the mind of little David, when the Beastie was born.

The Beastie was the most evil entity that the human mind could conceive. In David's twisted psyche it had the mouth, jaws, and razor sharp teeth of a dinosaur. It could walk upright or on all fours. It ate raw meat and drank only blood. At night, David and the animal inside him would hunt stray cats and dogs to keep the Beastie in a fresh supply of blood. When this animal personality was in control, David's body would go into convulsions and assume the physical characteristics and posture of an animal hunting for his prey. Many times, the silence of the night would be broken by the cry of the Beastie. When a prey could not be found, the Beastie actually drank the bowl of blood he provided for himself. The neighbors complained, police published a notice to beware of stray dogs known to be in the area but no one ever saw the Beastie except David and Gaylord. In David's mind the Beastie was totally subservient to David's commands. It would kill on command. In fact, David only had to think about killing and the Beastie would attack.

In the living room of the apartment, the mantel clock struck midnight. Automatically, almost like sleep-walking, David arose and walked to Gaylord's door and knocked.

"Gaylord, its time for our session."

"For crissakes it's God damn midnight you stupid fuck." Gaylord shouted back. David shook his head in frustration. He had to go through this with Gaylord every time Doctor Michaels has a session available.

"Gaylord, you know this is the only time Doctor Michaels has open."

"I don't give a fast fuck what he has available, go away!" Gaylord answered. David's body began to twitch. He twisted and contorted his body until he was on the floor. The Beastie had emerged. His nails clawed at the door. Then a chilling howl roared from David's throat.

"Okay, okay, I'm coming. Knock it off before you wake the whole damn building. With that assurance the Beastie disappeared as quickly as it had appeared. David straightened up, and calmly walked to the utility room adjacent to the washer and dryer and wheeled out the wheelchair. Sitting fully dressed, with coat, tie, faded white shirt and a stethoscope still around his neck was the decomposed body of Dr. Michael A. Smith a prominent psychiatrist who had disappeared from Seattle General over two years ago. David wheeled the corpse into the kitchen and sat it at the head of the table. David turned two chairs facing the corpse.

"Now I believe we are all comfortable." David said as he sat in one of the empty chairs. Looking at the other empty chair as if Gaylord was there, David asked, "Well, are you gonna just sit there or are you gonna talk to the doctor? These sessions are not cheap." Gaylord surfaced and answered, "This was your idea not mine. If I had my way I'd go back to bed."

"See, what did I tell you Doc, no cooperation.

Suddenly, another voice, clinical, totally matured, with a completely different inflection, emanated from David.

"Gaylord, we have to get at the root of your problems with David. So, if you could, please try to answer my questions as truthfully as you can. Did David ever get into trouble when he was a kid?"

"Yeah, but only when I'd get him into it. The little brat always did what I told him."

"What did you tell him to do?" The doctor's voice asked.

"Lemmie see... I told him to put gasoline on Agnes's flowers and set fire to it," Gaylord said smugly.

"Why did you want him to do that?" the Doctor inquired.

"I was mad at the old bitch. She didn't like the way I made love."

"You mean had sex." The doctor retorted.

"Yeah whatever."

The voice from the corpse continued the questioning. "Tell me about the fire."

Gaylord in total control of David's body continued. "He set it in her best garden plot next to the old oak." David stood up and stepped back while still talking in Gaylord's voice. His voice took on a vicious tone. "He put it out! He got too scared! Chicken! I told him to let it burn! Let it burn!" Gaylord emphasized the words with true hatred in every syllable.

"Who were you angry at?" the Doctor's voice asked.

"Who do you think?" was Gaylord's angry reply.

"You tell me."

"Agnes! You stupid shit. What the hell are we paying you for?"

The Doctor's voice did not change expression as he continued. "Were there any other fires?"

"No, the candy-assed David was too scared." Gaylord glared at the corpse and didn't see the toothy grin of death on the decomposed body of the doctor. He only heard the Doctor's voice. "What other things did you make David do?" Gaylord answered smugly. "Lotsa things, steal, I made him break into houses, lockers at school." He sneered as he spoke about Agnes and David's mother. "They never knew. Those stupid women never paid any attention to him. Agnes only wanted him when she wanted sex." Hatred dripped from Gaylord's voice. "Neither of those bitches cared about David. I was the only one who could protect that little brat." The voice from the grinning corpse asked, "Didn't David ever get caught?"

"Once. At the K-Mart. The police brought him home. The little shit was terrified. But, I told him don't worry, she won't do nothin."

"She?"

"His mother." Gaylord's mouth twitched under the questioning. "She don't care I told him. She just cares about herself, and having sex with Agnes."

"What did David's mother do when the police arrived?" the Doctor asked.

"Nothing, she opened the door in her bathrobe. You knew she had been giving Agnes head. She embarrassed me!" Gaylord shouted. "All she cared about was herself." Gaylord paused, then a sly grin come over his face. "I knew I could fix everything. That night I really showed Agnes what I could do. I had sex with both of them."

"You mean you had sex with your mother." The voice stated coldly. Gaylord began to shake his head violently. "No! She's not my mommy. She's David's mommy." David's childlike voice interrupted. "I think Doctor Michaels has covered enough ground for this session."

"Good!" Gaylord replied. "I'm getting tired of his stupid questions. We've been over this a hundred times." David, who was now in control stood up, and carefully began to wheel the corpse of Doctor Michaels back to the closet. In a careless moment he bumped the side of the kitchen table causing the head of Doctor Michael's corpse to fall in his lap. "Oops!" David remarked and placed the head back into its proper position then carefully returned Doctor Michaels to his resting place until the next session.

A stationary tropical low was sitting off the coast, pumping water over the state in a seemingly never ending deluge. It'd been like this, on and off, for the past three days. Torrents of rain, interrupted by moments of calm, was continuing into the third day. Somebody, jokingly, had put out an APB on some old guy with a beard sailing an ark down the Expressway. With Studs safe and dry inside Beau's car, the window sufficiently lowered to let fresh air in while keeping the moisture out, Beau sat in the airport's cocktail lounge impatiently nursing a drink as he waited for the flight that was now thirty minutes overdue. He stared out at the sparkling wet tarmac as a bolt of lightening struck, immediately followed by a loud kettle-drum clap of thunder and he became increasingly convinced that it was definitely not a night to fly.

"Flight 231 from Washington is now arriving at Gate 4", a voice boomed over the terminal's loud speaker system. Beau rose from his bar stool, shoved the change still on the bar towards the bartender and exited into the main terminal, sure that the guy the FBI had sent was happy to be back on terra firma again. Beau picked up his step, moving through the airport's main lobby quickly. Hopping on the escalator for the upper level, he heard his name over the airport paging system.

"Lieutenant Gasteneau, please report to the information counter. Lieutenant Gasteneau, your party is at the information counter on level one." Beau reached the second level on the escalator, turned in schoolboy fashion, and went back, the down side.

Approaching the counter, Beau saw a well dressed man in a one button tailored business suit carrying a briefcase. He had "agent" written all over him. Beau asked, "Agent Thornton?" Before the man could reply, and from another direction, a young woman's voice interrupted, "I am Special Agent Thornton."

Turning, Beau came face to face with Agent Sally Thornton. She was a handsome woman, auburn hair with eyes the color of bright topaz, a strong jaw, and the most desirable lips he'd ever seen in his life. She was in her middle thirties, dressed in a tailored suit, with matching shoes and carrying a Gucci briefcase. He wondered, "How come all agents looked alike?" Male or female, they all looked like they were stamped out of the same mold. They must have a charm school hidden somewhere in Virginia just to train these people how to dress, and IBM is in charge. Under that beautiful face Beau could sense hostility. A quick prayer passed over his mind, "Please God, don't make her another Women's Libber. It would be a sin to have someone with that body be a Woman's Libber." Sally waited for some acknowledgment as the Lieutenant pondered his alternatives. Sally flashed her I.D. at Beau. Sure enough, she was an agent. He shook his head and blurted out, "I knew this wasn't my day."

Sally's eyes narrowed as she replied, "A woman, right?"

A reluctant smile came over the detective's face. "I'd say so. What do I call you? Mrs, Special Agent, Ms, Thornton?"

"Sally will do."

The Lieutenant shook hands with the agent and introduced himself, "Gasteneau, call me Beau. Welcome to Charleston." He politely reached for her bags when she cut him off.

"I can handle it."

Beau thought to himself, "Another attitude problem."

"Any bags checked?" He asked casually.

"No, just the carry-on."

"I dated a girl once. She couldn't even get her cosmetics in a bag that size."

"I'm not her and I am not your date." Sally replied looking Beau square in the face.

"Suit yourself. Car's outside," he said and headed for the front door.

The storm had intensified. The rain was now coming down in buckets and the busy street just outside the airport terminal building had become a torrential river. Beau held Sally back as a passing terminal bus drove by, sending up a sheet of water that splashed onto the sidewalk.

"Bad night. Surprised your flight arrived at all." Beau said, pulling up his collar. "You ready?" he asked, then not waiting for an answer, he checked the momentarily empty street, then darted across to where he parked his car. Fumbling for his keys, he quickly unlocked his trunk then signaled the stranded agent to join him.

"So much for chivalry," Sally mocked to herself. With a look of determination, she picked up her bag and struggled across in the downpour. Watching her, Beau figured she must have been cursed by the Frog Fairy. Not only did she manage to hit almost every puddle between the curb and the parking lot, she hadn't gone more than a half dozen steps when she broke one of her high heels, turned her ankle and put a run in her hose. Not completely dispassionate, Beau grabbed her luggage and tossed it into the trunk of his car, just as a departing bus gave Sally and Beau a shower. Beau slammed the trunk down and ran to the driver's side of his car and climbed in. Soaking wet, her make-up running, Sally hobbled on her sore foot to the passenger side only to find it still locked. If she'd had a hammer she'd have put it right through the window without a moment's hesitation. Seeing her plight, Beau reached over and unlocked the passenger door. She climbed in, yanking the door shut and sat back with her eyes shut, trying to hold back her anger. She was not going to let this big ape get to her. She'd been harassed by experts at the Academy, then at the Bureau. No podunk, hick cop, playing macho games was going to intimidate her. Sally had come up through the ranks the hard way. A rookie cop, night school and on up. She had a father who could see more as a blind man than most men see in a lifetime. She was the step-daughter of a career cop who gave her a love of the law. Her step-dad ran the Sacramento Police Department with a firm hand. Ever since she sat on his knee she dreamed of being part of law enforcement. When he died she vowed to make it her career. However, her dreams went beyond local cops. It was the FBI for her. At college she sacrificed her own social life to be number one in her class. She also put off all the macho ego centric types at the FBI academy to graduate number one. She had put all the numbers together only to find out that the field agents either came on to her or didn't take her seriously. Now she was going to have to go through all this bullshit again.

Beau had no sooner started the car and pulled out from his parking space, when a wet tongue licked the back of Sally's neck. Spinning around in her seat she found herself face to face with Studs who, this time, gently licked her nose.

"That thing belong to you?"

"Yep."

"Well, tell it to keep it's tongue to itself. Don't suppose you have a Kleenex or something?"

"Try the glove compartment. His name is Studs."

"What else," Sally chided.

"Usually he doesn't like Feds, but in your case, he'll make an exception."

"I'm thrilled. What kind'a name is Studs anyway?"

"What else would you call a dog who walks around with a hardon half the time?"

Studs barked happily.

Sally looked at him and then at Beau. "Is he bragging or complaining?"

"Just don't bark." Beau grinned, "Or you'll find out. How come they sent a woman?" he added, looking to change the subject.

"You have trouble dealing with that?"

"No, long as you can do what they sent you for."

They drove the next few minutes in silence, the only sound was Stud's panting and the flopping windshield wipers. Beau's eyes were riveted on the road ahead as they moved onto the Interstate. Sally eventually broke the silence. "I understand this Gray Lady Killer of yours struck again?"

"Numero seven and he's just as much your's now as he is mine."

"Glad you feel that way, Lieutenant. If he's black as we've heard, you're going to have a lot of trouble right here in River City," she commented.

"We aren't sure what his color is," Beau snapped sharply. "What you heard was one asshole reporter trying to sell more papers and get himself a bigger byline. The only weird thing about the latest one was that it's the first time he ever hit twice in one night.

"What about your partner?"

"The wrong place at the wrong time."

Sally glanced at Beau and saw the pain in his face. She suddenly felt sorry for the male chauvinist, with a badge, sitting next to her. She hadn't been close to anyone in the Bureau, but she had known other agents killed in the line of duty. She had seen what it did to their families and friends and it hurt. In spite of all the glitz of Women's Lib, she knew there was a bond that all law enforcement people shared, regardless of sex or race, and it hurts to lose one to the bad guys. With a concerned look, she commented, "He's sending you a message and it's not happy birthday."

"What do you mean a message?"

"Not sure yet." Sally answered, thinking about what she already knew about the case.

The quiet moment that followed was quickly interrupted by the car radio. "Mobil 271, this is Control Central, over."

Beau snatched up the mike and responded, "Control Central, 271, go."

"Roger 271, transmitting in the clear, be advised we have a double homicide, two females. Sgt. Bellamy is responding."

"Got it." Beau started to hang up his mike when Control Central continued, "271 Control."

"271, go."

"Lt., both victims are black."

There was a short silence. Beau looked at Sally. She saw a glimmer of fear in his face as he transmitted again, "Somehow that doesn't surprise me. What's the location?"

"Unit 272 is located on Route 61, one mile north of the 165 Interstate." Pulling the mike closer to his face Beau asked, "That's out of our beat. How come we responded?"

The dispatcher's answer came back, "272 said you'll know when you get there."

"On my way." The detective hung up the mike and looked at the wet agent. "You mind a side trip?"

"Like this?" She said, pointing at her blouse.

"You a cop or a woman?," came Beau's quick reply. Putting on the flashers, he hit a hard right at the next intersection and sped off into the rainy night.

The highway was lined with police cars and support vehicles. A Sheriff's deputy, controlling traffic, waved the police car through, while directing other traffic to the far side of the divided highway. This part of the Interstate meandered through rolling hills, heavy pulp pine and small farms.

There was a narrow gravel shoulder that fell off to a small, but steep, incline that led into the pine forest. The rain came down steadily, although it had lessened to a constant drizzle. Sheriff's deputies, in yellow rain slickers, moved down the incline, carefully swinging their flashlights over the area looking for crime-scene evidence, standard operating procedures for the county.

Beau got out, pulled up his collar, dipped under the yellow tape and worked his way down the slope making his way towards Jack who was talking to the County Sheriff. Jack did the introductions. "Sheriff Cullpepper, Lt. Gasteneau."

Beau had worked with the Sheriff before. He was a typical 'good old boy' country Sheriff, in his middle forties with a pot belly that strained the snaps of his yellow slicker. Leaning closer to Beau, the Sheriff reported, "We have two black females and positive IDs, Millie Fergerson, age 33 and a Gale Brisby, age 28."

A honking police car interrupted the conversation. Jack looked at Beau, "That our Fed?" Ignoring the noise, Beau nodded, "Uh huh."

"What's he like?"

"It's a she. How'd you get the ID so quick?"

Jack chuckled and the Sheriff smirked as the horn sounded again. Shrugging his shoulders, Beau resigned himself to the situation. "I better go see what Linda Lovely wants." With that, he struggled up the embankment, under the tape and opened the car door. The puddle of water that had accumulated along the rim of his hat dripped onto Sally's lap as he leaned into the car.

"You got a problem?" he asked smartly.

Using another Kleenex to clear away the water, Sally asked, "I'd like to know what's going on?"

"That's what I'm trying to find out."

"Is it our guy?"

"Donno, come on out. You're the expert."

Looking at the smartass detective in frustration, she answered, "It's raining."

Beau tilted his head mockingly. More water from his hat dripped into the car. "You've got a tremendous grasp of the obvious. You on this case or not?"

As far as Beau was concerned this conversation was over. He closed the door and disappeared down the hill. Sally looked at Studs sitting in the back and said, "Is he always like this?"

The agent thought, as she looked out, "If this was his game, she could play it too. She'd handled these guys who were constantly on some ego trip. This two-bit hick cop was about as subtle as a train wreck. "Okay, if Mr.

Macho wants to play games, I'll show him games," she said, nodding to Studs. Gritting her teeth, she opened the door and stepped out into the rainy night.

Totally unprepared for this kind of action, the high heel on her good shoe sank into the wet soil, and gave a sucking sound when she was finally able to pull it out. Her shoes were immediately filled with water, red mud and grass as she hobbled into the woods. Anyone with half an eye could have seen it coming. At the top of the embankment, Sally slipped and took a Three Stooges pratt fall. Moments later she found herself sitting upright in the mud as it flowed slowly down the incline. Every police flashlight followed her down as she tried desperately not to lose her dignity. It was too late, her dignity had already been compromised. She might as well stay where she was. The whole scene looked like a kid swishing down a water slide at an amusement park in slow motion. She heard the laughter but wasn't amused. She kept her arms folded in pride as she completed her journey to the bottom. Trying to control his own laughter, Beau made his way to her, held out his hand, helped her up, and escorted her to the murder scene. While trying to remove the excess mud from her expensive skirt, Beau introduced the embarrassed agent.

"Agent Thornton, Sheriff Cullpepper and Detective Sgt. Jack Bellamy. Jack goes with us."

Sally nodded, trying to regain her dignity. "Gentlemen."

Jack continued the briefing, "The victims are school teachers from Washington Carver High School. Everyone around here knows them. Two linemen from Southeast Power found them at 7:45 PM and reported it to the Sheriff's office."

Sally cut in, "Mind if I take a look? Anyone got a raincoat?"

The Sheriff snapped his fingers and a yellow slicker was quickly draped over her shoulders. Kneeling over the bodies, the Sheriff removed the tarp. The men looked at each other as they waited for some kind of reaction from Sally. What they saw was a clinical eye examining every detail of the victims. The men knew that she'd seen it all before. Sally didn't know it, but she'd passed the first test. She had been there. She was a pro. Kneeling next to the Sheriff, Sally looked up. "Each victim has a puncture wound on the right breast. They were tortured."

Taking out a stick of gum and popping it into his mouth, Jack remarked, "Yeah, but it was the 38 in the back of the head that ruined their day." From his raincoat pocket, Jack produced two evidence bags. In one bag was a set of bloody darning needles. The other bag contained a note written on brown shopping bag paper. Jack handed Sally the note.

"The note was pinned to one of the victim's breast with these." He wiggled the bag with the needles in front of his face and looked at Beau. "It's addressed to you."

Sally began to read the note aloud. "You had your chance Gasteneau. Now it's our turn. We will kill two blacks for every white woman. Justice is mine, sayeth the Lord. Remember the good book, an eye for an eye... The White Vigilante." Standing up, Sally handed the note back to Jack.

Wiping a drop of rain from the end of his nose, Beau bellowed in disgust, "The White Vigilante? Is he serious?"

The Sheriff covered the dead victims as Sally spoke, "I'd say so," nodding at the bodies, "so would they."

"We've got ourselves a copycat," came Jack's quick reply.

"No shit, Cochise." Beau blurted it out before he remembered that a woman was present. She shot him another stern look.

Hunching his shoulders to prevent more rain from sneaking under his collar, Beau looked up at the empty road. Trying to fill the embarrassing silence, he said, "That's all we need, another psycho running loose."

The only sound was the steady beat, beat of the rain as it hit the large tarp covering the mutilated bodies.

Jack broke the silence, "You wanna know how it's gonna go down from here? First, we've got what we think is a black psycho out there, somewhere, icing white old ladies. That means the Klan is gonna jump on this and accuse every black in Charleston of operating a hate group. The brothers will demand protection. They won't get it. So, we'll have gangs running loose all over the neighborhoods. By tomorrow night, if a white man is found in a black neighborhood, he won't have a snowball's chance in hell."

Beau took a deep breath, and stuffed his hands into his coat pockets. "If either of you got any ideas now's the time to come out with it."

Sally, thinking aloud, questioned, "You think this is a Klan hit?"

Jack took a hard look at the silent Sheriff. "Does Mick Jagger have lips?"

Beau asked rhetorically, knowing the Sheriff had Klan connections, "Sheriff?"

The Sheriff's eyes darted from the black detective, to the Lieutenant, then nodded affirmatively, "I'll check it out." It was obvious the Sheriff was embarrassed. This was his county and no one did anything like this without checking with him first, not even the Klan. "You better believe I'll check it out." With that assurance, the Sheriff stomped away leaving the three detectives staring at each other.

"I'll bet." Jack said with disdain.

Sally made the connection with the Sheriff to the Klan. Looking at Beau, she remarked, "Where'll he do that? At the next meeting?" Taking Sally by the arm, Beau started to help her back to the car. This time she did not refuse his help. He looked at her with concern, "At least he's a line of communication to the Klan. You tell me how to reach the psycho?"

The streets of downtown Charleston were full of water as the runoff rushed into the flooded storm drains. The rain had diminished to a light drizzle with patches of fog beginning to form in the low-lying areas. The green neon logo of the Holiday Inn was displayed in front of a revamped turn-of-the century hotel that maintained the old South's traditional architecture. It was a shame that the modern downtown office buildings didn't carry on this tradition of clean, functional lines, with a trace of the baroque, seen in the old white pillars and majestic cornices. However, that was the price you had to pay for progress.

The police car pulled up to the curb and stopped in a "No Parking" zone in front of the hotel. Beau looked at the young agent. Sally had remained silent for the return trip. Her hair was in her eyes. Her makeup had stained the collar of her blouse. The three hundred dollar tweed suit, along with her hose and shoes, were ruined. She blew a small puff of air from her mouth to her forehead to move a curl dangling between her eyes out of the way. She looked at the man who had kept her up until two a.m., ruined her clothes, and was a scum-sucking, ego happy, son of a you-know-what.

Beau's face was blank. He revealed no emotions, no shit-eating grin, no "I told you so" look, not even a twinge of smugness. He popped the trunk, handed Sally her carry on bag and said, "See you tomorrow, 08:30 sharp. 34th and Grand. Six blocks in that direction." He ended his statement by pointing his finger down the street and thinking to himself, "If she wants to be treated like one of the guys, so be it."

Sally was just too tired to argue. She'd been going since five-thirty this morning. She wanted to soak in a hot tub and a good night's sleep. She nodded, retrieved her bags and hobbled towards the front door. As she turned her back, Beau grinned for the first time. The sight of the tired and muddy agent was too much for him. He had to smile. She looked like a ruptured peacock with a broken leg as she waddled through the revolving door. Putting the car in gear, he drove off into the night.

Arriving at the squad room, Beau hung his wet coat on the stand by the door. Studs curled up in his usual place. Jack was on the phone with the Sheriff. Beau found himself getting to like his new partner. He was a professional doing his job and he was good at it. Pouring himself a cup of coffee, he stood in front of Jack's desk as he finished his conversation.

"Yeah, anything else? Well, we appreciate your help. You hear of anything, let us know. Thank you." Jack hung up and looked at Beau. "The Sheriff swears it wasn't a Klan hit."

Beau savored his coffee. "You expect him to say anything else?"

"Nope."

Jack picked up his cup and took a long swig of the bitter brew.

"Did you notice how the victim's hands were tied?" Beau asked, "Seen that before. Those were professional executions."

Jack nodded, put his cup down as the doors to the Operations room swung open and a pathetic, pissed-off, Sally entered, dragging her bag. Jack had to control himself or he would burst out laughing. To Jack, she looked like a rookie at the Police Academy who had just finished last on the obstacle course. He looked at Beau's expressionless face. What was going on between these two, he wondered. He waited for one of them to speak. Puffing a curl out of her face, in a tired voice with undertones of anger, Sally said, "The hotel's full!"

"I thought you had a reservation?"

"For tomorrow. They can't get me in tonight."

Jack could see it was time to bail out. "Would you two mind excusing me? I'd like to leave and reacquaint myself with my family."

With that diplomatic statement, Jack retrieved his coat and headed for the door. "Nice to see you again, Agent Thornton. Have fun." Popping Beau a quick smile, he made a hasty retreat. The two adversaries stared in silence as the swinging doors flapped in the breeze.

"I can't believe there're no rooms. Couldn't the clerk get you into another hotel?"

Sally let her bag drop to the floor, "I asked, but I didn't know Charleston was the Mecca for conventions. You've got three in town right now. I can get a room in East Podunk, but that's it."

For the first time, she saw that male chauvinist, shit-eating grin on the Lieutenant's face. "Cup of coffee?"

Limping over to the detective, she put her dirty face in front of his. While puffing at that persistent curl hanging in her face, she let it all hang out. "Look!, (puff) I've been going since five-thirty this morning. (puff) I'm tired, wet, dirty, and definitely pissed. I want a bath, (puff) a soft pillow, (puff) no bullshit, and my share of Z's. Now, you got any ideas?"

This little confrontation had Studs up, panting as he sniffed at Sally's muddy skirt. Beau glanced at the dog as though asking his permission, "How about it Buddy? Think we can put her up for the night?"

"No way, Jose!" came Sally's reply to the obvious solution, "I'm not sleeping with any dog."

"Yeah, I guess you've got a better shot with me."

47

"In your dreams Buddyboy. I'd take the dog first."

Setting down his cup, Beau put on his coat and opened the door, then gestured like Sir Walter Raleigh. Sally resigned herself to the situation and picked up her bag. Talking to the ceiling, she made her way towards the door. "The Incredible Hulk and his dog. Why dear God are you doing this to me?"

The door to Beau's apartment opened. He flicked on the lights as he ushered Sally into his private domain, still reflecting his "early slob" motif. This time Sally allowed him to carry her bag. Rushing ahead of her, Beau hastily picked up discarded newspapers and a few stray sports magazines.

"Make yourself at home," then seeing the expression on her face as she observed the apartment he said, "Suppose I better tidy up a bit."

"What are you gonna do, call the Sanitation Department?"

"Well it doesn't have matching wallpaper, drapes and cutsie-pie slipcovers but I call it home."

"I'd call it a disaster area. I suppose there's a beer in the 'fridge?"

"Bear to the right and hang a sharp left. Second shelf."

As Sally headed for the kitchen, Beau made a fast dash for the bedroom. Moving like a professional hockey player, he swept across the floor kicking empty beer cans under the bed as he gathered up jockey shorts, shirts, socks and an assortment of women's undergarments and stuffed them in his closet. Next stop the bathroom, where he snatched some drying socks and T-shirts from the shower rod and dropped them into an already overflowing hamper. This done, he scooped up his shaving gear and deposited all of it into his travel kit. Grabbing a towel, he quickly wiped down the sink, and erased a few dried sprinkles from the mirror. Giving the surroundings one last look, turned out the light.

"Yuck!" Sally muttered to herself as she eyed the sink full of dirty dishes. The inside of the 'fridge wasn't much better, it's ingredients bore the look of a garbage disposal gone amok. Gingerly, she reached in between a half loaf of moldy bread, a plate of week-old chili, a bottle of kosher pickles and grabbed two cans of cold beer, drawing her hands out quickly before they became contaminated.

"Mind if I take mine to bed with me? It's been a long day."

"The bedroom's right this way," Beau said, picking up her bag. "One king-size bed and private bath. Bathrobe's on the bed."

Poking her head inside the bedroom, she surveyed the now somewhat acceptable accommodations when Studs took the hem of her skirt in his mouth and began to tug her inside.

"You teach him to do that?"

Beau shrugged and grinned, "He's got a mind of his own."

"I'll bet." She shot Studs a look that he immediately understood. This was a no-nonsense lady. She looked at Beau.

"Is there a lock on the door?"

"Hey, we're professionals…"

"It's not you I'm worried about. It's him!"

Beau glanced at Studs, shrugged and pointed to the door. Studs was not too happy about it but out he went.

"Thanks," Sally said, offering a small smile. "Oh, and thanks for the bed, bath and beer."

"Nothing you wouldn't do for me."

"I doubt it," she replied wryly and closed the door. A moment later Beau heard the lock to the bedroom door click shut. Minutes later, he heard the bathroom shower running full out.

Not feeling a bit sleepy, he looked around the room and decided that the place could use a little spit and polish. It took him all of ten minutes to prop up some pillows, pick up some old newspapers, toss them down the compactor chute, stacked the dishes in the dishwasher and put some fresh coffee in his Mr. Coffee machine.

"Is that fresh coffee I smell?" Sally called from inside the bedroom.

"Sorry, no room service. You want some, come and get it."

He had just poured the second cup when Sally entered wearing his blue terry cloth robe, toweling her hair. Without a stitch of makeup she was even more beautiful than he remembered. A number of Charleston's available women had visited his abode but none had ever filled his robe as well as Sally did. He handed her a cup, picking up his own, they moved into the living room.

"I see you've been busy," she smiled, glancing around the room.

"It needed to be straightened up," he admitted, "Been a little preoccupied these past few weeks."

"So I see," she said, plucking a size 36C cup brassiere from behind a couch pillow where Beau had hastily stashed it only minutes before.

"Sorry," Beau swallowed, his face reddening as he snatched the bra from Sally's hand and quickly plunged it into the first vacant drawer he could find.

"Question is, was she in a hurry when she got here or when she was leaving?"

"Frankly, that's none of your business." He hesitated, "If you must know, it was my therapist."

"Sure it was," she said trying to stifle her laugh at Beau's discomfort. "My apologies. You're absolutely right Lieutenant. It's none of my business," she chuckled, sitting down on the couch. "So let's talk business."

"Good idea. How long have you been a shrink?"

"I'm not a shrink," she corrected, "I'm a Behavioral Scientist. I don't try to cure'em, I just try to figure them out."

"Figure any out so far?"

"I worked the Hillside Strangler and the Lucas cases. That and a few others. Why don't you get to the point. You want to know how much help I can be, right?"

"You've got it."

Cradling her cup in both hands, Sally rose and walked around the room casually studying the various photos and police awards.

"Okay, my job's going after serial killers and I'm good at it, or does that bother you that a woman can be good at her job?"

"The truth? I don't care if you're a gorilla as long as you get the job done. You've read the reports. You know as much as we do. Why's he killing old ladies?"

Sally's gaze continued to roam the room as she spoke, addressing him as if she were lecturing her students at Quantico.

"That's your problem, Lieutenant. You're a cop and think like a cop. The first thing a cop always looks for is a motive when the first thing you should start with is the man. Serial killers don't have motives. Find out what kind a person he is. What's he like? How does he think? Try to build some sort of a psychological profile with whom you're dealing. For example, Carlton Gary, Remember him? His killings were ritual reenactments of a horrific experience as a child. Only this time the killer reverses the roles he occupied in his childhood experience. This way he reverses the suffering and reestablishes his own power and identity. To make my point, another case comes to mind. A guy named Edmund Kemper killed his mother whose nagging voice had dominated his every thought throughout his childhood. As his final act of murder, again to symbolize his victory, he cut out her vocal chords, threw them in the garbage disposal and brought her head to his apartment and used it as a dart board for several days. My point is, there is a common thread that ties the murders together. We have to find that thread."

"And just how do you find that when you've nothing to work with?"

"We look for patterns," Sally replied. "For example, most serial killers are male. Usually between twenty to forty years of age. The fact that the one we're looking for performed two sexual acts, each with ejaculation hours apart, would lead me to conclude that our killer is both young and healthy."

"But he had sex with his victims after he killed them."

"Or.. while he was killing them. Serial killers often have the need to maintain a high degree of control over their victims but seldom get any gratification from the sexual act themselves. More often, it's the act of killing that really gets them off. I'd say our killer is on the shy, mild side, afraid to confront anyone normally. Thus the sex during or immediately following death."

"Go on."

"They're often elated by their power and their deed and are so fascinated with their kill that they'll maintain records, photographs, newspaper clippings of their crimes and of their victims. They're mostly sociopaths with little or no friends or family and they usually like to move around. He's been in trouble before. I suggest one of the first things we do is check the M.O. of our killer with as many other police departments as possible.

"Which is icing little old ladies." Beau replied rhetorically.

"Serial killers aren't born, they're created," Sally said, seating herself on the couch and crossing her legs, causing the robe she was wearing to separate and show just enough leg and thigh to momentarily distract Beau. She adjusted the robe and continued. "They're products of their environment. Almost all of them were abused children.."

"Are you saying that maybe this guy is killing his mother over and over again?"

"I don't know," Sally shook her head. "What's throwing me is the ritualism of these murders. Mainly, the serving of tea to his already dead victims. However, be forewarned that the disease could very well be in the process of development. The symptoms and the M.O. may change as he does. That's about all I can tell you right now until I visit some of the crime scenes."

"What do you expect to find there that we haven't found already?"

"When you're looking for the man and not the motive? You'd be surprised. Take you for example. I know you're a man in a hurry. Strong willed, opinionated, distrustful of women, unable to sustain a relationship for any protracted period of time. I know you're recently divorced and still carry some of the pain around with you."

"And just how did you come to all those conclusions?" Beau questioned sternly.

"Like I said, I don't try to cure anyone, I just figure them out." Sally said smugly. "All I had to do was go to your closet, see the food you ate, the way you keep house, listen to you talk, and find one woman's photograph laying in the drawer of your night stand, face down."

Beau nodded. "Okay, maybe I'm no behavioral scientist but now it's my turn. I'd say you have strong feminist feelings. You're the consummate upward, mobile yuppie type. You're 32 years old, give or take three years, drive a '92 maybe a 95 Buick, you're lousy at balancing a checkbook, determined to make a name for yourself, but so far you've been harassed every step of the way. You've been married, or had a serious relationship, which didn't work out either, and I believe you have a kid running around your house back in Washington."

Sally glared at him. "How the hell did you find that out?"

Beau smiled, "That's just good police work lady. Once a cop always a cop. I also listened and I went through your purse and your wallet. Saw the photo of your kid."

"You're a real smart-ass, aren't you?" Sally said.

"Depends on the company I keep." Beau replied with just a hint of a smile.

"Well, this company is going to bed."

Rising, she walked to the bedroom door. "Nighty-night Lieutenant," she said with a beguiling smile and closed the door behind her.

Beau and Studs looked after her, then hearing the click of the lock, Studs gave Beau a questioning look.

"Not tonight, fella, but I'm working on it."

Chapter Four:

The Unholy Alliance

It was an upper middle class neighborhood in the suburbs of west Charleston. The tree-lined streets with well kept lawns reminded you of a Norman Rockwell painting of middle America. It was predominately a black neighborhood, yet it had none of the trappings of the south side Charleston ghetto. Both blacks and whites, who resided in this community, worked together and took pride in who they were. The blacks were doctors, lawyers, engineers, the upper middle class professionals of greater Charleston.

The First Evangelical Baptist Church was constructed of red Virginia clay brick. It gave the building a bright, clean, new look when contrasted against the white columns that supported the steepled roof. Positioned on the roof was a tower that housed a bell said to be taken from a church that was burned at the Battle of Atlanta during the Civil War. The congregation, still hanging on to tradition, rung the bell every Sunday to signal the beginning of services.

The parsonage was a southern classic, two story red brick building that complemented the church. It was set aside from the main church grounds by a small garden cemetery that surrounded three large Charter oaks. No one knew the age of the oaks, only that they had been there long before the Civil War.

Jack Bellamy parked his car in the space next to the one marked "Pastor." Stepping out, he flipped his coat over his shoulder and walked towards the parsonage. In mid-stride the door opened and two children, an eight your old boy Michael, and a six year old girl, Malissa, both dressed in jeans and football sweatshirts, came running out yelling, "Daddy, Daddy". Jack scooped them up and placed one on each shoulder. They giggled and gave each other the high five while perched precariously on dad's shoulder for the short ride to the door. After promising to come out and play later, he put them down, shooshed them away, then entered the parsonage.

Emma Joe Bellamy greeted Jack from the kitchen, "Is that you, honey?"

"Yeah," Jack responded as he headed in the direction of Emma's voice. Emma Joe was a strong woman, who had stood beside Jack through college. She did without so Jack could finish the University of Pennsylvania with his degree in Criminal Justice. She gave up her education so he could get his. After the kids arrived, she never had the time to go back. To her, it was better if the kids had a full time mother. Jack reluctantly agreed. Emma had been a determined child who kept her dignity while growing up, struggling to get out of the Charleston ghetto. With a father who deserted her, and the

Reverend Jesse Baxter as her stepfather, she made her way to the University of Pennsylvania on a scholarship and met Jack. She had seen her share of adversity and leaned on her mother for advise, which was always there. With a loving hug and a pat on the head, Mary Rose Baxter cared for Emma during those troubled years of the sixties.

Emma sat at the kitchen table nursing a cup of coffee, trying to hold back the tears.

"What's a matter?" Jack said, knowing that Mary Rose had had another bad day.

"We almost lost her."

"How bad is it?" Jack questioned as he put his hands gently on her shoulders. Emma kissed his hand struggling for her words. "She isn't going to last. I mean, they say it's only a matter of time. If she'd gone to the doctor when she first felt ill, maybe," She searched for the right words, "Maybe we could'a saved her. It's too late now."

"I know," Jack acknowledged, gripping her shoulder a little tighter, to let her know he felt her pain too. "It's always the good ones. She's worked too long and hard. She deserves more out a life."

"What are the kids going to do? What do we tell them about their Grandma?"

"You tell 'em the truth. They're good kids, they'll understand," Jack advised as he sat down in front of Emma.

"Suppose you're right, but I can't…"

"Don't worry," Jack interrupted. "I'll tell them."

The Reverend Jesse Baxter quietly closed the door to Mary Rose's bedroom then leaned against it with his head slightly bowed. Taking out his handkerchief he wiped the tears from his eyes with his shaking hands. It took at least thirty seconds for Jesse to regain his composure and walk towards the kitchen.

Emma looked at Jack, smiled, and gripped his hand, thanking him for being there when she needed him. Jack was her pillar of strength. With him, she could lick any adversity that came along. With Emma, Jack felt that he could do anything, and be the best at what he did. They were not only lovers but friends who had promised to meet whatever life gave them together.

"It's about time you showed up!" Jesse blurted out from the doorway.

Jack stood up and met his cold stare head on. "I'm sorry, I couldn't get away any sooner."

"You can never get away any sooner. Is that all you can ever think about is your job? What about your job to your family? Or, is that asking too much for the great detective from Philly?"

"Jesse, don't jump on Jack."

"You shut up!" Jesse roared as he pointed his finger at his stepdaughter.

Jack grew tense with a long felt hatred for this man, a man who held God on his sleeve for everyone to see. He hated hypocrites and this man was one of the first order. Jack still held himself in check as Jesse began his tirade.

"You've got a woman in there that loves you like a son and has been calling for you all day and you've been out pussy-footin around with your cop friends, Lord knows where, boozin and drinking and sinnin'."

Jack's eyes narrowed and took on a blazing fire. He glanced from Emma to Jesse as his jaws continued to tighten. Jack could see that Emma was afraid of Jesse. He had beat that into her mind at a very young age. Pointing out to her at every opportunity, how saintly he was for taking her and her mother in. All her life Jesse made her feel like poor swamp trash. He made sure everyone in the parish knew that he had been a good samaritan by marrying Mary Rose. The Reverend Baxter saw himself as another Martin Luther King but never had the personal integrity to pull it off. To most of the congregation he was a shining example, a man of God, a leader. To Jack he was just another professional black who raised racism to an artform.

The Reverend was sure he had the upper hand as he went on. "Where I come from, a man takes care of his family first."

"Bullshit!" Jack roared surprising himself, Emma, and catching Jesse in mid-sentence causing his jaw to drop open.

"You've got more shit in you than a Christmas turkey." Jack leveled his pent up anger at Jesse with spades. "You are the biggest fucking hypocrite who ever put on a white collar."

"How dare you swear in this house."...

Jack cut him off, "I'll swear any fucking place I feel like it and you can stuff it. I've worked all my life to get where I am and I took a two year drop in seniority to take this job so Emma could be close to Mary Rose. You wouldn't give up one Sunday for that woman lying in there and she is about as close to a saint as anyone can get. You! You Bible thumpin' son-of-a-bitch are going to be damn lucky to lick her boots when you get to heaven. Hell, I don't even think they'll let you in." Jack moved closer to Jesse, staring him down like he did when he questioned felons at police headquarters. Jesse hadn't seen this side of Jack and was taken by surprise.

"You stand up there on your pulpit and spout scriptures and you haven't got the slightest idea what it means. You haven't got one ounce of love in you. Ever since Emma and Mary Rose came here you've been putting them down. You haven't said it, but you've made them believe they're black trash, stupid, lazy. Well I've got news for you, Reverend," Jack caught himself, just in time. He hesitated, looking at the astonished old man who had just got his come uppence. Jack stepped back and took another breath before he went on.

"In case you haven't noticed, there's a God damn serial killer out there murdering the good people of this community and now we've got some hot head Klan guy with a sheet over his head murdering black women, and this town is gonna blow itself wide open, so pardon me if I'm just a little busy right now." Jack paused to get his breath, "You know something? Mary Rose would understand. That's the kinda woman she is." Jack moved in a little closer to Jesse, breathing into his face. "I'm only gonna say this once, so, as the big man says, 'read my lips.' If I ever hear you speak to Emma again in that tone of voice, Reverend or no Reverend, I'm gonna come down here and punch your lights out. You got that!? And if you ever lay a hand on her or any of my kids, I'll kill you right where you stand."

Jesse stood silent with his back braced against the wall. Jack backed off and looked at Emma who stood with her hands over her mouth.

"Now, I'm gonna go see Mary Rose." Slowly, Jack's tension eased. He took one gasp of air and walked out of the silent kitchen.

Mary Rose held out her frail hand and motioned Jack to her bedside. Trying not to show the pain, she smiled and asked, "How's my big black policeman?"

"Just fine Mary Rose, just fine." Gently taking her hand, he pulled the stool closer to her bedside. "How's my favorite girl doing?"

"Fair-to-middlelin; I guess."

Jack kissed her on the forehead and sat down. "You're not in any pain are you?"

"Pain and I are old friends, son. We are old friends." Mary said with a slight inflection in her voice as she tried to get comfortable. "What is all that hollerin going on out there?"

"I'm sorry, Mary, I kinda' lost my cool."

"Don't you pay a nevermind to that old man with the white collar."

"I'll try." Jack said, trying to calm Mary Rose.

"He means well. I know he's a pompous old fart, but he's done well by me and Emma. After all these years, I really believe I love him and he loves me." Mary Rose chuckled as if joking to herself. "Now's a hell of a time to find that out." She began to cough and motioned for a glass of water at her bedside. The hacking cough subsided as the cool water was drained from the glass.

"Detective Sergeant Jack Bellamy, soon to be Lieutenant, hmm, hmm, I am sure proud of you... Emma is finally happy and two beautiful grandchildren." Mary Rose shook her head in delight and smiled. "Son, don't you worry about me, where I'm going I won't be alone. I'll be happy knowin that Emma and the kids are happy." She gripped his hand a little tighter and looked at Jack as if it was for the last time. Jack knew. He held back the tears. They stuck like a lump in his throat. He bit his lip to hold his emotions in check.

"Now, go on, git, before you say something stupid and sentimental. 'Sides, I want to see my grandchildren."

Jack leaned over and kissed her on the forehead. He moved a small lock of hair that was out of place, gripped her hand tightly for one last time, got up, and walked out of the room wanting to look back, but afraid of what he might see. He wanted to remember Mary Rose as she was at that minute. He had seen too many dead bodies, twisted and torn by some ugly madness. Not Mary Rose. Her memory was going to stay just as it was, peaceful, a memory of a good woman, a good mother, and a deep friendship that was coming to an end.

Emma stood in the dining room with the kids. Malissa tugged at her mother's skirt and sucked her thumb. The child knew that something was wrong but was too frightened to ask. Her sad brown eyes looked up at her father hoping he would make everything all right. Michael clutched his mother's other hand. He stood tall and erect, trying to be a big boy but did a little side step to stay close to her. Jack wondered to himself if his kids would have it better than he had. How would they handle discrimination? When it happens to them, what do I tell them? Maybe, just maybe, we've grown up and these kids will be able to be the best they can be without regard to their color.

"Grandma wants to see the kids."

Emma nodded and walked the kids into the bedroom.

Jesse was standing at the bay window that looked out onto the small garden cemetery. Looking at Jack's reflection, he spoke to the window. "Mary Rose will be buried right next to that big old charter oak. A beautiful place, don't you think?"

"You told her what she was going to do all her life, there's no reason you shouldn't tell her what to do when she dies," came Jack' terse response. The remark didn't phase the Reverend. He continued to look out the window.

"You happy now? Anything else you wanna' get off your chest?"

Jack let the remark pass. The Reverend continued, "That was where she wanted to rest and I have a piece of ground next to her."

"Sorry," Jack answered.

"Don't be sorry for me, the Lord called me to take care of my children and I have."

"That's a crock and you know it."

"At least I don't have to be an Uncle Tom for the city."

Jack had been waiting for that remark to come out. Now it was time to clear the air. He responded to the Reverend's insult by telling him the truth.

"You have any idea what they call you downtown? You are the head spear chucker at the local welfare office. That's not just the white guys callin you that, it's the blacks too. You ever notice that your congregation is getting smaller each day? You haven't got anything to say to an intelligent blackman. You're not talking to a bunch of black sharecroppers anymore. Most of us have skills, we've been educated and we work for the system. You're still back in the sixties. You'll take some poor dumb bastard down to the welfare office and get him another handout and that's it... When the poor sonofabitch wants an education." Jack paused letting his words sink in, "Can't you see that you're not getting anyone out of poverty, just getting handout after handout. And you know what scares me? I think you want it that way. I think you get some perverse feeling of superiority out of being the Reverend Jesse Baxter."

Without looking back the Reverend walked out of the house and headed for the church. Jack didn't want it to be this way, but he just couldn't handle the lying anymore. He felt sorry for the man as he watched him walk away with his head down.

Brenner Woods was a small uncut stand of old oaks, walnut and hickory in the middle of a pulp pine forest. The Brenner Paper Company had left the area untouched and used it as a private campground for Brenner employees. It was a quiet area tucked away from the Interstate by five miles of winding dirt road.

Nestled in a small valley, it had all the conveniences not normally found at a state park, hot showers, club house, and a dance pavilion. Miller's Creek twisted it's way through the small valley creating picturesque fishing holes that would have made Huck Finn envious. At the far end of the valley, Miller's Creek emptied into Butler's Pond where the old grist mill still turned out a local buckwheat flour that was known throughout the state.

The grist mill was dark with all the doors securely padlocked. On the second floor, a small opening in the shutter scanned the picnic area, parking lot and the only road into the narrow valley. Detectives Bill Travers and Mark Stoner scanned the area with a night vision digital camera. The green images of cars and trucks moving along the road were displayed across a small screen. Strategically placed in the assembly area were highly sensitive miniature microphones that could record the slightest sound. "How's the camera working?" Bill asked as he adjusted the headphones and volume control on the tape recorder.

"Coming over five square, take a look." Mark replied. Bill bent over to look at the green tinted screen as several trucks passed the old grist mill.

"How about the sound?" Mark inquired. They had to make sure that they were getting both pictures and sound. A full blown intelligence effort had been put into effect. The Klan had been penetrated with undercover operatives, phone taps, and mail intercept operations, but they still needed more than Klan rhetoric, hard proof that the Klan was planning some type of reprisal.

"Looks like we've got the same old group. No surprises" Mark commented watching the little green screen.

"Oops! I spoke too soon. Here's one I don't recognize. It's an outta state." Bill stood up and took some quick still shots of the new arrival using a telephoto lens. Both detectives made feverish entries in their log book as the Klan arrived.

"You get the number?" Mark asked.

"Got it," Bill replied and made an entry into the log book.

The park was a long time meeting place for the Klan. No one really cared if the Klan held it's meetings in Brenner Park, it was out of sight and would attract little attention. The nasal twang of Willie Nelson, blue grass fiddling, and good old country music blared out into the night. It was a calm night, overcast, with the moon breaking through at irregular intervals. The weather forecast had no rain in it except along the coast, with fog in the inland and low lying areas. Cars, trucks, RV's, and tractors were parked on the edge of the outdoor pavilion. Men, women, and children in white Klan dress, moved about preparing for tonight's gathering. A robed man, with his white pointed hat tilted to one side, joked with friends, as he handed out beer from the back of an old pickup. On the side of the red truck in gold, bold lettering, was a logo that read, "Wayford Feed & Grain." Women laid out home cooked food on the big table as two Klansmen made final adjustments to the P.A. system. Young teenagers, dancing in their Klan robes made it look like a Pagan ritual was about to begin with some human sacrifice to be their reward. The revelers twisted, twirled, and kicked up their heels to the frenzied beat of the twangy country music. In the center of the meeting area a large bonfire was set. The flames leaped into the air, and engulfed the burning cross, growing higher and higher as the music increased it's tempo. The flames tossed it's flickering light against the twirling white robed dancers who were shouting their high pitched rebel cry. Old men, farmers, and kids clapped to the music as the square dancers took the tempo to an even higher level.

As the dance reached it's climax, the music stopped. Dancers, caught in mid-stride, stopped and turned towards the dirt road that approached the pavilion. Click!. Click! The stake out night vision cameras silently snapped instant photos of the big limo. The army of sheeted Klansmen crowded along the road to watch a long white limo turn into the parking area and stop. The crowd was hushed as it waited. The side windows of the car were mirrored as if to hide some celebrity. The front doors opened and two armed men, obviously bodyguards, got out and approached the Klan leader. They exchanged whispered words. Satisfied, they returned to the car, opened the back door and, bedecked in his purple robes, Duncan "Duke" Delchamp, the Klan's Grand Dragon, stepped out. The crowd went wild with cheers. Men rushed to shake his hand. Women presented their children to the Grand Dragon. He was like a politician on election day, shaking hands, and kissing babies as he greeted the crowd. Duke Delchamp was tall, blonde, blue-eyed, in his late thirties, with an athletic body. He looked like he stepped from the cover of Gentlemen's Quarterly. It was common knowledge that he was a lawyer, educated at Harvard Law School, and an unsuccessful candidate for Governor during the last election. What surprised the media was, he came close to winning. It was a foregone conclusion that he would run again and that made a lot of people in the state nervous. From the other side of the limo, another man, wearing a gray cloak, got out and moved to the side of the Grand Dragon. Duke, introduced him to the Klan elders. The crowd was silent as the man removed his cloak revealing a Nazi uniform. The swastika was prominently displayed on the arm of his brown military shirt. He wore high leather boots with jodhpur pants and a stiff military cap with an SS emblem of the thirties. An unknown voice from the crowd whispered, "That's Gerhart Meinich". With that acknowledgment, the crowd cheered. Gerhart Meinich was the Oberfurher of the Neo-Nazi movement in the United States. The crowd continued to cheer as the men made their way to the dais.

With his pointed hat turning in little circles above his head, the Klan leader raised his hands and asked for quiet over the P.A. system. As the noise settled to a murmur, the Grand Dragon stepped up to the podium and began to speak.

"You'al know why we're here. For the past seven months our families… our women have lived in fear for their very lives." He paused gathering his thoughts, then went on. "We are law abiden' people by nature. We let the law do its job. But they've been covering up on us. They knew all the time that the killer out there was black. But the black Mayor and those bleedin heart liberals were afraid to tell the truth. Well, we know the truth! and we're gonna do something about it before some judge sets the nigger free, if'n they catch him, right?" The crowd responded with a resounding, "Right!", followed by other racial slurs. He waited for his audience to calm, then continued. "It's a sad day when I have to come to you under these circumstances… It's an evil time in which we live my friends. We have a Jewish controlled media, more and more blacks are eroding our Federal Government." Making gestures with his hands, his voice building with resentment, he went on. "We are losing whole states to black politicians. Blacks are feeding on our welfare system, taking us deeper in debt while you break your backs trying to feed your family. Who pays for it?! You do.

The blacks don't pay. They demand this, and they demand that, but they don't pay... Those blacks that do work come in and take your jobs under some sort of a quota system. They take jobs they're not qualified for only because they are black." The crowd murmurs again in agreement.

"Your God given rights we fight for in the courts. Your dues are used to keep those rights, your rights, alive in the minds and heart of all white men. But this, what is happening to the good white folks in Charleston, cannot be fought in the courts and it cannot and will not be tolerated. The time for action is now!" The crowd erupted again in angry shouts of racial slurs. The Grand Dragon held up his hands and the crowd grew silent. "Folks, it is my pleasure to present to you, The Director of the White Aryan Society, Mr. Gary Meinich!" The crowd responded with a loud roar of approval. Moving to the mike, Gary waited for the crowd to calm before speaking. "Friends, Mr. Delchamp has eloquently summarized our problem." Gary paused gathering his thoughts. "As I pondered my visit with you tonight I thought that if my Creator could give me one gift it would be to connect you with the hearts and minds of the great men in our history who fought for their freedom. I want that gift now, to reconnect you with your own sense of liberty... Your own freedom of thought, your own sense of what decent law-biding white folks deserve." Gary paused, waiting for his words to touch each individual. "As I think back, I recall the words of Abraham Lincoln who said, "We are now engaged in a great Civil War, testing whether this nation or any nation so conceived and so dedicated can long endure."

Gary paused again forming his words carefully. "I believe that we are again engaged in a great civil war, a cultural war that's about to subvert your birthright to think and say what resides in your heart. I am here, my cause is here and now, my life is dedicated to this time because I fear you no longer trust the pulsating heartbeat of liberty inside you. That is the stuff our white forefathers had in their hearts. It was the love of freedom that made this country rise from the wilderness into the greatness it is today." The crowd responded with a loud applause. Gary motioned again for quiet and continued. "Think back, look at what you see on TV and read in the newspapers. If you read between the lines you'll come to understand that the cultural war is raging across this land, with a media-backed big-brotherism that tells you that only certain acceptable thoughts and speech are mandated. I remember last year I addressed an audience and told them that white pride is just as valid as black pride and they called me a racist. As God is my witness, then I am a racist because I believe this to be true and it is my right." The crowd roared with approval at his last words. Gary could hear the complementing remarks coming from the Klan gathering. He knew he was pressing all the right buttons. He began again. "I am a God fearing man. Like you I live by the Good Book. But when I told an audience that gay rights should extend no further than your rights or my rights I was called a homophobe." Half the audience applauded and the other half murmured to themselves asking, "what the hell is a homophobe?" Gary waited to make sure everyone understood his last sentence. He began again, "There seems to be an undertow of new customs, new rules, new anti-intellectual theories being pushed upon us from the black community and its media lackeys. Think about it, underneath, this nation a storm is about to break loose. Oklahoma is a vivid example. All white Americans know something without a name is undermining the nation, turning mushy rhetoric when it comes to separating truth from falsehood and right from wrong. You know if we were members of the National Association for the Advancement of White People, we would immediately come under the investigation of the FBI. The IRS would come down on us like a ton of bricks and the scum-sucking media like Sixty Minutes would descend on us like a swarm of locust. I ask you do you see anything like that happening to the NAACP? No you don't!! You don't like it, I don't like it, and its time, like our forefathers, to stand and fight! And I promise you, fight we will!"

Raising his fist in the air, he pounded on the podium as he spoke. "We are sick and tired of the lies. We are fed up with legalized black racism! We will not submit to allowing our good women to be murdered in their beds by some black animal who will plead insanity and be free in two years... It stops now! No more! We are one and we are with you!!" The crowd had worked itself into a frenzy as it cheered and fired guns into the air. Gary pushed his arms up into the air calling for silence. Again the crowd responded with calm.

"We will provide security patrols, busing, neighborhood watches, and we'll collect money from those good citizens who are sick and tired of our do nothing black police force... I can't tell you where, when, or how, but we will strike. The people of Charleston will know ten times the terror of Oklahoma City. Do you hear me?!! We will strike! We will strike!" The crowd picked up on Gary's words and began to chant, "We will strike!, We will strike! We will strike!." With every chant, Gary stood erect, with his chin protruding like Il Duche and gave the Hitler salute.

The detectives in the grist mill stakeout had every word on tape. Travers looked at Stoner and spoke. "He's good. He almost had me convinced." Stoner shook his head wondering how all this was going to turn out. "Shit, I sure wish I had a couple of months leave coming. I don't want any part of this." I think we're gonna have a pretty good idea of what Hitler was talking about in a few days." Travers replied picking up the cell phone then dialing some numbers. Stoner moved closer to the phone so he could hear Beau's remarks.

"Hello"

"Beau, are you awake?"

"Yeah"

"The shit has just hit the fan. Listen." Travers held the phone to the tape recorder, adjusted the volume, and played the last few lines of the speech. Beau could hear the words, "we will strike, we will strike." Putting the phone to his ear Travers spoke, "What did I tell you. Was I right or was I right. eh? We've got the Hitler Youth and the Klan joining up."

Beau barked his orders over the phone. "Okay, get some copies made, and get that tape over to the D.A and the Mayor. I want the FBI's Regional Director in on this. Then see that a copy gets to the Governor. You got that?"

"Yeah," Travers responded nodding at Stoner.

"And another thing. Get that video tape to the lab and see if you can pull some numbers from the cars."

"Gotcha. Oh, Beau, in case you didn't recognize the voice, that last speech was from our friend, the Furher, you know, Adolf from the last riots we had here. We didn't just have a bunch of speechafyin by some beergut rednecks. These guys are highly pissed. The head miffwick said it was gonna be ten time worse than Oklahoma City."

"Thanks guys, you've really made my day. Later."

The detectives cut off the conversation and began to pack their equipment.

It was a quiet, predominately white, neighborhood on the northeast side of the city. They were upscale homes that reflected the rich architectural history of Charleston. The clear night had given away to coastal fog. The police car moved slowly through the area flashing it's spotlight into the dark wooded areas between the old homes. Through the windshield the officers saw a black man get out of his car, go through an iron gate, and disappear into the fog. Taking his hand from the steering wheel, the driver nudged his partner. "That's him, I know it."

"Aw, come on Chet, you're seeing this guy everytime you turn around. That guy is not sneaking around. If he is he's not very clever."

The driver turned his vehicle down Bay Drive as he rationalized, "Yeah, then what's a black guy doing in this neighborhood this time of night? Remember, this guy can get in anyplace without so much as breaking a window." His partner sat silently thinking it over, then gave in. Handing the rookie a shotgun, he said, "Okay, if it'll make you feel better, we'll take his ass." Picking up the mike, he barked into the radio. "Unit 1224 has a ten-sixty six. A possible four sixty in progress at 781 Bay Drive, we'll be on foot for ten minutes."

"Ten-four", came the dispatcher's routine answer.

The old man was in his middle sixties. Slightly overweight and walked with a limp. He had rounded shoulders from years of hard work which had brought on premature arthritis. His hair was curly white and he peeked occasionally over his Ben Franklin glasses as he searched for the backdoor key, murmuring to himself. "Landsakes, that woman has the mind of a butterfly. Knowing her, she tells me the key is under the mat, I'll bet my britches it's above the doorsill." Reaching up, he found the key and chuckled to himself as he inserted the key into the lock.

"Hold it right there mister!" Came a sharp order. The flashlight beam blinded him. The old man jumped, dropping the key as he held up his forearm, shading his eyes. "You scared the living be-Jesus outa me."

There was a brief silence as the officers examined the suspect. The officer with the flashlight had his weapon drawn and his partner stood to the left with the shotgun ready. From behind the light, the officers continued to question. "Whatcha doin here?"

The frightened old man began to stutter, "Ah, sa, sa, Sir, I, I, I am…"

The officer cut him off waving the shotgun towards the door. "Spread'em. Face against the wall."

The confused old man tried to explain. "What do you ma.. ma.. mean? I.. I.. I.. work for Ma.. Ma.. Mrs. Moorehouse. I just went to the st.. st.. store to pick up her prescription. Look, it's right here." Moving towards the officers, he reached quickly into his coat pocket. In mid-stride a shotgun blast hit the man like a Mac Truck, lifting him up and punching him through the back door. The body slid across the white linoleum floor coming to rest in front of the kitchen table. With guns still ready, moving cautiously, the officers stepped through the splintered door. The police man, with the flashlight, felt for a pulse. The moving light revealed a bloody hole where the old man's chest used to be. A large trail of blood lay pooled on the white kitchen floor. The force of the blast had knocked the old man some ten feet into the kitchen. Holstering his weapon, the officer carefully looked into the coat pocket of the victim. Under the beam, the officer examined a wallet and a small paper bag containing medicine and a prescription receipt. The young rookie officer was shaking with fear as he watched his partner examine the contents. The kneeling officer lowered his head in resignation, then looked up.

"Geez! he was telling the truth."

"Hell, how was I to know," came the excuse from the young officer.

Without a sound, the kitchen lights snapped on with a hundred watts displaying the horrible, ugly scene. The old lady, in a blue terrycloth bathrobe, hair in curlers, stood in shock, both hands covering her mouth.

"My God! What have you done?"

The nervous rookie responded, "We caught him breaking into your home."

Clutching the top of her robe, the old lady's horror quickly changed to irate rage. "Breaking in, hell! That's John Blessing. He's worked for me for over twenty years. He lives in the Gate House out back during the week. I'd just sent him to the store."

The two officers exchanged looks. The older officer looked at the rookie with the shotgun waiting for an answer.

"Shit! I thought he had a gun."

Looking disgustedly at the young man, he turned to the old lady and said, "We're sorry."

The old lady began to weep and shake her head back and forth in anger. "Sorry?! You witless, good for nothing white trash. You wouldn't a shot him if he was white. He's got six kids and a wife. What are you gonna tell them?"

The heavy silence held as the trio stood alone looking for some reasonable excuse. The trembling rookie moved close to his partner and spoke, searching for some hint of approval. "Come on Dave, you saw it.. It was a legal shoot.. He could'a had a gun."

The old lady's hands covered her face as she leaned against the doorjam and wept. Dave looked at the rookie, "Chet, shut up. Why I ever let you talk me into coming back here I'll never know. Talk about bad timing." The officers stood in silence looking at the mistake lying in blood on the floor. Dave, what are we gonna do?" Chet asked nervously.

"How the hell do I know?" Dave looked at the frightened woman. "Ma'am, with all the killings going on we honestly thought your life might be in danger."

"That's nice. Don't you question the suspect before you shoot or is it open season on blacks?" Chet, not knowing, answered her rhetorical question. "Ma'am, please understand. He reached into his pocket when he was told to put his hands behind his head. When a perpetrator fails to respond and the suspect's action leads the officer on scene to believe his life is in danger, or the life of his partner, he is justified in shooting."

The old lady leveled her stern look at the young officer and said. "You better be prepared to tell that to a judge." Dave responded before the rookie got himself deeper into a legal debate. "I'm sorry Maam we'll have to call and report this and we'll need to get a statement from you. Let's go." The two officers returned to the black and white. Dave picked up the radio and was about to transmit when Chet stopped him.

"You did tell him to put his hands behind his head didn't you."

Dave looked at the nervous young rookie and shook his head in disgust. "Yes, I guess I did."

The Mayor sat behind his desk tapping his yellow pencil nervously as he listened. Standing at his side was District Attorney David Blackstone. David was a balding, overweight, political shark, as well as a top lawyer. He was the Mayor's right hand man and the city's chief prosecutor. The two large, leather, overstuffed chairs had been pulled up closer to the Mayor's desk forming a small arc. Seated in the first chair, wearing wire rimmed glasses and a black suit was the Reverend Jesse Baxter. Besides being Jack's father-in-law, he was the leader of the Black Christian Brotherhood and the appointed spokesman for the black community. To his right was Carl Hawthorne, a well educated black lawyer, representing the NAACP. Carl was a smooth operator, who knew the law inside out. It was common knowledge that he was being groomed for Congress. He was a master at negotiation and civil rights arbitration.

Carl shifted his weight in the chair as he addressed the Mayor, "So, what are you going do about it?"

The Mayor continued to tap his pencil as he replied, "Gentlemen, a full investigation is underway. Believe me, if there is any wrong doing, the men will be punished."

The D.A. cut in, reinforcing the Mayor's words, "And I'll see that they get the max, but, we're not railroading anyone. We will not provide the black community with a sacrificial lamb." Suddenly, the Mayor's office door smashed open as two rough looking black gang leaders paraded into the office followed by a complaining secretary, "Wait a minute, you can't go in there."

The gang leaders stood defiantly in the center of the room surveying the situation. Obbie and Willard Jackson were brothers, in their middle twenties, and absolute leaders of the Saints, the largest gang on the lower east side.

It was ironic, maybe even funny, how various organizations, be they gang members or FBI agents, all had a dress code. Obbie and Willard wore black berets, tight levis, boots, tanker jackets decorated with gang logos, and gloves with the fingertips cut away. Between them they wore more earrings and jewelry than Gypsy Rose Lee.

The secretary apologized, "I'm sorry sir, you want me to call security?"

The Mayor shook his head calmly, "No, that won't be necessary."

Gil Washington had pulled himself out of the ghetto with hard work and determination to become Mayor. He knew where the street kids were coming from and had spent hours of his spare time working with the gangs. He'd been able to make some progress with everyone except Obbie and Willard.

Obbie strutted around the room seeing it for the first time, then stopped in front of the Mayor's desk. Putting both hands on the desk, leaning toward the Mayor, he demanded, "I wanna hear it from the Uncle Tom here. What's he gonna do about the killings?"

The Reverend, insulted at this breech of good manners, stood up and protested, "How dare you come barging in here and"... The younger brother, Willard, pushed him abruptly back into the chair. "Cool it, Reverend," then gave him a cold stare.

Turning back to the Mayor, Obbie picked up the conversation while nodding towards the Reverend. "Asshole over there is gonna sit around all day praying and that slick lawyer will sell his mother to get black or white votes... Me, I don't give a shit." The lawyer tried to get up, only to be pushed back into the chair. Complaining, Carl said, "Obbie, you're only gonna make it hard on everyone." Obbie turned on the Mayor in anger borne of grief and frustration. "Hard?! Would ya listen to our black honky. Old man Blessin is dead. Two of our school teachers have been raped and murdered! They done nothin to no one. The Klan is puttin' on the sheets and you say I'm makin' it hard? We've got a white Mayor in a black skin, who can't take a shit without asking when or where and all you can say is, hard?" With rage breaking loose, he threw the Mayor's glass paperweight against the wall, smashing it to pieces. Pointing his finger in the face of the Mayor, he warned, "My people come to me, they don't go to them," he barked, nodding at the Reverend sitting uncomfortably in his chair. "You want'a war, you got it."

That was it as far as Gil was concerned. He'd been a gang member. He'd seen these punks come and go and no one was going to come in here and threaten the Mayor. Slapping Obbie's hand away from his face, he grabbed the heavy gold chains on Obbie's neck and twisted them tight, cutting off some of his air as he pulled him across the desk. Face to face, with his anger ready to explode, Gil explained to the punk. "Now, you listen to me you candy assed pimp. You wanna fuck with me, huh? You step outta line once and I'm gonna come down on you like a ton of shit." Shouting, he went on, "No one! I mean no one! is gonna step out of line. You or the Klan! I don't care if I have to call in the Guard and kick ass and take names, I'm gonna keep a lid on this... So, don't you ever come in here and fuck with me again... Now, take your idiot brother and get the hell out of my office."

A tense moment held as the two men faced off. The Mayor slowly let go of his chains and Obbie stepped back. With narrowed eyes and tight jaws, Obbie turned, and paraded out the door. Willard, following close behind, stopped at the door, made a make believe gun with his hand, took aim at the men in the room, and said, "Bang, Bang you'al", then closed the door.

Chapter Five:

The Task Force

Beau's unmarked car eased up to the curb in front of the old brownstone and came to a stop.

"Victim number one, "Beau said, nodding towards the house. "Amanda Hollingsworth's place. Don't know what in hell you expect to find in there that we haven't. The boys have been over this place with everything from a sniffer dog to a 20 ton magnet."

"You looked for clues, I'm looking for reasons."

"Okay, let's go." Beau shrugged, reaching for his door handle.

"No!" Sally snapped, holding out her hand for the keys to the house. "I want to go in alone. You have a habit of distracting this lady and I don't want or need distractions".

"That's nice to know," Beau grinned with a pleasant surprise. "I bother you, huh?"

"The keys please."

"That good or bad?" he asked, taking the keys from his pocket and handing them to her. "That I bother you."

"I wouldn't get my hopes up too high." Sally smiled back taking the keys, as she slipped out of the car.

He watched her as she approached the two stone pillars that supported the heavy New Orleans style wrought iron gate with a shiny brass coat of arms attached to its center. Beau tilted his head as though that would give him a better perspective of Sally's backside. Her athletic body, full hips, and strong thighs pressed against the tight skirt. She radiated sensuality. He thought to himself that if the right man ever turned her on she would be one hell of a woman in bed. He also knew that she wouldn't let herself go unless it was the right man. Beau smiled and said to himself, "It damn well better a man if he is to handle that".

Removing the yellow police crime scene tape that forbade entry to the premises, Sally moved up the stone paved path past an old magnolia tree that had laid a carpet of brown leaves and rotted blooms across the now unkept lawn. The slate pathway was bordered by a small planted area that had long since dried up. The path made a slow curve that led to the front door. Turning, she waved to Beau then inserted the key into the lock and disappeared inside the darkened house. Beau got out of the car and went to the front gate then stopped. He paced back and forth like a teenager on a first date. This lady was not your ordinary Fed. Her eyes although a beautiful deep blue looked straight through you as if she could almost read your innermost secrets. He didn't know for sure if he really liked that or not. But everything else he liked.

In the few seconds it took her to cross the outer threshold and close the door behind her, the lightness of the prior moment was quickly replaced by the darkness. The fresh morning air outside was now suffocatingly stale with the lingering ambiance of evil and death that had visited so violently some days ago.

Sally leaned against the door in the deadly silence, closing her eyes and letting her mind go blank in order to project herself into the past, into a place of shadows without dimension or substance. Since childhood she had known she had the gift of "second sight" as her mother used to say. A gift or a curse, it wasn't something she could turn on and off like a faucet or that she could call up on demand. It came when it wanted to and it wanted to, now. It was as if the house itself called out to her in outrage at the evil that had been committed here. Sally closed her eyes, then, quick, sharp flashes of light darted through her mind. She saw a beast that seethed evil in every breath. The beast grunted and hobbled to the mirror on the wall. Sally let out a stifling yell when she saw the beast's reflection in the mirror on the wall. She snapped out of her semi-trance and looked around the room. She spotted the broken mirror and positioned herself exactly where the killer would have stood. She touched the broken mirror only to see a hundred small fingers in the reflection. Sally stood back and closed her eyes again trying to project herself back in time to a point where the killer had been on the night of the brutal murder. The flashing pictures in her mind revealed another figure this time. A figure much calmer. A figure that seemed sad. She fought to get a clearer picture in her mind but only saw a distant figure with no face. But this time she had a feeling about this figure. It was a feeling of sadness. The figure seemed to be crying. There was something else about this vision but she couldn't put her finger on it. She spoke to her vision, "Hello." But the specter motioned her away. Sally realized, from the motion of the vision, it was a child. No sooner had the vision appeared then it was gone. Nervously, she realized that some horrific evil was still here. Soon the sounds and smells that the killer had experienced flowed back into the hallway becoming stronger with each step Sally took into the sitting room where Amanda Hollingsworth had been found. The tea service sat exactly where it had been placed by the killer along with a now decayed bouquet of flowers.

Although it was now too withered to identify, Sally knew what the vase had contained. From the records she had seen before she left Washington she knew they were Forget-me-nots. Sally extracted a dried stem and studied it.

"Forget-me-nots," she said aloud as if to another person in the room. "They mean "fidelity", did you know that? Of course you did. But you couldn't be faithful to all of these ladies. No, of course you couldn't. They were one to you, weren't they?"

David had just picked up the newspaper when he heard it. At first he scowled at the interruption then remembered he was alone in his small kitchen about to have his morning coffee. Yet the voice was there. A woman's voice. He'd heard it although it hadn't called him by name. Was he going mad? Hearing voices? Or was the voice he'd heard not meant for him but for the others? His eyes darted to the paper that carried a picture of Sally, identifying her as having been brought into the Gray Lady Killer case. The headlines were in bold black letters proclaiming the Gray Lady Killer had struck again the night before. He dropped the paper and reached for his cup with trembling hands. Lifting it, he rose and walked slowly into the first bedroom and stood before the mirror and studied himself. Or was it himself? Or was it little David whose face stared back at him? The image in the mirror blurred and began to change again. Lifting the cup, David flung it at the dressing room mirror above his dresser. The fracturing mirror sent back a spray of scalding hot black coffee. The remaining jagged pieces of the mirror distortedly reflected only one image, the Beast, and the room was soon filled with wild laughter.

"You're here. I can feel you. Talk to me. Tell me why you are doing this?" Sally moved to the other shattered mirror in the sitting room and stared at the jagged pieces of reflective glass in the ornate frame, and asked aloud, "You didn't want to do it, did you? Is that why you break the glass each time, so that you won't see the side of you that's so filled with hate? This is it, isn't it? Killing little old ladies and then fucking them isn't something you're very proud of, is it? Tell me, what's behind your looking glass? What is your secret?"

She turned and walked slowly out of the sitting room back into the foyer, climbed the stairs to the second floor, and entered what had been the Hollingsworth's master bedroom. The canopied four poster bed had remained the same as the day of the murder. The doubled wedding ring comforter was neatly folded down at the foot of the bed. The pillows still bore the impression of the victim's head where she was sexually assaulted after death. A cold shiver moved across her shoulders. Sally realized this was where it had happened. But there was no struggle. Everything was neatly in place as if the victim had willingly participated in the sexual act. But she had been dead when the sexual act had taken place. She noticed several small spots on the bedspread. From her visions she knew that those spots were probably dried semen. She made a mental note to check the crime scene folder for semen samples. That would give them a DNA link to the killer or killers. Sally glanced at the mirror over the dresser. It had not been smashed as the two downstairs. If anger had overtaken the killer, why downstairs and not up here? Why had he been so enraged as to smash only the mirrors in the foyer and sitting room? Was there someone else here? Whoever you are, you had rough sex for about an hour, climaxed all over the bedspread, then you brought her downstairs again. To have tea? It made no sense.

On the lower south side of Charleston the apartment that David shared with Gaylord was double locked from the inside, with a riot bar fully in place covering the full width of the door. The curtains and shades were closed giving the room a darkness of varying shades of gray. Candles were lit in the kitchen, living room, and in each of the two bedrooms. Sitting at the head of the kitchen table was the corpse of Doctor Michaels. The grinning detached skull sat lopsided on its torso. David sat sobbing in his regular chair. Doctor Michaels inquiring voice spoke. "What is it? Why are you crying?"

"I don't know."

"Yes you do or you wouldn't have asked for this session."

"I don't want to talk to anyone," was David's childlike reply.

"David, don't play games with me. You've had another bad dream haven't you."

"This always happens to me," David answered the corpes between sobs.

"What always happens to you?" the Doctor's voice asked without backing off.

"I do things that I don't want to do. I get myself into trouble, and they don't want me around anymore. They get mad at me, - especially Agnes.."

At that moment Doctor Michael's skull toppled from its position onto the kitchen floor. The noise startled little David. His instant reflex was to lift up his arms protecting himself. Gaylord instantly appeared. "Shit! You candy-assed pimp, stop that!! Gaylord now in control, picked up the skull and put it in its rightful place, bringing Doctor Michaels back into the conversation. "Thank you Gaylord, Now, if you don't mind let me talk to David." Gaylord sat down and David squirmed embarrassed in his chair.

"How do you feel right now David?" The doctor asked.

"Uncomfortable," David responded shyly.

"What did you think was going to happen?" The decomposed body of Dr. Michaels inquired silently.

David laughed nervously, "You'd slap me."

"Did I hear you right? You thought I'd slap you?"

"Yeah, in the face like my mommy did. Hard, really hard," David said in mumbled tones.

"When did she slap you?" the Doctor's voice asked.

"I don't know."

"Yes you do."

"She was always yelling and screaming at me. Always mean to me." David squirmed in his chair remembering the past. "She knew everything and she just let it happen."

"What did she let happen?" Doctor Michaels asked. David nodded his head back and forth denying the truth that was about to be told.

"The showers."

"What showers?" the voice from the silent corpse asked.

"Me and Agnes."

"What happened in the showers?"

"I don't remember."

"Yes you do." The voice from the long expired Doctor Michaels were questions the personalities of David and Gaylord were asking themselves. David's face showed anguish, mental torment that was dying to break out but couldn't. He continued. "She rubbed me all over. She touched me in all my private places." David pulled his knees up under his chin and crossed his hands in front of him in a gesture of self protection.

"Did you touch her in all her private places?"

"Yes," David answered shyly. "She put her fingers inside me."

"Where?" the Doctor inquired, David pointed to his anus.

"Did she ask you to put anything inside her?"

"Yes," David answered again almost in tears.

"What? Your fingers?"

"No," David said quietly. There was a short moment as David stared at the doctor's corpse. "What?" the Doctor's voices inquired again.

"My fist." With that, David started to sob when Gaylord came to the surface, took control of David's body and began to admonish the Doctor.

"That's it, this session is over. How in hell you call this therapy is beyond me. Sex is sex and its no big thing. I give' em what they want and they'll take care of me."

"Is that what you want, to be taken care of?" The grinning skull of Dr. Michaels asked.

"Oh no you don't, you're not analyzing me. This session is over, "Gaylord rose and wheeled the good Doctor Michaels back to his resting place.

The Mayor would be unavailable for the rest of the day. This was the statement that his secretary was supposed to say to anyone who called, especially the media. His visit to the Citadel commencement exercises was canceled with no excuse. He had called an emergency meeting of key members of his staff, city, and state officials… The Chief of Police, District Captains, City Engineer, Commander of the National Guard, FBI Area Supervisor, Coast Guard Commander, the Fire Chief and his deputy, a State Senator, a Congressman, and the Harbor Patrol Marine Captain. The Senator had arranged for a CIA Liaison Officer from Washington to be flown in. The men sat quietly around the conference table as the tape recorder played the rhetoric that had transpired at the Klan meeting in Brenner Woods. They hung on the words that another Oklahoma bombing would probably take place soon. As the tape ended the officials began to murmur between themselves. The Mayor sat upright, tapping his pencil on his notebook addressed the table, "Gentlemen, I take these threats very seriously". The Congressman answered, "Gil, you know we've had these threats before and they've been just talk."

"Three years ago I might have agreed with you. But not now, not after the Trade Center in New York and the Federal Building in Oklahoma City. Christ! We've got kids out there buying automatic weapons, making bombs and blowing away half the student body. No gentlemen, this threat is real and it won't go away until the killer, who ever he is, is caught. And God help us if he's black." The FBI agent nodded towards the CIA agent for comment. The CIA agent cleared his throat before adding to the conversation. "Gentlemen, historically we've geared our operations to counter external threats to national security. Right now, working with friends in the FBI we're rethinking our strategy for counter terrorist operations within the U.S.. Of course, you know its a matter of jurisdiction. I can tell you this. We will actively support any plan you come up with and we will coordinate that effort with the FBI. We want to prevent anything like the Oklahoma incident." The Fire Chief raised his hand. The Mayor recognized him. Heads turned to the Fire Chief. "Its obvious that this effort will require additional manpower for both the police and my department." The Police Chief nodded with approval. "I don't think there are additional monies in our discretionary fund to cover it." Gil responded, "you're right." then turned his attention to the Senator and Congressman. The Senator looking at the Congressman then to the CIA representative, asked, "Can you help us with funds from your internal security operation?"

"I believe that might be arranged. As to the amount right now, I can't say," was the CIA's usual evasive, but promising answer. Gil rose and nodded to Sam Mosely, the City's Civil Engineer. He opened a large case and rolled a large city street map onto the center of the table. Everyone stood in order to examine it more closely. Coffee cups were placed at strategic locations to hold the map in place. Gil spoke as he hovered over the map. "Gentlemen, I think its time to brainstorm as to what we are actually talking about. The Chief of Police spoke, pointing to a strategic location, "First, we should consider securing City Hall and Washington Square." Everyone nodded in agreement as the Chief continued, "we should define a restricted access area from Broad Street, to Meeting Street to Church Street and Queen Street. I suggest cement barriers here, here, and here." He moved his hand across the map then looked at the City Engineer. Sam replied, "No problem. We have plenty of barriers available.

"Do you have the manpower to cover these check points?" Gil asked the Chief.

"Give me the money and I'll get the manpower." The Chief said looking at the Mayor.

Gil continued, "Any problem using National Guard troops?"

"No, but we need a coordinated plan. I don't want anyone to go off shooting up the town." The National Guard Commander looked at the two silent politicians and asked, "Senator, you're on the Armed Services Committee aren't you?" The Senator answered, "Yes."

"Could you possibly get some additional funds for us to do some extra training this quarter?" The Senator smiled knowing the guard was on a limited budget and had to justify to the GAO every penny spent. "I will inform the National Security Advisor of the situation and see if he can release some discretionary funds. Can't promise, but I think this administration doesn't want another Oklahoma City incident on their hands. I'll keep you advised."

"Good." Gil said approvingly.

The Civil Engineer interjected, "I don't have a feel for what the target might be, but I am sure I can get the Army Corps of Engineers to erect more permanent barriers if need be. I'll have a traffic control plan on your desk in two days. One other thing, I think it might be prudent to have the corps put security patrols on the bridges leading in and out of the city. These are probably the most vulnerable targets around. As I see it, the most likely targets would be the Grace Memorial Bridge, the Ashley, the Pearlman, and the Old Towne Road Bridge. A little bit of plastic in the right place would bring any of them down. I think you know what that would do to the city's economy."

The Fire Chief interjected, "Make sure your traffic control plan will allow us to respond effectively."

"That goes for the police, too," the Police Chief said nodding in agreement.

"Another thing, we'll need additional foot patrols for City Hall and the Washington Square area." Gil said. Shaking his head again he continued, "However, I don't have the foggiest idea what other targets might be hit. Gentlemen, we can't cover them all."

Everyone acknowledged that fact before he addressed the Fire Chief," I want you to discreetly, I mean discreetly, coordinate with the hospitals to prepare for emergency medical services with designated triage centers at key points in the city. Tell 'em its a disaster preparedness plan that the government wants us to prepare."

"Tell 'em it means more tax dollars for us. They'll buy that." The National Guard Commander added, "My medical unit has four deployable units and one partial."

"Good." Gil answered. Everyone nodded approvingly. Gil picked up the buzzing intercom, "Yes." The secretary's voice announced that Lieutenant Gasteneau and Sergeant Bellamy were here. "Send them in."

The door opened and the two detectives joined the officials at the table. Gil introduced the officers and then outlined their security plans. "What do you think so far?" the Mayor asked. Everyone waited for the detectives answer.

Beau studied the notes on the map, then spoke as he moved his hand across the map. "So far, so good. Their main objective will be to kill as many blacks as they can, or," Beau looked directly at the Mayor, "kill one important black. You've got City Hall covered. I suggest additional security at the Avery Research Center of African American History. It's the easiest to get to and has a high probability of killing blacks."

"Good idea," Gil answered. Jack chimed in, "May I make a suggestion?" Everyone stopped and looked at the usually stoic black officer. "Go ahead Jack." the Chief of Police answered. "In about two weeks, the Serenade Music Hall will be having Diana Ross and her Motown Review. That's the target they'll go for." Everyone stared at the two officers in silence. Beau looked at Jack. Jack was not sure if had spoken out of turn. The Mayor smiled and said, "You know, I think he's right. Let's give that target top priority."

"How about calling the concert off?" the Police Chief inquired.

"Are you kidding? We're trying to avoid a riot, not create one." was the Mayor's answer, as he turned to Sam Mosely and issued another order. "Put the Disaster Control Center on alert with 24 hour phone service, and tie in to 911 and all other agencies." The Mayor looked at his watch, "Gentlemen, not a word of this leaves this room. It's gonna be impossible to keep all this away from the press. We want to keep them in the dark for as long as we can. Okay, take time for lunch and meet back here at one thirty."

The Charleston Police Operations room was packed with officers waiting for the morning briefing. The grapevine already had the word out on the copycat killer and that the Klan had some heavies in town. Something was coming down soon. That's all they knew. The Klan and the Skinheads would be the perpetrators, but no one knew for sure, what, where, or when. The Charleston PD hadn't felt this much tension since the Civil Rights movement back in the sixties.

At one end of the room, desks had been hastily pushed aside and a podium was set up. The overflowing crowd filled the seats, sat on edges of desks, or stood along the wall as they waited and listened to the tape of the

Klan meeting. They hung on the words that another Oklahoma City bombing would probably take place soon. As the tape ended, officers began to murmur among themselves. The rear door opened. Beau, Sally, Jack, and the Duty Sergeant inched their way through the crowd to the podium. As the room hushed, Beau stepped forward, looked at his notes, and began. "Okay, all leaves and time off are canceled, as of now." Moans of disappointment, not surprise, came from the officers.

Beau continued a hard stare until groaning stopped, "You all know we have a copycat hitting black women, two for one. I hope to hell he doesn't play catch up ball... You all knew Harry. It's official, this guy is now a cop killer." The room was silent as they watched resentment build inside the Lieutenant. With undertones of anger, he went on, "No one! I mean no one! is gonna kill a cop and get away with it, not in this town. We're gonna nail both these guys, fast... Anybody got a problem with that?" The Lieutenant's determined eyes, surveyed the room. He had everyone's attention.

"We have Special Agent Sally Thornton from the FBI on loan to us for the duration. This lady knows what she's talking about. She's already picked up on a few things we missed, so listen up."

Stepping up next to Beau, Sally began, "Gentlemen, ladies. Let me start with the Strangler. I'm not telling you anything new when I say this guy is sick. We're going back to square one and try to lock in on his psychological profile. Okay, let me run a few things by you. Be very careful with this guy." Sally took a quick glance around the room. "On the outside he's gonna look very normal, maybe even a Casper Milquetoast type of guy. On the inside he's ready to explode. Don't ever forget what happened when one of your fellow officers got too close."

She looked at the officers standing along the left wall. One man stood with his coffee mug frozen in mid-air halfway to his open lips.

"From the pattern of the murders, we're dealing with an episodic behavioral disorder which means he's a regular sort of a guy until someone pulls his chain the wrong way and boom, off he goes. He is a psychopath, which means he has absolutely no remorse about the act of murder, in fact, just the opposite, he gets off on it."

Sally walked around to the side of the podium, took a moment to gather her thoughts, and said, "Now, lets talk about the murder scene. First, it's not just a murder scene, it's a stage, it's a place where some sort of a grotesque play or sacred ritual has taken place. Don't look for the obvious. The ritual is a repeated observable pattern. It's what you might call a psychological skeleton that provides a framework for the killer's fantasies. We've seen decapitation, mutilations, and sexual molestation with the corpse, even cannibalism. With our guy, it's sex. Henry Lee Lucas and Charles Manson, they all had their fantasies. Starting today, every man, woman, or teenager brought in will be interviewed before being booked. I want you to use this." Sally held up a stack of forms. "We are going over every case file from the beginning and transpose the info to this format. In ninety percent of our cases, the serial killer has had some sort of encounter with the law. If we can make a link we might have our man."

Beau cut in with the assignments as Sally stepped back,

"As of today Sergeant Bellamy will be in charge of the copycat investigation. Bradley, Mitchell, you work with Jack. Coates, Brockman, Farley and Singletary you're on the psycho case with us."

Sally moved forward and spoke. "Is forensics here?" In the back, a man raised his hand. She nodded, then continued, "You have any of the victim's clothing that may have semen on them?" The answer was affirmative.

"You haven't got any info back from the Bureau, right?" Sally acknowledged another affirmative nod.

"Get with me after this and we'll get it off for another priority one DNA match."

She moved away from the podium as Jack got up, looked at his notes and spoke, "This guy Delechamp, the whatcha-call-it, Purple Dragon, and this Nazi cat are probably tied into the black hits or knows who is." Holding up two pieces of paper, he went on, "I have two court orders for phone taps. Bradley, get with the mechanic. I want those bugs in place ASAP. Mitchell, get on the wire. I want a list of all Neo-Nazi types and Klan members in the area. Get some uniforms to cross check local campgrounds, motels, hotels, flophouses, you name it. I want to know who we've got in town. Check these guys for priors."

Raising his voice slightly, Beau read from his notes, "Brockman, Farley, run a check on all men black or white in the state under the age of 65 undergoing mental therapy on an out-patient basis. Also, check for priors, who knows, maybe we'll get lucky. Coates, Singletary! You and Agent Thornton will go over the case files. Another thing, any collars, for any reason, cross check these guys for Klan or Nazi affiliations. I wanna know who these guys are and what they're up to."

Beau paused, waiting for questions when Sally spoke, "Sergeant Coates, get a hold of an Almanac. Check the dates of the murders with cycles of the moon, or astrological dates. Remember, we're looking for a pattern. Who knows? This guy may bark at the moon for all we know." Everyone chuckled at the morbid, but funny, thought. Sally continued, "Oh yeah, check the back issues of the newspapers to see if there were any conventions in town at the time of the murders. Oh, Coates, either you or Singletary check out the banks for any account for the Christian Brotherhood, or Christian Fellowship. Check to see if any of the victims made any checks out to any of these organizations. If that doesn't work out, check with the

IRS to see if anyone like that has applied for tax exempt status." Coates nodded as the other officers continued to take notes.

The Duty Sergeant moved forward and announced, "You all heard about the shoot last night. The officers have been put on desk duty pending hearing... We have a new directive and you all know where it came from. As of today, all units will be composed of black and white officers."

Hushed grumbling was heard as the officers talked to themselves. The Duty Sergeant continued, "I think you don't have to be a rocket scientist to realize that by tonight this city is gonna be a war zone. Everyone! I mean everyone! Wear your flak jackets. I'm sorry gentlemen, that's it." The Duty Sergeant gave a slight smile, "One of those golden be-bees out there might have your name on it. The new schedule is posted outside. Another thing. Stay visible. I want the community to know we're fully integrated, so watch your partner's back."

The Lieutenant, with his hands on his hips, moved in front of the podium, "Questions?... Let's get with the program." With that command, the room emptied.

In the days that followed, every felon booked had a detailed interview and an FBI form entered into his record. There was no problem in obtaining a court order to examine records of all the men using state mental health facilities on an out-patient basis. The data was fed to Quantico for analysis. Sally, Detectives Coates, and Singletary had reviewed the case files of all the victims with no significant results. Mountains of data were fed over the wire to Quantico. It was analyzed, sifted, processed, and examined but nothing turned up that would lead directly to the killer.

It was a quiet night. The killer hadn't struck in three weeks. So far, there had only been one copycat killing and maybe, just maybe, the pressure being put on the Klan would hold it down. The street was dark and misty as the midnight fog gave way to the early morning. In front of police headquarters the sign displaying "Charleston Metropolitan Police" was well lit as an occasional car moved in and out of the enclosed parking area. A blue and white van turned the corner and drove slowly down the street. A few feet from the front of headquarters, the van gunned it's engine; the side door slid open, and a body, tightly coiled in barbed wire, was pushed out as the van sped off. The body rolled to a stop in front of the steps leading to the main entrance.

Billy Jo Trimble, a white foreman at the Brenner Paper Company, had been severely beaten. The letters K.K.K. had been burned into his forehead with a hot iron and his Klan robes were tied around his legs. A young black officer, emerging from the station, caught a fleeting glimpse of the whole affair and ran to the victim. The sight of the mutilated body turned his stomach. Looking into the night, the black officer thought to himself, "God help us, this is how it starts, and Lord only knows how it will end."

The Operations Room was vacant. The night shift had gone home and the day shift wasn't due for another thirty minutes. Beau hung up his coat. Studs went to his regular spot by the window and curled up. Beau was surprised to see Sally in so early. He hoped the undeclared war between them was over. She didn't have to prove herself to anyone. The Lieutenant, and everyone on staff, knew she was good at her job. She was more than good. When she got her teeth into something, she wouldn't let go until she knew why. If anyone could make sense of all this, it would be Sally. Jack was a good cop with good instincts, but when it came to getting inside the killer's mind, no one could do it better than Sally, even Jack knew that. The FBI agent was studying a case file when Beau approached with a cup of hot coffee in each hand.

"You're in early."

"Yeah," she said continuing to read.

"Coffee?"

"Thanks", she looked up and took the hot brew, then sat back to smell the aroma. Reaching for a folder on her desk, she remarked, "Oh, we got the DNA analysis back." Handing the report to Beau, she went on, "We got a match on five out of seven. So, it's not one hundred percent. At least we know the same guy did all five, probably seven."

Beau sipped his coffee as he glanced at the report, "It's hard evidence, that's more than we had before." He paused, looking for the right words to apologize, "Ah, look, I'm sorry if I came on the wrong way. Ah…"

She cut him off, "What are you trying to say Lieutenant?"

"Beau. Call me Beau."

"Okay, Beau."

"I just wanted to say, I think you're doing a great job." The agent stopped sipping her coffee. Her deep blue eyes looked across the top of her cup, "What brought this on?"

Beau, slightly embarrassed, countered, "Hey, don't ruin it."

"You mean you have trouble admitting you were wrong?" She said with a sly grin.

A wry smile came over his face as he took another sip of coffee. The phone rang interrupting Beau's answer. Sally put the phone to her ear as the Ops Room doors swung open.

Jack and two detectives entered with the usual good morning jokes. As the chuckles faded, Jack made a bee-line towards Beau and Sally.

"You're not going to let me off the hook are you." Beau remarked, seating himself on the edge of the desk.

Putting her hand over the phone, "I might," she said with a twinge of glee on her face.

Putting his cup down, he said, "Forget it."

"Forget what?" Jack questioned, looking at a quick smile on Sally's face. "What hook?", he said looking at Beau, "You mean this guy actually apologized? Oh, this I gotta see." Jack smirked, noticing Beau's embarrassment.

Sally turned her attention to the waiting phone. "This is Agent Thornton…Yeah, what time? I'd like to talk to him too. We can use all the help we can get… Right. We'll be there, ten o'clock sharp. Thank you sir." Hanging up the phone, she sat back with a smug smile.

"Well, what was that all about?" Beau asked.

"Wait a minute, you were going to say something," Sally said, leaning forward, putting her elbows on the desk and cradling her chin in her hands, waiting.

Jack, knowing this must be a first for Beau, pressed the issue, "Yeah, what were you going to say?"

Jack and Sally waited for the answer as Beau squirmed, slightly embarrassed. "Okay guys, come on, let's get on with it." Both detectives waited for more of an apology. Beau began to study the DNA report as if he really cared what it said. Looking at Sally, Jack shrugged, "Sorry kiddo, that must be as good as it gets."

Standing up, Sally took a deep breath, "I guess I'll have to settle for that. We have a ten o'clock meeting with the D.A. and the FBI's District Director."

The two men stared blankly at each other. Jack said, "Fine, I give up." They both looked to Sally for an explanation.

"Well, if our Nazi guy, or this Purple Lizard…"

"Grand Dragon", Beau said, correcting her.

"Whatever. If he crossed state lines with the intent to foment riot, that's a federal rap. We might be able to get some more manpower and Uncle Sam will pick up the tab."

Both detectives smiled and said in unison, "Isn't she sweet."

"Don't thank me. It seems as though someone lit a fire under the District Director."

Glancing at his watch, Jack announced, "I'm gonna check Vice to see if they've turned up anything new on the copycat." Jack started to leave when Beau cut in, "I need you and Sally to brief the Governor before he takes off for Washington tonight. Can you handle it?" Both detectives nodded.

"What about you?" Sally asked Beau, with a curious note in her voice.

"Sorry, I promised the kids. It's the final game tonight."

Jack said, "Later", and made a hasty exit.

She was still waiting for an explanation to Beau's curious comment when the phone rang. Punching up his line, Beau picked up the phone, "Gasteneau... Yeah, she's here... It's for you," he said, handing her the phone.

"Agent Thornton," Beau watched her blue eyes move with interest as she listened. "Bring that by again? It's on the FAX? ... Just a minute." The agent picked up her pencil, turned over her note pad, and began to write as she spoke, "Go, Yeah... Okay... Right. What else?.. Got it. Thanks a lot. Appreciate it." Hanging up the phone, she smiled that infectious smile, then broke the news. "Bingo!... That was Quantico. We've got a match on our profiles. Two possibles from Salt Lake City, three from Seattle, and get this, two from Houston and two from Dallas. I've got the number of a Lieutenant Finley from Houston, and a Macklinberg from Dallas."

Beau put his cup down, then flopped into the chair next to Sally. "We went out on the wire before with no results. What makes you think this is going to be any different?"

"Our database. We've been putting this together for the past ten years. She leaned forward as she explained. "Serial killers do not emerge in a vacuum. There has to be a history floating around someplace on this guy. I'll lay you ten to one he's been in trouble before. The database is linked to every police department in the country. We can tie into every unsolved murder case over the last fifteen years. We are tied into the national missing persons net. Besides that, we've got MO's and psychological profiles on over a hundred and sixty serial killers in custody. We can identify common traits, and believe me, some of them are pretty spooky. For example, we had one cat who cut off the heads of his victims and used them as trophies. He preserved them in pickle brine. Nice big glass jars all in a row. He told the officers they all argued among themselves and he finally couldn't stand it. They were all women who were domineering, like his mother. He was killing his mother over and over."

Beau cut in, "Hey, you've convinced me. But what happened last time?"

"For some reason, your MO didn't get flagged by us. Believe me, these cases have been pulled after extrapolating one hell of a lot of data."

The Lieutenant sat up and casually moved the phone in front of the agent, then gestured politely. "Okay, go for it. Put it on the box."

She smiled, picked up the phone and dialed. The Lieutenant put his feet up on her desk and took another sip of coffee as he heard the phone buzz again.

Lieutenant Finley, Houston Homicide, was a short, heavy set man with a bull neck. He looked like a gorilla in a business suit. He had a rough dark stubble that left the lower half of his face blue no matter how close he shaved. To complement his appearance, the soggy remains of a half-smoked, half-eaten cigar dangled from his mouth. Picking up the phone, he growled hoarsely, "Finley, Homicide."

Sally picked up the conversation from her end. "This is Special Agent Thornton, FBI. I have Lieutenant Gasteneau with me, Charleston PD. Did our office flag two of your cases?"

Lieutenant Finley searched the top of his desk, then his in-basket, as he spoke, "Let me see, yeah, I have a note. They said you might call. What can I do for you?"

Sally began to read the case numbers, "Reference case number 6421-85 and case 6873-85. The victims were old ladies, sixty-five and seventy-two, both raped and murdered."

Finley shifted his cigar to the other side of his mouth as he hit the intercom switch on his desk. "Hold on a minute. Hampton! get the case files on those two old ladies iced back in eight-five." Addressing the phone again, he went on, "Let's see, yeah, I remember those. Sergeant Hampton handled the investigation. We believe the same guy did both hits. As I recall, there was no evidence of a psycho being involved."

Sergeant Hampton, a black officer who had been Finley's partner in the old days, entered and dropped the case files on the desk. The Lieutenant motioned his partner to stay. "Just a minute, I'm putting you on the box. Sergeant Hampton is here... Now, on both these cases we had money and jewelry taken and the victim's car was stolen. Found abandoned, no prints, no forced entry, nothing."

Beau sat up and asked, "Did you notice any tea cups, cookies, flowers, or anything like that?"

Sergeant Hampton spoke into the box from the other end, "Yeah, as a matter of fact, there were some cups laying around. No prints other than the victim's."

Sally looked at Beau, then asked, "Do you have any of the victim's underwear that might have semen on them?"

Lieutenant Finley took the stubby cigar from his mouth and spoke hesitatingly, "Yeah, it'd be pretty old though."

Sally answered quickly, "Will you send it to Quantico for DNA analysis and info copy us?" She adjusted the volume on the box as Finley came back, "Sure, whatcha got going?"

Hearing the voice loud and clear, Beau answered, "If we get a match, we'll let you know."

On the other end, Sergeant Hampton looked at Finley, then questioned, "Lieutenant, you think our boy has hit your town?"

"Could be," Beau replied, followed by a short silence.

Hampton added, "Something you oughta know. We had a witness."

The statement jolted Sally and Beau to the upright position. Sally blurted, "You what?"

Hampton went on, knowing he had peeked the agent's attention,

"Not really a witness. We picked up a David Delongpre, on possession. He said he knew the guy who hit the old ladies. He said this guy bragged about it."

"What happened?" Beau responded eagerly.

Hampton went on, "We found some stolen articles along with the dope. None of the items belonged to the victims. For his cooperation we let him cop a possession plea. He spent eighteen months in the slammer with three years probation. He jumped parole, let's see, last year sometime. We have an outstanding warrant on him for parole violation."

Beau asked quickly, "Did he have a Jamaican accent or a foreign accent?"

"Naw, he was a white guy. He was about as far from an English accent as you could get.. He was a southern boy. He's what you guys call white trash."

"Who was white trash, the killer or the scumbag?"

"The scumbag," came Hampton's reply followed by a chuckle.

Sally cut in anxiously, "Can you send us a copy of his file?"

Finley shuffled through the file on his desk. Moved his cigar to the front of his mouth and spoke around it, "We can do better than that. I've got it right in front of me... He gave us a composite on one Gaylord Harcourt, age 33, white male, five feet seven inches, one hundred and seventy pounds, wore jewelry, smelled like a French whore and you're right, according to this, he had some sort of accent. Does that fit?"

"Great," came back loud and clear. Finley went on, "We had an APB on Harcourt. He never turned up. You think Delongpre and Harcourt have hooked up again?"

The Lieutenant gave Sally a big grin as he answered, "Maybe, this is the best lead we've had so far."

Sergeant Hampton was the next voice on the box, "This guy, Delongpre, according to our records, is from your town. Something else, he hated Harcourt's guts. He took us around to his hangouts. Spent seven days going over line ups, mug shots, you name it, we did it. I mean this guy was bent on getting even with Harcourt. I'm surprised they've hooked up again."

"Thanks, I'll remember that." Beau said.

Sally made one more request, "Could you also send us his case file from his parole officer? Appreciate it. We'll get back to you if anything turns up. Talk to you later."

Punching off the box, she smiled smugly at the Lieutenant. She saw a faint smile as he spoke, "Don't you say it... I hate it when a woman gets you into an, 'I told you so 'position."

It was one of those few nights, this time of year, Charleston had a full harvest moon. The humidity hung in the air like a wet blanket, sticking to your underwear, allowing it to creep up into your crotch. Everything clung to you, like hot honey to cement. The slightest movement started you sweating. The local folks called this "mosquito weather".

The Governor's briefing had gone well. Beau's absence was duly noted by him, but he said nothing. However, he did ask the agent if she was getting the support she needed. Her answer was positive without going into specifics. A typical political answer that could be construed either way. The Governor didn't like the answer, but he decided not to pursue it. With the racial tensions running high, he didn't want to be misquoted in the press. Overall, Jack and Sally had given a good briefing that left everyone on a positive note. The only one who wasn't convinced about the progress on the Gray Lady Killer case, was the Mayor. He had good reason; he was sitting on a powder keg with a short fuse and his town was on fire.

The unmarked police car pulled up in front of the Holiday Inn. Sally and Jack got out and walked towards the door. Moving close to Jack, taking his arm, she said, "Thanks for the ride home."

Jack looked at the Agent with understanding, "No sweat. Things any better between you and Beau?"

They continued to walk slowly towards the lighted entrance. Sally sighed and spoke, "Sometimes yes, sometimes I don't know. Something bothers him."

Jack answered, "Yeah, you bother him."

"Me?"

Jack went on, "You look like her...his ex-wife, tall, good looking and smart, so I hear."

Sally looked at Jack wanting more. He went on.

"Well, it's no secret. Heard it all the day I became his partner. They had a three year old boy, named Mark. He died of leukemia. She blamed him. She couldn't handle being a cop's wife. Maybe it was guilt, anger, who knows what? He caught her in bed with another cop and that did it. So, she took off. Not so much as a goodbye, go to hell, or anything. Beau blames himself. Anyway, that'd kinda dampen a guy's outlook as far as women goes. As for the kids, he refs for the police junior basketball league. I guess that's his way to make up for Mark." Sally looked sadly at the detective as they stopped at the door. She said gently, "You know something?.. you guys are not too bad... for cops, that is." She stood slightly on her toes and kissed Jack on the cheek. "See you in the morning."

Jack watched her go through the doors. He thought to himself, as he walked back to the car, "Where will all this end? Beau and Sally are good folks. It seems kinda natural that they should be together. Maybe she's what Beau needs to turn his life around?" Jack sensed that Sally also had her crosses to bear. She had a deepness to her that you couldn't put your finger on. She'd been hurt and it gave her a tough veneer that if you didn't look deep enough you might get the wrong idea about her. She was the kind of woman that wouldn't let you get close to her unless she wanted you to.

As Jack stepped into the street, a red pickup with bold, gold lettering reading "Weyford Feed & Grain" pulled up and stopped abruptly, cutting him off from his car. Three men jumped out and walked menacingly towards him. The black detective looked up and down the empty street and saw no one. The three men were obviously Klan goons. They had picked their spot. An empty downtown street and a black guy with a white girl. That was the only excuse they needed. Their leader was a big guy, grossing out at about two hundred and thirty pounds, six four, and hands that looked like meathooks. His Neanderthal look made Jack think, "If ignorance is bliss, this guy's in hog heaven." He had a typical "good ol boy" beer belly that looked like a watermelon hanging over his belt. Jack knew where this was going and saw that big belly as his first target. The second punk was a skinhead with earrings in both ears and a shaved head. Jack knew from his youth gang days, you never went to a rumble with earrings. The last guy was smaller than the other two and held back. He was the weakest of the three. If he could drop the other two quickly, he'd have no problem with this asshole. The little guy was the kind that fed off the remains of the victim, a bully and a coward. If he could, Jack might be able to scare them off with his badge.

"Hey, Nigger. I see you prefer white women to your own kind." The big guy scowled as he closed on Jack. The detective stood his ground. "Gentlemen, I suggest you back off before you get yourself into trouble."

The guy with the earrings looked at his leader, "Hey Harvey, did you hear that? The Nigger is going to give us trouble."

The third punk smiled, showing one big tooth where two should be. Jack thought to himself, "That would come in handy opening beer bottles." The little man looked nervously at his two buddies, sensing it was time for him to speak. Gathering up courage that wasn't really there, he said, "You want trouble, you're looking at it."

Jack moved toward the one toothed punk who suddenly realized he was too close and started back pedaling. Before he could show his badge, the big goon on his left hit him in the gut with a hard right coming from nowhere. Jack folded up and dropped to one knee trying to catch his breath. He had to slow the big guy down so he could work on the other two. He wasn't going to last at this rate. Bad guys, one: Jack, zip. The big guy, taking charge and enjoying his advantage, stepped back to deliver a left hook, just as Jack ripped a devastating elbow into his balls, feeling them crunch under the blow. The big man let out a howling bellow as he grabbed his crotch and limped away. The closest adversary was the little punk who was trapped between him and the wall. With the heel of his hand, Jack gave him a judo shiver shot to the bridge of the nose, breaking it and sending blood all over his white sports shirt. The crybaby fell immediately, covering his face and cowering behind the car. Jack turned to meet the skinhead, just as he hit him with a solid haymaker right. The bad news was, he was wearing brass knuckles and put Jack down, hard. Dazed, trying to recover, the brass knuckles followed up with a combination of lefts and rights to the body and head. Blocking a hard right with his forearm, he locked up his opponent's arm tight into a judo bridge. Giving it a hard jerk he felt it snap like a toothpick at a Sunday picnic, then brought his forehead crashing down into the face of his opponent. That move caught the punk off guard and dropped him hard. Jack was still trying to take charge of the situation when the big guy hit him from the back with a 2 X 4 wooden club, taken from the truck. The last thing Jack remembered was lying there, being kicked, and finally, crawling under his car where everything went black.

Chapter Six

Close Encounter

Beau pushed through the swinging doors like a freight train hitting sixty miles an hour on a downhill grade. The overhead neon tubes pointed down the hallway to County General's Emergency Room. With a scowl on his face, and clenched fists, he marched with a storm trooper's gait down the corridor and turned the corner.

Jack sat on the edge of the operating table as the intern put the last stitch into his forehead. Besides a few sutures and a fat lip, he was fine. The doors flew open with a resounding whack! Chipping the paint from the walls as they bounced closed again. Jack saw an expression on Beau's face that he hadn't seen before. Beau was frightened, angered, and pissed off all at the same time. He was frightened to think he may have lost another friend, angered to think anyone would do this to a cop, and pissed off to think that Jack went and got himself hurt in the process. Jack knew that an unsaid bond had developed between them. It was not just one cop caring for another, it was a bond between friends. The expression changed to one of relief, as Beau spoke, "Who did this?"

"Don't worry about it. Haven't you heard? black bashing is becoming a major sport in this area."

"The hell I won't," came Beau's angered reply as he took a closer look, making sure Jack was all right. Jack held his head still while the intern snipped off the last suture.

"I dropped two of those bastards before I went down."

Beau began to pace around the room like a coach at a playoff game. "Why didn't you show them your badge?" Before Jack could answer, Beau interrupted himself, "Don't tell me, I know, you just felt like decking a few assholes before you went home."

Jack grinned, then stopped as he felt the stitches strain.

"Did you get it outa your system?"

Jack shrugged. Beau continued to shake his head,

"You're punchy that's what you are," Beau said admonishing his partner but also admiring him.

Rounding the corner in a fast walk, coming to an abrupt halt, was a slightly out of breath, FBI Agent. Jack picked up on Sally's expression, which was the same as Beau's. Both men saw the relief in her face as she surveyed the situation. "I just heard. Hotel Security brought me down. You all right?"

"I'm okay."

"He's punchy, don't believe anything he says." Beau cut in, pacing in front of Jack. Sally stepped closer to see for herself. "I mean it, are you okay?"

Jack began to button his shirt, "Yeah, I'm fine. Things are a little terse out there with a white girl on your arm."

Sally unconsciously picked up the pace behind Beau as she asked, "Can you ID them?"

Jack walked to the mirror and began to tie his tie. Examining his stitches, he said, "Weyford Feed and Grain on the side of the truck. Forget these guys, we've got bigger problems, besides, I needed the exercise."

Beau had calmed down. He had his anger under control when he said, "Let me take you home."

"No thanks, my car is outside. You two go on."

Beau looked at Sally, "You need a lift?"

"Yeah, thanks."

A short silence prevailed as the three detectives examined their feelings. Jack motioned with his hands, as if sending his pet dog outside, "Go, both of you, go, git,"

Waiting for Sally, Beau said, "See you tomorrow, or, whenever. Don't come in if you don't feel like it."

Jack nodded and pointed towards the door, then smiled, "See you guys tomorrow."

The fog had fallen on the city like a white shroud. It was as if the old Sea Witch had put a curse on the city. Maybe the killer was some evil beast conjured up by the ancient mariners. Maybe, like in the movies, the phantom was some sort of retribution for a past injustice. Beau put these crazy thoughts out of his head and inched the car slowly down the road, keeping a close eye on the centerline. Oncoming headlights looked like the eyes of sea monsters rising up from the mist, then disappearing into nothingness.

Sally broke the heavy silence, "Where's Studs?"

"Wednesday night is his TV night."

A quick smirk crossed her face, "I thought he was man's best friend? Does he watch Monday Night Football too?"

"Only if the Dolphins are playing."

Sally kept the silence, staring into the night. Keeping his eyes on the road, Beau began to think aloud, "I wish I could get a handle on this guy? Sometimes I get the feeling I'm close to him, then I lose him."

Sally looked at Beau with renewed interest, then spoke, "Don't try to put this guy in a box. Stay loose, go over what you already know. Think about him long enough and you might get an idea where he's headed."

Beau looked at Sally and smiled, "I'm always loose, at least my bowel movements are, and what do we already know?"

"How nice for you," Sally retorted. "I really needed to know that."

"Okay, lets go over what we already know. Maybe we can brainstorm our way into what the killer is all about." Beau said looking into the white mist still in front of the car.

Sally answered, nodding in agreement, "Lets start with the basics. What is a murder?"

Beau still carefully watching the road answered as though reciting from the police manual, "Murder is the willful and unlawful killing of one person by another." Sally nodded. Beau continued, "This does not include death by negligence, suicide, attempted murder, accident, or justifiable homicide." Sally started to speak when Beau interrupted, "Furthermore, murder can be subdivided into first degree, second degree and so on."

"Good," Sally answered. Beau smiled as he slowed down entering another area of dense fog.

Sally broke the short silence with a further definition of murder. "You also know that murder or homicide, usually happens for a very few basic reasons, right?"

"Right," Beau answered nodding his head.

Sally began again, "And we can put these in general categories. Let's see, category one is the spontaneous outcome of an event, a quarrel, rage, a reaction to an insult, like a bar room brawl where someone is killed by a jilted jealous lover."

Beau nodded again as Sally went on, "Category two is the murder for gain or profit. It could be revenge, protection of one's self, or to gain power."

"So far so good," Beau answered.

"Once you step outside these familiar motives for murder, you step into the realm of the serial killer. The why and wherefore of this type of murder has given law enforcement fits since Jack The Ripper."

"Okay, lets continue on with Crazies 101. What is your definition of a serial killer?" Beau said turning to look at Sally momentarily.

"I don't know if there is a complete and concise definition of a serial killer. However, serial killers have several common elements. The first one of course is the most obvious. Multiple victims. At least three or more. So, our guy more than qualifies. The serial killer will continue to kill and he won't stop unless he or she is made to stop, or some event causes him to stop. For example, we had a guy arrested on a totally different charge only to find out we had a serial killer on our hands. We had another in a mental hospital who also confessed to killing twenty four women."

Beau shook his head then brought the car to a brief stop at an intersection, then proceeded slowly as the mist engulfed the car again. "So far so good," he said acknowledging Sally's definition.

Sally continued, "The serial killer will have dormant periods, but the killings will continue. He may even wait a year of more before taking another victim. The point is, there will be more killing."

Beau interrupted, "I hope he doesn't go dormant or we'll never get him."

"Yeah, you're right, the other thing is that most murders include people who knew each other or had daily contact. Serial killing is a stranger to stranger crime. The perp and the victim usually do not know each other, and most likely have never had any previous contact. What bothers me about this case is that serial killers usually work alone. But we seem to have two guys involved in these murders if the info we got from Houston is correct."

"Yeah, I've been wondering about that myself," Beau commented.

"The motivation for the serial killer is not about money, or property, or the outcome of the event. The killer is simply motivated to kill for the sheer pleasure of it. Just like you or I need water, or should I say in your case, sex." Sally smiled at Beau.

"Make that booze and sex and you've got a deal." Beau said jokingly.

"You know something?" Sally said looking straight ahead.

"No."

"I think the booze and sex thing is just a macho come on. Either for your benefit or for the boys at the station."

"Please, don't analyze me, we've got other things to think about."

"Okay, lets get back to the basics again. I think you know from your experience and training that the killer seems to need the control, power, and dominance during the ritual preceding the actual murder. So the killings are not as obvious as the killings for gain or reaction murders. Their motives are internal. This is the mystery we have to solve if we are going to figure out who our guy is."

"I have no problem with that," Beau answered.

Sally was beginning to like Beau. He was the first cop who didn't know it all and wasn't trying to hit on her all the time. She also knew instinctively that he had seen his share of grief. He tried to hide it, but he couldn't. She wondered when he would open up to her and let her inside that tough exterior. Sally went on with her discussion by testing Beau's knowledge, "Okay, from what you know, who is your typical serial killer?"

Beau automatically began to rattle off his reply, "He's male, between the ages of 25 and 35, usually white, and will normally kill people of his own race. Now that's blowing a hole in our logic. Do we or don't we have a black guy killing white old ladies?"

"Or two black guys," Sally corrected.

"Yeah, two black guys. I agree he doesn't know his victims, but they symbolize something for him. His mother, an aunt, some family member.

However, I've got a feeling our guys is a loner. I think he has a regular job, but he's a loner."

Sally smiled and said, "See you already know more than you thought. You know what? I think you'd make a great profiler."

"Thank you, but no thank you. I prefer the normal everyday murder."

Sally chuckled, "See there you go. Like most cops you have a lot of misconceptions about serial killers."

"How so, oh little Agent of great knowledge?" Beau asked jokingly.

"Yeah, go ahead, oh Flat Foot of little faith." Sally went on testing the detective, "How many serial killer types do you think there are?"

"I didn't know they had types." Beau said, egging her on.

"Let me see, I'd say there are about four types.

"Just four," Beau remarked sarcastically.

"Well, more or less." Sally said. She held up one finger, "There is the visionary type. This guy is probably insane, psychotic, probably hears voices telling him to go and ice old ladies." Holding up the second finger, she went on, "There is the Missionary or Save the World type. This guy displays no outward psychosis, but on the inside he is trying to rid the world of something he considers immoral or unworthy. The killer will select groups of people like politicians or prostitutes. The Uni-bomber and that guy that bombs abortion clinics are good examples."

Beau acknowledged her explanation. Sally held up her third finger and began again, "Then we have the Thrill Oriented killer. This guy is the most dangerous. He gets his rocks off by simply killing. He's a sadist of the highest order. He's into it for the simple fun and excitement." She held up her fourth finger, "Then we have the Lust Killer. This sickie kills for the pure sexual pleasure. For him, the amount of pleasure is directly proportional to the amount of pain he can inflict on his victim. These guys will take great pains in developing different methods of torture. The more hideous the torture the more aroused they become. This guy is in touch with reality and is able to have relationships. Did you know that we have thirty-five active serial killers in the United States today? The majority of these guys are Lust Killers."

"Beau sat silent for a few moments thinking about what Sally had said. Sally looked at him knowing he had a deep hatred for this animal feeding on the people of Charleston. But the real danger would be that the racial hatreds that have existed for years would be coming to the surface. They could very well destroy this town if the killer was not caught and caught soon. Beau looked at Sally and asked, "Which one do you think our guy is?"

Sally thought for a minute then answered, "I think our guy is a cross between the visionary and the lust type."

"You're assuming that its just one guy."

"Yeah that's what's bothering me."

Beau nodded, then replied, "This whole investigation has turned into a political circle jerk, pardon my choice of words. If this guy spooks and we lose him, I'm the fall guy."

Sally thought to herself before she spoke; she knew the pressures of the job. She had to live with politics every day in the Bureau. "This might sound funny coming from a so-called scientist, but don't let a mob of politicians mess up your thinking. Listen to the little man twisting your guts. Go with your feelings."

Beau looked at her with a growing respect, then responded, "I've been doing it for sometime. What does your gut tell you?"

Sally closed her eyes for a moment and sat, as though in a trance, trying to communicate telepathically with the beast. "It's been too long."

"Hmm?"

"He's overdue. What's he waiting for?" Sally said with her eyes still closed.

Beau pulled the car over to the curb and parked under a lone street light that made a halo effect in the night mist. Turning off the engine he studied Sally for a moment.

"What?" She asked.

"You're more than a profiler aren't you."

"What do you mean?" She said opening her eyes.

"I mean you have all the training, all the right words, and all the right diplomas, but you've got something going for you other than profiling."

"Okay, yeah, I might."

Beau took a long hard look at Sally. "You're psychic aren't you."

"I don't believe in psychics." She responded calmly.

"Please don't bullshit me. Let me rephrase that. I don't really care one way or the other. But I think we know each other well enough to tell the truth."

Sally gave a sigh of resignation. "Okay, yeah, I do have the ability to get inside other people's heads now and then, but I'm not psychic."

"Go on," Beau said searching for some more insights to this strange and probably unreachable woman.

"I was recruited and trained as soon as I finished college. I figured this ability or curse depending on your point of view, might as well be put to some good use."

Beau started the car again and let it sit in idle. They both looked at each other trying to put the conversation back on track.

Beau wondered aloud, "Maybe our killer took some time off after killing a cop?"

Sally sighed, then asked, "Do me a favor."

"Yeah."

"Make the rounds of the previous murder scenes."

"Now? Tonight?"

"Please, something we've forgot." She said, as a new idea crossed her mind.

"What?" He noticed that something had just clicked in her head.

She looked at Beau as if some mathematical solution had just come to mind. "Maybe our guy only' hits when it's foggy? We didn't check the murder dates with the weather service."

She had a point. He knew the serial killer had a pattern that they hadn't locked onto yet, but there was still doubt. Beau put the car in gear and moved into the night fog.

"That's kinda reaching, isn't it?"

Sally looked at the detective slightly irked and asked pointedly, "You got a heavy date?"

They both smiled. At the next intersection he turned off onto the side street leading to the residential area.

Azalea Heights was a collection of old antebellum homes, remodeled and upgraded with all the modern conveniences. The homes were situated in an oak and pine forest over looking the harbor. The fog had become patchy, with intermittent clear areas moving slowly inland like misty waves covering some enchanted forest. The police car crawled down the street, stopping, shining it's spotlight into the night. The on shore breeze had picked up and the fog left tiny water droplets covering the car. Beau turned on the wipers to clear away the accumulation of water. Sally was searching with not only her eyes, but her mind, and it was turning over a thousand ideas a minute. "He's here, I can feel it. He's going to hit tonight. Don't ask me how I know."

Beau believed her. "It's a good night for it."

Sally rolled down the window hoping it would improve her visibility, when she spotted it. "What's that?" she asked nervously. Beau slowed the car to a crawl, bent over, and looked up from her side of the car.

From the second story of the old house, a light pushed it's bright finger out into the night. The curtains had not been fully closed. It was like a beacon in a white void with no up or down, just mist enclosing everything.

"A light," came Beau's typical ho-hum answer.

Slightly perturbed, Sally came back, "Very good, Lieutenant. It's outa place. Who'd be up at this time of night?"

Beau stopped the car by the curb, put on the parking brake, turned off the headlights, then looked at the Agent, "How about an insomniac? or worse, someone with loose bowels."

She gave him a look with a twinge of spunkiness in it, "Lieutenant!"

Beau let a quick smile come across his face. "Just a minute." he said, as he picked up the radio mike and transmitted, "Control, this is two seven one."

The alert voice of the dispatcher came back, "Two seven one, go."

"I need a rundown on a dwelling at 5416 Azalea Lane."

"Standby, two, seven, one."

As the Lieutenant waited for the request to come back, he asked mockingly, "You always get these fits?"

"Like I said, sometimes you have to go with your guts. Humor me."

"It's two a.m. and the lady wants humor. We don't need humor, we need some Zs'."

The open channel crackled with the dispatcher's scratchy voice, "Two seven one, control." Beau put the mike to his lips. "Two seven one, go."

"I have a rundown on your request. The owner of the house at that address is one Henrietta Wentworth."

The Lieutenant answered, "Roger that, we are going on foot for ten minutes, you copy?"

"You require assistance?" the scratchy voice inquired.

"Negative, two seven one, out." Beau put down the mike, looked at Sally, and said nothing.

Waiting, she asked, "Well?"

"Henrietta is the founder of the Wentworth Academy for Young Girls. Everyone in town knows her… She happens to be 65 years old." The detectives immediately got out of the car and walked toward the old house.

Surrounding the old house was a six foot stone wall topped with heavy wrought iron pickets. Old Charter oaks with Spanish moss dripping from the limbs stood majestically on either side of the mansion. Two massive red brick pillars with iron gargoyles perched on top held a heavy baroque cast iron gate with a goldleaf "Wentworth" crest displayed in the middle. The iron gate gave a rusty creaking noise as Beau pushed it open. The two detectives walked toward the imposing oak doors with their large ornate brass door knockers. It was another pre-Civil War antebellum home for which Charleston was famous. Stately white columns held a large slate roof two stories high. The large oak door had a white cornice typical of the colonial south. Well kept potted plants were strategically placed on the porch to enhance the beauty of the impressive front door. As they approached the door Sally grinned and spoke, "If you make any crude jokes about what nice knockers those are I'm gonna punch your lights out."

The Lieutenant chuckled, "Well, you just took all the air out of that punch line. You're really a party-pooper, know that?"

Sally tried the brass door handle. To her surprise, the door swung open with little effort. Beau pointed to a large piece of ducting tape covering the deadbolt. Alertly, both detectives took out their weapons and stood clear of the door. With her adrenaline beginning to pump, Sally said, "You take the back."

Automatically, Beau started to move, then stopped and asked in a hushed voice, "Wait a minute, how come I take the back? Why don't you take the back?"

Irked, trying to hold her voice down, she answered, "Okay, I take the back and you take the front. No wonder you've never caught this guy. He's probably going out the back door right now."

Before turning away, Beau said, "Okay, ladies first. Next time it's my call."

Sally inched her way into the foyer. It was a large room with a winding staircase leading up into the darkness. The interior was again typical old south with antiques at every glance. She thought that Scarlet O'Hara could come waltzing down the staircase and she'd be right at home. The door to the parlor was open and embers of a dying fire sent a glowing light into the foyer. Sally moved to the staircase, put her back against the wall and listened, with every nerve in her body, for the slightest sound. Her eyes probed the blackness at the top of the stairs. She was hoping for a noise, a creaking board, anything that might give her warning of danger. There was nothing, just flickering light. Yet, in her mind, call it intuition, or a sixth sense, something told her that the beast was near. With both hands on her weapon she took one step at a time, moving slowly toward the top of the stairs. Her total concentration was focused on the landing. She knew if anyone was below her Beau would have confronted him by now. The threat, if any, would be upstairs. Hesitating, she stopped to catch her breath and to muster up more nerve before turning the corner and moving down the dark hallway. Without warning, the noise of a crackling ember distracted her. A dark gloved hand shot out from the corner and knocked her gun free as a nylon noose slipped around her throat and cut off her air. Clutching the smooth garrote with both hands she fought for air. The beast had her by the throat, lifting her up. She dangled almost helpless as the twisted pantyhose tightened, cutting off her scream as well as her air. She fought, kicked, and turned as the Beast dragged her into the darkness of the upper hall. She could feel his hot breath on the back of her neck. Putting both feet against the wall, in a last ditch effort, she pushed him back against the opposite wall, giving her a moment to get her hands under the garrote. She gulped as the new air rushed into her lungs. Her mind raced with ideas about what to do next. He was too strong for her. Grasping for straws, not knowing why, she shouted, "Gaylord, stop! You hear me? Gaylord, stop this at once!"

The taunt noose relaxed. It was as if the Beast had been told to "heel". She knew she had only a second to make a decision before the animal would recover from the surprise. There was only one avenue open to her and she took it. Spinning hard, she threw herself headlong down the stairs, taking the surprised killer with her. The two figures tumbled and rolled down the incline and spilled out onto the foyer floor.

Beau had finally picked the lock on the back door. He slipped into the kitchen with his weapon ready. A crashing noise from the front of the house alerted him that Sally was in trouble. Speeding up his movements, he stepped into the formal dining room. Looking for the slightest movement, or hint of danger, Beau kept his gun extended in front of him as he moved. He put his back against the wall next to the door leading to the foyer. A quick peek revealed Sally lying face down on the floor. The fear that he had felt at Harry's death flashed through his mind. Throwing caution away, he ran to the Agent's side. Carefully rolling her over, she let out a soft whimper and reached to feel a goose egg on her head. With relief in his voice, Beau asked, "Are you okay?"

"Did you get him?" came Sally's groggy reply as she tried to sit up.

Beau took a quick glance around the room. He noticed that the downstairs hall led to the kitchen. The noise of breaking glass confirmed his suspicions. The killer had circled around him and was in the kitchen. "Stay here," Beau commanded, and ran down the hall towards the kitchen. Putting his back against the wall, he readied his weapon, then spun into the open doorway ready to fire at anything that moved. The French doors in the kitchen had been shattered from the inside and were swinging free.

"How stupid," Beau thought. The door was already unlocked. The intruder could have left undetected but he panicked. Racing out the door the detective spotted a dark figure leaping from a small tree grabbing the iron pickets on top of the wall and pulling himself up. Assuming the firing stance, Beau shouted, "Police Officer, halt, or I'll fire."

The 9MM Colt automatic bucked in his hands as the bullets missed the phantom disappearing over the wall.

In less than 15 seconds the detective leaped from the top of the wall to the ground outside the estate. Beau could feel his body ache as he took off in an all out dash after the killer. He was sorry now that he'd let himself get so far out of shape. He was sucking dry cotton as he ran, not gaining an inch, and not always able to keep the assailant in visual range.

The old cemetery was an historical landmark of old Charleston, honoring the Civil War dead. Beau had chased the man for more than three blocks and had finally lost sight of him. He knew, unless the killer was an Olympic runner, he would be sucking wind too. He was here. It occurred to him that he now had entered the killer's world. Instead of the hunter, he was being hunted. He could feel the evil stalking him in the mist. The Lieutenant knelt by an old tombstone and slowly surveyed the area gulping more air.

The dream that chased him since Harry's death hung in the back of his mind, that someday soon, he would face death in the fog. Beau desperately tried to pierce the fog with his eyes. The dream that haunted him was fast becoming a reality.

"What an appropriate place to meet death," Beau thought to himself, "A cemetery."

The Lieutenant's eyes scanned across the rows of weatherworn headstones. They looked like nameless soldiers marching into battle in a tight dress right formation. Occasionally, one or two headstones were cocked, lopsided, or had fallen over. He remembered the old wives tale, "If a headstone falls away, a soul has gone to hell." His thoughts were interrupted when a night owl hooted, "Whoo! Whoo!"

Beau gave himself a nervous chuckle and said, "I wish the hell I knew who?", then moved out in a slight crouch ready for anything.

The leafless old oaks were decorated with Spanish moss and mistletoe as they stood like guardians of the dead. An old bronze statue of a Confederate General rode a black stallion in the fog. For a brief minute, it looked like the statue was alive. It had to be the moving mist. His eyes were playing tricks on him. The angry bronze horse, prancing up on his hind legs, with his forehoofs striking at the air, reminded Beau of a passage from the Bible, "And I looked to behold a pale horse riding; and his name that sat upon him was Death." For a fleeting moment it looked like the bronze face wore a mask of death. The detective blinked and the face faded away. Another thought crept into his mind. Was he living a self fulfilling prophecy? Was this the time and the place he would meet his death, like Harry? No! He was wasting time. He had to move. Fate had dealt the hand; let's play it out. The Lieutenant moved deeper into the mist searching for the slightest movement.

The beast had fallen into an open grave, and for the moment, was too weak to move. He gulped at the air. His adrenaline pumped his heart at an astounding rate. As if on command, or by self hypnosis, David closed his eyes and concentrated on slowing his heartbeat and intake of air. In no time, he was breathing normally. The adrenaline that fed his body was still running in high gear as he searched the night fog for his enemy. Picking up a heavy tree limb, the crazy man climbed out of the grave and disappeared into the mist.

Beau thought he saw movement to his right. With his weapon extended, he maneuvered himself to an old family tomb. The ornate structure was made of aged and yellowed white marble. On each corner of the tomb, weathered gargoyles grimaced at the night. A bronze cross at the apex of the roof had tarnished green with age. Stepping around quickly, Beau turned the corner in a slight crouch ready to fire. He was met by more empty space.

The Lieutenant eased up and made a quick sigh of relief. Behind his back, a dark figure rose up from the grave, as if Lucifer himself had commanded it, and struck Beau from behind, sending him tumbling over the short gravestones. The blow had caught him totally off guard, causing him to lose his gun in the darkness. Beau tried desperately to catch his breath as he rose to one knee. Quickly, a webbed belt was slipped over his neck and pulled tight with a jerking force, cutting off his air. The detective grabbed at the garrote as he twisted and turned. Lifting the killer on his back, Beau charged backwards into the granite wall smashing his opponent between him and the wall. The grip loosened only slightly. That was enough for Beau to get his fingers under the belt. Using the back of his head, he butted it against the face of his unseen assailant. The beast still hung on, tightening his grip at every turn. Beau knew it was only a matter of time and he'd be too weak to fight. From the swirling fog a shot rang out, chipping away at the corner of the white marbled tomb. In the mist, he could see Sally kneeling with her weapon ready. The next shot missed his head by a few inches, tearing into an old oak tree. From the gray mist he heard Sally say, "FBI, you are under arrest."

Keeping Beau off balance, the beast pulled him upright. Using him as a human shield, the killer began to move towards the river. Sally couldn't shoot for fear of hitting Beau. She followed quickly to close the gap so that she'd be within range to take a shot if the opportunity presented itself. At least this way, Beau was alive and she planned to keep it that way.

The rolling mist enveloped Beau and the killer as he inched his way backwards. It was a Mexican standoff. Sally had no choice, she had to play it out. Beau's life was in her hands. Although she'd been trained in hostage tactics, she'd never been faced with a real life situation. A murky cloud momentarily obstructed her view. When it cleared, both men had vanished. It was as if the night had swallowed them whole, leaving nothing but a vacuum where they once stood. Rushing to the spot, the Agent had to catch herself before plummeting over the cliff that descended into the river. With her weapon moving from left to right, she listened for the slightest sound. There it was, to her right came the sound of a man grasping for air, as he swam towards the shore. Moving down the embankment, Sally met Beau struggling to climb out of the water in his wet clothes. Holstering her weapon, she reached out to him. The Agent totally forgot that a two hundred pound detective in wet clothes weighs a little more than two hundred pounds. About half way out of the water, she slipped and both detectives fell headlong back into the river. It looked like a remake of the old Keystone Cops movie as the two detectives continued to struggle out of the water and lay exhausted on the ground.

"Where did he go?" she asked exhausted, looking at the black water in front of her, not attempting to stand up.

"I hope he went to hell." Beau answered, laying flat on his back ignoring his wet clothes.

As the heavy breathing subsided, Sally began to laugh, "You really know how to show a girl a good time."

Beau chuckled as he caught his breath. "It's funny."

"What?"

The Lieutenant propped himself up on one elbow, "Us, this, it reminds me of a Laural and Hardy comedy. No, I take that back, a Saturday Night Live skit."

She turned to face him, "Come to think of it, it is kinda ridiculous."

"I seem to be always getting you wet."

"You are really hell on a lady's dry cleaning."

Beau sat up trying to get the water out of his ear, and said, "That was pretty good shooting back there."

Struggling to a sitting position, Sally wrung the water out of her hair, "Not really, I was aiming at his leg." They both laughed, then Sally turned dead serious as she announced, "It was Harcourt." That statement caught Beau off guard, "How'd you know?"

"I called out his name and he stopped. I mean the guy had me by the throat and he stopped when I called his name."

"Well, now we know who we're after."

"Yeah, but I only saw one guy." Sally remarked.

Beau couldn't help but notice that Sally's blouse was soaking wet. Her breasts made a deep impression on the fabric with every breath. Unable to take his eyes off her Beau said, "Thanks."

"For what?"

"For saving my life."

"You're welcome. You did the same for me." She said feeling her attraction for this handsome cop. They both moved slowly towards each other. Beau moved a curl from her forehead. The excitement of the moment had her still breathing hard. Slowly, she realized her breathing was no longer from excitement. It was from pure sexual desire. To hell with the killer. To hell with the danger that held their fears just moments ago. At that moment, at that time, she wanted to have him. It was as if some hidden desire mixed with adrenaline had overtaken them. They both eagerly clutched each other as their lips met in a passionate kiss. Sally parted her lips and met his tongue with hers. She clutched at his body wanting to tear off his clothes. She wanted him inside her, she wanted to feel him on her. He felt her full breasts which were hard and erect with desire. Suddenly, the passionate embrace was broken with the sound of grinding metal.

"What was that?" Beau said, moving to put Sally out of harm's way. Sally drew her weapon and moved to Beau's side.

"It came from over there," she said pointing at a dense part of the woods near the river's edge. Carefully, they moved into the woods.

The iron grate covering an underground runoff aqueduct built before the Civil War, was partially open. It was part of a an old sewerage system under the city that allowed for excess water from storms to drain either to the Ashley or Cooper rivers. It was still in working order and had helped to reduce the flooding significantly during hurricanes. Beau examined the grate closely.

"He went in here. See, he moved it back, then tried to close it again. There had to be two of them. One guy couldn't move that by himself."

"Don't be too sure about that," Sally remarked.

The iron grate was old and rusted. Beau brushed away some more leaves, kneeled down and give the grate a tug. It moved slightly.

"Give me a hand."

Sally gripped the grate, then together they moved it to one side revealing a black pit with steel step bars protruding from the side leading down into blackness. Beau gestured, "Ladies first."

Sally pushed him forward, "Go Mr. Macho."

He smiled and started down the ladder. At the bottom of the pit he looked up at the only source of light to see Sally close behind him. They held each other not sure of their footing, or in what direction they should proceed.

"Now what?" Sally asked.

"Your guess is as good as mine," he answered.

"Wait a minute," She reached into her jacket pocket and produced a penlight. The dim light barely illuminated the floor.

"Oh, that's nice," Beau said sarcastically.

"Hey, you want something better? Wait here and I'll run back to the car," Sally answered in rebuttal.

"Okay, which way?"

"How should I know. I got you the light, the rest is up to you." She could play this game with the best of them. This time she knew that Beau was just trying to take her mind off the fear that would have gripped any normal person.

"Wait a minute, you're the psychic," Beau quipped.

She smiled and nudged him in a direction. It was a large sewerage system. You could have driven a Mack truck through there and not even scraped a fender. The dim light revealed a construction of river rock with patches of red clay brick that had been used to repair the aging system. Beau held up his hand, "Shhh!" They both froze in mid stride and listened. There it was, the tell tale splash of footsteps echoed down the large tunnel. The killer was in the tunnel ahead of them by about a hundred yards.

"Come on," Beau said as they both picked up the pace. The two detectives were almost in a dead run when they tripped over an object laying across the bottom of the now narrowing tunnel. Both detectives ended up face down in the slimy sewage. The penlight had dropped and they were in total darkness. Beau groped around searching for the penlight.

"Hey, that's my leg your grabbing," she said trying to find Beau's hand.

"Sorry, you okay?" He asked in a whisper.

"Yeah," was Sally's whispered answer.

Reaching his hand deep into the pool of sewage up to his elbow he was finally able to retrieve the penlight, but could not get the light to work properly. After hitting the light with the palm of his hand a few times it lit. Turning the light on Sally he saw that she was sitting in the middle of a dead and rotting corpse. Noticing the expression on Beau's face, Sally turned to come face to face with the smiling skull. Her scream echoed throughout the sewer. Moments later, another iron grate slowly moved closed as the killer disappeared into the night.

Beau and Sally returned to the open manhole from which they had entered. They climbed out, moved the grate back into position, and sat reflecting on their first encounter with the killer. They were both ragged looking, clothes torn, tired, and filthy. Sally's hair was wet and hung down in her face. Beau brushed bits of feces out of her now flattened curls.

"Thanks," she said, picking more indescribable items from her hair and clothing. Sally looked at Beau. He wasn't a pretty picture either. She thought to herself, "How ridiculous, minutes ago we were two hot and passionate people and now we look just like we've been flushed down a toilet."

They both started to laugh when Sally suddenly stood up straight and shouted, "Oh my God! We forgot."

"What?"

"Ah… What's her name?"

"Henrietta?"

"Yeah, we don't know if she's alive or dead."

He took Sally's hand and they disappeared quickly into the fog.

Beau opened the car door and grabbed the mike as a wet Agent shivered at his side. "Control 271, this is Gasteneau. The suspect was last seen in the vicinity of 5416 Azalea Lane behind the cemetery on Wexford. Seal off the area. We have a dead body in the Ashley aqueduct. We will need a crime scene unit ASAP and portable lights, lots of 'em. Also patrols on either side of the river for three miles, from the cemetery to the Ashley river front. And get some K9 units out here; I want them to run the aqueduct from the cemetery to the river. One more thing, get forensics to 5416 Azalea Lane, ASAP. We still don't know what we'll find inside. Oh, one last thing. Could you bring some clean clothes for Agent Thornton and myself?"

"That's a ten four, two seven one." came the dispatcher's excited reply.

After resetting the main circuit breaker panel they entered the house. Sally and Beau began to turn on the lights as they proceeded upstairs, down the hall, stopping at Henrietta's bedroom door. Knocking gently, Beau asked, "Henrietta, are you there?"

There was no response. A worried look met Sally as she looked at Beau.

"Henrietta, it's Beau, are you there?" Still they heard nothing from the other side of the door. Beau's hand gripped the locked door knob and gave it a hard twist. From the other side of the door came a feisty voice with a solid warning. "You come through that door and I'm gonna wrap this hickory bat around your ugly head. Now, go on, git!"

Beau leaned his forehead against the door in relief. She was alive. Smiling, he turned to Sally, "That's Henrietta." The Agent was surprised to see Beau's extra concern for this woman. The Lieutenant leaned his shoulder against the door frame as if talking to an old friend, "Open up Henrietta, it's Beau Gasteneau, Rowland's boy." There was a momentary silence from the other side.

"How do I know who you say you are?"

Beau smiled again at Sally as if he were playing a game with the voice. "Didn't you use to spark around with my Pa? I seem to remember about the time you and he went skinny-dipping at Butler's Pond one night."

This time there was no silence, no hesitation as the door swung open and a gray haired old woman, with eyes of blue fire, stood there. At age 65 she was still her own woman, outspoken, and full of life. She smirked as she reprimanded Beau like one of her own kids, "That no account good-for-nothing fathead told you about that? My God, you're the spittin' image of your Pa, God rest his soul." She observed his filthy clothes, "you even dress like him. Well, don't just stand there. I don't care what you two have been up to, come here and give me a big hug."

The Lieutenant did as he was told. He held the old lady tenderly, with relief, knowing she was alive. Then he introduced Sally. "Henrietta, Special Agent Thronton, FBI."

Henrietta took Sally's hand in a firm shake as she examined her like a mother looking at her son's first date.

"My, my, things have sure changed haven't they." Nodding at Beau, she added, "Look out for this lad. If he's like his Pa, he'll steal your heart away."

Beau put his arm around the little woman and spoke, "Sorry Henrietta, he got away."

Looking at Beau, Henrietta responded bluntly, "He gave you two a run for your money didn't he. Don't you worry, as long as I have my hickory bat and Big Bertha." The old lady displayed a big Civil War saddle gun and her hickory club before she continued, "He won't be giving me any trouble."

Scratching the top of his head, Beau asked jokingly, "Are you sure you can handle it?"

The determined look never left her face for a minute as she sang out her answer, "Son, I've been handling it before you were a gleam in your daddy's eye."

Sally chuckled out loud as she saw Beau blush for the first time. The Lieutenant was actually at a loss for words. Beau kissed the little woman on the top of the head and announced, "Sweetheart, I'm gonna have to bring some boys to go over the house just in case he left something."

Tightening the belt on her bathrobe, Henrietta looked at the detective, "Well, I better get downstairs and put on a pot of coffee." Taking Sally by the arm, she marched out of the room talking to her like a daughter.

"Come on child, we're gonna get you into a shower and then you can tell me why in the world you are trapsin' around with the likes of him."

At three A.M. Henrietta's old house was lit up like a Christmas tree as police officers moved in and out. Yellow tape cordoned off areas of the house as photographers and forensic experts searched for prints. Beau had showered and put on some clean clothes Henrietta had laid out for him. Beau had a t-shirt, a pair of bib overalls and a blue jean jacket that made him look like a local farmer. Sally and Beau side stepped policemen as they moved out the back door and walked towards the old magnolia tree situated in the center of the back yard. The early morning air carried a chill that made Sally sneeze.

"Bless you," came Beau's automatic reply.

"Thanks."

He looked at the attractive Agent at his side. She was dressed in a patch quilt squaw dress. He hair was still wet. Even with wet hair in her face, she was gorgeous. She wasn't just pretty, she was smart pretty. She was not a good looking air-head, with a vacuum for a brain; she had set high standards for herself and went after what she wanted. The Lieutenant respected that. It frightened him a little, but he could understand it. She was unlike any other woman he had ever met, not even his ex-wife. He had met career minded women before. They let no man get in their way. They were women, who in business or bed, came on like a steam roller. But, Sally wasn't like that. She was kinder, gentler. She proved herself before demanding anything.

"I'm sorry, you're cold." Taking off his jacket, Beau draped it over her shoulders as he spoke, "Listen, I… I want to thank you.".

Sally interrupted, "For what?"

"For saving my ah…" Trying to be polite, the detective changed his choice of words in mid sentence, "my bacon, back there."

Sally looked up at the handsome man, then pulled the jacket up around her neck, "You did the same for me."

Beau moved her closer under his arm and asked, "Back there, by the river," he paused, "I wouldn't have let it get out of hand." He said looking directly at her. "I respect you. And I'm not just saying that. I really mean it." He thought for a moment. "Mind if I ask you a question?"

Sally nodded.

"Is there anyone special in Washington?"

"No. Why?" She said smiling at his shy bumbling attempt to find out more about her personal life.

"No reason," he said looking at one of the patrol men guarding the side gate.

"You have a reason. Everyone has a reason." Sally wanted to press Beau for some honesty and at the same time help him over his shyness.

Beau squirmed getting a little uncomfortable with his personal questioning. "You answer my question and I'll give you my reason."

Sally thought quietly before speaking. "You mean the kid in the wallet photo?"

Beau nodded politely.

Sally answered, "That's Katie. She's the light of my life. Like most college kids I had too many hormones and too few brains. When my boyfriend found out I was pregnant he took off. My Mom, bless her soul, kept me going to school and the rest is history." Sally looked lovingly at Beau for the first time. This is more than she has shared with any man. "Now, your reason."

Beau hesitated like a shy schoolboy on his first date, "Back in the house, when I saw you laying on the floor, I thought… I thought I'd lost you and…"

For a long moment their eyes locked in a silent embrace. He didn't mean for this to happen. It was totally unprofessional, but he had fallen in love with Sally. This wasn't just another lustful encounter, another "whim-wham thank you ma'am deal." Sally had really gotten to him. This was the kind of woman he could spend the rest of his life with. Sally saw in Beau a man who wanted and needed commitment in his life and that was the void she had in her life. Nobody in Washington was committed to anything but self interest. She wanted him but she knew there had to be respect on both sides for it to work. Unconsciously, Sally moved closer to Beau as a chill sent a small shiver into her body. She wasn't cold. Her shiver was one of physical excitement. Beau held her tighter, then broke the silence as he turned her around and rested her back against the trunk of the old magnolia.

"Look, I'm no Mr. Suave as you've noticed. I'm about as subtle as a train wreck. I believe you've heard that before, but I say what I think, and I have this tremendous urge to kiss you."

Sally brought her lips up to meet his and whispered, "Sounds like you need therapy."

She opened her mouth and met his lips tenderly at first, then with pent up passion, their tongues touched and searched each other with building excitement. Sally broke the long kiss and looked at Beau,

"On second thought, maybe I'm the one that needs the therapy." Letting the excitement of the moment subside, Beau kissed her softly again and said, "You're the doctor... Look, you are a very desirable woman. I'm not going to jump on you until you say, jump, all right? So, let's get out of here before I change my mind."

Sally's mind raced with the idea of making love to Beau. Right now, she needed that, wanted that. After being so close to death, she wanted to feel alive. He made her feel alive. Her mind said, "Jump, Jump, Jump," but she only nodded in agreement as Beau lead her towards the back gate.

The Police Chief stepped carefully over the broken glass as he exited the back door and moved expectantly towards Beau and Sally. He caught up to Beau and Sally at the back gate. Lighting a cigarette, he asked, "Okay, give me a rundown. You had him. What happened?"

Keeping his arm around the shivering Agent, Beau replied, "We lost him in the sewer behind the cemetery. We'll get him next time."

The Chief took a long drag on his cigarette, then blew the smoke away from Sally, "Whose the corpse in the sewer?"

"I haven't the foggiest," Beau answered.

The Police Chief took a long drag and blew the smoke into the air, "Next time? This guy is like trying to catch smoke. Are you any closer?"

With a chill in her voice, Sally replied, "We know who the guy is,... Gaylord Harcourt. He's probably teamed up with a David Delongpre. We've got Delongpre's file. We find Delongpre, he leads us to Harcourt, it's just a matter of time."

"How much time?"

The Agent shrugged her shoulders and left the Chief with a blank expression as they stepped around him, walked to the police car, and got in.

"Good question, no answers," was Beau's parting remark. The Chief threw his cigarette butt down and stomped on it in constrained frustration, as the car drove off into the night.

Chapter Seven:

The Child

The low marine clouds were just beginning to break up. It was going to be a bright day. The heat and humidity were already taking their toll on the demonstrators in front of Police Headquarters. The heat became merciless. It clung to your skin, making you break out in a running sweat at the slightest movement. This was the kind of weather that brought tempers to the surface and the black community, already steaming, had turned out to demonstrate. Women, children, old men, grandmothers, and grandfathers marched with hastily made signs held aloft, chanting slogans demanding police protection and recall of the Police Chief. Some of the signs asked for immediate prosecution of the policemen involved in the death of old man Blessing. Other posters were even more blunt, calling white policemen Klansmen.

The chanting protesters took turns parading in front of the TV cameras. It was almost comical to see young black teenagers as they tried to occupy center stage, chanting, waving fists, showing off their Malcolm X T-shirts, behind protesters being interviewed by TV news teams. It was a well organized demonstration designed to get as much coverage as it could from a liberal press. The black demonstrators were confined to the left side of the street. On the right side, the Klan had gathered to muster a counter demonstration. It too, had protest signs showing a black man killing white women, and demanding the recall of the black Mayor. The skinheads displayed signs with the Nazi swastika and slogans promoting white Aryan supremacy. They shouted insults at the news media for not hearing their side of the controversy. In between the two factions, three police cars with riot control squads were strategically placed to prevent any confrontation.

The police Operations Room was a beehive of activity. Beau entered and poured himself a cup of coffee. Studs curled up in his favorite sunny spot near Beau's office door. Jack was standing in front of the main city operations map. Looking at notes in his hand, Jack placed colored pins at specific points then turned and met Beau's concerned look. He nodded his head at the window. "It's starting again. At least they agree on one thing. Both sides out there want to recall the Mayor."

"I've noticed. Whatcha got?" Beau said, gulping at his coffee.

"Mostly fire bombs tossed from a moving vehicle. So far, we've been able to keep it down. I've put extra fire extinguishers in all patrol cars."

Beau nodded, "Good idea. I want vests and helmets too, the works."

Detective Sergeant Bradley reached across his desk and handed Jack a note. Scanning it quickly, he handed it to Beau, and announced, "Last night,

Weyford Feed & Grain was blown up. We've got two victims in four rubber bags, ID unknown." Putting his free hand on his hip, Jack shook his head, "We're at that point, payback time."

"Afraid so," Beau said, moving his attention to the city map.

Detective Sergeant Nancy Coates, a sharp, aggressive, detective who Beau had sponsored through the ranks, joined the group and added, "Our girl was right. Checked the murder dates with the Weather Service. He hits his victims only in the fog or rain."

Beau looked at her notes, "See that this gets posted on the MO board. What about Delongpre's file?"

Coates responded, "Sally's working it. The photo they sent isn't worth diddlely squat. It came over the wire as garbage."

"Get Houston to FAX another one." Beau turned to study the situation map.

Jack picked up the conversation. "Okay, the red pins represent arson responses. We have eight Federal Marshals teamed up with our riot units, here, here, and here. All units have a black and a white officer. That doesn't sit too well with some of the guys."

"That's tough."

Jack smiled, then went on, "The orange pins are known demonstrations planned for the next three days."

The Lieutenant took another sip of coffee, "What about intel?"

Jack sat on the corner of his desk as he answered, "The Purple Lizard, or Wizard…"

"Dragon," Beau interrupted.

"Whatever," Jack said, taking another sip of coffee before he went on. "He's too smart to use the hotel phones. No joy on our Hitler friend either. So, we've bugged the pay phones for a one block radius around their hotel. By the way, we've already got a man on the Weyford bombing. Maybe we can get a tie in."

Beau nodded in agreement, "It's there. These guys were Klan muscle as you found out and everyone else in this town knows it."

Jack went on, "We have two tag teams from Vice posing as teachers working the east side school district"

"Be careful, I don't want any more dead cops."

"They're covered."

"Anything else?" Beau questioned as both men walked towards his office. Jack was hesitant, which was not his style. He always knew what he did and why he did it. However, he knew he owed Beau an apology for jumping on his case back at the apartment. At that time, he didn't understand how close Beau had been to his partner. Although Beau tried to keep everything inside, he wore his feelings on his sleeve when it came to people he cared about. Everyone in the department knew Harry's death had hit him hard and he felt responsible for not being there fast enough to back up his friend. Any normal person would have come down hard on himself. Beau didn't. He mourned his friend with a week long drunk, then went on with his job and quit the heavy boozing. Some of the guys at the station told Jack that Beau doesn't get mad, he gets even. Jack didn't like the sound of that and he wasn't quite sure how Beau had taken his harsh words. That was history and he had to know where he stood. Jack spoke warily, "Ah, the other day, you know back at the apartment, I didn't mean to dump on you."

Beau cut him off with a knowing smile, "Yes you did. I deserved it. I screwed up, so forget it." Beau took a long look at the black detective at his side, then remarked jokingly, "You was the dumper, I was the dumpee, that's how it works. You is going to be the dumpee next time, Slick."

The Lieutenant and Jack chuckled as they entered Beau's office. Sitting on the leather couch, Sally hovered over Delongpre's file. Small notes were scattered around the floor next to her foot. Without looking up she said, "There's a hot cup of coffee on the desk. Pull up a chair."

Beau looked at the empty cup in his hand, the full one on his desk, then at Jack. Jack smiled, with an "I told you so" look on his face. As ordered, Beau sat down and Jack rested on one corner of the desk with one foot slightly off the floor. Still reviewing her notes, Sally asked, "Have you had a chance to look at Delongpre's file?"

"No." Beau made a pucker with his lips as he tasted the strong black coffee. "You make this coffee?"

Sally nodded.

"You could float a horseshoe in it," he said taking another sip.

"That's the only kind," she said and went on, "David lived right here in Charleston with his mother, then with his aunt... an Alma Winslow. It lists her number... David has been in and out of trouble ever since he left home."

Taking another sip, Beau puckered again before asking, "What kind a trouble?"

Sally rummaged through several notes, then continued, "Drugs, armed robbery, assault, was a pimp for awhile...and he's handled more powder than Max Factor."

"Nice kid," Jack remarked, setting his other foot on the floor.

Looking up, the Agent went on, "I talked with Delongpre's aunt a few minutes ago. They lived with her for a while."

Beau put his cup down, "And?"

"His mother, before she turned pro, worked for a Henry and Agnes Gladlow at 1624 Park Lane as a housemaid. She said young David used to work around the yard for a few dollars. As far as I know Mrs. Gladlow was a gardener and took a liking to little David."

Beau shrugged his shoulders, "So, where does that take us?"

Sitting back, looking at the ceiling, Sally began to rationalize about what she had learned. "For one thing, the Gladlow's address is smack dab in the middle of all the other murders."

"Go on," Beau said, sitting up.

"About that time Agnes would have been in her early fifties."

"So?"

"Alma Winslow said David ran away in April, 1970."

Beau looked puzzled. "Is this suppose to be going somewhere?"

Still looking at the ceiling, she went on, "Yeah, according to Delongpre's aunt, the Gladlow's pulled up stakes and moved to Florida two months later, in June of '70." Sitting up, shuffling through her notes, she found a passage she had highlighted, "Let's see. Yeah, here it is. Agnes died of a heart attack two years ago. She's buried here in Charleston someplace."

Beau sat back in his chair and put his feet casually on another corner of the desk, "What's the point?"

Tilting her head as though asking the question to herself, she said, "Doesn't that strike you as odd? David running away, then the Gladlow's sudden move to Florida?"

"Not really, there could be a hundred reasons."

Sally stood up and paced around the room as she hypothesized.

"Try this on for size. People are being murdered in the same place where the Gladlow's lived. The victims all fit Mrs. Gladlow's description and according to his aunt, Agnes Gladlow is the only woman to have paid any attention to David as a child. Now, that's not just coincidence."

Beau started to speak when Sally cut him off.

"And why did the Gladlow's move at that specific time? Why did they abandon their home, give up their friends, and leave town in such a hurry? Why? I've been told that Agnes was on about a half dozen civic committees, belonged to the National Charity League, worked for the Governor's re-election, and the list goes on. She just wouldn't walk away from all that without a good reason."

Beau and Jack exchanged a puzzled glance then looked at Sally. "I thought we were pretty much convinced that this fella Gaylord was our killer. Would you kindly tell me what all this business about the Gladlows and David as a child has to do with these killings by Gaylord?"

Sally looked at Jack and Beau. "I think there's a connection."

"Based on what?"

"Intuition."

Beau broke into a big smile and nudged Jack. "I knew that little thing you have an over abundance of would show up sooner or later."

Sally reddened. "Okay, joke all you want but I know there's a connection. I hit it on Henrietta's house didn't I? and I'll bet my sweet bippy on this one."

Jack and Beau looked at each other with condescending grins then spoke in unison. "What's a bippy?" Jack answered his own question, looking smugly at Beau, "I donno. Probably goes with that intuition stuff."

In a condoling manner Beau remarked, "If she has a bippy, I bet it's the sweetest bippy in all the world."

Jack answered jokingly, "I think she has at least a bippy and a half, maybe two bippies."

Putting her hands on her hips Sally retorted, "Okay guys, are you finished?

"Do I get more information on the Gladlows, or don't I?"

Beau sighed then getting up, looked at Jack. "C'mon. Let's go win ourselves a bippy." Studs happily followed the group out the door.

The Charleston Post Courier was located on the corner of Magazine Street and Trado. It was late afternoon in the lower west side of Old Charleston. Picket Street, one block west of the Courier's office building, was the dividing line between the black community and the business district. At this moment Picket Street was, in every sense of the word, a battle line. The unspoken war that had broken out between the black and white community was coming to a head. The forward edge of the battle area, was Picket Street. The city's "no man's land" lay between Picket Street and Trado. Two large mobs had gathered for a final showdown in front of the Courier's office building on Magazine Street.

This crowd was not like the earlier demonstration in front of Police Headquarters. The demonstration uptown was peaceful, with women, children, and leaders of the black community. This mob was comprised of black gang members facing off against Klan muscle. It was as if some prearranged battle plan had designated this area as the location for the first bloody encounter. They came to rumble and when the time was right, they would have at it.

Both sides of the issue, black and white, were playing the media for every inch of coverage they could get. No one on either side could think of a better place to rumble, than in front of the Charleston Courier's office. A TV mobile news van was situated a little too close to the planned activities. However, in search of true life, hard hitting, sensational news, the evening news reporter was totally oblivious to his predicament as he went about interviewing mob leaders on both sides. An uneasy silence held the two mobs apart. The outnumbered police did not attempt to disarm either side for fear of kicking off a riot that was bound to happen.

The late afternoon had dwindled into early evening as the street lights automatically flickered on. The Lieutenant moved his car to the crowded curb and parked. A uniformed patrol officer dressed in full riot gear approached the car with a concerned look. The detectives, leaving Studs in the back seat, got out. Beau surveyed the situation as the young officer spoke, "Lieutenant, I wouldn't go in there right now."

"We have to get to the news office."

Lifting the visor of his riot helmet, the officer replied, "They're locked up. The only way in is through the front. As you can see it's fight night for your local TV news. Rumor has it our friend O'Brien has made up protest signs for both sides."

Looking disgruntled, Beau smirked, "That's show-biz."

Moving slowly toward the crowd the detectives eyed both sides of the upcoming rumble. On the black side, young gang members were dressed in football helmets, shoulder pads decorated with feathers, voodoo talismen, crudely painted rank and gang logos. They were armed with chains, knives, baseball bats, and other lethal devices. On the white side, Klansman, Skinheads, and Hard-hats were similarly dressed and armed. Some men used garbage can lids as shields while holding clubs in their other hand. It seemed to Beau that someone had laid down the rules of combat and that rule was, that there were no rules. He also knew that when the fight started it was every man for himself. The result would be brutal and it would settle nothing.

Glancing across the street Jack saw the Reverend Baxter moving to the front of the gang with his battery operated bull horn shouting scriptures to the blacks. Shaking his head in resignation, Jack muttered, "Shit!" and moved to confront his father-in-law with Beau and Sally following closely behind.

"What the hell are you doing here with this street scum?" Before he could answer Jack roared again, "You just couldn't resist another spot in front of the TV cameras could you... Well! Go ahead, they are all here just for you."

"These are all God's children." The Reverend's expected answer just enraged Jack more.

"Bullshit! These aren't your parishioners. Look at what the fuck they've got in their hands. Are you into bashing the Honkies? Is that it? What happened to your Christian beliefs? What happened to the law?"

"You mean Honkie law. What do you know about anything?" Raising his voice as though giving his Sunday sermon, "These are all God's children."

Jack's jaws tightened every time Baxter hid behind the pulpit. Pointing across the street towards the Klansman, Jack shouted, "Are those God's children too?"

The Reverend hesitated, "Yeah, but misdirected children."

"So, what are you gonna do, kill 'em? What does your good book say about that?...After the blood and the pain, you gonna pray for forgiveness? You think that is gonna make everything all right? Nobody is gonna win. Don't you understand that? Look at that white collar. You... you wear it like some sort of badge of righteousness. You're nothing but a fucking racist, you're no better than that white scum across the street. You know what your salvation is really gonna be? It's gonna be that black cop over there and that white cop putting his life on the line and living the letter of the law. Honky law or not, it's the only one we've got and it's gonna prevail. That's the only thing that's gonna give my kids a future, and you, you pompous sonofabitch, are not going to fuck it up."

Sally and Beau had never seen Jack go off like this before. He was right, but he had never been so verbal about his feelings. Beau wanted to step in and end the confrontation but remained silent as the two men shouted into each other's face.

Before the Reverend could gather his thoughts Jack spoke in a lowered tone, "I don't believe you. Rose is on her death bed and you're down here prancing around like a soul saving tent preacher in front of the cameras."

The Reverend Baxter calmly answered, "Rose sent me down here and by God I am gonna do my best, for both sides."

"Then get out there and put a stop to this." Jack demanded.

Dave Bently, the local TV Anchorman, followed by a grinning Danny O'Brien, broke off their interview with a tattooed skinhead across the street and moved toward Beau. Poking the boom mike in Beau's face, the newsman asked, "Lieutenant, you have any statement for the evening news?" A hundred different answers raced through his mind as he hesitated, "Yeah, why don't you take that boom mike and stick it up your ass? Or maybe, If you don't haul your ass outa here right now, you got about as much future as a cake of ice." None of these words were spoken as Beau searched for an answer that could be put on the evening news. From the corner of his eye, he caught sight of a Molotov Cocktail falling his way from an adjacent building. It's trajectory headed the falling fire bomb directly into the news van. That was the signal that would start the rumble. Looking at the two smiling idiots standing in front of him, Beau calmly said, "Yeah, duck."

Both sides rushed into the middle of the street swinging their weapons with vicious intensity. Beau grabbed Sally and moved to the edge of the riot. The TV news truck was immediately engulfed in flames. Danny O'Brien and Dave Bently, along with his two camera men, were trapped in the middle of the melee. The two cameramen continued to get as much of the fight on tape as they could until both of them were laid out with a baseball bat. O'Brien with all his quick wit could not talk his way out of this situation. In mid-sentence he was hit in the face with a gloved fist that had brass spikes protruding outward. His teeth broke outward as his lips spattered blood all over his attacker. Both Jack and Beau grimaced at the brutal blow. Dave Bently was hit in the gut with the end of a heavy piece of water pipe and he folded up like a newspaper. Before he could hit the ground, a knee to the chin straightened him upright, splitting his tongue, and he nearly choked on his own blood. Beau and Jack could handle themselves in a fight. However, this was getting a little rough. Beau started to move Sally to safer ground when she stopped and announced, "Wrong way, we have to go over there," pointing to the Courier's doorway on the other side of the fight. Bending down, Sally picked up a large piece of a brick that had missed it's mark, and put it into her purse. Taking out a can of mace and drawing the purse straps up tightly, she politely remarked, "Gentlemen, follow me." With that, Sally flailed her way through the mob taking on all comers with deadly expertise. Jack and Beau smiled in admiration as they followed quietly covering her blind side. One of Sally's opponents hesitated for a second, surprised to see a woman in a man's fight. That was his last mistake. The mace caused him to grimace in pain as he covered his eyes. This was followed by a purse swung swiftly into his testicles. He crumpled to the ground. Beau and Jack took out two clumsy fighters, easily disarming them before breaking their noses with devastating judo chops designed to inflict heavy damage on an adversary. Being momentarily unchallenged, Beau barked to Sally over the noise as though it were a New Year's Eve party, "I like your style. What do they call it?"

"It's my own, I call it a testicle reduction," she said, ducking a wild swing then bringing her purse up between the legs of another unsuspecting adversary. A brute of a black man confronted Jack, then froze in the middle of a swing, "Hey brother, whatcha doin' with these Honkies?"

That was the break Jack needed as he unloaded on the surprised rioter. "First, I'm not your brother." A smashing left hook stopped the big man in his tracks. "Second," a brutal right cross dislodged three teeth from the right side of his mouth, "You're breaking the law." The final uppercut sent his lower jaw into his upper lip and he sank to the ground. The mace kept the rest of the would-be attackers away as they made it to the front door. Flashing their badges at the hesitant security guards the Ledger's front door reluctantly opened then quickly shut as soon as the detectives were inside.

The lobby of the Charleston Post Courier was over waxed, over marbled, and reflected the lack of architectural imagination that followed

World War II. It didn't reflect the rich southern heritage of the other buildings seen throughout the city. It would have been a blessing if the building had burned to the ground. There were four armed security guards standing in the lobby. All of them were underpaid, untrained, and overweight. They had never had to deal with a riot before. If anyone was going to be trigger happy it would probably be one of them.

Beau and Jack took a few seconds to catch their breath as they watched the FBI agent rearrange her purse. Taking out the brick she handed it to an amazed security guard standing at the desk.

"Hold this 'til I get back."

The three detectives started up the stairs as Beau commented, winking at Jack, "Remind me lady, to never get you mad at me."

Jack chimed in playing the same game, "That FBI sure has some strange training?" The black detective stopped in mid-sentence, "I better stay down here and see if I can get some more troops on the job." Sally knew the real reason. Even though he didn't agree with his father-in-law he was worried about his safety. Beau nodded in agreement as the two detectives went on.

The newspaper's archives were as unimaginative as the rest of the building. Heavy oak files, probably rescued from some old library, were positioned along the walls. Stacks of papers that needed filing laid heaped on one table. The only interesting object in the room was W.C. Haskins, the librarian. He bore a remarkable resemblance to W.C. Fields. Like the old time film comic, his eyes sat above a big bulbous red nose that had blue veins covering the lower part. A big belly hung over his belt and he constantly chewed on an unlit cigar. Obviously, this man loved his booze. W.C. knew everyone in town, and at one time, back in the fifties, had been the top reporter on the Courier. Some say that he is a major stockholder in the paper. That's why he'd been there for so long. With his friends, W.C. took special time to play the part of the comic actor by adopting his mannerisms. Seeing the detectives enter his private domain, he picked up his old top hat and spoke in the drawl of W.C. Fields, "Aaah! as I live and breathe, if it isn't Charleston's answer to Sherlock Holmes, Dick Tracy, and Charlie Chan rolled into one."

Smiling, Beau answered his old friend, "Hi W.C., this is Sally."

Tipping his old hat, mimicking the actor, he went into his routine, "Aaah, my Sweet Chickadee, welcome to Haskins Hall of History. Don't tell me, ah, let me guess, you are seeking knowledge and enlightenment... Come to think of it," he looked at Sally and nodded toward Beau, "That lad hasn't had an original thought since puberty." Haskins took Sally's hand and kissed it gently before going on. "What do we have here, a gem, a beauty who could inspire Keats, a flower about to be plucked from the garden of love?"

Sally found him amusing. He was someone who could kid a kidder and always get the upper hand. Beau turned his head as though he didn't quite hear Haskins correctly, "What was that again?"

Haskins, seeing Beau's meaning, replied, "I said plucked."

"Nice save W.C.."

Haskins, disregarding Beau's attempt at humor, took Sally's hand again, "Ah, my Little Petunia, let's fly away to some forgotten land and escape this cesspool of society."

"Careful W.C. She's FBI."

With Beau's announcement, Haskins quickly withdrew his hand, comically moved his cigar to the other side of his mouth, tipped his hat again, and exclaimed, "Gadzooks! Federal fuzz!"

With the game playing over, Beau leaned against the counter, "We need to look at the obits from two years back."

Haskins sat back, "You have a date?"

Sally smiled politely and answered, "No, we're looking for a funeral that happened two years ago."

Walking to a rack of small shelves, Haskins began to thumb through some old shoe boxes. "You're in luck. This paper, for some God forsaken reason, likes to keep track of who kicks the bucket around here." Taking two boxes from the shelf he placed them on the counter then nodded toward the two microfiche machines in the corner. "Have fun kids."

Haskins enjoyed the shocked look on their faces. Taking the boxes in his arm Beau and Sally walked to the machines.

"When are you guys gonna get a computer in this place?"

"Tell me about it. I only work here you know. They don't ask for my opinion." Haskins sat back, took another puff on his newly lit cigar, and chuckled to himself.

Two hours later Beau still sat in front of the machine that was obviously designed to make him go blind. The words were beginning to run together. He was wondering if he could recognize the article even if he saw it.

"Whoops!" Sally remarked moving her slide back down to the previous paragraph, "Just a minute. Here it is. Agnes had a sister, a Mrs. Norma Pierce, 7421 Bayshore Drive."

Beau shut down his machine and read the article over Sally's shoulder. He smiled and said, "Lets do it. I'm about to win myself a bippy."

By the time Sally and Beau left the newspaper office the outside riot had dwindled to just a few rioters being loaded into the wagons and hauled off. The remnants of sunset glowed on the western horizon. The couple walked to meet Jack who was giving the last instructions to the patrol sergeant. Jack turned and gave Beau a beleaguered smile, then nodded toward his father-in-law the good reverend.

"How's he doing?" Beau asked trying to hold back a chuckle.

"He shaken but not stirred." Jack replied trying to keep a straight face.

"How is he, really?" Sally asked, concerned and a little peeved that these two cops had no heart for their own folks.

"He'll be fine. I'm gonna take him down to the station and scare the hell out of him," Jack replied letting out a frustrated sigh.

Sally and Beau looked at each other, turned and said in unison, "Be gentle."

"Outa my face you two," Jack said jokingly and pointed his finger.

The group watched the patrolman put the reverend in the back seat of the black and white. Jack climbed into the right seat and rode off.

The sun had completely set and the night fog was beginning to creep in.

"We better get going if we want to get this thing done." He motioned Sally to follow him to the car.

Bayshore Drive was a quiet little street, set on a small wooded peninsula area adjacent to the inland waterway northeast of Charleston. The house was a typical upper middle class, three bedroom, Cape Cod Colonial, with small white pillars supporting a shingled porch roof. A white swing held by chains swung in the evening breeze. Potted marigolds and mums provided a brilliant array of color that stood out against the red brick walkway. The garden was well kept, with azaleas grouped beneath the pulp pines that dotted the front lawn. Beau and Sally exited the patrol car and strode up the curving red brick walk to the colonial front door and rang the chimes.

Norma Pierce was in her middle sixties. She was a well dressed lady with graying hair tied in a tight bun behind her head. She was a handsome woman for her age. She stood erect with no dowager hump as you would expect for a woman her age. One would expect to see her in the local library checking books in and out.

When the door opened the detectives displayed their identification as Beau introduced himself and Sally, "Lt. Gasteneau, Charleston Police and this is Special Agent Thornton, FBI. May we talk to you for a minute?"

The old woman looked confused, "What about?"

"It's about your sister, Agnes," Sally responded in a calm voice. Norma Pierce was obviously shaken by the announcement and started to close the door, "I have nothing to say."

"Mrs. Pierce," Beau injected, "This has to do with the serial killer. Now, talk here quietly, or we can go to the station. Down there I can't guarantee that the news people won't get involved."

Norma resigned herself to the situation and opened the door allowing the detectives to enter. With a stern upper lip, she ushered them into the parlor and offered them a seat before she spoke. "I can't see what my sister has to do with these killings. She's been dead for the past two years."

"Does the name Delongpre mean anything to you?" Sally said, looking for the slightest reaction. She saw it in her eyes and noted that she nervously twisted the handkerchief held in her hands.

"Why should it?"

Leaning forward, Beau cut in, "Mrs. Pierce, we know that his mother worked for your sister and her husband."

"Yes, come to think of it, I do believe that a David did, but that was years ago. That whole incident couldn't have anything to do with.."

"What incident?" Sally quickly remarked, picking up on Norma's slip.

"Nothing."

"Mrs. Pierce, we know that when David came back to town the murders started. We also know that he's involved with another man named Gaylord Harcourt. They have already committed four murders in Texas, and have killed seven elderly ladies here," Beau said in his stern police voice. "Do you understand? He's killed seven well respected ladies in this community. Some of them may have been friends of yours."

Sally cut in with her calm counterpoint to Beau's demands, "Mrs. Pierce, I'm a Behavioral Scientist by training. I know that something, or someone, has turned our killer on. David is connected to the killer. Either he's protecting him, or the killer is killing these people because David wants them dead. Please listen to me, in some way David is the key. Please, I beg you, tell us what you know about Agnes and David."

Norma Pierce sat on the verge of tears and panic as she twisted her hanky around her fingers repeatedly. Sally went on, "I promise you right now, what you tell us will stay in this room."

A deep sigh of resignation came from Norma as she lowered her head in shame. "All right, Lord knows I've tried all these years to keep this buried, but it just won't go away...I knew little David. Far as I know his mother was the worse kind of white trash, a prostitute. She never knew David's father. He died of an overdose. Alma was his only relative... He was an innocent, loving child that needed a mother desperately." Norma hesitated.

Sally leaned forward, "And?"

The welling tears finally broke through and as tears trickled down Norma's face she continued, "Agnes was sick, she was under a doctor's care. She really didn't know what she was doing with that little boy..."

"She was a child molester," Sally said finishing the sentence. Beau and Sally silently looked at each other.

This was too much for Norma to handle. She broke into a sob and continued, "She molested that poor child for over three years. You know what's ironic?...David loved Agnes. He gave her his little body. All he wanted in return was her love. But, she treated him like the lowest kind of dirt." Norma took out her twisted hanky and tried to clear her eyes. "Finally,

David ran away. Left Alma a note telling the whole ugly story. Alma confronted Agnes with the letter and Agnes ended up buying the note from Alma. Then Agnes moved to Florida. I guess everyone has their price. I'm just as guilty as Agnes. I should have said something, but I didn't. For God's sake she was my sister, what could I do?" The tears continued to pour out of this tortured woman, "What could I do? What could I do?"

Sally knelt next to her and embraced her with understanding. Beau held his next question until she had regained her composure.

"One more question. Did Agnes grow Forget-me-nots?"

"No, David did," Norma said, taking a final sigh of relief.

Sally put her arm around the sobbing woman. "Mrs. Pierce, I know this has been hard for you but you've been a great help. Hopefully, we can get David some help. Is there anything else you can think of?"

Norma thought for a moment. "I got a letter from David."

That triggered a quick reply from Beau, "You got a letter. Do you still have it?"

"No, that was a long time ago." Norma hesitated again, thinking back, "But the letter was posted from Seattle."

The detectives made notes in their books. Norma continued remembering, "He said he was getting help."

"What do you mean help?" Sally queried.

"A doctor of some sort."

"Do you have a name?" Beau asked.

Norma closed her eyes thinking back, "I think it was a Doctor Michaels. Yes, that's it. Doctor Michaels."

Sally looked sympathetically at Norma. "I'm sorry we've had to put you through this but you've added another important piece of the puzzle. Thank you."

For Norma Pierce her final torment had ended. She had let her dark secret out to the light of day. It was said and done. She could say that the whole incident was finally over, and if it helped bring David back to his senses, it was worth it. That was her consolation. There was a weight finally lifted from her shoulders as she closed the door behind the departing detectives.

Beau put the car in drive and moved slowly down the street glancing back in the rear view mirror at the clean, neat little houses all in a row with well manicured lawns. A place you would think least likely to have a scandal that would twist a child's mind into that of a serial killer. Both detectives held their silence until they had turned on to the main interstate. Sally turned her attention from the passing landscape to Beau.

"You realize the hell that kid must a gone through?" She looked out the car window again as she spoke, "As a poor rag-a-muffin kid, what was he gonna say? Who was gonna believe him? You know how they treat white trash around here."

Beau was unsympathetic, "I've got some news for you kiddo, there are some pretty nice people around here. And that doesn't give him the right to go around killing people. You think he's the only kid who was ever abused? Remember, he killed a cop, too."

"Yeah, I know."

Beau tried to get her heart off her sleeve and her brain back in high gear when he began to rationalize about what they had learned. "Okay, the tie in to David is that he was abused as a child. Now he's getting even with Agnes by helping Gaylord kill other women."

"Not quite. He's getting even because of rejection… As I see it, he went along with the sex, he couldn't handle the rejection. Remember, David never really had a mother."

"So now, he gets Harcourt to ice old ladies."

Sally nodded confirming Beau's assessment, but she was still asking unanswered questions. "Yes, but why? Why have someone else even the score? Something is still missing. The pieces aren't all together yet."

"What do you mean?"

"How does David get Harcourt to do the killings?"

"Beats me, but Houston PD's convinced. David passed the lie detector. Even gave them a composite of Harcourt."

"Yeah, but nothing turned up on the wire. Nobody, including ourselves, knows anything about Harcourt. Why?"

"You think David made him up?"

Sally focused her attention on the road before she answered, "Oh no, Harcourt's real all right, I just don't know how he fits."

Beau put the pedal to the metal and increased his speed, as they headed back to town.

"What about this Doctor Michaels in Seattle?" Sally inquired.

"That's another lead that needs a follow up. Thanks to you there may be light at the end of the tunnel."

With a satisfied smile on her face, Sally sat back and enjoyed the ride back to Charleston. The FBI agent popped Beau a sly look, "You got time for a detour?"

Beau stared momentarily at the headliner of the car, "Let me guess, you want another tour of the city?"

"Like I said before," Beau cut her off before she could finish the sentence and they both finished the sentence in unison, "You gotta heavy date?"

The patrol car turned off the interstate as Beau took a short route towards the center of the city.

Chapter Eight

The Gathering Of Fools

An emergency meeting of the Charleston Action Committee was called by the Mayor. Confrontations, small fights, a labor boycott, fire bombs, sniper fire at the ACLU offices, cars vandalized, church bombings had brought the city to the brink of chaos. The Mayor was searching for some hint of progress in finding the serial killer. He was eager to get this issue out in the open and into the courts. He knew that this was the only way the rioting could be controlled. Getting the killer, or killers, into the court system would remove the race issue once and for all. He would see to it that the public would see the criminal as a deranged killer and nothing more and that would tell everyone on both sides that the city government is more than capable of handling this situation just like any other situation. It would also defuse the propaganda. It would cutoff the issues these radical elements feed on to incite civil unrest, and promote their own agenda.

The D.A., Chief of Police, FBI, National Guard Commander, City Civil Engineer, and the Fire Chief were seated around the conference table. All heads focused on Beau as he finished his briefing. He brought the panel up to date and advised them of the latest information obtained from Norma Pierce. Everyone nodded approval, but the consensus was that the investigation was progressing too slowly. Agent Thornton rose to her feet and began to speak, "Gentlemen." The panel stopped their internal discussion and focused on Sally.

"Let me see if I can explain what is happening here. Maybe I can put some of what we are dealing with into perspective." Sally began to walk around the table as though she were lecturing back at Quantico. "When a murder is committed, normally, the detectives gather what evidence they can. They trace the victim's identity, try to reconstruct the crime from what they know to determine the victim's movements during his or her final hours. You interview witnesses and so on. Now, these procedures will probably work seven out of ten times in solving most homicides. It doesn't work solving serial killer murder cases. The reason is simple, he isn't like other killers." She could see that she had their attention. Before they could interrupt her train of thought with a question, she continued, "His motive for murder is not dependent upon a particular situation, or a particular individual, it is pure compulsion that drives him. That compulsion is an ever repeated pattern of violence." The men at the table had stopped drinking their coffee. A burning cigarette was left unattended in the ash tray. Sally had to make sure that they clearly understood the situation, and hopefully, that would take some of the pressure off the task force. She continued to circle the table as she went on. "I think we are all aware that the normal homicide investigation depends on the weight of evidence accumulated, clues at the crime scene, the relationship, if any, between the victim and the murderer, involved witnesses, and finally, the fear and guilt of the killer himself. In cases where the murder is a secondary act, solve the first crime and you've solved the second. Statistics today show that a large percentage of murders take place as a result of other actions, such as a drug deal gone bad, a car-jacking, or whatever. These murders have well defined motives and are very traceable. Since 1980 over twenty-five percent of all murders have been stranger murders. Gentlemen, these are murders where the killer has no rational motive, and no apparent connection to the victim." Sally had made the complete circle around the table and was standing at Beau's side when she began again, "The other problem we are dealing with, is time. The killer, if he follows his normal pattern may only be in this city for a short time. Usually, he'll run up a score of victims and move on. I'm sure he thinks that the Charleston Police are a bunch of hick cops. Gentlemen, I think he'll begin to take victims from neighboring counties. He knows that you could care less about Sheriff Ledbetter's problems. He's counting on this. The other thing he's counting on is that we won't take the time to trace his movements in other cities or states. The information given to us about a Doctor Michaels in Seattle is something he hadn't counted on. That's why we need to follow up on this as quickly as possible. Questions gentlemen?"

It didn't take five minutes for the Chief to authorize the trip to Seattle. With the city fathers staring at him coldly, his only recourse was to say, "yes". Beau smiled to himself, he loved to see the Chief squirm. He considered him a product of political patronage, not a cop who earned his rank by dedicated service. He thought maybe someday Charleston would get an honest politician that would pick a man to lead the force whom the men would follow eagerly.

Sally sat next to Beau as the Boeing 747 set contrails westward towards Seattle. They were airborne for the better part of thirty minutes when she nudged Beau awake and asked, "How did we rate first class?"

"After that sterling lecture, what else? Besides, I told the Chief that the Feds only travel first class."

"You didn't", she chuckled.

"I did, why not? I don't get many perks so I take'em where I can get'em."

"Am I a perk?" she inquired coyly.

"Definitely." Beau smiled thinking to himself, is she a perk? She's smart, honest, and she's with me.

"May I ask you a personal question?" she asked looking at Beau, searching his eyes for an honest answer.

"Sure."

She waited, trying not to be blunt or too harsh in her question. He waited, having a pretty good idea what the question was going to be.

"You want to know what happened with my marriage," he said before she could ask.

"No, well, not if it's none of my business."

"What happened to us. I mean the other night. The feelings we shared. I want things between us to be as honest as we can make them. So, yes I owe you that." He leaned his head back against the seat, thought back over the years, and began. "Maybe it was my fault. I don't know. Maybe if I'd paid more attention to her. I really don't know. I've thought about it a hundred times and I still don't have an answer. Maybe people just grow apart. Or, maybe things can be so traumatic, that the relationship just can't recover.

"You mean your son," she answered in a serious tone.

"He was wonderful. He made our marriage complete. We went fishing, camping, Alice and I went to all his games. I was a Little League coach. The whole works. Alice was on the PTA. You know, the perfect all American family."

Beau looked down sadly, "Then Mark got sick. He was a brave little boy. He didn't complain, didn't whine. He tried not to be a burden on us. We took him to every Doctor, every specialist. It took all of our energy. We even tried some scam cure in Mexico. I knew it was a scam, but when you are grabbing at straws, you'll take anything that comes your way. I even prayed for some miracle that didn't come."

"Leukemia." Sally stated calmly.

"Yeah. As the disease progressed Alice couldn't handle it. I had to sit there and watch him slowly slip away. Anyway, Alice couldn't cope, she drank, took pills, let herself go. I'd come home and she'd still be in bed. When I tried to get her to get some help, she just went to bars and drank even more. The arguments became more frequent, we said things we didn't mean. Then I couldn't handle it anymore and started staying late at the office." Beau gave a sigh of sadness and continued, "Then I came home and found her in bed with another guy. The rest is history. It must be some sort of record. In less than two years I lost my whole family." He sighed again. This time Beau felt that a big weight had been lifted from his shoulders. He had never been this open with any woman before. He went on, "You know what's sad?

Sally nodded and waited.

"We never seem to know what life has in store for us. I had my life all planned. I'd watch my son grow up. We'd be buddies. Alice and I would be grandparents, have the kids over for Christmas. Have a house with a white picket fence, a garden, you know, all the normal stuff." He paused again thinking about what could have been before he continued. "You know something? When Mark was sick and our marriage was in the garbage. I actually prayed. I went to church and prayed. Even lit a candle. Hell, I must have lit fifty candles." Beau looked out the window, "It didn't work. I arrived at a final conclusion, either there is no God, or I've done something to piss him off, or the candles only work for good Catholics."

Sally sat quietly waiting for him to finish this painful part of being honest. Beau went on, "I think she knew, that this was the only way to end it. Knowing Alice, she probably planned every move."

She touched his hand tenderly and said, "I'm sorry."

Beau looked at her seriously and said, "Hey, now that your feeling sorry for me, will you sleep with me?"

She hit him playfully on the shoulder, "You're bad, you're really bad."

The 747 broke out over a high overcast as it began its letdown to Seattle's Sea-Tac International Airport. The blue Pacific water that surrounds the city and the plush green forest that approached the city from the Cascade Mountains gave the city a green glow. It reminded Beau of the Emerald City in the Wizard of Oz. The space needle stood alone at the edge of the 74 acre park that surrounded the Seattle Center. Beau turned his attention to the landscape below as the aircraft continued its descent. The Lake Washington ship canal that cut the city in half, came into view. He could see the Hiram M. Chittenden locks cradling ships waiting to move forward. He concentrated on the locks trying to see the salmon ladders that continue to allow for the annual migration of salmon to their natural spawning grounds. He thought to himself that one day he would like to come out and fish in the salmon derby. But that would have to wait for another day. Beau looked at Sally, "Do you like to fish?" He asked, expecting the typical female reply.

"I love it. My step-dad took me to Mexico and got my first Marlin before I turned sixteen." She noticed a grin of satisfaction on Beau's face.

"What?"

"Nothing," he said, and closed his eyes, and thought, "she's got to be putting me on."

The Seattle-Tacoma International Airport was midway between Seattle and Tacoma just off route 99. It was a modern structure that displayed dark marble and an abundance of glass. Even though it was a contemporary structure it didn't look out of place. It was a well planned terminal with arriving passengers claiming baggage on the lower level and the departing passengers buying tickets and checking bags on the upper level. Both detectives carried only walk-on bags. They'd been told that they had only the weekend to run down their lead and get home. They were met by Lieutenant Clarence Darrow of the Seattle Metropolitan Police.

"Agent Thornton and Lieutenant Gasteneau?" he asked as they approached the information counter.

"Yes," Sally answered as the group shook hands.

"I'm Lieutenant Clarence Darrow. I'm your liaison while you're here. Anything you need, just ask."

"Lieutenant?" Beau asked, but was cut off before he could finish.

"No, I am no relation to the real Clarence Darrow." He'd been asked that question so many times it was standard procedure for him to clear that up at the beginning.

The three engaged in small talk as they stepped outside the terminal to a waiting police car. Clarence popped the trunk lid with his remote as they approached. The detectives quickly deposited their luggage and hopped in the back seat. Clarence moved the car smartly into the Seattle traffic. Clarence broke the momentary silence with the first question.

"I understand you're doing some follow up on your serial killer."

"Yeah." Beau answered with an air of frustration in his voice.

"And you have a feeling he was in our fair city."

"It's more than a feeling." Sally answered curtly.

"Well, we'll give you whatever you need. We hope maybe we can close a few open cases ourselves."

"Maybe." Beau answered.

The Seattle Police Headquarters was a modern multistory building with an abundance of windows. The squad room was like any other police squad room except everything was newer. Beau wondered where they got all the money for the facility. The detectives immediately felt at home. With Darrow leading the way they skirted the hustle and bustle of people going about their business of policing a city like Seattle. The sign on the door read Director of Intelligence Captain Mike Shannahan. Big Mike as he was called by other members of the force, came from behind his desk to shake hands with the detectives. Introductions were made and Mike said, "Sit down, make yourself comfortable. How about some coffee?"

"Thanks." Beau replied automatically.

Mike pressed his intercom and held it down. "Ethel, we need four coffees black, and all the usual stuff on the side."

"Okay," came the scratchy reply.

Seated behind his desk Mike picked up a folder and began to scan through it. "I've been reading up on your case. The MO you describe could fit some of the open cases we had a few years ago. I'd love to get some closure on these, so anything we can do just ask."

Ethel entered carrying the coffee on a small tray with sugar and cream. Sally took a sip of the strong coffee then addressed Mike.

"We know that David Delongpre lived here two years ago and was seeing a Psychiatrist Doctor Michaels. We were hoping to contact him to see if he could tell us more about Delongpre."

"Is he your prime suspect?"

"Could be. Or he knows or has had personal contact with the killer." Sally responded.

"Houston had him on a minor drug rap and let him go when he helped Houston ID the killer of two elderly women. We think Delongpre has hooked up with the killer again and is in our fair city." Beau explained.

Mike took a long gulp of coffee. Put it down and turned a page in the folder. "We've got two open cases of elderly women strangled, and sexually assaulted. However, money, jewelry, and a car were stolen. We found the cars abandon a few hours later." Mike looked at Sally knowing she was one of the FBI's top profilers. "What do you think?"

"The MO is close. Sometimes events may require quick money. But the method of killing and the sex is ritualistic. Did he have tea with the women? Or Were there any flowers at the crime scene?"

Mike thumbed through additional pages of the folder. "You're right. Not tea but coffee, and sex."

"He's probably our boy. But something spooked him and he needed money fast. My guess is he had to leave town, fast."

Beau remarked, "We might be able to give you some closure. We'll send you the results of our DNA examination. If they match what you have, then you'll know."

"Good idea." Mike said as he picked up another folder. "Now, you said you were looking for a Doctor Michaels who was in practice at that time."

"Right." Sally responded.

"We had no Doctor Michaels in practice at that time . Here's the list of all psychiatrists and psychotherapist working in Seattle at that time."

Sally and Beau looked disappointed as they both scanned the list. Mike continued, "Now, you've noticed that I've underlined a Doctor Michael A. Smith. About the time your guy was in town, this guy disappeared. There was no plausible reason for this guy to leave. He had a nice family, no debts, socially active, country club and all that. Nothing in his background that would indicate he wanted to or needed to leave. I was wondering if this guy whose first name coincides with your request might have a connection."

"Never thought about it. We assumed that Michaels was his last name." Beau commented. Sally stared at the name on the list. "We better check this out." She said with her finger still resting on the name.

"We'll need to take a look at his records." Beau added.

"When he went missing we got a court order and impounded his records. They are down stairs in the evidence room. That looks like a good place to start." Mike said standing up and gulping down a last bit of coffee.

The police sergeant had already set four large cardboard boxes aside as Clarence signed for the materials. Clarence led the way across the hall carrying two boxes to the interrogation room. Beau and Sally followed each carrying a box. The room was drab with two small tables in the center. A two-way mirror adorned one wall. The group began to unpack the boxes setting folders in piles according to date. Clarence suggested, "Since I'm familiar with our marking system I'll sort and you guys can read." Picking up a stack of folders he added. "Lets start off with the patient list starting four years back."

It took about two hours of sorting, reading and then dropping the unneeded files in the empty box on the floor. Sally looked at Clarence and said, "I'm up to the dates where the murders were occurring in Houston. Our guy would have left town by then."

"I agree." Beau responded scratching his head, searching for other options. "Is there anything we've overlooked?" He asked looking at Clarence, then to Sally. She stared at the remaining unopened files. "Did the good Doctor do any charity work? Have you seen a file where he may have worked outside his office, say for the city, state, or even a hospital?"

"Funny you should ask," Clarence said with a hint of levity in his voice. He moved a pile of folders and produced a rag torn brown folder with an orange index tab on the top edge. "Here we go. Saint Jude Free Clinic. It looks like he volunteered his time. From what I see here it looks like one day a week. Nice guy," he said handing the folder to Sally. She quickly scanned the document then smiled.

"What?" Beau asked noting her expression.

"I'm sorry to say there is no name like David Delongpre here, but we do have a Gaylord Harcourt."

Beau stopped his reading and Clarence sat down assuming that the quest was over but not knowing why. "Anybody want to fill me in?"

"Gaylord was David's buddy." Beau answered.

Sally continued to leaf through the file. "It seems that our Mr. Harcourt was part of an encounter group" She said as she continued to read quickly flipping through several pages.

"Okay, here it is. They met on Wednesday nights and we have, lets see, yeah, five more people, a Mr. Brian Hadley, Dora Philburn, Mr. Keith Blackman, Ms, Carla Dawn, and a Bruce Hickman." She went on scanning the Doctor's notes. "There seems to be notes about everyone in the group. But I don't see anything on Gaylord."

"I wonder if he took those notes with him when he left?" Beau answered looking randomly at some other files.

"Who?" Clarence asked, "Doctor Michaels or Gaylord?"

"Good question." Sally responded.

"I guess we know our next step." Beau said looking at Sally.

"We need to have a talk with the group." Sally said looking to Clarence.

It was a small conference room on the third floor near the executive offices of the Police Commissioner. Clarence had been able to contact everyone involved with Doctor Michaels encounter group. Each had agreed to attend that night except Carla Dawn who worked at nights. Clarence had enlisted the help of Doctor Gary Pullman a police psychiatrist. He felt Gary might be able to keep the group at ease just in case some one got out of hand. The conference room was warmly decorated with a coffee bar at one end. Comfortable chairs were arranged in a circle at one end near the coffee bar. The Doctor recommended a tape recorder be set up and running. The coffee bar had an assortment of cookies, and jelly donuts displayed.

After several introductions, and a fresh cup of coffee everyone took their seats. Before the session started Doctor Pullman had briefed Sally and Beau on each member of the group. Brian Hadley, was a salesman for Pacific Sales and was suffering from a chronic sleep disorder and hyper activity. He was constantly twitching his eye and it was impossible for him to sit still for more than five minutes. He had the vulgar habit of twisting his nose hair. Dora Philburn was an overweight widow suffering from deep depression. She was on constant medication and the group, despite the insults, made her feel like she wasn't alone. She was timid, mild mannered and would usually go along with anything anyone in the group had to say. Keith Blackburn was a retired railroad worker who had lost his left arm in an industrial accident. He suffered from acute migraine. Although it was psychological, he could still feel the pain in an arm that was no longer there. Doctor Michael's notes revealed that he was looking for sympathy. Blackburn thought every one was lazy and they had never done a hard days work in their lives. Carla Dawn was a night club dancer and had nymphomania tendencies. She was undergoing drug therapy as well as counseling. It seems she had a love fixation on her father. As a young child she would secretly watch her father and mother have sex. At age twelve she had sex with her brother and anyone else that asked her. Before entering this program she has had three abortions. Bruce Hickman was a Baptist minister who had been charged with child molestation. To keep the whole affair quiet, the church settled out of court and the case was dropped provided Bruce took one year of therapy at a facility designated by the court.

Everyone sat quietly except Brian who twitched and played with his nose hair. Doctor Pullman broke the silence, "I'm Doctor Pullman and I'd like to thank you for showing up this evening to help us out. We believe you may be able to help these detectives in their investigation. If you have no objection, we will record this session for later review. This is just a preliminary investigation and is not legally binding so anything you say will not be used in any litigation. So you can speak freely and say anything you want. I would like to introduce Agent Thornton, FBI, Lieutenant Gasteneau, Charleston Police, and Sergeant Darrow from Seattle." Everyone nodded as they acknowledged the introductions. Sally opened her notebook and began. "Thank you. We are hoping you may be able to help us locate a past member of your group. A Mr. Gaylord Harcourt."

Dora blushed. Bruce, Keith and Brian all snickered at each other.

"Would you mind telling me what all the snickering is all about?" Beau asked.

"He was a Romeo." Brian said smirking.

"He was an asshole." Keith retorted with a scowl,

"I didn't like him and I was glad to see him go." Bruce added with a hint of anger in his voice.

"Yeah you did. He wanted to kick your ass every time you opened your mouth." Keith said staring angrily at Bruce.

"You see this holier than thou preacher is a child molester and Gaylord hated that." Keith said venting his anger. "But Gaylord was a blowhard. You challenge him and he becomes a pussy cat."

"How come?" Sally asked searching Keith's face for the truth.

"I told him I'd kick his ass with my one good arm when he tried that shit with me and he started to cry like a baby." Keith said sitting back in his chair with a macho expression on his face.

"Dora, what about you?" Sally questioned.

Her face turned slightly red. She looked at her shoes as she answered. "He was a fine gentleman, polite, courteous, loved art and music, and was deeply religious."

"In other words she had the hots for him." Brian said, as he went back to unconsciously playing with the hair in his nose.

"We were going to take a vacation together. We were going to tour Europe. Enjoy the art, the food."

"I betcha I know who was going to pay for it. She was hoping he would ask her to get married." Brian said. Brian and Keith both started to laugh.

"Drop about fifty pounds and inherit about a million bucks and you'd have a chance." Keith said, disregarding the fact that he was being cruel.

"Why do you say that?" Sally asked, looking hard at Keith then to Brian.

"Because he had the hots for Carla." Brian said smugly.

The detectives looked at each other.

"Obviously, you haven't seen Carla?" Keith said with a knowing smile. Brian and Keith gestured indicating that she had large breasts.

"If Carla had winked twice at little Brucie over there he'd given up playing with little boys in a second." Keith said with venom dripping from his words.

"Okay, gentlemen, ladies," Beau said. "Lets get back to our Mr. Harcourt. Are you saying that Harcourt and Carla had a thing going?"

The men in the group looked knowingly at each other while Dora frowned and continued to look at her shoes.

"I'm surprised they didn't do it right on the floor." Keith said, looking around the group for agreement. Bruce spoke out for the first time. "We had long talks about religion."

"What did you talk about?" Sally queried.

"Life, death, heaven, hell, God, and angels." Bruce paused for a moment thinking back. "He asked about the angel of death. He wanted to know what he looked like. Was he a good angel or a bad angel?"

"Is that all you noticed about Harcourt?" Beau inquired.

"No, there was something else."

"What?" Sally said turning her complete attention to the preacher.

"I can't really put my finger on it. But, sometimes I had the feeling I was talking to two different people.

"How do you mean?" Sally said softly.

"Well. Some of the time I had the feeling I was talking to a child."

The detectives looked again at each other and waited for Sally to phrase her next question. "Did you ever hear the name David Delongpre used?"

"Maybe, I'm not sure." Bruce answered thinking back.

Beau examined the group's reaction to Sally's last question. He noticed that Dora looked up and he thought for a moment Dora wanted to say something but changed her mind.

"Dora, something you want to say?" Beau said, pressing Dora to open up.

"No." She said squirming slightly in her chair.

"I think you do." Beau replied pressing her further.

Dora looked up, still hesitating, Sally spoke, "We're just trying to find Gaylord. Remember, nothing you've said will be used in a court of law. You are just helping us in our investigation."

Dora looked sadly at the detectives and said, "He wanted me to be his new mother." With that statement Keith and Brian burst into laughter. Dora's face reflected how deeply her feelings had been hurt. It was hard for Sally to see how cruel these people could be to each other. Looking at the Doctor she asked, "Are they always like this?"

The Doctor explained, "In therapy it is imperative to be bluntly honest. Its not the easiest way or the happiest way but its the only way one can face his or her problems. Once you realize how ridiculous your idea may be, and you can handle the criticism, then you can begin to deal with it."

Sally turned back to the group and focused her attention on Keith and Brian. "What was so funny?"

Keith answered with a snicker, "Dora there, with the hots for Gaylord wants to have him jump her bones and he wants her to be his mother. Don't you think that's funny?"

"That's sad." Bruce added.

Turning her attention back to Dora, Sally asked, "Did Gaylord ever talk about David Delongpre?" Dora thought back trying to recall events that had taken place over two years ago.

"I believe he referred to a David. But as I recall it was his son. I think he died or something."

Beau had been listening intently before he spoke. "Do any of you happen to have a photo of Gaylord?" Everyone except Dora shook their heads negatively.

"Dora?" Beau asked. She took a small snapshot from her purse and handed it to Beau.

"I took this at the hospital's Memorial Day picnic. That's Doctor Michaels in the front."

"You mean Doctor Smith." Sally corrected.

"Yes, but we all called him Doctor Michaels. That's Gaylord in the top row third from the left." Dora pointed to a small face in a group of thirty hospital staff and patients.

"Can we keep this," Beau asked.

Dora nodded. Beau looked at Sally then said, "Is there anything else you can think of?" Sally opened her notebook to an empty page. "Can you tell me where Miss Dawn works?"

With a lecherous grin Keith answered, "At the Body Shop. Sixth and Weller. You can't miss it.

The Body Shop night club was a typical flesh market where horny men went to get their jollies when in Seattle. The outside was decorated with an abundance of neon lights advertising the new sex shows now on stage. Two big muscle bound mental retards stood at the door to keep the riff-raff and the occasional women rights advocates out. Clarence, leading the way, flashed his badge and motioned Beau and Sally to follow him past the two stoic bouncers.

The inside was dark, dingy, with strategically place blue and red neon lights. It reeked with stale cigarette smoke. It was a large room with a bar extending along one side that contained three busy bartenders. Cocktail waitresses almost dressed in string bikinis scurried about the room delivering drinks, fending off drunks, and getting pinched in every conceivable place. One table had a group of rowdy college kids, while another table entertained out of town business men. One well dressed man whispered in the ear of the cocktail waitress, folded a twenty dollar bill and stuck it in her bikini, then walked into a back room. Sally whispered to Clarence, "Is that a drug buy that just went down?"

Clarence smiled at Beau knowingly.

"What?" Sally asked looking at one detective and then the other wanting immediate information.

"He went to get an air start." Beau said with the hint of a smile on his face.

"A what?" She said with a blank look. Both men smiled and said nothing. They had assumed that the FBI Agent had some idea of what vice was all about. Apparently, that part of her training had been left out. Finally, it dawned on Sally what had happened and then she felt stupid but still tried to get a better look at the back door.

The center of the room displayed a raised, well lit stage that led two-thirds of the way across the room. Four tall metal posts protruded upward from the stage floor. Spot lights and strobes moved, and flickered intermittently in synch with the rock music. A nearly topless cocktail waitress with too much make up, too little string bikini, sauntered over to the table. Clarence and Beau's eyes were glued to the approaching platinum blonde Dolly Parton look alike. Sally noted the attention her two associates were paying to the blonde air head with rather large tits that swayed when she walked. She rolled her eyes and shook her head, "Is that all it takes? Tits and ass to get your attention?"

Beau smiled and looked at Sally, "What did you have in mind?" Sally snickered and said nothing.

"Good evening gentlemen. Welcome to the Body Shop what can I do for you?"

"That was the wrong question to ask," Sally mocked and nodded towards her two male companions.

"Don't mind her," Beau said, "She's Seattle's regional recruiter for NOW. She's into anti female exploitation."

"And these guys have more horns than a six-headed moose," Sally chided smiling at Clarence then Beau.

"I'll have a scotch on the rocks." Clarence declared, "We're now officially off duty."

"Sounds good to me," Beau answered. "I'll take a cold beer, you know, that stuff that comes from Tumwater." Sally chimed in, "Give me a gin on the rocks with three olives." The waitress took the order and was about to leave when Beau asked, "Do you know Carla Dawn?" The waitress smiled knowingly, "Sure, she's up next." The waitress nodded at the stage.

From the loud speakers the hidden voice announced, "Ladies and gentlemen, here she is, the blonde beauty that has turned on more lights than General Electric. Miss electricity herself, Carla Dawn!"

The loud bump and grind music started its pulsating rhythm when the stage curtains parted and a statuesque blonde stepped into view. She was tall for a dancer. Her face gave a youthful impression as though you were watching a young virgin exposing herself for the first time. She wore a short rhinestone jacket with a white string bikini exposing an athletic body. She strutted around the stage then removed her jacket and tossed it to the table with the young college studs. They whistled and shouted sexy remarks which she totally ignored. Her breasts were the color of fresh milk and stood erect as though she was slightly aroused at showing herself to these panting male animals. The waitress arrived and distributed the drinks. Beau and Clarence were totally engrossed in Carla Dawn. Knowing that in these situations chivalry was gone, Sally paid for the drinks.

"Just a minute," She said, grabbing the waitress's arm. "We'd like to talk to Carla after she finishes her bit."

"I'm sorry but customers aren't allowed..." Sally flashed her FBI identification, "I don't think the management wants to interfere with an official police investigation."

The waitress looked somewhat stunned to see a female FBI Agent in this kind of place. She nodded and left. Sally's gaze followed the waitress to the bar where she whispered into a well dressed man's ear. He eyed the table then nodded approval. Sally turned her attention back to center stage. Carla had stripped away everything but her make up. She did have a small patch of fabric held by two G-strings between her legs to keep her last bit of modesty. She spun gracefully around the pole then stopped. Looking at the two detectives, she moved to the edge of the stage, squatted and began to rub herself in a suggestive manner. Other men yelled and stuffed twenty dollar bills under the small patch between her legs. With twenty dollar bills erupting from her G-string she rose and straddled the large pole near the edge of the stage. The music changed tempo. With her gaze fixed squarely on Beau she began rotating her hips humping the pole with every beat. Beau looked at Sally and asked, "What do you think?"

"Anyone can fuck a pole." She answered. Both men reacted to her bluntness, chuckled and returned their attention to the stage.

Back stage was crowded, hot, dirty, with an abundance of cheap perfume hanging in the air. Fully dressed, partly dressed and completely naked women moved in and out of the one dressing room shared by all the strippers. Modesty was not an issue here. However, getting dressed and meeting your stage cue was. Clarence, Beau and Sally bumped and punched their way down the hall to the dressing room. A big bouncer stood at the door. Clarence flashed his badge, whispered into his ear. The big man nodded, then motioned to Carla to come to the door. This time she had a bathrobe covering her scanty costume.

"Yes, what can I do for you gentlemen?"

"Is there a quiet place we can talk?": Clarence asked.

"Look, I'm not into drugs. I haven't seen anyone around here doing drugs. None of the girls do drugs and…" Sally cut her off, "This is not about drugs. It's about murder. Now we can talk here or down at the station. Your choice."

Carla waited. Looked at the two men. "You cops too?" Clarence and Beau nodded.

"Okay, over here." Carla led them down the hall to the prop room and opened the door. An overly fat woman with a thin cigar hanging from her lip looked up.

"Bessie, we need some privacy. You mind?" With some effort the fat seamstress extracted herself from the table and left the room. Carla sat on top of the sewing table and spoke. "Okay people, before we start I want you to know, I do my show and I go home. I don't know about anything that goes on around here. I also don't know anything about a murder."

"Do you know a Doctor Michaels?" Sally asked stepping forward. That statement brought a long silence from the exotic dancer.

"Why should I know a Doctor Michaels?"

"We've already interviewed the other members of your encounter group." Beau said cutting to the point. Carla resigned herself to the questions that would follow. "Okay, what do you want to know?"

"Did you know Gaylord Harcourt?" Beau questioned.

"I suppose those two-faced bastards told you a bunch of lies about Gaylord and myself."

"No they didn't, that's why we're here." Sally added. Carla no longer looked like a sex goddess. She looked like an ordinary woman trying to cope with her situation. "Gaylord was nice to me. He treated me like a lady. We went to dinner, concerts, talked about books, and art. He wasn't like those other animals who just wanted to jump on you for a quick hump. He was great with my little Tina."

"What do you mean?" Sally asked.

"Tina was my little girl. Her father dumped us thirteen years ago. So here I am like most of the girls in that dressing room. Trying to make a life for my little girl and myself. Gaylord was the only one I've met that took an interest in her. I mean he got down on the floor and played with her.

Sometimes he was like a kid himself. He and Tina would play hide-an-seek, fly kites in the park. You know all the things a father should do."

"Tell me more about being a kid." Beau queried trying to focus on Gaylord's behavior. Carla smiled fondly, "He and Tina made up a playmate. You see Tina didn't have a chance to play with normal kids her age so Gaylord made up a playmate for her."

"What do you mean exactly, a playmate?" Clarence asked becoming interested in the story.

"You know, he'd pretend to be Tina's age."

The detectives looked at each other. Carla noted the concerned look on the group. "You know, he'd talk like a thirteen year old. It was only pretend you know. He was great. It was hard on Tina when he left."

"Why did he leave?" Sally questioned, moving closer to Carla searching her face for a hint of a lie.

"I guess it was my fault. I'm not sure. I thought he'd make a perfect father for Tina."

"So you slept with him." Sally said interrupting.

"Yeah, except."

"What?" Beau said, pressing her for a quick answer.

"He wanted some kinky kind of sex. He liked to pretend he was raping me. I went along. I mean we all have sexual fantasies. This was his."

"So, what happened?" Clarence said with anticipation.

"Well, he'd pretend to strangle me. I'd play dead while he had sex with me. When I would respond he'd get mad and say that I'd ruined it for him. I had to lay absolutely still until he was finished or he'd be mad at me. Then one time he actually did strangle me. If it hadn't been for Tina coming in I don't know what would have happened. It scared me. I hadn't seen him like that."

The detectives sat silently and looked at each other. Sally had finished her notes first. "Are there any more questions?"

Beau looked up from his notes, "Did Tina ever tell you the name of his make believe playmate. I mean the one Gaylord pretended to be?"

Carla gazed at the ceiling thinking back. "No he never did say what his whole name was. The only name I heard him use was David. No last name."

"May we speak to Tina?" Beau asked politely.

"No you may not." Carla replied sternly.

"Why not?" Sally asked pointedly.

"Cause she's not here."

"Why?" Sally asked again.

"None of your damn business?" Carla replied raising her voice in contempt.

The detectives jotted down their last notes. Then Clarence looked up. "Thank you Miss Dawn, you've been a great help. I'll need your address and phone number just in case we have to contact you again." Sally smirked as the two men wrote down the information.

The detectives finished the report for Big Mike. Beau and Sally Wrapped up any loose ends required by the Seattle police and checked out of their hotel. Clarence drove them to the airport. After hand shakes all around and a promise to come back to Seattle for a fishing trip they were on the red eye flight to Chicago with connections to Charleston. The American Airlines flight out of Chicago cruised at 25, 000 feet. It was a smooth flight. Drinks and snacks had been served, lights dimmed, and everyone settled down for the final flight to Charleston. The overhead light was focused on Beau's lap as he finished reviewing his notes.

"What do you think?" Sally asked noticing Beau's expression of concern.

"Well, we know now that we are looking for one person not two." He answered.

"That is if you assume the David your stripper mentioned is in fact David Delongpre" Sally stated trying to look at the broadest scenario.

"What do you mean, my stripper?" Beau replied, verbally sparring with Sally.

"I saw you drooling over her. My God, you were looking at her cleavage so hard I'm surprised you could even ask a question." She said coming back at him with a smirk.

"I thought I was pretty good. I didn't pussy foot around by trying to analyze her psyche. I got to the point."

"You were analyzing her body that's what you were analyzing," she retorted.

"I'm hurt that you would even think that's all I was interested in was sex."

"You wouldn't be a man if you didn't." She responded smugly.

"You're jealous." Sally smiled and said nothing. Beau changed the subject because he knew that Sally was just putting him on. He knew she wasn't like that but it was fun kidding each other.

"So, you think Tina's David is our David. Right?" Beau confirmed.

"Personally, I do. We need to get the photo digitally enhanced and enlarged. We compare it with the photo Houston sent, then we will lock in another piece of the puzzle. However, I have a feeling we didn't get all of the information we wanted." She replied with an intuitive look.

"Why, who was lying?" He inquired. Beau had come away with the same feeling.

"All of them. They were all leaving something out."

"Is this another one of your psychic guesses?"

"Yeah, She replied then closed her eyes.

"He's our boy. You can lay money on it." Beau confirmed lightly. With that statement he closed his eyes, folded his arms across his chest and napped his way into Charleston.

The weather at Charleston International Airport was clear with ten miles visibility. There was a full moon that made the Ashby River sparkle like diamonds in the night. However, a coastal fog still hung over the lower half of Charleston. Beau's police car was parked in the airport staff lot which gave an easy exit from the airport. Turning onto route 26 it was a slow easy drive to the center of Charleston. Beau drove and Sally sat back to enjoy the wonderful summer night. It was one of those nights where the aroma of magnolia filled the night air. Sally opened the window slightly and took a deep breath then relaxed. Beau smiled looking at a contented Sally. "I kind a like you being jealous."

"When?" She answered keeping her eyes closed.

"You know. Miss Boobs of 1999.

"I was not jealous." She reaffirmed.

"You were too."

"Not."

"Too."

She smiled at the kids game they were playing.

"Okay, maybe only slightly. Is that what you wanted to hear?"

Beau nodded and smiled. Sally looked fondly at Beau.

"Now that you've got you ego pumped up again. What are you going to do about it?" She asked with a sly smirk.

"Oh, that's nice, when I've got both hands on the wheel, and you know you're safe, you ask me." She sat back and closed her eyes again and said, "You betcha Chester."

He smiled and turned his attention back to the road.

It was about 11:30 pm when Beau's patrol car slowed to a school zone speed as the mist of the inner city began to close around the vehicle. Beau turned off Magnolia and headed for Park Lane one of the more exclusive areas of Charleston.

Queensland Park was a small residential park bordered by quaint old red bricked walkups that dated back to the turn of the century. It was a visual delight if it could have been seen through the fog. The park gardens displayed ageless old charter oaks. A rose garden at the center of the park contained a gazebo covered in climbing roses that displayed light pinks and subtle shades of yellow. The older families of Charleston still gathered every Sunday after church for a picnic during the summer months. This tradition had been carried on since the Civil War. The park was meticulously maintained by the Queensland Ladies Garden Club. Park Place, Magnolia, Azalea and Wexford streets covered all four corners of the park. These were the original narrow cobblestone streets of the old city. The converted gas street lights in the park shown like misty globes in the night fog. A small group of hard hats, skinheads and men wearing Klan robes moved from the shadows across the lighted parkway path to an old charter oak dragging two frightened black men. The mob was drunk and rowdy, probably survivors of another rumble that had taken place earlier.

Beau quietly parked his car and turned off the lights. The two detectives watched the mob from a distance. Beau had seen it all before. He remembered as a young man seeing the riots of the sixties and seventies. He knew a lynch mob when he saw it. In a matter of a few days it had come down to this, lynching and vigilante violence. Sally had read about this kind of mindless killing. She had seen photos in her training manuals at Quantico, but she never thought she would see this kind of mob hysteria in real life. Beau rested his forehead on the steering wheel for a few seconds, then commented, "How come we always seem to fall into shit. I mean you're in the mood, I'm in the mood and now this. The whole situation sucks."

Sally opened her purse, took out her service weapon, checked the safety, chambered a round, put some extra clips into her jacket pocket then looked at Beau, "This just isn't your night I guess."

Getting out of the car Beau pulled the Agent close to him keeping them both in the shadows. "Last time you got the front door now it's my turn. Stay low, stay outa sight and move around to the back."

There was no argument from the Agent. She knew the Lieutenant had been through this exercise before and she wasn't about to argue the point.

The gang leader was an over tattooed brute with a shaved head, except for a Manchu pigtail, and tight levis, that slipped under his belly so that his Harley Davidson T-shirt never quite got tucked in. Tattoos ran up both arms, from his elbow to his shoulder. There were about fifteen men in the mob. They ranged from die-hard Klansmen to hard hats, who for some reason, had to strike out against some kind of enemy even though it was wrong. As Beau moved into position he thought to himself, "Fear makes fools of two kinds of men; the one who is afraid of nothing, and the other who is afraid of everything. If I can take down the leader, the others will follow."

The skinhead strutted around like a rooster in a hen house. He was in charge and he had two niggers dead to rights. The niggers were caught in a white neighborhood after dark and obviously up to no good. The mob reasoning rationalized that most likely, one of them could be the Gray Lady Killer. If they were innocent, well, that didn't really matter.

One of the frightened blackmen was dressed in U.P.S. coveralls. The other had levi's and an NFL jacket on. The two hostages were held with their hands folded behind their backs by four white men. Panic was seen in their eyes as the brute put his face up close to the tallest of the two. "Whatcha doin in this neighborhood, boy?"

Both men tried to answer at the same time and their words came out like jibberish. The brute grabbed the throat of the closest man, "I'm talkin to you nigger. Whatcha' doin' here?"

The frightened man coughed and cleared his throat and spoke in a pronounced Jamaican accent, "I'm sorry man. I'm just deliverin packages… It's my job, man."

The blackman remained silent, too afraid to say more. The gang leader's eyes moved to the next blackman who cowered at the thought of what was going to happen next.

"Now, we told you what would happen if we found you here after dark didn't we. You like gettin' it on with white old ladies? Huh, nigger?"

Both men were on the verge of tears. They shook their heads negatively then held their silence. Stepping up next to the skinhead, a smaller man, holding a coil of rope interrupted, "Hey man, you gonna talk all night or are we gonna decorate this tree?" Another man holding the arms of one of the black men added, "Yeah, if we decorate enough trees, maybe our killer will get the idea." There was a deadly silence that held for a few seconds then the brute smiled and nodded to the little man. The fanatic dangled the noose in front of the two hostages taunting their worst fears. He tossed it over the lowest and strongest limb of the Charter Oak. Suddenly a shot rang out. The slug tore a big piece out of the old oak about two inches above the gang leaders head.

Beau moved into the open with his gun aimed at the leader's head. "Hold it right there."

One of the Klansmen turned the black hostage around and placed a shotgun under his chin, then spoke. "Come any closer and I'll blow his fucking face off."

Beau held his position as the mob waited for the Lieutenant's reaction. A wild, crazy expression crept over Beau's face. With eagerness in his eyes, he cocked the hammer back on his 357 magnum and aimed it point blank at the mob leader. "You guys are gonna have to excuse me. I'm tired, unhappy, and definitely pissed. Now, that gentleman over there has threatened to use lethal force." Beau leveled the gun again at the fat skinhead and smiled, "Which gives me the legal right to blow that pimple, you call a head, clean off… Just think about that for a minute. Do you really think I give a damn if you blow that nigger away?" Beau nodded to the shaking hostage with the shotgun under his chin. It was the ultimate poker bluff and the Lieutenant was an expert at this game. "What I need is an excuse and you just gave it to me."

The mob was frozen in dead silence. All eyes were focused on Beau as he held his ground. "At this distance I can't miss."

The Klansman holding the shotgun shouted at the now shaking skinhead, "Are you gonna just stand there and…" The detective cut him off abruptly, "Tell ass-breath to shut the fuck up. You've got five seconds, then I'm gonna plant you right here. Then numbnuts is gonna be next."

"And I'm going to plant a few more." Sally's voice cut in from the other side of the clearing. The men turned to see the Agent standing in a crouch with her snubnosed thirty eight cocked and ready. The men began to whisper among themselves. Beau decided not to let them talk things over. It was at this point the mob was most vulnerable. With their leader neutralized, they wouldn't act on their own.

"On the ground, Now! Move!". Beau's voice was demanding, not debating. The men slowly did as they were told. The bully with the shotgun tossed it aside and laid face down next to the fat skinhead who was just about to piss in his pants.

"Call for backup."

The FBI Agent holstered her weapon and moved to the car to make the call that should have been made in the first place. Sally, thinking to herself felt that Beau wouldn't normally make a mistake like that, not calling for backup first. Maybe he was grandstanding for her sake? That thought scared the hell out of her. On the other hand, maybe he enjoyed it. Maybe he enjoyed playing the ultimate poker game with the mob. She remembered for a split second the crazy smile Beau had on his face. She whispered to herself, "God, I hope we're not all crazy."

The two blackmen remained frozen against the tree. It took a few minutes for them to realize that it was all over. Before they could move, Beau said, "You two stay here. I need you to sign a complaint and I'll need statements."

The Charleston police headquarters looked like a scene from a disaster movie. It was jammed to the doorway with hookers, rioters, felons, drunk drivers, vagrants, and teeny-boppers in trouble with enraged parents waiting to get their kids home. The park lynch mob leaders along with a few bystanders sat, with plastic cuffs securing their hands behind them, on a long bench in the hallway. The two blacks sat nervously across the hall from the men that had almost killed them. The interrogation and booking process would take all night at this rate.

The interrogation room was a dark room void of all but the barest amount of furniture. Six hardback chairs, a table, an overhead light, and a recording machine occupied most of the space. A smaller table with a coffee urn and a stack of paper cups sat in one corner. On the wall next to the table was a city map pinned to a cork bulletin board. Sitting in front of the table was the skinhead. He wasn't quite as cocky as he was in the park. A little of the air had been let out of his bubble as the interview grew more intense. Sally stood silently in the corner and observed the interrogation. She had been briefed to stay out of local police interrogations. Beau and Jack knew instinctively how the interrogations were suppose to work. In this case, with Jack being a black police officer, he was going to be more effective if he took the lead in intimidating the suspect. Beau paced back and forth, with his notebook in his hand, before putting one foot up on the seat of the chair next to the suspect, "Okay Hitler, let's do it again."

"Go screw yourself. I have rights you know. You don't scare me."

Jack moved to the coffee table and poured himself a hot cup of coffee. The mere sight of the skinhead pissed him off. He had to do something with his hands or he might just tee off on this bigoted asshole. Stepping closer, Jack put his cup on the table and his face in the face of the skinhead, "Oh? I bet you like to strut around, don't you. I bet you even practice the goosestep."

The silence that followed was interrupted when the door opened and a young rookie stepped in holding a fax photo.

"Lieutenant, we got the fax on Delongpre from Houston."

"Put it on the board."

The rookie, slightly nervous, pinned the photo to the board and left before another word could be spoken. Beau continued, "Fritz."

"The name is Hans."

"Fritz", you know, you disappoint me… I wanted to blow your ass away so bad it hurt. But, when I saw you loading your pants, I changed my mind… I know any one of ten guys who'd blow you away for ten bucks. All I gotta do is say the word. Now, you got anything to tell us about the copycat that's out there?"

The bully tried to pull off his last gesture of bravado. "Me? I don't know nothin'. If I did I wouldn't tell a faggot Jew cop."

Jack could hold his composure no more. With uncommon strength in his hands he picked the scum up by the collar and braced him against the wall surprising himself, as well as Sally and Beau. In the next few seconds Sally and Beau held their breath hoping Jack wouldn't do the wrong thing and blow their case no matter how right it seemed at the time. Jack smiled, dusted off his non-existent collar then picked up his hot coffee. "Well, it seems as though we have a communications problem." With that announcement, he pulled out the waistband of the bully's levi's and poured his boiling hot coffee down his pants. Sally grimaced at the pain that the man was enduring. Beau chuckled quietly to himself. Beads of sweat popped out on the forehead of the brute. Jack grabbed the poneytailed man, spun him around and pushed his face into the bulletin board on the wall with a force that would break a normal man's nose like a pretzel. One of the many pins strategically place on the map stuck up his nose. His face was only inches from the fax photo of Delongpre.

"Oops! I spilled my coffee, sorry."

Ignoring the pain the man exclaimed, "That's him!"

The detectives remained silent and exchanged surprised looks.

"Is that the killer?" The skinhead asked in a strained voice.

Beau pulled him away from the wall so he could get a better look at the picture. The Lieutenant raised his voice in disgust,

"You guys are so bent out a shape you wouldn't know the truth if you fell over it. Yeah, that's the killer, or one of em."

"Both the black guys in the park had Jamaican accents"

"So what?" Jack answered angrily.

"But the newspapers and the TV said." Jack cut him off.

"Fuck the newspapers." The black detective glanced at Sally with an unsaid apology for his language. The skinhead began to laugh and shake his head as he sat back down.

"You guys are a friggin' joke. That's the guy in the park… He was one of us. He's sitting out in the hallway, you assholes."

Beau ripped the photo from the wall and rushed out of the room with Jack and Sally close on his heels. As Beau rounded the corner of the hallway his eyes quickly scanned down the line of men on the bench and saw an empty place were David Delongpre had been sitting just a few minutes ago.

"Gone."

Jack gave a big sigh, "Like you said, a phantom."

Beau looked at the crumpled fax in his hand and yelled for the young rookie who had delivered the photo. "Mason! Mason!. Get your buns over here." The Lieutenant was pissed that the officer didn't have the presence of mind to check the felons when he had the picture in his hand. He had to end his frustration by chewing someone out and Mason was the chosen candidate. Beau started to lay into the innocent young officer when he changed his mind and said, "Get copies out to all the beat officers. And I want a new APB, now!" The officer knew he was in trouble but he wasn't sure why. Rather than ask a stupid question, he took the photo and left on the double. The skinhead was still sitting with a smirk on his face when the detectives returned to the interrogation room. With the veins sticking out on his neck, Beau marched over to the suspect, picked him up, and shoved him towards the map.

"Where'd you pick him up?"

The scum bag shrugged his shoulders, "I donno'… near the park someplace."

"What street? What was he doing?"

"Come on man. Just hanging around that's all."

Jack stepped in restating Beau's question, "What street?"

Beau pointed to the map, "Park Place? Magnolia? Azalea? Wexford? Which one?"

The man paused thinking back, "Wexford, he'd just turned on Wexford from Azalea. Yeah, Wexford and Azalea."

Jack asked, "What do you mean, turned on to Wexford. What kind a' car was he driving?"

"He wasn't driving a car? Like a said, he was just hanging around. Come to think of it, he was wearing Sears coveralls. He was some kind of maintenance man. You know, one of those guys that comes out to fix your garage door or something. "Yeah, I thought it was funny at the time, the black dude had U.P.S. coveralls and our guy had Sears."

Sally broke her long silence, "Did you ever see a Sears man without a truck?" The room held it's silence as the detectives realized they had their third break in the case and nothing to show for it.

Chapter Nine

Closing The Ring

The Charleston police headquarters was the scene of a media frenzy. A small army of foot patrolmen, and motorcycle police held the TV News and other reporters at bay not allowing anyone who wasn't authorized in. It was the tightest security the metropolitan police had ever enforced. As the Mayor's car arrived he was quickly ushered into the building pushing by all the microphones shoved in his face. The questions about the Gray Lady Killer were shouted and ignored by the Mayor and his party. "Mr. Mayor is this just another cover up or is the killer really white?" Was shouted by one reporter.

"Your Honor, is it true you actually had the killer in custody and let him go because he was black?" Was another pointed question shouted from the crowd.

"Your Honor, if the killer is white how can you explain a black man's pubic hair found on the victim?" Was shouted so it could be heard above the noise of the crowd. The Mayor and the District Attorney led by the Chief of Police continued to ignore all the questions until they were safely inside police headquarters. Looking at the Police Chief the Mayor asked, "Did we find a pubic hair on the victim?" The Police Chief responded, "To my knowledge we have not recovered any evidence of that sort."

"Cut the God damn politics I want to know for sure." The Mayor responded with a stern look at the chief.

The squad room was packed with the morning shift seated in their assigned seats. The Mayor, chief of police and the District Attorney stood in the back. The Beat Sergeant gave the final assignments then Jack Bellamy stood up to give his part of the briefing. "Gentlemen, we have an update on the Gray Lady Killer. As the scuttle-butt has it, we had him right here in the station and he just got up and walked out. He was picked up on a misdemeanor charge with some other people and walked right out the front door. Be alert out there! This guy looks like any other hard working stiff, but he'll slit your throat if you so much as look at him the wrong way then stand around in the crowd of on-lookers and you won't even know it. The stiff we found in the sewer is still a John Doe and he's been dead a long time. Looks like natural causes. We won't know until the autopsy is complete. Also gentlemen, our killer is white. He's not black. Let everyone know on your beat know that this is not a race issue. Lets keep everyone calm. We have a photo from Houston police of a Mr. David Delongpre. There is an APB out on this guy. He could be the perp. If you see him call for back up. Don't approach him alone. Got that? Now Lieutenant Gasteneau has some more information for you." Beau stood up and approached the podium. "Before you leave this room I want everyone to take a copy of the Houston photo. Ask the people on your beat if they have seen this man anywhere. The Seattle Police know this man to be a Mr. Gaylord Harcourt. So, he may answer to either name. He also can change his looks and can be anyone he chooses to be. Now, we have another photo from Seattle of a Dr. Michael A. Smith. He was treating Mr. Harcourt at a mental facility in Seattle. He disappeared at the same time we believe Mr. Harcourt left Seattle. He may be being held against his will. He could be working with the killer, after two years he's probably dead but we don't know. If you see this man report it to the task force immediately. Do not apprehend. Maintain surveillance. He could lead us to the killer. Now, we've told the press that we know the killer is white but we do not want his name all over the front page. So, keep it to yourselves. No! I mean No! statements to the press by anyone. We believe he is suffering from a multiple personality disorder. Do you all know what that means?" One patrolman raised his hand and said, "Yeah, its like talking to a crowd all at the same time." The rest of the room laughed at his observation. Beau smiled, "Yes, but remember one of those guys has killed seven people and he may be fond of even numbers." The room chuckled again.

"Is he gay?" came another voice from the rear of the room. Beau looked at Sally. She approached the podium and stood next to Beau and answered the question, "He could be. In fact, he could be a cross dresser. So when you're playing Mr. Macho with some Linda Lovely on the street she just might circumcise you when you least expect it." Everyone broke into laughter. The shift Sergeant interrupted, "Okay Gentlemen, if there is no more questions let's get out there and take care of business." With that statement the room began to empty.

Beau, Sally and Jack moved to the back of the room and met the Mayor head on.

"Okay, no bullshit. Fill me in." He demanded.

"Well, what we know for sure is that David Delongpre and Gaylord Harcourt are one and the same." Beau said. "Houston police were kinda unhappy that their snitch was leading them around looking for himself."

"How can a guy pull that kinda shit and get away with it?" The Police Chief asked even though he knew it was a rhetorical question.

"Because he really is two people." Sally said.

The Mayor looked at her wanting to hear more. She continued clarifying what she'd just said. "He really believes he's that particular personality."

The Mayor gave her a questioning look of disbelief. She went on to explain her last statement, "He may not know that the other personality exists. He truly believed he was helping the Houston police find the other personality that he obviously doesn't like. If you put him on a lie detector he'd be telling the truth."

"So, you're saying that one of these guys is the killer and the other one doesn't know it?" The Mayor repeated having trouble believing the story.

"Right." Beau stated, "and one other thing."

"What?" the Mayor questioned continuing to shake his head in disbelief.

"Usually, a multiple personality disorder has more than two entities at work."

"Oh that's nice," the Mayor said sarcastically, "We are looking for Murder Incorporated all wrapped up in one guy." There was a short moment of silence while the Mayor digested what he'd just heard. "What does this guy look like?"

Jack handed two photos to the Mayor. "This is the Houston photo of David Delongpre and here is a blow up of the Seattle photo. This is a photo of his encounter group. Here he was known as Gaylord Harcourt." Jack said displaying the two photos for the Mayor to take a closer look before he continued. "And this is Dr. Michael A. Smith, his shrink who disappeared about the same time Gaylord left Seattle."

"We believe there is a connection." Beau added.

"He's probably dead." Sally said.

The squad room doors swung open and the desk Sergeant approached the group and handed Beau a note. Everyone waited for Beau to read the note. The Mayor impatiently asked, "What's the next step?" Looking up from the note Beau answered, "Our John Doe in the sewer, there's a guy at the morgue who can ID him. Excuse me Gentlemen, our next move has just arrived." Beau leading the way, Sally and Jack left the Mayor in the squad room still wanting more.

The interrogation room was almost identical to the one in Seattle. It was as if the same architect had designed both rooms. The only difference was the furniture. Beau, Sally and Jack gazed through the two-way mirror attached to one wall. Pacing back and forth was a street bum. He was a homeless blackman who had made Charleston his home. The man was dressed in shabby torn blue jeans, with a tee-shirt that had turned yellow with age, sweat, and body dirt that had accumulated over time. A ragged and faded Navy P-coat hid most of the yellow tee-shirt. A stocking cap sat on his balding head. The bum walked to the mirror and began examining his face moving his fingers through his beard, twitching his nose to the left and then to the right. He raised his upper lip and examined his yellow teeth which were topped by red inflamed gums. The homeless people in Charleston were a different breed than other homeless people. They were there but you never saw them. The city was always pristine clean waiting for the next tour to go walking by absorbing all the history and architecture of the old city. At night however, the homeless would appear, go about their business whatever that was and be gone. You never saw anyone begging on the streets.

Jack opened a police folder and began to read aloud. "We have a Mr. Jojo Jones. He's a regular around town. Never been in any real trouble. He was picked up with a shopping cart once. He's a user and has been for some time. If he had any money to buy the stuff he'd be dead by now. So, he's opted to drink himself to death and take a hit whenever he can afford it, which is almost never. His sheet say's he's related to a prominent family here in Charleston. They gave up on him a long time ago. He has no address, no job, except he cleans up at St. John's for food on occasions. The only other thing is, when it gets cold outside he gets himself arrested in order to have a warm place to sleep it off."

"Why doesn't he go to St. Michael's or St. John's shelters that care for these guys?" Beau commented.

"You got me. Who knows why any of these people do the things they do?" Jack said.

"They're sick and they don't know it. And for the most part no one cares as long as they're out of sight." Sally responded sadly.

Beau moved out the door, "Okay, lets see what we can find out."

Jojo turned and met Beau as the group entered the interrogation room. "Look, I've done nothin wrong, so you can't hold me."

"Take it easy, ah, Mr. Jojo is that right?" Beau said glancing at the folder Jack had given him.

"Jojo Jones, and I'm a citizen and I have rights"

"Relax, here is a ham and cheese on rye, and a cup of coffee," Jack said setting the food on the table. Jojo eyed the food suspiciously, then sat down and took a large bite. With a mouth full of sandwich he said, "It's probably drugged. The jokes on you guys I don't know nothin."

Sally stepped forward. Jojo hadn't noticed her before and was surprised to see a woman in the interrogation room. "Take it easy. We just need your help in identifying the body in the sewer. After that, you've got five bucks and you're free to go."

"What's the ketch? I already identified him a few minutes ago."

"We want to know a little more about this gentleman." Sally answered.

Jojo's suspicions eased and he sat back in his chair. "You got a smoke? he asked.

"Smoking is not allowed anymore." Jack replied.

"Shit, what is this world comin' to. The damn government is takin' what pleasures we have and dumpin' them in the trash."

Beau moved closer to Jojo but not so close as to be intimidating. Casually, he asked, "What can you tell us about the body you identified?"

146

Jojo replied sadly, "We call him "Doc". As far as I know his real name is Danny Beamer."

"Did you know him very well?" Beau asked.

"Yeah, we hung out for a while. Come to think of it, I was probably the only real friend he had."

"What can you tell us about him?" Sally questioned as Jack began to take notes.

"Well, it's kinda' sad. Of course you ask any one of us and we all have a sad story." Jojo took another bite of sandwich and washed it down with a big gulp of coffee before he continued. "You probably already know he was a user. When that didn't chase away the nightmares there was always booze."

"What nightmare?" Sally responded trying to lead the conversation to any area that might have a relationship to the killings.

"He was a Nam vet like I was. A medic, that's why we called him Doc'. He took care of us when we had nothing and no one gave a shit."

"What were the nightmares all about?" Beau said glancing at Sally hoping this might lead them a little closer to the killer.

"Yeah, he told me once. He use to be part of a rescue team. You know, those guys that go in and rescue downed pilots." Beau nodded indicating that he understood.

"It seems as though he went in on one mission and they had to leave him due to enemy ground fire. He found the pilot. Carried him 'round on his back for three days staying just ahead of the V.C. As he tells it, he came across a Vietnamese mother and a baby. The mother was dead but the baby was still alive. He tried to save the baby, too, but it was crying. When the V.C. were close he couldn't stop the baby from crying. He held his hand over the baby's mouth to keep it quiet. A few minutes later he realized the baby was dead. He had killed it. He never got over that. They gave him a medal but he was never the same. He thought the V.C. were still chasing him. That they wanted to kill him for killing the baby. He hid out in these woods for four years before getting up enough courage to come into the city."

"What was he doing in the sewer? Beau asked. He watched Sally get up and walk to the corner of the room. He could tell that she was crying.

"Oh, you mean the pit. When you want to shoot up that's where we all go if it isn't raining. Doc liked to go down there. He said you could tell if anyone was coming a mile away."

"Did Doc tell you anything else? I mean, did he have any relatives, a family, or any other stories he might of mentioned?" Jack asked, looking up from his notes. Jojo thought for a moment then a smile crossed his face as another story popped into his mind. "He did talk about the Beastie."

147

"The what?" Jack replied. Sally turned and joined the group upon hearing the last statement. Jojo tilted his head remembering Doc's exact words. "He said there was a man beast that lived in the sewers."

"I don't understand." Sally said, "What did he mean by man beast?"

"You've got me. I aint never seen it. But he said it moved on all fours, or walked upright. It could move in and out of the sewer as if he owned it. He said he'd never seen anything move so fast in the dark. For some reason the Beastie seemed to ignore him. Oh yeah, it grunted and I guess snarled as it moved and he said it was dressed just like you or I, well, not like me. He had better clothes than me. Doc told me he liked it because it would keep the V.C. away. As far as I'm concerned he was strung out, had one too many hits. You know, head candy, Angel snuff that sort a stuff."

"Is there anything else you can think of?" Jack asked closing his notebook and looking at Beau and Sally. Everyone nodded negative.

The Bayview Mall was one of those structures built in the middle sixties. It was a monument to concrete slab construction and completely out of style with the other businesses in the area. Somehow the mall was still a huge success with the baby-boomers but was slowly deteriorating with age. The main entrance to the mall displayed a large fountain. Over it was a towering glass covered atrium with a myriad of hanging plants that presented an array of color to the passers by. Radiating from the fountain were four wings housing smaller shops that invariably sprang up at these malls. Like most malls, it had a big Sears store situated at one end, a K-Mart, a Delchamps market, and for more selective customers a Macy's Department store.

Two police cars pulled up to the main entrance and parked. The officers, including Sally and Jack, got out and huddled around Beau as he motioned them his way. Beau began to distribute the photos. "Okay, this is the latest on our boy, David Delongpre. I want you to spread out and cover this area like a blanket. Agent Thornton and I will take Sears. Jack take K-mart. This guy was last seen wearing Sears, workman coveralls. He may be posing as a delivery man, a service attendant, a customer, who knows. Brockman, you take the service ramp in back of Sears. Coates, run through the small shops. See what you can find out. Farley, take Delchamps, maybe he's working in the back."

The last detective to be assigned was Sergeant Singletary, an old friend of Beau's. She was Harry's daughter's Godmother and had been on the case from the very beginning. Beau always had an extra comment for Singletary. It was sort of a game they played. It was a game born of love and mutual respect but the orders wouldn't be orders if Beau didn't throw something extra for Singletary. "You take Macy's. No shopping! It's business."

Singletary was ready as usual with a comeback, but before she could get it out, Beau piped in, "Forget it, you're the only woman I know with a black belt in shopping, so hold the urge. I don't care how long it takes, we need a make on this guy for sure." Everyone chuckled to themselves as they broke the huddle and went their way. Beau was back to his old self again, and everyone knew it.

The Sears Automotive Service Center was Beau's last stop. They had been on every floor of the big store, and interviewed everyone from the floor manager to the credit clerk. Like most Sears Auto Centers, the floors were cleaned to a pristine shine. Detailed lines marked off repair area on the main shop floor. Safety signs were posted on every corner. What was absent were those sexy calendars with the naked women that you would see in a less organized establishment. Beau wondered to himself if that was why he took his car to Pender the Fender Bender. It was a two-bit repair operation run by an ex-con. Pender always gave him a good deal with a shot of rye while he waited for his car. Yeah, that was it, he missed the calendars. It didn't seem right to repair cars and have no naked women hanging around. To him this was an orderly, well organized, over priced car mill that specialized. Everyone seemed to specialize these days. They had a brake specialist. He was more versatile than the rest. He also did tires. An electrician did all of the accessories and timing work. Some young summer hires did the detailing. Beau always wondered how they could stay so clean after working on cars. Pender was always covered in grease and oil. These guys looked like they'd just finished brain surgery. He thought they must have a wardrobe mistress hidden in the back. The man behind the counter could hardly be in his twenties. He wore slacks, white shirt and tie. What kind of auto shop had a guy with a tie to wait on the customers? Another thing Beau could never quite figure this out. What could Sears have in mind when they would put a teenager at the front desk in a tie? Maybe it was to influence the women who came in. Whatever the reason, it seemed to work.

Beau and Sally identified themselves to the young man and showed him a picture of David.

"Have you seen this man?" Beau questioned.

The young man took his time examining the photo. "Don't look familiar to me?"

"He was last seen wearing Sears service coveralls." Sally commented.

The manager looked at the photo again. "We had some uniforms stolen right outa the shop a while back and I caught hell for it."

The chattering noise of a pneumatic power wrench echoed as the door to the main shop floor swung open. A short, stocky mechanic in Sears coveralls entered the room. He was neat as a pin. Beau commented to Sally in a low voice, "He looks like he works for IBM. How do these guys do it? They work all day and I never see a smudge of grease anywhere."

"Jimmy, I need a starter generator for that '87 Camero." The mechanic ordered leaning casually against the counter.

Beau held up the photo for the mechanic. "Have you seen this man around here?"

The mechanic studied the photo, tilting it slightly. Hey! Yeah, last month sometime. He came in for a tune up or something."

"Do you remember what day." Sally said.

The mechanic kept looking at the photo as he nodded negatively. Beau questioned. "What kind a car?"

"You kiddin'? You know how many cars we get in here everyday? All I know is he hung around all day and watched TV. I remember thinking, I wish I had his job where I could sit around all day."

Beau looked at the young shop manager. "You got copies of all the work orders for the month?"

"Yeah, you never know when a customer has a complaint or a part fails under warranty. We stand behind our work", the young manager announced proudly. Beau picked up a tablet of blank work orders laying on the counter and began to examine it closely. "Did you fill in all the info?"

"Absolutely, its company policy."

"What about a license plate number?"

"Sure, for insurance purposes, we record the license plate numbers of every car that goes through here. In fact, if he used a credit card or a check we'd have those numbers too."

Beau smiled and gave a quick nod to Sally and announced to the manager. "Don't let me keep you. If I had them now they'd be late."

The manager paused for a moment thinking about the demand Beau had levied on him. "Let me ask you something. This guy could be the Gray Lady Killer, right?" The detectives nodded affirmative.

"The photos in the paper. I mean he really is a white guy?"

"Yeah, you can put your sheets away. Forget about any cross burnings you've got planned for tonight. He's white." Sally answered with a tone of sarcasm in her voice.

The tempo at the Special Task Force Command post hadn't changed in the past 24 hours. Beau had recalled the officers from the mall on his car radio. Sally and Beau were the last through the door. Detectives Coates and Singletary watched as Beau marched toward them carrying a shopping bag full of Sears automotive work orders. Pouring the papers on Singletary's desk then leaning over with both hands firmly pressed on each side of the pile, he announced to the two detectives. "I know Dirty Harry never had to do this, but good police work is 90% drudgery and 10% panic, so take the license numbers off these work orders and run them through DMV."

Sighing, Coates whined, "Come on, Lieutenant."

Singletary put in her two cents jokingly, "I've been doin' so much reading even the bags under my eyes have got luggage."

As he had a habit of doing when he wanted to, Beau pulled out another quote from who knows where? "Didn't you know that the soul of a murderer is blind?"

"Good for him." Coates said mockingly, "We are already on our way to a good set of bifocals. So what are we looking for?"

"The killer's car." Sally added as she watched these three play their word games.

Beau butted in, "I want the name and address of every man that had his car worked on. Get on to DMV. Cross check for plates or licenses issued in the past 24 months. I want any connection to Houston, or Seattle. I want this yesterday. If we get him, dinner's on me and you name the restaurant."

Coates exclaimed pointing to Sally, "Sally, you heard that, you're our witness."

"Yeah, yeah, now go on move, move it."

The girls smiled and started to sort through the pile of receipts and work orders.

An eerie calm had fallen over the city. The streetlights had been on for over an hour. The light mist created a dreamlike halo around each of the glowing globes that dotted the streets of the old town. After all the riots, demonstrations, and mayhem, the city seemed overly calm. It was like the lull before the storm. Like the moment before an earthquake where everything stands still or in the eye of a hurricane when nothing moves.

Sally was in the operations room standing in front of the city map sipping her coffee. Sitting dutifully at her side, Stud's eyes followed her every move sensing that something was bothering her. Over the past few weeks Studs had adopted Sally. Maybe he sensed she was a female, or that she was something special to Beau. Somehow he knew when Beau said to look out for her that was exactly what he was suppose to do. Sally's fingers began to trace a pattern across the map moving from one colored pin to the next. Sitting back on the edge of the desk she patted Studs on the head and took another gulp of coffee.

The operations room doors swung quietly open. Beau entered. Stepping up to the coffee table he poured himself a cup of the black brew and brought the pot over to Sally.

"Want a warm up?"

"No thanks."

Beau put the pot back on the warmer and sat on the edge of the desk next to the Agent. He studied Sally for a second. "I know that look. Something is turning around up there and it's not romance."

Sally gave him a sly smile, "Everything good comes to him who waits."

"Him doesn't have my hormones."

"You think you're the only one with hormones? Besides, we've got other things to talk about." She put her coffee down and walked to the city map and began to examine the pins more closely.

"Where did that guy say he picked up Delongpre?"

"Which guy are we talking about.?"

"You know, 'Curtis Cute' with the pig tail." Sally turned and smiled at Beau. "You know what they say about schizos?"

"What?"

"They're never lonely."

Beau chuckled at her lame attempt at psycho levity.

Sally began to talk, thinking out loud, to Beau, "We know we have a sociopath, right?"

"Right."

"We now believe he is a multiple personality, right?"

"Right."

"One of these entities is the killer, right so far?"

"Right." Beau answered following Sally's reasoning.

"Now, let's lock in on the killer's personality." Beau nodded in agreement.

"This serial killer personality has an addiction to his crime."

"Okay so far." Beau added.

"He also has an addiction to a specific pattern of violence and this becomes his way of life. We know that Gaylord is a ladies man and David is probably the child ego. I think something happened to Gaylord or David and his defensive mechanism made up the other personality in order to cope."

"So far, so good." Beau said taking another sip of coffee.

"One of these personalities has put the act of killing into a ritual of psychological survival that has meaning to one or maybe both personalities. Most likely, the preparation for the capture and torture of the victim, even the moment of death, and the disposition of the remains each have some sort of perverted significance to our killer. This ritual sets him apart from other killers."

Beau started to speak when Sally cut him off continuing with her train of thought.

"Wait, hear me out. These ritualistic acts lead up to, at least for one of his personalities, experiencing a murder high, or a sexual orgasm, maybe he even gets off on a power trip. He could experience all of the above at the moment of the murder itself."

"Agreed, but do all the personalities go along with the ritual?" Beau asked.

"I don't think so because we know the killer has sex with the corpse. I don't think he knows he's killed the victim. Remember what Carla said about the choking." Beau thought back over everything he'd learned about the killer. "There is one other possibility."

"What?" Sally thought she'd covered a lot of ground.

"There could be a third personality doing the killing. Think about this. If David is a scared little boy, and Gaylord is a lover, neither of these personalities are likely to be our killer. So where does that leave us?"

"Thanks Cochise, you just blew my theory. But you are really getting a handle on this guy and your point is well taken." She continued her analysis, "No, it still works. Lets press on with what we know." Beau gestured for her to continue. "Okay our studies indicate the pattern of serial killing usually follows seven phases. First, we have the aura phase."

"What happens? Does our guy get a halo or light up or something? I hope so that would make it easy to pick him out of a line up." Beau mocked.

"Very funny, shut up and listen. This is where he withdraws from reality. This is a precursor to a personality change. Maybe this is where David, Gaylord or someone else becomes dominant. Sounds, smell, even colors become more vivid. This is the time he feels the compulsion to find a victim to act out his role in the killing ritual." Sally moved to the coffee service. Dumped her cold coffee into the trash can then refilled her cup and returned to the map.

"Now, this phase can last for a moment or two or it can go on for months. As he moves into the next phase whatever humanity he had, recedes. Here he enters the shadowy world of reasoning about death, life, laws of common decency, and threats of death or punishment. This would explain why he asked about the angel of death to the preacher in his encounter group. The morality, mores, or taboos that we take for granted and even life itself have no meaning to him." Sally took another sip of coffee. Beau sat back in his chair and stared at the city map as Sally continued. "Next we have the trolling phase. This is a compulsive phase. He actively begins searching for his next victim. These are not accidental or random patterns. These are deliberate conscious patterns of cruising for his next victim. He will stake out territories were he can find the most vulnerable victims. In this phase the killer is very alert and focused. Now, he may no longer be functioning as a normal sane individual. He is nevertheless, instinctively reacting to daily stimuli. He is now operating at a higher level of behavior programming which will direct his every move."

"So, that's where we are. He's trolling" Beau said still gazing at the city map. "Okay, don't stop there. What are the other phases? If we miss here what will he do next?"

"The next phase is what we call the wooing phase. He has some way of winning the victim's confidence. This is why we never see any evidence of a break in. He has some method of getting the victims to let him in."

"That we've already figured out. We just don't know how." Beau replied at the obvious conclusion.

"Then the next phase you and I are also familiar with. That is the capture. This is usually as quick as the snap of a finger. What does our guy use to capture his victims?" Sally asked her question seeking Beau's input.

"A silk stocking garrote." Beau injected touching his neck.

"Right, now this starts his psychological high. He'll savor this moment because he knows his victim has no chance of escape. He can rape and torture or just taunt his victim."

"And the last phase is the murder itself." Beau said completing the train of thought. "So for right now he's trolling."

"That's right. He'll pick a widow, spinster, or someone's grandmother, most likely white and rich."

"You know what? This is where he is the most vulnerable, because he's predictable. And, you've just described Agnes. Our next victim will be another Agnes." Beau said, setting down his coffee cup.

"Right," Sally replied moving to the city map, "And he's going to hit someone near Azalea and Wexford."

Sally picked up a black pin and put it on the map. She looked back at the map. "Azalea, Azalea, why does that ring a bell?"

Beau shrugged, "Donno, Henrietta lives on Azalea."

"That's it, What's her address?"

"5416 Azalea."

Sally put another pin on the map. "I'll bet you 2 to 1 he was going to hit Henrietta again. Look at that, he was only two houses away from Henrietta's."

"You think the Klan scared him off?"

"Maybe? But he'll be back." Sally looked at Beau. He was looking into his empty coffee cup as he spoke. "So our guy has a big ego."

"Most of em' do…You open to an idea?"

"What did you have in mind?" Beau replied looking up from his coffee cup.

Sally turned from the map and faced the Lieutenant squarely, "Pull his chain a little. Let's put Henrietta on TV. Stake out the house and see what happens."

"What about Henrietta?"

The silence was about as subtle as an earthquake. It didn't take Beau long to figure out that Sally wanted to take Henrietta's place in the house. "I know what you are thinking. No way Jose!"

"Yeah, who you gonna get to do it?"

"A regular police officer."

That statement touched a much abused nerve in Sally as she shouted bluntly, "What the hell do you think I am?"

"You know what I mean."

The Agent had been put down so many times before she had almost become use to it. But with Beau she thought it would be different. She thought that with all they'd been through together, it would make him see that she was a damn good police officer, not just another skirt with a badge. If he had any feelings for her, he would see that this is what a relationship is based on, respect, mutual respect. Before you can be serious lovers, you have to be friends and that means respect for each other.

Sally replied angrily. "No! I don't know what you mean. You got another Behavioral Scientist with police training?"

Beau was getting uncomfortable with the voices being raised to a gut wrenching level. Studs didn't take to kindly to the tension either as he uttered a seldom heard whimper. Taking her arm by the elbow tightly, he escorted her to his office. Closing the door firmly behind him he lowered the venetian blinds that looked into the command post then braced her up against the back of the door. He searched her eyes for some sign of giving in. Beau looked desperately, for some sign to say, 'Talk me out of it.' It wasn't there. He groped for the right words. "Look, I don't want to have the loss of a Behavioral Scientist on my conscience."

"Bullshit! What's the real reason?" They both stared at each other knowing the truth. Beau had fallen for her and couldn't put her in harm's way. He needed an excuse. "The reason is, we've got one, two or more crazies out there who know how many and you want me to set you up?"

"It goes with the job."

"Now that's bullshit, it doesn't go with the job."

The Agent waited for the real answer. Beau sighed and relaxed his grip on her, "All right, the truth. I like you a lot. I'd like to keep liking you a lot."

"Then don't take my self respect away. I have to put up with that crap everyday." Sally moved up and pressed her body close to Beau's. One of the rare moments of passion he knew Sally was capable of was coming to the surface. "I'm also a Federal Agent. That's what I do. I've worked damn hard to get here. I am not going to be just another broad you've managed to get into bed. It's got to be more than that. Who I am, what I am, goes with the relationship. You're gonna have to accept that goin in or it won't work. Is that the real reason your wife left you? She couldn't accept what you are. I'm probably the only one around that can… I'm a cop too. Get use to it."

Beau knew she was telling the truth. He brushed away that persistent curl that hung over her forehead when she got mad and pulled her close. Her lips parted and their tongues met as he kissed her with the passion of two young lovers hungry for the pleasures of the flesh. Beau pulled her firm body close to him. Sally parted her legs slightly as he stepped between them and rubbed her thighs with his knee. The passion was beginning to grow when they both broke it off realizing where they were. They both knew they wanted each other now, but place and circumstances prevented it. Beau sighed controlling his passion. "If you go and get yourself hurt I am going to be highly pissed, you got that?"

Sally smiled and lovingly bit his ear before they broke the embrace.

"I turned you on, didn't I." She said with an impish grin of satisfaction.

"Yeah, that's not fair." Beau replied with a slight pout on his face.

"That's what you get for being a horny old man."

The TV blared out in full color to an empty apartment living room. It was the apartment on the south side of the city that was the home of two distinct and different people, David Delongpre and Gaylord Harcourt. The living room was a mess with rotting TV dinners sitting in various locations. The kitchen was infested with cockroaches while the bathroom was spotless. Gaylord insisted that the bathroom always remain spotless, otherwise David would have to leave. Gaylord always ate out, so he gave the kitchen area to David and the Beastie. In the kitchen next to the refrigerator, there was a large doggie bowl with the half eaten contents of a can of Pedigree dog food.

The TV set continued with the evening Charleston talk show, News Scene 8. The show's host was a well known local newsman who coupled the local news with comments from the local viewing audience which were always colorful but most of it was dull rhetoric. News Scene 8 had covered everything from presidential elections, and hurricanes, to the crowning of Miss Gay America which was a parade of transvestites who'd had too many sex operations.

The voice of the newsman echoed to an empty room. "Last night the Gray Lady Killer, struck again. This time he missed his mark because not all of his victims are helpless. His last intended victim was one of Charleston's most distinguished citizens, Henrietta Wentworth, who, even though the killer out weighed her by a hundred pounds, successfully fought him off." The camera panned back from the host to reveal Henrietta sitting upright with all her spunk readily apparent. The newsman asked, "Henrietta, most women your age have either left town or hired professional bodyguards. You haven't, how come?"

Realizing she was on national TV didn't slow Henrietta one bit. Without hesitation she answered the question. "My daddy, my grandaddy and his daddy have lived and died in Charleston and I'm not about to change." Reaching to the side of her chair, picking up what looked like a knitting bag, the fiesty old lady went on, "Besides, I've got my hickory bat and Big Bertha right here." With that statement the old lady took out a 45 caliber cap and ball Civil War antique saddle gun and held up her bat. Rebel yells came from the audience as she beamed with pride. Henrietta turned and faced the camera, "I know you're out there. I'm giving you fair warning. You mess with a Wentworth and it'll be the last woman you ever touch."

The audience had erupted into wild applause when the TV screen disintegrated with the thrust of a policeman's night stick. David, dressed in a policeman's uniform marched to the wall mirror and examined his new self. Strapping on his belt and gun he turned to his left profile, then to his right profile. Satisfied with his reflection, he began to hum 'Tea for Two" as he adjusted his tie. Bringing himself to full military attention, he saluted his image as a patrol officer and paraded out of the apartment.

Chapter Ten

The Entities

The weather phenomenon that had been attacking Charleston for the past three months still persisted. It was a bad night for a stakeout. The thick fog rolled in like the breath of some evil thing, not seen, not heard, with no form, yet felt in a cold shiver that went to your very soul. Beau was positioned across the street from Henrietta's house with a stake out team. He sat down uneasily on his hardback chair, propped his feet on the window sill, and stared aimlessly out the window looking for the slightest movement along the front of Henrietta's house. The white void had a hypnotic effect. His mind drifted off into a misty realm, a kingdom without dimension, without time, and space. A place where things beyond description might dwell. It was as if time, for a brief moment, stood still. He wondered what was going through the killer's mind at this very moment. What was he thinking? Who was in charge of his mind? What was he feeling? What compulsion was driving him out into the streets? What kind of high did he feel at the moment of his victim's death? How close were we all to that thin line between sanity and madness? He wondered about all the victims who had died since this insanity started. He wondered about his own mortality. About how he was afraid when the killer had him by the neck. He closed his eyes and wondered about Harry. Was he all right? Was he looking after Lori? Was he somehow, some way, watching over him? He thought back to when he was a little boy and his grandfather was slowly dying in the upstairs bedroom. He remembered climbing the stairs and peeking in on him. He motioned him to come in and sit by his side. Beau remembered telling him that he would miss him and asked him why he had to die? Grandpa Gasteneau said, "When the angel of death tugs at your sleeve and whispers into your ear, live, for I am coming. You live each moment as if it is your last and you know that when it ends you will go to a better place. I've met him. We've talked. He's a nice fellow not at all like the stories you've read. Remember son, when you're born the time for your passing has already been decided. So out of each hour of each day, get the most out of every minute you can. If you can understand this you'll no longer be afraid and you will begin to live your life." He also remembered the open casket funeral for grandpa. He was a frightened little boy and afraid of this unseen destiny called death. His father saw him crying, cowering in the corner of the funeral home. His father picked him up and carried him to the wall of the funeral home and said, "Touch it." Beau touched it and his father asked, "what did you feel?" Cold, and dry." The frightened little boy answered. His father took him to the casket where grandpa laid in state and said, "touch him." He was afraid at first but complied with his father's demands. His father asked, "what did you feel?"

"Cold, and dry."

"You see son, grandpa no longer occupies his body. It's like the wall over there. He's gone from this form to another and more brighter future." Beau had never forgotten what Grandpa and his father had told him. After that he was never really afraid again.

Beau knew instinctively that the killer would be out tonight. If not here, he would strike somewhere. Before first light, someone would die. A quick flash, illuminated Beau's vision, it was the old bronze statue, the dark horseman in the cemetery on Wexford. It wasn't a clear picture, just a flash and it was gone. Why the flashback? Was that his way of being afraid? Or, was there some meaning to his visions? As he did on the night he met the killer, he began to put together pictures with bits and pieces of poetry running through his mind. In a monotone voice he spoke to the fog, "Hydra, has released the Jabberwocki and it has descended upon the land of Nod."

"What was that?"

The awkward question came from across the room as Sergeants Brockman and Farley entered carrying two large jugs of hot coffee and a bag full of sandwiches from the deli.

"Huh?"

"Who's this guy Hydra? Did we get a make on him?"

Farley, who is usually the last one to get with the program asked, "Is there another perp working with these guys? I haven't seen anything in the files on a Hydra."

Beau had no idea how he knew. The answer just popped out from somewhere. "Hydra is a mythical creature, a beast with nine heads and no matter how many times you chop off it's head it grows two in place of the one."

"Wow, that's what I call a real collar."

"Farley! Sit on it, would you." Brockman growled.

"By the way, Lieutenant, where is this place, ah, whatcha call it?"

"Nod?"

"Is that sort a like OZ?" Farley asked with childish enthusiasm.

Again, Beau knew the answer. "Nod lies East of Eden. It's where Cain was banished by God for killing his brother Abel. The legend says that it's the land of sleepless souls. The place where evil meets evil. Where the beast sleeps until returning to our world."

"Whoa! Lieutenant, that's pretty far out stuff."

"It's not my idea, it's legend."

"And this Jabberwhat's it?" Farley added jokingly, "It reminds me of my first wife. Now, that was a jabbermouth. She could put you down in three languages in less than 30 seconds."

"The Jabberwocki is a winged dragonlike beast that goes around killing people."

"Yeah, that sounds like my first wife all right. Except she had a breath that would melt a tank."

"Sorry Lieutenant, I never got past Snow White and the Seven Dwarfs." Brockman remarked with a chuckle.

Beau returned his gaze out the front window. It was impossible to see more than ten feet in front of your face much less across the street to 5416 Azalea. Why had he let Sally talk him into such a crazy scheme? Of course he knew. She was right. He couldn't take away her dignity, yet he couldn't protect her without losing the mutual respect they had for each other. If he was going to have a relationship with Sally he couldn't risk damaging the one good thing they had going for each other, respect. Why did he always have to go for the kooky dames? Naw, that was wrong, Sally wasn't kooky. She was for real and like all of us wanted to be the best at what she does. Who could blame her?

Brockman and Farley stood next to Beau and gazed into the heavy mist. "Wow, that's as bad as I've seen it. You couldn't cut it with a hacksaw." Farley muttered taking a deep breath.

"Naw." Brockman added, "You should see the fog were I come from. One time the fog was so thick when I opened my mouth to yawn, I chipped a tooth."

"Funny. Very Funny." Farley took a sip of black coffee from his paper cup and looked at the Lieutenant. "What do you think Lieutenant?"

"We can't see shit from here. I need you closer. Take Henrietta's car in the garage. Stay put, keep your eyes open and your mouth shut."

"You've got it."

With that remark and one look at Brockman, Farley picked up a thermos of coffee and left. Beau looked at Brockman then held out his hand. It was time for a radio check. He tossed the Lieutenant the hand radio followed by a ham and cheese sandwich which he caught in rapid succession without taking his feet from the window sill. Putting the radio to his ear, he commanded, "Sally, how do you read?"

The radio cracked with slight background noise, "Read you five by."

"Okay, TAC 7 is clear. Remember, you don't have a wire, so the first sound you hear get on the horn. You got it?"

"I know." Sally said with a stifling yawn.

"Two clicks on the hour every hour."

"I know, I know."

160

"No hero stuff, understand? You're not the voice of experience. By the way, how many times have you done this?"

"This is my first."

Exhaling a disgusted sigh, Beau looked at Brockman, then spoke. "Remember, Henrietta is a night owl, watch TV for awhile. Go through her normal routine."

Sally answered with two clicks on her radio. Beau unwrapped his sandwich, took a bite and keyed his radio again. "Bradley?"

"In position and nothing moving." Sergeant Bradley had positioned himself in the garden area of the home adjacent to Henrietta's.

"Michaels?"

"Same here Lieutenant." Michaels was positioned in a parked van on the corner so that he could see both approaches to Azalea.

Before Beau could speak, Farley broke in on the radio conversation. "I'm snug as a bug in a rug."

"Okay, stay put and listen up. If you see anything, or think you see anything, let me know." Everyone signed off with two clicks on the radio.

Beau took another bite of his sandwich followed by a gulp of coffee then turned his attention back to the window. The fog seemed to have a mind of its own, moving down the street, swirling and churning at will, oblivious to the killer who hid in the shadows. Beau thought about when he was a kid, looking up into the sky and seeing faces in the clouds. The 'thunder bumpers' as he used to call them all made some sort of face. He would make up stories about the strange faces in the thunder bumpers. Maybe that's how he came to know about all the legends, the ogres, gorgons, and dragons. On a warm summer day he could lay on the hillside, and count the faces. But now the fog began to transform itself into faces, forming, moving, grinning, laughing, crying then disappearing. He saw Harry's face laughing at his own joke before he delivered the punch line. Yeah, that was Harry, never did know how to tell a joke. He saw Lori crying kneeling over Harry's grave. Harry's ghost, seemed almost transparent, standing beside her. The specter looked at Beau, "See what you did. If you'd been on fucking time, none of this woulda' happened." Harry's image thought for a minute looking around the graveyard, "Ah, what the hell, it's not so bad. At least my God damn feet don't hurt anymore. But, Buddy, you're gonna have to get yourself out of this one." The scene vanished and in it's place the gorgon Hydra stood laughing at him. The image had nine heads, each having snakes instead of hair. Seven of the faces were those of the dead victims. The sixth head was that of Sally pleading for help. She had purple lips, white skin, and blood red eyes. The center, and larger of the heads, was Hydra himself, taking his hand and forcing Sally's head to kiss him. Every time she tried to scream, his grotesque purple lips covered hers and smothered her cries. It was as if the beast was sucking the very life out of Sally. She grew weaker with each embrace.

A voice from the doorway, broke the nightmare. A young uniformed officer looked in. "Lieutenant, you have a phone call."

Still recovering from his ghoulish vision, Beau got up and walked warily to the hall phone The young officer took over his observation at the window.

Beau let out a stifled yawn as he spoke, "Gasteneau."

On the other end of the line Detective Coates asked, "You awake?"

"I'm working on it. Whatcha got?"

"Lobster at the wharf."

"In your dreams, Sergeant. You only get six points after the touchdown."

"Let's see if this makes a score. Last month, Sears worked on approximately one hundred cars. Sixty of these jobs were for women. I never realized that women went to Sears that often. Anyway, that leaves forty men. The printout on those forty from DMV has twelve of the men living out of state. Of the 28 left, eighteen live upstate. Unless our guy commutes, that leaves us with ten."

"Go on."

"You said our guy was in Houston two years ago, right? Well, of those ten, we have only one man who has had a license issued within the past two years. A Scott Stapely. Last known residence, 1976 Brookside, Apartment 21. I crossed checked his statement of auto insurance. His insurance company, Texas Mutual in Houston."

"Get a warrant."

"Already working. It'll be there by the time you arrive. Jack's getting an unhappy Judge out a bed right now."

"You just got yourself a dinner."

Beau had an uneasy feeling creeping up the back of his mind. Tonight was going to be the night. He just knew it. He was going to come face to face with the killer. Looking into the guest bedroom, he nudged Brockman who had just shut his eyes. He had the twelve to seven watch.

"Wake up, Sunshine."

"Talk about a short nap. What time is it?"

"You can get your beauty sleep later. I've got a line on the suspect. I want you to keep your eyeballs caged on that house. Tell Farley if Sally doesn't check in on the hour, you guys are through that door in two seconds. I'll be on TAC Common. We think we know where our boy lives."

"You've got it." Brockman said, sitting up and slipping into his shoes and jacket.

The fog was even thicker on Brookdale, which was one block west of Azalea. It was if some disemboweled ogre was spewing forth its white breath on the ground, devouring every image in its path. Only shadows, here and there could be seen as an occasional car moved slowly down Wexford just one block away. The rat-tat-tat of David's police night stick clanged as he dragged it along the old iron fence in front of the brownstone building. A strange and lonely whistle came from the shadows. Then a humming of some old Gregorian chant broke the silence of the night. If anyone could have seen David, he would have looked like any other officer on patrol. The chant was suddenly cut off and the image of David had disappeared. Moving along the side of the brownstone, David climbed the fence, crossed the alley, and entered the backyard of 5416 Azalea. He sat in the shadows behind the hedge row and watched the house for what seemed like hours, training his ears and eyes to the slightest sound or movement from any part of the house. He saw Henrietta turn out the upstairs light and come down to the living room and turn on the TV. "Yeah, Henreatta likes the TV", he said to himself. "I wonder if she'll like TV tomorrow when she sees her dead body?" His body began to twitch and Gaylord spoke, "David, dammit, I don't want you to hurt Agnes again."

"I never hurt Agnes, the Beastie does and you know it."

"Bullshit. You've always look out for number one. When you get yourself into trouble you come crying to me and I end up getting you out of trouble, especially with Agnes. You just use the Beastie as an excuse. Remember Houston? When you got the urge you started going out to all the gay bars. When that didn't work you called out the Beastie and I had to bail you out again. When we were kids you were such a skinny shit, you'd never go out and play ball and all that other stuff. You were a damn sissy. Always afraid the other kids would take your toys. I always had to come and take care of business. The closest you ever came to manhood is jacking-off somewhere behind the compost heap."

"I don't wanta' hear anymore of this so just fuck off." David said raising his voice then bringing it back to a whisper. "Just go off and comb your hair, look into a mirror or whatever you do."

David changed expression, hunched his shoulders over, growled like some wild animal then moved cautiously out of the darkness toward Henrietta's garage.

Sally was dressed in a gray wig and cotton floor length sleeping gown. She had used a white makeup base to age her face and with a deep red lipstick, she had managed to age herself considerably. She looked at herself in the bathroom mirror rubbing the back of her neck with a cold rag. Taking a big yawn, straightening her wig, she picked up her radio and gun, turned off the light and went downstairs.

Across the street Brockman sat at the window trying to stay awake. A half smoked cigar dangled from the edge of his lip teetering up and down as his head rocked. The hot ash from the cigar dropped on his shirt and began to smolder. Feeling the sudden pain he jumped up and brushed away the debris.

"Shit", he mumbled as he looked at the hole in his new shirt. Inside Henrietta's garage sat a yellow 1972 Ford station wagon. It was one of those big machines that had false wood decaled sides to give one the impression that it was an old 'Woodie" wagon of the thirties. Farely, liked stakeouts. He was one of the few who would volunteer whenever this kind of duty was required. The reason was, he grossed out at two hundred and thirty pounds and loved to eat. He had this thing for double cheeseburgers and coffee, topped off with a chocolate shake or something sweet. Beau understood Farley. He used eating as an excuse. In reality, he could not bring himself to hurt a sole. How he ever got on the police force was beyond Beau's comprehension. He knew that stakeouts usually ended up with hours and hours of nothing and that was just what Farley wanted, nothing. Wiping his face with a paper napkin, Farley looked at the selection of double chocolate doughnuts sitting on the seat of the car. Without hesitation he woofed down a chocolate double cream within three bites.

Henrietta's kitchen was neat as a pin. Everything in its place and organized. Large copper pots hung on an iron rack above the kitchen island that supported a heavy butcher's block. A large double door fridge sat opposite the large stove on one end of the island. Sally rummaged through the various canisters looking for some instant coffee. She looked at the kitchen clock that read 1:57 am. She picked up her radio and transmitted, "Any movement?"

"Nothing out here." Brockman replied crisply.

"Nothing back here." Farley snapped jokingly.

"It's almost 02:00. I don't think he's going to show." Sally added.

"We're on it until the Lieutenant says, 'off'."

"Where is he?"

"He's not here now." Brockman's filtered voice came back.

"Look guys, I'm fading fast. Anyone got any coffee?"

"Farley answered quickly, "Yeah, I've got some."

"We should stay put. I don't think anyone should move."

"Look, I don't think he took the bait. The night's almost over."

"Okay, make it fast. We'll stick it out until first light."

Farley laid his radio on the front seat of Henrietta's car. He rummaged through his sack of goodies and brought up a double meatball sandwich he'd take to Sally along with the coffee. The back door was only thirty feet away from the garage so it would only take a minute. Balancing the thermos and the sandwiches in one hand he opened the car door. Before he could stand up straight, a knotted hemp garrote was silently slipped over his head and pulled up tight. The noose had two heavy knots positioned to crush the windpipe in one easy jerk. The police officer didn't have a chance. His body was arched back over the hood of the car and the rope twisted until the last breath of life left the victim. He looked like a big whale draped over the hood of the car, like some trophy about to be displayed to the neighborhood. Farley's eyes bulged out as blood streamed out of his nose. The victim vomited over himself just before death.

David's face beamed with sexual excitement as he witnessed the moment of death. He twisted the knot again in order to hear some bodily gases escape from his bowels. Looking on the floor, the killer picked up the short wooden handle of a toilet plunger, slipped it into the twisted knot and torqued the garrote until he heard Farley's neck snap. The orgasism wasn't complete until he heard that final snap. The Beast's panting slowed until the orgasm had passed then he looked at the dead detective. This moment, this perfect experience, was better than sex. The Beastie knew what the ultimate pleasure was. It was the act of passing on to death. It was being in absolute control. With the twist of his hand the Beastie could give or take life. The victims would eventually thank him for the release of their souls to a better place... He would meet them in the beyond, and then they could thank him, but for now, the experience was the final pleasure, the narcotic of a troubled mind.

The Beast perched the dead man on his back and carried him piggyback to the big car and sat him upright in the back seat as though he was off on a Sunday picnic. Picking up the thermos of coffee and the radio he slipped quietly out of the garage and approached the back door of the house.

A soft knock at the back door alerted Sally to the expected coffee. Picking up her radio and gun she stopped short of opening the back door.

"Who is it."

"Hot coffee Ma'am."

Sally peeked through the curtained back door and observed an officer in uniform holding a thermos of coffee and a paper bag. If she had taken the time, she would have wondered what a uniformed officer was doing at a stakeout? In plain sight? So intent on getting the coffee, she didn't observe any of the normal precautions. Putting her gun and radio on the sideboard, she opened the door. The officer stepped in from the mist and handed her the coffee keeping his face somewhat hidden.

"Thank you. I really needed this," she said fumbling with the plastic top while looking into the bag. "A sandwich, thanks. I'm starved." Sally turned slightly as she unwrapped the sandwich and was preparing to take a bite when she caught sight of David's face. Nothing registered at first, then something clicked in her mind. She recognized this officer from somewhere. David beamed with pride, knowing that he had fooled these dumb-assed pigs. He was with Agnes and no one knew about it. Sally stood frozen. With the sandwich halfway in her mouth when intuition alerted her to the fact that she was face to face with the killer. Out of nowhere the officer's nightstick was thrust into her stomach taking most of the wind and all of the sandwich from her mouth. A hard backhand slap sent Sally plummeting back onto the kitchen floor. David stepped in quietly and locked the door.

"You know Agnes, you said some bad things about me on television. The Beastie isn't happy with you."

"Who's the Beasties?" Sally said gasping, trying to catch her breath.

"It's Beastie, not Beasties. There's only one. For God's sake you know that Agnes."

"How would I know?"

"Cause you killed it."

"How'd I kill it?"

"It's Snipper. He's all grown up now." David's voice took on a childish tone. "Don't pretend with me. You know what you did."

"What did I do?"

"You locked Snipper in the refrigerator and don't say you didn't, cause you did."

"Did Agnes do that?"

"You're not gonna trick me, you know you did. You always hated Snipper. You kicked him and when he cried you got madder and you were gonna kill him if he didn't stop. You put him in the 'fridge to keep him quiet. You said I didn't need a dog, but I loved him and he loved me."

Sally realized at the onset of the conversation that she was talking to a completely different personality. She had read about multiple personalities, she'd even seen clinical reports on behavioral patterns but she'd never been up close. Nor had she seen a serial killer case involving a true multiple. Now she was up close and personal. The key to her survival was to unlock that common bond of terror that linked these entities. She was running out of time. At any moment, the wrong word, a gesture, a diversion could set him off on a killing spree. Maybe she could distract him long enough to make it to her gun sitting on the counter by the back door. Between Sally and her weapon stood a killer so complex that the slightest inconsistency in her behavior could mean her death in a matter of seconds. She had to stay calm inspite of her stomach hurting from the hard blow he had struck with his police baton. The Agent began by carefully phrasing her questions.

"Who are you?"

"Are we playing games again?"

"Do you like games?"

166

"Yes."

"Okay, we'll play games and you can show me how smart you are. How old are you?"

"I am 12."

"And what does your mommy call you?"

"David Arnold Delongpre. These aren't hard questions. Besides, when you adopt me I'll change my name so it really doesn't matter."

"Why would I adopt you?"

Sally could see the rage building inside the killer before he roared back. "Because you promised, Bitch."

The child's voice was gone in an instant and in it's place was another, more mature voice. Sally noticed his eyes looking at the butcher knife rack. Sally distracted him with another question.

"Who are you?"

"What are you trying to do Bitch, play fucking mind games with me?"

"No, and I'd also like to know how old you are."

"I am Gordon Arnold Delongpre, I am 29. I'm the asshole that let you fuck over my mind when I was a kid."

Sally sat up with her back against the kitchen wall and took a deep breath. The killer's eyes followed every move.

"I want to talk to little David."

"You mean the brat?" He paused. "I don't know if I'll let you."

"Little David wants to talk to me," Sally responded quickly.

His body began to squirm and his head rocked forward then back as he looked momentarily at the ceiling fan. David blinked his eyes, then frowned. Sally asked, "David is that you?" The Agent heard the child's voice again.

"Yes."

"Where were you?"

"In my secret playroom," The child answered.

"Who was I talking to?"

"That was Gordon. He doesn't let me come out and play very often. He gets nervous when I'm out."

"Tell me about the puppy, ah, Snipper. Is that it?"

"He's my very bestest friend. I love him…"

"Is he in your playroom?"

"Yes."

"David,…I'm sorry if I hurt Snipper. I didn't mean to."

"Yes, you did. You used to hurt me, too. Just like Snipper."

"What did I do?" Sally asked sympathetically.

David began to squirm. A tormented expression covered his face. Little David was feeling pain. Sally had to press on with this line of questioning. She had to get to the heart of the problem and she had to do if fast. There

167

was no sparing his feelings. To add a subliminal thought, she referred to Agnes as third person.

"David, you can remember. You can remember the times when Agnes was alone with you. What did she do? You don't need to be afraid anymore."

"My head hurts," he said, pressing his fingers to his temples.

His eyes remained closed. Sally thought that this might be the moment to make a break for the gun but she was in no position to get a quick start. Sally softened her voice in sympathy.

"I know. You get a headache when you try to lock away all the voices, don't you. Let the memories come out and the pain will go away. Let's go back to the times with Agnes."

David pouted. His eyes rimmed with tears. "I don't remember."

Sally urged him on softly, "You remember. Tell me about the times when just you and Agnes were alone. When Mr. Gladlow was gone."

David's body twisted, he squirmed and hunched his shoulders.

"Why are you wiggling like that David?"

"Cause it hurts," he said controlling some unseen pain.

"Where does it hurt?"

"My back and my wrists."

"What's wrong with your back?"

"She tied me up by my wrists and hung me from the rafters and beat me until I did it."

"Did what?"

"Played the game."

"What game?"

"She said she wouldn't let Snipper out until I played the game."

"What game, David?"

"The slave game."

"I don't understand?"

"She'd lock the shed door, turn out the lights then light the candles."

"Candles?"

"Yes, lots and lots of candles. It was pretty."

"And after that?" Sally questioned, not really wanting to hear the details she had no other choice.

"She would take off all my clothes. Then I'd take off all her clothes."

"Then what?"

David's body contorted and his voice drifted away to a mumbled inaudible sentence.

"David I didn't hear you."

His body straightened up as if on some specific order and the child spoke, "She made me lick her between the legs. Then she would bite me and lick me, too."

"I don't understand? Where did she bite you?"

"On my neck. Then she'd put my thing in her mouth." David's breathing became heavier. Sally watched the boy in a man's body squirm from pain to excitement."

"Did you like playing games?"

"Mostly."

"What did you like?"

"Mommy would hold me."

"Was Agnes your mommy?"

"She promised."

"Agnes was going to adopt you?"

"Yes."

"So playing slave with Agnes was mostly fun."

"Not always." David grabbed his stomach in pain and pleaded. "Please Mommy, it hurts. Oh no, don't poke that thing in me again, please!" David's words drifted off to a whimper…He seemed to be in a self induced hypnotic state. Still standing, his body went limp. Sally felt sick to her stomach as she listened to David sob in pain. With no warning, David's body snapped to attention. He stood erect, alert and more confident. The words dripped with venom from his mouth, "That piss-ant kid couldn't enjoy himself in a whorehouse with a fistful of hundred dollars bills if his life depended on it, and I told Gordon to stick his head up his ass and disappear. I'm the one that turned Agnes on. After me, everyone else was history. Shit!, even her husband couldn't satisfy her."

The Agent was taken aback by the sudden emergence of this new personality.

"And who are you?" Sally asked, afraid of what she might hear.

"Gaylord Douglas Harcourt, at your service, and I do mean service." Gaylord moved closer to Sally who was still sitting against the kitchen wall. She noticed the bulge in the crotch of his pants. This guy had an erection. The Agent took a deep breath. She knew she had to be careful. At this point she had no idea what part each personality played in the ritual of death. The reality was fast sinking in. This was the beginning of some elaborate game the killer played before he killed the victim. If she didn't panic she knew she had one advantage. She knew about the killer's past and her training, for whatever good that would do now, was the only thing she had going for her. Sally believed she had Harcourt figured out. What to do about it and where it would all lead she had no idea. She had to stall for time.

"So, you liked playing the game."

Gaylord held out both hands and helped her to her feet then pushed her against the wall before he spoke. "Agnes, all you ever wanted was a good suck and fuck.. and I was the best...Admit it, you couldn't get enough of me."

"Why would I want to?" Sally asked, trying to find out where this ego came from and why was David displaying it now?

"You cut me to the quick." Gaylord said, moving closer to Sally pinning her shoulder tightly against the wall.

"I'm sorry," Sally responded trying not to upset this new character who was now in charge of David's body.

"Here, you can judge for yourself." Gaylord unzipped his fly and his erection stood stiffly forward. The Agent tried not to look. This was the wrong time for this sort of thing. She had to get back to the more vulnerable personalities in order to weaken Gaylord. The smiling Gaylord pressed his erection into her stomach then grabbed Sally by the throat with one hand.

"Take it!" he commanded.

Sally tried to resist, covertly, to no avail.

"Take it," he commanded again. This time his grip on her throat tightened. He put her hand on his erection and began to move it up and down slowly at first, then with deeper thrusts. He was making Sally masturbate him. She had to say something to slow him down without turning him completely off. She realized she needed Gaylord fully functional in order to see what part of the puzzle he fit into.

"That's not bad. I'm impressed." She stroked his erection more firmly as he took away his hand. "There's more to sex than having a big dick," she said, trying to divert his excitement.

"You're right. You name it and you and I did it." Sally removed her hand from his erection and asked, "What did we do?"

"It's safer to say what we didn't do." Gaylord's hands moved to Sally's breasts. Strangely, they were firm and erect. The Agent did not try to remove Gaylord's probing hands. That, for sure, would have set him off.

"What I mean was that lovers do other things. Sex is over too quickly. What did you and I talk about?"

To Sally's surprise, Gaylord smiled then stood back and zipped up his pants before he spoke. "Aaa, we talked of sailing ships and ceiling wax and cabbages and kings."

"So you like poetry. Did you recite often?" She asked politely.

"Yes, you and I have so much in common. It was as if something, some higher authority, had preordained our destiny." Gaylord said with an air of snobbery in his voice.

Sally stiffened as Gaylord rubbed his body against hers. His hands began to slowly apply pressure to her breasts. He was becoming aroused again. The Agent could feel his erection pressing against her. She thought, to herself, that it didn't take much to get this guy turned on. She had to distract him again.

"Does David know you?"

"You bet your sweet ass he does."

"Why? Did little David ever get into trouble?"

"Why? I'm the one who'd get him into it. The brat would always do what I told him."

"Like what?"

Gaylord thought for a moment, then a smirk came over his face. "I told him to pour gasoline over some flowers and set them a fire."

"What kind of flowers?"

"I donno, ah, the whatchamacallems? Forget-me-nots, yeah that's it Forget-me-nots."

"Why? What was the reason?"

"I was mad at the old Bitch. I knew it would piss her off," Gaylord retorted.

"How did David feel about that?"

"He cried. But now it's time to light your fire."

Gaylord began to unbutton the nightgown revealing more of Sally's breasts. She had to keep him turned off.

"I hear David calling me," she said. Gaylord stopped and listened. He stood almost frozen.

"No you don't."

"Yes! David wants out and he's mad because you won't let him."

The killer stood back and a vacant stare looked past Sally as she rebuttoned her gown. Gaylord was gone, and the lone man stared at the kitchen clock. The behavioral scientist in Sally was fascinated by this complex personality and wondered how many other personalities might be locked up inside this twisted mind.

"David? Are you there?"

"Yes," he said, in a bashful manner as though he shouldn't be there.

"What's wrong?"

"I donno."

"What were you doing?"

"Playing with Snipper."

"Snipper? Do you play with Snipper?"

"Yeah. You want to play with him?"

"Sure. If he'll be nice?"

Slowly at first, then with more vigor, the killer's body went into convulsions. His face began to transform itself into some grotesque mask. His skin actually grew darker. His hands seemed to contort themselves into animal-like claws. Not really claws, rather twisted and gnarled fingers. His back hunched over and his voice took on a menacing low pitched growl. The mouth dripped saliva from what appeared to be canine, yet human teeth. If she hadn't seen it with her own eyes she wouldn't have believed it. It was a man, but barely recognizable as a man. It reminded her of an old black and white werewolf movie. The Beastie moved menacingly towards Sally who was still pinned against the wall in fear. Snipper had grown into something so terrible that the sight of him must have panicked the victims. Sally wasn't going to panic. She had to stay in control. So far she'd been able to manipulate these personalities, but a beast, a monster, how can you reason with a monster. What do you do? Throw it a bone? She had to tell herself that it wasn't all beast, it was part man..

"Snipper? Is that you?"

The Beastie, stopped, as if on command.

"Snipper, what a nice doggie." The Beastie cowered in front of Sally. She began to pet the man as she talked, "I'm sorry for all the trouble. You are really a nice fella. Don't you worry. I'm gonna take care of you. I'm going to let you sleep in our bed. David and I will always have you right beside us. You'd like that wouldn't you?"

Sally began inching her way slowly to the left, away from the wall as she continued to pet the man-beast. "Nice puppy." She was about ten feet from her radio and weapon. One problem, she had to go around the kitchen island and then down the other side to get to the radio.. The Beastie just had to move around his corner and he would be there… But could the Beastie reason that fast? What sort of response would she meet from the Beastie if she didn't make it in time?

It was as if fate were working against her. At the very moment she was planning to make her move TAC 7 sprang to life with the crackling voice of some unit checking in..

"Control Central, this is unit 546 approaching Main and Harbor."

The dispatcher's voice came back quickly, "Unit 546 keep TAC 7 clear, QSY TAC 2. Over and out."

Sally had pulled away from the man-beast and was racing down the other side of the kitchen island. She was within two feet of her objective when a pair of hands grabbed her by the throat and pulled her upright, then slammed her against the opposite wall of the kitchen. She was momentarily stunned by the hard blow against the wall. When she opened her eyes again Gaylord had almost instantly returned to his grotesque demeanor. Although still in a police uniform, he was a totally different person…

"Now, we wouldn't want to disturb anyone at this hour, would we Agnes?" From nowhere, Gaylord shot a ripping backhand slap across Sally's face that sent her spinning back to the other side of the kitchen. His ring had cut her cheek. Blood began to spill down her face. Gaylord opened the 'fridge and put her gun into the ice tray and slipped the radio into his belt... Sally's knees were weakening. Stay alert, keep cool, don't panic! She kept reassuring herself as Gaylord walked broodingly towards her. Another brutal forehand slap spun her around hitting the pot rack on the kitchen island. The pots swung like bells in a belfry clanging into each other. Without thinking, Sally grabbed a pot and hit Gaylord squarely on the side of the head stopping him dead in his tracks. She pushed past the dazed killer and raced into the dining room. If she could just get through the dining room there was the foyer and then the front door. Once in the street she'd be okay...She knew that the stakeout would see her. Her adrenalin was beginning to kick in... She was hurt, oddly there was no pain but she wasn't moving. She couldn't make her body move as fast as she wanted to.

Before she could get to the foyer, a hand snatched her hair and pulled her back forcing her to stumble onto the dining room table. Gaylord's other hand clutched the back of her neck and smashed her face headlong into the dining room mirror hanging on the wall above the lowboy. The fractured glass dug into Sally's face sending blood spurting everywhere. Her body went limp as the killer laid her down on the dining room table.

In a low panting rhythm the madman's breathing returned to a normal pace. Reaching into his pocket the killer twisted a pair of pantyhose into a tight cord and held it up in front of the unconscious agent...Seeing the limp body and bloody face, he hesitated, then put the garrote back into his pocket. The killer's strong hands picked her up and held her in front of him like a rag doll being played with by some giant child. Sally was barely conscious, drifting on the edge of reality. This was some bad dream. In front of the shattered mirror she could see Gaylord holding her. She must be hallucinating. The bloody face and gray wig couldn't be her. It was as if each of the pieces of glass had a small image each with it's own mind and voice.

"Why are you doing this?" Sally sobbed. She really couldn't see for sure who was holding her. She could only look into the broken mirror for the answer.

"Me? Agnes, how could I possibly harm you? It's David. He's the one that hates you." Gaylord replied.

David's voice responded with a child's anger. "The old Bitch is no good. She doesn't care about anything.. She ever take you anyplace? She ever introduce you to any of her friends? No, she just keeps you locked in the shed." It was David's images now reflected in the broken mirror. In a tantrum voice he shouted, "I hate you I hate you." The personalities were coming and going so fast that Gaylord's physical countenance could not keep up. It was as if each of the small mirrored images were arguing with each other. Gaylord spoke, "He's always hated you Agnes because he's jealous of us."

"That ain't true!" David paused, "I wanted a brother…and a mommy too. But you always forgot my birthday 'cause you liked him best." David whined sadly, "I did all those things. I played all the games, didn't I? You didn't have to go and like him best?"

Sally's heart went out to this abused child locked in a tormented man's body. "I'm sorry David. I never wanted you to hate me."

Gaylord interrupted, "That's 'cause she doesn't think about you at all. You're just a dumb stupid piece of white trash. That's all you'll ever be." The grip on her throat began to tighten.

"Please David stop."

"Go ahead, kill her. Ruin it just like you always do." The Beastie's grip loosened.

"David, I love you just as much as Gaylord. That's the truth," Sally said, trying to muster sincerity in her voice.

"You're lying. You've always lied to me."

The Agent was growing weak. She didn't know how long she could remain conscious. She had to protect herself. She must get David's mind away from this subject. She had an idea. It might buy her some time. "David, take me home. Let's go home and I'll show you how much I love you." Those were the last words Sally uttered before she passed out.

The night fog hadn't let up. The whole city of Charleston was socked in. It had taken Beau longer to get to 1976 Brookside than he had thought. The building was just this side of becoming a slum. It was a two bedroom walkup flophouse in the black ghetto of Charleston. Drug dealers, pimps and two-bit whores used this part of town to do business. Beau parked his car behind Jack's and climbed into the front seat next to Jack. Before he could get the first word out a hot cup of coffee was put into this hand.

"Thanks."

Taking a sip out of his paper cup, Jack nodded at the building.

"Second floor, third window to the left."

Beau looked at the window. He could see a window with the shade drawn shut and it appeared to have someone in the room moving around. "We have two in the back." Jack commented.

"What are we waiting for?" Beau inquired.

"I was hoping he would leave and we could ID him before we did the collar."

"I'd like to put him in the nickel seats right now," Beau quipped.

"He might not be the right guy."

"I know. What I'd like to do and what I can do are two different things."

Beau took another long gulp of coffee. "This is cold already, what about yours?"

"Sorry about that. What the hell, let's do it." Jack put the mike to his lips, "Okay, troops we're going in. Be careful."

The front door of apartment 21 of the old brownstone exploded into bits and pieces as the detectives entered with guns ready. Jack moved into the living room, while Beau took the kitchen. Jack noticed a dangling sticky fly strip hanging from the floor lamp. A portable fan in the corner passed a gentle breeze through the room causing the pest strip to move in front of the light. Beau checked out the bathroom and Jack moved into the bedroom. The bedroom held the key. It was not just a bedroom. It was the museum of a sick and twisted mind. Photos of the victims were pasted up on the walls. Soiled underwear, bra's, slips, perfume, and other articles of the victims were nailed to the wall as though they were some magic talisman that held special sexual powers. Jack shouted to Beau, "Take a look in here."

Beau entered the room and stopped. His mouth dropped open in disbelief. He began to study the items on the wall. He found newspaper clippings of the murders from Dallas, Houston, Seattle, and Salt Lake City. The killer had taken photos of himself having sex with the corpses. He posed with tea cups in his hand as though it was an afternoon social. Each victim seemed more brutalized than the next. Beau found sex videos and pornographic materials of every description. He even found a book about how to garrote people written and published in India some 60 years ago. One particular photo caught Beau's eye. He moved closer and began to study it. Without taking his eyes from the picture he sang out, "Jack, take a look at this." Jack stepped to Beau's side.

The photo was an eight by ten black and white portrait of David. Half of the face was covered with a chalk image. The other half of the face had a mustache, and the eyebrows had been thickened with a pencil. Next to the face was a photo of the movie idol, Errol Flynn. There were several other photos of leading men of the forties. Clark Gable, Cary Grant, Spencer Tracy, and Gary Cooper.

Jack opened the closet door and looked in and came face to face with Doctor Michaels. The remains of Dr. Michaels was still in his wheelchair and his skull was sitting in his lap cushioned by two skeletal hands. He looked like a grinning headless horseman. Jack reached into the vest pocket of a faded, rotted pin stripe suit and removed a wallet. Thumbing through the wallet he announced, "We've found our Doctor Michaels." Beau stood in front of the wheelchair looking sadly at the corpse. He glanced at the ID in the wallet and gave it back to Jack. Jack observed the empty shelves and the vacant coat hangers dangling above the corpse and said, "He's outa here, his clothes are gone."

Beau didn't take his eyes from the photo. He smiled and shook his head. "She's really good. She knew it was a multiple right off the bat and this photo is the final touch." He said searching the room for more evidence. "Our killer is one each type schizo with a group of guys calling the shots."

"Remind me to buy her a beer." Jack said stepping away from the wheelchair. "Which one is the leader? Gaylord or David?" Jack asked, taking out his hand radio and pressing the transmit button. "Okay gentlemen, let's wrap this up. We need a crime scene unit out here ASAP. If there is so much as a dimple on a pimple on an ant's ass I want to know about it."

"My vote is for David. At least he's the one with the Charleston address." Beau remarked.

"What do you mean Charleston address?" Jack asked, looking at Beau. "Our perp rented this apartment under an assumed name, Scott Stapely."

"Yeah, but this guy lived at the Gladlow's on Park Lane. That for all practical purposes is the only real home he's known." Beau replied as he eyed the rest of the room.

A young black officer looking in from the door announced. "Lt. I checked with the landlady. The suspect left about two hours ago." Beau acknowledged with a nod.

Jack began to look through a stack of papers sitting on the dresser. His eyes were drawn to a receipt that was slightly larger than the rest of the papers. He spoke with a foreboding undertone, "Beau, check this receipt. Our boy has rented a cop's uniform."

Beau snatched the paper from his hand, "Jack you got your cell phone?"

"No, its in the car."

"Where's the phone?"

"In the hall."

Beau hurried to the hall phone. It was a pay phone and no change. He could run down to the unit and call but it would take time. He needed to call now. "Jack, I need a quarter." Jack leaned out into the hall and tossed the coin. Beau quickly dialed the number of Control Central and waited as the dial tone rang.

"Charleston police, Control Central."

"This is Lt. Gasteneau, get me a patch to Brockman, fast!"

"Yes sir." The operator manipulated the communications switching console with the dexterity of a concert pianist.

Brockman, sitting at the front window at the stakeout house was lingering on the edge of sleep when the phone rang. He sat up, stretched, yawned, walked into the hall, placed his forehead against the wall, closed his eyes and answered sleepily, "Brockman."

Henrietta's house was engulfed in a white mist so thick a moving van could have pulled up, parked, loaded a ton of bricks and no one would have seen it. Henrietta's garage door automatically opened and the yellow station wagon, with no lights crept out into the street turned on its low beam lights and disappeared into the night mist.

Beau raised his voice on the other end of the line.. "Brockman, you awake?"

"Yeah, sure, go ahead."

"Heads up, our guy is dressed like a cop."

The news got Brockman's immediate attention. "He's what?"

"He's in a uniform. Get the word out. I'm on my way."

"Right, I'm closing this operation down, now!" The detective raced into the front bedroom and picked up his radio. "All units, be advised, our guy is dressed like a cop. Does anyone have any movement?"

Transmitting from his van Bradley announced, "Had a station wagon go by a few minutes ago. That's all."

Mitchell, sitting in the bushes on the other side of the house, chimed in. "Nothin my way, Shit! King Kong could walk by and I still wouldn't see him."

Brockman transmitted again, "Farley? Farley, do you read me? Thornton, do you read?" The transmissions were followed by dead silence. "Move it, go, go, go, it's over, get her out of there." Brockman was cussing to himself as he raced across the street. Mitchell met Brockman on the front porch. Both men without hesitation smashed Henrietta's front door. With weapons ready they searched the house. Brockman moved into the dining room and saw the blood, and the broken mirror. He worked his way into the kitchen and saw more damage. Mitchell joined Brockman. "Nothing upstairs."

Bradley knocked on the back door. Brockman opened it hoping that Sally would be with Bradley and that this was some cruel joke. Bradley reported, "Nothing out back."

"What about Farley?"

"That's what I mean, there's nothing out back. Farley's gone, the car's gone." Bradley waited. Brockman answered, "And Agent Thornton is gone."

"That must have been Henrietta's car that went by."

Brockman answered angrily, "No shit hot dog. What the hell's a'matter with you? Didn't you get a make on Henrietta's car?"

Bradley answered defensively, "Hell yes, I did. All I saw was two headlights, it could a'been a tank for all I would a known. And where in hell were you? You were just across the street."

Brockman realized they all had screwed up and they were now wasting time arguing.

Chapter Eleven
The Evil Entity

Beau and Jack, with Studs leading the way, moved quickly down the stairs of the old brownstone walkup as Detective Coates entered the front door.

"What's the deal?" she asked, dodging the group as they hurried past, then following them to the front porch. Beau glanced back and shouted his orders. "Check with Central. Make sure forensics and the whole team are out here now! I want this place taken apart. Also, we'll need a tag, a bag, and a meat wagon, we've got a body or what's left of one."

"It's pay dirt, right?"

"You've got that right." Beau answered, still heading toward his car.

Coates shouted back, "You owe us a freebie at the wharf."

"Let's get this son-of-a-bitch first, then it's Miller time."

Coates smiled and disappeared into the building. Returning to the car, Studs jumped into the back seat. Beau and Jack dropped into the front seat. Before Beau could start the car the radio cracked with an emergency alert call, "Units 277, 275, and 281. Officer requires assistance. Unit 377 is in pursuit of 2 armed suspects. The suspects have entered the old Waterford dry dock facility at 3714 Bayfront Drive. Suspects have Officer Meyers as hostage. Shots have been fired. Proceed with caution. I say again, suspects are armed, and believed to have officer Meyers as a hostage. Swat 31 has been scrambled. All units acknowledge."

"277, that's a roger."

"275, copy. Who is officer on scene?"

"Officer, Willcox and Adams are on scene. 281, you copy that traffic?"

"281 that's a ten four. If it's Meyers, she's a black officer, then these guys could be our copycats..281's ETA is in ten minutes."

The dispatcher responded with added instructions, "All units report to Officer Willcox for deployment orders. Units 277 and 275 what's your ETA?"

The radios snapped back with a quick reply, "277 is one block west, two minutes." Unit 275 followed, "We're about five minutes away."

The detectives listened to the unfolding pursuit. Beau bit his lower lip as a thousand possibilities ran through his mind. He picked up the mike but before he could transmit the dispatcher cut in, "271, Control."

"271, go."

"271, the officer in charge on that Code 3 wants to talk to you on TAC one, one.."

"Roger, 271 will QSY TAC one, one." Beau quickly changed channels. "Willcox, this is Lt. Gasteneau. How's it going?"

The crackling voice over the radio was surprisingly calm. He was a ten year pro and not much rattled Bud Willcox. If anyone could handle the situation, Bud was the man to have on the job.

"Sir, we have one suspect down, and two in the old Waterford dry dock. I have units on three sides and their backside is against the water. Unless they can walk on water or are a pair distance swimmers, we have their ass."

"What about Officer Meyers?"

"Don't know, Lt. As far as I know, she's still with them."

"Don't take any chances. Alert the harbor patrol. I want a boat out there ASAP. Get some light on that building as soon as you can. You can't see shit out there tonight. When SWAT gets there give the snipers the high ground and keep the attack team at your side."

"Roger that. Do you want a hostage negotiator on scene?"

Beau looked at Jack. He shook his head negative. Beau nodded in agreement. "Okay, get one for show only. Don't let her near that bull horn."

"What about the Chief on this one?"

"As far as I know he's at a fund raiser with the Mayor. Hold on that until I get on scene."

"Ten four."

At that break in the conversation the dispatcher cut in, "Unit 271 QSY TAC 7, Sergeant Brockman has an emergency call for you."

Beau immediately switched channels then keyed his mike. "Brockman, this is the Lieutenant, go ahead."

"Sir," Brockman searched for the right words to break the bad news, "Ah, aa, Sir, be advised, Sergeant Farley and Agent Thornton are missing."

Beau screamed back, "What? What the hell happened?"

"Sir, we don't know. We didn't see or hear anything. We only saw one car go by. The fog is so thick here, we couldn't get a make on it. We thought it one of the locals on his way home. Nothing suspicious. As soon as we got your call, we shut down operations, and they were gone. That's all I can tell you. Henrietta's car is gone. It must have been her car. We don't know for sure."

"I want an APB now!"

"Already done Lieutenant."

"I'm telling you right now Brockman, if anything happens to Thornton or Farley, I'll have your ass!" Beau slammed the mike back onto the dash and exclaimed, "Shit! Is the whole friggen' world coming apart all at once?" Both men locked on to each other's gaze thinking about the situation and coming to the same conclusion at the same time. Jack spoke first. "I'll take the guys in the white sheets, you get Sally."

"Go for it." Beau started the patrol car as Jack jumped out and raced towards the closest black and white. The Lieutenant laid ten of feet rubber on the street as he fish tailed the police car into the foggy night.

The old dry dock hadn't been really active since the Korean War. At one time it had been a major industry in Charleston employing over 3,000 workers. Everything from an apprentice welder to a marine engineer worked at the Waterford dry docks. It was a two story structure tattered and torn with time and emptiness. Two massive cranes with rusted fingers swung freely in the night mist. The old dry docks seemed like a ghost town. It was as if you could hear the workers, laughing, swearing, telling dirty jokes, and in the distance, the old noon steam whistle might call them back to the drudgery of backbreaking work. The water lapped at the large pilings adjacent to the large boat slips. Twisted pieces of scrap metal still laid about the old building and dock area.

Three large flood lights were positioned to illuminate three sides of the building. Two police cars were stationed at each end of Bayfront Drive to cordon off the threat area. Sergeant Bud Willcox stood by the side of his black and white with his brick in his hand directing the operation with the cool efficiency of a professional police officer. Lieutenant Davenport, SWAT Team leader, stayed at Sergeant Willcox's side. Even though he outranked the Sergeant, he knew that this was his show and as the on-scene officer, he would take his orders until the Sergeant was relieved. Bud keyed his mike and ordered, "SWAT two, call in position." The reply came back with a crisp professional voice, "Unit two is in position and my shooters are locked."

"Unit three, check in."

"Unit three is in position. Ready to rock and roll."

"Okay you Rambos, nobody shoots until I give the word. Remember, they've got an officer hostage. Nobody pulls down on a blind target." A cold sweat beaded on the Sergeant's forehead. He looked at the Lieutenant dressed in his black combat fatigues. "You've got the attack team in position?"

Without cracking a smile the SWAT team leader replied, "Cool it Sarge, you sound like a twenty year traffic cop with heartburn."

For some strange reason that struck Wilcox as funny. He knew that this wasn't the time for jokes, but it did lessen the tension. Bud chuckled to himself and keyed his hand radio. "Unit 275, tell them to put one of those floods on the second floor window." The beam of light moved up the old building and locked on to the window in question.

Jack's squad car pulled in behind Willcox's vehicle and parked. Jack moved to the Sergeant's side and questioned, "What's the scene?"

"We've got one mackerel over there and one dude high on head candy over there. That's their truck over there," Wilcox said pointing.

Jack saw a red pickup with Wayford Feed and Grain painted on the side. This was the same garbage he had a fight with just a few nights ago.

Sergeant Willcox continued, "He's got Officer Meyers with him." He ended his remarks by nodding at the warehouse.

Jack looked at the dead body with it's feet sticking out from under a yellow police rain jacket. "Anybody hurt on our side?"

"No, but this cat is shooting at anything that moves. We're just lucky that this asshole couldn't hit the broad side of a shithouse if his life depended on it."

"What about Meyers?"

"Don't know. I think he's planning to use her as a shield."

"What's he carrying?"

"A .45 as far as I know. Nothing heavier."

Jack looked at the old building and said nothing for about three minutes, then calmly said, "Get me a vest. Everyone else back off."

Sergeant Willcox hesitated, "Sergeant, Lieutenant Gasteneau told me to hold until he got here."

Jack reached pass the policeman and took a vest from the hood of the car. "Sorry to break your bubble, the Lieutenant put me in charge and the longer we wait, the harder it gets. I want this scene over before the press gets here. Who knows, these guys might have friends with their own white sheets and their own guns, too. I want you guys in the black jammies, to hold off. He can't watch all the exits by himself. One guy has got a better chance." Jack waited for a rebuttal and only heard silence. "Okay, let's do it." Staying in the shadows Jack dashed quietly to the side of the old machine building and entered. The flood lights painting the outside of the building seeped through the cracks in the walls leaving small beams of light radiating into the black interior. Rusted steam pipes ran helter skelter through the high ceilings like stiff spaghetti in a half opened package. A constant drip of water laid pools of water on the dirty cement floor. The bright fingers of light from the outside spotlights seemed to distort the blackness, giving it no dimension, no space, no time, just a void interrupted by beams of light. Jack paused next to a partially dismantled lathe and listened for the slightest sound. A large evacuator fan spun freely in the breeze sucking in the night fog depositing it on the floor of the old machine shop. The fan made a strange humming noise, like some forgotten ritual chant. Jack strained his ears and listened again. There it was, footsteps in the loading ramp above. The overhead ramp was used to house heavy steel which was lowered by a large crane onto the keel bay below where it would be welded and riveted into the skeleton of the ship being built. It was a large empty area that opened to the back bay pier. In the distance, the Charleston lighthouse fog horn repeated it's low growling warning in a monotonous tone. Jack heard the footsteps again. Two people moving along the steel grated ramp just above his head. As they walked, rust and debris fell below leaving droplets in the puddles on the floor. Jack could follow them from below and pick his spot for the final showdown.

The killer kept Officer Meyers in a choke hold as he drug her along the gantry. "Move, you black Bitch, or I'll blow your fuckin' tits off." The killer was beginning to panic. He moved back into the shadows trying to figure out his next move. The only route open to him was into the black waters of Charleston Bay.

Jack heard the commanding voice. He was right. The killer was the big brute that he had met in front of the hotel. If fate had ever been kind to Jack now was the time. It was his turn to play at this game of terror. Maybe it was his adrenaline, but Jack had to hold back a chuckle. It was that same giggly glee one gets when he sees that the hunter has now become the hunted. The bottom line was "get even time." Jack spotted a maintenance ladder that moved up one of the support beams twenty yards to the left of the killer. Silently, Jack scaled the ladder and waited for the killer, with his hostage, to move in his direction.

The brute clutched at Meyers then faded back into the shadows. Meyers, was crying, and choking back the tears, trying to get her emotions under control. Even with all her police training, she found she wasn't prepared for this situation. The killer put his gun in her stomach and growled, "Listen, Bitch, you're my ticket outa here. If I go down, you're going with me. You got that?" Meyers nodded affirmative. Before the killer could move Jack's voice echoed from the blackness, "You are under arrest." The words bounced from ceiling to wall to floor and back. The killer fired wildly into the black with no effect. He had no way of telling where the voice was coming from. Jack politely repeated his words, "Asshole, I said, you're under arrest."

The killer put his gun to Meyers temple and shouted back, "Come on out, pigface, or I'll blow her fucking tits off."

Jack stepped out into a beam of light and then into the shadows. His gun was leveled at the killer. The police spotlight on the second floor highlighted the loft outlining the killer and his hostage. He showed his smoked stained teeth as he laughed at the detective. "Well, as I live and breathe. What do we have here? A black pig!" The killer was getting careless as he lowered his arm. That was all Jack needed. "Assbreathe, you shouldn't have said that." Jack fired one shot that hit the killer between the eyes. The slug left a small hole going in and took half of the back of his head away going out. The brute stood frozen in death, momentarily, then crumpled to the ramp.

Meyers stood trembling in a pool of blood. Part of the killer's brain had spattered, covering the right side of her face with blood. Meyers was on the verge of complete collapse when Jack caught her and held her tight to his chest as she sobbed. The crying was not of fear, but rather tears of joy. Tears of life, tears of knowing that you've gone though hell and came out alive. Jack understood Meyers. He understood that at some time every police officer, every soldier, has cried tears of relief. The ordeal was over.

"Meyers." Jack said waiting for the tears to stop. She looked up at him. "You done good! You done damn good!! You didn't loose it. I'm proud of you."

Beau clutched at the steering wheel of the speeding patrol car until his knuckles turned white. Why did he let her talk him into this mess? He knew from the beginning that something like this would happen. No, that wasn't right, he didn't know. His worst fears had been realized. Maybe he knew from the moment he looked into the night fog at the stake out. Maybe the thought was parked somewhere in his mind? Maybe it was male intuition? Hell yes, men have intuition. You never hear anybody talk about it, but they do. He felt like some evil had come over the city of Charleston for the past seven months. The fog for one thing. Why did it persist? By ten o-clock in the morning the fog would move out to sea and lay off the coast until night and then, as if on some satanic command, would come back and embrace the city. He remembered hearing about the phenomenon from the old fisherman's tales when he was a kid on the docks. It comes about every one hundred years. Fishermen told about boats that went out to sea and never came back, cows not giving milk and hens laying eggs and the yolks would all be black, about children born dead or deformed, about strange sounds and the beast from the sea who would walk the night in search of victims. It was so much hogwash, or was it? What was the sea story that old Captain Webster used to tell when he was a kid? That there was some kind of mythical sea monster who could only come ashore with the fog and would have to leave with the fog in the morning. The Indians had a name for it but he could never remember it.

"Come on Beau", he said to himself, "Get a grip. This is reality, this isn't some ghost story being told to a twelve year old kid."

Why did he always start thinking about these old wives tales when things didn't go his way? Or, were they remnants of a bad dream he had after being on a week long binge?

The police car left a swirling vortex in the mist as it tore a tunnel through the fog. Beau knew his way through the city instinctively even if he couldn't see the street signs. It came out of the fog with no warning. It had two bug eyes like some mythical monster. Beau had only a second to make his move. He spun the wheel to the right starting the car into a partial spin then reversed his course causing the car to fish tale in the opposite direction, barely missing the on-coming car whose driver honked and swore at the idiot driving that fast at night. By avoiding the collision the Lieutenant lost control of his car. It spun out ending up half on the empty sidewalk and half in the street. Coming to a dead stop the Lieutenant thought to himself, "If it had been at any other time the side walk would have been full of pedestrians." He was lucky. The other motorist, seeing the blinking police light gave Beau a "thumbs up" and went slowly on their way.

The adrenaline had been pumping so hard Beau felt like his eyes were going to pop out. His hands were still clutched to the steering wheel. He slowly relaxed his grip and buried his face in his trembling hands. That was too close for comfort. He couldn't afford any mistakes at this time. He had to keep his cool. He had to think about what he was doing and where he was going. He needed a drink. Just one shot to get him through this crisis. He reached under the seat where he always kept a hidden bottle for just such an occasion and pulled out a fifth of Southern Comfort, unscrewed the cap and put it to his lips. Before Beau could take a drink a wet tongue licked him on the cheek. He had forgot. Studs was in the back seat. The dog whined, then squirmed with a concerned look on his face.

"What?" Beau questioned. Studs answered with a small yelp and nodded in almost humanlike fashion at the bottle in his hand.

"What this?" Beau raised the bottle a little higher.

"What are you, my keeper?" Studs nodded again as if he understood every word Beau had said.

"You know you're beginning to sound like Harry. It would be just like Harry to come back as a dog." Beau took a closer look at Studs. "Is that you Harry? Naw!" He looked at the dog, then at the bottle and shook his head. He couldn't do it. Not to Sally, not to himself. Not to Harry. He'd leaned on the bottle too many times. Not this time. He needed every everything he could going for him. He remembered that every time things went to hell in a hand basket, he went on a binge and Harry covered for him. Harry wasn't here now, or was he? It was his show. He couldn't hide anymore, all the excuses were gone. It was up to him. Maybe that was what Studs was trying to tell him. Beau threw the bottle out onto the street then sat and looked at his trembling hands. A cold sweat made his whole body tremble. He put his forehead on the wheel and closed his eyes.

"Think! You stupid Son-of-a-Bitch. Think!" Beau came up blank. There was something missing. Something the killer was trying to tell him. It was right in front of him but he couldn't see it. What was it? The detective sat up and looked ahead, staring at nothing. He saw the droplets of water that had accumulated from condensation on his windshield. Another set of hazed headlights poked through the fog. The droplets in front of him lit up like sparkling diamonds then faded as the car passed. From the other direction a big eighteen wheeler lumbered slowly through the fog. The big headlights and the multi-colored trailer lights sparkled an array of reds and yellows on the droplets, then passed. Then the seed of an idea began to form in his mind. "Come on boy, up front." Studs stepped between the bucket seats and sat next to his partner. Beau began to talk to Studs the way he use to talk to Harry. "What to you think Buddy? What was it she said? Don't put this guy in a box. Go over what you already know. You might get an idea where he's headed." The last words seem to echo in Beau's mind. "Where's he headed? Where's he headed?" Beau continued to speak the words to himself. "Where's he headed? Where's he headed? David loved Agnes. David was abused by Agnes. That's it!." Studs barked approval as if he got the same idea at the same time.

The police car still sat half on the sidewalk and half in the street. Beau started the car, turned on the lights, flipped on the windshield wipers, put the car in gear and laid the pedal to the metal as he ripped off in the opposite direction.

A green and white patrol car marked 'Metro Security Inc.' moved slowly down Park Lane. Metro Security Inc. was a private security company that the local neighborhood association had hired to maintain a night patrol in the area. Park Lane was an exclusive area of Charleston with homes valued from half a million to over five million dollars. Most of the homes and estates included from three to twenty acres of land and gardens. It was natural that the community would be concerned about protection. Even more so now that the Gray Lady Killer stalked their streets. Metro Security had stepped up the number of nightly patrols in order to stem the fears of its clients.

The Gladlow estate at 1624 Park Lane was the only eye-sore in the neighborhood. It was a classic old home surrounded by eight acres of woodlands. It had been vacant for a number of years with window and doors boarded shut except for places where vandals had come in and ransacked a home which was once the pride of old Charleston. The beautiful gardens that so many of the residents remember had long ago gone to weed. The people complained to the city about the disreputable conditions of the property to no avail. The whole estate was still tied up in the courts and probate was being contested by family on both sides.

The Gladlow's place looked like a set from a Hollywood horror film. An old weather vane creaked above a broken down widow's walk. Remnants of old lace curtains flapped through a partially boarded broken window on the second floor. The paint had faded long ago leaving only exposed shingles that were slowly rotting away. The estate, with a circular drive, was enclosed by a brick wall topped with a rusting wrought iron fence. To the left of the house was a creeping vine that wound it's way to the second floor. It was a Carolina Jasmine that had died from neglect leaving it's spiny fingers still attached to the side of the house. Spanish Moss hung from the old Charter Oaks and swayed in the night breeze.

The bug eye spot light from Metro Security's patrol car scanned the old estate. The guard strained to see through the fog. There had been reports that vandals were defacing the old place. The brass gate house bell had been stolen by some college pranksters last month and was finally returned to the estate. The moving spot passed over an object, stopped then returned and locked on to the top of an old station wagon. The guard shook his head and picked up the mike. "Base one, this is unit four."

"Yeah Burt, whatcha got?" Was Metro Base's sharp reply.

"I think I've got some kiddies in the old Gladlow place again. Maybe not. I want to check it out. I'll get back to you in about ten minutes"

"That's a ten four unit four."

The security guard guided his car into the estate and parked behind Henrietta's old station wagon. Stepping out of his car he put on his hat, flicked on a large flashlight and examined the abandoned car. Nothing, maybe someone stole it and left it here. He jotted down the license number and put the note in his shirt pocket as he headed towards the nailed and boarded front door. He sensed that something wasn't right. He smelled something. He turned his head left, then right sniffing. There was some kind of odor, like perfume in the air. It seemed to be coming from the house. Someone was burning incense. It was a pleasant smell but out of place. Some kids were probably having a beer party and he would have to scold them and send them on their way. This would be the third time he had to chase kids away from the old Gladlow place. Checking the front door he noticed that it appeared to be boarded shut, but upon closer examination only one nail held the door closed. With a good tug the door squeaked open and he entered.

The inside of the foyer was overflowing with cobwebs. Dust, broken furniture and debris lay strewn about. The foyer was a tall room extending upward to the third floor with a large chandelier hanging midway from the ceiling. The massive baroque framed mirror by the stairway had been smashed to bits. The guard moved the beam of his flashlight around the room. Every mirror in the room had been broken. Bits and pieces of glass covered the floor and staircase. The odor was stronger now. It was definitely coming from inside the house. If some kids were playing around they could easily burn this place down. He had to find out what was going on. Standing with his back to the door the guard continued to scan the room with his flashlight. The staircase was directly in front of him. It spiraled to the second floor then to the third floor. The parlor was to his left. A quick glance revealed an elegant room with discarded sheets that had been used as dust covers over priceless antique furniture. The hallway to the immediate right of the staircase turned to the right and led to the kitchen area. To the far right were two large oak sliding doors that opened to the dining room. The guard noted a soft glow coming from the crack under the doors.

That was it. The kids were in there with their beer and chips and probably destroying some of these priceless antiques. Kids these days have no appreciation for the craftsmanship of the old masters. Didn't they know that this furniture dates back to the 1720s' and was made from oak, walnut and cherry wood? It's priceless and they don't give a shit. The whole idea pissed him off. But, he didn't own it so what could he do? The guard put his flashlight in his belt and walked to the door. He was going to scare the hell out of these kids before he took them in. Standing in front of the doors, he grabbed both knobs and rapidly slid the doors open only to come face to face with some horrible man-beast. The grotesque figure dripped saliva as it roared. For a brief moment it resembled Quasimoto from the "Hunchback of Notre Dame". His body was twisted and bent over like some wild ape in a tattered uniform. The beast lunged at the horrified man and sank his teeth into his neck. The guard was knocked back into the foyer with the man beast still clinging to his throat. The two figures rolled on the floor, one defending himself and the other biting, scratching, and clawing. The guard managed to hit the Beast with his flashlight causing him to retreat momentarily. The bleeding guard stood up and grappled for his gun. He was in total panic as he fumbled with the snap on his holster. The last thing he saw was this human freak charging him with the spear shaped curtain rod. The lance hit the man in the chest and split his spine as it came out the other side. The force of the blow lifted the guard up and impaled him on the wall three feet above the floor. He hung there with his face frozen in death and a surprised look still in his eyes. Blood poured from his mouth and down his shirt to a small puddle on the floor.

"Nan a nan a nan na," came the mocking cry of David as he danced in front of the impaled corpse. The Beastie was gone and the little child in a man's body spun around mocking the dead man. Little David said melodically, "I won't tell if you won't tell. We're gonna have a tea party. Nan a nan a nan na."

The dining room was lit with a hundred candles which cast waving and distorted shadows against the faded wallpaper.

The Beastie danced about laughing and singing. The madman changed from Beast to boy and back to Beast as he continued to dance gleefully around the dining room. He stopped in front of the impaled corpse pinned to the wall. Then quickly spun around revealing Gaylord in all his sophistication who spoke to the corpse. "This calls for a celebration. No, a toast to this auspicious occasion. You, my fine friend, will get to see an expert at work. Now, lets see, where did she put it?" Gaylord began to examine the walls of the dining room closely. Stopping next to an oak carved face of an angel, he paused then twisted the decoration to the right. A latch clicked and Gaylord opened a panel revealing a small hidden liquor cabinet. He retrieved a bottle of wild Muscat wine, removed the cork and sniffed the bouquet of a fifteen year old vintage. He poured himself a drink from the dusty bottle, raised his glass to the corpse and said, "To your health sir." Gaylord displayed an evil smile and remarked, "No, I don't think that toast is relevant to you Sir considering your present condition. However, I will give you the pleasure of watching an expert in action. That young lady laying over there wants me to ravish her body. Now, you just don't ravish people, that's not done in polite society. You don't just have sex. Animals have sex. What you do is make love. When you make love you are tender, loving and precise. You let the woman experience the ultimate climax. You take her to her ultimate and final fantasy." Gaylord, now fully in control, turned and faced the large dining room table that occupied the center of the room. He raised his glass again and downed the tart wine in three quick gulps then poured himself another.

Sally laid semi-conscious on the end of the table. Her legs hung over one end and dangled inches above the floor. Her gray wig, bloody face and nightgown hid her identity from Gaylord. To him she was Agnes Gladlow and his reputation, his personal ego depended on how well he performed sexually with Agnes. This would be his best performance yet because he had a witness and that witness could tell the whole world that Gaylord was the best there was. Taking a small sip of wine he moved to the end of the table. Gently, he separated Sally's knees so she was spread eagle before him. Moistening his lips with wine he bent over and kissed her gently on the lips. Setting the glass on the table he began to unbutton Sally's night gown. He slipped her arms easily from the night gown exposing her full breasts pressing against her bra. Picking up the wine glass he slowly let droplets of wine trickle down her cleavage. He began to lick the wine from her breasts.

"My darling you are so beautiful. To me you'll never grow old."

Gaylord removed her pajama bottoms exposing her firm stomach and long thighs. Again, he let droplets of wine trickle down her flat stomach and pool in her navel. With his tongue fully extended he slowly licked the wine moving lower until his head was fully between her legs. Gaylord moistened his fingers and began to fondle her deeply. With each penetration he became more excited. The third penetration jarred Sally awake. She felt his fingers slide inside her again. Terror raced through her mind. What should she do? She weighed her options quickly. If she opened her eyes he would most likely kill her immediately. If she played dead he would rape her. Being raped was the lesser of two evils but she vowed never to let any man rape her. She thought to herself, "My God, what am I doing, I'm just laying here letting this madman have his way."

The sound of a whistling tea kettle broke Gaylord's concentration and jostled Sally into a decision. She recognized her naked condition. She didn't dare move. She was safe as long as she played dead. Gaylord was gone. She could hear him in the Butler's pantry. Looking to her right she saw a small tea service set with cookies, fine china and a flower vase with decayed Forget-me-nots sagging over one edge of the glass vase. She had to act. She couldn't let this go any further. Gaylord poured the hot water into the tea kettle to let it steep then returned to his position over an exposed and vulnerable Sally laying motionless on the table. Keeping her eyes closed she spoke in a low calm voice.

"I want to speak to David." At that moment Sally fully expected a nylon noose to cover her throat and that would be the last thing she'd remember. Strangely enough, nothing happened. Gaylord answered as though he was talking to Agnes.

"Why?" Gaylord answered still touching her thighs and probing her gently.

"Because I'm afraid I've hurt his feelings."

Gaylord's head twisted left to right before he answered, "So what. He's nothing but poor white trash. You can buy a hundred of his kind." He shoved her knees further apart and ripped her panties off exposing all of herself to the madman.

"He never did satisfy you. I was the only one who could really do it."

Still holding off panic Sally raised her voice slightly and demanded. "I want to speak to David, right now."

Gaylord's probing stopped. He twisted and turned rotating his head to the left and then to the right, then silence and stillness came over his form.

"David? David are you there?"

"I don't want to talk to you. You're dirty and you hurt me."

David was now in control. She knew she had to be careful because Gaylord was laying just below the surface of this child's personality and God help her if one mistake would hasten the return of the Beastie. "How did I hurt you?" Sally asked in a motherly tone while holding her exposed body perfectly still.

David stepped back from between her legs as tears began to well up in his eyes. He spoke in a childlike voice, "You locked me in the shed. You, you took away all my clothes. You spanked me with a strap then you made me touch you." The sobbing accompanied by childish anger came out and he shouted, "Mommies don't do that!"

Still motionless Sally waited for the crying to subside.

"David, listen to me. You have to make Gaylord go away. I'll love you and want to take care of you. I'll never hurt you again."

Opening her eyes slightly Sally watched this tormented madman fight the entities for control of his conscious self. David spoke again in a strained voice, "I can't, he's too strong."

"Try David. You have to try. Agnes loves you. Agnes will always love you." She had to keep David in control. If she could keep the child ego in charge she would be safe from Gaylord and hopefully the Beastie.

Beau had slowed the police car to a crawl as he turned onto Park Lane. He shined the patrol car spotlight onto the street sign to insure he was on the right street. "That's it. The house will be down in the middle of the block on the left", he said to Studs who licked his face. The spotlight moved from house to house checking the address on the mailbox. Beau brought the car to a stop and adjusted the spotlight backwards about ten feet. There it was, 1624 Park Lane. Henry and Agnes Gladlow could still be seen on a faded address plate hanging from the mailbox by one rusted screw. Beau picked up the car microphone and transmitted, "Control, 271, I'm at 1624 Park Lane, request backup."

"Roger 271." Was the dispatcher's firm reply. Beau noticed the security patrol car parked behind Henrietta's old station wagon. Thank God, he'd guess right. The killer is here. Patting Studs on the head he said a little prayer to himself, "Please God let Sally be alive." Studs whined concern as if he understood the prayer. Beau took out his .357 magnum handgun and put an extra fast-load clip in his pocket. With Studs at his side he moved cautiously to the white security patrol car and peeked in. Nothing. Checking Henrietta's car there was also nothing. Studs sniffed the ground and took off toward the house. Beau commanded in a low voice, "Studs, come here." The dog returned obediently. He knelt down and talked into the dog's ear. "Slow down Buddy. Quiet, I don't want to tip our hand." The dog knew what his master wanted and heeled faithfully as they moved closer to the big house.

David stood trembling in front of Sally. He twisted as though his body was experiencing severe convulsions. He bent over, hunched his back, took up a Quasimoto stance and growled. Sally could see David's face change into some animal like creature from some horror movie. She remembered about a case study and a film she saw in school about a mental patient in Germany who thought he was a Werewolf and when he had a seizure and reverted to an animal state he could actually change some of his external physical and facial features. This was happening right in front of her eyes. The Beastie hobbled about the room growling at the corpse pinned against the wall. The Beastie, in an apelike fashion, ambled to the table and began to closely examine Sally's naked body. She laid absolutely still holding her breath. The Beast nudged her and looked for a reaction. It was like an animal examining his kill to make sure it was dead. The Beast poked her in the side with his hand. It hurt, but she remained limp and motionless. With evil in every breath and saliva dripping from one side of it's mouth, the Beast put his face close to Sally's trying to sense the slightest breath, the slightest indication that she was alive. Satisfied, the Beast left. She didn't dare open her eyes. The Beast could be trying to trick her. There was a minute of silence. It felt like an eternity. She had no idea if the Beast would tear out her throat or a nylon garrote would be slipped around her neck and it would be all over. Instead, a soft and delicate kiss was placed on her lips. A tongue penetrated her open mouth.

"Agnes my love, I'm back."

She squinted slightly and saw Gaylord standing between her open legs. He began to rub her stomach gently and hummed his favorite tune, "Tea for Two". He walked his fingers slowly around her body as he repeated the tune over and over.

"Remember? You always told me not to rush it. To take it slow. Oh so slow."

Sally could feel his fingers. He was getting ready to probe her again. Gaylord stopped, took off his shirt and policeman's belt. He unzipped his pants and revealed his erection. "See what I have for you. See? David could never give you that." He walked around to her side and placed his erection in her hand. Sally did not respond but laid absolutely still with her eyes closed and said in a calm voice, "I want David. Where's David?"

"Gone. He has a secret hiding place."

She had to keep David in control. She had to delay Gaylord, buy some time until she could make her move and she didn't have the slightest idea what that was. She was alert and was determined to play the game.

"I want to speak to him," she said still keeping her voice in a casual monotone. "David, listen to me, you're not bad. It's Gaylord who's making you hurt people. The madman began to spin himself around. He looked like one of those Whirling Dervish dancers from the Middle East. Finally, he stopped with both hands hiding his face. It reminded her of a child playing hide-an-seek. Slowly, David lowered his hands and said, "Peek a boo, it's me." Gaylord was standing between her legs holding his erection.

"It's time my darling. You've waited long enough. He moved closer pointing his manhood at the point of penetration. Sally was at the point of panic, live or die she was not going to be raped by a madman. As he started to insert himself into her, Sally was left with only one option. She had to fight for her life. She prayed that she still had the strength to pull it off. Taking a deep breath, waiting for the right moment she cupped her hands and froze. As Gaylord looked down to make the final penetration Sally slammed both hands against his ears as hard as she could, trying with all her strength to rupture his ear drums. Gaylord screamed in pain and straightened up. She quickly place both feet against his chest and kicked him violently backwards. The surprise blow lifted him off his feet, through a glass patrician into the servant's pantry. The cabinet doors shattered spilling white flour over Gaylord's prone figure. Sally rolled off the table and stumbled to the floor trying to correct for the dizziness that was slowing her down. Her stumbling exit caused her to knock over several candles as she flung open the dining room doors. One candle rolled along the floor setting the decayed curtains on the east wall of the dining room on fire. The fire jumped up the curtain almost immediately. Her fast exit was halted when she saw the impaled security guard pinned against the wall.

"Oh my God!" she cried and began to run. Panic was taking over what was normally an orderly mind. "I've got to hide." She traversed the staircase in six giant running steps. Looking back she could see the fire jumping to the faded curtains on the adjacent window. Maybe that would work to her advantage by keeping the madman occupied. Turning right moving down the upstairs hall Sally fell, grabbing at the sharp pain she felt in her bare feet. Straining to see in the dark she removed bits of broken glass from her foot. She tried to stand but fell again with severe pain and now blood was rushing from the bottom of both feet. She looked about the hallway and noticed that all the mirrors had been broken. The hallway was littered with broken glass and she still had glass in her feet. Walking was out of the question for now. Sally began to crawl. She had to find a hiding place or get outside whatever opportunity presented itself first.

Gaylord sat upright with a jolt. The glass partition to the Butler's pantry had splintered and cut his face creating red streaks running down his cheeks and across his mouth. The bloody red lips combined with the white flour covering his face made him look like the Joker in a Batman movie or the evil clown in a B grade horror film. His mad expression and grimacing smile added realism to this fictional character. It was as though he had come alive and the reality was here and now. Sally could hear the mad chuckling which was a constant undertone that dominated his voice. To this insane Beast this was some sort of game Agnes was playing with him. The David entity remembered playing hide-and-seek with Agnes, the Harcourt personality remembered that sex should be planned, deliberate, and every fantasy explored before the ultimate climax. Just beneath the surface was the Beast waiting to come out at the slightest hint of anger by either personality.

Gaylord stood up and looked at himself in the shattered dining room mirror. He saw a hundred small images laughing back at him.

"Hello folks. It's show time." Taken with his strange image he spun around to face the mirror again and said, "Boo!" followed by a laugh that came from the depths of insanity and echoed throughout the old house.

Gaylord was totally oblivious to the fire that had leaped to the ceiling of the dining room. The madman walked about the room knocking more candles to the floor as he looked in every corner for Agnes.

"Peek-a-boo." He said opening the small closet door in the butler's pantry.

"Come out, come out, where ever you are," he sang as he moved into the foyer looking for Agnes. By now the dining room was totally engulfed in flames. Stopping in the foyer the madman picked up the gray wig that Sally had been wearing as part of her disguise. Holding the hairpiece in his hand the madman began to sing, "Oh where, oh where has Agnes gone, with her hair cut short and her throat cut long, oh where, oh where could she be."

The maniac held up a large butcher's knife as if it were a trophy. This was not Gaylord, it was not little David, and for sure, not a grunting, hunched over Beastie. Somehow, some way, the trauma of this night or maybe the events over a period of years had created another monster, one that was a combination of all three personalities and far more deadly. The madman continued to play the game, but there was no childlike voice of little David. Instead, there was a new voice with melodic venom in each syllable. The maniac noticed a bloody footprint on the stairs leading up to the darkness of the second floor. He slowly began to move up the staircase.

"Agnes. I know you're up there."

Sally, with terror clutching at her every breath, put the pain in her lacerated feet out of her mind, stood and hobbled down the hall trying each door as she went. They were either jammed or locked. She didn't have the time or the energy to force one open. She spotted a small closet door adjacent to the hallway alcove. She quietly turned the knob. Yes, it was open. Slowly opening the door she came face to face with detective Farley's corpse. He had a grayish face that seemed to have a smile on it as if the angel of death had arrived in the middle of a joke. The rolls of fat almost obscured the garrote still around his throat. His body began to tilt forward. Sally leaned her body against the bulky body and covered her mouth to stifle her scream. The heavy detective and her lacerated feet sent a shot of extreme pain through her body, but she did not let out the slightest whimper. If she had, it would have meant certain death. She pushed the body back and closed the door.

The grinning madman was halfway up the staircase, still singing his deadly song. He ran his fingers over the long butcher knife blade. "With her ears cut short and her throat cut long, oh where, or where could she be?" The maniac looked behind him to make sure his prey hadn't doubled back. Then, in anger, shouted, "Agnes, you ungrateful Bitch. It's over between us. You're dead. You hear that Agnes? You're fucking dead."

Listening to every word Sally realized what she was hearing was Gaylord's alter ego who for the first time had been rebuffed by Agnes. The final bit of sanity must have snapped when a corpse got up and ran away from his sexual advances. That was the ultimate insult and too much for him to bear. In every sense of the word, Gaylord had gone berserk taking the other entities with him. By now, the fire had totally engulfed the dining room and moved into the lower foyer racing up the west wall towards the second floor. The foyer drapes exploded into flames. Sally still fumbled in the dark trying in vain to remove the glass splinters from her feet. She hobbled a few more steps and took cover in the hallway alcove. It was futile to try to move again. Besides, there was no place to go. She noticed a southern Civil War saber hanging on the alcove wall. She tugged at the weapon until it pulled loose bringing chips of plaster onto the dirty floor. This was it. This would be her last stand. She would do as much damage as she could before she went down. Sally thought about her lovely innocent Katie. What would she do without her? Who would be there to take care of her? "No dammit!" she said to herself, snapping out of her self pity. "This isn't going to solve anything. I have to survive this by doing as much damage as I can on the first few blows." Sally put her back against the wall and held the sword tightly with both hands. She knew that Gaylord would be unable to see her until the last minute. By then, she would have swung her first blow. After that it would be up to good old luck.

This new entity, the madman, had reached the top of the stairs. He stood with his back against the stairwell wall and spoke to the dark hallway.

"Yoo-hoo, where are you? Sweetheart, I was only kidding. I wouldn't hurt you. I want to love you. Now, come on, your tea is getting cold. I brought those scones you always liked."

Beau had tried to enter the house from the rear kitchen entrance but the fire was spreading too fast. He elected to move to the parlor and try to force one of the windows. He had to hold back the onset of panic. He knew that Sally was inside and he prayed to God that she would still be alive. Using a broken tree branch he pried off three of the boards covering the door, punched out one of the window panes then unlatched the French doors and slipped inside, with Studs following sniffing the air for signs of Sally. The only odor that hit Studs was the fire which made him nervous but he stayed at his master's side.

Sally moved the sword back. She stood poised, like a batter at home plate. The first blow had to be her best. The madman moved slowly down the hallway testing the locked doors as he went. She could hear each approaching footstep on the broken hallway mirror glass that littered the hallway floor.

The flames from the fire in the foyer cast fingers of light down the hallway. The evil entity stopped just short of the alcove to admire himself in the broken hall mirror. A hundred more cracked images smiled back at him. Tilting his head to the left, then to the right admiring himself he said, "Welcome folks. Welcome to my world. Are we having fun yet?" He smiled and a hundred faces smiled back. Satisfied, he said, "Good," and went on. He hadn't taken two steps when Sally swung her sword slashing at Gaylord's midsection. She realized that the sword was a replica, made of cheap pot metal, and couldn't have cut butter on a warm day. It shattered on impact. An astonished look covered Gaylord's face. He clutched at his midsection and fell to his knees gasping for breath. He began to cry as David appeared to take control and moaned, "Mommy! Mommy!, Help me, please help me. Agnes hurt me again." The madman who just seconds ago was so enraged he was ready to kill anyone in his way was now weeping like a child. Sally, actually felt sorry for him and held short of delivering another blow.

He knelt quietly almost angelic holding his stomach. Sally lowered the sword and was about to step around the figure when Gaylord's hand shot out knocking the sword from her hand. With the other hand he grabbed her by the throat. A cry of rage came from the madman who now pinned her against the wall. His maddened face was only inches from hers. He stared at Agnes not believing that she wouldn't die. That she had ran from him, Gaylord, who had always satisfied all his women. Now, this one ran from him. Why? This was more than he could tolerate and he slapped Sally unconscious. Her body laid in a limp pile on the floor. Searching the floor the maniac picked up the knife and moved toward Sally. He hadn't taken two steps when, from the darkness of the hallway Studs leaped on the madman sinking his teeth into his arm. The knife fell helplessly to the floor as the man and dog fought. With the adrenaline of two men the Beast threw Studs against the wall. Studs laid unconscious next to Sally.

"Hold it, right there." Beau was standing at the end of the hall with his gun ready. "Police, you are under arrest," He shouted.

The madman at this point had no sense of right or wrong, or crime or punishment. He only had his insane rage. Billows of smoke came up from the foyer below. The fire was moving up to the second floor toward the east wing. Beau was momentarily engulfed in smoke masking his view of the madman. Seizing the moment the Beast pulled Sally up and held a knife to her throat.

"Come one step closer and I'll kill her," he warned.

Beau moved closer to get a clearer shot if the situation called for it and it looked like it was going to end in someone getting killed.

"I said I'll kill'er," the maniac challenged.

"You wouldn't kill Agnes would you? You love her, remember?" Beau retorted.

These words coming from a total stranger confused the madman and aroused Gaylord's personality. These entities struggled for control as he twisted his head back and forth. Beau could see that Sally was now awake but remained perfectly still. Beau stepped closer then stopped short seeing a trickle of blood on the knife at Sally's throat.

"I mean it." The madman nodded at Beau's gun. "Throw it away or I'll put her head on the floor right here and now."

"Okay, okay," he replied in a calming voice. Beau laid the weapon on the floor. There was a tense moment of silence as the madman tried to determine his next move. Suddenly, the hall was filled with a blinding white light as the police chopper circled outside. Gaylord was distracted momentarily and that was Sally's cue. The knife was lowered slightly as he turned to look out the dormer window. With her last bit of strength she brought her elbow hard up against his testicles feeling them crunch under the blow. Sally ducked as the knife was slashed cutting thin air just inches above her head. Gaylord brought his knee up hard against her head forcing Sally back against the wall. She sank again to an unconscious heap on the floor. By this time Beau was already in the air, leaping on the knife slashing madman. He was able to disarm him with three bone crushing blows to the head and body. From that point on Beau took out all his anger and frustration on the madman, who was running on pure adrenaline. He moved methodically around the man delivering punishing blows at will. He had moved the man away from Sally, down the hallway to the head of the stairs. At this point, below was the fiery foyer and behind the madman was the east wing which was also on fire. His only way out was through Beau. Without warning the madman fell to his knees and cried, "Don't hit me anymore, please."

Beau stopped his next blow in mid swing. Little David was in control reliving the beating he suffered as a child. What Beau didn't know was that Gaylord used little David when things weren't going his way. Groping on the floor Gaylord grabbed a table leg and brought it up against Beau's rib cage. He was able to deflect part of the blow with his elbow. Beau fell to the floor trying to catch his breath. Looking up he could see the madman heading toward Sally again. Gaylord tried in vain to find the detective's gun. Picking up the knife he raised it high for the final plunge into Sally's limp body. A strong grip grabbed his hand and a fist smashed his face breaking his nose. Beau was so enraged that now it was one madman against another. The difference was Beau's madness was clearly calculated with one thought in mind, killing. Two more rapid blows to the body and a spin kick sent Gaylord smashing through the dormer window onto the slanted roof, rolling off the guttered side into the garden below.

The broken dormer window sucked the smoke down the hallway at an ever increasing rate and changed the direction of the fire in the east wing toward him. Fortunately, the black billows of smoke pouring out the window hung to the upper part of the ceiling. By crouching his visibility improved. He knelt next to Sally's limp body. Her face was still filled with dried blood. One eye was swollen shut and her split lip protruded. She moved her head and moaned. "Thank God." Beau said to himself, "At least she is alive". He picked her up and carried her to the head of the stairs. The flames that hung to the east wall of the foyer were now leaping across in his direction. The stairway and a path to the front door was still clear but not for long. Beau propped Sally's naked body against the wall. Taking off his jacket he covered the upper part of her exposed body. That was the best he could do. He'd have to be quick. He lifted her upright and said, "I'm sorry sweetheart, this is the only way." He hoisted her on his shoulder in a Fireman's carry and dashed down the stairs with the leaping flames licking at his left shoulder. There was no time to think about the locked front door. With running momentum he kicked the front door and to his surprise it splintered off its hinges and fell before him. Choking and coughing he ran with Sally still perched on his shoulder to a safe distance. Setting her down gently, he knelt next to her coughing and gasping, his lungs taking in every millimeter of fresh night air. He rubbed his eyes as the coughing thankfully subsided.

The two red fire engines and the Fire Chief's car came rolling up the curved driveway with lights flashing and sirens screaming bringing every curious neighbor to their windows. Firemen jumped from the vehicle and moved about unloading, connecting and dragging hoses into the most advantageous position to attack the fire.

"Over here." Beau shouted. One firemen approached. "Get me some oxygen, fast." He ordered. The fireman removed his backpack and handed Beau his oxygen mask. He covered Sally's bloody face and felt for a pulse. The fireman quickly shouted orders into his hand radio. "We need a medic up here. Get an ambulance out here, now!"

Sally opened her eyes and saw Beau hovering over her. His head was bent down. She realized he was praying. She touched his hand gently. Beau pulled her close to him and kissed her on the forehead. Sally smiled, then looked around.

"Where's Studs?" she whispered.

"Oh shit!" Beau shouted, then took one step toward the burning house before turning back. "Are you okay?"

Sally nodded. Turning to the confused fireman Beau demanded, "Gimme your coat."

"You're not going back in there?" The surprised fireman asked.

"The hell I'm not. The coat, now!" The fireman complied immediately. Placing his helmet, nomex jacket, face mask and tank on Beau's back, he slapped him on the shoulder and gave him a thumbs up. Beau grabbed the fireman's ax and took off on a dead run leaping onto the front porch and into what looked like a raging inferno.

It was a lucky break that Beau had the practical sense to pick up the oxygen and face mask. Without it he would have been totally lost. By crouching low he could see that part of the stairway leading up to the second floor was still intact. The helmet and fire jacket gave him the protection he needed as he moved up the fiery staircase. Half way up the staircase collapsed, leaving a gaping hole revealing a raging fire pit below. The fire was beginning to climb the west wall of the foyer. He had to get over it and he couldn't wait. Maybe there was another way up through the kitchen? Looking back, he saw the staircase behind him give way to the raging fire on the first floor. He was trapped. His only option was to go up. There was no turning back. He needed some leverage in order to make the jump across the burning gap. Taking his ax in one hand, he swung it with all the energy he could muster against the west wall of the foyer. The sharp ax buried itself into the wall. Yes, it felt strong enough to hold him for the second he needed to leap across the gap. With one arm on the ax he took a step back and leaped taking extra leverage from the ax. It worked. He was across the gap and at the top of the stairs. An explosion from the kitchen below ripped up the balcony on the east wing and knocked Beau on his backside. Rolling over in his prone position he spotted Studs still laying in the hallway of the west wing. He quickly crawled to his old pal. "You okay buddy?" Studs didn't move. Beau felt his chest for a heart beat. "Yeah, you're still with us, aren't you," he said with a sigh of relief. "We're gonna get you outa here." Beau grunted as he picked up the limp dog. Cradling the dog in both arms he edged his way along the wall to the broken dormer window on the west side of the house. Looking back, he could see that this was his only way out. Kicking out the rough edges of the broken window Beau squeezed his way through the window and in a sitting position slid slowly down the roof until he could see the scampering firemen. Beau let out a screeching whistle and got the closest man's attention. Beau raised Stud's limp body. Fireman understood Beau's problem immediately. A second fireman noticed the predicament and ran to the side of the second man. They locked arms looked up and shouted, "Drop him." Just at that time an ear splitting explosion rocked the west wing of the old mansion knocking Beau forward. Studs was gone and he was barely able to grab the storm gutter at the edge of the roof. Fortunately, the gutter held Beau's weight. He hung there swinging like a trapeze artist some thirty feet above the ground. Using every bit of energy he could muster he swung his foot up on the edge of the roof and pulled himself back to the roof line. Fearing the worse he looked over to see that the men had caught Studs. Thank God, he was safe. The top of the roof was totally engulfed in flames. Fingers of fire were shooting from the dormer window. It was a matter of minutes before the whole roof would give way. There wasn't time to get a jump net. He had to find a quick way down. Moving along the edge of the roof to his right he spotted an old Magnolia tree reasonably close to the house. One limb stuck out toward the house. It was a good twelve foot leap to catch the limb. He wasn't sure if he could make it. There was no way to get a run at it. It would have to be a leap from a squatting position. Beau took off the cumbersome heavy fireman's equipment and tossed it down to the waiting firemen. He looked at the very spot where he could grab the limb. That was it, that was the spot he had to get to. Giving a couple of spits into the palms of his hand, he took a step back and sprung into mid air. To Beau it seemed like he floated in slow motion. About halfway to his objective he realized that he was going to make it. Both hands had a firm grip on the limb when it broke under his weight. From the sound of the break, Beau realized that the tree was stone dead like everything else around here and full of termites. "Shit!" He shouted as his feet swung up in the air and his body plummeted towards the hard ground. Fortunately, he was close enough to the tree that his back broke several smaller limbs slowing his fall on the way down. After about six branches snapping under his weight he suddenly came to a firm stop. The last branch of the tree held his weight. Looking like a clumsy Tarzan, he examined himself. There were no broken bones, no cuts, maybe a few bruises but what the hell, "I'm here", he thought to himself. A fire ladder was quickly put in place just under the limb and he calmly came down to safe, firm ground. The smiling fireman asked, "Are you okay?"

"Yeah, but I'll need a change of underwear." He answered jokingly.

"We took your dog to the ambulance. He needs oxygen." The fireman said pointing to the end of the driveway.

"Thanks." Beau said tapping the man on the shoulder as he took off in a quick run.

By now the area was crawling with firemen, police, TV news trucks, and spectators who gawked from the flickering shadows. The medics had just finished attending to Sally's needs and were getting ready to depart. A slightly out of breath detective approached the medic and grabbed his arm. "Did you take care of my dog?"

"Sure did, you want to see?" he answered opening the door. There they were the two most important people in his life. Sally and Studs. It was funny, Beau always thought of Studs as a person. He used to say that Studs was a dog who thought he was a person. "Will they be all right? he questioned as he climbed in between the two stretchers.

"I've seen worse." The medic responded.

"Is that suppose to make me feel better? I asked you if they are going to be okay." Beau asked again with an angry tone in his voice.

Sally's hand touched his and her eyes opened. "My aren't we the tough one." She said in a faint voice.

"How do you feel?" He asked, tenderly kissing her forehead.

"I'll be okay. I'm just tired."

"God dammit, this is the last time I let you talk me into anything as crazy as that again. Do you understand young lady?"

"What do you mean, let me? You're not my husband. I'll do what I damn well please."

"Well, we can take care of that right away. Dammit, I'm not going to have you doing this sort of thing."

Sally looked momentarily confused, then smiled. "Did I miss something or did you just propose to me?"

Beau looked at the smiling medic who shrugged his shoulder and waited for Beau to answer the question. Beau nodded and also shrugged his shoulders, "Yeah, well, I guess I did. But it's not an official one. So don't go bragging around the station."

"That is the damnedest proposal I ever got. By the way, what makes you think you're worth bragging about?" She said and grabbed his hand.

A whimper came from the limp Studs as he struggled to sit up. The medic removed the oxygen mask so everyone could see the big smile on Stud's face. He immediately began to lick everyone within licking distance. Beau gave his best friend a big hug. Both Beau and Studs hovered over Sally and smiled.

"You two are undoubtedly the ugliest two guys I've ever seen." She said fighting the sleeping medication she had been given. "Now, will you go and cuff that guy so we can wrap this thing up?"

"Sure, I'll take care of it, and I'll see you when you wake up." He gave her one more kiss as she closed her eyes.

Beau had stepped down from the ambulance when Jack arrived. "How is she", he asked looking at the departing ambulance.

"She's going to be okay. Now, lets take what's left of our asshole and get this thing over." The two detectives made their way back to the house. The fire was at its peak. The last remains of the house were ablaze with smoke billowing up into the night sky. Moving through the old oak trees they made their way to the spot where the killer had fallen only to find an empty space where his body was only minutes ago. The two detectives looked at each other in utter amazement.

Chapter Twelve

Face To Face

"Shit!," Beau shouted looking around at the mob of firemen, singling out each man's frame for some tell-tale clue. He could see nothing out of the ordinary. "He couldn't have survived that fall."

Jack looked around and found a broken limb from the oak tree directly above the spot. "Looks like this limb broke his fall. He got his ass saved again."

"I can't believe it. This guy is a fucking phantom or he has a shitpot full of luck going for him." Beau looked over the fire scene and spotted three black and whites with their lights flashing and four patrol officers making their way through the hustling firemen. Beau yelled at the first man on scene. "Spread out and search the area. Our killer is still in the area." Dusting himself off, not waiting for an answer, he commanded, "Come on Jack," as he moved quickly down the hill to a group of firemen unrolling hoses.

"Did any of you see anyone come down this hill?"

"No," the fire boss responded, "Not from our unit."

A young rookie unrolling a hose said, "There was a guy who called in the fire and tried to help with a garden hose. Looks like he had a ton of bricks fall on him. You might want to talk to the captain."

"Thanks." Jack said, as he followed Beau who had already darted down the hill toward the captain's car. The captain was on the bullhorn directing movement of his units attacking the fire. Beau attempted to talk to him but was waved off. He tried again and was silently rebuffed. Getting a little pisssed, he grabbed the Captain by his equipment harness and stood him up by the truck and shoved his badge in his face and screamed, "God dammit, talk to me now."

"Who in the fuck do you think you are. Get your fucking hands off me and get that piece of tin out of my face. I've got a God damn fire to put out."

"Fuck the fire!" Beau screamed. "I've got a killer running around out there and I need some answers, now!. Did you see anyone around here that shouldn't be here?"

"All right, just hold your fucking horses." The surprised captain said defensively, pushing Beau's arm away. "No, all my guys are accounted for. If you'll get all that fuzz outa my face I might be able to get this fire out."

Beau snapped back. "I don't give a shit if that whole fucking house burns down. I've got a cop killer around here and I haven't got time to put up with your shit. Now, give me some answers or your gonna be spitting some teeth out right here."

"You have any idea who you're talking to?" The captain growled.

Beau put his face close to the fire captain and sneered, "I don't give a damn if you are the fucking Pope. I want some answers now."

The fire captain stopped his macho dialog with Beau. He knew this guy had a problem and wasn't impressed with rank. Taking his eyes from the fire scene he looked directly at Beau and said, "Yeah, there was this civilian who called in the fire and tried to put it out with a garden hose. He looked like a ton of shit fell on him."

"Yeah, I've heard that before. Where'd he go?" Beau asked with a leveling tone in his voice.

"I told him to go to the hospital." The fire captain said looking away at the fire scene still in progress.

Beau took a deep breath and mocked, "I truly believe you are the stupidest asshole I've ever met. Did it ever occur to you that this could be arson? That your arson investigators might like some witness information? Or that the water has been cut off to this address for the past 4 years? You dumb fuck, you were probably talking to the arsonist and didn't even know it. Where did he go?

The surprised fire captain responded awkwardly, "I sent him to the hospital. He climbed into the front seat of the ambulance that just left."

Beau shoved the bewildered man against the fire truck and cocked his right arm to give him a shot in the face when Jack stopped him. "Not now, later."

Both detectives ran to the nearest black and white and laid ten feet of rubber as the black and white fish-tailed down the street with lights flashing and sirens screaming.

The ambulance raced through the city winding its way to Charleston Memorial Hospital. The driver was a paramedic who was unlucky enough to catch the third shift which was usually quiet except on weekends. Starting about 2:00am the drunks and bar fight victims would get called in. He would make about a half a dozen trips and he would be off. But that would only be about 4 hours of busy time not bad he thought to himself.. Tonight was a little bit out of the ordinary. He hadn't had a fire call in some time. The driver gave a big yawn and gazed at the injured man riding in the seat next to him. He had checked him over and determined he had a few stitches coming along with a mild concussion and maybe a few cracked ribs. But all in all, he'd be okay. The driver, from time to time, couldn't help but notice a smirk on his face.

"Are you okay?" He questioned while glancing at the road.

"Yeah, I'm fine," Gaylord answered glancing into the side view mirror to see if anyone was following.

"Looks like you took a nasty fall," the driver inquired.

"Well, you know what they say, shit happens," Gaylord remarked with a sly grin.

"You got that right," the driver responded. "By the way, what's the name of the lady in the back?" The officer forgot to tell me."

Gaylord slid open the back window and gazed at Sally and Studs resting on the stretchers. A sinister smile came over his face and he began to sing softly. "Oh where or where has my little girl gone, oh where or where could she be. That's Agness Gladlow. That was her house back there."

The driver thought to himself, "What the hell do I have here? There are some weird people roaming around Charleston. I think he's had one sniff too many."

"Did you get her out?" the driver asked again, interrupting his melody.

"Yeah. Just happened to be in the neighborhood and saw the fire."

"A lucky young lady," the driver acknowledged, nodding his head.

Gaylord slid open the rear window again and mumbled, "and that's about to change."

"What?"

"Nothing." He said and gently closed the window.

Jack was at the wheel of the patrol car with tight jaws and white knuckles as he gripped the wheel snapping the police car quickly in an out of sharp turns. Beau picked up the radio mike, held it close, and transmitted. "Control Central this is 271 over."

"Go 271, Central."

"We need back up to meet us at Charleston Memorial Hospital ASAP. The suspect is believed to be enroute to that location. Alert hospital security."

"That's a roger 271."

"Central, there will be an Agent Sally Thornton to be admitted. I want a police guard on her right away. No one comes close to her unless he's approved staff. Got that?"

"Roger 271 copy."

Charleston Memorial Hospital was a monument to red brick. It was a classic example of southern architecture built just prior to World War II. Over the years the building had been expanded to include a modern state of the art cardiac care center, cancer research laboratories, cardiac rehab facilities, a new 500 bed hospital wing and the newest addition, the emergency trauma facility. The hospital was surrounded by parks, green areas with flowers and a new covered parking lot. The trauma center had a circular driveway that allowed several ambulances to off load at the same time. Although the outside of the hospital looked classical, the inside was a first rate modern facility with all the modern conveniences including a restaurant that served food that didn't taste like prepackaged garbage from the food court at the local mall.

This night was not your usual night in Charleston. The shit hit the fan about 11:30 pm when catastrophe struck an Orel Roberts revival at the local high school. As the crowd reached fevered pitch by being born again, the bleachers collapsed and 20 good God fearing Christians were rushed to the emergency room at Charleston Memorial. It was bedlam as stretchers were unloaded and rushed into various emergency care centers. Sally was barely conscious as she waited to be pushed through the door. Gaylord wanted to disappear into the mob but knew that he needed medical attention if he was going to cover any distance between him and the law. It would only be a matter of time before they would figure out where he had gone. Then there was Agness. Agness had ran from him and that had infuriated him. She could never be allowed to get away with such an insult. Hadn't he always done what she wanted? Now, she was just throwing him away. Why? His twisted mind had to know why. There must be another man. He had to take his revenge. God dammit he's gonna slit her fucking throat. She was just like all the rest. Use a man then just throw him away. Well as far as he was concerned she was gonna pay. These thoughts continued to race through his head as he pushed Sally's stretcher down the busy hallway. The driver pushed Studs who was barely awake still sucking oxygen. The oxygen mask hastily placed over his nose prevented him from picking up on the scent of the killer. He was also preoccupied with the people moving around him to notice the evil that was so close to him. Victims from the shoot-out on the water front were laid out on a gurney with tags on their toes in a quiet corner of the emergency room as the nurses and call doctors attended to the more needy patients.

A nurse rushed to the front of the stretcher and stopped the driver. "That dog can't come in here." She ordered.

"Look, ma'am I was told to keep this dog with the patient. It's gonna be my ass if I don't."

"Who told you to do a dumb thing like that?" She blurted.

"The police ma'am. This dog is a material witness and needs attention."

"I don't care if its Sherlock Holmes he's not coming in here."

The charge doctor looked up from his patient and moved to the argument ensuing in the hallway. "What's the problem?"

The nurse firmly stated, "This animal poses a health hazard in this area. We have no means of caring for a dog. He needs to see a vet."

The doctor looked examined Sally then looked at the dog. Turning his attention back to Sally he examined her eyes with a small penlight. She regained consciousness and murmured, "Don't touch my dog. He stays," she whispered. The doctor smiled, held her hand and said softly, "He stays. He will be all right."

The nurse looked stunned at the doctor's announcement and protested.

"Sir, you know that this is a health issue, and…" the doctor interrupted her in mid sentence, "This is also a police officer," nodding toward the dog, and he's been hurt in the line of duty and needs emergency care and I intend to give it to him and that's the end of if. Now, get her into surgery and clean her up right now."

"And the dog?" she questioned smugly.

"The dog too." The doctor ordered.

Gaylord began to push Sally's gurney following the stern faced nurse when the doctor spoke again, "where are you going?"

Gaylord turned to face the doctor with an innocent look, "I was going to see that she is all right and …"

The doctor cut him off again, "No you not. You're coming with me. You need surgery right now. You are frightening my patients and you've lost a lot of blood." The doctor motioned him to follow him but he still hesitated.

"But sir."

"Don't worry, you can come back later," he said with an understanding smile. "Come on, lets go."

Gaylord had no choice with everyone watching and moving about he had to fit into the crowd if was going to complete his mission. It took about 20 minutes for the doctor to put the last stitch into Gaylord's face.

"Okay, get undressed and put this gown on," The doctor ordered.

"I'm fine, I can make it home all right," Gaylord assured.

"No, you're staying the night for observation."

"No, really, I'm fine," Gaylord said again.

"Let me see those ribs," the doctor asked.

Gaylord held up his shirt. The doctor began to feel the bruised area of his chest when Gaylord grimaced.

"Just as I thought, You've probably got a few broken ribs," the doctor announced. "Now slip into these," he ordered tossing him a patient's gown. Before he could put on the shirt the doctor interrupted, "Wait a minute. I'm going to tape those ribs. Sit over there he commanded." Gaylord had no choice, he complied. The doctor began to apply the tape, "Now, I want you to go down to X-ray and have some pictures taken. I'll call them and tell them you're on the way. You could have punctured a lung or have some internal damage we don't know about. You'll have to stay the night and we'll take a look tomorrow, okay?

Gaylord nodded as he tied the string on his hospital gown.

"East wing, second floor is X-ray. Just take the elevator and follow the signs. When you've finished go up to the third floor west wing and the nurse will admit you."

"Where will Agness be.? Gaylord questioned.

"Agness?" the doctor hesitated, "Oh, the girl you came in with. She'll be in surgery a while. Then we'll put her in the first available room. We are getting booked up fast. The floor nurse in your area will know what room she's in. Now, get down to X-ray. I want to see those pictures before I go home."

Gaylord reluctantly complied, slipping on a bathrobe and limping out the door. Stepping into the busy emergency room hallway he made is way to the elevator and pressed the button for the second floor. The doors began to close when a hand stopped their closing motion. Two uniformed hospital security guards stepped inside. Everyone stood silently as the elevator moved upward.

"Excuse me." Gaylord said politely, "I came in with a Mrs. Agness Gladlow. She was in surgery a few minutes ago. Do you know what room she might be in?"

The older security guard responded automatically, "Recovery is on the third floor west wing. Talk to the charge nurse. She'll know."

"Thank you." Gaylord answered with a sinister smile that quickly vanished when the officers looked his way.

Surgery room four was large compared to other operating rooms in the hospital. It was used primarily by the trauma center for emergency procedures and doubled as a surgical classroom. It's interior included modern up to date equipment that was conveniently placed around the well lit table. Sally had been washed, cleaned, and dressed in the drab green hospital gown. The chief surgeon had scrubbed, put on rubber gloves, examined her new x-rays and moved to Sally's side. The surgical nurse and the anesthesiologist where all set for the procedures that were to follow. Sally opened her eyes to a glaring light. The doctor leaned over casting a shadow over her face.

"How are you doing?" the doctor inquired.

"Fine. Where's my dog?" She could hear the doctor chuckle under his surgical mask.

"He's doing fine. We'll put him in the same room with you if that is all right."

"Thank you." Sally said calmly.

The doctor took a closer look at her face. "Now Agness, you have a broken cheekbone, and a few lacerations on your face. These are all minor. By the time we're finished you'll look like Cindy Crawford. Okay?"

"Okay," she mumbled hoarsely. Suddenly she grabbed the doctor's hand.

"What did you call me?" she exclaimed.

"Agness. Your name is Agness isn't it?"

"Who told you my name was Agness?" she demanded.

"the fireman outside, he's the one who brought you in."

The doctor nodded at the anesthesiologist.

"Oh my God. He's here." Those were her last words as the gas mask was placed over her face and the lights went slowly out.

The lights were flashing and the siren going at full tilt as Jack continued to maneuver the patrol car through the streets of Charleston.

"Can't you go any faster?" Beau questioned nervously.

"We'll get there just hold your horses," Jack answered with a typical cliché. Beau began to argue out loud to himself. "I was against the whole fucking idea in the first place. It was too loose. Not enough attention to detail. The wrong night, the wrong place and the wrong girl."

"You can't say you didn't get results." Jack reassured him then slipping the car into another tight turn.

"I must of had my head up my ass and firmly locked. I should of never let her do it. She's a schrink not some one who has been trained to do that sort of thing. This is the last time I let personal feelings get in the way." Beau said broodingly.

Jack took another quick glance at Beau. "As I live and breathe you're in love. Mr. hardass is in love." Jack replied with a chuckle.

"Fuck off." Beau growled picking up the radio mike. He paused then hit the transmit button, "Control, 271."

"271, Control, go," came a scratchy reply.

"What's the status of the hospital backup?"

"We have three units in route to that location now."

"Alert hospital security that they have a killer roaming around there someplace. I want them to block off all avenues of escape. Detain and hold all suspicious personnel until we can check them out. Allow no one to leave the building. Use any excuse you want. Quarantine or whatever. I don't want any panic over there."

"That's a ten four 271."

Beau returned the mike to the cradle. "What are we doing, taking the grand tour of Charleston?" Beau blurted sarcastically.

"One more block and we're there." Jack announced as he put the car into another screeching turn.

"The driveway to the emergency trauma center was packed with ambulances and private automobiles off loading injured personnel. The patrol car came to an abrupt halt. The detectives could see one man pick up an injured child from his car and rush into the trauma center.

"What the hell is going on? Looks like the whole fucking city is falling apart. This isn't gonna hack it." Beau announced bluntly. Both detectives got out of the car and pushed their way through the hustling crowd.

The charge nurse in the trauma center was in constant motion giving directions and taking calls and initialing paperwork. Phones rang continually and papers were pushed in front of her by passing doctors. She was shouting orders to nurses, nurses aids, and anyone who'd listen and was able to lend a helping hand.

"We are looking for an agent Thornton, Sally Thornton. She was admitted just a few minutes ago." Beau asked nervously.

"Just a minute," she responded waving them off as she barked orders over the phone. Beau and Jack both displayed their badges then Beau pressed the phone button cutting her off in mid sentence.

"This is a police emergency. You have an agent Thornton, Sally Thornton who was just admitted to the hospital. I need her room number. Now!. Beau roared glaringly.

"Just a minute." The nurse did a quick search on the hospital computer checking the current database. "Sorry, we have no record of a Thornton being checked in." she advised.

"Bullshit! She must be in surgery right now."

The nurse calmly replied, "We have a Thompson, Tyler, and a Thomas admitted and assigned rooms as of about 20 minutes ago."

"What about surgery? Who's currently in surgery? Do you have a record of that?"

The nurse entered additional keystrokes and scanned the screen on the monitor. "When did you say she was admitted to surgery?"

"Within the last hour." Beau responded nervously, trying to be calm. The nurse shook her head negatively as she read the names, "We have a Baxter, Carlin, Gladlow, and a Harcourt in the last hour."

"Yes!" Beau shouted, "Gladlow, that's agent Thornton. What's her status?" he demanded. The nurse picked up the phone and called surgery. Beau tapped the counter nervously waiting for the answer.

"Hello, Shirley? What's the status on the Gladlow woman?" There was a nervous silence as both detectives held their breath. The nurse nodded and said, "Yeah, uh huh, okay." Jack interrupted, "Find out the status of the Harcourt patient too." The nurse nodded, "What about the Harcourt patient? He came in about the same time." Again the two detectives waited like two runners at the starting gate.

"The Gladlow woman is still in surgery. She'll be out in a few minutes. The Harcourt patient is out of surgery and is in room 306A."

"What's the room?" Beau commanded starting to move down the hall toward the elevators.

"306A," the nurse shouted."

"No, surgery, what's the room number for surgery?" He shouted.

"There's only two on the third floor west wing." The nurse replied shouting even louder.

"Get hospital security up there now and I want any officer you can grab to get up there ASAP."

Jack grabbed Beau's arm, "I'll check out Gaylord's room." Beau nodded as he closed the elevator doors.

Gaylord limped slowly down the hallway toward the X-ray lab. The doctor had given him some pain killer but it wasn't working. Each step of the way caused him to grimace in pain. His concentration was broken when the hospital public address system announced, "will security report to X-ray?" Gaylord tried to move faster but that was out of the question. Turning to look behind him Gaylord spotted two security guards running toward him. That was it, the game was over. He hadn't been able to take his revenge on Agnes. It wasn't fair he thought to himself. After all he had done for her, to reject him for someone else. To just be lying there in a cozy warm bed while he had to run and hide. It wasn't fair. Hadn't he given little David to her? Didn't he just sit there and watch her have sex with David. Now, she just throws me on the dung heap for someone else. These thoughts had barely passed through his mind when the security guards ran passed him turning into the X-ray lab down the hall. Gaylord laughed to himself and whispered, "Those dumb shits don't know what I look like. How stupid of them." He had one lucky break. He wouldn't get another. He had to make himself invisible for now. There would be plenty of time to take care of Agness. He had to clear the hallway those guards would be back and would be asking questions he couldn't answer. The only avenue to get out of sight quickly was the woman's restroom. He entered the restroom silently then held the door slightly open to observe the hallway. He was right. the guards reappeared from X-ray and began checking the doors in the hallway. It would be a matter of minutes and they would be here. Gaylord looked around. The restroom was empty. He would take the last stall, curl up his feet under his chin, hold his breath, and sit silently. Minutes passed and noting. No one came in. He'd lucked out again. He was just about to step out of the stall when a new visitor entered. She was a young blue-eyed blonde nurse's aid about eighteen years old. Gaylord resumed his position on top of the toilet and remained absolutely quiet. The attractive young woman made a quick check of the stalls bending over to look for feet. Satisfied, she went to the door and told the guards that no one was there. Satisfied, the guards moved on down the hall. How stupid he thought to himself. If he had been a police officer he'd come in and check each stall personally, to hell with embarrassing someone. The young girl began to wash her hands. She hummed a little tune as she went about washing off her makeup. She opened her purse and set a lipstick and two bottles of makeup on the counter. Gaylord watched from the stall directly behind her. He was beginning to get excited watching the young woman remove her makeup. He flashed back to when little David was forced to wear makeup and dress in woman's clothes. Then Agness, dressed as a man would grab him, tear off his clothes and rape him anally with some type of plastic dildo she would strap to her waist. He remembered how it took days before he could walk like a normal boy. He would never get the humiliation and pain out of his mind. She hurt him so severely that he had to sit in a hot bath until the pain subsided. The whole episode infuriated him and at the same time excited him.

Gaylord slipped out of the stall grabbed the young woman by the hair and smashed her head into the stainless steel shelf. She immediately went limp. He was moving automatically with the feeling of hate and lust driving him on. He shoved the girl into the stall, tore off her blouse, and brassiere. Throwing her skirt up he tore off her bikini underpants with one quick grab. The young woman laid motionless against the back of the toilet with her legs spread open and fully exposed. Taking her by the throat he pulled her up and kissed her passionately then began licking her face and breasts like some child with a lollipop.

"Agness, I want you to watch." Gaylord lifted his chin and looked around as if performing for an audience. "I'm going to show you how to really fuck, do you hear me?"

The young woman groaned momentarily. Gaylord stuffed her panties in her mouth stifling any possible crying. Untying his robe he inserted his manhood inside the girl and rammed it inward pushing her back against the wall. "Does that feel good Agness?" He rammed himself into her again and again. The young woman's head flopped back and forth like a rag doll being impaled on a large spear. On the final thrust he held the spread-eagled unconscious girl on him until he had spent his passion. He calmly stepped out of the stall and adjusted his robe, and stood in front of the mirror proud of his sexual power over women. Looking at himself in the mirror he grinned then spoke, "You've still got it." His eyes looked up through the ceiling of the restroom as if he could see to the third floor. "Now, you bitch, you're gonna get yours."

The hallway was momentarily clear of traffic. Looking in both directions Gaylord slipped out of the restroom and entered room 206B just across the hall. It was dark, he could hear the constant blip of the heart monitoring machine at the head of the bed. The steady stream of the EKG graph moved across the screen blipping intermittently with each heart beat. An old lady with white hair slept quietly, not knowing that a killer stood at the foot of her bed. Gaylord looked adoringly at the old lady then tenderly straightened her covers and tucked her in. Gaylord's revelry was interrupted when he heard voices just outside room 206. Gaylord quickly stepped into the bathroom as the door opened. The floor nurse looked in, then quietly closed the door.

Inside the small bathroom Gaylord noticed a stainless steel IV stand with large rollers extending down from each leg. An IV bag half full hung from the top. He smiled to himself, then taking some surgical tape from the medicine cabinet, he taped the IV to his wrist. He was beginning to experience a new high from the game of hide and seek. This was his game. Those stupid people would never catch him. They'd been trying for years and just like Seattle and Houston, he was going to fool them again. He had only one more mission to accomplish and that was to kill that bitch Agness who had the unmitigated gall to turn him down. Me, Gaylord Harcourt, she turned me down, and she was going to pay with her life. Then, he thought to himself, "the ghost would disappear into the night and maybe next year he would be up in Canada, or Alaska or maybe even Mexico. Where ever Agness went he'd find her." These thoughts continued to race through his demented mind as he stepped into the hallway and moved slowly toward the elevator blending in with other personnel now in the hallway. Pushing the IV stand Gaylord ambled unnoticed, as hospital personnel moved quickly up and down the hallway paying no attention to the patient in a hospital robe and slippers. Stopping at the elevator he pushed the up button. It seemed like and eternity before it would arrive at the second floor. When the door moved open Gaylord came face to face with two police officers. He hesitated. The officers held the door back and asked, "are you coming?" That statement jolted Gaylord to react, "Yes. This going to the third floor?" The officer made room for him and the IV stand. Inwardly, Gaylord was laughing to himself, "What stupid people they have in uniform these days." The elevator doors crept open as the elevator leveled itself on the third floor. The officers raced down the hallway and paused momentarily at the floor nurse's station. One officer stationed himself in front of room 317A and the other officer stood at the nurse's station. The sign on the wall read, "Surgical Recovery." He smiled inwardly and said to himself, "thank you you dumb fucking cops for telling me that Agness is in room 317A.

Two large metal swinging doors separated the surgical recovery room for the main hallway. Adjacent to the doorway was the Surgical Recovery Supply room. Gaylord knew that he needed time to figure out how he could get to Agness. The supply room offered a temporary safe haven away from the searching security officers who had passed him in the hallway earlier.

Moving cautiously, he opened the door and scanned the room to see if he was alone. "Great", he whispered and removed the taped IV from his arm setting the stand to one side. "I've got to think", he said, cracking open the door to observe the nurse's station. For now he was out of luck. The two officers were firmly in position. The officer at room 317A had a chair set to one side of the door and a newspaper firmly in his hand and could see anyone approaching from either the west or east hallways. The other officer was leaning on the nurse's counter talking to the charge nurse. The surgical recovery night shift consisted of a charge nurse, three intensive care nurses and two male orderlies who moved in and out of the rooms at various times taking blood pressure, and administering medicine or taking blood samples. Gaylord closed the door slowly. He sat quietly and began to form a plan. Not rationalizing, but letting his ego personality Gaylord take charge of the whole process. These are basically stupid people and stupid people are able to follow routines and so he would blend into the routine. But how? How would he blend in? He began to search the supply room checking each locker and cabinet. "There had to be something", he remarked to himself opening each cabinet door and examined each item on the shelf. Opening the last locker he found the answer. Gaylord grabbed a doctor's smock, took off his robe and quickly buttoned up the smock and hung a stethoscope around his neck. He looked into the small mirror that was attached to the locker door and murmured, "What do you think guys?" There was no answer, nothing but a nod of approval.

The side door of the supply room opened onto operating room number four viewing balcony. This was a theater room from which medical students could observe surgical procedures. The darkened glass provided Gaylord with the invisibility he needed to look down on the proceedings below. There she was. Sally was on the table with the doctor putting in the last suture. Looking up with satisfaction at the two nurses the doctor said, "She's going to be great. A work of art if I must say so."

"Quit your bragging, I think you did a better job on the dog." the older nurse answered with a nod of approval.

"I get no respect," he joked imitating Rodney Dangerfield. "Okay ladies she's all yours."

The nurses tucked her in, moved her to the gurney, and wheeled her out. Gaylord moved silently back into the supply room searching every corner again. Picking out a hospital push cart he assembled several syringes, bottles of saline solution, glucose drips, IV plastics and put them on the cart. He hung a clipboard on the end of the cart and moved back to the hallway door. He saw the gurney from the operating room carrying Sally enter room 317A. The nurses paused and exchanged a few words with the security guards then left. It was now of never. This was the time of make his move. Gaylord waited quietly until the hallway traffic had subsided. Opening the supply room door he entered the hallway pushing the hospital cart. He had to control his anxiety. He had to force himself to act normal. To act as if this is just another routine job, not the crowning achievement of his career. He was going to kill Agness right under the nose of those stupid people who protected her. He pretended to scan the clipboard checking fictitious names and room numbers as he approached the officer guarding the door of room 317A. He glimpsed momentarily at the head nurse who was making small talk with the other officer at the nurses station. Her brains were in her boobs he thought to himself, She could have cared less about anything out of the ordinary.

"What's the problem officer? You've got some VIP in there?" He said nodding at the door. The officer stood up and examined Gaylord closely before he spoke.

"You must know the routine. I'm just a mushroom in the scheme of things. They keep me in the dark and feed me shit". Gaylord smiled at the cliché and answered.

"I'm suppose to start an IV on," he paused looking at a blank piece of paper attached to the clipboard, "A lady in 317A. Lets see, yeah, Agness Gladlow."

The security officer was quick to reply. "I don't know about your orders but mine are that no one goes in there unless they have written approval form the Chief of Surgery."

"I assume that these are his orders?" Gaylord retorted shaking his shoulders in frustration.

"You betcha," the officer responded smiling, "Unless they are written and signed by Dr. Milton we can debate this all night. If you'll run up to the 4th floor I'm sure you'll find him in the office."

With every fiber in his body Gaylord tried to put on a front that he didn't really care. "Okay, I'll do the rest of my rounds and get back to you." Gaylord casually pushed the cart forward and entered room 318A. Room 318A was a dark room with only one table lamp casting a low yellow glow throughout the room. He opened the bathroom door and scanned the inside momentarily, then closed it. He tried the connecting door to room 317A only to find it locked. Pulling back the curtain to bed number two he saw another elderly lady asleep. He paused and looked at the old lady with tenderness. It was amazing that this killer who in a rage had killed Agness over and over again could find a few moments of sympathy and kindness to a dying white hared old lady. Gaylord moved to the window and looked out. He could see the park, the emergency room entrance and the police cars strategically placed blocking any possible escape. Looking to his right Gaylord observed a ledge of concrete connecting all the third floor windows. That was it. If they weren't going to let him through the front door he'd go through the window. He slipped a surgical scalpel into his smock and cranked open the window. It was going to be touch and go but he could make it. The red bricks above the ledge gave him a firm hand hold as he edged his way toward room 317A.

The doctor had given Sally a mild sedative that was hardly sleep inducing. She tossed and turned reliving her nightmare. The shock of the Beastie that had almost killed her caused her to bolt upright in bed with a muffled cry. Sally looked around the darkened room seeing evil in every shadow. She placed her hands on Stud's head, breathed a sigh or relief and laid back down staring at the shadows on the ceiling that streamed in from the window. It was over she thought and it was time to get some rest and not think about tomorrow or the next day for that matter. She thought about Katie and how she missed her. She took a close look at her life. Where she'd been and where she was going and how would that affect Katie's life. Had she done the right thing? Katie needed a father but could she handle another man in her life? Would Mr. Right ever come along? Was Beau Mr. Right? Her thoughts were interrupted by a low growl from Studs.

"What is it boy?" Another growl, this time more menacing as though he could sense some evil close by. Sally turned towards the partially open window just in time to see a shadow of an arm reaching for the edge on the window pane. The window shook firmly as the hand now griping the window from the outside tried to force it open.

"Oh my God, he's here," she whispered to Studs who stood crouched ready to pounce. Still shaky, Sally eased out of bed only to be stopped short by the IV connector still in her arm. Making no sound Sally pushed the IV stand with her. If she tried to get to the front door the Beastie would see her. Her only avenue of escape undetected would be to the bathroom. She shut and locked the bathroom door then sat in the corner waiting for the Beastie to crash through and kill her. This nightmare would never go away. He was going to finish what he had started. She covered her mouth with her hand as she sobbed openly trying to muffle her panic. This whole episode brought back memories of a dream she had as a child. She remembers this terrible beast of unspeakable horror that chased her. No matter how far she ran or where ever she hid the beast would always find her. Maybe her childhood dream was the foretelling of her fate and it was all coming true tonight. The thought of death put her stomach in knots, or maybe it was the drugs or the ordeal she had just gone through that brought it on but she began to shake out of control, unable to hold in her silence. She had never cried since childhood but she could not stop. It was a cry of fear, helplessness, coupled with total exhaustion. She hated herself for not being in control of her feelings, but she couldn't control it. She hated the idea that she was giving up. She was just too tired to fight anymore. She knew deep inside that she was just going to sit there and let herself die.

Gaylord had quietly force the window open and stepped inside the darkened room. He moved to the front door and quietly locked it from the inside. In a low murmur Gaylord began to hum and sing to himself, "Oh where, oh where has my little girl gone, oh where oh where could she be? With her hair cut short and her throat cut long, oh where oh where could she be?" Holding the scalpel high, ready to strike he moved to the first bed curtain and flung it open only to meet Studs leaping at his throat. Studs who was in the attack mode caught him completely by surprise knocking him down upsetting Sally's bed pan sending it clanging to the floor. The guard outside the door sprang out of his chair and reached for his gun and he tried the locked door.

"Frank!" he shouted to the other guard, "Someone's in there. The door is locked from the inside." Frank seeing Beau and Jack exit the elevator, shouted down the hall,? "Lieutenant! We've got a problem." Beau and Jack sprinted down the hallway and pushed against the door with no luck. They could hear bottles and glasses falling to the floor and Beau recognized Stud's bark. Studs was attacking the killer. The men moved back three steps to get a run at the door. "All together now," Beau commended. The men hit the door at full speed splintering it on impact. The light streaming into the room revealed a stunned, frustrated and maddened Gaylord. He charged at Beau with his slashing scalpel screaming like some banshee gone mad. This is exactly what Beau wanted. He stepped into the first blow of the beast and blocked it then quickly spun around bringing his elbow with full force into the killer's Adam's apple cutting off his wind momentarily. He followed up with a fast forearm to the bridge of his nose, crushing it and sending blood spattering onto the bed curtain which he grabbed helplessly trying to right himself. The beast let out another cry of rage ignoring the pain. Beau was not finished. With three quick steps he dropped kicked the beast sending him crashing through the third floor window. Beau, slightly winded, looked at Jack and remarked, "Lets see him survive that." Beau and Jack casually walked to the window only to find the killer clinging to the edge of the overhang with his feet dangling three floors above the hard pavement and certain death.

Beau screamed at the dangling beast, "You fucking scum bucket don't you ever die? You, you son-of-a-bitch go ahead and let go, die and save us a whole lot of fucking time." As his fingers began to weaken and slip Gaylord's expression changed and the little boy David began to sob hopelessly as he pleaded with Beau.

"Please Mister, don't let her kill me. I don't want to die."

Beau automatically grabbed the wrist of the sobbing killer and was slipping further out the window when Jack grabbed his shoulder with one hand and his belt with the other. The two security guards quickly had a firm grip on Beau's legs giving him more leverage to hold onto the killer. Beau could now use his other hand to get a firmer grip on Gaylord. Losing his grip on the ledge the killer swung freely in Beau's hands three floors from certain death. Beau gave the killer a cold stare and said, "I don't care if you're Don Juan or Little Boy Blue you're still apiece of shit as far as I am concerned so stop the bullshit. You know something? My hands are beginning to sweat. I don't think I can hold on for very much longer. You know something else? Nobody is going to give a shit. All I have to do is to let go and nobody will have a problem with that."

Jack stretched out his hand to help Beau hold on to the killer. Looking at Beau Jack grunted, "Yeah, you will."

"Bullshit!" Beau shouted in anger.

"Call it bullshit or whatever you like but you won't do it." Jack answered, gripping the killers arm with one hand.

"Yeah, just try me. You spend a few weeks with a guy and he becomes Mother Teresa." Jack trying to calm the situation lightly remarked, "You took an oath to serve and protect didn't you?" Beau chuckled then tightened his grip as the killer's hand slipped a sweaty inch. "Yeah sure, I'll serve the community by letting this asshole go. I can protect them by not letting this scum cop an insanity plea."

"That's not for you to decide," Jack answered, raising his voice slightly. "Beau, you're a lot of things. You may even be an asshole from time to time but you're not a killer. You're a good cop and you've done your job, so lets cuff this piece of shit and go suck down a Miller."

The killer's expression changed again as he relaxed and calmly stared at Beau. He spoke, not as the egotistic Gaylord, or grunted as the uncontrollable Beastie. Instead of the childlike little boy David, there was another personality who had finally made it to the surface. "Do it. For God's sake do it. Give us all some rest. Just let us go, please. I'm tired of fighting. I just want to die. I know at least then we'll be at peace."

"Who in the fuck are you?" Beau asked angrily, tightening his grip as the killer's hand slipped another inch closer to death.

"My name is Gordon. They've kept me locked up and wouldn't let me out. I've begged and pleaded but they pushed me back into that dark place."

"Why now?" Jack interrupted as he moved his hand to get a better grip and grabbed the killers arm just below the elbow.

"They're scared. They're out of answers and ideas. They think I can help them."

Beau cut in abruptly, "You actually think we're going to buy this line of bullshit?"

"All you have to do is let go and it's over," Gordon replied.

Beau looked at Jack who was now almost out of the window with two more police officers holding his legs. "What do you think?" Jack smiled through the beads of sweat rolling down his forehead and replied, "I think you have a young lady in the bathroom who needs some reassuring." Beau shook his head, "I'm sure I am going to regret this."

With that statement both men gave one big tug and pulled the killer back into the room. Beau smashed his face into the cement floor. Putting his knee firmly in his back he twisted his arms behind his back and snapped the cuffs on him then stood up and looked at Jack. "You know how long I've waited to do that? Get this piece off shit out of here."

Beau watched as they drug the killer out. Jack tapped Beau on the shoulder and nodded toward the bathroom door.

The commotion in the next room and cuss words flowing from Beau's mouth brought tears of relief from Sally who was crouching in one corner of the bathroom. Unable to control her tears now mixed with laughter she stood up and put her back to the door and waited for her emotions to calm down. Beau and Jack stood outside listening to the muffled sobs coming from the bathroom. They smiled at each other knowing that this horrible nightmare has finally come to an end. Beau tapped his knuckle on the door gently and calmly said, "You can come out now." There was a long silence before Sally answered, "How do I know who you are?"

"It's Beau." He replied winking at Jack.

"How do I know?"

"I've got Studs with me."

"You could be the killer making me think you're Beau."

Jack murmured to Beau, "Do you guys always play these games?" Beau nodded as he spoke again, "How can I convince you that I'm him?"

"Who?" was Sally's quiet reply from the bathroom.

"Him."

"Him who?" she said quickly. Jack rolled his eyes at the ceiling as Beau answered.

"Him Beau."

"Or maybe him Gaylord?" She answered.

"Okay, I can prove it because I am the only guy who knows that you've got big feet and an ugly temper. Oh, by the way, the girls say you've got great boobs too."

There was again another brief silence then the door opened. Sally stood half naked in her surgical robe holding her IV stand. Beau struggled to hold his emotions in check. He could see she'd been crying. Trying to ease a tense situation he asked, "What was that all about?" Sally smiled and answered, "Just testing."

Without another word being said they grabbed each other in a tender embrace. They held each other as tight as they could for as long as they could realizing how much they really cared for each other. All the come on lines were over, all of the smart repartee of a man trying to impress a woman was over. This was pure emotion, honest feelings and love. The security guards and two uniformed officers smirked at each other knowing that this kind of emotion you never saw coming from the hard nosed lieutenant Beau Gasteneau. Jack turned to the smirking men and said, "What are you looking at?" The policemen dropped their smirks and marched out of the room. Jack looked back at Sally and Beau still embraced and closed the door to room 317A.

Chapter 13
Coming Together

It had been more than two weeks since the "Night of the Beastie", at least that's what the newspapers and the media called it. The capture of Gordon Delonpre had occupied the media blitz and the circus had just begun. Everyone with a morbid curiosity was waiting for the trial of the century to begin. The TV and radio interviews bombarded the airways. Chief Wexford and Captain Peterson were both interviewed on "Twenty-Twenty" by Barbara Walters. He didn't realize how they singlehandedly zeroed in on the killer. Beau was thankful that Jack had refused to be interviewed just as he had.

Beau couldn't think about that now as he pulled his car into the Charleston Memorial Hospital parking lot. For the past two weeks his thoughts, his time, and his emotions were centered on Sally. He was at her side every waking minute. He had neglected the mountain of paperwork that went with documenting their investigation. Today was Sally's "coming out" day. The bandages on her face were to be removed and she would be able to see herself for the first time since her ordeal. Sally was now in room 327A. After that fearful night she didn't feel safe in her old room. Studs was her constant companion. He wouldn't leave her side until he knew she was safe. To be on the safe side, in case any of the extremists or news media animals had any ideas, a 24 hour police guard remained outside her door. The guard took Studs outside to do his business then brought him back to be with Sally. The police officer's standing orders were to let no news or media people in the room. Captain Peterson who was always interested in getting his face in the news and taking credit for something he didn't deserve complained. He was about to counter Beau's orders when the Mayor stepped in and told the Captain to politely piss off.

Beau opened the door to Sally's room only to find her sitting on the edge of her bed gazing at the wall mirror gently touching her bandages. Studs was sitting by her side with his head resting comfortably in her lap. Studs rose and trotted to his master's side and sat with a satisfied look on his face. He had done his job and was waiting for his reward.

"Okay fella I wouldn't forget you," Beau said, patting his dog on the head. He removed a can of beer from a small paper bag then finding a small plastic dish poured the beer into it and put it on the floor. Studs eagerly lapped at his favorite brew.

Sally had been lucky, considering she had had her face smashed into a mirror. The only major damage to her face was a broken cheekbone and a few minor lacerations. The doctor was able to get to her early and repair the damage. The best plastic surgeon in the state had been called in.

"Well, what do you think?" Beau said, closing the door.

"I'm afraid," she answered turning her head to get another angle on her reflection, looking closely as though she could see through the bandages.

"You've got nothing to worry about," Beau commented, pulling up a chair next to hers, examining her closely as though he were the attending physician.

"Yeah, that's easy for you to say," She replied cautiously.

"You could be the 'Hunchback of Notre Dame' and you'd still be beautiful." Sally smiled at him and smirked, "That's because you want a quick roll in the hay. I've heard what the guys say about you. If it's a she, and breathing, you'll jump it." Beau feigned an arrow to the chest. "I'm hurt, that's the old me. I've changed."

"I'll believe it when I see it."

Beau took her hand gently and kissed it. "I don't blame you. I wasn't the nicest guy to be around. I was hurt, I was mad at everyone. I'd lost my family, my son, and my best friend. I thought I'd never care about anyone again. That's all changed now."

Sally recognized Beau's sincerity and gave him a kiss on the forehead. She started to speak. Beau put his fingers gently to her lips stopping her. "Please understand, when I thought I had lost you I was pissed at you for letting you talk me into it. Then I realized I was pissed at myself for letting you get too close to me. But now I'm glad. I know now that I can care about someone and I don't want to lose you. Look, I don't care how any of this turns out. I mean you can walk out that door and not look back and I'll understand. No hard feeling. But I just know I want you to be a part of my life. I want to belong to someone again. I want a home, a white picket fence, Sunday dinners with the family, and everything that goes with it. I want to feel normal again."

She had known almost from the beginning that she wanted Beau. Not just for the physical attraction, but deep inside she knew they both needed each other. She had finally found a man who actually needed her and was willing to make a commitment. It reminded her of how much love her mom had for her dad and when her mother met her stepfather it was the same total commitment. Casey told her how she felt blessed again to know God had sent her another man to love and would love her in return.

Sally never thought she could ever find a love so complete, so honest, but there it was, a man sitting in front of her opening his heart unconditionally.

The tears in her eyes were beginning to flow down her cheek when the door opened and Doctor Lance Morgan stepped in. "Okay troops knock off the billing and cooing. It's time to get down to business."

Beau relinquished his chair and stood behind the doctor as he examined the bandages. Turning Sally's head left then right he asked, "Are you ready for the unveiling?" Sally nodded bravely. Taking his surgical scissors from his vest pocket he carefully began to remove the bandages. As the last piece of gauze was removed the doctor nodded and winked at Beau.

"What do you think?" Standing back, tilting his head as though looking at a painting, going along with the doctor's put on, Beau answered, "I don't know? The nose looks a little out of line."

"Yeah, I don't know what we can do about that."

"What! What!?" Sally asked with rising concern in her voice. "She won't win any beauty contest but at least you can take her out in public," Beau said trying to keep a straight face.

"I want to see a mirror," Sally demanded. It was hard for Beau and the doctor to hold back the laughter.

"Do you think she can handle it?" Beau questioned, grinning at the doctor. "It's now or never," he answered reaching for a small hand mirror.

"Come on, whatever it is I can handle it." Sally said with a worried look. Doctor Morgan gave Sally the mirror. She held it up to see her face for the first time in over two weeks. She turned her head back and forth touching each cheek. She was beautiful. Not one blemish. Doctor Morgan had worked pure magic on her face. He had even taken her age wrinkles from around her eyes and neck. She looked ten years younger. The remains of her injury was a small almost unnoticeable scar on her right cheek. She touched it.

"That scar will be gone in a couple of weeks," the doctor commented. A sigh of relief came over Sally as she looked at Beau. He snapped his fingers and Studs jumped to his side and followed Beau's every move.

"Okay gorgeous let's blow this place," Beau said opening her closet door then putting a small suitcase on her bed.

"I'll sign the papers and you're out of here," Morgan said standing up and opening the door to the hallway. Sally was wheeled down to the back entrance where Beau had his car waiting. Even then the press was there popping photos and shouting questions at Sally. Several patrolmen pushed the reporters back giving them a clear path and a quick departure.

It was a quiet Friday morning in Charleston. The sun was still low on the horizon but it was going to be a scorcher. Studs curled up in the back seat and closed his eyes. Sally also closed her eyes and laid her head back and gave a sigh of relief. Beau drove slowly moving across town to highway 26 north then picking up 256 and crossing the bridge to Daniel Island. It was a beautiful drive. The lush green trees came down to the roadside casting intermittent shadows over Sally's face. Beau looked at the small scar that remained on an otherwise perfect face. He wondered if she would come out of this with a much deeper scar. He would do everything in his power to be there for her. "A penny for your thoughts," He asked. Sally kept her eyes closed and answered, "That's what I was going to ask you."

"I asked first," he replied.

"I was wondering. Have you ever been afraid of dying?" Beau remained silent wondering how to answer her question. He knew too well that when you come close to death you wonder about your own mortality. "Yes and no."

"What's that suppose to mean?" Sally questioned opening her eyes.

"We all think about dying. We all have to do it sometime. No, I'm not afraid of dying but your real question is, is there a heaven? Or, maybe is there someplace we'll all go after we die?"

"Yeah, that thought had crossed my mind," Sally stated turning to face Beau as he glanced at her, then back to the road. "You've had a brush with death and now you're looking for some answers." She nodded affirmatively looking at the deep green forest passing by the car window.

"I've never considered myself a religious person", He continued. "I went to Sunday school and church on Sundays. My father had strong religious beliefs. After he died I haven't been a regular member of the parish. Being a policeman, dealing with human garbage on a daily basis I'd just about given up on the human race. My wife ran off with another man and I had a son dying of Leukemia. I thought God had shit on my life. Or, I'd done something to piss him off. Finally, one night I got called to the hospital. My son was dying. These were going to be his last few moments on earth." Beau's voice was becoming labored with emotion. He went on. "My son, the boy I had taken to ball games and gone on fishing trips, this beautiful, loving little boy had been reduced to a mere skeleton. Even with all he'd been through he was still bright and cheerful. He knew that his mother had left him alone to die. He knew that I had the hate of a hundred men weighing me down. He motioned me to come close to him and in a soft voice said, "Please promise me that you'll be with me in heaven. Make your peace with God". I could not control my sobbing. It all just broke loose and I cried and cried. I knelt by his bed and prayed to God for forgiveness. I can only hope that in some way God heard me. After that, I took his frail, small body in my arms and held him for the last time. I cried and told him I'd be there, I'll meet you in heaven I promise, I promise." Beau had tears streaming down his cheek as he concentrated on his driving. "Then he just closed his eyes and he was gone. So you asked if I believe in God I'd have to say yes." Sally gently touched his hand and looked away. Her reflection in the car window revealed her tears and a mountain of emotion ready to burst out. She wanted to hold him, comfort him. She knew she loved him deeply.

The car turned off Highway 256 on to Clements Ferry Road. Both Sally and Beau had remained silent for at least fifteen minutes, each thinking about the conversation when Sally asked, "Where are we going?" noticing the majestic antebellum estates passing by. "It's a surprise," Beau replied recovering from his thoughts with a smile and a happier tone in his voice. "Your bags are packed and you've been checked out of your hotel. In fact, you've been out of your hotel for the past two weeks." Sally gave him a sly look. "What does that mean?"

"It means that your are moving in with me."

"Oh, just like that. I'm moving in with you," she said sternly sitting up straight and looking around.

"Yep!" he answered smugly.

"Boy, you really take a girl for granted. What makes you think I'm moving in with you?" She uttered defiantly

"You'll see," he replied like some school kid ready to play a joke. With that statement Beau made a right turn at a country road that had a massive hand carved wood sign spanning the entrance. The sign was held upright by two massive pine trees. The ornately carved letters on the sign read, "Falconbrair". Beau brought the car to a slow stop, grabbed his cell phone, and dialed a number then announced, "We've just turned off the highway. Is everything ready?" She looked at him and said, "Come on, what's going on?".

Studs jumped up with a happy smile on his face and licked Beau's face then Sally's. "What's the matter with him?" Sally asked, scratching Studs behind the ears. Beau smiled again reaching for the door handle. Studs leaped into the front seat with both feet landing on Beau's crotch. He moaned slightly as Studs bounded out of the car and took off running down the road. "Where's he going?" Sally asked laughing at Beau's predicament. "You'll see," he said closing the car door then driving slowly down the road.

The forest gave way to acres of well kept pecan groves, then groves of flowering peach trees that stretched across the small valley. When the car made it's last turn, it came into sight. There it was, 'Falconbriar.' It was a classic antebellum mansion that sat on a grassy knoll. Leading up to the home was a small country lane that was once used for horse and buggies. The lane was lined with massive 100 year old oak trees that cast intricate shadows on the dirt road. The Spanish moss hanging from the old oaks swayed gently in the afternoon breeze. The home was a classic monument to the Civil War. It had 6 statuesque white columns that supported a two story home under a red tile roof. Brightly colored azaleas surrounded the house.

The pathway to the right of the house meandered by the biggest magnolia tree Sally had every seen. She gasped at the sudden majestic beauty that had miraculously come into view. "This is Falconbrair?" She asked. Beau nodded with a grin beginning to cover his entire face. "It looks like Tara", Sally joked. "I expect to see Scarlet O'Hara waiting on the porch." She quipped.

As the car approached the front of the house Sally's expression changed. On the porch she could see her mother, Casey Thornton, and Katie, her little girl, the real love of her life. Standing next to them was a tall gray hared well dressed lady. She knew instinctively, that was Beau's mother. Her presence could never go unnoticed in a crowd. She automatically commanded your attention. Beau had those same qualities

Sally had tears of joy ready to burst when she stepped out of the car. Katie took only two big hops before she was off the porch running for her mom. Sally scooped her up with one big hug and kissed her. They just held each other. Josey put her arm around Casey and they both smiled at the reunion that had been so long in coming. Katie looked at Beau, then at Sally and said, "Group hug, group hug." With that command, Beau, Sally and Katie hugged each other as Sally cried and laughed at the same time. Studs was not about to be left out off all the fun. He stood up on his hind legs and pawed his way into the group hug. Sally put her arm around Stud's head, and scratched his ears while everyone laughed. Josey and Casey joined the happy group. Casey, with concern in her voice said, "Come on, let me take a look." She tilted Sally's face left then to the right. Satisfied, she remarked, "Is that all? Just a little scar.?"

"That's it," Sally responded giving her mom a kiss on the cheek. Sally turned her attention to Josey. "You are Beau's mother aren't you." Josey held open her arms and said, "My child, you don't know how long I've been waiting to meet you. You are beautiful." With that, she gave Sally a motherly hug as though she'd been a long lost member of the family.

Beau noticed that Casey had been disfigured at one time. The scars on her face had almost disappeared. However, you could still see that she had been burned badly. Casey Thornton still had touches of the fiery Irish red hair even though most of it had softly turned to gray. Beau knew where Sally had inherited that Irish temper. Casey had it but at her age of 66, she was able to keep it under control. However, from time to time it surfaced and she told people exactly what she was thinking and devil take the results. In the brief time he had known Casey, they had become close friends and Beau took joy in teasing Casey. There was an immediate bond between the two.

Katie tugged at her mother's arm, "Mommy, come on I want to show you my kids." Sally looked puzzled at Katie and Beau smiling at each other. They had cooked up some sort of secret to surprise her.

"Come on, what's going on?" Sally questioned. Katie taking Beau and Sally by the hand led them down the path past the old Magnolia tree.

"What have you guys been up to?" She insisted again being tugged along by an excited Katie.

Katie smiled and answered, "You'll see, you'll see," then bounded down the path toward a large barn. The barn was painted snowy white with a bright red tin roof. It looked like it could have been in a Norman Rockwell painting or classic photo seen on a feed and grain calendar. Attached to the barn was a chicken coop, holding pens for livestock, stables, and a spacious hay loft. Sally put her arm around Beau and laid her head on his shoulder. "It's beautiful and its totally out of character for you."

"What do you mean?", he answered kissing her on the forehead. "I mean the image, Beau Gasteneau, the tough cop, womanizer, drinker, and that garbage pit you call an apartment. Now this, It doesn't fit." Sally noticed that Beau's attitude had completely changed. He was calmer, at ease with himself. Maybe it was the Beau he always wanted to be? "This is where I come to get away from the mess we have to deal with every day. Here I can shutout the rest of the world. I feel safe here. This is where I grew up."

"So why the cop?" Sally asked.

"I needed my own money. I wanted to make a difference so I became a cop." He paused, collecting his thoughts. "Then I found out I was good at it and here I am." She kissed him on the cheek as they continued to walk toward the barn. "You are the only woman I've brought her since my first wife". Sally considered that an honor. Or, at least Beau was telling her that she was not just another conquest. This was a relationship he was taking seriously.

Katie was in the third stall on the right. When Sally and Beau arrived they saw Katie with a baby's milk bottle feeding a newly born lamb as several other lambs nudged in waiting for their turn on the bottle. Sally's heart melted as she knelt down and began to pet the little babies. "Aren't they wonderful?" Katie exclaimed. Laughing, Sally nodded. Beau had retrieved another bottle from the chiller box and gave it to Sally. Together, Katie and Sally fed the lambs and laughed. It was pure joy watching both of them enjoying the simple pleasure of tending to the young helpless lambs.

It had been the most wonderful weekend Sally had ever known. For the past 3 days Beau, Sally, Katie, Casey and Josey had been just a family doing those simple things that hold a family together. The women puttered around the kitchen baking bread, making brownies, fixing family dinners while

Katie and Beau made ice cream the old fashion way, mixing fresh cream and sugar with spices from an old family recipe. After dinner no one watched TV. They all sat on the porch in wicker rockers and watched the summer fire flies light up the soft summer night. It was a time Sally would never forget and hoped deep down in her heart that it would never end.

It was one of those lazy summer days. A buttermilk sky covered the picnic area cooling the hot Charleston sun. It was as though someone had ordered a perfect day for a picnic. Beau had found a secluded spot just off Beresford Creek overlooking the Wando River that meandered down to Charleston Bay and out to sea. The old oak trees protected a small grassy meadow where Beau had spread out two large blankets under the biggest oak they could find. Beau immediately flaked out putting his baseball cap over his face and ordering, "Don't call me, I'll call you."

No one in the group heard him because Casey, Josey and Sally were off to pick blackberries for the evening's dinner while Katie was running through the meadow chasing butterflies.

The women walked through the blackberry patch, carefully selecting only the ripest berries. Sally knew she loved Beau but she had to know how Josey felt about her relationship with her son. She also knew if anyone would know how Beau felt about a single woman, with a child, closing in on forty she would. "Josey?" Sally asked causing her to stop picking and look up. Josey smiled knowing that the berry picking was only an excuse for a one on one talk with Josey. "Yes dear," Josey responded resting on a stump of an old tree. Sally was hesitant trying to phrase her words carefully. "I guess I better come right out and say it. I love your son." Josey smiled putting her basket down holding her arms open to Sally motioning her to come and sit by her side. Josey put her arm around her and said, "You want to know how I feel about you and Beau?" Sally nodded.

"It's not important how I feel. What's important is how you both feel." Josey said giving Sally a motherly hug. Casey stepped out of the berry patch and sat next to Sally. "This was going to be a girl to girl talk". Josey announced. "What you want to know is how Beau feels, right?"

"Yes." Sally answered softly waiting for the truth.

"Did Beau tell you about Mark's death?"

"Yes," Sally answered sadly.

"Well here's something he hasn't told you. In the first few weeks after his death he was numb with grief. Unable to cry, to feel anything. After he got passed the initial shock he was on the verge of a nervous breakdown. He would get drunk, then he would cry. It was like he couldn't stop crying. He would stay away from work. He dreaded meeting anyone. Harry stood by him, covered for him. Beau didn't want pity and he didn't want his grief to make anyone uncomfortable so he stayed away. One night coming back from one of his drinking binges he remembered Mark's last words, 'Make peace with God'. He happened to be passing St. Michael's church. He went in and sat alone in an empty pew. No one was there, not a soul. It was late. He knelt and prayed. He knew that if his grief overwhelmed him he could always slip away and there would be no one there. As he prayed he thought of Mark, the loneliness, the void in his life and his grief was about to explode. Then quietly, almost unnoticed, a small girl entered the pew and sat next to him. He glanced at her through his tears. Her crystal blue eyes were framed by dark brown tresses of curly hair. She was dressed in a blue and white print dress with lace at her neck and on the sleeves. The little girl was looking up at him as though she knew him. Then she picked up a hymnal book and began to hum a soft lullaby. For some strange reason, the music began to calm him. A sense of well being came over him. The little girl nudged closer and closer to Beau until she took his hand in hers. At that very moment he felt like he knew everything was going to be all right. He felt his grief ebbing away. He never thought for a moment that this could ever happen again but he began to feel happy. Then the little girl kissed him on the cheek. Beau knew at that very moment that this was the end of his grief. He would be happy again. He looked down at the little girl and she smiled with all the sweetness and love God has ever given anyone. But who was the little girl? He smiled again at her. She looked at him with the most penetrating blue eyes as though she knew him. The little girl kissed his hand and walked away. Now this was one o'clock in the morning and he was concerned. What was a little girl, with no adult, doing in a church this late? He followed her to the door. When he opened it she was gone."

Casey and Sally sat quietly listening transfixed to her story. "I've heard of things like this from the old country," Casey commented.

"Did Beau ever find the little girl again?" Sally asked. Josey sat quietly for a moment as Sally and Casey waited for an answer. Looking directly at Sally she said, "Yes." Again Casey and Sally sat upright waiting for Josey to answer. "It's Katie."

"What?" Sally and Casey asked simultaneously.

"The little girl that comforted Beau that night in the church was Katie. So, if you're asking how I feel," Josey took a deep breath, "You and that little angel are a Godsend. You and Katie are what I've been praying for."

Sally began to cry as Josey held her tightly. From the berry patch deep in the woods near a quiet running stream you could hear three happy women crying tears of joy.

These tears quickly changed to laughter and small talk about wedding plans. They returned to the big oak tree to find Beau snoozing quietly with Katie nestled in his arms fast asleep. Studs with his eyes closed rested his chin on Beau's legs. The women stood over them smiling when Josey commented, "Now that's a site."

It had been another perfect dinner topped off with a deep dish blackberry cobbler and some homemade ice cream. Of course Katie and Beau bragged to everyone how dinner would not have been so good if it wasn't for their ice cream. The evening passed with small talk on the porch while Beau and Katie caught fire flies and put them in a bottle.

Casey and Josey had retired for the night and Katie had said her prayers, and with her bottle of fire flies sitting on the bedside table, was tucked in for the night. Beau was in his old room unable to sleep thinking about the past. The grandfather clock in the hall chimed eleven times. He thought to himself that he would never get to sleep. There would be some changes coming in his life and he hoped he would make the right decisions.

Slowly, his door opened and Sally, dressed in the sexiest piece of lingerie he'd ever seen, entered and silently stood in front of his bed.

"Are you awake?" She asked softly.

"Yes," he said resting both arms under his head. Inwardly, Beau was smiling. He knew where this was leading. He also knew that Sally would never do anything like this unless she was serious about him. There was a short embarrassing silence. Slowly and very seductively Sally slipped her shoulder straps off and let her nightgown drop to the floor. She was absolutely the most beautiful woman he'd ever seen. She had athletic shoulders, a thin waist, voluptuous hips with perfectly formed breasts that stood erect. Beau's eyes continued to feast themselves on the sensual sight standing before him. This wonderful woman was ready to give herself to him. Somehow, it seemed all right. It was a natural thing after what they'd been through. Sally waited before asking, "Well, this is what you wanted isn't it?"

He knew that this wasn't going to be a one night stand. This was the beginning of a commitment. He smiled and said, "Does this mean we're going steady?" The retort caused Sally to break out laughing as she answered jokingly, "You rat." Breaking the seductive mood she took one big dive and landed totally naked on top of him. They held each other, kissed passionately and talked about love, commitment and plans for the future. Then slowly, naturally, they made love until the wee hours of the morning.

Chapter Fourteen

Beyond The Looking Glass

Sally looked back pensively focusing on the beauty of Falconbriar as Beau maneuvered the car slowly down the country lane. She could see Katie, Casey, and Josey waving goodbye. She kept staring at them as if this would be the last time she'd ever see them. When they were out of sight she turned around and sat silently for a few moments then took Beau's hand and said, "Thank you for a wonderful weekend. I hated to see it all end."

"What do you mean end?" Beau retorted trying to cheer her up. "We'll be back Friday and no one is going anyplace." Sally smiled and looked straight ahead.

There was a question that had been sitting in the back of Beau's mind. He was looking for the right time to ask. He finally broke the silence. "Can I ask you a question?"

"Sure," she said resting her head on the headrest looking up at nothing. Beau went on, "I noticed your mom had been scarred in the past. You want to tell me about it?" Sally sat pensively for a few moments gathering her thoughts. "It's a long story do you want the short or long version?"

"Whatever turns you on," he answered, focusing on Sally, waiting for an answer to his question. Sally began to tell Casey's story. "Well, you know my step-father died about five years ago. He gave me a love of the law. However, my real father died when I was fifteen. I loved him deeply. He was a wonderful, kind man. He was a full professor at Georgetown University." Sally paused, thinking back to the stories her mother had told her when she was growing up. "I guess it all started in Ireland about four years before I was born. At that time in Northern Ireland there were more than twenty-four sectarian murders that year. Catholics killing Protestants, and Protestants killing Catholics. You know the story.

My father came from a good Protestant family, you know, the kind that goes to church twice on Sunday. My grandfather worked in the shipyards and my grandmother kept a tidy house, according to dad, and baked the best cakes in the neighborhood. She had a sharp tongue and an iron fist. You can see where my mom gets it. Her mother and dad were what you might say cut from the same Blarney stone." Beau smiled and nodded in agreement.

"Dad was an excellent scholar and made good money working at the publishing house. He liked to take long walks in the country side. He enjoyed the coming of the green. He liked to sit by the fireplace with a good book when the storms would come. Then on his twenty second birthday, when he was walking home, a terrorist threw a bomb at him from a passing car. It left him screaming with excruciating pain and totally blind. He was rushed to the hospital. They operated but he would never see again. The other wounds healed but the scars on his soul were heard in every word he spoke. He hardly ate or drank. He just simply laid in bed with depression eating away at his heart for almost four months. However, there was one nurse who could get a rise out of him. Guess who?"

"Your mom." Beau answered smiling.

Sally continued, "My mom. She came from a good Catholic family. Her dad was a merchant mariner and was away most of the time. Grandpa was a good man and loved his family. Now, as for Grandma she wasn't what you'd call a good house keeper but wow, could she put out an Irish stew.

My Mom was a staff nurse at Belfast's biggest hospital. She never had time for a lot of boyfriends but seeing dad, the lost little boy who was fighting darkness for the first time, brought tears to her eyes. She knew he couldn't see her tears but she was always afraid her voice would give away her emotions. Her warmth, the strength in her words, her jokes, prodding, and laughter brought him back from his deep depression. After four months dad was incurably blind but he had fallen in love, and that love would give him the courage to carry on.

Their families were appalled. The idea of getting married was out of the question. Even the priest was against it. All kinds of pressure, constant arguments, threats and even lies were thrown at them from both sides of the family. Eventually, they were driven apart. One night they quarreled and said harmful things that they didn't mean and mom just walked away. They both withdrew into their work. Months drifted into a year. One night there was a frantic knock on dad's door. My aunt, Hester, with tears choking her words said, A bombing… she's trapped, half dead. She's screaming for you, please, for God's sake help her'. Hester led dad to the scene. A bomb had blown apart a small cafe where mom and some other nurses were eating. The others got out but mom was trapped. Both her legs were pinned under some debris. There was a fire and it was spreading in her direction. They could hear her screaming but couldn't reach her. When dad arrived he moved into the carnage. The policeman controlling the crowd said, 'He couldn't see the hand in front of his face. You'll never find her.' Dad said, 'What the difference does it make. I'm blind anyway.' He moved toward her screams, using all the instincts of a blind man, and found her. He held her and told her that he'd always loved her. If God was going to take her he would be with her. She passed out just before the firemen got to them. She recovered, but her face would always be scarred. Mom always told me that the only man she loved would never see her so she didn't need fancy plastic surgery. Anyway, their families continued to fight their love every step of the way. Then one day when they'd had enough, Mom took dad's hand and they walked away from both their families, got married and came to America. A year later I was born."

Beau continued to drive quietly thinking about the story. "I can see why she was so concerned about your face."

Beau eased the car into a roadside rest area and parked. It was a picturesque little nook surrounded by a green forest of pine, walnut and acacia trees. A small wooden picnic table was nestled among flowering azaleas. They both sat quietly in the car taking in the beauty of the area. Sally knew something was on his mind and she was waiting for it to come out. Beau looked at her with a warmth she hadn't seen before. "The other day when we were down by the river do you know what I was thinking about?" He asked. Sally nodded and quietly said, "No".

"I was looking at every leaf, every blade of grass as though I was never going to see it again. I was looking at Katie, trying to put each little image in my mind. How she smiles, how her dimples deepen when she's happy, just like you. I tried to burn into my mind every bit of laughter, the way you look when the sun is hitting your hair just right. Watching you when you are asleep, sitting on the porch watching the sunset. The other night, when we made love, held each other, and talked about what we wanted to do with our lives, I was so afraid that I might never have a time like that again. I am not going to let that happen. I know we've got careers, and ambitions, but I don't think that will stop us. I love you so deeply that I ache every time I look at you. I want you to marry me." Beau looked at Sally searching for a reaction, praying it wouldn't be some last minute rejection. He could see tears welling up inside her. She burst out crying, weeping with joy, "Oh my God I love you, I want you so much." She hugged him and showered him with kisses and sobs. After a long tender embrace, Beau handed her a Kleenex from a box in the glove compartment then started the car and let it idle. Sally looked at him lovingly and sniffled again. Beau embraced her once again kissing her lovingly then passionately. Putting their foreheads together Beau said, "you know something else?" Sally nodded negatively and pulled another tissue from the box. "We could be a family again. I couldn't think of anything more wonderful than being Katie's dad". Another outburst of tears and sobs flowed from Sally as she held Beau again.

"Can I take that as a yes?" he said, smiling and clumsily putting the car in gear with Sally still clinging to him. Beau took control moving the car back onto the highway. Sally sat back, with tears replaced by a smile

"You're a rat but I still love you. You sure took your time," she said, taking another tissue from the box.

Sally looked up at the third floor of Annex C at Charleston Memorial Hospital as Beau pulled the car into the parking lot. A cold shiver went through her at the thought of seeing the psycho that tried so hard to kill her.

Beau took her hand, "Are you ready for this?" he asked. With a determined look on her face she responded, "Yes, it goes with the job."

"It's not going to get any easier. We'll have to testify at the insanity hearing, then arraignment and the trial. Your face is going to be on every TV channel for the next six months."

"Yeah, I know, so let's take care of business," she said stepping out of the car. Beau smiled at the Irish courage bred into her. She was going to be okay.

Beau and Sally stood in front of the elevator door that led to the third floor psychiatric ward of Charleston Memorial Hospital. Beau pressed a red button marked "Access". The TV camera above the door whined and adjusted itself to focus on them. A crackling voice on the intercom asked, "Yes?"

"Agent Thornton FBI and Lieutenant Gasteneau, Charleston Police", Beau advised. Both detectives held their IDs up to the camera. The light above the elevator door indicated up as the doors swung open. The elevator ascended as another TV camera monitored the passengers. Sitting in front of the barred hallway to the ward was another security guard. He re-examined their credentials then pressed a button and the glass lined iron gate rolled away.

Outside the holding cell stood another guard armed with a stun gun and pepper spray. His job was to monitor the activities in the padded cell through a peep hole in the door. He motioned the detectives to another door adjacent to the cell.

The observation room resembled a small theater with comfortable lounge seats lined up in theater rows. In the darkened room, seats faced a large two-way mirror that opened onto the holding cell. The room would comfortably seat ten people. A small coffee bar was conveniently positioned in one corner of the room. The unbreakable two-way mirror was made of glass two inches thick. It seemed to magnify objects on the other side of the mirror. A sound system and automated recorder took down every word. The cell was a well lit fifteen by fifteen foot padded room with a table and three chairs in the middle.

It came as no surprise to Beau that the observation room was filled with a retinue of concerned individuals. They had assembled to get a good look at the animal that almost brought the city to it's knees. The pathetic, sick, simple man had brutally murdered elderly women in three states, then had sex with the corpse. Through mistaken identity and media hype these twisted, perverted acts had fostered killings of both blacks and whites. Now, this simple man could only murmur and babble to himself as he paced around the room with his face only inches from the wall. At each corner of the room he would stand as though he had been a bad little boy then move on to the next corner and repeat the same exercise in a low continuous babble. This little man brought to the surface all the old hatreds and biases dating back to the Martin Luther King era. The terror was over, everyone was here to view this pathetic individual. Beau wondered to himself who was really pathetic. The man on the other side of the looking glass or the politicians who gathered like vultures to gawk. The politicians who would now make plans for the whole world to see a choreographed display of justice cleverly disguised as seeking the truth. Of course, it was all for political expediency and vote getting in the next election.

David Blackstone, Charleston's District Attorney, introduced the detectives. "This is Barbara Starky, she's the court appointed counsel for the defense. Homer Canfield, prosecuting attorney". The Mayor and Police Chief Wexford stood and shook Sally's hand. "You did a great job," Chief Wexford said approvingly.

"Thank God it's over," the Mayor commented. Blackstone continued, "And this is Dr. Thomas Crum. He is the court appointed forensic psychiatrist." Sally and Beau both shook his hand.

"Come, sit by me young lady. I understand you've had a close encounter of a third kind, so to speak". Dr. Crum pointed at an empty seat in the front row next to the mirror. He had a clipboard and was taking notes as he observed David Delongpre.

"There's coffee over there," Chief Wexford uttered, nodding at one corner of the darkened room. Beau poured two cups and returned to the seat directly behind Sally and Dr. Crum. "Here you go," he said, handing her a warm cup of coffee. The doctor turned to Beau and inquired," I understand that you've had a chance to observe several of these personalities under very trying circumstances".

"Yep, we had a few misunderstandings," Beau replied taking a gulp of coffee. The doctor looked at Beau quizzically and asked, "From the reports I've read you could have dropped him and saved the state a lot of money. Why didn't you?" Beau sat back and took another long swig of coffee before answering. "I've asked myself that same question."

"And your answer?" the doctor questioned in a low voice.

"Well, if I'd dropped him she'd been pissed at me and I'd never get to first base with her," he said looking at Sally who smiled nodding her head. The doctor smiled and looked at Sally. "Did it work?" Sally took a knowing look at Beau. "It worked."

"Good choice," the smiling doctor responded in a low voice.

The other observers were focused on the being pacing around the padded cell in a straight jacket, and totally oblivious to the doctor's discussion with Sally and Beau. The D.A. took a sip of his cold coffee and asked aloud, "What do you think? Is he nuttier than a fruitcake, or is this a big put on?" Everyone looked at Dr. Crum. "I have not finished my evaluation. However, as of now he is suffering from a multiple personality disorder. He has a personality trait disorder with sociopathic and passive aggressive features, emotional instability, and is unpredictable by acting out unconscious impulses."

"Sounds like a few politicians I know." Beau said sarcastically. Barbara Starky gave a small laugh and remarked, "The Lieutenant has enlightened us on the political situation, and you Doctor, you've just summarized my defense".

"Or, he could be faking it," Homer Canfield snapped.

"Gentlemen, ladies, that hasn't been determined yet," the D.A. interjected, then looking at his young associates, he continued, "This is all well and good but it's moot. What you're going to have to prove in court is at the time of the murder, did he, or didn't he know right from wrong."

"Well, I'll tell you what I want." The Mayor exclaimed taking a deep sigh, "I want a show trial. I want the citizens of this state to see that justice is being done. That we take care of our own, and we won't tolerate vigilantism from either side".

"I understand your problem, but what about a fair trial? Where in hell do you think we'll find a fair and impartial jury?" the D.A. interjected.

"Right off the bat I'll ask for a change of venue." Barbara stated harshly.

"Oh, that's great!" The Mayor scowled. Canfield held up his hands like a referee in a football game. "Hold it! Time out troops! I think this type of conversation should take place in the Judge's Chambers." Canfield announced trying to calm pre-trial nerves. "There's going to be a trial all right and it's going to be right here in Charleston even if I have to go to the Governor," the Mayor stated bluntly, tossing his paper coffee cup in the waste basket.

Dr. Crum looked at Sally, "I know you've had training in this area. Do you think he's faking it?" Sally's gaze was focused on the lunatic on the other side of the looking glass. Her eyes followed each movement. She listened closely to his mumbling over the intercom. The Gaylord Harcourt personality rounded the room stopping at each corner, mumbling some unintelligible incantation then stopped in front of the mirror facing Sally in the observation room. He stared face to face with her while admiring his own reflection. It was almost as if he could see through the looking glass into her very soul. Suddenly, Gaylord demanded, "What are you looking at?" Sally jumped back in her seat momentarily startled by the sudden outburst. Dr. Crum sat back and observed both Sally's reaction and the madman facing her.

In his reflection Gaylord could see Gordon who was forcing his way to the surface. "You dumb shit. I asked you what the fuck you're looking at," Gaylord again demanded from his reflection. In a totally new more aggressive voice Gordon replied, "You, you asshole, you're the dumb shit around here. You couldn't keep it in your pants could you. You have to fuck every thing in sight and now that you've got us all in deep shit you want me to get you out. Well, It ain't gonna happen". Gaylord answered his reflection, "I didn't do it, that God damn Beastie did it. You think I can control that fuckin' thing? That fuckin' piss-ant little brat, he's the one that screws it all up. A little fuck never hurt anyone. No, he just has to fuck up every God damn time Agnes and I get together.

"Liar, liar, pants on fire," The little David personality answered, The madman suddenly humped over and grunted like some man beast. His face contorted into a snarl. He showed his teeth and saliva dripped over his chin. The Beast had taken control over his physical actions. He resumed his pacing around the padded cell mimicking a caged animal.

Everyone sat absolutely spellbound by the antics they'd just witnessed. He's not only lost his marbles, he's never had any in the first place," Chief Wexford exclaimed.

"When will the judge set the competency hearing?" Canfield asked. "We have a hearing in Buckner's chambers tomorrow, nine o'clock", Blackstone announced.

"What's your opinion?", the Mayor asked thoughtfully, looking at Dr. Crum. "I don't know yet. We have some more tests and I want to do some more one on one interviews." The doctor replied.

"He's faking it!" Beau announced bluntly. Everyone turned their attention to Beau. The Chief started to admonish him for his premature statement but Dr. Crum raised his hand stopping the Chief before he could speak.

"Why do you say that?" Dr. Crum asked politely.

"Have any of you gentlemen heard of 'Travis Bickle'?" Beau questioned. Everyone looked around with no response. Dr. Crum was amused. He knew Beau was highly intelligent, and intuitive. That's what made him a good cop. He never made a statement without a good reason. "That's right out of the movie 'Taxi' and it was done for our benefit. Robert DeNiro did the same act in front of a mirror. However, in the movie he said, 'You talking to me? You talking to me?" He was playing a lonely, friendless, and girlfriendless man alone on the streets of New York. No gentlemen, that little charade was pure acting done for our benefit. In my opinion he is a manipulative, calculating, cold blooded killer. Beau looked at the stunned spectators. "He knows exactly what he is doing. Right now, he is looking for your sympathy."

"Remind me not to put you on the stand," Barbara said stifling a laugh.

"He has a point. That's why we need to gather more information on this subject," Dr. Crum said, crossing his legs and taking a few short notes on the pad.

Sally momentarily looked away from the Beast in the holding cell. "Have you had any luck getting through to the other entities?" Dr. Crum shook his head, "No. The controller as of now, is Gaylord. He is reluctant to let me talk to the others. I get a rise out of one or two of them then he cuts me off."

"What have you got in mind?' Beau asked, looking at Sally. He could see the wheels turning inside her mind. Her intuition and psychic capabilities were uncanny and often put her inside the mind of the killer. "Can we switch the intercom on and talk to him from here?" she asked, looking at the switch panel in front of her. "Yes," Crum replied, pointing to the a red switch on the panel then handing her a microphone. She held it close to her lips and slowly began to sing the lilting lullaby she heard him sing that night. "Where, oh where, has my little dog gone, oh where, oh where could he be? With his hair cut short, and his tail cut long, oh where, oh where, could he be?"

The Beast in the cell stopped abruptly. His shoulder slumped submissively. He returned to the chair in the center of the room and began to cry. The little David personality was now in control. He put his forehead on the table and continued to sob remorsefully, totally out of control. "Now would be a good time to interview him again", she announced. All eyes were now focused on Dr. Crum. He rose calmly and walked to the door.

"Doctor," Sally interrupted before he could leave. "I might suggest that you get yourself a wheelchair and have the guard wheel you in." Crum thought about her words then the meaning clicked into his sharp mind. "You think he'll open up if he thinks I'm Dr. Michaels?" Sally nodded affirmatively. "Good idea, thank you. Let's see what happens'. He left the room closing the door.

"Well, I've seen enough," the Mayor advised getting up and following Dr. Crum's exit. Chief Wexford was at his side. "Ladies and Gentlemen, I suggest you get your act together. It's going to be show time in a few weeks," the Chief announced just before stepping into the hall.

Barbara Starkey sat back in her seat and looked at Sally, then mocked, "Politicians are like Bike Helmets, handy in an emergency, but otherwise, they just look silly."

"Fowl!" Canfield grinned, commenting jokingly.

It took about ten minutes to locate a wheelchair. The guard wheeled Dr. Crum into the cell. The sobbing killer kept his forehead on the table mumbling at the floor. The guard then took up a position inside the cell near the door.

"David? David, do you want to talk?" Crum inquired gently. "No!" came a tearful response from the killer.

"Who am I talking to?" the doctor asked politely.

"Who in the fuck do you think, you stupid shithead," came a curt reply from Gaylord.

"Do you always talk like that? I mean, is it necessary for you to be so aggressive?" Crum questioned. The sobbing had ceased as Gaylord continued to hold his forehead on the table. "How do you expect me to feel when I'm wrapped up like a Christmas Turkey". He flailed his elbows in the straight jacket. "Do you actually think I'm gonna hurt some one?" He said contemptuously. "I've told them over and over again, It's that damned Beastie." With that statement the killer raised his head and saw Dr. Crum sitting in the wheelchair. The sight caught the madman off guard. He froze unable to finish his statement. Dr. Crum remained motionless as he observed the killer's personality reaction. A calmness was heard in his voice before he asked, "Dr. Michaels, is that you?" Dr. Crum nodded before he spoke, "We haven't talked in a long time." A relaxed easiness seem to control the killer's body. He was at ease with Dr. Michaels. Gaylord spoke leaning forward as if to preclude the guard from hearing their conversation. "Can you get me out of here? You can tell them I'm not crazy. You know my only crime is getting laid from time to time."

This was the biggest opening into the killer's mind the doctor's had since starting his investigation. "I know what you're going through and I'll try to help but I'm going to have to talk to all of you." Crum answered, leaning forward in the wheelchair playing the killer's game. The Gaylord personality sat back, disappointed, thinking about his alternatives. But he knew Dr. Michaels was his friend and understood his problem.

"Please Doc, not like this," he nodded at the straight jacket. Crum motioned the guard over to his side and whispered into his ear. The guard removed the jacket then put handcuffs on the killer.

"Comfortable?" Crum inquired.

"Oh yeah that's great," Gaylord said, stretching then turning his head back and forth getting the kinks out.

"Now, may I talk to David?" the doctor asked. The killer went dormant for a few moments searching inside himself, then the personality Gordon appeared. "He won't come out," Gordon advised. "Why?" was Crum's quick reply.

"You didn't bring it," Gordon answered.

"Bring what?" The doctor replied trying to find the key to the door that might lead him deeper into the killer's mind.

"Come on, Dr. Michaels, you know," Gordon said with a small chuckle. "Gordon, remind me, I've forgotten," Crum muttered with teasing smile.

"Remember, you use to give him a 'Baby Ruth' candy bar. Have you forgotten how he'll do anything for a 'Baby Ruth'?"

"Of course, how silly of me to forget." The doctor replied glancing up at the mirror.

Inside the dark room Sally turned quickly to Beau, "Check out the candy machine in the waiting room. See if you can find a Baby Ruth." She exclaimed. "You've got it," Beau said bounding quickly out of the room.

"Gordon?" Crum asked, trying to hold this personality in his active conscious.

"What?"

"Can you tell me anything about your father?"

"No!" came an immediate reply from Gordon.

"How come?"

"Because my mom screwed everything in sight. She's just like Gaylord. As far as I know I'm the result of a one night stand, a 'whim wham, thank you maam." Gordon paused, and stared at Dr. Crum before continuing. "That makes me a bastard. You know something else? None of this, I mean all the trouble we're in now would a' never happened if my mom had gotten an abortion. Gaylord wouldn't be here, David wouldn't be here, I wouldn't be here and the Beast would a' never been born." He sat quietly thinking about his fate.

A short rap at the door alerted the guard who gazed through the peephole in the door. A Baby Ruth candy bar was poked through. The guard took the candy and handed it to the doctor. The killer eyed the candy bar sitting in Crum's lap. He began to twitch nervously when Crum began to play with the bright colored wrapper. "What does David want now?" Crum asked knowingly. The killer's shoulders slumped slightly, and a childlike calmness came over him.

"David?" the doctor inquired. A shy timid voice answered, "Yes."

"Will you talk to me?" Crum questioned gently,

"Dr. Michaels I don't like talking to grown ups."

"Yeah, but we're friends. Didn't I get you a 'Baby Ruth'?" The little David personality nodded putting one of his fingers in his mouth shyly.

"Remember, we use to have long talks, didn't we." The little boy in a man's body nodded again. "Now, so I can remember, I want you to tell me all about your mother and when you were growing up." The little boy held out his hand for the candy. "If I give you the candy now you might not tell me everything I want to know". Crum said, pulling the candy bar few inches out of his reach.

"I promise and double cris-cross my heart," David assured making a crossing motion with his cuffed hands, then reaching again for the candy.

"I'll tell you what I'm gonna do. Here's half." Dr. Crum snapped the bar in two pieces giving the smaller piece to David. The little boy personality savored the candy bite by bite until it was gone. He licked each finger then sat back satisfied.

"Now, tell me about Gordon," Crum inquired.

"The killer's eyes close momentarily thinking back, turning to his thoughts locked deep inside his mind. He was reaching out to his other personalities. "He's nice."

"How come?" Crum questioned softly.

"Cause he takes care of me when I'm hurt. She hurt me."

"Who?"

"Agnes," David responded with tears beginning to well up inside.

"What did she do?"

"She tied me down." David's voice became labored and tense reliving his abuse as a child.

"Then what?" Crum asked taking furious notes as the little David personality related his story.

"She put her fingers inside me." A small tear dripped down his cheek. He trembled as he continued. "She made me kiss her down here," little David pointed at his crotch. "She put things inside me. It hurt," David whimpered.

"How did Gaylord feel about that?" Crum asked.

"Oh, he liked it. He would not let her stop. He'd do anything she asked. He would put my fist inside her until she screamed. She liked that."

"Then what?" The doctor inquired.

"Then there was the good time. After Agnes was satisfied, she would hold me and tell me how much she loved me. I would get ice cream and presents. Agnes loved me."

"What about your mother?" Crum asked puzzled.

"She would watch," David said, knowing sexual performance meant approval from both Agnes and his mother.

"What about Gaylord?" Crum inquired shaking his head in disgust.

"Gaylord would brag about being a sexual athlete, whatever that is," David stated shyly and went on. "Gaylord said, 'they should have an Olympic event for sex. Then he would laugh."

"What was Gordon doing all this time?" Crum inquired.

"Gordon didn't know what was going on. He was in the playroom." David said nonchalantly.

"What's the playroom?" Crum asked quickly taking more notes.

"It's safe. It has no windows so no one can see in. It has a secret entrance that no one knows about," David answered proudly.

"Anyone else in the playroom?" Crum waited for an answer. He had to see if he could identify all of the alter egos present in David's mind.

"Yes, that's the Beastie's playhouse." David said smartly.

"Do you talk to the Beastie?"

"Yes."

"What's his name?" David remained silent for a few moments. "We use to call him 'Snipper'".

"Who is Snipper?" The doctor asked watching the killer's body language and reactions to his questions.

"He's my puppy. He sleeps with me and he's my friend."

"Tell me about Snipper." Crum inquired with a new curiosity.

"She killed him."

"Who?" Crum asked.

"Agnes!" David began to sob out of control as he screamed, "And she just stood there and watched her do it. I hate her!"

"Who?"

"Mommy."

"Do you hate your mommy." Crum questioned again, quickly completing several pages of notes. David waited calming himself before he spoke, "No, Agnes made her do it. Just like me Agnes made her do it."

"What did Agness make your mommy do?" Crum asked sympathetically.

"She put Snipper in the 'fridge and closed the door. She said Snipper could come out after we've performed."

"You mean had sex." The doctor said filling in the blanks. "You said we've performed. Did all three of you have sex together?" Crum demanded tolerantly. David's sobbing welled up again as he stammered trying to get the words out. "Yes, I, I, I'm sorry, please, p, p, please don't hurt me any more." The doctor sat motionless watching the child personality weep shamefully. He felt a compassion that he rarely felt for a patient. He'd worked on incest cases, and seen the results of child abuse first hand, but never to the extent related by David. If what David said was true, this was the worst case he'd ever seen.

"So, what happened to Snipper?" Was Crum's next sympathetic question.

"We went to the 'fridge. We were too late. He was gone. I took him to bed with me. I prayed to God. Please bring Snipper back. Then, the next day I buried him in the garden. He's taking care of the forget-me-nots. I know God likes that." David sat back calmly. The crying had ceased and the frown was replaced by a sly smile, "then God answered my prayers," David announced, folding his hands as if to pray, then looking up. "When I went to sleep the next night Snipper came and got in bed with me. This time God made him stronger so no one could ever hurt him again. Snipper said, 'he'd always look after me and protect me'. Snipper had big teeth like a dinosaur. I didn't want Agnes to find him so I hid him in the playhouse and gave him a new name, 'Beastie.'"

"What do Gaylord and Gordon think about the Beastie?" Crum inquired, turning to a fresh note page.

"Gaylord hates him. Blames him for everything. Gordon? Yeah, he likes him. He understands. They get along.

"David, have you ever taken drugs?" Crum asked bluntly. The killer's body stiffened. He took up a more secure posture, then Gordon spoke, "No, David would never take drugs."

"Have you taken drugs?" the doctor questioned tonelessly." The Gordon personality thought quietly for a few moments before replying. "Well, I get this voice," he said continuing thoughtfully, "It's really me I know. It's coming from the inside my brain. He keeps telling me to do things. I mean angry, awful things. Things I would never do… but he won't stop. He won't let it go. I get so tired of listening. I try to ignore him, but most of the time I can't."

"When can't you?" Crum inquired gravely.

"Mostly at night. In my apartment when no one else is around. When there is nothing else to do but try to fall asleep."

"Is that why you take drugs?" the doctor questioned sadly.

"It's easier to ignore him when I'm high, but sometimes I give in. Like on Holloween night he laid out some angel dust on the table and told me to take a sniff."

"You mean cocaine," Crum responded.

"He kept telling me to take a sniff. I tried to resist. I didn't do it at first. He kept insisting, always insisting." Gordon paused and took a deep sigh. "I ended up doing what he told me. I was just too tired to resist anymore." Gordon sat quietly with his head down looking at his cuffed hands before continuing. "He gave me another hit, then another. I was so out of it I didn't even have sense to go to the bathroom. I peed in my pants." Dr. Crum looked up at the two-way mirror knowing that this session was going to be a successful one and everything would be on tape. "Gordon," Crum asked softly. "Who did this voice belong to?"

"Gaylord," Gordon said in a whisper eyeing the guard suspiciously. "Was that when Gaylord took control?" Crum asked.

"Yes and no," Gordon responded, then continued. "He told me to go to the balcony and jump." Gordon's jaws tightened and anger crept into his face. "The son of a bitch was trying to kill me."

"What did you do?" the doctor demanded eagerly.

"I almost did it. I stood out there for, I don't know how long. I could have ended it all. With one step I could have erased all those voices."

"Why didn't you?" Crum asked taking a deep breath.

"Because that's exactly what he wanted, and I wasn't going to let him get away with it."

"What did you do?"

"David told me about the playhouse. David said Gaylord couldn't get in, and the Beastie would protect me even if he did." The Gordon ego sat back in his chair satisfied that he had defeated Gaylord. Dr. Crum took furious notes almost filling up his note pad before looking up. "Can I talk to Gaylord?" Crum asked softly, turning to the last clean sheet of paper. The killer sat quietly, relaxed, at ease with himself for a few moments, then his body stiffened and assumed a swaggering posture.

"Gaylord, is that you?" Crum demanded gently.

"Oh, come on Michaels, who do you think I am, Mother Teresa?" He said angrily.

"Have you been listening?" the doctor inquired.

"No, those damn shitheads had me in the playroom."

"You mean you can't get out of the playroom when you want?"

"Hello! Where have you been? Of course I can't." The Gaylord ego replied contemptuously before continuing. "That damn Beastie thing won't let me near the door."

"So you didn't hear anything David or Gordon said."

"No!" Gaylord answered spitefully. The doctor noted that the killer has episodes of amnesia between alter personalities. "Did you get Gordon on drugs?" Crum asked directly.

"I was just trying to help that asshole," was Gaylord's snarling reply. He sat up smugly and announced, "A little head candy never hurt anyone. He was having these dreams and he needed an easy fix. So I gave it to him. Look, I'm not totally a bad guy. Why does everyone get on my shit?"

"What kind of dreams was he having?" Crum questioned not looking up from his writing.

"Shit, I don't know," Gaylord paused, then spoke, "I remember he said he had a dream about some one chocking. He said dead people talked to him."

"Who?"

"Some old ladies, They all wore scarf's, They yelled at him to stop."

"Did he stop?"

"Shit no. He wouldn't take a crap unless I told him to." Gaylord exclaimed smugly sitting back in his chair crossing his legs casually.

The observation room was quiet. Everyone was focused on the subject and the doctor's interview. Barbara Starkey had her laptop in front of her entering her observations as quickly as she could. Looking up at David Blackstone, she asked inquiringly, "I don't think this guy will get by a competency hearing. What do you think?" Blackstone answered bluntly, "Oh, he'll get through the hearing all right. And, if you want to keep your job you won't fight it too hard." Barbara leered at Blackstone. "shit, why don't we just go and lynch him. You know, string him up to the nearest tree. I believe that's been a common practice in this state for a long time." Canfield retorted angrily, "Do you realize how many people he's killed? Not to mention three police officers."

"Three?" Barbara asked confused. Blackstone interrupted, "the body they found in the Gladlow house was a private security officer. That makes three." Barbara sat quietly gazing at her laptop. She clicked off the computer and looked remorsefully at Sally and Beau. Blackstone interrupted the short silence, "and one of the officers killed was Beau's partner."

"I'm sorry Lieutenant," Barbara said compassionately

"To err is human, to forgive is against department policy," Beau answered, looking at Blackstone. The D.A. acknowledged Beau's comment with a small nod. Barbara threw up her hands and remarked, "Okay, so we go to trial. Lieutenant I am truly sorry about your partner. But I will put on the best defense I can. I truly believe that if the defendant didn't know right from wrong at the time of the criminal act he's not guilty by reason of insanity and deserves treatment not the hangman."

"We don't hang em' in this state," Canfield mocked.

"That was a figure of speech, you know what I mean," Barbara said glaringly.

"You know what I have a problem with?" Beau snapped, then taking a deep breath before continuing, "this guy killed, I don't know for sure how many people. We have positive forensic evidence that he's killed people in three states. Now, he'll be declared innocent by reason of insanity. The state will put him in an institution for a long time. During that time he'll have a roof over his head, a warm bed, three meals a day, all the TV he wants while some poor drunk who is just as mentally ill as this asshole will die of pneumonia in some cardboard box he calls home, in some back alley. The difference is that this poor drunk never killed anyone, obeyed the laws, and tried honestly to deal with his illness. He'll die before his time, and if he's lucky he gets a pauper's grave with a wooden stake driven in the ground in some forgotten weedy part of a two-bit cemetery. The wood will rot away and no one will ever know he existed. And that ladies and gentlemen sums up our justice system." Everyone remained silent knowing the hidden truth in Beau's words. They knew he'd seen the alley people of Charleston. The people who go unnoticed by the community. The people who rummage through garbage cans to feed themselves, or search the trash for some small trinket that they can sell for another bottle of wine or shot of straight bourbon."

Barbara Starkey listlessly closed her laptop. Put it in her carrying case, then walked to the door. She turned and frowned, "I didn't make the rules," then calmly stepped into the hallway. The door had no sooner closed when Doctor Crum entered. "What's the prognosis?" Blackstone asked. The doctor sat down and fingered his notes. "Well, the verdict is still out. We have to do more tests, and there are ways to verify if he's lying. I'll need to interview Agnes's sister. What's her name?" "Norma Pierce," Sally advised. Dr. Crum put his notes aside. "For now, he has all the characteristics of a multiple with extreme schizophrenic tendencies. Let me explain what I mean. There are several types of schizophrenia. Catatonic schizophrenia, paranoid schizophrenia, disorganized schizophrenia, and something I call undifferentiated schizophrenia. I would have to say that our subject has undifferentiated schizophrenia. This type of illness is manifested by delusions, hallucinations, incoherent speech, disorganized behavior. It's sort of the hodge podge of several types of schizophrenia." Blackstone interrupted, "Is he capable of understanding the seriousness of his crime? Can he stand trial? Is he competent? Dr. Crum looked up from his notes, "Oh yeah, he knows."

Chapter Fifteen
The Ground Rules

The Charleston courthouse was another classic monument to Southern architecture. The four story edifice with massive Corinthian columns at the front, supported a gray slate roof. The courthouse faced one of Charleston's many picturesque parks. The well groomed grass and gardens surrounded a small pond that harbored a family of city ducks and pigeons that turned most of the statues white. The city maintained the park in pristine condition. It was the gathering place for the elders of Charleston. The good old boys could be seen playing checkers under the shade of a spreading oak, while white clad seniors citizens lawn bowled on manicured greens. Behind the courthouse was a modern three story parking garage. This structure was totally out of step with the dated architecture of the courthouse. The broad front entrance of the courthouse led to a marbled foyer. The traditional newspaper stand was located next to the elevator doors. Adjacent to the elevator was a large winding marble stair case leading to the mezzanine. The mezzanine walls hosted a gallery of paintings of past governors and court notables. To the rear of the foyer was an information desk. The information secretary busily directed people to their desired locations while handing out forms and registration permits. The busiest office was usually that of Social Services who processed marriage licenses. However, today the whole courthouse was buzzing with activity. The biggest trial in South Carolina's history was about to take place. The world's media giants would be surrounding this building to cover the "Gray Lady Killer" trial. Directors, producers and news media personnel were already surveying the building to determine where cameras and media crews would be located to give the world total coverage of the trial.

Judge Horace Buckner had been chosen the presiding judge. He was a feisty fire breathing legal icon in South Carolina. He had taken time to teach at the prestigious Harvard Law School for two years before returning to the bench. Since then he had become a prominent lecturer at legal seminars throughout the South. He had a tendency to lecture council, or anyone who'd listen on the finer points of the law. Everyone had a pretty good idea as to what areas the prosecution and the defense council would pursue in court. They also knew that this meeting with Buckner would indicate which of these areas would be favorably received by the bench.

The community also knew that with Buckner presiding it would be a fair trial with no frills, and no nonsense allowed.

The judge's chambers consisted of a small outer office housing a legal secretary and a young law school intern. This was his small, but motivated staff. Buckner's office was a larger oak paneled office lined with legal books and reference material that reflected a long and distinguished career. The west wall was decorated with photos of family, U.S. presidents, and several Supreme Court Justices, many of whom often called him seeking advise and opinion. There had been several occasions when Judge Buckner had been assigned "Amicus Curiae" (appointed by the court) to research and present legal opinion. He was a living encyclopedia of the law.

District Attorney Blackstone, accompanied by Canfield, counsel for the prosecution, and Starkey, counsel for the defense, entered Buckner's outer office. Blackstone jokingly stood at attention and quipped, "We are hear for Buckner's sermon on the insanity plea." Before he could speak the secretary frowned, then giving him a snide look replied, "Maybe you'll learn something remotely connected to your job." Using her pencil she pointed at the conference room door adjacent to the judges chambers. Blackstone gave a jovial salute and marched through the door.

The conference room was well appointed. A large oak conference table, that seated fifteen people comfortably, was centered in the room. As usual Buckner was getting his ducks in order before the highly publicized show trial began. Sitting at the head of the table Buckner was listening to the arguments from the media representatives. Sitting to his right was Les Averson, the ABC network news media executive for the southeast area. Next to him, was Ron Thompson, representing CBS, followed by Avery Compton of CNN, who was also an entertainment media lawyer. On Buckner's left was Dick Dickerson, from the Charleston Ledger and Stan Rush WXFC's anchorman. The judge motioned Blackstone and his associates to take a seat. They quickly located themselves at the other end of the table. It seemed like an unconscious symbolic gesture to distance themselves from the media.

Buckner spent a few more minutes in silence studying the petition from the media lawyer to have live TV coverage in the courtroom. Buckner looked up from the paper and took off his glasses. "Okay Gentlemen, let's hear your arguments, why I should even consider having TV coverage of this trial after the Simpson circus."

Avery Compton of CNN glanced at his media colleagues before speaking, "Your Honor, with all due respect, we do have first amendment rights to free speech and freedom of the press on our side, and we all know it's not without precedent." Buckner gave Avery a cold stare, "Son, are you trying to lecture me on constitutional law?" Avery backed off from his original statement, "No sir, I'm well aware of your qualifications."

"Good!" Buckner exclaimed, "Now that you've brought the subject up of constitutional rights, what about the sixth amendment that allows the defendant to a fair trial by an impartial jury of his peers?" Thompson of CBS interjected before Avery could answer, "I think the sixth amendment reads, 'a public trial'. Sir, this trial has peaked national public interest. The only access the public will have is through the media." Buckner smiled anticipating his statement. In fact that was the very statement he needed to unload his philosophy on the media. "You know Gentlemen, in politics, no matter how bad the polls, you never tell the candidate that the public doesn't like him. You tell him the public doesn't understand him. It's a public relations problem. Now, those of us in the business of law have a public relations problem. The attorneys that are promoted in the media, the ones that get spots on talk shows are not the best at what they do. Quite possibly, they are the worst. He is the lawyer who would say and do the most outrageous things to let his client get away with murder. It is this type of counsel we do not wish to parade in front of the camera. We in the legal profession do not celebrate our own heroes. The ones dedicated to seeking the truth and justice, hell, we don't even allow them to appear on television. How many of you remember Sheppard versus Maxwell 1966?" Les Averson of ABC was the only man to raise his hand. Buckner smiled and continued, "Sheppard was accused of murdering his wife. The media was allowed full access to the courtroom and turned it into a circus." Buckner's piercing eyes focused on each executive as he went on emphasizing each word with inflection. "They weren't interested in truth, or rule of law, they were only interested in ratings. They tainted their presentation with their own biases and bombarded the public mind with analysis and speculations which had little or no concrete basis, and disrupted the trial proceedings. My God Gentlemen, There were cameras scattered across the courtroom. Witnesses were harassed by reporters while testifying. You know what really gets to me? I look at TV news today and I do not see factual reporting. I do not see both sides of an issue. What I do see, is convenient editing and editorializing, not news. Now, in this case we have another important issue to consider," Buckner paused and looked at the counsel for the defense. Barbara Starkey felt his penetrating stare and it made her feel uncomfortable.

"We have to consider the pretrial publicity that this case has already received. When the media has saturated the public with innuendo, and describes evidence and facts not admissible at trial it makes it almost impossible to find jurors who have not formed biases, or who have not been exposed to inadmissible evidence. Hell, half the stuff I've seen or read about this case is inadmissible" Buckner shuffled through some papers on the table looking for a Xerox copy of legal text. Positioning the text in front of him he began to read aloud, "For your edification and mine let me read to you what Chief Justice Holmes had to say about this issue. 'Any Judge who has sat with juries knows that, in spite of efforts taken to establish an unbiased panel, they are extremely likely to be impregnated by the environing atmosphere.' Gentlemen, we all know that this environing atmosphere that Holmes refers to is created by the mass media. It is especially prejudicial to the defendant if the media has published information that may not be legal evidence at the trial, such as the existence of a confession which I may later rule inadmissible. I know before we open trial there'll be a change of venue petition. The other side of the coin is how do we allow defense counsel to challenge potential jurors for cause when they admit that their minds are already made up on the basis of what they've read in the newspapers, or heard on the radio or television? Can any of you tell me where we are going to find an unbiased juror? And you, the media have provoked a situation in this city without regard for the truth. You have brought this city to a racial crisis that rivaled Los Angeles. Unfortunately, the law states that prospective jurors who indicate they have some prior knowledge of the case or may even have formed an opinion on the ultimate issue of guilt, does not necessarily suffice to require the Judge to accept the challenge for cause. So, where in hell do you think we're going to find one man or woman in this state who doesn't fit that definition? Therefore, Gentlemen you have just screwed yourself out of first amendment rights."

Everyone at the table sat in silence waiting for Buckner's ax to fall. Buckner rubbed his eyes, thinking, reaching for a fair course of action. One that would give the defendant a fair trial and placate the media. He cradled his chin in his hand and surveyed at the expecting faces at the table. "Gentlemen, and Ladies," Buckner said, giving a quick smile to Barbara, "Since the Simpson circus a lot of my colleagues say that I'd be stupid if I allowed TV coverage at all. That's unfortunate. In most courtrooms, cameras may well improve the way the criminal justice system works. The media could, if it wanted, promote the rule of law," Buckner gave a stifled laugh, "Of course authoritarian judges like myself tend to behave better when they are being watched, and defense lawyers at least get to make their arguments. Who knows, the public might even learn something." The judge folded his hands and gave a stern look at the media representatives. "But the power to decide which cases can benefit from television coverage resides in the hands of the man responsible for running the courtroom, me! It doesn't rest with the cable or TV executive. I'm not going to make the same mistakes Ito made. Ito is a fine lawyer. He has an outstanding reputation on the bench. I think he was a little out of his league when it came to the media. Now, understand this, the primary function of a trial is not to educate the public, or entertain them, but to assign responsibility. Doing it fairly and honestly, according to the law is more important than doing it on television. It is precisely in these high profile cases with headlines, instant celebrity status, that the dangers of lawyers, and even jurors, playing to the TV camera is the greatest. In my courtroom, I will not tolerate it." Buckner paused again, giving a cold stare down the table. He put on his glasses, took a piece of paper from his folder and began to read aloud. "This is my decision. I will allow only one camera in the courtroom. The signal will be pooled by all media and they may direct that signal any way they wish. The courtroom camera will have a cameraman appointed by the court. At no time will the camera expose any of the selected jurors. It may cover the bench, counsel, audience, and the witness stand, nothing else. If any of the media attempts to contact any of the selected jurors I will slap a contempt of court on you so fast you won't know what hit you. And, if you really piss me off, it'll be an obstruction of justice charge. Do I make myself clear?" The media representatives nodded and began to collect their paperwork. "One other thing Gentlemen, you will not take photos, interview or harass any member involved in these proceedings in the confines of this building. When they're outside, what can I say, it's a free country." Buckner closed his folder and looked at the disappointed media executives. "Any questions?" The response was a cold blank stare. "Gentlemen, that concludes this meeting." The men quietly collected their papers and filed out of the conference room. Buckner sat back and stared at Blackstone and the young lawyers.

Buckner rocked in his comfortable chair tapping his pencil lightly on the table thinking. He glared at the waiting lawyers and said, "Barbara, Homer nice to see you again." He smiled knowing the antagonistic firebrand type of courtroom drama of which these two young lawyers were capable. He remembered the legal debates these two had in his class and seminars. "Homer, you're going for the throat right off the bat aren't you." Homer smiled knowing that was exactly what he was going to do. "And you young Lady you're going to embarrass this court by quoting some precedent originating from Caesar, or the Rosetta Stone aren't you." Everyone at the table smiled. Buckner knew his students too well. Regardless of their antics, they always fought for the truth using their wit and the courtroom to find it. The Judge reached into his briefcase and laid two legal books on the table. Then looked at the two young lawyers. "Have any of you ever been involved with an insanity plea? I assume Barbara, that is the way you're going to pursue your defense." Barbara nodded. Buckner's eyes searched the other counselors and found blank looks. He still had their undivided attention. "Do any of you remember examples from law school? How about case studies?", Buckner mocked. He shook his head and opened one of the books to a pre-marked page. Let me give you some background he said, taking a deep breath then looking up, he continued. "I would say since the 19th century the insanity defense has come and gone like the plague. It comes, then disappears until a case like John Hinckley's. Probably, the most famous case occurred in England in 1843. A man named Daniel M'Naghten was a Scottish woodcutter who suffered from the delusion that he was being persecuted by the Pope, the Jesuits and Prime Minister Robert Peel. He set out to shoot Sir Robert, but by mistake shot Peel's secretary instead. Nine medical experts testified for the defense, and the prosecution offered none in rebuttal. M'Naghten was found not guilty by reason of insanity. This caused a public outrage. Queen Victoria, addressed Parliament disapproving with the verdict. She feared that the acquittal would bring all the radicals out of the woodwork gunning for the first official in sight. As a result of all this, fifteen ranking Common Law judges were asked by the House of Lords to answer the basic question about the insanity defense." Buckner lowered his glasses and looked at the young firebrand lawyers. It was like talking to his kids. His storylike rhetoric held their undivided attention. Buckner continued. "With one dissenting vote, they stated the law passed down from the 12th century Canon Law, which was practiced by Henry III, who, had pardoned murders of unsound mind. So, we can say from the King's acts of grace, the first recorded insanity verdict occurred in 1505. The answers of the judges three centuries later to the Lord Chief Justice became known as the M'Naghten Rule. This rule states that a man is not responsible for his criminal acts when, because of a disease of the mind, he does not know they are wrong." Buckner lifted two more dusty books on the table. The book on the top was the Bible. He put his hand on the Bible before speaking, "We can trace this concept to biblical law, Genesis 2, Verse 9, about good and evil. We can see it in Talmudic records of the Jewish faith. Their law about special treatment for deaf-mutes, idiots, and minors who injure someone without intent. We can go even further back to Greek philosophy and Roman law which stated that a society should not hold a man criminally responsible or morally blameworthy for unlawful acts he commits because he lacks the capacity to tell right from wrong." Buckner pushed the books aside and took a long stretch. "So much for ancient history. See Barbara, I've already researched ancient law so please don't be bringing it up in court." He quipped, stifling a laugh. "Now, lets take this idea of insanity a little closer to home. Later in the 19th century we had the Durham case. He had been convicted of housebreaking and other offenses. He had a long history of mental illness and on his 3rd appeal the court ruled not guilty by reason of insanity. The new ruling stated that the accused was not responsible because his unlawful act was the product of a mental disease or mental defect. So at that time what the court was saying, that a man could know right from wrong, and either lacked the emotional appreciation that

what he did was wrong or lacked control because of his derangement."
Buckner put both elbows on the table in a childlike fashion and continued,
"So, we have a puzzlement," he announced mimicking the character from
the King and I. "Under the M'Naghten right and wrong standard he could be
convicted. Under the Durham rule he could be acquitted." Buckner reached
into his briefcase and retrieved a pack of gum then offered it to his
captivated listeners. He savored his gum casually before returning to his
story. "Now, with the Durham rule I have a problem. We've had other cases
where defendants hid under this rule by citing irresistible impulse, a
volitional test or a cognitive standard. The bottom line is that under the
Durham rule a man could be acquitted if his acts resulted from brooding,
reflection, and not from a momentary seizure. Hell, he could be an
alcoholic, compulsive gambler, drug addict and qualify under the Durham
rule. That idea cast too broad a net. Counselor," he said, focusing on
Barbara, "I suggest you stay away from this approach. I won't buy it and the
jury won't. The other problem I have, is this rule allowed psychiatrists to
testify about all evidence on a defendant's mental condition, not just about
his ability to tell right from wrong. Counselors I don't want you to waste the
court's time. I want you to get to the issue of did he, or didn't he, know right
from wrong when he committed the crime. I will give you all the latitude I
can but do not stray from your objective. Now, there are some subtle
differences between the M'Naghten rule and the Durham decision. Under
M'Naghten the defendant has to raise the insanity issue, and prove his
insanity. Under the Durham test, the defendant still raises the insanity issue,
but once raised, Homer, it's up to you to prove him sane beyond a
reasonable doubt." Buckner saw the concerned look on Homer's face. Then
chuckled and said, Had you going for a minute didn't I. Fortunately Homer,
you're off the hook. The Durham rule has been rejected by most of the
federal courts and it doesn't work in this state either. Barbara, I know
you've researched this but once you bring up the insanity plea, you better
have your facts in order, you're going to have to prove insanity beyond a
reasonable doubt."

Buckner continued to chew his gum as he sat upright in his chair
stretching his shoulders. "All of this history still fails to solve an age old
question. What is a mental disease and what is it's connection to a crime.
Frankly, I don't know. It's up to you to convince me and the jury." Buckner
stood up chewing his gum faster. He put his hands in his pockets and paced
slowly in front of the table looking at the floor in deep thought. "The
problem with the Durham decision is that it gave no rule in addressing the
scope of expert testimony. I don't like the psychiatrists talking about the law
and reasonable guilt, that's for the jury to decide. Unfortunately, the
definition of mental disease or defect is at the heart of the law's test of

insanity. The American Law Institute addressed this problem and adopted the approach of a British Royal Commission on Capital Punishment published in 1953. You might review that before your day in court." Buckner still paced back and forth looking at the floor as he reached into the back of his mind searching for all the facts he could find. He stopped and looked again at the young attorneys, "Have any of you heard of the Brawner Rule?" He still saw blank faces. He resumed his pacing, staring at the floor as he continued. "As I remember, Archie Brawner killed a man, firing a gun through a door. As the story goes, he had been drinking all day then went to a party. He was pretty well shit faced when he got into a fist fight. He came out on the short end with a broken jaw. Being totally pissed off he went home, got a gun and returned to get even. Witnesses said he looked out of his mind. Experts testified that he had psychiatric and neurological problems. He was acquitted on that basis. The court held that a man is not responsible if, as a result of mental disease or defect, he lacks substantial capacity to appreciate the wrongfulness of his conduct, or to conform his conduct to the requirements of the law. What I have a problem with, under this test, knowledge of his act has been replaced with 'appreciation.'

Buckner stopped, put both hands on the table and looked directly at the counselors, "What that means is the defendant could be acquitted if he knew right from wrong but his thinking was severely disordered and he lacked emotional appreciation of the difference. So what we have here is the idea of irresistible impulse, the inability to conform, the lack of self control. This approach has been successful in some courts, and it doesn't apply to sociopaths and it probably won't be successful in mine. I suggest this approach would not influence the jury in the slightest. You would be beating a dead horse. Okay, lets get down to the nitty gritty, under the 1984 Insanity Defense Reform Act, the Federal Statutes for the insanity defense requires the defendant to prove by clear and convincing evidence, that at the time of the commission of the acts constituting the offense, the defendant, as a result of a severe mental disease or defect was unable to appreciate the nature and quality of the wrongfulness of his acts. So, here we are, we've come full circle, we're back to knowing the right from wrong standard."

Blackstone interjected, "Your honor, with all due respect, I believe counsel has already done a lot of research on this subject. "Buckner stood erect, pacing with his hands still in his pockets and smiled. "There's an old lawyer joke that goes, ninety percent of the lawyers make the rest of us look bad. Don't make us look bad." The young lawyers looked at each other and grinned.

Buckner stopped his pacing and leaned against the back of his chair. "Our first step after indictment and of course your plea young lady will be a competency hearing. Now, we have Dr. Thomas Crum appointed by the court. Barbara do you have anyone in mind?" She opened her small notepad and read, "Dr. John Hopper. I believe both men have excellent credentials." Buckner nodded, "Good, how much time will you need to complete your examination on the defendant as to competency?" The counselors looked at each other then whispered among themselves. Blackstone looked up and announced, "Three weeks."

Buckner made a notation in his book, "Okay I'll schedule the hearing three weeks from next Monday." The lawyers quickly flipped through their day planner and entered the date. Buckner looked up from his planner and added, "I'll hear your arguments for competency. Counselors, I'll also review your petitions on competency. Barbara, I know you'll petition for a change of venue. I'll hear both arguments. If I disallow your petition I'll be as fair as the law allows. What I will do is bus in all potential jurors from the outlying counties. They will be sequestered at a secure location, no press, no TV. I will give each of you the greatest latitude I can for challenge, but please, lets not drag this out. The press will not have access to any juror for the duration of the trial."

Buckner closed the folder on the table, collected his notes, looked at Barbara and Homer, then announced contentedly, "Okay everyone, this spectacle will begin in three weeks. Look forward to seeing you two in court, and please remember," He paused, then taking a deep breath said, "I'm an old man, and you're not going to get an Academy Award even if you are on TV."

Chapter Sixteen
Meeting of the Minds

It had been two weeks since the meeting in Buckner's office. Barbara Starkey had contacted Dr. John Hopper, another well known forensic psychiatrist, three days before the meeting with Judge Buckner. Dr. Hopper and Crum had been jointly testing, interviewing and reviewing data on the killer for the past week and a half. She knew Buckner would follow the letter of the law. He would demand an opinion from the psychiatrist for the defense. She also knew he couldn't trust these doctors when it came to the letter of the law. But with two doctors both testing, and interviewing the defendant we might find a middle ground closer to the truth and not clinical speculation.

Barbara had asked for a meeting with Sally, Beau, Canfield, and Dr. Crum at Charleston Memorial. She wanted to confirm findings and establish an opinion from both sides of the issue. She also wanted Hopper to talk to the only two people who had close contact with the killer and lived to tell about it. Dr. Hopper had also been briefed about Sally's intuitive instincts and her ability to get inside the killer's mind. It was that ability, and calm resolve that saved her life that fateful night.

Sally and Beau had been through the same routine, as they did on their last visit, showing IDs and watching doors slide open and close. When they entered the hospital observation room the light from the hall beamed into the darkened room highlighting Barbara Starkey. She introduced them to Dr. John Hopper. Canfield waved his acknowledgment then returned his attention to observing the killer through the looking glass. The padded holding cell had the same table and chairs. However, a comfortable bed had been added to the room giving it a more homelike atmosphere. The straight jacket had been removed from the killer and replaced with handcuffs.

Dr. Crum, who was always neatly dressed, and the epitome of politeness, shook hands then gestured for Sally to have a seat between the two psychiatrists. Beau retrieved two hot cups of coffee. Giving one to Sally he sat directly behind the trio. Barbara leaned against the looking glass and folded her arms before speaking, "First question, is he capable of standing trial?"

"You mean is he competent?" Hopper answered. Barbara nodded. The two doctors glanced at each other, then Hopper answered, "Yes." Dr. Crum nodded in agreement. Hopper continued, "You know I've seen him and it's obvious that your next question is, 'Is he faking it?'" Canfield and Barbara both nodded again.

"First, we need to discuss the multiple personality disorder. M.P.D., we call it. I want you both to understand where we're coming from." Dr. Hopper looked at Dr. Crum who motioned him to continue, "It is a disassociative disorder in which two or more personalities or personality states exist within a person. Now what happens is at least two alter egos recurrently take full control of the patients behavior." Dr. Crum added to Dr. Hopper's statement, "I'd say in the last twenty years there has been new studies, focusing on the diagnosis, and treatment of this disorder. We have some very professional in-depth studies that we can refer to on the psychological, and physiological differences among these alter egos." Dr. Hopper waited for Crum to finish before he began. "We know that the MPD demonstrates a consistent symptom pattern and reveal traits that are not replicable by fakers." Homer Canfield interrupted, and stated with a hint of contempt in his voice, "Gentlemen, so there is no misunderstanding, let me tell you where I am coming from. I can show you literature by your own respected colleagues that states a very good case that the disorder doesn't really exist. That it's really a sham to keep one out of the death penalty." Barbara quickly answered Canfield's argument, "Yeah, but the law nevertheless agrees that this disorder exists and recognizes that it is a treatable disease. Do you want me to quote you chapter and verse?"

Beau and Sally had remained silent listening to the debate about MPD. But it was time to get to the bottom line. Beau questioned, "In how many of these cases have you presented expert testimony?" Dr. Hopper thought for a moment. "In the past ten years, three." Hopper closed his eyes thinking back to past experiences, "MPD disorders are, for the most part rare. The insanity defense I would say based on MPD is even rarer. Having said that, I must admit I know of about twenty times that this MPD issue has been used as a defense."

Canfield asked smugly, "How many got away with it?" Dr. Crum interrupted before Hopper could answer. "Four."

"Yes, four acquittals," Hopper added. Dr. Hopper opened his briefcase and retrieved some notes before continuing, "From what I've heard I can see Judge Buckner's concern. The courts today are not sure how to handle the MPD defense."

"How do you mean?" Sally asked. Hopper began referring to his notes. "From my experience the courts can address only three positions. One, is that the multiple is not guilty by reason of insanity, only if the alter ego committing the crime was itself insane. What I mean is that it met the legal insanity test of the particular jurisdiction. In our case that would be South Carolina. Another view is the sanity of each of the individuals personalities when one of them commits a crime. Do they all have to be insane? Another issue is, do the alters communicate with each other and are they cognizant of each others actions." Dr. Crum added to Hopper's observations, "The courts are really confused on this issue. They are trying to fit MPD into the traditional categories of the insanity defense. That's a mistake. The law written back when, who knows when, was not formulated with the MPD in mind." Hopper picked up on Crum's idea, "How are you going to present your case? Do you see him as different people, as different personalities? Or, parts of one deeply divided personality? The analysis will differ based on what theory you adopt."

"Good luck," Canfield quipped smugly, "If you're going to approach the jury with this kind of bullshit you're out of luck." Barbara unfolded her arms and put her hands on her hips defiantly, "Sit on it Canfield." Everyone chuckled at the rivalry between the two lawyers.

Hopper motioned with his hands, "Wait a minute, let me explain what I'm talking about. Let's say we have a multiple with two alter egos. Jim is the good guy and Jack is the bad guy. Jack is aware of Jim. Jim, on the other hand, is not the least bit aware of Jack. He does know that he loses time now and then. One day Jack, acting consistently with his personality, kills a man. The police quickly arrest him for the crime. The problem is that Jack has fled the scene psychologically and it's Jim who is charged with murder. He swears on a stack of bibles that he hasn't killed anyone. Let's say now we put him under hypnosis and are able to talk to Jack. He proudly confesses to the crime. Now, can Jim argue that he is not guilty, because it was not he who committed the crime, but Jack? Is there a legal basis for a multiple exoneration?"

Barbara Starkey pondered the hypothetical analogy. "So, you're saying, that if I can convince the court that these personalities are in fact different people, we cannot hold Jim liable for Jack's actions?"

"Fat chance in that arena. You're reaching," Canfield advised contemptuously, "Do you really think the jurors will buy that? There is only one body sitting in the courtroom and one person committed the crime." Barbara replied to Canfield stubbornly, "Okay smart ass, Beau, did you read him his rights?" Beau smiled, "Sure did, counselor." Barbara quickly retorted smugly looking at Canfield, "Who did you read the Miranda rights to? Gaylord, David, maybe Gordon? You sure as hell didn't read them to the Beastie. I have grounds right there to push a hell of a lot of crap on the court. And one other thing, any confession obtained while the defendant is hypnotized is inadmissible."

"You're so full of crap I can't believe it. Buckner will crawl all over you with that approach." Canfield answered raising his voice.

Dr. Crum motioned the two young lawyers to cease, then crossed his legs and thoughtfully continued along the same theory reinforcing Hopper's logic. "You both have a point, if you subscribe to a bodily criteria of personal identification. If the Jim I met today is the same Jim I knew ten years ago, that's fine. Now, if we use the psychological criteria it becomes less clear. The Jim I met today is the same Jim I met ten years ago only if he remembers most of the past of Jim's experiences, and for the most part, has the same psychological characteristics."

Dr. Hopper picked up on Crum's assessment and carried the idea of MPD culpability to a philosophical level. He smiled then continued to philosophize, "All of us, and that includes the Judicial System in our ordinary day to day living do not require us to decide between these two concepts because bodily and psychological continuity go together in ordinary life." He took his pencil and pointed at the two young lawyers, "For example, our criminal justice system is based on the idea we are autonomous beings who can justly be punished for criminal behavior. However, modern science suggest that some, if not all behavior, is determined by biological or environmental forces, which can render us non-responsible under the law. Why? Because the law assumes we have free will. The other fallacy is that, for the purpose of punishment, the law assumes that this will is not manifested until the person acts. So, what if the defendant had no free will? Do we try him based on physical identification or psychological identification? Who actually did the killings?" The lawyers remained silent. Sally and Beau were amused at the philosophical debate that was beginning to take shape. They knew that the psychiatrists were leading them on, getting deeper and deeper into legal arguments versus philosophical arguments.

Canfield threw up his hands and broke the momentary silence. "The law couldn't possibly work on the idea of psychological culpability. Can you imagine stopping Henry Smuck for drunk driving, 'Oh, officer, that wasn't me driving that was the other me, Henry Ellen Lewellen, the bad me'. Come on guys lets get a grip on things." Barbara Starkey poured herself a cup of coffee, returned to the looking glass and observed the killer for a few seconds then turned to the doctors, "Let's look at this situation again, If a multiple is one person who now acts like Jim, then all of a sudden acts like Jack, the question to put before the court, is the person currently acting as Jim, the good guy or guilty for the actions of Jack, the bad guy."

"Now I am beginning to lose you guys," Beau interjected. Both doctors smiled and nodded at Barbara's assessment. Dr. Crum picked up the conversation again, "There are two arguments to put before the court that say no. Remember, Jack's acts do not reflect Jim's character and Jim does not know the nature of Jack's act, or he knows and cannot control it. This is one area you should pursue, at least based on what we know about the defendant so far." Dr. Hopper held up his pencil like a student in a classroom. "Now, we do know that the defendant had a long history of using drugs. We are not sure of what, where, how, or when, but the fact that he did use drugs brings up another possible scenario." Hopper closed his eyes momentarily thinking back, "Okay, suppose some junkie slips a drug into Jim's beer, that turns him into a mean and vicious criminal. Jim in a moment of hallucination kills someone. Jim is not literally a different person from the old Jim. In this short lived stupor he is not a different person. He is just Jim transformed by a drug into a mean vicious personality. I believe the jury would still want to spare the good Jim from punishment. The reason is that the defendant lacked the capacity or a fair opportunity not to offend."

"Objection!" Canfield declared as if they were in the courtroom. "Merely changing Jim's character did not deprive him of either capacity or opportunity to restrain himself. We don't turn drunk drivers free who kill people on the road. If we buy that idea any junkie out there has reasonable excuse for murder. Besides, not all drugs change a man's character. A real junkie is more apt to kill himself rather than someone else. No gentlemen, I don't buy that. The whole idea is bullshit. If one's character compels him to act, he does not get an excuse. Jim should have risen above his character and let reason be his master." Barbara Starkey folded her arms again and looked at her shoes thinking about a rebuttal position, "Wait a minute," She interrupted, "Jim does have an excuse. An act has to reflect one's character, there has to be intent, at least for murder in the first degree. Now, let's take the example of entrapment."

"Of what?" Canfield exclaimed in disbelief.

"Yeah, entrapment," Barbara said curtly, I can quote you chapter and verse if you want. Entrapment is an excuse because the act of an entrapped person does not reflect on his character. He has responded to overpowering inducement by doing something that his normal character would protect against. Jim's act does not support Jim's character therefore Jim is innocent." Both doctors clapped as if watching a Perry Mason TV show. After a small chuckle Crum spoke, "So, now to prove your point in court you have to assume that the multiples alter egos are in fact different personalities and not just parts of one deeply divided personality."

Sally interrupted the doctor, "This is all well and good. I enjoyed the debate, and I look forward to our day in court. But what factual evidence do you have to prove that these are truly different and separate personalities?"

Dr. Hopper answered, "That's what we have to find out."

Crum added to the discussion, "I can tell you what we do have that supports this idea of individual personalities. That is amnesia between personalities." Canfield interrupted again, "Wait a minute, we've seen the text, and the interviews, and we know that David, Gaylord, and this guy Gordon talk to each other, I don't see any amnesia there."

"Yes, but none of them seem to know what the Beastie is doing when he does it." Sally asked quietly, "In your view how does that equate to the law?"

"Crum gestured with his pencil again as he spoke, "First, true multiples have fully developed and separate personalities. The defendant for example, Gaylord Harcourt, has a separate driver's license, social security number, voter registration, and has a job. The Gordon personality has essentially the same thing in his name. David on the other hand is about 12 or 15 years old and has none of these. Just look at his apartment. Two distinct life styles. Gaylord is a lady's man and David is the typical adolescent and Gordon is somewhere in between. So, in essence, if one alter does not have access to what's going on in the other personality's life, it is in part, what describes it as another personality. You can show that in court."

Beau commented quickly, "That doesn't change the fact that they both knew right from wrong."

"You're right," Hopper commented affirmatively, "However, what about the Beastie? Did he know right from wrong? From what we've learned so far, he was the killing instrument."

Canfield jumped in recapping, "So, Gaylord knew both Gordon and David, he approved of the killing because it made sex easier, it boosted his ego but didn't control the Beastie, David did. That clearly shows collusion between David, Gaylord and the Beastie. Right there you have culpability."

"What about Gordon?" Barbara asked. Crum answered the question glancing at some hand written notes. "Our interviews indicate he was locked in the playroom with no way in or out." Barbara Starkey smiled and said with inflection in her voice, "Therefore there was a conflict between Gordon and the other personalities and he indicated that while locked in the playroom he didn't know what was happening. He had no opportunity to act in a correct manner. So there is our amnesia and the lack of free will."

Beau and Sally smiled at the debate. They were getting further away from the facts and more into the philosophy of right and wrong and the law concerning insanity. Beau quipped, "So, what happens now? This is going to be one hell of a trial."

Sally joked, "Think of it as an upscale Judge Judy." Hopper added, "We need your help during the hypnosis session. Agent Thornton, you probably know more about how to get to him than we do."

"Whose going to put him under?" Sally asked.

"I will." Crum answered. Everyone remained silent as they gazed through the looking glass at the killer. "Who's in control?" She questioned.

"Gaylord seems to be in charge most of the time." Crum replied. "That's because they feel threatened. Gordon is a nice guy but he doesn't have the guts that Gaylord has. You can get to David with a candy bar. I think you're telling me you haven't been able to get them to cooperate so you can put them under. Correct?" The psychiatrists nodded at Sally's observations. "What about drugs?" Beau asked.

"We have him on tranquilizers." Hopper added. Sally looked at Dr. Crum, "Do you want to try the wheelchair again?"

"That worked the first time but I think he's getting a little tired of Michaels." Crum answered. He glanced at Hopper who nodded in agreement. Sally was staring through the looking glass at the killer. She wondered to herself how a person could be so mentally disturbed that he would be compelled to kill so many people. He hated Agnes with every fiber in his body. His hate was so extreme that it compelled him to kill Agnes over and over. Agnes was the key to the inside of his mind. Sally looked at the two psychiatrists and said, "Let's try with Dr. Michaels putting him under with a little help." Hopper was confused, but Crum knew that she had an idea of how to get through again to the complex and private mind of the killer. It took fifteen minutes to get a wheel chair and several Baby Ruth candy bars. The guard wheeled Dr. Crum into the cell then positioned himself inside the door.

Sally looked around the dark observation room then pointed at a small office trash can and asked, "Beau, could you empty that and hand it to me?" He quickly dumped the paper on the floor and handed her the empty trash bucket. Picking up the mike, turning on the PA system, then holding the can in her lap she spoke into the empty can. "David," The voice echoed through the PA system. It sounded like a voice from the other side of the unknown. "David," came another low melodic monotone. The killer sat upright in bed and searched the ceiling for some specter, a ghost, an image from the past. "David, I miss you," came another mournful statement.

"Agnes?" David had come to the surface. "Is that you?" was the little boy's question.

"David, Dr. Michaels is here. He wants to help you. Will you let him?" The killer assumed the posture and gestures of what seemed like a little boy. It wasn't obvious, it was nothing you could put your finger on or describe. But you knew instinctively that you were talking to a little boy. The little boy nodded his head. Crum wheeled his chair closer to the bed and handed the killer a candy bar. The killer rocked happily back and forth as he devoured the candy. With the last bit of candy in his mouth, little David asked, "Do you still love me?" He continued, looking at the ceiling, seeing nothing, but waiting for an answer. The deep echoing response said, "Yes David, I've always loved you. You are the son I've always wanted." The childlike killer smiled smugly at Dr. Crum. Sally's echoing voice announced softly, "I want you to lay down, close your eyes and listen to Dr. Michaels". The killer promptly did as he was told.

Dr. Crum spoke in a low soothing voice, "David, this is Dr. Michaels, can you hear me?"

"Yes," was David's timid reply.

"You know we've always talked and I've always wanted to help you. You know that don't you?"

"Yes," David replied automatically.

"David, I want you to close your eyes," Crum waited momentarily. "I want you to think back. Think back to a warm summer day. The sun is shining, birds are singing and you are happy. I want you to think about a cool running stream with bubbling water and a warm summer breeze. You're floating, so softly in the stream. Your are relaxed, just floating and floating, so at ease, so at peace. Everything is flowing so easily." Dr. Crum noted that the killer's body was becoming more relaxed as he brought him deeper into a hypnotic state.

"David, are your eyes shut?"

"Yes."

"How do you feel?"

"I feel like I could sleep forever."

"Good, I want you to sleep so you'll feel better. Your eyes lids are getting heavy. They are so heavy that you can't open them. Just sleep and relax. David, I want you to keep your eyelids shut but open your eyes. Can you do that?"

"Yes, Dr. Michaels."

"They are open, but everything is still dark isn't it," Crum advised.

"Yes, I can see, but it's still dark". There was a relaxed tone in the killer's voice as he went deeper into the hypnotic trance. Dr. Crum glanced at the looking glass and nodded. Sally checked the tape recorder while the rest of the audience watched silently.

"David", Dr. Crum began again in a slow monotone voice. "David, I want you to turn your eyes inward and focus on the center of your mind." Crum watched the killer's body make a slight movement. "David, you will see a small white light. Do you see it?" The killer nodded, and the David personality calmly said, "Yes."

"I want you to walk toward the light. The light will get bigger. As you get closer you will see a door. I want you to go through the door and into the sunlight." A satisfying, relaxing smile came over the killer's face.

"David, no one can hurt you in here. God will protect you. However, you must always tell the truth. Can you do that?" Dr. Crum waited for an answer.

"Oh yes, I love it in here," was the little David personality's answer.

"David, did you ever use drugs?"

"No, but Gaylord did."

"What kind of drugs?"

"You name it, he took it. Smack, coke, marijuana, ecstasy, uppers, lowers, opium."

"What about Gordon?"

"Oh no, Gordon would never do anything like that. Gaylord tried to sell him some but he turned him down."

"Did Gaylord sell drugs?"

"Yeah, but he didn't sell on the street. No, he sold in the night clubs, and at all the in-parties. He only sold to the rich bitches who could afford it. Carla got him into that."

"Was Carla a dealer?"

"No she was a slut. They had sex parties for the rich dudes. They all got high and screwed each other until they passed out." Dr. Crum shook his head sadly before going on. "Tell me about the Beastie." The killer laid quietly for a few moments. "David, tell me about the Beastie." Crum asked again.

"I love him." David responded tearfully.

"What happened?" Crum asked calmly, then sitting up in his chair so he could catch every word.

"He was my puppy."

"Your puppy?" Crum replied softly.

"Yeah, she killed him."

"Who?"

"Agnes."

"Why would Agnes kill your puppy?" The killer had completely assumed the demeanor of a 9 year old. "Snipper, she took Snipper away from me. I couldn't get him back until I performed."

"What do you mean performed?"

"I was the girl."

"The girl?" Crum questioned having a pretty good idea where this was headed.

"Yeah, panties, bra, wig, lipstick." David said with his voice straining with every word.

"Then what?" Crum asked knowing it wasn't going to be pretty but he had to find out all the details no matter how painful.

"They would bend me over the table. Tie my legs apart and have sex with me."

"How do you mean?" Crum asked again taking notes on his pad.

"They would put that thing on and stick me."

David, you said they. Who else did this to you?"

"Mommy." Was David's tearful reply.

"You mean Agnes and your mother had anal sex with you?" The killer broke out in uncontrollable sobs as he answered, "Yes."

"That's all right David, I'm here. You'll never have to do that again." The sobbing subsided as Crum waited. "So, what happened to Snipper?" The sobbing had not completely subsided when David answered, "He died in the 'fridge."

"So Snipper is the Beastie," Crum announced looking at his notes.

"Yes, he's not going to let anyone hurt me again."

"So, Snipper, I mean the Beastie does only what you tell him."

"Yes."

"So the Beastie kills Agnes whenever she hurts you," Crum waited for an answer. The killer remained in the trance not responding. Crum questioned again, "Does the Beastie kill Agnes when she hurts you?"

"Sometimes," was David's cautious reply.

"What do you mean, sometimes?" Crum asked curiously.

"Sometimes Gaylord makes me."

"You mean Gaylord tells you to have the Beastie kill Agnes?" Crum glanced again at the looking glass hoping everyone on the other side was hearing what he was hearing. "Why would Gaylord make you kill Agnes?"

"'Cause."

"'Cause why?" Crum added quickly.

"'Cause it makes the sex easier. He doesn't like anyone to say no."

"What about Gordon? Can't Gordon stop him?"

"No, Gordon has tried, but he's too weak. He just hides in the playroom. He doesn't want to know what's going on."

"Does he know what's going on?" Was Crum's next quick question.

"Yes, but he doesn't care anymore. He just goes to the playroom and waits until it's all over."

"Did the Beastie kill Amanda Hollingsworth?" The killer lay perfectly still for almost a full minute before the David personality answered, "Gaylord said that was Agnes. She tries to get away. You know, like she did before, move to another city, change her name, but that was Agnes all right."

"I see," Dr. Crum said politely. "Why does Gaylord try to find Agnes?" There wasn't a moments hesitation before David answered, "Gaylord loves Agnes, and she loved him. But she ran away and left us. She took everything and just left us." The sadness was now replaced with anger. "Gaylord is all hung up on Agnes. He will not let her get away with it. He knows once he makes love to her she'll take us back."

"Why do you have the Beastie kill Agnes if you want her to take you back?" There was a momentary stillness in the killer's demeanor before the David personality answered, "I don't, Gaylord does."

"Why?"

"'Cause, she won't run away if she's quiet. Then they can talk, have tea, and listen to music together."

"So, the Beastie makes them quiet." Crum announced sadly.

"Yes," was David's solemn reply. Dr. Crum waited a few minutes before asking his next question. "You know it was wrong to hurt Agnes like that."

"I didn't hurt her, Gaylord did." David said defiantly.

"But the Beastie does what you tell him and the Beastie kills." Crum continued to press the little boy personality.

"Gaylord made me. If I didn't let the Beastie do his thing he'd make life a living hell for me."

"I know, Gaylord is a bad person isn't he." Crum said condescendingly. With eyes remaining shut the killer nodded in agreement. Crum remained silent for a few minutes reviewing his notes before he asked, "Why did the Beastie kill the policeman?" There was no hesitation in David's answer, "Oh no, you're not gonna blame that on the Beastie. Gaylord did all that on his own. I told him not to do it. But he was mad. He didn't like anyone to interrupt his sex." The killer shook his head denying anything to do with Harry's death.

"Did you tell Gaylord that killing the officer was wrong?" Crum asked.

Oh yeah, I told him. I screamed at him but he didn't care." Dr. Crum waited for the David personality to calm down before asking his next question. "What about me? Why did you make me come along? Why do you keep me locked in the closet?" Tears began to well up. He became remorseful and said, "I'm sorry. You were the only one we could talk to. You were the only one who understood. We needed you. We couldn't let you go. Please forgive me." The child personality began to cry. The spectators from behind the looking glass watched in amazement as this grown man, lying on a bed with his eyes closed, sobbing and repeating, "I'm sorry, I'm sorry, I'm sorry." Dr. Crum waited until the David personality had calmed himself before he spoke, "That's all right David. We are going to make everything better. Now, before we can do this you're going to have to answer all the questions from now on truthfully. You promise?" The killer nodded affirmatively in a childlike fashion. "Now, you've been very helpful. I want you to relax and sleep. I want you to rest. Put all your problems behind you. Think about the warm sun and beautiful trees. I want you to count from ten backwards to one. When you get to the number one, I want you to listen for the door to slam shut. When you hear the door shut you will wake up and you will feel totally rested. Do you understand?" The killer nodded again. "Okay, start counting," the doctor ordered. The little boy in a man's body began to count. "Ten, nine, eight," Dr. Crum motioned for the guard to wheel him out. At the door Dr. Crum waited for the killer to say number one, then he slammed the door shut. The killer rose, rubbed his eyes and began to strut around the room. Gaylord, was now in charge. He stopped his strutting and gazed into the looking glass. He admired himself as though he had no worries in the world.

Chapter Seventeen

The Wake

Preservation of the stately mansions and antebellum homes decorated with intricate wrought-iron is a way of life in Charleston. This city, that is over 300 years old, has been at the heart of Southern art and culture. Charleston is one of the last cities to reflect Southern pride that runs deeper than the Ashley and Cooper rivers which cradle the city.

Charleston's Historic District encompasses more than 2,000 buildings, 73 of which predate the Revolutionary War. One hundred and thirty six date from the late 1700s and more than 600 other buildings were built in the early 1800s. So many church spires poke their noses up over the city's skyline that at one time, it was called the "Holy City". Crowded into this small peninsula is Charleston. It's old narrow streets are often one way and parallel each other. However, Meeting Street, which is U.S. Route 52, is a two-way street that runs through the Historic District and the heart of the city.

Within walking distance from City Hall at 135 Meeting Street is the Gibbes Museum of Art. It houses an excellent collection of Japanese woodblock prints, early American paintings, sculpture and engravings that is a major tourist attraction. Located across the street from the museum is Murphy's Stake Out Bar and Grill, a favorite watering hole for the police and most of the city employees. Everyone from the Mayor to the local garbage collector manage to hit Murphy's on a Friday night.

The bar had been an old, and now defunct, Newberry's 5 and 10 cent store. About 15 years ago Murphy bought the building, gutted it and turned it into an Irish pub with all the trappings, decorations and elegance from the old country. The outside of the building blended perfectly with the Southern architecture of the Historic District. Once you stepped inside you immediately felt at home when you were greeted with a warm smile and a pat on the back by Murph, the owner and chief bartender.

The Stake Out Bar was a large expansive room. At the back was a large horseshoe shaped bar that housed an array of beer taps. The bar was finished in finely lacquered oak. Every kind of liquor imaginable was displayed behind the bar in front of a mirrored wall. At one end of the room was the snooker area that contained three pool tables and a small seating gallery. Murph had been the precinct pool champion three years running. At the other end of the room was the dining area and dance floor. On the west wall, overlooking the dining area, was a collection of police badges. Murph had been collecting badges for the past 30 years. His display consisted of over

1500 police badges from law enforcement agencies all over the world. Murph even had a badge from the Moscow Central Security Police. Of the 1500 badges displayed 300 had a black strip of tape over the badge signifying that the officer who wore that badge had been killed in the line of duty. It gave policemen a sort of immortality to have your badge displayed at Murph's Bar.

Almost nightly an old retired lawman, from another state or even another country for that matter, would visit the bar and remember the sacrifices that these men had made. In the center of the badge display was a small black frame that stood out from all the other badges as a place of honor. In the middle of this frame, with a black stripe across the front of the shiny piece of tin was Harry Mackland's badge. This badge would be displayed here in this homemade shrine for as long as the Stakeout Bar and Grill existed. It was already arranged that when this era has passed, when these souls are long forgotten the badges will then be displayed in the Charleston Museum across from Marion Square. Murph had seen to that.

Even in his seventies, Murph was a mountain of a man. Six feet six inches tall, weighing 250 pounds with a heart made of sweet honey. He hadn't always been like that. He was a strapping young Irishman who never walked away from a fight. He had a great sense of fairness and honesty and a genuine concern for his fellow officers. He rose quickly to Chief of Detectives. Murph was like a second father to Beau and Harry. When they were young, the two of them were going to single handedly, bring law and order to Charleston. He quickly showed them the reality of working the streets, being tough when you had to, and compassionate whenever possible. When he married Jessica, his wife for over 25 years he began to mellow. Jessica was the planner in his life. She saved every penny she could. She went without whenever possible, had her vacations at home and was perfectly happy. Come retirement time they had enough money saved to open the bar, which had been his dream since coming to this country. The rest, as the say, is history. Five years ago Murph lost Jessica. He went into a deep depression. At the bottom of his depression Murph went to church and prayed. It was as if a light had suddenly been shown to him. He finally realized that Jessica had given him the bar. The bar was Jessica's gift to him, to keep him in his loneliness. In the years that followed every customer was like family and it filled his loneliness. He was the Guru of the force. Young rookies sat at the bar for hours, captivated by his stories and the wisdom he passed on.

Tonight was the night. The Gray Lady Task Force had made a solemn promise not to have a wake for Harry until the killer had been caught. It was a Friday night and everyone from the Lt. Governor to the local tax collector had turned out to give Harry the send off he deserved. They also knew that

Murph would go all out for Harry. And, they wouldn't miss that for all the world. It was like a holiday for a local hero. Harry and Beau had been Murph's surrogate sons. He was as proud of them as if they were his own.

When Beau and Sally entered the bar it was wall to wall people. Loud music, smoke, and laughter. They were immediately met with smiles, hugs, kisses, and handshakes. Sally thought Beau must have had a photographic memory as he introduced her to everyone who came his way. He could even tell you about their family, their job, kids, wife's name, how long they'd been together and what they had planned for their future. Between hellos and introductions Beau and Sally nudged their way toward the big horseshoe bar. As soon as Murph caught sight of them he waved above the crowd, smiled, and pointed at two bar stools that had been especially reserved for them. Sitting at the next stool was Jack Bellamy and his wife, Emma Joe. All three began to wave and point at the stools. Sally and Beau waved back then made their way across the dance floor to the bar.

Murph scurried from behind the bar and gave Beau a fatherly hug and without hesitation gave Sally a big hug too. Standing with Sally held at arms length, looking her over he smiled with great satisfaction and in an exaggerated Irish brogue stated, "It's a fine Irish girl you'll be marrying." Sally chuckled, then playing with Murph's put-on she replied, "Aye, that he is, and he's marrying me with a fine hot tempered Irish mother. So you best be remembering that."

"Oh bucko, you are really in for it." Murph commented as he swirled Sally around then gently put her on the bar stool. Sally liked Murph immediately. It was as if she'd known him all her life. She kissed him on the cheek as he adjusted her stool.

"'Tis Himself honoring us with his presence," Came another put-on Irish brogue from Jack. Smiling at the two partners Murph laughed and replied looking at Sally and Beau, "How about that. May the Saints preserve us, a black Irishman." Beau chimed in, winking at Jack, "Don't worry, he's from Southern Ireland." They all laughed. Sally turned on the bar stool and observed the mass of humanity dancing, huddled in small groups, laughing and telling jokes.

Nodding at Beau then looking at Sally, Murph asked, "I know what he's having, what can I get for you?"

"I'll have a glass of white wine," She answered politely. Murph quickly pulled a beer and poured a wine for Sally then remarked, "You are truly a beauty and Beau doesn't deserve you."

"Thank you," she replied taking a sip of wine then looking down the bar, taking in every face. Most of them she knew, some she didn't and wondered what connection they had with Harry and Beau. There was Starkey and Canfield, who were at each others throats just hours ago now huddled together still debating the legality of the insanity defense. At the other end of the bar Sally observed the Mayor, Police Chief, and the Fire Chief all discussing politics.

A loud voice from the end of the bar came from a young rookie cop. "Hey, Murph, give us one of your golden rules." Before Murph could answer Beau explained to Jack and Sally about Murph's golden rules. "Murph is the Guru of the force. He's got a rule for just about anything or anybody especially when it come to law enforcement." Sally looked admiringly at Murph. Jack had heard rumors about the legendary Murph. The old grand dad of the force. He was also curious about his ability to simplify almost everything into a rule, and in some crazy way, it made sense. "Okay Murph, give the rookie a golden rule," Jack remarked, jokingly gulping down the last part of his beer. Murph pulled another beer for Jack, thought for a moment, then pointing down the bar to the rookie, said, "Never search an empty warehouse with a partner named, 'Boom Boom'."

Sally was about to sip her wine when she erupted into laughter, spewing wine all over the bar. Beau broke out in laughter, not at Murph's patter, he had heard it all before, but at Sally's reaction. Jack was beside himself with laughter. The Police Chief shouted from the end of the bar pointing at the Mayor, "I bet you don't have one for the Mayor." Murph didn't hesitate a second before he answered, "The Mayor will always get a traffic ticket the day before the department negotiates a salary increase." Everyone at the bar gave a jovial 'boo'. The Mayor lifted his glass in a mock toast and replied, "Okay, now give us one for the Chief, pointing at Wexford. Murph lifted his beer mug acknowledging the Mayor's request, "To err is human, to forgive is against department policy." Another yell of approval came from everyone at the bar. "Come on Murph, you can do better than that," the Fire Chief commented, with everyone at the bar urging him on. Murph took another gulp of cold beer before he continued, "You'll be decorated for stupidity, and busted for brilliant work, and that is also department policy." The bar broke into loud clapping as Wexford gave Murph the finger.

Beau raised his hands and said, "Hold it, okay Murph, how about a rule for Jack our new super dick?" Jack smiled as he knew it was his turn to take one of Murph's quips. Murph smiled, patted Jack on the head and said, "Remember, your bullet proof vest was supplied by the lowest bidder." Wild laughter and applause broke out. Sally could see looks of approval from the bar. Murph poured everyone a new round of drinks. The dancing had stopped and everyone was assembled at the bar listening to Murph's humor. It always had a ring of truth in it. Jack pointed at Beau before he asked, "Okay you've got to have one for Beau." Remarks from the crowd agreed, "Come on Murph one for Beau." Murph took on a saddened stance as he looked at his only remaining son. "Eat right, exercise right and die young anyway." With that statement the room went silent. Not a word, a movement, a cough, just pure reverent silence. Murph and Beau sadly embraced.

Resting in a place of honor, at one end of the bar, was a large beautifully polished brass bell given to Murph when he opened the bar. It was the fire bell that hung in the first fire station in Charleston. Murph clanged the bell getting the full attention of all the revelers. Murph raised his hands, along with his voice, "All right, everyone get your drinks and gather 'round the bar." He waited until he had the full attention of the crowd. "You know we're all here to give Harry the send off he deserves." Murph paced up and down the bar handing out drinks, pumping beer, making sure everyone had his fill in order to toast Harry's final goodbye. Satisfied, he stopped, bowed his head, remained silent for a few moments gathering his thoughts. "This is something Harry and I used to talk about when he came in here for his Friday night dram." He held up a bottle of Bushmill's Irish whiskey. Murph lined up an empty shot glass in front of everyone seated at the bar, then sat two bottles of Irish Whiskey on the bar before continuing. "Harry said that life is like a fine bottle of vintage wine to be savored and enjoyed for as long as it lasts." The crowd at the bar hung on Murph's every word. They all knew that Murph was a man of few words but when he spoke he usually meant it. "What he meant was that each moment we live is new, and to be enjoyed. It's unique, and when its gone it won't come back. The important thing is what we do with that time. When we were kids we learn math, geography, all the things that are suppose to get us by in life. Harry wanted to know, do we ever teach ourselves who we are? Do we know what we are? I asked him if he had the answer and he said, 'Yes'. He said, you are one of a kind, you're unique. In all the time that has passed, all the time that is yet to be there will never be another you. Your eyes, your smile, the exact color of your hair, your capacity to love are all uniquely yours. You have the ability to be anything you want. You could be a doctor, lawyer, heaven forbid," the crowd chuckled approval at that comment, "'Even a cop'. Harry passed this idea along to kids, to anyone who'd listen and that is part of the man we honor tonight. So, hoist em up to Harry." Murph took his shot of Irish whiskey with one gulp and followed it with a beer chaser. "Well?" Murph said motioning everyone at the bar to do the same. Mechanically, like a common understood ritual, they all gulped down the whiskey and followed it with a beer chaser.

Murph smiled then filled their glasses again winking at Sally. "We all have a story to tell about Harry. Whose next?" he announced. Gil Washington, Charleston's Mayor, to everyone's surprise, raised his hand. Murph acknowledged the Mayor with a nod. "Well, this happened sometime ago. I've never spoken to anyone about it. But now I think it's time I told someone." The Mayor fondled his drink before continuing, "You remember when you and Harry were recruiting kids for the Police Athletic League?" Gil looked at Beau. Beau acknowledged the Mayor with a smile and a nod recalling those good times. "Do you remember a little runt of a black kid too small to play football, too short to get on the basketball team, too shy to have many friends?" Beau answered immediately, "Yeah, little Jimmy Washington."

Gil smiled, "He's my kid."

"I know," Beau answered, "He's a nice kid. I like him a lot." Gil looked at Beau with an expression he hadn't seen in the Mayor before. It was as if he was about to confess to some dark deed in Jimmy's past. "Do you remember a clumsy kid with an arm full of books, a baseball bat, a boom box and a load of junk that tripped and fell outside of Central High?" Beau thought for second, then nodded. "You and Harry stopped, helped him load the stuff in the car and gave him a lift."

"Sure."

"Do you remember how depressed he was? He was having trouble with his school work. All the girls laughed at him. You and Harry took him to Baskin and Robbins, bought him a shake and talked to him about his future."

"Sure." Beau responded again, "He wanted to play sports but no one wanted a runt."

"And what did you and Harry tell him?" Gil asked already knowing the answer.

"We told him that no matter how small he was, or what kind of limitations God gave him there was a sport for him." Beau answered happily, thinking of how much Harry loved little Jimmy and how he had faith in him.

"Then you got him into boxing and he became the Feather Weight champ of the league three years running." Gil added, "Did you know that Harry went to every one of his bouts?"

"No!" Beau answered in disbelief. "Harry seldom talked about what he did on his days off."

"Harry went to Jimmy's high school graduation and Jim was the class valedictorian. Then Jimmy went off to college. Harry stayed in contact, either on the phone or E-mail. I'm sorry to say that I was too busy running for Mayor to give Jimmy the father he deserved." Gil was having trouble getting all the words out. He struggled on, "When Harry died, Jimmy was at the funeral, do you remember?" Beau nodded. Gil continued to struggle for the right words. "He told me about that day, when you two guys picked up his books and gave him a lift. Did you know he was on his way home to commit suicide." There was a stark silence in the crowd. Here was the Mayor revealing something that was personally painful. He was exposing his failure as a father. Tears came to Sally's eyes. Gil continued, "But you guys took the time to be his friend."

The Mayor quickly commented to the silent crowd, "By the way, he graduates from law school this year." The crowd erupted into a huge roar shouting, "Here's to Harry. God bless his soul." Then, as if on some divine command they downed their whiskey and chased it with another beer. Beau glanced at Sally and noticed she was getting with the program and little by little losing her inhibitions.

Murph held his hands up again, and said, "Whose next?" Everyone at the bar looked at each other then the Fire Chief slowly raised his hand and said, "I've got one," Again the crowd was surprised that the Fire Chief would also have a story about Harry. He looked at Beau as he spoke, "Remember when Mark first went into the hospital?" Beau nodded sadly. "Harry and Mark both knew that his condition was terminal even though Harry never discussed it with you. Remember when you had to go to Washington for the Law Enforcement Action Committee meeting?" Beau answered, "Yeah."

"Harry went to see Mark every day. They talked, laughed, watched TV together."

"That sounds like Harry," Beau commented.

"Mark told Harry that he always wanted to be a fireman."

"Yeah, Mark told me that's what he wanted to do. He thought I'd be disappointed. I told him I only wanted him to be his own man. To do what's best for him," Beau added. The Fire Chief acknowledged Beau then took another gulp of beer. "What you don't know was that Harry gave me a call and told me the story. He arranged for a wheelchair, then got our rescue unit to the hospital and took him down to the fire station. He spent the whole day with us. He ate with us, went out on a minor fire call, the whole nine yards. We got him a real fire hat, yellow slicker, rubber boots and hoisted him up on the fire truck and zipped around the city full blast, sirens going and a smile on that kid's face that would melt your heart." There was a momentary silence before Beau said, "I saw all the equipment and I thought it was nice of you guys to bring it to him, but I had no idea you guys did all that for him." Beau wiped a small tear from his cheek and said, "Thanks guys." The Fire Chief replied, "Don't thank me it was Harry's idea." Sally handed Beau her handkerchief and Beau covered his eyes.

"Okay, lets hear it for Harry" Murph shouted raising his glass as a signal for everyone to do the same, then downing another whiskey. "Whose next? Murph demanded, pouring another round of whiskey in each of the shot glasses. "We're gonna keep this up until those bottles are empty. Excuse me, this bottle is empty." Murph threw an empty bottle in the trash and held up another half empty bottle.

"I have one," Came a soft voice from the other end of the bar. It was Lori Mackland, Harry's daughter. She came to the center of the bar, stood next to Beau, gave him a warm hug. Murph moved her drink next to Beau's and motioned her to continue. She began thinking back to a time of innocence, a time of wonder, when a father and a daughter shared those precious moments. "Do you all remember when hurricane Hugo hit?" Everyone nodded. How could they forget the damage that devastated South Carolina and miraculously spared Charleston. "Dad took me down to the beach to see what had washed up on shore. He said, 'Sometimes you find interesting things. This is the only time the sea gives up some of it's treasures.' It was low tide. As we went along Dad would stop at these tide pools, scoop up a bunch of minnows, and toss them back into the ocean. I asked him why he was doing that? He said, 'If I don't throw em back they'll die from a lack of oxygen.' I thought he must be crazy. I told him, Dad, there must be million of these fish up and down the beach. What possible difference could that scoop make? Dad scooped up another bunch of minnows into the palm of his hand, then tossed them into the sea and said, 'It made a difference to those 'little guys.' So we spent the next few hours scooping up fish and tossing them back. I mean we were really a weird sight."

"That sounds like Harry," Murph said, interrupting Lori. Lori tucked her arm under Beau's and said, "I never forgot that." This time, Murph silently held up his glass. Everyone followed Murph's lead, and put down another shot of whiskey.

By this time there wasn't a dry eye in the crowd and not a sober soul in the bunch. Stories about Harry were coming out spontaneously. Murph filled glasses again and again. Then, looking at the last empty bottle, he threw it in the trash and declared, "That's it. One more story and we get back to the party."

"I've got one," Homer Canfield yelled. "You haven't got one," Barbara Starkey said contemptuously.

"Yes I do," Homer insisted.

"Okay, give Homer a chance," Murph demanded, as everyone at the bar laughed. "This is getting a little maudlin so it better be a good one," Murph said bluntly. Homer thought back to the first time he saw Harry. Homer began slowly as though he might be in court, "This story, well it's not really a story. At the time I didn't give it much thought.

Let's see, it was about three years ago. I was the new guy at the DA's office. I was driving to my first trial as a buck lawyer for the DA. I wanted to give a good impression, and I was on the verge of being late for my first appearance. So I was kind a in a hurry. I came screaming up to a stoplight somewhere on Meeting Street. I was all ready to peel out of there. I figured I could beat the next two lights if I got ahead of the other cars. Guess who pulled up next to me riding in a patrol car? Harry Mackland. I sat there tapping my thumb on the steering wheel when a young couple, both blind, with a white cane came walking by arm-in-arm. The man held the hand of a little boy and the woman had another kid in a sling, or whatever you cail it? A shoulder pouch, that's it! They were walking across the street tapping the cane in front of them trying to navigate across the intersection. At first, I was a little peeved. Who would let people like this out on their own? I mean, they should have had a guide dog at least. Then I thought how horrible it must be to be blind. Anyway, as I watched, I noticed that the couple was veering out into the intersection with on-coming traffic. Harry jumped out of his car, and ran into the traffic. In fact, he almost got hit himself. He stopped traffic instantly. I mean a lot of guys laid rubber on concrete that day. Now, here's the funny thing. No one honked, or swore, they just watched Harry. You'd think he'd take them by the arm and lead them back to the crosswalk. No, Harry walked along next to them and casually said, 'To your left.' When they were safe, he jumped into his car and took off. These people simply wanted to get to the other side of the street safely. Their problem was eight lines of cars aimed straight at them. With Harry's quiet reassuring voice, he passed the time of day with the couple and no one panicked. It was my understanding that Harry sponsored a proposal at a city counsel meeting to put those raised dots on the crosswalks. It never got approved." Everyone looked at Gil Washington, the City's Mayor. "What?" He asked defensively, "That was before my time, remember? Maybe we should try it again?"

Barbara Starkey looked suspiciously at Homer. "You're not making that up are you?"

"Why is it you always think I'm lying?" He responded, looking sternly at Barbara. She smiled and said, "Cause your lips are moving."

"Okay ladies and gentlemen," Murph interrupted, "The last one to send Harry on his way." Everyone raised their drinks and said in unison, "Bless you, Harry." A roar of applause followed.

"Hold it! Hold it!" Murph shouted, "We're not done yet." Everyone turned their attention back to the bar. Murph motioned for complete silence before he spoke, "We have one more item on the program." Everyone looked around for something crazy to happen. Murph was known for his stunts and pranks. "Sally Thornton here, if you don't know is Federal fuzz." Everyone chuckled and made hushed remarks to themselves. "Now, she single handedly captured the killer. Isn't that right Beau?" Murph winked at Beau and Jack. They both nodded and faced Sally with a big grin.

"Tonight we have an special guest. A distinguished member of the force with many of faithful years of service and one who was also instrumental in capturing the perp." The crowd murmured among themselves. Looking at Sally, Murph said, "Would you please stand up?" Surprised, she complied with Murph's request. "Beau?" Murph motioned for Beau to do the same. He also complied. Murph put two fingers in his mouth and let out a loud screeching whistle. The swinging doors to the kitchen swung open and Studs, finely groomed with a mock police uniform on, came trotting into the bar. Smiling with confidence, Studs jumped up on the bar and picked his way to his master and planted a wet slurp on his cheek. The crowd noticed that Studs didn't nudge, tip or knock a single drink on the bar. Studs turned and gave Sally an equally wet kiss who returned the affection with a big hug. Studs then gave a loud burp resulting in immediate laughter. Murph commented, "He's been into the beer again." Okay, Beau, it's your turn." This was the first time Sally had seen Beau embarrassed. His face had turned slightly red. He stammered like a shy kid asking a girl out on his first date. "Sally, Studs has something for you." She was taken back. This was a total surprise to her. She looked closer at Stud's harness. Attached in a prominent place, was a diamond engagement ring. She covered he mouth with both hands and gasped, "Oh my God." Beau removed the ring and placed in on her finger and half whispered, "Will you marry me?" Sally broke out in joyful tears, "Oh yes, yes, yes." She threw her arms around Beau and gave him a warm, loving, tender kiss. The couple was immediately surrounded with revelers offering congratulations, hugs, and kisses. Murph shouted above the happy roar, "Okay folks! Your heard it here first, so he can't back out." While all the attention was centered on the happy couple, Studs casually walked down the bar lapping beer from every mug big enough to get his snout into.

The party went on into the wee hours of the morning. With Murph's urging, the Police Chief provided two paddy-wagons to haul the drunks safely home. The Fire Chief provided an emergency rescue vehicle to pick up the overflow. The bar was almost empty. Studs slept in the corner. An occasional burp woke him up. He would look at Sally and Beau dancing alone then close his eyes.

Murph had seen to it that the couple in love had plenty of coffee before sending them on their way. Murph watched the couple like a proud father. "Hey, you two," He softly commanded, "Drink your coffee and lock the door on your way out. Oh, and don't forget that drunken dog of yours." Murph took off his apron, turned off the lights, and went out the back door. It had been a great wake and engagement party.

The autumn night was warm. A bright harvest moon hung high in the midnight sky as they drove slowly out of the city toward Falconbriar. Studs was fast asleep in the back seat of the car. For Sally, life had come full circle. She finally felt at home. Her head was still spinning from all the excitement, not to mention the greatest consumption of booze she's ever had in one evening. However, tonight had been a special night. She had finally found a man, a real man who loved her and was willing to make a commitment. She rolled down the car window slightly to let in the cool night air. Beau looked quietly at Sally, "You know something?" he asked. "No", she responded, keeping her eyes closed letting the cool air flow over her face.

"I bet Harry is up there laughing his ass off." She looked at Beau lovingly, "I think he's up there saying he's going to look out for us. He's going to see that everything works out." Beau kissed her hand and turned his attention back to the road. Sally gazed up at the harvest moon and smiled, "You know that rest stop? You know, the one where you proposed? The one where you actually made a commitment?" Beau nodded. Sally smiled, "You know you didn't have to. You already had what you wanted."

Beau slowed the car and pulled off the road at the same rest stop. "Here we are," he announced. Sally sat up straight, surprised and looked around. The forest at night was even more beautiful than she had imagined. The soft moonlight on the trees gave it a magical atmosphere. Beau looked softly at Sally, "Sweetheart, I've had plenty of sex since my divorce. It was only animal sex. You're the only real woman I've known. You are my pal, my friend, as well as being the most desirable woman I've ever met. I want to have kids, I want to be Katie's dad, I want to take her to Disney World and do all those things that a family does." Sally moved next to Beau, touched his face tenderly and gave him a soft kiss that quickly turned passionate. "Come on, I want to show you something," he said opening the car door.

He led Sally down a winding path through pine and moss covered oak trees to a small pond with a bubbling waterfall that cascaded softly into the pond. The moonlight caused the waterfall to sparkle like falling diamonds. She was taken back by the natural beauty of the hidden pond. Beau put his arm around Sally. "This is where I used to go swimming," he commented. Beau pointed to a limb that overhung the pond, "Look." She saw the remains of an old rope that had been tied to the tree. "We used to swing out and drop into the pool when we were kids. We called this the skinny-dip pond." Sally looked mischievously at Beau, took off her shoes and dipped her toe into the water. She stepped back and looked at Beau in a quiet sensual manner then began to strip. Maybe it was the booze, the total loss of inhibitions, or the magic of the night, but Sally had decided she was going skinny dipping. Beau watched hypnotized by her beauty. Her broad shoulders held two perfect breasts which stood erect and firm. Her small waist and flat stomach were actuated by full hips and athletic thighs. The moonlight made her skin appear milk white. Beau hadn't moved a muscle as he watched her wade slowly into the pond. She lifted her hands up and let the water trickle down over her shoulders and between her breasts. "This is great," she remarked sensually. "Are you coming in or not?" Sally asked facing Beau with her arms at her side. Beau tore at his clothes, kicking off his shoes, ripping buttons from his shirt. Taking off his Jockey shorts he revealed a giant erection. Sally laughed at Beau's predicament. "I didn't know I had that kind of effect on you?" She said stifling a small laugh. "You know damn well you do," he said, wading into the cool water. Sally moved close to Beau, kissed him passionately, with her tongue searching for his. She broke the embrace. He saw in Sally's face pure animal desire. Raw animal passion was coming from inside her, "You said you like animal sex, so do I," She reached into the water, gently took Beau's erection and inserted it into her. She straddled him and began to impale herself on him as fast and as deep as she could. Sally was rapidly approaching her climax when a bright spotlight illuminated the nude copulating couple standing in the middle of the pond. On the other end of the light was Sheriff Cullpepper who shouted, "What are you two doing out there?" Beau knew instantly from the voice that Cullpepper was making his nightly patrol of all the teenager make out spots. Without a break in his rhythm Beau shouted back, "We're having sex. Now turn off the light before I shove it up your ass." The light went out immediately followed by uncontrollable laughter from Sally who uncoupled herself and hugged Beau until she could regain her composure.

Sheriff Cullpepper being your typical dirty old man, got some sadistic pleasure out of finding young teenagers having sex. He often read them the riot act before letting them get dressed. That gave him time to ogle the young innocent bodies. One young girl offered to have oral sex with him if he would let her go, and not tell her parents. That episode turned him on to his nightly sex patrols. Occasionally, he would brag to young rookies about all the offers he'd had for sex from these young girls. No one knew for sure if he'd ever taken anyone up on the offer. However, there were no records of a young lady having sex in the make out park. Most of the men in the Sheriff's Office believed he had, but no one talked about it. Tonight however, was a total surprise to Cullpepper as he returned to his patrol car with a young rookie waiting to hear all about it. Cullpepper got into the patrol car, slamming the door, and looked straight ahead. "Well, what happened?," the young rookie asked, waiting for another juicy story.

"Don't ask, just shut up, and drive." was the Sheriff's stern command.

Falconbriar glistened in the midnight moon reflecting a time when this old house stood as a hallmark of southern culture and chivalry. This dreamlike vision reminded Sally of a Grant Wood painting. The night was filled with soft pastel colors and the aroma of night blooming jasmine and magnolia blending together to create an atmosphere upon which lovers kiss and dreams are made. The fire flies had long turned out their twinkling lights and gone to bed.

The porch light had been left on to welcome the lovers home for the weekend. Brightly colored crepe paper streamers were strung across the porch and a paper banner hung above the door stating "Congratulations". Sally smiled and gave Beau a warm hug. Beau put his arm around her and said, "We're home." No sooner had he closed the front door when Sally put her arms around his neck, kissed him gently and said, "You don't know how wonderful those words sound." Arm in arm they went upstairs and checked in on Katie who was fast asleep in her own room. Sally was surprised to see that Katie's room had already been redecorated with a children's theme. She smiled and whispered, "Those two are pretty sure of themselves aren't they." He smiled, "You know how mothers are." He gently put the covers back on Katie, kissed her on the forehead, and shut the door.

It had been a long eventful day. Beau stepped into the shower, closed his eyes, and let the warm water run over his head. He had a habit of taking long showers. It was a place he could relax and forget about almost everything. Beau put his head against the cold tiles to allow the water to run down his tired back. The steam from the shower filled the bathroom making the cold mirrors misty. The glassed shower door slid silently open and Sally stepped in and began to message Beau's shoulders. He didn't move but enjoyed the moment. There was nothing sexual in this encounter, it seemed like a normal, natural thing for two lovers to do. Sally lathered her hands and began to wash his back. Her strokes were gentle and soothing to the touch. Slowly, her strokes moved lower and lower until she touched his manhood with her soapy hand. Beau turned and looked at her. Sally was totally aroused. She wanted him and she wanted him now. Her wet body moved closer to his until they were touching. She still stroked his manhood lightly. The two lovers changed positions and Beau began to soap her back. He couldn't help but notice the athletic shoulders, small waist and desirable hips. Facing the cold tiled wall she put both hands on the shower head allowing him free access with his soapy hands to explore her body. Each stroke resulted in a moan of satisfaction from Sally. His hands slowly moved down her back to her hips, thighs, then toward her womanhood. She opened her legs further and arched her back inviting him to go deeper. She wanted him. She wanted to give herself totally to the man she desperately loved. Sally turned and kissed him passionately opening her lips waiting for his tongue. She whispered into his ear, "I'm going to make sure that you'll never want any other woman but me." She kissed him harder then knelt in front of him and inserted his manhood in her mouth allowing him full penetration. Beau was her love, her passion, she was giving herself to him totally.

A light tap, tap on the steamed shower door and a little girl's voice saying, "Mommy?" Another tap, "Mommy?" revealed little Katie standing there holding her teddy bear. Sally stood up then looked sadly at her man. Beau smiled back understanding the irony of the situation. Sally slid open the shower door and looked lovingly at Katie, "What is it Sweetheart?"

"I can't sleep."

"Okay Honey, you go back and hop up in our bed and I'll be right there. The little girl with long dark curly hair, skipped into the bedroom, hopped up on the bed and sat with her legs crossed Indian style. The two lovers quietly stepped out of the shower, quickly donned terry cloth robes, came into the bedroom, and sat next to Katie. "What's the matter Sweetheart?" Sally asked, putting her arm around the child.

"I had a bad dream."

"Pretty little girls shouldn't have bad dreams. They should only have happy dreams." Beau said reassuringly.

"I dreamed that the bad man came and took you away," Katie remarked softly taking Beau's hand, then looking sorrowfully at him. He put his arm around the child, "How would you like to stay here with Grandma, and your Mother and me? Of course you'd have to take care of the animals," Beau winked at Sally. "You'd have to take care of a pony I am thinking of buying." Katie's eyes opened wide with excitement as she looked at her mother, "Can we mom? Please, pretty please. Katie was bouncing with excitement waiting for her mother's answer.

"We'll see," Sally answered with a smile. "Now you're going to have to hop back in your bed. I have to dry my hair." Sally walked to the bathroom door then turned to Katie and said, "Okay." She turned and went into the bathroom. Katie looked up at Beau with her big almond eyes, "Does that mean we can stay?" "I thinks so." He answered, putting both arms around her. Katie gave Beau another big hug and held him close for a few precious moments then asked, "Would you tell me a bedtime story? Mom always tells me a story, but I know all of hers. Can you tell me one?"

Beau smiled, and picked her up, opened the bedroom doors to the balcony, and stepped outside. He sat down and put her on his knee and they both looked at the bright harvest moon. After a few moments of silence Katie looked up at Beau and asked, "Are you going to be my Dad?" Beau responded gently, "Would you like that?" Katie snuggled closer to Beau, and looked up searching for a father's love. "Would you? Would you really?" He kissed her on the forehead and gave her a warm hug. "You know, I've always wanted to have a little girl like you." Katie cuddled closer to her new Dad, then turned and looked at the harvest moon.

"Lets see, I believe you wanted a story?" Katie nodded and smiled. Beau began slowly, "Once upon a time in the land of Nod, which is a kingdom beyond the land of Oz. Do you remember the Wizard of Oz?" The little girl nodded with a smile of contentment.

"Well Nod is another kingdom just like Oz. However, Nod had a rich prince and everyone in Nod was happy. They had enough to eat, the crops were always plentiful and the weather was always just right. Only one thing marred their happiness. The young prince of Nod was ugly, had been scarred, and had a deformed leg. When he went out he scared the children and the women could not bare to look at him. One day when he was deep in the forest he saw a beautiful young maiden. Her name was Angelica. The ugly prince fell hopelessly in love with her. The prince, while in the village would take every opportunity to pass by Angelica, but she refused to look at him and ran away. One day the Prince followed Angelica into the woods. He had to tell her how much he loved her. This was going to be his last chance because Angelica and her father were moving away to another village. When Angelica knelt down to take a sip of water from a forest stream the prince quietly walked up behind her and said, 'Don't look up. Just look into the water. Now, as Angelica looked into the water she could only see the prince's reflection. In the reflection he was young and handsome. She was overtaken with love for the handsome prince's reflection in the water. The ugly prince asked, 'Do you believe that marriages are made in heaven?'

'Yes, I do,' Angelica answered, still looking into the water.

'I do too,' the ugly prince replied. 'You see in heaven when a young boy is born, God announces which girl he will marry. When I was born God showed me you. You had ugly scars and a deformed leg. I called out to God, Oh Lord, a scarred deformed bride would be a tragedy. Please, Lord, give me the scars, give me the deformed leg, let my bride be beautiful.' When Angelica turned away from the reflection in the pool she saw only a handsome prince. She reached out and gave him her hand and she became the Queen of Nod."

When Beau had finished his story Katie was fast asleep in his arms. He carried her into the bedroom and laid her gently on the bed then settled in beside her.

The whining hair dryer was turned off as Sally examined the results in the bathroom mirror. Satisfied, she returned to the bedroom to find Beau fast asleep with Katie tucked securely under his arm. She smiled wiped another small tear from her eye, and crawled into bed next to her family.

Chapter Eighteen
The Fetish Club

It was a sunny Friday afternoon. Beau and Sally had collected their case notes and headed for the Stake Out Bar and Grill. Murph had insisted that Sally try his Irish stew. She could not have the right of passage into the Charleston Police Force unless she'd eaten at least one bowl of his Irish stew.

Being an incurable romantic Murph had set up a private table with soft candlelight and a bottle of wine in a quiet corner of the bar. Murph gave Sally a big hug then folded the bar towel over his arm and elegantly escorted her to the table. After seating Sally he gently kissed her on the forehead and announced, "Your dining pleasure is about to commence." Sally started to comment when Murph put his finger over her lips and said softly, "Shhh." Sally smiled, looked at Beau as Murph scurried off. She slid her hands across the table and sighed contentedly. Beau took her hands in his and kissed them gently, then announced, "A toast." He lifted the bottle of wine and filled their glasses. "To what do we toast?" she asked. Beau touched her engagement ring, "You notice that your diamond is surrounded by blue sapphires." She nodded looking lovingly at Beau. "The sapphire is the stone of fidelity. So here's my toast. To my love, to my friend, to my pal, to my lover, to our family. I now promise to love and cherish you forever." Sally was moved by the sincerity in his voice. She knew he meant every word. They slowly sipped their wine.

"Don't believe a word of it," Murph growled as he brought a large piping hot bowl of Irish stew. "This guy has more malarkey in him than I do," Murph joked as he served the stew. The stew had a thick gravy with chunks of tender beef, large pieces of carrot, onions, celery, potatoes and all covered with a brown biscuit crust. It didn't take much to fill you up and put a warm feeling in your stomach.

"Where do you think you're going?" Sally questioned as Murph started to leave. "Oh no you don't! You're not gonna leave us with all this stuff." Sally served another bowl of stew and pointed to an empty chair at the table. Murph quipped, "You don't really think I eat this stuff? It's for the tourists." Sally continued to point at the empty chair. Murph smiled and sat down. Beau poured Murph a glass of wine. Murph held his glass up and toasted, "To the sweetest fuzz I've ever known, and this guy is damn lucky to find you." With that, they all took another sip of wine. "That's good wine," Sally commented. "Take a look," Murph said, and proudly handed the bottle to Sally. She scanned the label. "'Falconbriar Red,'" she said out loud looking at Beau. "Yep!" Murph interjected, "You are looking at an entrepreneur. Let's see, there are Ragin Kagin restaurants, Falconbrair Red wines, and Granny Smith's candies. You are going to become a pillar of the community." Sally looked amazingly at Beau who was actually blushing like some shy schoolboy. "I'm just the owner, it's my mom. She's the big boss. After dad died she wanted something to do and the rest is history."

"History, right." Murph interjected like some proud father. Sally looked at Murph, "Tell me about Beau's father. I can't get Beau to tell me." Murph beamed from ear to ear and with a big smile he started, "Now there was a man. Frenchy, we called him. He swept Beau's mom off her feet. In fact, you two remind me of how they were. I was a young stud, hot for action, always getting into trouble. Frenchy said, 'I better get you on the force before they arrest you'. So he put in a good word and here I am, an over the hill, fat, ex-cop, with a world full of wonderful memories." Murph put his arm around Beau, "When Frenchy passed on, I promised him I'd look after Beau. If I'd known how much of a problem he'd be I'd never have volunteered."

"Yes you would," Beau interjected giving Murph a nudge. Murph ruffled Beau's hair as he stood up. "You two have work to do, and so do I. Now, enjoy your lunch, do your work, go home and make babies." Murph smiled at the blushing couple, picked up his bowl of stew and walked away.

Sally leaned over and gently kissed Beau on the lips, "I like the idea of making babies."

"You're a brazen hussy, you know that?" Beau said jokingly, "and I wouldn't have it any other way."

"You'd have it any way you could get it," she smirked, clearing dishes away from her place then opening her briefcase. Beau put the rest of the dishes on the next table, then removed the case folder, thumbing quickly through the pages. "Okay, let's take a look at the inventory from Delongpre's apartment." Beau suggested. Sally quickly began to scan her copy of the inventory. "Is there something we've overlooked?" she asked. "Don't know. There's always something," he responded. Sally's attention was drawn to the contents of the killer's address book. Her eyes locked on to an entry, "Padre Joe". She couldn't take her finger from the entry "Padre Joe". "Was Delongpre a baseball fan or a religious nut?" she asked.

"Not to my knowledge." Beau answered, still looking down the list of items found in the killer's apartment. "Take a look at Item 152 on the list of names in his address book. The name "Padre Joe" sounds like a San Diego baseball player to me."

"Bingo!" Beau quickly retorted. "Father Joseph Marchello, St. Mary's, that's just down the street a few blocks."

"Are you sure?"

"I'm sure, Father Joe has been there forever."

"Okay," she answered, "we've got another loose end to check out." Sally underlined Item 152 with her pen.

The front door of the Stake Out Bar swung open. David Blackstone, the district attorney handling the Gray Lady Killer case, entered, followed by his entourage, Homer Canfield and Barbara Starkey. They walked hurriedly toward Beau and Sally. "There goes the neighborhood," Beau whispered.

"Good afternoon everyone," David announced, "Mind if we join you?" Not taking no for an answer they pulled up chairs in a circle around the small table.

"Isn't there a law against invasion of one's privacy?" Beau said sarcastically. No one paid any attention to the remark. "Look, you two can bill and coo later," Blackstone replied. "We are getting closer and closer to show time. I've got two hot shot lawyers here who are going on national TV and they argue like two beginning law students."

"Sounds like a personal problem," Beau retorted.

"I want this trial to be fair and resemble a presentation that might, in the slightest way, be considered intelligent."

"If we're smart we won't let it get to trial. The Judge rules him incompetent, we put him in the funny farm until this cools off and then we try him," Barbara interjected interrupting Blackstone.

"Oh that's smart!" Homer answered sarcastically. "So we just keep the National Guard hanging around for a year or two. No, the public wants closure. They want a trial and they want it now." The DA sat back in his chair, crossed his legs, shrugged his shoulders, then gestured at the two young lawyers as he spoke. "See what I mean? Now, as I see it, you haven't got a snowball's chance in hell of keeping him away from a trial. We've got a lot of forensic evidence as to proof of guilt. But, to keep it fair, we need some more data on the killer's state of mind. Frick and Frack, or whatever their names are, can only comment on what they know from testing."

"You mean Hopper and Crum," Barbara corrected.

Blackstone gave Barbara a cold stare, and continued, "There seems to be a big chunk of evidence missing that may substantiate the insanity plea."

"Like what?" Sally asked. The DA leaned forward, "Like we don't have a detailed interview from Norma Pierce." Barbara Starkey quickly interrupted, "If anyone would have information about the relationship between Agnes and the accused, she would. Why the tea? Why the flowers? Why the sex with a corpse?" The doctors can give us clinical reasons. But what are the underlying reasons? I need to know what pushed him over the line of sanity to insanity. Everyone remained silent. Barbara searched for a response, "Come on folks. I can't go to court with just statements of two doctors who think all killers are crazy and should be in a hospital. If I'm going to defend this guy I've got to have a history that connects to his state of mind."

"What do you want from us?" Beau questioned. The DA answered, "First, I want you to interview Norma Pierce again. Dig a little deeper. She's going to be called as a witness, but we need a deposition from her."

"Why us?" Sally asked, "We still have to get our report finished. You've got staff people to do that." Homer answered Sally's question. "Yeah, we've talked to her but she won't say anything without her lawyer. You guys she trusts. We need something to work with."

"Whose side are you on? Beau said, smiling at Barbara.

"I didn't say he didn't have a heart. A brain maybe," Barbara answered with a sly chuckle. The DA raised his voice slightly, "One other thing, we need to look at Dr Michael's notes on Delongpre. Think about it. If this guy they whacked, kept his body in a closet, then talked to it whenever they felt like it. He must have some damned interesting notes." Again, everyone sat silently. That was a big piece of evidence that had been totally overlooked. The DA pointed at Sally and Beau. "I want you two to go back to Seattle and see what you can dig up."

"Dig up is not a good choice of words when talking about a serial killer," Beau quipped. Everyone chuckled.

"Whose nickel?" Beau asked.

"Don't worry, I've got a budget that would choke a horse," Blackstone answered.

Satisfied with the outcome of his quest the DA stood up, pushed his chair under the table. Homer and Barbara followed suit, picking up their briefcases like Wall Street lawyers. Beau questioned the DA before he could leave, "Your nickel, right?" The DA nodded, "Yeah, my nickel."

"Good, would take care of this on your way out?" Beau handed David Blackstone the lunch check. The DA rolled his eyes and let out an angry grunt then snatched the check from Beau's outstretched hand and marched away with Homer and Barbara close behind. Barbara turned back to Beau and Sally and whispered with a grin, "I love it."

St. Mary's church was located between Meeting and King Streets, at 89 Hasell street. It was a large gray stone structure with a tall spire that rose above the Charleston skyline. It was established in 1839 and was the mother church of the Catholic diocese for the Carolinas and Georgia. It was a short walk from the Stake Out Bar to Hasell street. Two large oak doors addressed the front of the church. The arched slate roof towered above small gargoyles at each corner. The front of the church housed a stained glass rose window that mimicked Notre Dame. Four large stained glass windows depicting creation, the Virgin Mary, the crucifixion and the resurrection occupied each wall of the church. The inside of the church was dark, with light streaming in on the altar highlighting Christ on the cross. To the right of the altar were several rows of candles each flickering, giving some light to a prayer left by some unknown soul. It could be a prayer of need, or a prayer of forgiveness, no one really knew, or cared, Beau thought to himself.

Beau and Sally walked slowly down the main isle each looking at the serene beauty that the church radiated. Sally looked at Beau, "You are Catholic aren't you? I forgot to ask."

"Are you Irish?" he retorted lightly. "Did you ever meet a Frenchman who wasn't?"

"Come to think of it, not really," she answered with a warm smile.

"What do you think? Would you like to be married here?" he asked. She smiled at the idea and moved closer to Beau. "Yeah, that's fine with me. I've got to tell you I'm not a good catholic. I mean, I've had a child out of wedlock, remember?" "That won't matter," Beau said reassuringly. The two detectives sat in the pew next to the confessional. Beau had grown up in this church and knew that Father Joe would be taking confession this time of day. He pointed to the confessional and spoke, "See those crosses above the two doors?" Sally nodded. Beau continued, "Father Joe puts them up when the booth is occupied and takes them down when he's finished. He'll be out in a minute." He had no longer said those words when the doors opened. A young bashful girl darted off after giving Father Joe a kiss on the cheek.

"Father Joe," Beau called softly. The priest beamed at the sight of his old friend. He moved quickly toward Beau with both arms open and gave him a warm hug. Pushing Beau gently aside he stepped over to Sally. "And this is the beautiful lady I've been hearing so much about." Sally blushed slightly.

"Boy, the news travels fast around this town." Beau quipped.

"I hope you two have come to discuss wedding plans. This old church needs a wedding." Suddenly realizing an unanswered question, the priest put his hands over his mouth and looked momentarily at Sally then lowered his hands and asked, "You are Catholic aren't you?" She held her hands out to the padre, "Have you ever met an Irish girl who wasn't?"

"Saints be praised! We're gonna have a good old Irish Catholic wedding." The father was beaming with enthusiasm.

"Father Joe," Beau motioned for him to sit down. "That's not why we are here." The priest's smile was cut short. His expression changed to one of concern.

"We will be back to talk about a wedding. We want to be married here and we want you to perform the ceremony." Sally assured. Father Joe restored his ear to ear grin. "What can I do for you?" he asked.

Beau took out a photo of Gaylord Harcourt and handed it to the priest. "Have you ever seen this man before?" Father Joe studied the photo, then sadly shrugged his shoulders, "Yeah, I know him." Beau and Sally sat on each side of the saddened priest. Beau spoke softly, "You saw him in the papers. You know what he has done. Why didn't you come forward?" Father Joe fingered the photo before he answered, "Because I couldn't believe it."

"You mean you didn't want to believe it," Sally interjected.

"I only know him as Gordon Delongpre," Father Joe said, then continued, "I have never met a nicer, kinder, or gentler man in my life. I mean, if he were any nicer he'd be a saint."

"How do you mean?" Beau questioned.

"What ever the church needed, he did it. I mean all the dirty jobs. On top of that, he taught Sunday School, Bible classes. He had a way with kids that was uncanny. I mean, they loved him. He made meals for the homeless, raised money for the church. Whatever you needed, he did it."

"Father he's murdered five people and raped a young girl." Beau stated harshly.

"I know," the priest said sadly, "I still don't believe it. Even if I did, I couldn't tell you anything he might have said in confession."

"We know," Sally affirmed quietly, "But you can tell us about your relationship with him outside the confessional," The saddened priest nodded. Sally continued, "Molly Philburn, Amanda Hollingsworth, are those names familiar to you?" The priest put his hands over his eyes and mumbled, "Yes. They are members of our congregation."

"How about Henrietta Wentworth? Is she also a member of your congregation?"

"Yes." Father Joe mumbled.

"Did you know that he tried to kill her? Not once, but twice?"

"No, I didn't." the priest acknowledged sadly.

"How can you say you didn't know? It was in all the papers and on TV?" Beau asked, with an air of sternest in his voice. "Did you know that he was using your flock to select his next victim?" Beau stated firmly.

"Look!" The priest interrupted, "I'm sorry, I've been in Rome. I also don't believe everything I read in the papers and nothing I see on TV. All I know is, that he gave love, he could take the most down trodden wretch and make him feel good about himself. Now that is a gift that he gave these people."

"The scriptures tell us that evil has many faces and this man is pure evil. Believe me, I've been close to him," Sally said sternly, "He was like an evil serpent feeding on these people. Selecting a helpless member of the flock each day for his next meal."

"Father Joe," Beau said calmly, "I know how you must feel. You feel betrayed, hurt. You befriended the wrong man. Now, we need you to go down to the station and talk to a detective, Jack Bellamy. Give him whatever statement you can. Would you do that?" With his head lowered in sadness Father Joe murmured, "Yeah, sure."

Sally put her arm around the priest and spoke reassuringly, "Father, when we get this finished, and behind us, would you marry us? Right here in this beautiful church?" The priest lifted his head and struggled with a smile, "I'd love to. God bless both of you."

The drive to Norma Pierce's house was an easy one. The traffic was light, and it was a warm fall day. The green pine forest poked its green fingers up among the yellow, orange, red and brown leaves of ash, black walnut, and water willow trees. It was that time of the year where the color of the leaves herald the coming of winter. Corn stalks were tied, dried and stood like soldiers in the brown fields. The tobacco had been cut and sold, and the haystacks were trimmed neatly in the fields. The countryside was quiet waiting for the winter cold to set in. Norma Pierce was dressed in faded Levis, with a long sleeve shirt, and a gardener's apron tied neatly around her waist. Wearing leather gloves and carrying a pruning shear she was patiently tending to her roses.

Norma put her hand above her eyes to focus on Beau and Sally stepping out of the car. Sally waved to Norma as they made their way up the garden path. Norma stopped her pruning, took off her gloves, and slowly walked down the garden path to meet the detectives. Sally held out her hand as she greeted Norma, "Sorry we have to bother you again."

"You should have called first. I could have saved you a trip. I'm not saying anything without my lawyer," was Norma's firm answer.

"I can understand how you feel," Sally answered in an understanding tone.

"We were just in the area and thought you might clear up a few points for us," Beau said, showing Norma a pleasant smile.

"Help you with what?"

"Last time we talked I know you felt sorry for little

David Delongpre. Isn't that true?" Beau asked. Norma nodded, "Yeah, that child suffered for years. My sister and I had an argument over the little boy and we never talked after that." There was a small garden bench sitting to one side of the garden pathway. Sally motioned for Norma to sit down. "We're trying to help little David and we were hoping your knowledge of what went on would help him during the trial. You tried to help before, now he needs your help more than ever."

"What do you want from me?" Norma asked with a sigh. Sally opened her handbag and took out a small tape recorder. "We just want to put together the facts as you know them about little David. We want to get them on tape that's all."

"Okay," Norma answered, resigned to her fate. Sally laid the recorder on the bench next to Norma and pressed the record button. "This is the 20th of October 1999. Please state your name." Sally pointed at Norma.

"Norma Pierce."

"Are you aware you are being taped?" Sally pointed at Norma again.

"Yes."

"Do you agree to this tape being used in the on-going investigation? She nodded at Norma

"Yes."

"The investigating agents present at this recording are Agent Thornton, FBI, and Lieutenant Gasteneau, Charleston Police." Sally sat back and nodded at Beau to start.

"Let's start from the beginning. What can you tell us about Agnes Gladlow and her relationship with the Delongpres?"

"She was sick. They both were sick."

"What do you mean, both?" Sally inquired.

"Her and that beast she called a husband. They were perverts, both of them."

"How?" Beau asked quickly.

"He'd let her have sex with other men so he could watch. Hell, she could have sex with anyone or anything just so he could watch." Norma said angrily.

"How do you know all this?" Sally asked, trying to be as tactful as she could. Norma became nervous. She was afraid she'd gotten herself in too deep. She was being recorded and self incrimination was fast becoming an issue in her mind.

"Norma?" Sally said reassuringly, "We're not here to pass judgment on anyone. We just need to know the whole story in order to help that little boy who was abused by the Gladlows. Please." Norma sighed, her shoulders slumped in resignation. "I want your promise that anything I say about my part in all this will not be used against me."

"We can't make that promise," Sally said looking worriedly at Beau then at Norma. "If there is anything that doesn't pertain directly to the case we will erase it." Norma was satisfied with Sally's statement. "I have your word, right?" Both detectives nodded before Norma went on. "I know because I was there. At least for the most part. Now, before you say anything or pass judgment, let me explain. Agnes was my older sister. I worshipped her. However, she was sexually active long before I was." Norma hesitated, "We had sex together when we were growing up. We both dated in high school. Then after the date we would have sex in bed with each other. She would pretend to be my boyfriend, then I'd pretend to be her boyfriend." Norma looked at the stoic detectives answering the next obvious question. "Yes, we had oral sex, and lesbian sex together, but we weren't dikes. Agnes just loved sex, and I'd do anything she asked."

"How long did this last?" Sally asked showing no emotion.

"All through our teen age life and beyond. It even kept going after Agnes was married. They even invited me on their honeymoon, and we became a threesome."

"So you had sex with Agnes's husband," Beau reaffirmed.

"Oh yeah, he loved the idea. We played sex games. I was their sex slave. He had plenty of money and I was treated well. I could have anything I wanted."

"So what happened?" Sally questioned glancing at the tape recorder to see if it was still recording.

"I met and fell in love with my husband, and I told them that the whole thing had to come to an end."

"How did they react?" Beau asked.

"They didn't like it, but they accepted it. In fact, Agnes asked if I wanted her to sleep with my husband? She said, she'd be my sex slave if I'd be hers. I said no. It was time to go our separate ways. I wanted kids, a home, white picket fence, brownies, PTA, you know, the whole nine yards."

"So what happened then?" Sally demanded softly.

"That's when Leah Delongpre came on the scene. The Gladlows had a habit of picking up whores and going through the sex slave fantasy. They found out that Leah had kids and a bad drug habit."

"What do you mean kids?" Beau responded quickly.

"Yeah, David had an older sister. I don't remember her name. Oh yeah, Alice was her name. As I recall she was about 13 at the time."

"So what happened?" Sally asked gravely knowing that the story was only going to get worse.

"The Gladlows made a deal with the mother. She moved in as a housekeeper, and gave herself and her kids as sex slaves to the Gladlows. Can you imagine, she did this just to feed her drug habit."

"Go on," Sally uttered.

"Henry Gladlow, the Stud Beast, Agnes used to call him, took the girl and made her his personal sex slave. Agnes did the same with little David. Henry tried to get the little girl hooked on drugs but she out smarted him. She pretended to take pills then threw them away when he wasn't looking or forced herself to throw up in the bathroom."

"How do you know all this?" Beau questioned, looking sadly at Sally.

"One night, no, it was the girls night out before my wedding. Agnes threw me a party, or so I thought. I showed up at the house. No one was there. Henry took me upstairs to the bedroom and demanded sex one more time before I got married. When I went in he had Alice tied to the bed naked. She was out cold. He had slipped her one of those date rape drugs. He forced me to have oral sex with her while he had anal sex with me. I tried to resist but I couldn't. After it was all over he took me to Agnes's room where she had little David walking around on the floor with a dog collar on. His backside was red with blood. I know he'd been whipped. Henry held my arms back while Agnes forced David to have oral sex with me."

"Why didn't you report this?" Sally questioned angrily.

"Because my sister and her husband had a video tape of the whole episode. In fact, they had tapes of us together for the past two years. Henry threatened to show it to my new husband if I did. I told Agnes that I never wanted to see her again. Soon after I moved away and I never spoke or wrote to her again."

"So what happened to Alice Delongpre?" Sally questioned sadly.

"I don't know. I heard, I don't remember how I heard, but there was a rumor that she ran away when she was 16. She probably ended up like her mother on the streets doing the only thing she knew how to do, sell her body."

"What about Leah Delongpre?" Beau asked taking a long breath.

"She overdosed. They found her in some cheap motel on one of the county roads. If you want to know what I think. I think the Gladlows dumped her there after they'd finished with her."

"Do you have any idea at all what happened to Alice Delongpre? I mean did little David ever see her again?" Norma rubbed her forehead thinking back. There was something that stuck in the back of her mind that kept trying to get out. What was it? She stammered searching for the right words. A sly smirk came across Norma's face before she spoke, "After all that, I was made executor of her estate. There wasn't much left after probate but a box full of personal letters. The house on Park Lane is still being contested in the courts. I think I saw some letters written to David from Alice. Agnes hid them from him. She kept them in a box."

"Do you have them?" Beau said inquiringly.

"Let's go see." Norma answered.

The basement was a damp dark cinder block room with one incandescent bulb with a pull chain that swung back and forth in the drafty cellar casting moving shadows across the room. Norma pointed to four boxes sitting on a top shelf. Beau lifted each one carefully and set them down on the floor. Norma sorted quickly through the faded papers and old family photos. She suddenly halted her quest and held up a packet of four letters tied with a blue ribbon. Sally quickly held them under the cellar light and read the return address. "Alice Delongpre, 2443 Queen Anne Way, Seattle Washington. The two detective looked at each other and smiled.

"Another piece of the puzzle," Beau quipped. Sally comforted Norma and assured her that they would cut any self incriminating statements from the tape before they gave it to the DA.

On the return trip to the city Sally picked up the cell phone, waved it in the air then looked at Beau. Keeping one eye on the road he asked, "What?"

"Shall we give the DA the news or should we leave him hanging?" Sally commented with a sly smile. Beau returned her smile, "Decisions, decisions. We could wait until we got back. But, what the hell, he did pay for lunch,' he quipped. Sally nodded and dialed the number.

The secretary, in a slightly snobbish tone, answered, "District Attorney's Office."

"District Attorney David Blackstone please," Sally responded in her official sounding voice.

"I'm sorry he's not available. He's in conference."

"Young lady, I suggest you get him out of that conference if he wants some important information concerning the Gray Lady Killer case."

"Whom may I say is calling?"

"Tell him agent Thornton, FBI," was Sally's curt reply. It was only a matter of 3 seconds before Blackstone's voice asked, "What have you got?"

"I want to thank you for picking up our lunch tab."

"Okay, okay, consider it a wedding present. It ain't gonna happen again."

"David, David," Sally said condescendingly, "I thought you're suppose to work with the FBI?" Beau and Sally were holding back a laugh.

"Yeah, you've been brainwashed by that over-sexed, and over the hill flat foot. Pardon the pun," Blackstone stated rhetorically.

"Is it true what they say about you?" Sally asked holding the cell phone away from her ear so Beau could hear his answer.

"What?" Blackstone responded.

"That the only time you come out from behind your desk is to overreact?" There was a momentary silence on the phone. Sally could picture the tight jaws and red face replacing the DA's normally smug expression.

"Okay, so who lit the fuse on your Tampon?"

"Wow, that's a low blow." she responded.

"Well you know more about low blows than I do," the DA said smugly.

"Okay, here it is. The defendant had a sister who we believe was also sexually abused as a kid."

"Where?..." Sally cut Blackstone off before he could complete his question. "Last known address was 2443 Queen Ann Way Seattle. And yes, we'll check it out when we get to Seattle. By the way, we have the interview with Norma Pierce on tape. However, we will edit it before we give it to you."

"No you won't!" Blackstone demanded. Sally held the phone closer to Beau's ear as an irate DA began to rant, rave, and expel a few choice swear words. Beau took the phone from Sally to listen to a thoroughly pissed off DA.

"Blackstone!" he commanded, "Practice safe sex. Go screw yourself." He punched off the connection and handed the phone back to Sally.

Beau and Sally caught the red eye flight out of Charleston with a connecting flight to Seattle from O'Hare International. American Airlines Flight 714 nonstop from O'Hare to Sea Tac airport leveled off at 31,000 feet. It was now 2am Charleston time. Sally had a small flight blanket up under her chin and snuggled close to Beau resting her head on his shoulder. Beau looked out of the window. There was a full moon that reflected a milky glow down on the high stratus clouds. It was like being in another world, cut off from all the madness and pressure that we endure in our struggle through life. He remembered reading about pilots getting this same feeling of detachment. It was comforting and at the same time just a little bit frightening.

He looked down at Sally sleeping quietly on his shoulder. She was so beautiful, he thought to himself. What was so nice about her was that she had no idea of how beautiful she really was. Beau wondered if everything happens for a reason. It was as if God had some master plan for him. He had lost his son only to find a little girl who loved him. It was almost like love at first sight when he met Katie. Along with Katie came Sally, the only woman that could fill the void in his life. The one who could make him feel like a whole man again, not just a man going through the motions of living. He took satisfaction in knowing that finally all the dreams he had for a family were going to come true. He knew that some higher power had sent Sally and Katie into his life. He thought that Harry might be looking down and saying, "See, I told you so."

Beau kissed Sally lovingly on the forehead. She moved her head slightly then opened her eyes and smiled, "I liked that. But you're going to have to wait until I can get you in bed," she said with a sexy tone in her voice.

"Once a hussy, always a hussy," he whispered. Sally closed her eyes again and smiled, then snuggled a little closer. Beau thought for a moment before he asked her a question that had been sitting in the back of his mind. "Am I coming on too strong?"

Sally looked up. "How do you mean?"

"I mean, telling you how I feel. You don't think it's a line do you?"

"Well," she realigned her answer in her mind before she spoke, "Well, if was sex you were after, you've already had that. So you weren't just out to jump my bones. Then there was Katie. I've seen you with her. You love her as much as you love me." Sally paused, then pulled his arm a little closer to her. "Don't ever stop telling me how much you love me. I need that. Katie needs that too." Beau kissed Sally on the forehead then out of the blue announced, "I want to adopt Katie after we're married. I want her to have our name."

Sally opened both eyes and looked up at Beau. "You know something? I think she'd love that."

American Airlines flight 714 touched down at Seattle Airport at 6:40am. The eastern horizon was showing the light of the coming new day. At this time of the morning Sea Tac Airport was relatively quiet. There was the hustle of ramp activity as ground crews serviced the aircraft for the early departures.

Beau and Sally emerged from the passenger tunnel only to spot police Lieutenant Clarence Darrow smiling at them. "Welcome back you two," he said warmly. Everyone shook hands before Clarence asked, "Do you have baggage checked?"

"No, just one carry on," Sally said, as she pulled up the handle on her tow-bag and walked quickly toward the street exit. "By the way," Clarence announced, "Congratulations, you two."

"Did the DNA check out on your cases?" Beau questioned.

"Oh yeah. You've got our guy. I think it's going to close a few files for us. No, I mean congratulations on you two, you know, getting hitched." He said smiling at Sally. "Let me see the ring."

"Can't anyone keep a secret anymore?" Beau commented humorously. Sally smiled and displayed the big diamond ring.

"Wow!" Clarence remarked jokingly, "You sure this guy is not on the take? I could never afford a ring like that." Looking at Beau, Clarence scratched his head, "Are you rich or something?"

"No, I took out a second mortgage on my pad," Beau said, winking at Sally.

The electronic terminal doors swung open and the cold, damp Seattle air hit Sally and Beau in the face. "Oh, that feels good," she remarked. Lt. Darrow led them to the waiting police car. After depositing their luggage in the trunk, Clarence maneuvered the car cautiously into the Seattle traffic. Glancing at the two detectives in the back seat, he said, "Okay, we're on our way to 2443 Queen Anne Way."

The Lieutenant knew his way around Seattle. He avoided the downtown traffic, passed the famous Space Needle, and up into the Queen Anne Hill district. Making a left turn onto Queen Anne Way he slowed the car to a crawl as they checked the house numbers. Slowly bringing the car to a stop the detectives stared across the street to a public parking garage with bold numbers indicating 2443 Queen Anne Way. Sally sat back in her seat with a disappointing expression. "Well, nobody said it would be easy." Clarence pulled the police car into the lot in front of the parking attendant. "Yes sir?" The attendant asked with a concerned tone in his voice. Rolling down the window, Lt. Darrow questioned, "Didn't there use to be an apartment house here?"

"Oh yeah, it was a dump. The city tore it down about 2 years ago and put in the lot," the attendant replied. Clarence nodded, "Thanks," then backed the car out and drove quickly down the street. "Never fear, Clarence is here," Lt. Darrow exclaimed. He picked up the car radio and barked his command, "Tac Ops, this is unit 677."

"Unit 677 Tac Ops, go," was a quick scratchy reply from the radio operator at police headquarters.

"I want you to run a DMV check for me on an Alice Delongpre, 2443 Queen Anne Way. Check about 2 to 4 years ago," Clarence thought for a moment, "In fact, give any and all names answering to Alice Delongpre regardless of the address."

"That's a roger 677." The Lieutenant quickly maneuvered the patrol car through Seattle traffic as he headed back to precinct headquarters. Clarence looked back at the two detectives, "Well, when is the big day?"

"What do you mean?" Beau said casually.

"The wedding. Do I get an invite?" Clarence asked glancing at Sally, then at Beau. Sally chuckled at the frustrated expression on Beau's face. "Doesn't anyone have any privacy around here?" he asked with an abrupt sigh.

"Hey, what can I say? You guys are famous. You're all over the news and TV. You know, how you two captured the killer and falling in love at the same time." Sally chuckled again at Beau as he rolled his eyes in frustration.

"Clarence," Sally said with a smirk, "He just wanted to get in my knickers and this was the only way he could do it." Clarence turned onto the expressway then glanced back at Beau and remarked, "That's kind of a high price to pay. Was it worth it?" Beau looked at Sally who still had a small grin on her face.

"You know what they say," Beau answered, "I've always wanted to marry a police officer nympho maniac whose father owns a liquor store." He paused, "Two out of three isn't bad." Clarence laughed as Sally gave Beau a playful punch.

"You guys have got to invite me to the wedding," Clarence said emphatically.

The kidding patter was interrupted by the scratchy voice on the radio, "Unit 677, this is Tac Ops."

"Tac Ops, go." Clarence adjusted the volume so everyone could hear. "We've got a make on your subject. We have an Alice Delongpre with a new license issued about 3 years ago. She has Farmer's Insurance on a GS500 Lexus. Address 1624 McGraw St. Apartment 22A."

"That's a roger," the detective answered, pulling the car off at the next exit. "Did you copy that?" Clarence asked. Sally penned the address into her notebook.

"We're only six blocks away from that address," the detective said turning onto a short east to west cross street. 1624 McGraw was a middle class, slightly run down, stucco, 4 story apartment complex with Manager displayed on apartment 1A. Clarence rapped on the manager's door. A balding, overweight, middle aged man appeared at the door. He reeked of garlic, and his T-shirt was stained with tomato sauce. He let out a grotesque burp as he said, Yeah?" Clarence displayed his badge. The manager didn't seem the least bit impressed. He looked like a candidate for a beer commercial. "Do you have an Alice Delongpre living in apartment 22A?" Clarence asked in a polite but official tone.

"Why?" The manager replied lazily. Apparently Clarence had a short fuse. He had dealt with this kind before. He probably had a criminal record someplace downtown. The detective stepped closer to the man, getting in his face. "I am going to ask you one more time. Do you have a lady named Delongpre living in 22A?" The manager backed off. Clarence was good at subtle intimidation. The manager nervously answered, "No." The detective inched closer to the manager's face showing a cold stare. The manager backed up and answered nervously, "Ah, she moved. She was a nice kid. Too nice if you ask me."

"How do you mean?" Sally questioned.

"Anyone stacked like that," the manager made a sexy motion with his hand. "However, she was a straight arrow. As far as I know she went to school at night, worked during the day. She paid her rent on time, I'll say that."

"That must have disappointed you," Sally said sternly knowing that the manager would have loved to take the rent out in bed. The manager looked nervously at Sally before continuing. "The only thing I can tell you is that she went to work for a big fancy dancy law firm downtown."

"Do you know the name of the law firm?" Beau inquired.

"'Na," the manager nodded, "Wait a minute, she gave me her card." The manager walked to a cluttered desk in a messy living room and rummaged through the drawers. "Yeah, here it is." He returned to the door and handed it to Clarence. The card read, "Sidney, Wolfe and Dunlap, Attorneys at Law." Clarence's expression turned to one of surprise.

"What?" Sally questioned looking at Clarence curiosly.

"These guys are big bucks guys," he said, turning the card over, looking for a notation on the back.

"How big?" Beau asked.

"I know they just collected from a big oil company for an oil spill that happened a few years back. These guys are connected. I mean they get Governors elected, people appointed in the right places. How big, I don't know. But I'd say big with a capital B." The manager interrupted, "Are you finished with me? My dinner is getting cold."

"Okay." Clarence said, satisfied with this new bit of information. The manager started to close the door when he stopped. "Oh, I almost forgot. I heard she got married not long ago to some big shot." The manager closed the door.

The law firm of Sidney, Wolfe, and Dunlap was located in the ARCO building in downtown Seattle. The building had 35 floors and was a monument to glass and steel construction. Lt. Darrow knew you just didn't walk into this law firm without being announced. Seattle's District Attorney had taken the time to call ahead and make an appointment with the senior partner William H. Sidney.

The elevator rose silently to the penthouse office suites on the 35th floor. The doors rolled open and the three detectives were confronted by a middle aged well groomed secretary. "May I help you?" She inquired politely.

"Yeah, Lt. Darrow, Seattle Police, Agent Thornton, FBI, and Lt. Gasteneau, Charleston Police. We have an appointment with Mr. Sidney." The secretary looked at her calendar then pressed the intercom key, "Sir, we have some police officers here to speak to you."

"Yes, Miss Hornsby, show them in," was the scratchy reply. The secretary opened a large oak door revealing William H. Sidney's office. A large bay window spanned one wall of the office. From this vantage point you could see almost across Puget Sound. William Sidney rose from behind his ornate, desk and shook hands with the officers, "Please, call me Bill," he said, in a warm personal manner. He immediately set everyone at ease. "Can we get you some coffee?" he asked politely. The detectives all politely declined. Beau noticed that Bill couldn't take his eyes off of Sally. "Now, what can I do for you?" he said seating himself behind his desk.

"Sir," Sally started her question when Sidney stopped her. "Please, Bill. And you are?" he asked turning his complete attention to Sally. "I am Agent Thornton, FBI," she replied.

"I'm impressed young lady. The FBI is recruiting beauty as well as brains. I've been reading about your part in the defendant's apprehension."

"Can we stop with the bullshit and get to the issues?" Beau interrupted harshly. Sidney turned his attention to Beau. He quickly realized that Beau was a hard nosed cop and charm wasn't always in his make up.

297

"I'm sorry, you're right," Bill said, sitting back in his expensive leather chair.

"I take it you've read that the Gray Lady Killer case is about to go to trial in Charleston." Sally asked looking for a reaction from Sidney. She had an intuitive sense about most people, but this guy was a blank.

"Yes, only what I've read in the papers," Bill said leaning forward resting both elbows on his desk. "What does that have to do with this law firm?" Sidney's eyes searched the detectives for some clue as to why they were here.

"Do you, or have you ever, had an Alice Delongpre working here, or associated with this firm in any way?" Beau questioned pointedly. Sally read Bill's changing expression immediately. She was sure he knew her.

"Well, Lt. We have over 1500 employees. It's possible we may have had an employee by that name. I don't know. If this person happens to be a client, you know I couldn't provide you with any information without her permission." Bill said defensively.

"Mr. Sidney," Sally replied in a reassuring voice, "this person, who by the way, has a social security number and a tax form showing that she is, or was, employed here has not been involved in any way in criminal activity. We believe she may have information as to the background of the defendant." Clarence and Beau remained expressionless. Sally was lying through her teeth. There hadn't been time to research tax records much less Social Security numbers. She was bluffing. Sally gave Sidney an innocent smile before continuing. "If we could have just a moment of her time we could put all this behind us and we'd be out of your hair."

Sidney rubbed his forehead as he rocked in his chair. "You know that we must protect the privacy of both our clients and our employees."

"Mr. Sidney," Beau interrupted politely, "If we could talk to her, maybe get a deposition, we wouldn't have to call her as a material witness. You know the publicity she would get in the press if she was called." Bill Sidney nodded, picked up his phone, and dialed. On the other end of the line a voice announced, "Judge Schooling's office." Lt. Darrow raised an eyebrow looking at Beau and Sally. Bill Sidney spoke, "Mary, Bill Sidney, I need to talk to Jacob."

"Just a minute." A low click and Judge Schooling said, "Hi Bill are we on for golf this Saturday?"

"I hope so. Jacob, I have some detectives in my office and they say that Alice may have some information concerning their ongoing investigation." There was a silence on the other end of the line. "What sort of an investigation?" Schooling inquired. "It's pretty big. I think they ought to explain it to you," again silence.

"How's Alice involved?" the Judge asked. "From what I understand she isn't, but she does have knowledge relevant to their investigation."

"Okay. We'll do lunch, as they say in Hollywood." the Judge answered with an empty jest. "I'll meet them at Dalley's Crab House on Market Street. Let's say in about 2 hours. If that's okay with the other party. I'll be at my regular table." Sidney nodded to the detectives before he spoke, "Sounds good to me. If you need anything just pick up the phone." Bill said calmly.

"Thanks Bill," the Judge replied, then a quick click ended the connection.

Dalley's Crab House was in the middle of the famous Seattle fish market along the waterfront. The restaurant was known throughout the state for crab cakes, and stuffed crab, along with the finest salmon steak you ever wrapped your lips around. The fish market buzzed with activity as brightly decorated fish stalls displayed their catch of the day. Mounds of halibut, grouper, salmon, and brown shrimp were piled on stacks of crushed ice. Buyers from restaurants and hotels quickly made their selections. The fish mongers dressed in smelly bloodstained aprons tossed the selections to the packer who caught them in mid air with all the expertise of a professional football player.

Dalley's Crab House was a small, unobtrusive restaurant tucked in the middle of all the market's activity. As usual, the house was packed with its regular customers who had made Dalley's a tradition in their daily routines.

The detectives entered the dining room with Lt. Darrow leading the way. In the corner, next to a bay window was a large booth with one well dressed, distinguish looking gentleman. As Lt. Darrow approached, Judge Jacob Schooling rose and shook hands with the detectives while introductions were made. He motioned for them to sit down.

"I took the liberty of ordering a pitcher of beer." The Judge began to pour beer for everyone. "Now, what can I do for you?" he asked, filling the last glass.

"We're not sure. Mr. Sidney didn't elaborate about your association with Miss Alice Delongpre," Sally said, ignoring the large schooner of beer sitting in front of her. The Judge smiled, "Bill's like that. He's a cautious man." The Judge took a sip of cold beer then wiped some of the condensation off the glass with his finger. "Before I answer that, I want to know what you need from her?"

Beau interrupted, "Have you been following the Gray Lady Killer Case? It's been in all the papers, and on TV. Because of some foolish misunderstanding it has resulted in race riots as well as a series of brutal murders and rapes. The case has received more attention than the O.J. Simpson case."

"So, what's that got to do with Alice?" the Judge asked politely.

"She's the killer's sister." Sally answered bluntly. The Judge froze, but displayed no emotion. Lt. Darrow broke the short silence. "Your Honor, you know what's involved here. These officers need a statement from her as to the relationship with her brother, that's all." The Judge gave a cold stare at the detectives before he spoke. "Alice Delongpre happens to be Mrs. Schooling, and I assure you I will take all the legal means available to keep her out of this mess."

"We're sorry sir, but Judge or no Judge, you know the court could compel her to testify," Beau said sternly.

"Lt. Don't try to impress me. I've forgotten more law than you'll ever know. I could legally delay that demand until her testimony would be moot," the Judge replied, returning Beau's cold stare.

"Your Honor," Sally stated calmly, "Did you know she was sexually abused until age 16. Then she ran away, lived on the streets, and who knows what else she's had to do to stay alive?"

"We all have our crosses to bare officer," the Judge said concentrating on Sally. "I think she did all right. She went to school, got an education, a good job and she is the most kind, loving person I know. That's why I married her. I will not let you drag her through the embarrassment of a trial."

Lt. Darrow took a sip of beer before entering the conversation, "Look, no one wants to embarrass anyone. I think the FBI and the Charleston police would be satisfied with a deposition." Darrow looked at Beau and Sally.

"Why don't we let Alice decide for herself," the Judge said, looking at a well dressed, distinguished looking lady entering the restaurant then walking smoothly toward the Judge's booth. Alice slipped into the booth next to her husband and gave him a kiss on the cheek.

Alice Delongpre was completely different from what Sally had pictured. She was a handsome, well groomed, sophisticated, professional looking lady in her early forties, and about 20 years younger than her husband. She also noticed that Alice was deeply in love with her husband. This wasn't some gold digging sugar daddy relationship. Sally could sense that she really loved her husband.

There was a quiet moment while Alice waited to be introduced to her husband's lunch guests. The Judge held her hand tightly under the table. She sensed something was wrong. Her happy demeanor slowly changed to one of concern. The Judge spoke politely, conveying that this was just a normal occurrence. Alice knew otherwise. "Sweetheart, I want you to meet Lt. Darrow, Seattle Police, Agent Thornton FBI, and Lt. Gasteneau, Charleston Police." Alice Delongpre's face turned ashen white. She looked at her husband worriedly and saw a blank stare. Sally, trying to be as comforting as she could, said, "We'd like to talk to you about your brother." Alice held her emotions in check as she looked at her husband. She could read no emotion in his face at all. Alice returned her gaze to the detectives, "What brother?" She asked nervously.

"David or Gordon Delongpre, whatever his given name." Sally answered.

"What makes you think I have a brother just because we have the same name?" Alice asked defiantly. Beau interjected, "Please, Mrs. Schooling, we've spent a lot of time and leather running this down. You can save us a lot of time if we can get what we came for."

"I have no idea what you want or who you think I am." Alice insisted. Sally opened her handbag and laid the packet of letters tied in a blue ribbon on the table, turned them around so she could see the handwriting and address. She sat back in the booth. All of the denial was immediately drained from her demeanor. Alice looked at her husband sorrowfully. The tears began to well up in her eyes. "I'm sorry Sweetheart," She said looking at Jacob. "I love you so much. I wanted you so badly," Alice hesitated, grasping for the right words. "I thought if I told you, you wouldn't want me." Jacob embraced his young wife as she began to sob. The Judge looked sternly at the detectives, "So what is it you came for?"

"May I call you Alice?" Sally asked softly, handing Alice her handkerchief. Alice nodded. "Look, we're not here to dig up dirt on anyone. Anything that is not directly impacting the case we could care less about. We need to find out what went on at the Gladlows and if you had any contact with him while he was in Seattle? If anyone can tell us what his state of mind was then, you can."

Alice looked at Jacob, he nodded, then kissed her on the cheek. "Okay," Alice said, handing the handkerchief back to Sally. "Do you mind if we make a recording during the interview?" Beau questioned.

"No!" Alice clamored, "In this place, with all these people?" looking at Jacob for help.

Beau interrupted quickly, "This is the safest place I can think of. No will hear us or pay any attention to us. Any question you do not feel comfortable answering you don't have to. It's a quiet conversation over lunch. This won't be one of those police interrogations you've probably read about. No yelling, screaming, just a quiet talk and a glass of beer." Beau took a sip of his beer with a smile.

"I'll tell you what we'll do," the Judge said, like a banker ready to make a deal. "We'll let you make the recording provided we keep the tape. Then we'll edit and transcribe the tape and submit it to the court. Otherwise, no deal." The detectives looked at each other. The Judge added, "I want your promise that the court will not call her to appear as a material witness."

"We don't have that authority," Beau replied.

"I'm sure you don't," the Judge answered. "Here's what we'll do. We will do the tape. We'll edit it and give it to our attorneys. If you'll get a written commitment from the court, and our attorney's agree, we will release the transcript. Otherwise, gentlemen, our business is concluded." The detectives reluctantly agreed.

"One other thing." Jacob added, pointing directly at Lt. Darrow, "This tape will not be used in any litigation pending in the state of Washington without our lawyers approval." Lt. Darrow shrugged, "I guess so."

"I'll have my people contact the DA to iron out the same deal." Jacob added, then looked at Alice.

Sally inserted a new tape into the machine and made the standard memo for record introduction. Beau looked at Alice then questioned, "Tell us your version of what went on when you were living with the Gladlows."

"How much do you know?" Alice asked.

"We've talked to Norma Pierce," Sally said, searching Alice's face for a reaction. Alice smirked before she spoke, "There was a weak soul whose heart was in the right place."

"How do you mean?" Sally answered quickly.

"I was forced to have sex on a daily basis from 13 to 16 years of age. Norma was kind enough to get me on the pill before anything happened. She showed me how to take the pill and how to keep myself clean."

"How do you mean, keep yourself clean?" Lt. Darrow interrupted slightly embarrassed having asked the question.

"At age 13 I had sex with whoever Henry Gladlow wanted me to. You name it, I was forced to do it." Alice gripped Jacob's hand tighter. She looked at him sadly before continuing. "I had oral sex, anal sex, I was whipped, had sex with Norma and Agness at the same time. I was raped repeatedly for a whole week in a mountain cabin by some of Henry's fishing buddies. That's why I had to keep myself clean. Do you want to hear anymore?" Alice asked, with anger in her voice. "I was forced to have sex with my own brother, and he'd been beaten into submission."

"Tell me about David? Is that his real name?" Beau asked calmly.

"Yes," Alice closed her eyes recalling all the horrors she had managed to shut out of her mind over the years. "David,.. somehow David managed to cope." Alice looked at the detectives who were engrossed in her story. "Little David was more impressionable than I was. He was so used to role playing in those sex games that he began to take on those specific personalities."

"How do you mean?" Sally questioned quickly.

"David became the sex object. Totally submissive to whatever sexual demands were made on him. He would call himself Gordon when he tried to

302

rationalize what he was doing, when he knew it was wrong. Then, as he was rewarded by the Gladlows for sexual performance he called himself Gaylord, and Gaylord enjoyed what he was doing. He bragged about it constantly. You see, that was the only way he could cope." Everyone remained silent as they digested what they'd just heard. Beau rubbed his forehead before asking, "Is David a multiple personality, or is he just acting?"

Alice sat quietly thinking about Beau's question.

"I don't really know. He's so used to acting, and playing out roles, he would actually believe in those roles. Then again, he was taught at a very young age that by using his wit he could get what he wanted."

"What made you finally get out of this situation?" Sally inquired. Alice covered her eyes and sat silently before she answered, "The Beast," she said with hatred in her answer.

"You mean Henry Gladlow." Beau said.

"No, Henry forced me to have sex with a dog."

"A what?" Sally answered in disbelief.

"He got a friend's Great Dane and forced him on me. I was so degraded. I thought whatever was out on the streets, even death was better than what I had. So I left. I really think God was looking out for me. I picked Seattle because it was about as far away from Charleston as I could get. I had saved enough for bus fare. Got here, got into a halfway house. I had to lie to get in. Then Sister Margret became my friend. She turned my life around and here I am, married to the most wonderful man in the world," Alice kissed Jacob on the cheek and looked at him tenderly.

"What happened when David came to Seattle?" Sally inquired.

"He tried to contact me. Finally, we had dinner a few times but he had changed."

"How?" Beau asked knowing that they were getting to the end of the story.

"He was hard, manipulative. He knew how to use people. He was into drugs and sex. He tried to get me involved and I told him no. He had this thing going with the stripper and her daughter."

"Daughter?" Sally questioned, surprised by another fact that Carla failed to reveal when she was questioned.

"Yeah, I think Tina was her name."

"Gentlemen," the Judge interrupted, "I think my wife has covered the whole story. I don't think there is anything else she can add that would be of help." Sally turned off the tape recorder and the Judge held out his hand for the tape. As promised, Sally handed the tape to the Judge.

"Off the record." Lt. Darrow asked as he stood up. "Did you know, or did your brother ever mention, a Dr. Michael J. Smith? He was a psychiatrist, I believe."

Alice looked up at Clarence as she thought back, "Yes, I believe he did mention that name once or twice. In fact, he told me that he was the only other person he could confide in."

"Did they meet socially?"

"Yes, I think David or Gaylord turned him on to sex and drugs."

Sally and Beau slid carefully out of the booth then Sally shook Alice's hand. "I know this wasn't easy." Then turning to look at the Judge, she commented, "You have a wonderful wife, treasure her." The detectives walked away. Jacob and Alice held each other warmly and watched the detectives make their way through the crowded cafe.

Sarah Smith had been married to Dr. Michael J. Smith for 13 years before the Gaylord personality came on the scene. She lived in an upper class posh suburban neighborhood of north Seattle. Sarah had filed a missing person report on her husband some two years ago. Lt. Darrow had been the investigating officer and had several meetings with her during his investigation. Lt. Darrow knocked on the front door of the sprawling two story Tudor home. When the door was opened the trio met a trim, neatly dressed woman in her early forties. She had a tight black mini-skirt and a body you could kill for. As soon as the men moved their gaze up her body they couldn't help but notice that she had a low cut blouse revealing a cleavage that rivaled the Grand Canyon. Sally immediately noticed that Sarah was overly nervous. There was something lying beneath the surface in Sarah Smith's actions that was bothering her. She had the feeling that Sarah needed a Father Confessor to get this burden, whatever it was, out in the open.

Lt. Darrow made the introductions and Sarah led the detectives into a comfortable family room lit by a warm fire in the fireplace.

"I am very sorry to hear about your husband," Lt. Darrow said in a kind, gentle voice.

"Thank you," Sarah replied, "At least now I can have some closure. Lt?" Sarah asked, looking at the detectives, "I'd like to bury my husband next to his family here in Seattle if that can be arranged." Beau answered assuringly, "Yes Maam, Dr. Michael's remains will be released as soon as possible. I'll take care of it." Sarah looked at Beau with renewed interest. Sally interrupted, "Do you have your husband's papers concerning his patient, Gaylord Harcourt?"

"Yes, I had my lawyers go through them. They're over there." Sarah pointed at several folders laying at one end of the coffee table. "I can probably tell you more about Mr. Harcourt, or Delongpre, or what ever name he chose, than those papers over there."

"How do you mean?" Sally queried.

"Mike, I mean Dr. Michaels was totally taken in by Gaylord. So was I for that matter."

"Go on." Beau commanded politely.

"Mike broke every rule in the book with Gaylord. You do not, and I mean, do not socialize with your patients. But Gaylord had this magnetism about him. He was sort of like Charles Manson. He was the guru of sex and hedonism. He offered the both of us a life style that we've only read about. He took us into the world of fantasy sex, drugs, fetishes, and alcohol." Sarah wasn't like Alice Delongpre, sorry for her actions. Mrs. Smith seemed to be able to accept that lifestyle. What she needed was to get it off her chest and get on with life. This is what she was trying to convey to the detectives.

"I take it that you went to those sex parties that Gaylord and Carla gave." Sally inquired.

"Yeah, we went. I take it you've talked to Carla. By the way, none of this will be used against me in a court of law will it?" Sarah said without emotion. The detectives nodded leading her on. Sarah began to unload her burden on the detectives. "We had a free sex type of thing going on. There was Carla, Tina and an occasional whore, with Mike and myself. You name it, we did it. After we got high on drugs we'd be taken to the dungeon, stripped, bound by our wrists and ankles, or put in some leather harness, then raped by whoever, Gaylord invited over."

"What did your husband think of that?" Sally asked with an air of disgust in her voice.

"He loved it. He liked to watch. He liked me to watch him fuck Tina." Sarah noticed the expression on Sally's face. "I'm sorry if this is embarrassing to you, but everyone there were consenting adults. The only illegal thing were the drugs."

"Did you know that Tina was only 13?" Beau demanded sternly. Sarah slumped back in her chair sadly. "No, I didn't. She never told me. She didn't look 13 either. She had a body... Well you know what I mean."

"Did you take drugs?" Lt. Darrow asked.

"Not really. Maybe that drug Ecstasy, but I would have nothing to do with the hard stuff. Now, Tina, was a whole different story. Gaylord did a number on her. He had her so doped up she didn't know if she was coming or going. That way, she'd fuck every man in the place before the night was over."

"How many men would be at these parties?" Beau questioned with a harshness in his voice.

"About 15 to 20. One night Tina took on the whole defensive line of some football team. After a while I knew that this wasn't going anywhere. Mike was going to break it off. He was about to recommend another psychiatrist to Gaylord when he disappeared. All this time I thought Mike had just taken off with Gaylord to go on some sort of a sex spree. Gaylord could be very convincing. Maybe he talked him into starting another sex cult someplace. Anyway, that's what I thought." Everyone remained silent. Sarah searched the detective's faces for some sort of reaction. "Hey, it isn't pretty. At that point in my life I would have done anything to hold on to my husband. It took me a while to wake up, and I won't apologize for it. Now, all of Gaylord's clinical records are in those folders, and I hope they help."

The detectives stood up and thanked Sarah for her honesty and bluntness then left. Lt. Darrow remarked as they moved into the Seattle evening traffic. "Wow, can you imagine having something like that in bed on a regular basis?" Sally smirked, "You couldn't handle it. You'd probably have a heart attack."

"Yeah, but what a way to go," Clarence answered, followed by a chuckle. "Okay folks, we can catch Carla at the club before it opens if we hustle."

The Peppermint Elephant Strip Club was alive with behind the scenes preparation for tonight's show. Starting at 6pm it was nonstop stripping until midnight. There were 12 strippers each putting on a 30 minute show. Each stripper had her own theme. Everything from dancing with a dildo to a homosexual duet between two hard bodied beauties. At the other end of the club was a mud wrestling arena that sponsored a full fight card.

The detectives were led backstage to the women's dressing room. The dancers were in several stages of nudity yet no one was in the least bit concerned that there were men in the dressing room. Carla sat topless in front of the mirror applying the final touches to her make up. Gazing into the mirror Carla remarked, "To what do I owe this honor?" Then turned and faced the detectives. Lt. Darrow and Beau immediately locked their gaze onto Carla's breasts. They were perfect, erect, with a piercing ring in each nipple. It was obvious that Carla was proud of her body and was eager to show it whenever she could. Standing close to Beau, Sally secretly pinched his butt to get him back to reality. "Miss Dawn," Beau said, clearing his throat, "We would like to talk to you a little more about your relationship with Gaylord Harcourt or David Delongpre."

"I don't know about David, but Gaylord was my man and still the best lover I ever had."

"Do you have many lovers?" Lt. Darrow asked with a sly grin, knowing that it had no bearing on their investigation.

"Right now, I'm kinda off men." Carla replied moving her eyes to Sally. Sally pulled up an empty chair, sat down and asked, "Would you tell us more about the sex and drugs that went on at your house?" Carla became defensive, "I don't know anything about drugs. The sex, hell, we were all consenting adults. We didn't go out on the streets or anything like that. We just had parties where you could let yourself go, that's all."

"Carla," Beau interrupted, "We know Gaylord sold drugs. We have a statement from someone who was there."

"You can have statement from the Pope for all I care. I had nothing to do with what Gaylord did." Carla scowled defensively.

"Look, Miss Dawn," Beau said, trying to calm the situation, "We really don't care about the drugs. We're hear to find out more about Gaylord and his relationship with you." Carla didn't respond to Beau's quiet request.

"Do you know he murdered Dr. Michaels?" Sally asked. "We could hold you as a material witness. Now, you could hire a lawyer, it would be expensive, and of course it would make all the papers. I haven't even mentioned child endangerment. So, if you want all this to come down on you, cut the crap. Believe me, we can make it happen." Sally sat quietly hoping she'd pressed the right buttons. Carla's defiant attitude quickly changed. She slumped back in her chair and lowered her head before she answered, "What do you want to know?"

"Tell us what went on at those sex parties you mentioned." Beau demanded calmly.

"It was called the 'Fetish Club'. We had a select group, an inner circle so to speak. Gaylord took a lease on a hunting lodge about an hours drive from here. The girls would, for a very big fee, play the love slave bit. You know, the leather straps, mouth bits, hands tied, and sex. The big money came on being whipped, or on the rack." The whole place was one big dungeon, and of course very private rooms." Clarence and Beau sat stone faced, Sally on the other hand, leaned closer to Carla with a new expression on her face, "Tell me about Tina?"

"Who told you about her?" Carla said defensively.

"Don't worry about that, just tell us about your daughter." Carla put her hands over her eyes momentarily before answering. "I suppose you've heard some things but the truth is, I tried to keep her away from all this. She was 13 when Gaylord got to her. She fell madly in love with him. He lavished attention on her. Then being the rat he was, took her one night to a church, gave her a ring, and in a very convincing manner, spoke wedding vows to her and made her believe that they were married. He promised to make it legal as soon as she turned 18. That was the night she lost her virginity. He also convinced her that she was to do whatever he demanded. So, at age 13, she became the star of the Fetish Club. She was whipped, gang raped, had sex with other women."

"Why didn't you do something?" Sally interrupted glaringly.

"Why? Because he had me too. I loved him, and I wanted him as much as Tina." Carla snapped back.

"Go ahead," Sally said, leaning a little closer to Carla.

"Tina and I were the stars of the Fetish Club. We were on the web site. We had people, I mean sick people, from all over coming to the club. I remember we had one demand, I mean a sick demand for Tina to have sex with some animals."

"Bestiality you mean?" Lt. Darrow asked astounded.

"Yes. Tina was bound in a harness and ravaged by a stud horse." Carla paused catching her emotions. Gaylord got $10,000 for that gig. Tina got $1,000. That did it for me. That was too much. I confronted Gaylord, and ended up in the hospital. Gaylord took off when the police came looking for him. Then Tina blamed me. Can you imagine? Here I go and get the shit beaten out of me, all for her, and she's pissed at me."

"So, what happened to Tina?" Lt. Darrow asked.

"She took off. I haven't heard from her since."

"Did you file a missing persons report?" Clarence questioned.

"No, to hell with it." Carla answered defiantly, "I don't care if I see any of them again."

"What about Tina's father?" Sally asked shaking her head in disbelief.

"Hell, who knows? Probably a one night stand gone wrong. I don't know," Carla answered defensively.

"Carla," Beau said sternly, "You're not telling the truth. Now, come on, level with us." Carla shrugged her shoulders in resignation. "All right, so I was young, in love, and I met a sailor. You don't need to know his name. We were together for about two weeks. We were going to get married as soon as he finished his last sea duty. I went down to the pier. Watched him put to sea. He blew me a kiss and I never saw him again. I called the Navy, they checked their records. He was discharged in Norfolk, Virginia six months later. His forwarding address was a post office box that had been vacated. I didn't know that the kiss he blew me was a kiss off not a goodbye." Carla paused choking back the tears that she'd shed a hundred times since that day. Carla straightened up and looked at Sally. "So, I thought to myself, if men can use me, I'll use them. That's when I realized I had a body, men wanted sex, and nothing else. I came to work here and have done all right by myself. Gaylord was the only one who knew how I felt. I guess he's the only other man I've had any kind of feeling for. As far as I am concerned they are all animals."

Everyone sat quietly. Carla turned back to the looking glass and continued to apply her makeup. Sally reflected on Carla's story knowing that it was similar to hers. The only difference was that she chose a different course. She remembered, when she was young and foolish, that she thought about becoming prostitute after her affair. However, if she did that it would mean that the bastards of this world would have won, and she was not about to let that happen. She knew that she'd made the right choice.

On the red eye flight back to Charleston the passengers for the most part, had turned out their lights, and pulled their blankets under their chins to grab a few winks before landing. Beau and Sally's lights burned brightly as they poured over Dr. Michael's files. Turning over the last page Sally remarked, "Do you have any idea how many lives this guy has ruined?" Beau glanced up from his reading, "Yeah, it's sad. You know what else is sad?" Sally nodded as Beau pointed at his file. "Take a look at the last few entries from his notes." Beau handed the papers to Sally before continuing, "His final conclusion was that Delongpre wasn't a true multiple, rather a very good actor who could turn it on when he wanted to." She quickly scanned the notes then handed them back to him. "I guess we're back to square one," She commented folding up her papers then turning out her light. "We're not back to square one, but Starkey is going to have a problem in court with the insanity plea." Beau put the papers into his briefcase, spread a small blanket over Sally, then turned out his light. Sally cuddled close to Beau and whispered into his ear, "I love you so much. I am going to make sure that you never want to look at another woman again."

"Hey, haven't I told you how I feel?"

"I saw how you looked at Carla," she answered coyly.

"Well, she had a great set of tits. Men notice things like that," he said defensively.

Sally pulled Beau towards her then kissed him passionately, opening her mouth to receive his tongue. In the dark, beneath the blanket, Sally put her hand on his manhood only to find it erect and excited. She looked up and said, "See what I mean." Beau took a deep breath looking around to see if anyone was watching trying to contain his excitement. Looking down at Sally, he smiled and remarked, "All that sex talk has really turned you on."

Sally closed her eyes, nestled her head on his shoulder and said, "Let's go home, get married, and have lots of kids. And do you know something else?" She continued before Beau could answer, "I'm going to turn you on like you've never been turned on before." The lovers slept the rest of the way home.

Chapter Nineteen

Competency

With a three hour layover in Chicago, the redeye flight from Seattle touched down at Charleston International Airport at 2:30 in the morning. It was too late to drive to the farm. Beau and Sally decided that the best alternative would be to stay at Beau's Charleston apartment. They had an early morning call at the office and they needed the extra time to complete their report for the D.A.

Sally had moved from her hotel to Beau's apartment more than six weeks ago. She had also taken the time to tidy up the bachelor's pad transforming it from a contemporary pig sty to a home away from home. Beau enjoyed every minute of Sally's redecorating, although he protested from time to time. Beau opened the apartment door and turned on the lights. Sally pulled her bag into the bedroom and kicked off her shoes. She looked at Beau and smiled, "How long did it take you to get me in this bed?" she asked.

"Too long." he jested, then kissed her on the forehead before untying his tie. Sally felt comfortable in the apartment, but she felt at home when they were at Falconbriar. She could hardly wait until the weekend when they could get back to the farm. She missed Katie, her mom, and the warmth that Beau's mother showed her. To Sally it was like having two mothers. She felt as though after all these years she was finally home. It was as if all this, the love, the coming together of these two families was preordained. Sally hung up her coat in the hall closet and announced, "I'm going to take a shower. You need to use the john?" Beau sat on the edge of the bed scratching the bottom of an itching foot, "No, you go ahead."

It was a large bathroom for a city apartment. One wall above the wash basin was fully mirrored. Sally turned on the shower and let it run full hot. She stripped down, folded her clothes neatly and placed them over an empty towel rack. She admired her naked body in the mirror. Sally had the perfect body even though she always thought of herself as skinny. She had strong athletic shoulders, a small waist, hardened and tight thighs evenly placed above beautifully sculptured legs. Her breasts stood high and erect as she turned from side to side examining herself from every angle. Satisfied by the image she saw in the looking glass, she stepped into the steaming shower and slid the door closed. The warm soothing water ran lightly over her head and down her body as she began to soap herself. She closed her eyes and leaned her forehead against the cold tiled wall. Her thoughts wandered back to the statements made by Carla about the Fetish Club. She knew that all women have some sexual fantasies and she was no different. The interview had definitely turned her on. She wondered what it must have been like to have taken part in those sexual encounters. To let all her inhibitions go, to experience every sexual desire that had ever crossed her mind. Unconsciously, Sally lowered her hands to her breasts and began to manipulate her nipples. She envisioned how Carla had been a sex slave for hire. Being tied spread eagle to a bed, unable to move, and then ravaged by several men. Sally lowered her hands to her flat stomach and rubbed gently before inserting her fingers inside herself. She moaned with pleasure opening her legs wider then increasing the in and out motion with her hand. She was nearing a self induced climax when she realized what she was doing, and turned on the cold water. "What am I doing?" she asked herself. "I've got a loving man out there, and I can have sex whenever I want. Why am I so caught up in all these fantasies?" Still excited, Sally turned off the water and stepped out of the shower and began to dry herself in front of the steamy mirror. She knew that Beau was in the next room waiting for her and she was sure as hell in the mood. "Tonight I am going to totally let my self go," she said, looking at the misty image in the looking glass. "I won't be embarrassed. I'll tell him how I want it and I'll give him anything he wants. I will not hold back."

Sally searched her handbag for her hand cuffs then wiped a clear spot on the mirror to examine herself one more time. Twirling the handcuffs around her finger she stepped totally naked into the bedroom. To her surprise, the lights were out, and Beau was fast asleep. She could only see a snoring lump beneath the covers. She frowned with disappointment, put the cuffs on the night stand, then smiled lovingly, and sat on the edge of the bed admiring her sleeping lover.

She touched his hand gently and whispered, "Do you have any idea how much I love you?" A snoring grunt and a slight movement from a sleeping Beau was the only answer she got. "You have no idea what I've gone through to finally find someone who is willing to live life on his own terms, not like some of those political pimps at the bureau who would screw their own mother to get promoted." She sat quietly looking at her lover. "You know, I wonder sometimes, I mean I'm not a religious person, I know what it is to lose something you love. But I really think that maybe God, in some way, may have given you Katie, and given Katie what she's prayed for, for so long, a father. And maybe, just maybe, given me what I've wanted, a man I could love."

Sally tucked Beau's hand under the covers and said jokingly, "What has a girl got to do to get laid in this town?" She stood up, moved to the other side of the bed and slipped her naked body under the covers, and cuddled next to Beau, "Are you going to be pissed when you find out what you just missed," she said softly.

The Charleston Ledger had been running front page feature stories about the Gray Lady Killer case for the past four weeks. The indictment before the Grand Jury went as expected. The Ledger outlined the indictment in great detail. The article read that the defendant David Delongpre, AKA Gaylord Harcourt, AKA Gordon Delongpre on July 1998 murdered Amanda Hollingsworth and Molly Philburn. The defendant on that same, night while resisting arrest, did assault and kill detective sergeant Harry Mackland of the Charleston Police Department. The defendant on the night of 17 August 1998 did kidnap and assault with the attempted rape of Ms. Sally Thornton, a Federal Agent assigned to the case. On that same night the defendant brutally murdered officer Henry J. Farley a member of the Charleston Police Force and Mr. Joseph Mac Ginney, a security guard who attempted to rescue Agent Thornton. At 1:30am on August 18th the defendant, while avoiding capture, did assault and rape a 17 year old nurse's aide named Judy Hampton at the Charleston Memorial Hospital. As expected the prosecution asked for murder in the first degree.

The defense asked for a change of venue which was denied. The defense then pled not guilty by reason of insanity. Judge Buckner set the date for the competency hearing and remanded the defendant to the state mental hospital for psychiatric examination and evaluation.

Courtroom 3A was a small room located on the third floor of the Charleston Court House. Normally, this courtroom was not used for a trial of this magnitude, however this was going to be a competency hearing only, and Buckner didn't want a media circus parading through the Court House halls. It was going to be hell when the trial started and he wasn't about to start this circus any earlier than he had to. No cameras or media personnel were allowed other than sketch artists and one reporter from each major news service. A court recorded tape of the proceedings would be provided to the media at large. There was no jury. The competency hearing required only a ruling from the bench after all testimony and arguments were presented.

The courtroom was packed when the manacled killer was seated next to Barbara Starkey. Sally and Beau took their seats next to David Blackstone, the DA. Looking down the row of seats they could see Dr. Thomas Crum, and Dr. John Hopper, the consulting psychiatrists. On the other side of the oak rail Homer Canfield sat ready to present his arguments for the State. Sally nudged Beau, then nodded toward the other side of the small courtroom. Alice Delongpre and Judge Schooling surprisingly were in attendance. Beau whispered into Sally's ear. "Homer talked them into sitting in. He wants her opinion on whether he's faking or has really lost his cookies."

Sally focused her attention on the killer. He was quiet, sullen, with his hands and feet securely chained to restrict his movement. She felt strangely sad with her sympathy directed at the defendant. How ironic she thought. I feel sorry for the man who tried to kill me. Delongpre placed his forehead on the edge of the table and gazed at his chained ankles. Her attention was interrupted when the court Bailiff announced, "All rise, the 12th Circuit Court of the State of South Carolina is now in session. The Honorable Horace Buckner presiding." The courtroom stood in silence as Buckner paraded sternly to the bench and seated himself. "Please be seated," he ordered, and the audience quickly complied.

Delongpre assumed his previous position with his forehead on the edge of the table looking at his shoes. Judge Buckner noted the defendant's lack on interest. He directed his statement to the defense, "Counselor, if you think the defendant's antics will in any way influence the decision of this court you are gravely mistaken."

"Your Honor," Barbara stood at her desk, "If it please the court? The defendant is currently on medication. He can hear the proceedings in this position, and this position keeps him calm. I would not want him to embarrass himself or this court. One other thing your honor," Starkey commented taking a Baby Ruth bite size candy bar from her briefcase then handing it to the defendant. The David Delongpre personality sat up smiled, unwrapped the candy bar, and savored it before returning a big smile to the judge. With the court's permission, I would like to provide my client with this candy from time to time. This also helps calm him."

"All right. I will allow it."

The judge held the courtroom in silence while he examined his notes. He removed his glasses and gazed at the audience. "Now, before we start these proceedings, and because there is substantial public interest in this case, for the record, I want to make the Court's position perfectly clear." He paused momentarily putting his hand under his chin. "Under Title 17 Criminal Procedures for the State of South Carolina, one must be competent to stand trial, plead guilty, or make a valid confession. If one is not competent a guardian may be appointed to manage his affairs and treatment may be administered involuntarily. Now, when we look at the law, pertaining to legal competencies we see a common structure consisting of several elements. First, the inquiry is always directed toward functional abilities which refers to mental tasks or beliefs. For example, an individual must be able to assist his or her attorney in preparing for and litigating the case, as well as having some capacity to understand the trial process and charges. Second, legal competency constructs require causal inferences to explain the individual's abilities or deficits. What I mean by this is that the functional deficiency must be a result of a mental disorder or developmental disability. Third, the Court is required to examine the interactive capacities in the defendant's particular situation." Buckner took a quick sip of water then folded his hands before continuing. "So, Counselors, let's boil this down to simple language. The legal test of competency has two facets, whether the defendant is able to assist the attorney in his or her defense and whether the person understands the nature of the charges and the trial process. We are here today only to determine competence. I hope I've made myself clear." Buckner eyed the defendant momentarily with his forehead now on the edge of the table gazing at the floor. He then turned his attention to the prosecution. "You may call your first witness."

Homer stood up and announced, "The State calls Dr. Thomas Crum." Crum was conveniently seated on the aisle. He made his way to the witness stand were he was quickly sworn in and seated comfortably. Homer scanned his notes before beginning.

"Your Honor, if it please the court, I would like to present Dr. Crum's credentials, and, for the record, I call him as an expert witness." Homer handed the credentials to the Bailiff. Before Homer could begin his presentation the Judge stated, "The Court will also accept Dr. Hopper's credentials and recognizes both gentlemen as expert witnesses." The Judge looked at Barbara who responded, "The defense has no objections to the learned doctor's qualifications."

"You may proceed Counselor," Buckner said, looking at the prosecuting attorney. Homer moved casually toward the witness as he spoke, "Dr. Crum, how long have you observed the defendant?"

"Approximately six weeks." Homer nodded affirming Dr. Crum's answer. "How many personal interviews have you had with the defendant?"

"Approximately 13."

"You said approximately. What do you mean by approximately?

"I mean I've had several conversations with the defendant outside of a clinical evaluation format."

"You mean you just passed the time of day."

"Yes."

Homer paced slowly in front of the witness before asking his next question. "Did his conversations with you seem rational?" Dr. Crum nodded affirmatively while saying, "Yes."

"All in all, how many interviews did you have?" Homer asked stopping to face the witness.

"Twenty."

"So, in twenty interviews would you say you got to know the defendant pretty well?"

Dr. Crum looked at the defendant who did not acknowledge his presence but continued to look at the floor.

"Yes." The Doctor answered with a sad tone in his voice.

"Dr. Crum, for the record. What would you say is the mental state of the defendant?" Homer questioned, leading the witness to reveal what he had read in the psychiatrist's report. Dr. Crum referred to a small note pad before answering. "Overall, he is suffering from a Multiple Personality Disorder. We call it MPD."

"MPD." Homer mused, looking casually at the defendant then turning his attention back to the witness.

"Please explain to the Court what MPD really is."

"MPD is when two or more distinct personalities, which coexist or alternate in the same individual, each more, or less dissociated from the other. MPD is a form of schizophrenia. This disorder is characterized by distorted thoughts and perceptions, atypical communication, inappropriate emotion, abnormal motor behavior, and social withdrawal."

Homer barked another quick question at the Doctor. "Does the defendant display all these characteristics?

"Yes, with the exception of social withdrawal." Crum replied.

"How do you account for the defendant maintaining his social contacts?" Homer inquired.

"The trauma suffered as a child and his personality makeup demand it."

"What do you mean?" Homer asked leading the witness toward his final point.

"In order to obtain his next victim he must maintain his social activity." Crum answered realizing the direction the prosecutor was headed.

"In profiling isn't this behavior called 'trolling'?" Homer questioned, looking at Buckner as though he already knew the answer.

"Yes."

"So,' Homer curtly said, "from these observations we can say that the defendant is capable of some rather sophisticated reasoning in order to get closer to his next victim?" Crum nodded, "obviously, that was our conclusion."

Homer faced the witness again. "How many personalities did you observe in the defendant?"

"Four. I was able to observe four distinct personalities.

"What can you tell us about these personalities?" Homer questioned.

"Gaylord Harcourt as he called himself appeared to be the dominant personality, Gordon Delongpre was the second, a more stable personality, and David Delongpre was apparently a 12 to 14 year old child." A low murmur moved through the courtroom audience.

"Dr. Crum, did the defendant undergo a physical examination upon entering the mental hospital?"

The witness flipped to a new page in his note pad. "Yes, the physical examination upon admission revealed a well developed white male, with several superficial scars on his face, two missing teeth, a cracked rib, a scar on his left knee, otherwise all other findings were within normal limits." Dr. Crum again turned to another page in his notes.

"The laboratory findings were within normal limits including a nonreactive VDRL."

"Excuse me Doctor." Homer interrupted, "What is a VDRL test?" The Doctor smiled, "That is a test for syphilis. Given the nature of the crimes we thought that this test was warranted." Both the Judge and Homer nodded, slightly embarrassed by the question. Dr. Crum continued his report to the Court. "The skull x-ray revealed a little irregularity at the outer side of the left antral sinus, and this might possibly be the result of an injury suffered as a child. Otherwise, the bony structure was normal. The chest x-ray was normal, and the electroencephalogram was normal."

"So we can conclude that there are no physical abnormalities affecting the defendant." Homer walked back to his table picked up another piece of paper. "Doctor, what other mental tests did you and Dr. Hopper perform on the defendant?"

"Our psychological testing on Gaylord revealed a full-scale IQ of 98, which places the defendant in the average intellectual functional level."

"Excuse me?" Homer interrupted, "You said Gaylord. Are you saying you tested each of the personalities?"

"We tested all the personalities but one. Gordon tested in the 98 scale and the David altar tested at the normal level for a 12 to 14 years old adolescent." The Doctor looked up from his notes. Homer moved closer to the witness stand, "So, you are telling us that three out of the four supposed personalities are normal?"

"Yes."

"Can the Court safely assume that these alter egos you refer to are competent enough to stand trial?"

"Objection!" Barbara declared raising her voice then standing by her table. "The learned doctor is not the Judge here your Honor. Only you can rule on what the Court may, or may not think about legal competency."

"Sustained," Buckner replied. Looking at Homer he responded, "Counselor, rephrase your question." Homer nodded before rephrasing his question.

"Doctor, can the defendant understand what is being said in this courtroom? Can he understand the nature of the charges against him?" The

Doctor remained silent momentarily then answered, "Yes." Homer went back to his table and said, "I have no further questions for this witness."

Buckner looked at Barbara Starkey and announced, "You may cross examine." The defense counsel stood and glanced at her notes then approached the witness stand. "Other than the syphilis test," Barbara said sarcastically, pausing so the Court could enjoy the irony of such a test, "and the standard IQ tests, what other test did you and Doctor Hopper perform?" Dr. Crum re-examined his notes. "The Competency Assessment Instrument, we refer to this as the CAI test. This test allows us to assess competency by looking at several different functions focusing on the defendant's ability to testify relevantly. We don't just rely on one test."

"Did you give any other tests?" Starkey queried.

"We also administered The Interdisciplinary Fitness Interview."

Barbara quickly interrupted, "Don't give me a hint. That test you call the IFI." The audience laughed. Buckner glared at the Defense Counsel.

"Yes, we call it the IFI," Crum said grudgingly. "Like the first test, we examine the defendant's ability with respect to legal items, capacity to appreciate the nature of the alleged crimes, and to disclose pertinent facts, events and motives to counsel. The examination also covers items such as 'Psycho-pathological issues like delusional mechanisms, disturbances of memory, and amnesia."

Barbara glanced at the Judge before asking her next question. "Am I correct in saying that these tests are given primarily to determine competency?"

"Yes," Dr. Crum answered, then quickly continued, "Finally, we administer the Competency Screening Test or CST." Dr. Crum smiled, and waited for the counselor to make light of his last statement. "Now this test consists of 22 sentence stems which the defendant is required to complete. Let me give you an example. A sentence might read, 'When I go to court the lawyer will...', or we might say, 'When a man is innocent until proven guilty, I...' Then we grade his answer."

"How did the defendant score?" Barbara asked inquiringly. "A score of 19 and below statistically indicates that he's incompetent or needs more in-depth evaluation.

"What was the defendant's score?"

"The defendant scored 29." Crum answered bluntly.

"Which means?" Defense Counsel asked quickly.

"Which means he's competent," Dr. Crum answered with an air of smugness in his voice. Barbara Starkey turned away from the witness stand and faced the courtroom audience before asking her next question. "Who did you administer this test to?"

"What do you mean?" The Doctor asked cautiously.

"I mean, you gave IQ tests to three different personalities. Who did you give this test to? To Gaylord or Gordon? Maybe you only gave it to David, the little boy, personality?"

"We gave the test to Gaylord, Gordon, and David and the test only varied a few points. All within the legal test of competency," was Dr. Crum's defensive answer.

"I would hope so. You were giving it to the same person. Isn't it possible Gaylord gave the correct answers to the other personalities?" Barbara began pressing the Doctor. "Isn't it possible that the three tests have little relevance to competency when you are giving it to the same man who may or may not be telling the truth, or under the influence of the dominant personality?"

"It's possible, but not likely." Dr. Crum said looking beyond Barbara at Dr. Hopper. Turning quickly and walking back to the witness stand she asked sternly, "How do you know for sure who was taking the exam?

"Counselor," Dr. Crum answered leveling his voice before he continued, "Each personality is integrated with its own personality patterns. It has it's own pattern of perceiving, relating to, and thinking about his environment and self. We can quickly discern from the answers who we are talking to. Even if he's lying." The Doctor sat back smugly.

"Okay," Starkey acknowledged, "How about the other altar as you call it, the Beastie?" The Doctor looked at the Judge with a blank stare, then directed his attention to the question. "Ah, we have no way of approaching the Beastie personality."

"How do you know it exists?" she questioned.

"We've observed the personality."

"And what have you observed?" Starkey quickly asked, moving closer to the witness, waiting for his answer.

"We observed grunts, groans, erratic posture, salivation, and other abnormal behavior."

"So," Barbara stepped back, and looked squarely at Judge Buckner. "So, if you couldn't communicate with this personality, how in hell am I going to talk to it during a trial?" The courtroom broke out in restrained laughter. Buckner rapped his gavel once, and the court room fell silent waiting for the Doctor's reply.

"Counselor, please refrain from using expletives in the court no matter how appropriate," Buckner ordered with a sly smile.

"Yes Your Honor," Barbara answered, having made her point.

Dr. Crum straightened his tie before answering. "To answer your question Counselor, the Beastie is a minor personality, and he, or it, only surfaces when the defendant is under severe stress."

The Defense Counsel paced in front of the witness as she spoke, "So, I cannot know for sure, if the stress of a trial might induce the defendant to call up the Beastie, who can only grunt, and salivate. How do I put him on the stand? How do you swear him in?" Before the Doctor could supply the answer, Starkey continued, "I have no further questions for this witness."

"Redirect Your Honor," Homer interrupted, raising his hand like some student in class. Buckner nodded, "Your witness." Dr. Crum resumed his position on the witness stand. Homer approached the witness before asking his question. "Dr. Crum, isn't it true that some of your colleagues believe that this so called MPD doesn't exist?" That it cannot even be considered as a mental disorder?"

"Yes, but"... Homer cut him off firing out another quick question. "Dr. Crum isn't it true that in 1930 dissociation ceased to be a subject for legitimate scientific investigation and was clinically demoted to the role of an obscure phenomenon?" The Doctor acknowledged Homer's statement with a nod and a soft, "Yes."

"Sorry doctor, I didn't hear that." Homer said, putting one hand behind his ear leaning toward the doctor.

"Yes," Crum repeated in a louder tone, obviously uncomfortable with this line of questioning.

"Isn't it true Doctor that some of your learned colleagues believe that this MPD behavior is nothing more than good acting?"

"Yes," Crum answered with his face twitching slightly.

"Isn't it true that you've seen or read about bazaar cases that challenge credibility? That may, or may not, have been acted out? Let me give you an example. How about the woman who tries to tear her clothes off with her right hand while making an effort to keep them on with her left? It doesn't take a Freud to figure out she's identifying herself with a man raping a woman and a woman being attacked. And for all practical aspects this woman was normal, able to ask questions, and aware of her environment."

"Yes, this is a classic case."

"Do you think the defendant is any more inhibited than this woman?"

"No I don't."

"No further questions Your Honor." Homer returned to his seat. Buckner looked at the Defense Counsel before speaking. "I think we've more than adequately covered the testimony as to the mental abilities of the defendant. I have the report from the consulting psychiatrists. Do you feel the need to call any additional witnesses?" Both counsels remained silent.

"All right, I will entertain closing arguments." Buckner nodded at Homer to begin. Homer rose and stood at the corner of his table, "Your Honor, statistically, relatively few patients with genuine MPD demonstrate this phenomenon in an overt manner. These medical statistics indicate that over 1% of the U.S. population has this disfunction in some form or another, and yet they live effective and productive lives. Additionally, the testimony has indicated that this MPD could possibly be nothing more than accomplished acting. The test results indicate that the defendant is mentally capable to stand trial, and we feel he should be prosecuted to the fullest extent of the law."

A hush fell over the courtroom as Homer sat down. Judge Buckner looked at Barbara. She stood, looked down at her notes before beginning her summation. "Your Honor, lets face it. MPD does exist. The Federal Court for the most part, recognizes it as a disorder that may, and has in the past, resulted in criminal behavior. How can, or should the criminal law deal with the multiple personality? Should the defendant suffering from MPD be deemed competent to stand trial, or be able to assert the insanity defense, or diminished capacity? Not only in the legal profession but the medical profession recognizes MPD as a bona fide condition although it's quite uncommon. Granted, there are those who would feign MPD in order to achieve a goal within the criminal justice system. I agree, it's not always easy to determine the fakers or malingerers because sometimes the doctor initially diagnosing the condition may be the one who has encouraged the person to have one or more personalities. We only know what the doctors tell us. If we accept the defendant as a rational yet suffering from this disorder, then we have to approach the legal aspects of this case and ask ourselves these questions. Can the law give recognition to more than one personality per human body? In order to have due process can the law regard each personality as though each were a different person? Should each personality of the defendant be afforded separate legal representation? I've observed the defendant and I know he has at least two separate personalities diametrically opposed to each other. This creates a conflicting legal situation." Barbara Starkey faced the Judge as she continued her summation, "Let me pose this question to the Court. If separate legal counsel can represent estates and corporations, why shouldn't separate legal counsel represent a personality whose internal coherence and competence has been established? Let me put it this way, one personality may wish to plead insanity, a second may wish to confess to the crime, and a third may wish to claim a lack of capacity due to age. Your Honor, we have all these complexities in the defendant." Barbara gestured at the defendant who was looking at the floor with his forehead resting on the edge of the table. "If we do not declare him incompetent and we go to trial other legal issues will come into play. For example, should the Court have issued a search warrant for each personality before searching his apartment? Should the arresting officer have given warning 'that anything you say can be used against you' to each personality at the time of arrest? Would each of the personalities have to waive his or her rights, or would one waiver suffice? Does the doctrine of double jeopardy bar the trial of a personality when another has been put on trial? The other question that comes to mind is, should each personality testifying at trial be sworn in and administered the oath? Believe it or not Your Honor some trial judges have demanded it." Starkey paused momentarily to take a sip of water before continuing. "I submit this question to the Court. Should the defendant who we've clearly established is suffering from MPD, even be put on trial. Your Honor, as you mentioned at the beginning of this hearing, the defendant must be capable of understanding the nature and purpose of the proceedings taken against him. I think it's been well established that multiples are often self destructive and tend to emerge during periods of stress. Believe me, a trial for murder is stressful. So what happens to the defendant if the Beastie emerges and becomes dominant? How can an attorney communicate with a personality who is not even present? Your Honor, I respectfully request the court find the defendant incompetent to stand trial."

The courtroom remained silent. Judge Buckner held eye contact with Barbara Starkey momentarily then a sly smile filled his face as he spoke, "You did it again didn't you." Starkey smiled and quietly sat down. She knew that Buckner would say something when she got on her soapbox. She also knew that he respected her capabilities as well as her arguments.

Judge Buckner announced, "I will consider these issues and render my decision this afternoon. This Court is adjourned until two o clock." Buckner tapped his gavel once and quickly exited the court room.

The Stakeout Bar and Grill was packed with the city lunch crowd. It seemed to Sally that most of the city's administration was here out of some morbid curiosity about the greatest trial to hit Charleston in over 30 years. Lunch was the only a secondary consideration. These curiosity seekers hung on every hushed word being whispered around the room. Beau and Sally had seated themselves in a large corner booth Murph had especially reserved for them. As they scanned over the lunch crowd Beau pointed out the Mayor, the State Attorney General, the D.A., and the Chief of Police all sitting at one long table exchanging views in hushed voices.

"What's all that about? Sally questioned nodding at the long table. "Politics," Beau answered, "I think the Governor wants to make sure that these blowhards don't talk to the press unless his man is there."

"Your probably right." she answered.

"I know I'm right. Half the people in this room are media," Sally scanned the room again. "So what do we have here a bunch of sickies trying to get the latest dirt?" Murph approached toting two ham and cheese on rye specials. "Hi folks, how are my favorite people?" He said putting the sandwiches on the table then kissing Sally on the forehead. Beau continued to stare at the lunch crowd. Murph interrupted Beau's gaze, "Yeah, I know it's a bummer, but good for business." Beau looked up, "What?"

"The trial. Look at all these jerks, most of them don't know what's going on and the others are trying to dig up some dirt for the evening news." Those words had no sooner left Murph's lips when Linda Adams, and her cameraman, toting his shoulder camera, boldly walked up to Beau's table with the bright camera light glaring in Sally's face. She shaded her eyes with one hand as Linda asked, "Agent Thornton, you were the closest to the defendant, in your opinion is he a real multiple personality or is he just acting?" That did it as far as Murph was concerned. He'd always been a man with a quick temper. Without asking, his massive hand grabbed the cameraman's testicles and squeezed. The cameraman moaned. He was helpless having to protect his jewels and the expensive camera at the same time. Murph, maintaining a firm grip on his testicles, quickly led him through the lunch crowd and out the front door. The lunch crowd laughed at the short episode. Linda Adams wasn't laughing, with her microphone still in her hand she said, "You didn't answer my question." Sally stared at Beau ignoring the pushy reporter. From the other side of the room Detective Sergeant Coates strode quickly to Sally's defense. Coates by no means was a big woman. She was five feet two inches, 125 pounds of solid muscle, and pure hell when she was mad. Beau had seen her takedown some pretty tough individuals. She was the department's judo instructor, and loved a good fight. Beau closed his eyes and hoped that Coates would keep her cool. Coates hovered over Linda as she spoke in a menacing firm tone, "Excuse me. I think you need some fresh air." With that statement Coates grabbed the back straps of Linda's bra and gave them a twist almost cutting off her wind. Using only one hand she lifted the reporter up on her tip toes, and led her to the same front door. Murph laughed, gave Coates a high five, and said, You are a woman after my own heart Lass. Let me buy you a drink sweetheart." Coates and Murph promptly marched to the bar. Beau disregarded his lunch and looked thoughtfully at Sally.

"What?" she asked, holding her sandwich in mid air.

"The lady's question?" he said, with a serious look on his face. Sally put the sandwich down and folded her hands,

"You mean that Barbara Walters type that just left?"

"Yeah, do you think our guy is for real or is he faking it?" Beau asked taking a sip of coffee.

"You know what scares me?" she said, looking at the long table with the local politicians chatting among themselves. "I think he's crazy as a fruit cake. In spite of everything I feel sorry for him. You want to know why?" Beau nodded. "Because he hasn't got a chance in hell of getting a fair trial.

His fate is already sealed. Those men over there want their show and they'll get it."

"What about the victims?" Beau questioned trying to bring out her true feelings.

"That's the hard part. There are some crimes so horrible, so depraved, that there probably isn't any excuse for them. How do you feel?" Sally asked, as she took a bite out of her sandwich.

"Mixed emotions. Remember this guy killed my best friend and almost killed the woman I love. I'm not a forgiving man. The problem I have is that a serial killer whose killed, God knows how many, will be committed to a hospital, have a warm bed, three squares a day, and a roof over his head while some poor drunk or druggie who never broke a law in his life, will freeze to death in some back alley totally forgotten by you and me and those politicians over there." Beau nodded at the long table. Sally touched his hand tenderly, "I know, life isn't fair."

Promptly, at two o'clock Judge Buckner entered the courtroom as the Bailiff announced, "All rise, the 12th Circuit Court of the state of South Carolina is now in session. Judge Horace Buckner presiding."

Buckner adjusted his robes as he seated himself. "Be seated." The audience respectfully complied. Buckner reviewed his notes before addressing the courtroom.

"The Court recognizes the term mental disease or defect has various meanings depending upon how and why it is used and by whom. Counsel has pointed out that mental disease means one thing to a physician bent on treatment, but something different, if not somewhat overlapping in a Court of law. Our law provides a legal definition of mental disease or defect, and has held that it included any abnormal condition of the mind which substantially affects mental or emotional processes and substantially impairs behavior controls. The simple fact that a person has a mental disease or defect is not enough under the law to relieve him or her of responsibility for the crime. This hearing has established the fact that the multiple personalities alleged to be present in the defendant, with the possible exception of one, is rational, conversive, and under the legal tests of competency, is able to assist counsel in his own defense. Therefore, the Court finds the defendant capable of standing trial as prescribed by law. Trial date will be set at the earliest practical time." The judge flipped through his papers. "That will be, ah, November 5th. This court is adjourned." Buckner rapped his gavel once. The Bailiff shouted, "All rise," Buckner made a quick exit. The media personnel quickly displayed their cell phones as they barked the latest developments in the Gray Lady Killer case to their news desks. Delongpre stood, and faced Sally then glared at her with an evil leer as he was led away. She instinctively knew that Gaylord was in charge. Barbara Starkey closed her briefcase before addressing Sally and Beau. "No new surprises but I was able to get in a few shots of my own."

"You did a good job Counselor," Sally commented.

"Yeah, but they don't want me to be too good." Barbara nodded at the D.A. and the Mayor as they exited the courtroom.

"Come trial date I'm going to take my best shot." Barbara looked at the two detectives, "I know Harry was your friend. Everyone liked Harry, but I want to give my client the best defense I can. No hard feelings I hope."

Beau smiled, "A girl's gotta do what a girl's gotta do. I wouldn't have it any other way." Barbara shook hands with Beau then joined the departing crowd.

"Barbara," Beau called after her, raising his voice slightly, "I would have been disappointed if you didn't." Starkey smiled and left the courtroom.

Chapter Twenty
Confrontation

It was a cool, crisp October Friday morning. Beau and Sally had been given the day off and looked forward to the long weekend at Falconbriar. The competency hearing had gone as expected. The city fathers and the Governor were satisfied that the first step was over with no outcries from either side of the racial strife that brought the city to the brink of marshal law. There were no black or white demonstrators marching in front of the media cameras. It was rumored that one media representative was so disappointed that the streets were so quiet, he was considering hiring some locals to protest in front of the courthouse.

The Gray Lady Task Force on the other hand, had information that this could be the lull before the storm. The task force remained on alert status alpha. Although many of the National Guard units had been sent home, one full mechanized infantry battalion remained billeted at the armory. A complete city wide security plan remained in effect and was ready to be implemented on a moments notice.

Beau and Sally put all these problems behind them as they drove out of the city, and headed for Falconbriar. Sally laid her head back, expelled a sigh of relief, and looked at the forest that now surrounded the highway. The cool northwest wind brought an unusual chill to the air for this time of the year. The trees continued to splash their fall colors throughout the forest. The yellow, red and orange leaves danced in the morning sun.

"Am I glad to finally get away," Sally said, gazing at the Spanish Moss hanging from the Charter oaks. The sprawling limbs of the oaks hovered over the road and the moss cast intricate moving shadows giving the morning a dreamlike quality. They drove slowly into the countryside, not rushing, but lazily, taking in the natural beauty of South Carolina.

Picking up route 256 they headed southeast over the Cooper River Bridge. Sally stared out the window for some time before asking, "that Spanish Moss, does it hurt the tree in anyway? It's a parasite isn't it? I've seen some trees in pretty bad shape and its covered with moss."

She was about to learn from an expert. Beau was raised in this area and as a young man had covered almost every inch of the Francis Marion National Forest. After hurricane Hugo hit he volunteered to help the Army Corps Of Engineers come in and clean up the debris.

"First of all, it's not Spanish, and it's not a moss," Beau answered with a voice of authority.

"No kidding." She responded, surprised by his quick answer.

"It's all American, and believe it or not, it's related to the Pineapple"

Sally blurted out a loud laugh, "Okay, what's the punch line?"

"No punch line. You can find this stuff from North Carolina to South America, and it's not a parasite, it's an Epiphyte."

"A what?"

"An Epiphyte, that's a plant that doesn't have roots. It lives off the moisture in the air. When we get home I'll show you some. It has tiny scales on its.." He made a gesture with his hand as he gave a quick look at the trees.

"I guess you'd call them tendrils. These little scales trap rain and absorb moisture. They get their food from some cells that wash off the tree. The more cells they get from the tree, the fatter they get."

Sally stared at Beau amazed at this tidbit of knowledge. "Are you putting me on?"

He smiled, and gave the Boy Scout salute with his hand, "I swear that's the truth."

"I'll find out if you're lying," She joked. They both remained silent, and enjoyed the ride. She took a long look at Beau. This was a side of him she'd never seen before. Someone who was born here, raised here, loved the land, and so badly wanted a family, and a good home. Sally asked softly, "Are you going to teach Katie about the trees and the forest?" Beau took Sally's hand and kissed it tenderly.

"I am going to enjoy every minute of it." He had a sad tone in his voice as he continued, "I started with Mark, now he's gone. So, God willing, the three of us will go camping, picnicking and fishing whenever we can. You know something about Katie?" Beau questioned. Sally nodded, waiting for his answer.

"She has an instinctive love for all living things. That's a rare quality. I've watched her in the barn. Something else, the animals know that as well, and they respond to her." Sally was surprised by Beau's observations.

"I have a confession, no, we have a confession," Beau exclaimed gleefully.

"What do you mean?" She responded.

"Katie and I have a surprise for you when we get home."

Beau steered the car carefully from the highway through the main gate to Falconbriar. The massive wood carved sign hanging over the dirt road never failed to impress her. Sally was excited to get back to the farm, to see Katie, the family, and to finally soak in a hot tub. After about a mile down the road Beau's face turned to a smile. He looked at Sally and announced, "Welcome to your surprise."

Under a large oak tree Katie sat upon a golden Palomino pony waiting to surprise her mother. Beau pulled the car to a slow stop. Astounded, Sally stepped out, and walked up to Katie speechless.

"What do you think Mommy? Beau bought it for me. I've been practicing all week, and I am pretty good," Katie said proudly.

Sally looked impishly at Beau. "So, this was the big surprise." He put his arm around Sally, and asked, "How's the riding coming sweetheart?"

"Watch Mommy." Katie took off on a gallop down the road then stopped, spun the pony around, and quickly dashed back coming to a fast stop in front of the car. Beau stood with his chest out as proud of Katie's skills as any father could be. Sally had never seen Katie so excited about anything before in her life. He was right, she did have a way with animals. Katie went through a quick drill with the pony showing off for her mom. The pony side stepped, spun, and walked backward on command.

"What's her name?" Beau asked, petting the pony gently.

"Rose, I call her Rose because she's so pretty," Katie answered, bending over in the saddle to give her horse a loving hug. "I'll race you home," Katie shouted and she took off in a full gallop. As she headed for the short path back to the farm she looked back and waved. Katie, in the excitement of the moment broke her concentration. A small limb hung down from the large oak tree directly in her path. Beau could see what was coming, and ran in her direction. A loud smack was heard as the limb broke across Katie's back sending her plummeting to the ground.

Sally shouted, "Oh my God," and ran with Beau to Katie's side. The surprised little girl was beginning to cry. Beau scooped her up in his arms and held her gently, examining her to make sure nothing was broken. Satisfied that only her ego was hurt he began dusting her off. Katie clung to Beau, and wouldn't let go.

"Are you all right sweetie. I'd hate to tell you how many times I've been dumped." The teary eyed little girl looked at him curiously, "Yeah?" she asked wiping her eyes with her sleeve.

"Oh yeah," Beau said with a smile, "I've forgotten how many times. Look," he pointed at the pony who was quietly waiting for it's master.

"You know, when you get dumped on, you have to shake it off and step up and do it again." With Katie in his arms he inched back and sat with his back against the big oak tree. Sally positioned herself next to Beau. "You know there is an old story people around here tell." Katie had stopped crying. He had her full attention.

"Well, it's not really about a horse, it's about a mule. Do you know what a mule is?" Katie nodded affirmative.

"Let me see, how does it go? Oh yes, a long, long, time ago there was a farmer who had a mule. Now this was an old mule. It had helped him clear the land, and plant the seed. It worked hard and never complained. The farmer loved that old mule. There came a day when the old mule could no longer work. It deserved a rest. It earned the right to get the fresh grass, and enjoy the sun. Then one day the old mule fell into the farmer's well. The farmer heard the mule braying,"

"What's braying?" Katie interrupted, totally engrossed in the story.

"Braying is the noise mules make when they are in trouble. Anyway, they had no way of getting the mule out of the well. He had no ropes long enough, or strong enough to pull him out. It broke his heart, but he decided that neither the mule or the well could be saved so he called his neighbors together and told them what had to happen. He asked them to help him haul dirt to bury that old mule in the well, and put him out of his misery. Now, in the beginning that old mule brayed, and brayed. But, as the farmer, and his neighbors continued shoveling, and dirt hit his back, a thought came to that old mule. You know, mules are sometimes very stubborn. So every time a shovel-load of dirt hit his back he would shake it off, and step up. So, he did this after every shovel full. Shake it off, and step up, shake it off, and step up. No matter how painful the blows, or how bad the situation seemed, that old mule just kept right on shaking it off, and stepping up," Beau stood Katie up in front of him. "And guess what?" Katie shook her head not knowing the answer. Beau continued with the story, "It wasn't long before that old mule. Battered, tired, and dirty, stepped triumphantly over the wall of the well. So you see, what seemed like it would bury him was actually a blessing. It was a blessing because of the way he handled it. So, if we face our problems. If we get up, and dust ourselves off, and try it again we can over come anything."

Katie looked at her mom then at Beau. "Okay, I'm still going to race you home." The big smile that covered her face was marked by two dimples as she gave Beau another hug. Getting up, Beau gave her a lift back on the pony, and she took off in a fast gallop toward the farm. Beau remarked, "She's Irish all right." Sally smirked, "Someday you're going to run out of stories." They held hands and walked back to the car.

As the car pulled up to the front of the old antebellum mansion Josey and Casey were standing arm in arm on the front porch just as they had been when they left. The friendship between Josey and Casey had grown into something more than an occasional friendship. It was at this point in their lives where Casey was just what Josey needed and Casey had found the sister she'd always wanted. While Josey was out running the family business Casey was running the farm. She was up at the crack of dawn, out in the orchard tending to the slightest detail in the everyday operation of the farm. At night, Casey and Josey sat on the front porch in their rockers and talked mostly about their kids.

Sally ran up the porch steps, put her arms around them, and held them as though she might be torn away from their love at any moment. Beau lugged the two travel bags up to the porch, and joined the teary eyed mothers.

"Well, did you see your little girl?" Josey asked excitedly.

"She couldn't wait until you came home," Casey interrupted.

"She's a natural," Beau advised the proud grandmothers.

"We have a nice dinner planned for tonight," Casey announced proudly.

"We also have home made ice cream right out of the bucket made by none other than Katie Thornton herself." Josey said, mimicking an Irish accent, then nudging Casey.

"Let me have those," Josey commanded taking their bags and marching up the stairs.

Josey hadn't taken two steps up the staircase when Katie bounded through the front door shouting, "Come quick! She's in trouble!"

"Who?" Beau quickly questioned.

"Daisy Mae, she's down in the barn." With that announcement Katie dashed out the front door, down the porch steps, and took off on a fast run toward the barn. Beau and Sally ran quickly behind Katie followed by a surprised Josey and Casey.

When they reached the stall one of the ewes was laying on her side trying to give birth to her lamb. It was a small wood stall at one end of the barn. There was an opening to the outside coral. The big stud ram of the flock stood stoically in the doorway, confused by all the commotion. The ewe was obviously having trouble giving birth. Katie had piled hay around the animal to make it more comfortable and sat petting it trying to calm the animal. It was obvious that the animal was in pain. Beau noticed that the mere touch of Katie's hand on the animal calmed it.

"Please, you've got to do something. She's going to die. I just know it."

Beau knelt by the animal and examined the situation. The baby lamb was breached and having difficulty coming into this world. He had seen this before, and knew exactly what had to be done. "Get some clean towels from the TAC room," he ordered. Beau went to a small trunk sitting just outside the stall and donned a pair of rubber gloves. Opening a jar of petroleum jelly he applied it thoroughly over the gloves and returned to the stall. Kneeling behind the ewe he quietly said to Katie, "Now, you keep her calm. Let her know that everything is going to be all right." Katie nodded, and began to stoke the animal softly and whispered into her ear.

Beau inserted his fingers into the birth canal reaching for the unborn lamb. There it was, slightly turned not completely in the right position. Carefully, Beau's fingers turned the lamb into the correct position. Without notice, with one convulsion from the mother, the new baby was out. A new life had begun. He took the clean towels and cleaned the young animal as everyone smiled. Seeing the beginning of life restores ones faith in God. It is a holy event. It is a time of joy, a time of peace and reflection. The family stood in silence watching the miracle of life. Beau wrapped the little lamb in a clean towel and gave it to Katie. She held the new baby tenderly as everyone looked on.

"What are you going to name it?" Beau questioned. Katie thought for a moment. "How about Lamb Chop?" She asked.

"Oh, I don't know. Do you think she'd like that name?" Sally asked as everyone chuckled.

"Oh yeah, Lamb chop may not be the best after all," Katie looked at the little Baby lamb before answering, "She's so cute I think I'll call her Barbie."

"Here, I have something for Barbie," Casey advised, handing Katie a nursing bottle full of warm milk. The baby lamb eagerly took the milk and began nursing. The new born lamb immediately bonded with Katie.

The big ram hadn't moved one inch from it's original position. It continued to quietly take in the big event. Katie looked at the regal looking ram and asked, "Is that the daddy?" Beau took off the rubber gloves and wiped his hands with another clean towel before sitting next to Katie. "Yep, that's him. A handsome devil isn't he." A sadness came over Katie's face when she asked, "Does he love his little lamb? Beau leaned closer to Katie before answering, "Oh yes, he's very proud. You noticed that he didn't go away. He stood right there."

Katie thought silently for a short time. "Why did my daddy go away? Didn't he love me?" Sally held back her tears. Josey and Casey shook their heads sadly but said nothing. Beau didn't hesitate, but answered her question happily. "Oh that's easy," Beau put his arm gently around Katie, "You know that God works in mysterious ways. I mean you've heard people say that?" Katie nodded sadly.

Beau stroked the baby lamb, "You remember the story about the ugly prince and his love for a beautiful girl?" Katie nodded again, before Beau continued, "well you know I'm not the prettiest person in the world. You also know I lost my little boy. Well one night, I prayed to God to send me someone I could love. He told me that he had always meant for me to have you. It seems as though there was a mix up in heaven. So you see he had to make things right before I could have you, and your mommy."

Sally came to Katie's side and put her arms around both of them. Josey and Casey wiped the tears from their eyes. Then Josey spoke abruptly interrupting the tenderness of the moment. "You better put your money where your mouth is and come up with a wedding date."

Everyone laughed at Josey's bluntness.

"Anytime ladies, anytime," Beau said then kissed Sally lovingly.

"You heard him," Casey declared, "Leave it up to us. We'll make all the arrangements."

"Hot Dog! Josey and Casey exclaimed together, gave each other a high five clap, then marched hand in hand out of the barn. The two ladies had no longer left the barn when they returned. Josey, putting both hands on her hips asked defiantly, "Okay, what are you two up to?" Sally and Beau looked confused. "The police are here," She loudly announced.

Jack Bellamy and Detective Coates walked hurriedly toward the barn. Beau and Sally, followed by the two mothers, met them half way.

"We've got a couple of problems," Jack blurted out quickly.

"No, you're the one with the problem," Casey stated sternly with both arms folded across her chest.

"Mom, please," Sally answered, looking frustrated at her mother.

"We're about to plan a wedding here. Can't this wait?" Casey replied.

"I'm sorry for the interruption. By the way, congratulations you two." Sally gave Jack, and Coates a warm hug. "Thanks," Sally said, then looking at Casey and Josey asked, "Will you excuse us?"

"Okay, when this is over we want to talk to you two," Casey politely commanded. The two mothers marched into the house.

"Okay, what have you got?" Beau asked the detectives as the walked toward the old Magnolia tree adjacent to the house. Jack pulled out his note pad as the detectives huddled together.

"Once we've got our nut case I thought things would cool down but I was wrong." Jack flipped through his notes, "We `kept getting a lot of phone traffic on our Hitler guy, Jack scanned his notes again, "Ah, Gerhart Meinich."

"So, what's he up to?" Sally questioned. Jack explained, "I thought it wise to keep the phone taps in place as long as he was in town." Beau nodded, "good idea. What did you come up with?"

"This guy is really out in left field. He's laying down a bunch of bullshit about we've just picked out some white village idiot from the Funny Farm to put on trial to make the blacks happy."

"That figures," Beau replied.

"That's not all," Jack continued, "He's planning on making a statement. In fact, from what we can gather, he's made several statements about this.

"Go on," Sally said, holding back her Irish temper.

"On the phone they talk in and around things. We think there is a threat against you and your family."

Beau's eyes narrowed as his jaws tightened. It was easy to see that he was mad. However, he was not one to go off half cocked. He planned every move. Right now he had to deal with the hatred churning inside him. Jack could understand. If it was his family he'd feel the same way.

"Hear me out," Jack said before Beau could speak. "We've got some officers on the way out here. They'll provide security backup for your family 24 hours a day until this is over. Another thing," Jack inserted, "The FBI has someone on the inside."

Beau looked at Sally, "did you know anything about that?"

"It's news to me. But I'll find out. I don't like being setup." She answered. Jack continued the impromptu briefing, "Well, we've got two problems. They're going to have some sort of get together tonight. We think it's to plan their next move. The only thing we know is that the meeting place is called, 'Round Pond.' It's not on the map and no one seems to know where it is." Jack unfolded the map and laid it on the grass. The detective hovered over the map. Beau placed his finger on the map.

"Round Pond, not too many people know about it. United Paper Company used it to hold pulp pine for processing. They went belly up years ago. They still have a couple of old buildings there, and only one dirt road in or out. It's right here at the top of Beresford Creek." The detectives studied the map before Beau asked, "Do we have anyone still on Hitler?"

"Yep, we've got him covered," Jack answered quickly.

"How many men are available tonight?" Beau asked again as a plan began to form in his head.

"As many as you want. Everyone wants in on the action," Jack answered confidently.

"Okay, route 526 is the only road to the turn off. After Hitler passes in his limo I want you to put a road block at 526 and Clements Ferry Road. Except I don't want it to look like a road block."

Sally interrupted, "Why don't we turn over an empty semi and make it look like an accident?"

"Good idea," Beau responded, "I want Hitler as isolated from his goons as I can get him. Put up another road block on 526 south of the turn off at Devil's Creek Crossing. Tell them that the bridge has been damaged. You can't let anyone cross until it's been inspected. That will leave Hitler pretty much on his own. We'll need a few of our troops to set up at Round Pond under cover and wait for our asshole to arrive. Set up a new TAC secure frequency. I don't want anyone listening in or what's going down."

"Got it," Jack answered quickly with a smile realizing what Beau is planning to do.

"Another thing," Beau added, glancing at Sally, "don't tell anyone except our people. Not the Mayor, D.A., or FBI."

"How did you get this information?" Sally questioned suspiciously, "I don't think you got all this from the Hitler phone taps. He's not that stupid."

Jack smiled slyly, "Culpepper's phone. Oh yeah, we've been monitoring his radios too."

Beau cut in with some additional comments, "I want to know when Hitler leaves the hotel, when everyone's in place, and when he passes the first checkpoint."

Coates, who had remained silent through this whole conversation, interrupted, "What about the other problem?" Sally and Beau turned their attention to Coates as she continued, "These phone messages also mention that they are really going to make a statement for the media to see. They say, and I quote, 'they're going to cut the balls off that fucking bull, pardon my language." Coates looked at her notes momentarily, "Another phone caller mentioned that the big A is going to be tumbling down. You have any idea what all this means?"

The detective gazed at each other trying to recall any bit of information that might fit or give a clue as to their next target.

Josey and Casey returned to the group carrying a tray of cookies and steaming mugs of hot coffee. The women looked at the quiet detectives ignoring the treats placed in front of them. Curious by the silence, and blank stares, Josey asked, "What?"

"Nothing," Beau quickly answered politely, ignoring his mother, still staring at the map.

"I know it's not nothing. Tell me what's the problem," she demanded from the detectives.

"It's police business mom," Beau answered being as tactful as he could.

"You never know what a mother can do until you ask. I'm not stupid you know," she said defensively.

"It's not that."

"Then tell your mom. Maybe I can help." Knowing his mother wasn't going to let the issue drop, he answered, "We have these skinheads, you know, Hitler types, racists. They said they we're going to make a statement for the media. They said, they were going to cut the balls off the bull."

Coates interrupted, "They also said that the big A was going to fall."

Beau looked at his mother, "You have any idea what that means?"

Josey didn't hesitate one second, "That's easy." Everyone looked astonished at Josey as she answered the question, "Where is the media located?" Josey stated, asking a rhetorical question then answering it, "Charleston. So, the target, or whatever it is they are going to do is in Charleston. Now, the only thing I know in the city that fits is the Avery Research Center For African Studies. The big A is for Avery"

The detectives were awestruck as they stared blankly at Josey. "By the way gentlemen, the Avery Center is at 125 Bull Street." Josey said smugly.

Everyone began to laugh, Beau jumped up and gave his mother a big kiss. "You've got it!" He exclaimed, "We've got a bomb at Avery. Get the bomb squad over there quietly tonight. Keep the media out of it. If you can't, make some excuse to close the center. A gas leak, or something like that."

The group sipped at their coffee and smiled. The plan was in place. A lot was going down tonight. This was going to be a covert operation. No press, and no politicians if at all possible.

"We've got about six hours to make all this happen. Let's move." Beau commanded.

The detectives started for the house ignoring the tray of cookies. Josey shouted at the departing group, "Hey, what about the cookies?" Beau and Sally returned to Josey's side, "Sweetheart," Beau said calmly, "There's been a threat against the family. We're going to have three officers here for your protection."

"Well at least someone around here will appreciate what I do." Josey chided, as she picked up the tray, and accompanied Beau and Sally to the house.

"Just a minute," Beau commanded in a calm voice, stopping Sally before she could enter the house. "I want you to stay here."

"Bullshit!" She barked putting her hands on her hips coming face to face with Beau. "This is my collar just as much as it is yours."

"No it isn't!" He shouted back slightly surprising Sally causing her to move her face back a few inches.

"Your collar is in jail, and is going on trial. This is a local problem and I'll take care of it."

"Do you love me?" she demanded loudly, "are you going to marry me?" she asked bluntly. Before he could answer she shouted, "then I'm sure as hell family. What threatens you threatens me. Don't you dare go macho on me. I've had enough of the crap already."

Casey and Josey stood in the background observing their children in their first argument. Casey whispered into Josey's ear, then they shook hands. After Sally let her Irish temper cool down she spoke, "Look, we've been over this ground before. Either I'm part of the team, or I'm not. If I'm not, I'll pack my bags, and I'm out of here." The two strong willed lovers stared at each other in a tense silence before Beau answered, "Okay, if you're part of the team you know that I am the team leader, right?"

"Right," Sally acknowledged with a stern shout.

"Then God Dammit, learn to take orders."

"Bullshit! You're just afraid I'll damage a pinkie or something. Hell, what do I have to do to prove to you that I can handle any damn thing you want to throw at me?" She responded with the same intensity as Beau's demands.

Casey whispered again to Josey, "Damn, I sure like your son. No one has ever stood up to her like that."

"It's sure going to be in interesting marriage I'll say that," Both women chuckled to themselves.

Beau waited for their tempers to cool down before he spoke in a calm voice, "Look, I know you can handle anything. You don't have anything to prove to me or anyone else on the team." He moved closer to a calmed Sally. "I know these guys. They are going to make a move on this house and we've got Katie, my mom, and yours in danger. I want someone around here in charge I can trust. Someone I'd trust with my life. That someone is you sweetheart." Beau continued, putting his arm around Sally. "Everything I love in this world is here. I am trusting you to protect them until I get back."

She looked into his eyes. This wasn't some story just to keep her out of harms way. She felt he meant it. Reluctantly, she said, "Okay. I'll do it. But if you're lying to me I swear I'll get even."

Casey looked at Josey, sighed, reached into her apron pocket, gave Josey a dollar, then announced, "You win."

The western horizon had a soft glow of the after-day as the fog and swamp gas began to rise on Round Pond. Beau had positioned three Swat Team camouflaged snipers in strategic positions in the thicket that fronted the approach to the outbuildings. Beau and Jack scouted the area only to find empty buildings. Tire tracks told Beau that someone had been here recently. Beau and Jack had donned black Swat Team garb and equipped themselves with the latest Starlight Night Vision goggles. Moving into the forest cover behind the outbuildings Beau keyed his hand radio, and in a low voice commanded, "Check in. Let me hear it."

"Number one is in position."

"Two is in."

"Three is here, where's the beer?" Came the last scratchy answer. Jack smiled at Beau enjoying the happy chatter.

"You have the car covered okay?" Beau questioned.

"Yeah," number one replied, "It's covered, I'm not sure if I could find it in the dark."

"You couldn't find your dick in a whorehouse in broad daylight," came an anonymous comment from the team.

"Okay guys knock it off. Stay sharp," Beau commanded, "Hitler left his hotel 45 minutes ago. I expect him to come be boppin down that road any minute. I don't want any movement until I give the word."

"That's a roger," was a scratchy answer.

Jack and Beau sat in an observation position behind the outbuildings waiting for the rat to fall into the trap. Jack looked at Beau before speaking, "what if this is just a spoof to draw you away from the farm?"

Beau thought for a moment before speaking, "No, I don't think so. In any case we've got both possibilities covered." Beau's words were interrupted when the small hand radio announced, "Hitler has just passed the road block. ETA to your location in about ten minutes," The two detectives smiled at each other then moved into their assigned positions.

"We have lights on the road, and guess what? We have a nice long pimp of a limo," the hand radio barked on the TAC frequency. Beau turned the volume down slightly before talking, "Okay, after it goes by move to your new positions. The Swat Team acknowledged his orders with two clicks on the radio. Beau could now see the limo winding its way along the old logging road into the clearing coming to a stop in front of the largest outbuilding. The night vision goggles gave the images a green glow as they lit the candles in the cabin. There he was the would be Hitler himself, Gerhart Meinich. He had only one big bodyguard with him. This was going to be get even time he thought to himself as he adjusted his night vision equipment. The bodyguard gazed out the window looking for their expected visitors. Jack moved silently back to Beau's side and said, "I think they're getting antsy. We don't want them back in that car."

"Yeah, let's pull the plug," Beau answered confidently, "Okay gentlemen, lets make some noise, go!"

Immediately Beau saw the black and white patrol car come careening down the logging road with sirens blaring and lights flashing. It had the effect Beau was hoping for. The back door of the outbuilding flung open. Hitler accompanied by his favorite goon, came running out headed directly toward Beau and Jack's concealed position.

"I want Hitler. You take assbreath," Beau commanded nudging Jack. Both men positioned themselves behind two large oak trees directly in the path of the two fleeing skinheads. Beau removed his night vision goggles, took off his leather belt and wrapped it around his knuckles. The two panicked men charged into the forest on a dead run. Gerhart had taken one step too many when Beau, with every bit of hatred he could muster, hit Gerhart smack in the mouth knocking him on his backside. Hitler rose to one knee only to receive Beau's boot in his face. The kick drove his lower jaw up through his tongue into the roof of his mouth sending teeth snapping into the air. Cupping hands, Beau slapped both ears popping his eardrums leaving him with a ringing that would take several days to clear. Hitler had no idea what was happening to him. Everything was pitch black and happening too fast. Beau slipped his belt over the neck of his opponent pulling him upright next to his face. He increased the tension on his garrote. Gerhart's lips were beginning to turn blue when Beau whispered into his ringing ears, "I want you to know you son of a bitch if you ever threaten me or my family again I'm going to kill you. I don't care how many fucking bodyguards you have I will kill you. That is a promise. Now, take your sorry ass and get out of my state" Beau shook the garrote several more times to make sure he got the message. "Do you understand?"

A weak nod came from the skinhead leader. Beau let him drop to the ground. He gasped for air as Beau removed his belt from around his neck.

Jack had a similar encounter with Hitler's bodyguard. This guy was a walking hulk, 250 pounds with the IQ of a soda cracker. Jack picked up a hefty tree branch and swinging it like a baseball bat hit the goon right between the eyes. He folded like a newspaper dropping to one knee. Using the end of the tree limb like a pile driver, he delivered a vicious upper cut to the jaw lifting the big man upright. Jack followed up these savage blows with a devastating kick to his testicles. The hulk collapsed into a sobbing glob of bleeding fat on the ground. Jack stood over the bully and said before delivering the final kick to the head, "what goes around comes around asshole." Both men looked at the results of their few minutes of exercise with satisfaction. Jack took out his handkerchief and tore it in half. He gave half to Beau and said, "A blood sample is a blood sample, right?" Beau smiled, and wiped the rag across Hitler's bleeding face. Jack did the same to his opponent then gave Beau an evidence bag. After depositing the evidence in the plastic bag he clicked his radio and announced, "Okay gentlemen, we're finished here. Let's go home."

Sally sat at the bedroom window of the old manor house with a 12 gauge automatic shotgun cradled in her lap. She looked at her daughter sleeping oblivious to the dangers that now threatened the family. It's ironic, she thought to herself, throughout her career at the FBI she had gone after some of the most brutal killers that had ever walked the streets. In all that time she had never had to shoot to kill. The idea of taking a human life was repugnant to her. Even when the killer had Beau by the throat, and she had a clear shot, she missed. She knew she missed on purpose. It worked that time, the killer let Beau drop, and everything was all right. If the killers had Katie by the throat would she hesitate again? She had no answer that left her with a comfortable feeling. She wanted to avoid a confrontation with whoever it was that would try to do harm to her family. With this in mind she had deployed three Swat Team snipers in strategic positions to all approaches to Falconbriar. They were all outfitted with night vision equipment and a bull horn. She gave specific instructions to the shooters what to do when, and if, these goons arrived. They thought she was crazy but they went along with her plan. These ideas were still turning in her mind when the small hand radio scratched the message she was hoping she wouldn't have to hear, "We have a pickup pulling off the highway, parking, now the lights are off."

"How many?" she questioned

"Three," was the sniper's quick response.

"They are armed, and carrying some containers," the second sniper added to the radio chatter.

"I've got them," the third sniper commented.

"Okay, let them come this way. Wait until they've passed you. Then wait for my call," she ordered.

"Are you sure you want to do this?" came the calculating voice of the first sniper, "I can take them all out right now and they won't know what hit them."

"Aw, you're no fun," was the deadly comment for the second sniper, "you didn't save one for me."

"All right you guys. Knock it off," Sally commanded.

"Okay, they've passed right under us. They're about 15 yards in front of us," the sniper whispered over his radio. Sally keyed her mike, "Okay, remember how we rehearsed it. Make it sound good," she ordered. The first sniper, concealed at the top of an old Charter Oak, keyed his bullhorn, and imitating a recorded message said, "You have triggered the outside perimeter security line. Proceed any further and you will be shot." There was utter confusion among the three goons as the peered into the darkness.

"You have triggered the outside perimeter security line. Proceed any further and you will be shot." This bullhorn announcement came from another direction, then was followed by a third announcement from yet another direction. As Sally had hoped the trespassers panicked and ran blindly through the forest tripping and falling intermittently. To hurry their exit to the main highway, the snipers placed an array of bullets at the departing goons chipping away tree bark just inches from their heads. As quickly as the encounter had started, it fell silent. Sally waited nervously for the snipers to report. "They took off. I think they laid about ten feet of rubber on the highway," a sniper announced on the TAC frequency.

"I got their license number," was another sniper's scratchy comment.

"I think these guys are going to need a change of underwear when they get back to town." Sally smiled at the radio chatter. She could have easily killed three men tonight but didn't. The threat for now was over. She keyed her radio, "Thanks gentlemen." A quick response echoed over the TAC frequency, "you're welcome. Now what?" Sally answered the question by transmitting, "It's Miller Time."

Chapter Twenty One
Physical Evidence

It was a rainy 3 am morning. Sally drove alone through the vacant streets of Charleston unable to keep the killer out of her thoughts. The streetlights sparkled like diamonds through the raindrops on the windows of the car. She let the coming events run through her mind. In a few hours these streets would be crowded with onlookers; ACLU picketers protesting some unknown cause; media trucks with cables sprawling out, going who knows where, like some out of control octopus; police security; and traffic control officers who will try vainly to bring some order to the media generated bedlam.

She couldn't sleep. She had left Beau a note to meet her at the courthouse. Some underlying sense of dread, a feeling of non closure, kept pulling her to the mental hospital for one more look at the killer. The madman, who had her on the edge of death, had to have some logical reason for what he had done. Was he a real multiple? Or, a clever actor who was hiding behind the facade of the insanity plea. She had to know. She had to put these uneasy feelings to rest before the start of the trial.

The car skidded slightly on the rain slick street as Sally pulled into the parking area of the hospital. Bringing the car quickly under control, she parked, and turned off the lights. The misty rain filled the window with diamond droplets of water. She sat alone in the dark and thought to herself. "Is there something else I'm looking for in the killer's mind? Do I have some sick depraved need to know what kind of sexual pleasure he got from killing and raping women?"

Sally went through the standard security routine before entering the darkened observation room. The two-way mirror revealed a bed in one corner of the padded holding cell. An overhead hanging light cast a single spot over the table in the center of the darkened cell. Sally sat alone on the other side of the looking glass gazing at the sleeping killer. She wondered what sexual high did he get at the moment of death? "What sort of sexual games did he play when he was in control of the Fetish Club? How was he able to control Carla and her daughter? What sort of sexual relief did he give these women? What sort of devious logic did he display in order to corrupt and control Dr. Michaels and his wife? Is there some hidden madness in all of us that screams to be set free? He had the same effect on these women as Charles Manson did when he was the leader of his cult. As a woman, could I give in to this madness just to satisfy my sexual fantasies? For a moment while the killer had me spread open on the table before him, did I secretly want him to rape me? Do I have some sick desire deep inside me?" These thoughts raced through Sally's mind causing her, through her own hidden desire, to become aroused. Her face flushed, her breathing increased, and she felt a warm moist feeling in her groin.

It was as if, on some psychic cue, the killer suddenly sat erect in bed. He to gazed straight ahead as though listening to a hidden voice. He rose and walked to the table, seated himself and stared blindly at the looking glass. Sally was taken back. It was as if the glass wasn't there. Then he spoke. "I know you're there," he said calmly. "Are you the one?" he asked waiting for an answer that didn't come from beyond the looking glass. "I knew that someday you'd come to me. I knew that it would end with you."

Sally rose from her theater seat and moved to the microphone. It was uncanny, the killer's eyes seemed to follow her movements from the other side of the glass. She was entranced with his ability to see beyond the mirror, or, was it just acting? Sally keyed the mike, "I'm here," she answered in a slow echoing voice. The killer sat back satisfied that the one woman who would bring this misery to an end was finally here to talk to him. The killer rose again, took off his hospital robe and walked to the front of the table so that the single light kept him in full view. He wore only the bottom half of his hospital pajamas. His body was lean, and slightly muscular. There was a sensual quality to his body, almost feminine. Physically, he was quite attractive.

"What do you think?" he bragged, strutting in a small circle under the light showing off his body before sitting back on the table. "See what you missed?"

Sally remained silent watching the killer with intense interest. The killer walked closer to the mirror before speaking, "How did it feel Sally?" She was alarmed by the fact the killer had learned her name. "I could tell you wanted me to have you. I felt it when you opened to me. Why did you stop me?"

Sally didn't understand, but she was getting even more aroused. It seemed like the killer was getting inside her mind, raping her most private thoughts. She didn't realize she had been hiding these carnal thoughts in the back of her mind, yet the killer knew. He knew instinctively what she wanted. What she had told herself over and over again, that this wasn't what she wanted, when she knew she did. When she was spread open before him that night, on that table, she knew she secretly wanted him to rape her. God forbid, that was the thought had been haunting her for the past few weeks. What was it deep within her that attracted her to the forced sex he had offered? Why had she fought him off? Was it the fear of the inevitable, of satisfying his high? That had to be it. His high was death. She could see it in his eyes. His climax came only when he strangled his victims. The rest was just part of the ritual.

The killer smiled in a sensual manner before asking in a calm voice, "How did it feel when I touched you here?" he grabbed his crotch and began to manipulate himself, quickly bringing up an erection that pressed against his pajamas. "When I sucked your breasts I was in heaven," he said, as he continued to manipulate himself.

Sally continued to be aroused by the killer's sexual antics. However, she noticed that during the whole episode none of the altar egos appeared. She was witnessing a totally different personality. Suddenly, she realized that the whole multiple personality thing had to be an act. She wasn't hearing Gaylord, or David, or Gordon for that matter, it was someone else in control, someone evil.

"I was going to fill you so completely that you would cry for more," the killer stated with smug satisfaction. Sally remained mute. The killer laid back on the table, pulled down the lower half of his pajamas revealing a giant erection. The erection stood like a flagpole atop his prone body. The killer slowly began to manipulate himself coming to a quick climax. The erection spouted sperm like lava flowing from a volcano.

Sally, who had been aroused by his words was now disenchanted by his actions. He was a ham actor showing off before an audience of one. This wasn't anything more than taking a woman's fantasies to the extreme. If she was going to live these fantasies, it was going to be with Beau. It was going to be with her lifes partner, the father of her children. She had to find the truth. To come face to face with the realities of the situation. She had sexual desires just like any other woman but she knew where to draw the line. She keyed the mike and said calmly, "Get a life," then walked out of the observation room.

The city streets around the courthouse were jammed with media vans and reporters broadcasting their pretrial hype from the courthouse steps. Judge Buckner was not about to be intimidated by the press. The Associated Press ran a scathing article about Judge Buckner hinting that he was over stepping his authority by limiting the access of media camera coverage of the Gray Lady Killer trial. As a result, Buckner countered with a pretrial court order requiring all reporters to submit to a finger print, and background check by the FBI before being issued a press pass to the courtroom. Additionally, the journalists had to supply the court with valid press credentials and two ID photos before the final pass could be granted. Of the 50 journalists who had applied, and submitted to the proper background check, only 30 had been issued passes.

It was a running joke around the squad room. Danny O'Brien, the Charleston Ledger's loud mouth reporter, who had started all the racial uproar by falsely announcing that the killer was black, had a minor criminal record. That was all the court needed to deny him a press pass.

The media executives were furious and countered with a radio and TV media blitz. They aired interviews with First Amendment experts who denounced the procedure as unconstitutional. One TV interview with Stanley Norewood, General Counsel for the Washington DC First Amendment Coalition, stated, "That the court order requiring fingerprints is clearly in violation of First Amendment rights to a free press." He went on to say, "The U.S. Supreme Court has held, in numerous cases, that the press, and the public have a right to attend criminal court proceedings."

Buckner countered this publicity with his own direct tactics by allowing the issuing of public passes without a background check to selected citizens of the state. Buckner went on to say, "All personnel will have to pass through a security check for weapons. He answered his media critics by informing them that these same procedures were in place for other trials of this magnitude, and public interest. He used the Rosenburg Spy case, and the Uni-bomber trials as examples.

The newspapers and the TV stations continued to follow the pretrial legal maneuvering and debate over the upcoming conduct of the trial. The prosecution filed a pretrial motion to prohibit anticipated testimony by defense witnesses who would present evidence concerning the defendant's mental condition below the standard recognized by the M'Naughton Rule. The M'Naughton Rule would severely hamper the defense's capability to pursue the insanity defense by rigidly confining the testimony. The news articles publicly defined the M'Naughton Rule for its readers.

At the time of committing the act, the accused was laboring under such a defect of reason, from disease of mind, as to not to know the nature and quality of the act he was doing or, if he did know it, that he did not know what he was doing was wrong.

The defense quickly countered the state's petition with its own rationale for denial of the motion. The defense stated that if the court was rigidly limited to the M'Naughton Rule it would excuse only those totally deteriorated drooling hopeless psychotics, and congenital idiots. The defense went on to explain to the court that the insane mind is often rational, and can exercise sound, well-balanced judgment. To limit the defense to focus on merely cognitive impairment is incomplete. The defendant's ability to control his acts must also be considered.

Barbara Starkey expanded her rebuttal to the state's motion and argued that the precondition of moral and legal responsibility are, that the defendant is reasonably rational, and in control of his actions. The defense intends to prove that within the defendant's mind is several dominant personalities. One personality is a beast. An animal that is completely irrational, and a small boy who is in all legal sense of the word, a minor. The law clearly states that perpetuators such as small children, who lack reasonable cognitive or volitional control through no fault of their own, may be dangerous, but are not considered fully responsible as moral agents.

Judge Buckner denied the pretrial petition by the prosecution. His answer to the counselors was published in all the newspapers. Buckner stated that in order to give both sides their day in court he would use the American Law Institute's (ALI) definition as a guideline. The paper printed Buckner's interpretation of the ALI definition.

The defendant is not responsible for criminal conduct where as a result of mental disease or defect, did not possess substantial capacity either to appreciate the criminality of his conduct or to conform his conduct to the requirements of the law.

The Judge also warned the defense that he would also follow the guidelines outlined in the Insanity Defense Reform Act of 1984. He warned the defense that they must prove by clear, and convincing evidence, that at the time of the acts constituting the offense, the defendant as a result of severe mental disease, or defect, was unable to appreciate the nature and quality or wrongfulness of his acts.

Beau was waiting for Sally at their reserved courthouse parking space. She lowered the window and smiled at him as she set the car in park.

"How did it go?" he asked as she opened the car door and stepped out.

"What do you mean?"

"I mean, how was our local nut case?" Beau replied with a knowing smile.

"How did you know I went to see him?" she asked, surprised by his insight.

"If I had gone through what you did I would have to get some closure before all this gets started," he nodded toward the courthouse.

"He's out of it, and he's one hell of a good actor," she remarked, then gave Beau a kiss.

"Are you okay?" Beau searched her eyes for some glimmer of the truth.

"Yeah, I just want to get this over with so we can get down to business." Sally took Beau's arm as they walked toward the back entrance to the courthouse.

"I hope you mean monkey business," he said slyly with a wink in his eye. Sally didn't comment but continued to walk in silence.

"He turned you on didn't he," he remarked, as though he could see into her inner thoughts.

"No," she answered defensively.

"Yeah, he did, and you had to come to grips with it," Beau said confidently.

"No!"

"Look, it's all right. I understand," he added, "I don't know how many prostitutes I've booked that I didn't have some sexual attraction for." Before she could speak he continued, "I remember one hooker, she was only 15 years old. I mean you'd get an erection just looking at her. It wasn't her sexy clothes, cheap lipstick, or hair. It was her innocence. The look in her face. She looked like a virgin."

"How did you know I went to see him?" she inquired.

"Well, when you show up at a guy's bed naked with handcuffs he kinda gets the idea."

Sally hit his arm laughingly, "You rat! You were awake?" Beau stopped, turned her around, and gave her a warm loving kiss. Breaking the kiss he said, "Don't forget those handcuffs. When this is over we'll really get down to business."

"You'd better remember you've made a promise to your Mom, you've got to make an honest woman out of me," Sally responded, giving him another kiss.

When Beau and Sally entered the courthouse lobby, from the rear hallway, they were instantly deluged with rude reporters pushing microphones in their faces and shouting wild questions that had no bearing on the case. As Judge Buckner had predicted these American paparazzi weren't after good journalism, or reporting the facts, they were after sensationalism and ratings for the local TV networks.

"We understand that you could have killed the defendant, but you saved his life. Do you have any regrets?", one pushing reporter shouted at Beau as they nudged their way through the mob.

"Are you sorry that you didn't drop him?" was another question from the crowd.

"Agent Thornton, the rumor is that you were actually raped by the defendant. Is that true?", was another question coming from a female reporter with a crass New York accent. Sally pushed the mike away and ignored the question. Flash bulbs, and cameras clicked in their faces like a 4th of July fireworks display.

Midway through the media mob Beau noticed Judy Hampton, the little girl that had been raped at the hospital. She was surrounded by nagging reporters firing questions at this confused and frightened little girl. Tears welled up in her eyes. She was on the verge of a total breakdown. Her mother vainly tried to push the reporters away.

"Excuse me," Beau said to Sally, then pushed his way to the little girl's side.

"Back off!", he shouted as he stared the reporters down. The parana-like mob of reporters, who enjoyed feeding on the weak, and confused, broke ranks. Beau led the little girl, and her mother, to the safety of courtroom one.

"Thank you," Judy's mother said gratefully.

Courtroom one was the largest courtroom in the courthouse. It could easily seat three hundred people. A portion of the front two rows had been reserved for the witnesses. In the back of the courtroom was a TV camera. The camera had a blocking attachment which prevented it from accidentally panning to the jury box. The judge's podium was paneled in solid oak and rose above the courtroom. The witness stand was to the right of the judge's bench. This allowed the judge to confer with the witness and gave the jury a good look at the witness. A microphone was positioned at the witness stand in order that all testimony could be readily heard.

Homer Canfield sat at the prosecution's desk on the right side of the room while Barbara Starkey sat at her desk on the left side of the courtroom. The audience was separated from the trial counsel by a low oak railing that had a swinging gate in the middle.

Jack Bellamy waved at Beau and Sally when they entered the courtroom. He pointed to seats that had been reserved for them. Beau made sure that Judy Hampton, and her mother were seated before returning to Sally's side. Jack whispered to Sally, "Well, it's showtime. How are you doing?"

"I'm okay," she replied assuredly.

"It looks like everyone is here," Jack announced looking at the crowd.

"I think they've covered just about everything," Sally commented nodding at the bowl of mini Baby Ruth candy bars sitting on Starkey's desk.

"Yep, our wacko has his goodies. He's happy." Jack observed.

As the last observer was seated the security guards quietly closed the doors, then stood guard, limiting access to the courtroom. The side door to the courtroom opened and the defendant was led in. He was not dressed in prison garb, but had been given a gray suit. He was still handcuffed, and seemed extremely subdued.

This was going to be the greatest act in his life, Sally thought to herself. The killer was seated then took one of the small, bite sized, Baby Ruth candies, and popped it into his mouth. The killer turned slowly to observe his audience, then fixed his gaze on Sally. It was a cold smile emitting pure evil. The cold smile suddenly melted when his eyes met Beau's penetrating stare that reflected pure hatred.

"All rise!" the Bailiff announced loudly, as Judge Buckner entered the courtroom from his chambers.

"The First Superior Court for the State of South Carolina is now in session. The Honorable Horace Buckner presiding."

345

Buckner seated himself then commanded politely, "Please be seated." Buckner shuffled through his folder and removed one sheet of paper. He scanned it quickly. Lowering his glasses to the tip of his nose he looked at the two young lawyers ready to do battle in court, then spoke.

"The District Attorney's office has filed a petition of murder in the first degree naming the defendant as Gaylord Harcourt, also known as David Delongpre, also known as Gordon Delongpre. The Court has found that probable cause does exist for the prosecution of murder in the first degree. The Court has also determined that the defendant does possess the mental competency necessary to assist defense counsel in his own defense. Does defense counsel wish to present any further motions before the court before this trial begins?"

Barbara Starkey stood beside the defendant who tried vainly to provide an angelic look to the jury while munching a small candy bar. "No your honor," Starkey answered quickly, then seated the defendant who grabbed another candy and popped it into his mouth.

"Good," Buckner replied, then looked at Homer. "You may present your opening arguments." The judge sat back, and folded his arms waiting for Homer Canfield to start the prosecution's opening statement. Homer stood, gazed at his notes then began to address the court.

"Your honor, ladies and gentlemen of the jury. The state will prove beyond a reasonable doubt that David G. Delongpre, alias Gaylord Harcourt, alias Gordon G. Delongpre did, with malice of forethought, on the night of July 17th 1998 did willingly, and with premeditation, kill Amanda Hollingsworth, address 8557 Jefferson St, Charleston South Carolina, and on the same night met, and murdered, Mrs. Molly Philburn, address 2743 Kings Court, Charleston South Carolina. When the defendant was pursued by officer Harry Mackland of the Charleston Police, he assaulted, and brutally murdered this officer in cold blood. We will also prove that on the night of September 15th 1998 the defendant brutally attacked, and murdered, officer Franklin Farley of the Charleston Police Department. The defendant, dressed as a police officer, entered the residence of Henrietta Wentworth assaulted, kidnapped, and attempted to rape FBI agent Sally Thornton who was on assignment with the Charleston Police Department. Furthermore, the defendant while evading capture at approximately 2:00 am September 16th did assault, and rape Miss Judy Hampton a nurse's aide at Charleston Memorial Hospital." There was a low murmur in the courtroom as Homer paused to look at his notes. "Now, you've noticed that the Court, and I, have used several names when identifying the accused." Homer moved closer to the jury box as he continued, "Now, the defense will try to convince you that the defendant is not guilty by reason of insanity." He paused, the gestured with his hands. "Why not? These crimes are so horrendous, so repugnant, one would have to be insane to commit them." Homer turned, faced the jury box, and looked the jurors squarely in the eye, then emphasized, "don't let the defense fool you. The defendant carefully chose his victims, planned his approach, stalked their every move before closing in for the kill." Homer stepped away from the jury box and faced the defendant who had put his forehead on the edge of the table and gazed at the floor.

"Our judicial system has emphasized over the centuries that 'free will' is the prime postulate of culpability under our jurisprudence." Homer turned again to face the jury, and leaned on the railings of the jury box before continuing,

"Our concept is in the freedom of the human will, and the ability of the individual to choose between good and evil. This is our core concept that is universal, and constant in a mature system of law." Homer stepped back, and slowly walked to his table. "As we proceed with this trial I ask you to keep these principles firmly in your mind. Criminal responsibility is assessed when through 'free will,' when a man, such as the accused," Homer pointed at the defendant, "with malice, and intent, freely elects to do evil, he should be punished to the fullest extent of the law."

With a satisfied expression on his face Homer sat down and looked at Barbara Starkey.

Judge Buckner turned his attention to the defense, "Counsel, you may make your opening argument."

Barbara Starkey rose slowly from her chair and faced the jury. Barbara was a statuesque woman with long auburn hair that hung gracefully down to her shoulders. She had a body that most women would die for. She could have had a successful career as a model but chose the law instead. She was one of those rare women who was blessed with both beauty and brains. She had long muscular legs, a thin waist, and athletic shoulders. Her most sensual feature were her breasts that stood erect, and pressed against the top of her opened blouse. She wore a tailored suit with a white silk blouse. When she leaned over to talk to the jury she revealed a magnificent cleavage. Barbara had wisely chose, using her challenges, in order to have more men on the jury than women. She knew that she could have a significant effect on men if she could keep their attention. Her dignified sensuality was one way of doing it. Barbara walked to the jury box, put her hands on the railing giving all the men on the jury a good look at her cleavage before she began.

"Your Honor, Ladies and Gentlemen of the Jury. The standard of criminal responsibility is a political compromise enforced by law. That's all it is, That's the way it is, that's the way it's always been. That's also it's genius. The common law is a system for achieving compromise and common standards for deciding who gets what, when, where, and how, and giving legitimacy, or force of law, to those decisions. That's why we are here today, to decide the guilt or innocence of the defendant." Barbara moved along the railing of the jury box, stopping, leaning over before she spoke so the other men might gaze one more time at her cleavage.

"The law clearly states that choice is the core of criminal liability." She paused, allowing those words to register with the jury before continuing. "A person who chooses to kill is more blameworthy than one who acts out of foolishness, inattention, or laboring under a mental disease. Justice Holmes once said, 'Even a dog knows the difference between being tripped over, and being stepped on.' As this trial progresses I want you to keep one idea in the back of your mind. The capacity to choose sets the threshold of criminal liability. Small children are treated differently from adults. The law recognizes that the defendant must have the mental capacity to appreciate, and control his conduct before he can be held criminally responsible for it.." All eyes in the jury box followed Barbara as she walked back and forth.

"What is criminal intent?" was the rhetorical question Barbara asked, then immediately supplied the answer. "Criminal intent is divided into four basic categories. The first is purpose, I mean by this, he is acting with a lethal object, a gun, a knife, knowing that this object will result in death. Second is knowledge. Doing something you consciously know will have a bad result. Third is, recklessness. Knowing, and taking an unreasonable risk. Last we have negligence, taking unreasonable risk whether you know it or not. And, of course, what the prosecution, and the defense, will examine during the course of this trial will encompass all of these aspects. The intent of the defendant." Starkey turned, and faced the courtroom audience. "The hit man, who kills for money, he acts on purpose, he is worse than a drunk driver who acts recklessly. The reckless driver who deliberately runs a red light is worse than the careless driver who doesn't see the red light." Barbara calmly walked back to her desk, and looked at her notes then focused her attention on the jury.

"Why do we punish people? Why are we here? I mean, what is the purpose in punishment?" Barbara motioned with her hands as she spoke, "deterrence, we say 'hang him', so the rest of the people won't get the same idea, and it will deter the person from making the wrong choice in the future. Incapacitation, in other words we say, 'get him off the streets' so he can't harm anyone else. Rehabilitation, we say, 'train him', so he can return and function normally in society. And of course there is retribution, the man deserves to die. The victim's family is satisfied, the Bible tells us an eye for an eye, and the harmed have been given their justice." Starkey moved briskly toward the jury as she continued to emphasize her words, "To punish in the absence of choice is absurd. It cannot deter. How can you deter someone from doing something he didn't choose to do? As for retribution, aren't we all angrier at the person who intentionally runs down a child than at the person who does it by accident? To punish in the absence of choice is morally unjust. Punishment requires fault, and fault requires the ability to do otherwise. We will prove that the defendant, who for years was abused as a child; Who was physically, and mentally tortured; Who has a mental illness so severe, so debilitating, that he was denied choice. That he was responding to the sexual demands placed upon him as a child. The defendant who sits before you does not need your condemnation, he needs your help. Thank you." Starkey sat down and touched the killer's hand tenderly.

The courtroom remained silent. Judge Buckner slipped Barbara a sly smile. Deep down he was proud of his student. Someday she was going to be one of the best lawyers in the country. Buckner turned his attention to Homer Canfield, "You may call your first witness." Homer nodded, looked at his list then announced, "The state calls Corporal Gerald Caughlin, Charleston Police Department."

Officer Caughlin rose from his seat, made his way down the isle, through the gate, to the witness stand. The bailiff held a Bible in his hand and commanded, "Raise your right hand." Caughlin complied. "Do you swear to tell the truth, the whole turth, and nothing but the truth so help you God?"

"I do," Caughlin replied.

"State your name for the record," was the bailiff's order before leaving the stand.

"Jerry Caughlin," he answered.

"Be seated," Buckner said, in an even voice. Homer stood at his desk with a list of questions in his hand.

"You are a member of the Charleston Police Force. Is that correct?"

"Yes."

Homer slowly approached the witness stand as he queried the witness. "You were on duty July 17th 1998?

"Yes."

"Can you tell the court what happened that night?"

Caughlin referred to a small notebook as he spoke, "At approximately 10:30p.m. I responded to a call that a murder had taken place at 2743 Kings Court. When I arrived I was met by Mrs. Mildred Potts who found the body. She identified the deceased as Molly Philburn, Caucasian, female, age 63, gray hair, blue eyes, weight 125lbs."

"What did Mrs. Potts have to say?"

Caughlin looked at his notes. "She indicated that she saw a stranger departing the area just as she was arriving."

"Did she describe the stranger?"

"Not completely, it was dark and foggy. However, she did describe a male, in his late 30's or mid 40's dressed in a dark suit, 140lbs to 170lbs. She said the subject was whistling some sort of a tune."

"What else did you notice?" Homer asked.

"It was strange. I've never seen anything like it before. The victim was sitting nude in an easy chair. A tea service had been set for her. A knotted panty hose was found tied around her neck. She'd been strangled and her neck was broken. I also noticed a small vase with flowers in it sitting on the tea tray in front of the victim. There was two tea cups. It was as if she sat down and had tea with her murderer."

"Then what did you do?" Canfield questioned.

"I called in, and confirmed we had a murder on our hands. Then asked for a crime scene unit to be dispatched to my location. Took a statement from Mrs. Potts, and secured the area."

"How long before the crime scene unit arrived?

"Forty-five minutes," Caughlin answered, looking at his notes.

"Did you notice any other peculiar aspects of the murder scene?"

"Yes, almost all the mirrors in the house had been smashed."

"Are you saying that the killer broke all the mirrors in the house, then sat down and had tea with the deceased?"

"Objection your honor!" Starkey interrupted. "The officer should report only fact. He has no way of knowing who broke the mirrors, or in fact, who even made the tea for that matter."

"Your honor," Canfield rebutted, "Subsequent testimony will substantiate this line of questioning, and will connect the defendant with the other killings."

"That's all well and good," Buckner replied to Canfield, "when that time comes you may recall this witness. As for now, stick to the facts. Sustained."

Homer referred to his notes before continuing. "Did you observe any other peculiarities at the crime scene?"

"Yes, there was no evidence of forced entry. There were large sums of money found in the deceased's purse and dresser drawer. The motive was not robbery. To my knowledge, no fingerprints were found. The victim's body had several small bruises on her arms, legs, and back."

"Did you observe anything else?" Canfield questioned returning to his desk.

"Yes, the victim's body appeared to have been sexually assaulted." There was a moment of silence over the courtroom.

"I have no further questions for this witness," Canfield announced, then sat down.

"Your witness," Buckner said, looking at Starkey. Barbara rose and walked to the witness stand as she spoke.

"You said the victim's body appeared to have been sexually assaulted," She paused momentarily, "you must be pretty good at your job. How could you tell she was sexually assaulted without an autopsy?"

"I've seen these cases before. She was nude, obviously not about to take a shower. She had multiple bruises and I observed what I believe to be semen in the vaginal area and on her face."

"Do you always check the vaginal area of your victims? Barbara said sarcastically.

"Objection! Your honor! Counsel is badgering the witness with cheap shots."

"Sustained," Judge Buckner announced firmly, "Lets keep this clean counselor,"

"I'm sorry. I withdraw the question." Starkey returned to her table and said, "I have no further questions for this witness."

"The witness is dismissed," Buckner commanded. Caughlin quickly returned to his seat. Homer Canfield examined his notes again before announcing, "The prosecution calls Detective Sergeant Nancy Coates."

Detective Sergeant Coates was a strong willed woman endowed with an abundance of self confidence who strode to the witness stand, and was quickly sworn in. Homer continued to look at his question sheet walking slowly to the witness stand. "Detective Coates. You received a call to respond to a neighbors complaint about a loud noise at 8557 Jefferson street is that correct"

"yes."

"Is it usual for a detective to be called out for a domestic complaint?"

"No, not normally. But everyone of the units were unavailable so I took the call."

"I see. What did you find when you arrived?" Homer asked carefully.

"I found the radio, excuse me, it was a tape hi-fi playing loud music." Coates answered quickly, then continued, "I knocked, found the door opened. I announced myself as a police officer, then entered."

"What did you discover?"

"I found one dead female. Identified as Amanda Hollingsworth, age 65, gray hair, weight 145lbs." Coates paused.

"Go ahead," Homer urged.

"The victim was dead. She had been strangled with a silk scarf."

"What else did you discover?" Canfield questioned.

"She was nude, sitting upright on the sofa. There was a tray with a complete tea service, with scones and fine china as though she had just finished tea with the killer."

"Go on."

"Every mirror in the house had been broken. Also, same as the other murder scene, there was a small vase of flowers on the tray."

"Anything else?"

"Yes, no evidence of forced entry. No money was taken. The victim's car was still in the garage, and the keys were in the victim's handbag." Coates answered referring to her notes.

"Then what did you do?" Canfield asked, leading the officer as though this was a well rehearsed play.

"I notified the dispatcher that I had a murder, and needed a crime scene unit here ASAP.

"What was their response?" Homer asked, knowing the answer.

"I was told that the crime scene unit was already on a location just two blocks away from my location." Coates answered confidently.

"So, what we have here is two murders committed within hours of each other only 2 blocks apart. Is that correct?" Canfield surmised as he walked toward the jury box.

"Yes."

"And these murders were absolutely identical is that right?" Canfield asked, leaning on the jury box rail.

"Not quiet," Coates answered, surprising Canfield momentarily.

"Two different bodies." Coates added bluntly.

"Of course," Canfield smiled. "However, wouldn't you say that the victims were similar. I mean, they were in the sixties, alone, widowed, and vulnerable?"

"Yes."

"Now, officer Coates, you are a well trained investigative officer. What did you think about all this?"

"It didn't take a rocket scientist to figure out we had a serial killer in our town," She answered smartly.

"Thank you." Canfield was about to finish his questioning when he asked, "Oh, officer Coates, did you notice if the victim had been sexually assaulted?"

"Yes, the victim ha multiple bruises and semen on her stomach, vaginal area, and on her face."

"Thank you. I have no further question for this witness." Canfield sat down. Buckner looked at Barbara Starkey, "Your witness."

Barbara stood up and walked toward the witness stand. "How did you know that the fluid on the victim's body was semen? I mean doesn't that require a chemical analysis?"

Coates smirked, "I don't know about your sex life but mine is pretty good. I know semen when I see it. Besides, she's naked, in her home, at night, she sure as hell isn't getting a sun tan, she's getting laid."

The courtroom broke into laughter. Media artist scribbled their drawings as fast as they could to capture the brash police officer on the stand.

"Officer Coates, it's been established that you are a well trained investigative officer. From your experience, could you say that the same person committed both murders?"

"Yes."

"Could you also conclude that anyone in their right mind would commit two identical murders, hours apart, only a few blocks away from each other?"

"No," Coates said calmly.

"I have no further questions for this witness," Barbara said, and casually sat down. All eyes were on officer Coates as she returned to her seat giving Sally a wink of confidence.

Homer Canfield rose again from his chair, "The state calls Detective David Danelli to the stand."

Danelli took the stand quietly and repeated the oath in a professional manner.

"Your honor, the state would like to offer into evidence prosecution's exhibit A and B. The crime scene reports for both Amanda Hollingsworth and Molly Philburn." Homer handed copies of the two reports to the defense, and the court Bailiff.

"Now, officer Danelli, you were in charge of the crime scene investigation unit that responded to both murder scenes."

"Yes I was." Danelli responded curtly.

"Where the two murders identical?"

"Yes with the exception of the victims, and location, they were the same."

"Are you telling this court they were exactly identical?"

"Almost. One victim was strangled with a panty hose and the other with a silk scarf. The killer served the same tea, Orange Pekoe I believe, and served the same scones."

"I see," Canfield said, pacing in front of the witness.

"Were you able to determine how the killer obtained entry without breaking a window or forcing the door?"

"Yes, the victim let him in." Danelli announced

"Why would the victim let a man in the house at night when she was alone?" Homer asked, scratching the back of his head lightly.

"The murderer was either someone she knew, or the killer presented himself as a non threat."

"How would he do that?" Canfield asked pointedly.

"Our search of the defendant's apartment revealed several policeman's uniforms, a priest's white collar, a gold cross, and a rosary." Danelli answered, looking at his notes.

"So, it's your contention that in order to gain entry the accused posed as an officer of the law or a priest."

"That would be a logical explanation." Danelli answered calmly.

"Can you be more definitive. What was it a policeman or a priest?" Canfield said, carefully leading the witness.

"He was a priest," Danelli answered firmly.

"How did your arrive at that conclusion?"

"We found uncashed checks for the Southern Christian Association in a folder in the defendant's closet when we searched his apartment. There were two checks that were drawn on both victim's bank account. They were signed by the victims. They were dated on the day of the murders, and they had the defendant's fingerprints on them."

Canfield moved closer to the jury box before making his point. "So, the accused had received checks written, dated and signed by each of the victims on the night of the murder."

"Objection! Those checks could have been sent in the mail and received at any time after that date. That does not place the defendant in the house at that precise time."

"Sustained. We need some more substantial evidence." Buckner advised.

"Yes you honor," Homer acknowledged. He turned his attention back to the witness. "Is it possible that the killer could have posed as a priest to gain entry? Maybe asking for donations?"

"It's possible." Danelli replied.

Canfield went to his table and displayed two small plastic bags with uncashed checks inside. "Your honor, if it please the court, I would like to enter prosecution's exhibit C into evidence. Two uncashed checks found in the accused's apartment" Canfield handed the bags to the court Bailiff.

"You will note that the checks are made out to Southern Christian Association. Bank records indicate that the defendant is the sole owner of this account." Canfield produced another sheet of paper. "You honor prosecution would like to introduce state's exhibit D an inventory of the contents of the defendant's apartment. The search warrant was issued by Judge David Hornsby on the 15th of September." Canfield handed the papers to the court Bailiff. Turning his attention to Officer Danelli, Canfield continued, "Now, along with these checks, what else did you find?"

Danelli looked at his notes, "we found records of previous bank accounts from Seattle, Dallas, and Houston."

"What did these accounts reveal?"

"We found accounts titled 'Christian Overseas Relief Fund', 'The Christian Children's Book Association,' and the 'Catholic Relief Fund.'"

"Was the defendant in anyway associated with any of these organizations?" Canfield carefully led the witness in order to make an impact on the jury.

"No they were bogus," Danelli replied.

"So it was a scam."

"No not quite."

"How come?" Canfield asked, as he turned to face the jury, knowing what the answer would be.

"These were real accounts and the defendant was the administrator in charge. He also used these accounts to cover personal expenses. Also, three of the names on canceled checks to these accounts were murdered. Two in Seattle, and one in Houston."

"Can I assume you contacted the Seattle and Houston police in order to obtain this information? Canfield asked smugly.

"Yes," Danelli responded, flipping through his notes.

The confident lawyer marched to his desk, and produced two more pieces of paper. "You honor, I would like to enter into evidence state's exhibit E and F. Police reports from the Seattle and Houston police." He handed the papers to the court Bailiff and copies to the defense counsel.

"Now, I won't read these reports verbatim. However, officer Danelli you've read them. Can you summarize what they say?"

Officer Danelli looked at the jury before beginning, "They show that three names that appear in these ledgers have been murdered." A low murmur echoed through the courtroom.

"What else did they reveal?"

"The information we received from the Seattle, and Houston police confirms that Mrs. Shirley Vido, Mrs, Carol Manning, and a Maggie Smith were in their late 50's to 60's, alone, widowed, they were strangled, and raped."

"Now officer Danelli, this could be coincidence couldn't it?"

"Not likely. The M.O. was the same."

"Explain to the jury what you mean by M.O.," Canfield asked confidently.

"Each of the victims were strangled, sexually assaulted, served tea, and had flowers." Danelli said calmly. Ripples of whispers and head turning moved through the courtroom. Canfield stepped closer to the state's witness before making his point. "So, in each of these cities, three women were murdered in the same way as the women murdered here in Charleston?"

"That's correct." Danelli answered.

"Objection, your honor! This line of questioning is prejudicial to the defendant. The state has produced no definitive evidence that he was in these cities at the time of these murders." Starkey demanded.

"Your honor," Canfield rebutted, "If will allow me to continue I can substantiate the defendant's whereabouts."

"Overruled," Buckner ordered.

Canfield paced in front of the witness, "Were you able to place the defendant in Seattle at the time of these murders?"

"Yes." Danelli flipped a page in his notebook. "He was issued a Washington State driver's license at that time. He paid state taxes, and even got a library card."

"Objection your honor!" Starkey said in frustration, "The defendant is being charged for murder in the first degree in the state of South Carolina, not in Washington. This again is prejudicial your honor."

"Your honor," Canfield interrupted, "this goes to cause and shows a trend to substantiate that the defendant is a multiple killer, a sociopath, who preys on helpless women."

Buckner leaned forward," I appreciate where you are going with this. Unless you can offer more substantial facts I will have to rule for the defense."

"Your honor, my next witness will have substantial evidence to validate these claims."

"I hope so," Buckner replied, "let's get on with it counselor."

"Officer Danelli, what else did you discover in the defendant's apartment? Canfield quietly asked.

"In the closet we found the mummified remains of a man 40 to 50 years of age. The skull of the victim indicated a severe blow to the head which was the probable cause of death."

"Were you able to identify the victim?" Canfield queried, walking again toward the jury box. Danelli turned to another page in his book. "Dental records indicate that the victim was Doctor Michael Smith, reported missing by the Seattle police." Danelli answered mechanically.

"Let's see if I understand you? Are you telling this court that you found human remains in the defendant's apartment who you were able to identify as Dr. Michael Smith from Seattle?"

"Yes," Danelli stated bluntly.

"I have no further questions for this witness." Canfield said. He returned to his seat at the prosecution's table.

"Your witness," Judge Buckner said wondering what Starkey was going to do with this damaging testimony. Barbara rose slowly from her chair. Glanced at the defendant who sat quietly with his forehead still resting on the edge of the table as though he thought he could drown out all the bad words.

"Officer Danelli. How long have you been with the Charleston Police" She asked, walking toward the witness stand.

"Fifteen years," he answered proudly.

"How long have you been assigned to the crime scene investigation unit?"

"Nine years."

"How many murder investigations have you been actively involved in your nine years of experience?"

"I'd say fifty, give or take one or two."

"I see," Barbara acknowledged, turning toward the jury box. "In all that time have you ever seen a murder scene quite like the ones you've seen in this case?"

"No, not hardly," Danelli answered, shaking his head slightly.

"How come?" Barbara queried quickly, not looking a the witness but looking at the jury.

"Well, most murderers usually try to hide the fact that they've murdered someone. They hide, or get rid of evidence. Our killer was just to opposite. He kept souvenirs taken from his victims."

"What do you mean souvenirs?"

"Well, like underwear, photos, newspaper clippings, maybe some of the victim's hair."

"Did the defendant have any such items?"

"Yes."

"Like what?"

Danelli scanned his notes quickly, "Ah, he had Dr. Smith's wallet, ID cards, credit cards. We found underwear and a bra belonging to Amanda Hollingsworth along with some other personal items belonging to Molly Philburn. It is all in the report."

"In your experience, have you ever seen anyone in his right mind keep a dead body in his closet?"

"No."

Barbara Starkey chose her words carefully, and spoke slowly with inflection in every word. "Do you think the defendant is crazy?"

"Yes."

The courtroom erupted with hush murmurs. Buckner rapped his gavel, "Order in the court."

"Objection you honor," Canfield interrupted in a loud voice. "That calls for a conclusion from the witness. He is not a qualified psychiatrist."

Barbara countered quickly, "Your honor, this officer is a veteran crime scene investigator. He is more than qualified to make that judgment based on what he observed at the crime scene."

"You can't have it both ways counselor. I suggest you rephrase your question. Sustained." Buckner said, looking at Barbara. Starkey rephrased her question. "Looking at the crime scene evidence, and the search of his apartment what would you say about the defendant?"

"Either he wanted to get caught or he's very stupid. Nobody in his right mind keeps a dead body around for years."

"Move to strike your honor," Homer said, with a bored expression. Buckner looked at the court recorder, "Strike that last statement," Buckner adjusted his glasses higher on his nose then nodded at Barbara Starkey to continue.

"I have no further questions for this witness."

"The witness may step down," Buckner ordered.

Before Danelli was able to seat himself Canfield quickly announced, "The state calls Dr. Roger Mudd. Let the record show the Dr. Mudd is the Chief of Pathology for the state of South Carolina."

Dr. Mudd was a slightly plump man with a balding head. For a man who dealt with death on a daily basis was unusually jolly. He told jokes and played pranks on his fellow coworkers. It was his way of coping with the sadness in seeing the everyday waste of human life in his community. Some of his pranks were not always in the best of taste. When a reporter wrote an unflattering article about him in the newspaper, it was rumored, that at a charity banquet, he slipped the severed finger of a cadaver in the reporter's soup. Needless to say, no one ever challenged his abilities again. Mudd was a meticulous man, and took great care when conducting autopsies. He was the past president of the American Society of Crime Lab Directors, A contributing writer for the College of American Pathologists and had done research for the Forensic Science Technical Center. Dr. Mudd was sworn in, and seated himself comfortably in the stand. Mudd was a twenty year veteran and had forgotten how many times he had presented testimony in court.

"Dr. Mudd, you are the coroner assigned to the Gray Lady Investigation Task Force? Canfield said, examining his notes at his table.

"Yes I am," he answered, then glanced at Judge Buckner and commented, "And I would like to insure you your honor that I am in no way related to, or connected to, the TV news anchorman of the same name." The courtroom laughed at the irony of the name, realizing Buckner's on going battle with the media. Buckner smiled at the joke, and answered jokingly, "I am relieved by that disclosure."

"Dr. Mudd," Canfield quickly interjected, "you performed the autopsies on Amanda Hollingsworth and Molly Philburn?"

"Yes I did."

"Please tell the court what your findings were."

"Both victims died of strangulation. The victims suffered a crushed esophagus, and each had a broken neck."

Canfield retrieved another folder from his desk. "The state would like to enter into evidence State's exhibit E and F. Coroner's report on both female victims."

This time Judge Buckner motioned for the Court Bailiff to hand him the coroner's reports. Canfield positioned himself next to the witness stand, and handed Dr. Mudd a copy of his report.

"Dr. Mudd, I'd like to draw your attention to the item marked 2-1 titled 'Body Fluids.' Dr. Mudd knew the report by heart, and had no need to refer to the report while he waited for Canfield's next question. "What were your findings concerning both victims?"

"We found semen in the vaginal area, on the stomach, on the face, and in the mouth of both victims," Mudd answered tonelessly.

"Any other fluids found on the victims?"

"Yes, in the mouth of each victim we found a small amount of tea."

"Were you able to identify the tea?"

"Yes, Orange Pekoe."

Canfield walked to the jury box before asking his next question. "Did you perform a DNA test on the semen?"

"Yes," Mudd replied, knowing what counsel's next question was going to be.

"Were you able to identify the DNA?"

"Yes. The DNA taken from the semen found on the victims match the DNA taken from the defendant."

Another, and louder outburst of murmurs, head nodding and whispering swept through the courtroom.

"Order please!" Buckner commanded loudly. Canfield paced in front to the jury as he continued to question the coroner. "How accurate are the DNA tests?"

"They are 99.9% accurate." Mudd answered confidently.

"You honor," Canfield said, quickly walking to his desk. We would like to enter state's exhibit G into evidence to illustrate this point." Canfield produced two large charts, and a display stand so the court could see the DNA trace charts.

"Doctor, would you explain about DNA, and show the jury what you found?"

Dr. Mudd left the stand, and stood by the two large charts. Using a pocket laser pointer, he pointed at a particular part of the DNA diagram. He began slowly, knowing that the jury would have trouble following him. "DNA has a unique structure that consists of two chains like strands arranged in a twisted ladder, double helix form." He moved his laser pointer up and down the diagram. "The sides are made up of alternating sections of phosphate, and a sugar called deoxyribose. The inner strands are pairs of thymine, I've marked with the letter T, and adenosine, I've marked with the letter A, and guanine, the letter G, finally cytosine, the letter C. These bases are the letters of the DNA alphabet using a language of the genetic code. Each person's DNA code has about 3 billion locations that tell us all our traits. Because all of us belong to the same species, a large amount of our DNA codes are identical. Traits we have in common such as ten fingers and toes have identical DNA codes. Our individual differences are produced by unique DNA codes. Each person has a difference of at least 10 million spots along the DNA strand." The doctor continued to move the red pointer across the charts. "One in every three hundred locations will be unique. These unique places are called DNA markers and these are what we use in Forensic Science to identify people."

"Is there any possibility that two people could have the same DNA trace?" Canfield asked loudly.

"Only identical twins. The DNA of each person is unique. That's why it's so useful in identification." Dr. Mudd added. "We then isolate the DNA in question from the rest of the cellular material. We do this chemically. The DNA is then poured into a gel, such as agarose, or onto a sheet. An electrical charge is applied to the gel. Because the DNA is slightly negatively charged all the DNA will be attracted to one pole. The smaller genes move faster that the larger genes, and they will separate. The DNA sheet is blotted, applied to a paper, and then X-rayed. What you see on these charts are the X-ray comparisons." Dr. Mudd moved his red pointer from one chart to the other.

"If you will notice the chart on the left matches the chart on the right. Here and here," Mudd said, moving his laser highlighter. The chart on the left is a DNA semen sample taken from Amanda Hollingsworth, and the other is the defendant's DNA. The semen sample taken from Molly Philburn also matches the defendant's DNA."

"Thank you doctor." Mudd returned to the witness stand.

"Dr. Mudd can you say without reservation that the defendant raped Amanda Hollingsworth, and Molly Philburn?"

"Yes, with one reservation." Mudd said, but Canfield was not surprised by Mudd's last statement.

"What sort of reservation do you have?"

Mudd was ready to lay another bombshell in the courtroom.

"They were both dead when they were raped."

Buckner shook his head in disbelief.

"What else did you autopsy reveal?" Canfield asked.

"The victims were also dead when they had tea."

"So, what you are telling this court is that the defendant, with murder as his primary motive, strangled his victims, had sex with them, then calmly sat down, and had tea with them?"

"That's affirmative with the exception of the murder of officer Mackland and officer Farley."

"How were you able to determine that the defendant, in cold blood, murdered officer Mackland, and officer Farley?"

Dr. Mudd glanced at Beau before beginning his testimony. They both knew what he was going say.

"Officer Mackland was strangled with a piece of doubled stranded packing wire which was attached to a piece of wood that came from a packing crate found behind Fowler's Furniture store. The wood, and the wire had blood on it. When we analyzed the blood, some of it did not belong to the victim. We then did a DNA sample, and it matched the defendant's DNA. Agent Thornton discovered officer Farley's body at the Gladlow residence. He had been strangled in the same manner as the other victims."

"Your honor," Canfield addressed the judge, "I would like to enter into evidence state's exhibit H. Canfield displayed a large clear plastic bag. He held it in full view of the jury. "This is the wire, the killing mechanism that ended officer Mackland's life. If you will note, the blood stains on the wood. They belong to the defendant." After Canfield was sure that each member of the jury had a good look at the bloody wire he continued. "This bloody wire, the testimony of professional investigators, and pathologists show explicitly, that the defendant is nothing more than a cold, sexually motivated, sociopath, who has no regard for human life."

"Objection our honor!" Barbara shouted sarcastically, "would the prosecution please save the rhetoric for closing."

Buckner smiled, "sustained. You'll have your chance. Let's get on with it."

"Yes your honor," Canfield replied, as he moved again to the witness stand. "Dr. Mudd, other than the DNA was there anything else that tied the defendant to these murders?"

"Yes, we found pubic hair in the vaginal areas of both victims. They match the defendant's" Canfield paused, then went to his desk, and displayed a small clear plastic bag. Holding the bag Canfield approached Dr. Mudd.

"Can you identify this for the court?"

Mudd examined the bag quickly, "Yes, these are fibers taken from officer Franklin's clothing."

"That would be Officer Franklin Farley, correct?"

"Correct. We also found these same fibers on Agent Thornton's clothes, and in the defendant's apartment. Oh yes, we also found these same fibers in the car which the defendant stole."

"You honor, the state would like to enter into evidence state's exhibit I. Now, Dr. Mudd, were your people able to identify these fibers?"

"Yes, they are from a special woven fabric used in the manufacture of police uniforms. The dye lot number is that dye used only in police clothing."

"Is it safe to assume that the killer caught officer Farley off guard by posing as a police officer?"

"Objection, your honor. Counselor is asking for a conclusion of what may or may not have occurred."

"Sustained," Buckner stated quickly.

"Dr. Mudd," Canfield asked, rephrasing his question. "As a police officer. If you were sitting alone, in a car, on a foggy night, and a stranger approached you in a police uniform would you consider him friendly?"

"Yes."

Canfield paused, then went back to his desk and looked again at his notes before beginning.

"Lets go back to officer Mackland. What else did you note on your autopsy of the deceased?"

Dr. Mudd replied quickly, "He had been stabbed repeatedly with a kitchen knife."

Canfield held up another plastic bag. "Is this the knife?"

"Yes it is."

"Your honor, we would like to enter state's exhibit J into evidence."

Buckner nodded. Canfield approached the witness. "What can you tell the court about this knife?"

"It is a common kitchen knife, cheap, plastic handle. You can buy it at any Wal-Mart."

"Anything else?"

"Yes, on this item we were able to remove fingerprints but they were smudged. We were unable to get a positive match with the defendant. However there were similarities."

"So, this was the knife that killed Harry Mackland.

"No, not necessarily," Mudd answered surprising Canfield, "He may have been already dead."

"So, the killer with extreme malice, and hate, continued to stab a dead man, is that right?

"Yes."

The courtroom fell silent. Canfield held the knife high momentarily so the jury could get the full impact of Dr. Mudd's testimony. Then Canfield paced in front of the jury box looking thoughtfully at the floor. He looked up before speaking, "In all your years of experience, why would a man repeatedly stab another man repeatedly stab another man hanging from a wire by his neck, who for all practical purposes may have been dead?"

"The killer wanted to make sure the victim was dead."

"Could this have been done in a jealous rage?"

"Objection!, calls for a conclusion. The learned doctor has no idea what went through killer's mind anymore than I do." Barbara interrupted.

"I withdraw the question," Canfield said, with a sly smile knowing he had already made his point to the jury. Canfield continued. "Lets bring this full circle. Did you perform any other DNA tests?"

"Yes, we took semen from the rape victim Judy Hampton."

"Did they match the defendant's DNA?"

"Yes. All three women were attacked by the same man."

Canfield calmly walked to his desk. "I have no further questions for this witness at this time. However, as we may have to refer to forensic evidence as we progress I would like the right to recall."

"You may." Buckner looked at Barbara. There wasn't much she could do against the flood of physical evidence that the coroner had presented against the defendant but she had to use some of it to her advantage.

"Your witness," Buckner announced.

Barbara rose slowly glancing at the defendant who still had his head down. He reminded her of an ostrich sticking his head in the sand so he couldn't hear, or see, what was going on around him. Barbara walked toward the witness thinking of ways she might turn this testimony to her advantage or at least lesson the impact on the jury. If she couldn't make that happen maybe she could use it to cast doubt as to the sanity of defendant. But first, she had to blunt the effectiveness of the forensic evidence. She knew that the jury would have a tendency to take forensic evidence as gospel, as harbinger's of the truth. After all, it was science, and most of us failed high school chemistry.

"Dr. Mudd," Barbara Starkey began slowly, "did you do the DNA testing yourself?"

"No, We send that out to a lab who is licensed to perform that kind of procedure." He answered calmly.

"What lab did you send the evidence samples to?"

"Ah, we sent the samples to Columbia Medical Labs Inc, right here in Charleston."

"In fact, Columbia Labs does all the forensic testing for the state, is that correct?" Barbara asked, looking at her notes. Barbara continued before Mudd could answer.

"Do you own stock in that company doctor?" Barbara questioned, as she walked slowly to the jury box.

"I know what you are getting at counselor. Yes, I own stock. The mayor owns stock, the governor owns stock, and it might even be part of your 401K. That had no influence on the outcome of the tests." He replied angrily.

"I am sure it didn't. But we have to cover every aspect of such evidence presented by the prosecution. You know the jury will treat forensic evidence as overwhelming proof of guilt. But let's take another look at what actually happens to this evidence. Now, correct me if I am wrong. First, you collect the evidence at the scene of the crime. If you are not careful it could become contaminated at the scene."

"Not likely," Dr. Mudd interrupted.

"Isn't it true, that at one of the crime scenes, Lt. Gasteneau had his dog running all over the place?" She rebutted quickly.

"Yes, but he is a trained police dog, and we use him to pick up the scent of the killer." Dr. Mudd replied, getting slightly nervous.

"I understand. Then the evidence sample has to be packaged, labeled and stored evidence locker, then transported to the lab. That's three or more ways it could become contaminated. At the lab the evidence has to be logged in, labeled, and stored. Usually, it's given another identification number," Barbara said, going down her list of items while looking at the doctor. "Then at the lab it is removed, tagged again, mingled with other evidence, then be properly documented. All this is done even before the first, and as you pointed out, the complicated test begins. Then, this little minute piece of evidence," She held up the little plastic bag, "has to travel to a contamination free room where it must be properly unpackaged, this I am told is an art in itself. In most cases it will be photographed and weighed before any lab work begins. Am I right so far?" Barbara asked a frustrated Dr. Mudd. He nodded, then said softly, "Yes."

"Then you have to determine if you have the right amount of material to test. Was there enough evidence material to properly test?"

"Yes."

"Now, as you pointed out there is about five of six different steps to be performed in order to do the DNA test. Then a report has to be prepared and the evidence is sent back to the police evidence locker. Does that about sum it up."

"You honor," Canfield interrupted. This is all well and good, and we appreciate the counselor's knowledge of forensic procedures. What's her point?"

Buckner looked at Barbara. "You honor, my point is, no other type of evidence is exposed to anywhere near as many opportunities for destruction, mishandling, contamination, or any other conceivable catastrophe than this."

Buckner nodded in approval, "You point is taken. Continue."

Barbara went to her desk and picked up another folder and approached the witness, "Now, you have qualified lab technicians perform these DNA tests is that correct?"

"Yes." Mudd replied, slightly upset at this line of questioning.

"What type of written test are they required to take in order to be certified?" Barbara asked, pointedly.

"They take the test published by the American Academy of Forensic Sciences." Mudd answered smugly.

"Yes. Let me see if I am correct. This test covers, toxicology, ballistics, fingerprinting, fiber and hair identification.?" She said, referring to the notes in the folder.

"Yes, this is a composite test given annually." Mudd added confidently.

"The passing score is 70% is it not?" Barbara asked looking at the jury.

"Yes,"

"So, it is possible to fail, lets say, toxicology, and still pass the test?" There were murmurs throughout the courtroom. The media made quick notes and whispered to each other. Dr. Mudd looked embarrassingly at the camera.

"That's possible. But we have quality control procedures in effect. And, the technicians get blind tests throughout the year to insure proficiency in their lab work." Mudd said, trying to repair the damage being done by a well informed defense counselor.

"Yes, you're right. That brings me to this document." Barbara Starkey walked to the stand, and handed Dr. Mudd some papers. "These are the bench notes used in the DNA tests conducted on the defendant's DNA are they not?"

Dr. Mudd, now on the defensive, said, "Yes."

"Turn to page four and notice the notes handwritten by the technician who conducted the test." She asked, firmly.

Dr. Mudd flipped to the requested page and stopped.

"Please read the note to the court?" She requested.

Dr. Mudd hesitated then read the note. "This should convict that honky son-of-a-bitch."

"Was the technician that conducted the test black?"

"Yes." Mudd said, reluctantly.

365

"So, how can the court except the value of any DNA test conducted when we can't trust the biases of the tester?"

More murmurs rushed through the courtroom as they waited for Dr. Mudd's answer.

"Two reasons," Mudd said sternly, "First, each lab technician has a code of ethics that they must adhere to. Secondly, the same DNA tests were done by the FBI's forensic laboratory, and they also came up with the same DNA results."

"I hope you're right." Barbara Starkey paused. She realized she's gotten as much as she could out this line of questioning.

"Dr. Mudd," she said, standing next to the state's star forensic witness, "you testified that the killer had sex with the victims after they were dead. Is that correct?"

"Yes, that is correct."

"How were you able to determine that the accused actually had sex after death?"

"The semen in the vaginal area had not been absorbed by the surrounding tissue. When a person is alive the body automatically begins interacting with that substance. For example, we found tea and semen in the mouth of the victims. If she'd been alive at that time, some of the substance would have been found in the stomach, or in the lower esophagus. It was still in their mouths. Also, rigidity of the corpse indicated that the victims had been dead for several hours before sexual activity."

"I see," Starkey paused, "Have you ever heard of a man having sex with a corpse?"

"No, it's a little sick if you ask me."

"Sick? You mean crazy?" Barbara asked, leading the witness. This was where she wanted to take the witness. To get it on the record that the police thought he was crazy.

"Objection!" Canfield protested.

"Your honor," Barbara interrupted, "This information was volunteered by the good doctor, and the question leads to motive, and the prosecution has already opened the door for this line of questioning."

"Over ruled, I'd like to hear more. Besides, there will be plenty of time to present psychiatric testimony later. Go ahead," Buckner ordered.

"Would you answer the question?" Starkey asked calmly.

"Yes, I would say that the evidence points to a mentally disturbed individual."

"Thank you doctor," Barbara Starkey moved to the jury box before asking her next question. "Dr. Mudd, I refer you to states" exhibit J. The knife that killed officer Mackland,.. Excuse me, I mean the knife that killer used to repeatedly plunge into the body of a dying officer, right?"

"Right."

"How were you able to tie the ownership of that knife to the defendant if the fingerprints were smudged?"

"When we searched his apartment we found a set of knives exactly like the one removed from officer Mackland's body."

"That's a common brand isn't it? Hasn't hundred of thousands of these knives been sold?"

"Yes, that's true."

"So, it is possible that the knife introduced into evidence could have come from another set?"

"Yes, but not likely given the other evidence."

"I see," Starkey said, as she paused thinking about her next question. "How many times was officer Mackland stabbed?"

"We counted 15 wounds on the officer's body."

Barbara Starkey walked to the jury box, and placed both hands on the rail, before asking, "What do you think of a man who strikes a dead man 15 times with a butcher knife knowing that any one blow would be fatal?"

"He was either in an uncontrollable rage, or didn't know what he was doing."

Barbara moved down the rail of the jury box giving all the men another good look at her cleavage before continuing, "In an uncontrollable rage, or didn't know what he was doing. Thank you doctor Mudd. I have no further questions for this witness."

"Redirect Your Honor!" Canfield demanded.

"Your witness," Buckner replied.

Standing at his desk Canfield questioned, "In all your forensic experience have you seen any cases where the victim received multiple stab wounds?"

"Yes, several."

"In all those cases, were any of them found to be insane by the court?"

"No. None."

"Thank you doctor," Canfield said with a smile of confidence.

"You may step down. Please make yourself available for recall." Judge Buckner rapped his gavel hard getting the court's full attention. "It's getting late, and I am sure some of us have deadlines to meet. This court is adjourned until 10:00am tomorrow,"

"All rise," the Bailiff shouted. Buckner rose, and made a hasty exit to his chambers.

Chapter Twenty Two

The Realm of Madness

Beau sat pensively under the old Magnolia tree that stood guard over Falconbriar. The overcast sky had an orange glow that sat on the western horizon as sun made it's way to the other side of the world. Studs nuzzled his nose under Beau's arm, and laid his head in his lap. "Hello buddy," Beau said, knowing that Studs, through sheer love of his master, could understand. Beau often wondered if this dog, his pal, knew what was on his mind, knew when he was troubled. Studs looked up at his master as if to say, "I'm here. Maybe if you pet me I can make things okay for you."

"I've missed you buddy. I see you have a new friend. I want you to take care of Katie. Watch over her. Promise?" Studs lifted his head at the sound of Katie's name and gave Beau a big panting smile. "Go on, scram," Beau said calmly. Studs trotted off looking for his new friend.

"What are you thinking about?" Casey Thornton asked, as she sat down next to Beau.

"I don't know, just thinking I guess." He answered lazily.

"You aren't having second thoughts about your commitment to Sally are you?" Casey said, with a sting of Irish humor in her words.

"No, every moment, every second, with Sally and Katie I consider a blessing."

Casey put her arm around Beau giving him the motherly comfort and understanding, that for some reason, she knew he needed. Casey looked intently at Beau, "Do you have any idea how much Sally and Katie love you?" Casey answered the question before he could speak, "Your her knight in shinning armor, you're the answer to her prayers, you are the love that Katie needs," Casey smiled, and gave him a kiss on the cheek, "and if it makes your feel any better, I love you too, and your mom." Beau smiled, and put his arm around Casey. "I think you're pretty neat too." Beau said, then looked at Casey curiously, "Sally told me about you and her dad. I mean, all you went through in Ireland. If you had your life to live over would you do it again?" Beau didn't have to wait to hear Casey's answer, "In a moments notice", she remarked. "He was a fine man. He could see more with his heart than most men see with two eyes in a lifetime." Casey answered, closing her eyes for a moment thinking back to those memories that are engraved into one's heart, into one's existence.

"Tell me something," Casey asked, not looking at Beau, but looking at the orange horizon. "If you had your life to live over what would you do different?"

Beau sat silently for a few moments before answering Casey's question. "I would probably take fewer things more seriously. I would climb more mountains, swim more rivers. Take more time to enjoy what I have here."

"Anything else?" Casey asked trying to bring Beau out of his depression.

"I would eat more ice cream, and fewer beans. I would go to more dances, and ride a few more roller coasters, and take more time to smell the flowers." Beau looked at Casey, and smiled, "Then I would search every world, scale every wall, to find your Sally."

Casey laughed out loud, "who said the Irish have the corner on malarkey?"

They both hugged each other tenderly. "So, now that we've got you chipper again, why were you sitting out here so gloomy?" She questioned lightly. Beau's expression changed to a more serious demeanor as he spoke, "Oh, the trial, all the ugliness being brought out. It kinda gets to me." He paused for a moment remembering. "My father told me once that other people are merely mirrors of ourselves. You cannot love or hate something about another person unless it reflects something you love or hate about yourself. I wonder, looking at the killer, if I could see beyond the mirror, if there isn't a little madness in all of us."

Casey thought about Beau's concerns. "You know, there is an old Irish proverb, the answer to life's questions lie inside yourself. All you need to do is look, listen, and trust your instincts. If you know what is right, and you try to live by God's rules, even if sometimes you fail, you will leave your footprints in the sand. And, the people who follow will know you've been there." Casey gave Beau another warm, loving, motherly hug then said, "Lets go, dinners ready. Come and get it, or we'll throw it to the hogs."

As usual Buckner was true to his word. The trial resumed the next day right on schedule. Sally and Beau were in their assigned seats when she whispered into Beau's ear, "What did you say to my mom last night?"

Beau looked at her curiously, as she continued, "She thinks you walk on water. What did you do?" She said smiling at him.

"We're sole mates that's all."

"You know what she told me?" Sally volunteered, "she said, of all the boys I've brought home you are by far the best."

He grinned, "When you've got it, flaunt it." Sally gave him a playful nudge.

The whispering was interrupted when the Bailiff announced that the court was in session. Judge Buckner was seated and nodded to Homer Canfield to begin. Canfield stood and announced, "The state calls detective Sergeant Jack Bellamy to the stand."

Jack whispered softly to Beau as he rose from his chair, "It's show time." Jack was quickly sworn in and assumed his position on the witness stand. Canfield meandered to the witness stand as he questioned, "Sergeant Bellamy you are a member of the Gray Lady Investigative Task Force?"

"Yea I am."

"And what is your official position?"

"I am the Deputy Director of Operations for the on-going investigation," Jack responded calmly.

"Are you the only black on the team?" Canfield questioned turning his gaze to the three black men on the jury.

"No I am not," He answered firmly.

"You are aware of the racial tensions caused by this investigation, are you not?" Canfield said, focusing his attention back to the witness.

"Yes I am."

"Can you tell this court how the media got the mistaken idea that the killer was black?" Canfield snapped.

"No I can't," Jack answered, returning Canfield's cold stare with a stern look.

"Do you think the police deliberately released false information to the media?"

"No I don't," He responded, getting slightly angered at this line of questioning.

"Do you trust your fellow officers?" Canfield asked confidently, knowing he was getting to the witness.

"Yes I do. I would trust them with my life." Jack replied in an even tone looking at Beau.

"Even white officers?" Canfield questioned, probing him with the idea of racial bias.

"Even the white officers Jack answered, becoming angered yet holding his temper.

"So, with your life," Canfield said smugly, "Then let me ask you this. Do you have a locker room in the police station?," you know, a place where you hang your coat, maybe keep a few valuables before you go on your shift?"

"Yes sir, we do." He replied, wondering where he was going with this line of questioning.

"And you have a locker in that room. Is that right?"

"Yes."

"And you have a lock on that locker. Is that right?"

"Yes."

"Now, why is it, officer Bellamy, if you are so sure that the leak of false information didn't come from the police, and you trust your fellow officers with your life, why do you find it necessary to lock your locker in that room?"

Jack finally realized that this line of questioning was nothing more than a media show. Canfield was trying to gain a few points with the media while casting shadows at the police department. He wondered if there wasn't some political motivation behind all this. Barbara Starkey didn't mind because it had nothing to do with the case, and it took the jury's focus away from the defendant. Jack paused, choosing his words carefully to show Canfield that he could play to the cameras as well.

"Well, you see Counselor, we share that building with the court complex. From time to time, we have members of the D.A.'s staff, you know, lawyers, they have been known to walk through that room, and we all know about lawyers don't we."

The courtroom erupted into laughter prompting Buckner to rap his gavel. "Counselor," Buckner said, directing his attention to Canfield, "I suggest you move on to more pertinent testimony."

The embarrassed lawyer took another moment to refer to his notes. "Officer Bellamy. During the course of this investigation you were able to locate and search the defendant's apartment. Is that right?"

"Yes, that's correct." Jack noticed this time, Canfield was cautious, limiting himself to the facts, and not grand standing for the media.

"Would you tell the court what you found?"

"Yes, we found the human remains in the bedroom closet. We were able to identify these remains as Dr. Michael Smith from Seattle. He had been tied to a wheelchair using duct tape."

"I see, what else did you find?" Canfield queried calmly.

"It was a two bedroom apartment with a balcony. One bedroom was very neat clean, expensive suits, ties, shoes, and paintings. It reminded me of an executive's bedroom. This person had a neat freak fetish. We found receipts for the rental of a police uniform along with the checks from the victims that you've already entered into evidence. We found photos of Molly Philburn, and Amanda Hollingsworth, nude, laying on top of their individual beds. We found child pornography, and other photos of nude women. We were later able to identify these photos as murder victims from Seattle." Jack paused, and thumbed through his notes.

"Please continue, Officer Bellamy," Canfield urged politely.

"We found human waste on the balcony. DNA tests confirmed that the waste material belonged to the defendant. In the kitchen we found a dog dish, and a water dish on the floor. We did not find a pet on the premises so we did a DNA test on the saliva from the dog dish and it matched the defendant's."

"Excuse me officer," Canfield interrupted, "are you telling this court that the defendant ate out of a dog's dish?"

"That appears to be the case." Jack answered.

"What else did you observe in the defendant's apartment?"

"Along with the pornography he had literature on After Death Experience, Astro-projection, the Occult, we found a diary," Jack said, glancing at his notes.

"Your honor, the state would like to enter into evidence state's exhibit K. The defendant's diary." Canfield handed the diary to the court Bailiff, then continued, "Tell the court what was in the diary," Canfield demanded politely.

"We found detailed descriptions of the murders, and his feelings when he had sex with his victims. We found names of victims from Seattle, Houston, Dallas, and Charleston. They were all described in intimate detail including his sexual high when achieving death." Jack looked up from his notes waiting for Canfield's next question.

"So the defendant achieved sexual gratification from strangling his victims. Not from sex?"

"Yes."

"So, he didn't murder in some jealous rage. He killed solely for a sexual high?"

"Yes."

"What else did you find in the defendant's diary?" Canfield questioned, as he casually walked to the jury box waiting for Jack's answer.

"We found his conversations,…excuse me, his transcripts of his conversations with Doctor Michaels."

"And what did these transcripts reveal?" Canfield asked sadly.

"Apparently, he had Dr. Michaels, and his wife totally under his control," Jack replied quickly.

"How do you mean?" Canfield ordered, turning to look at the jury waiting for the expected response.

"From the text it was apparent that Dr. Michaels helped the defendant finance an illegal drug, and sex club in the Seattle area."

The media was going to have a field day with that story after the trial was over Sally thought to herself.

Canfield waited for the courtroom murmurs to subside before continuing.

"Officer Danelli testified that the murder scenes appeared strange to him. Did you notice any peculiarities in the defendant's apartment?"

"Yes, there was only one mirror. All the other mirrors were broken, even the bathroom mirror."

"Where was the one mirror located?"

"In the master bedroom," Jack advised quickly.

"What about the other bedroom?" Canfield prompted.

"It was a total mess," Jack answered.

"What do you mean a mess?"

Jack glanced at his notebook, "Two unmade bunk beds, clothes on the floor, unwashed underwear, comic books, colored posters of comic book hero's, drawings, and a collection of toy dinosaurs."

"What kind of drawings," Canfield inquired.

"Dinosaurs,…Ah, the Rex type, you know, meat eaters."

Canfield returned to his desk before asking, "What else did you find in the defendant's apartment?"

Jack flipped to another page in his small note book.

"We found a box in the defendant's closet labeled, 'Showtime Costumes Inc.,' Atlanta Georgia. Inside the box we found fibers that we identified with the fibers taken from officer Farley's car, and fibers taken from the clothing of Agent Thornton."

"Your honor, the state would like to enter state's exhibit L into evidence," Canfield held up another small clear plastic bag. Walking to the witness stand, displaying the bag, he asked, "Are these the fibers you retrieved from the box found in the defendant's apartment?"

"Yes they are. My identifying mark is here." Jack pointed to the tag on the bag.

"So, lets see if I understand your testimony. In defendant's apartment you found photos of the murdered victims taken while under the control of the killer. You found the defendant's diary, and in his own handwriting, he describes how he took sexual pleasure from torturing and killing his victims. You found the remains of Dr. Michaels. You were able to secure fibers from the police uniform that he wore the night he killed officer Farley, and attacked agent Thornton, and these same fibers were found in officer Farley's car, and on the clothing of agent Thornton. Are these the facts as you know them?"

"Yes they are," Jack answered sternly.

"I have no further questions for this witness." Canfield stated and returned to his desk.

"Your witness," Buckner responded, looking at Barbara Starkey. The attractive counselor for the defense rose from her chair, and approached the witness stand. "Officer Bellamy, all the officers who investigated the murder scenes said that they looked odd." She paused, considering how she would approach the overwhelming physical evidence being presented by the state. "I mean by that, that the mirrors were all broken, sex with a dead 60 year old woman, things like that. Did you notice anything else odd about the defendant's apartment?"

"I'm not sure I understand the question? I think I just answered that question?" Jack responded defensively. Starkey looked momentarily at the jury. "Let me put it this way, Let's say you were searching the defendant's apartment for drugs. Murder wasn't an issue. Would you think that two different people lived there?"

"Objection!, calls for speculation," Canfield interrupted.

"You honor," Barbara contested quickly, "The prosecution has already established the existence of two completely different bedrooms, and evidence of adverse behavior. I should be able to pursue this line of questioning."

Buckner responded thoughtfully, "Over ruled, I'd like to hear the witness's response"

"Officer Bellamy, would you like me to repeat the question?" Jack gave Barbara a sly smile before answering.

"Yes, the two bedroom gave the impression that two different people occupied that apartment. However counselor, there is one thing I haven't been able to determine."

"What is that?" Barbara asked cautiously.

"Was that done for our benefit, or, did in fact, two people actually live there?"

"Good question," Starkey responded, walking back to her desk to look at her notes. "Maybe we can answer your question officer Bellamy," she paused, "Lets look at the defendant's diary. That is prosecution's exhibit K is it not? Bellamy nodded affirmatively.

"Do you think anybody in his right mind would right down, in explicit detail, how he murdered all these people?"

"Objection!, speculation!" Canfield interrupted before Jack could answer.

"Sustained," Buckner ordered.

"Officer Bellamy," Barbara said, moving on to her next question, "What did you notice about the handwriting in the diary?"

"We had whole paragraphs printed neatly, very legible while other paragraphs were mere scribbles, barely legible." Barbara smiled. She had set the stage for the next question, "Did it appear that two different people had made entries into the diary?"

"Objection!, officer Bellamy is not a qualified handwriting expert."

"Your honor," Barbara answered, "we can call handwriting experts, but I don't think we need an expert to tell the difference between printing and scribbles."

"I will allow it," Buckner said. Barbara waited for Jack to answer.

"Yes, the text indicated that two different people did make entries in the diary."

Barbara turned her attention to the jury. "My learned colleague has aptly summarized your testimony for the jury. I believe it's only fitting that I do the same. You admitted that the apartment looked like two different people lived there. Yet, on the lease agreement there is only one name, Scott Stapely an assumed name. No one in the apartment complex reported seeing anyone other than the defendant enter or leave the apartment. You testified that the diary had two distinct sets of handwriting, yet only one person lives in that apartment. Am I correct so far?"

"Yes." Jack knew where she was going with her summary.

"Would anyone in their right mind keep a dead body in the closet, then write in his diary as having held conversations with it? These entries in the diary, some of them were dated after his death isn't that correct?"

"Yes, they were." Jack said softly.

"The good counselor forgot to point that out didn't he?"

"Yes,"

Barbara walked toward the witness stand then stopped midway, and turned back to face the jury again. "So, from all this, isn't it logical to conclude that there were two distinct personalities living inside one, mentally disturbed human being?"

"Objection!, Calls for conclusion, and it's blatant speculation."

Barbara smiled, "withdraw your honor," she looked at the jury, then returned to her desk.

"I have no further questions for this witness. However, we would like the right to recall."

"Granted, the witness will make himself available subject to recall," Buckner ordered.

Jack returned to his assigned seat. Buckner looked at Canfield who rose and announced, "The state calls Detective LT. Beau Gasteneau, Charleston Police Department, Investigative Division."

Sally squeezed his hand gently as he rose, and calmly walked to the witness stand. The killer lifted his head from the table. His crazed glare followed Beau to the witness stand. The rage that laid just below the surface of his expression revealed the perverted evil that laid deep within this man's disturbed mind.

After he was sworn in Beau seated himself, and waited for Canfield to begin. "Lt. Gasteneau, you are the Investigative Officer in charge of the Gray Lady Killer Task Force?"

"Yes I am."

"I understand you've had some face to face confrontations with the defendant," Beau nodded. Canfield began to lead Beau through his testimony. "During these confrontations do you believe that the defendant was trying to kill you while resisting arrest?"

375

"Yes I do."

"When was you first lethal encounter with the defendant?"

Beau sat silently, he would never forget that night. It still haunted him. He could not completely excuse himself for being late, giving the killer the opportunity to kill his best friend. "Officer Mackland and I responded to a crime scene on the night of July 17th at 8557 Jefferson St. A few minutes after our arrival we received a call that a prowler was seen entering the alley near the crime scene. We assumed that it could be the perpetrator. Officer Mackland went on foot while I drove two blocks north to cut off the suspect's avenue of escape from the other end of the alley. Due to the fog, and low visibility, I was late getting to officer Mackland's aid. I found him hanging by the neck from a low fire escape grate. He had a knife protruding from his chest." Beau was fighting for control of his emotions. He had to get through this calmly, with no sense of anger, or guilt. He waited for Canfield's next question.

"What did you do then?" Canfield asked sadly.

"I called in an emergency. Officer down." Beau looked at Sally. Her look told him to hang in there. Get through this. Get this behind you. I'm there for you. Canfield walked to the jury box before asking softly, "Did you examine the murder scene, and what did you find?"

"Yes I did. The wire that killed officer Mackland was wrapped around a piece of wood which was wedged between the fire escape grate. That device supported the officer's weight," He said, with controlled anger. Canfield paced in front of the jury box, "Am I correct in assuming that the defendant slipped the wire over the neck of officer Mackland, pulled him up then crammed the wood into the grate?"

"Yes, that's correct."

"That takes a lot of strength. How can you be sure that this in fact, was the way officer Mackland was killed?," Canfield asked, as he looked at the jury.

"He sure as hell didn't hang himself." Beau blurted out angrily.

"I am sorry, this must be painful for you Lieutenant. Please, take your time."

Beau brought his emotions back under control and continued in a level voice, "The defendant cut his hand on the wire when he lifted the officer up. The blood as you know, was found on the wood, and the DNA matches the defendant." Beau answered glaringly.

"So, the defendant in cold blood, with rage in his heart, in the dark of night, attacked, and brutally murdered officer Mackland."

"Yes," Beau answered emphatically.

Canfield paused, letting Beau's statement take full impact on the jury before he began. "Let's move forward. How were you able to zero in on the defendant? To Identify him as the killer?"

"Most of the credit goes to Agent Thornton of the FBI's Criminal Profile Division. She was able to provide us with an overview of the killer, his habits, his method of operation, and she had access to the FBI database on serial killers. She knew exactly where to look for the information we needed. Armed with that information, and a lot of legwork by the team, we were able narrow down the suspects." Beau said proudly.

"I see," Canfield responded, "So the FBI identified a pattern of behavior which led you to the defendant."

"Not directly," Beau answered, then quickly added, "Agent Thornton suggested that on nights where the killer would most likely be stalking his victims we should dispatch patrols in these areas. We knew he operated at night, usually in the fog, or rain. He selected middle, and upper class neighborhoods. The victims would be in their 50's to 60's, women, alone, and vulnerable. While on patrol, Agent Thornton and I noted a possible home invasion in progress at 5416 Azalea Lane, residence owned by Mrs. Henrietta Wentworth. We called it in, and Mrs. Wentworth's profile fit the victim's. We responded to the scene where Agent Thornton was attacked by the defendant. She was able to free herself, and I gave chase to the Charleston Memorial Cemetery where I was attacked the defendant."

The courtroom sat motionless hanging on every word. Canfield asked, "Then what happened?"

"As I was struggling with the attacker Agent Thornton responded to the scene, and was able to force the attacker to break off his attack, and flee the scene. We lost him in the night fog."

"So, Agent Thornton saved your life." Canfield remarked.

"Yes, she did." Beau smiled at Sally. She replied with a slight nod.

"How do you know that it was in fact the defendant who attacked you that night?" Canfield questioned, as he walked to his desk.

"During the struggle I tore a button from the defendant's shirt. When we searched his apartment we found the shirt with the missing button."

"Your honor, the state would like to enter into evidence exhibit M and N. The button recovered at the cemetery, and the shirt found in the defendant's apartment." Canfield walked briskly to the stand, and held both bags in front of the witness. "Do these match?"

"Perfectly," Beau answered, glancing at the jury.

"What did you, and Agent Thornton do after that?"

"We took a statement from Mrs. Wentworth. Thankfully, she did not open the door. If fact, I know Mrs. Wentworth personally, and it took me ten minutes to convince her who I was. Then she opened the door."

"A very cautious woman wasn't she."

"Yes," Beau replied, in agreement with Canfield's observation.

"So, at this point in time you had a pretty good idea of how the killer worked. Can you tell the jury more about how you were able to narrow down the search for the killer?"

Canfield was taking his time, building his case slowly, providing the jury with background to substantiate and provide weight to the evidence presented by the prosecution.

Beau quickly summarized the investigation, "Our queries through the FBI criminal database gave us three hits on the same M.O."

Canfield interrupted, "By M.O. you mean method of operation."

"Yes, the description of the victims, the murder scenes, sex, and the killing mechanism. We received responses from Dallas, Houston and Seattle."

"Then what did you do?" Canfield asked, leading his witness carefully through his testimony.

"Generally, serial killers have had some sort of trouble with the law. We asked for data on personnel who fit the killer's profile who had been arrested at the time of the murders, and had left the state. We crossed checked to see if any of them had migrated to Charleston."

"I see," Canfield acknowledged, "That's a lot of paperwork isn't it."

"That's why we have an investigative task force," Beau replied.

Canfield smiled. He wasn't about to take any glory away from the police department. "Please continue Lieutenant."

"Agent Thornton pointed out that the killer was probably trying to kill Mrs. Wentworth. That he may have a big ego."

"How did she arrive at that conclusion?" Canfield responded with interest.

"Well, for one thing, he murdered two women on the same night only blocks apart, and thumbed his nose at the police." Beau paused momentarily to allow his words to register with the court. "Therefore, we used the local TV to entice the killer to try again. This time Agent Thornton would pose as Mrs. Wentworth, and we'd stake out the house. It worked."

"However, your trap didn't workout the way you expected, did it?"

"No, not quite," Beau answered sadly.

"The defendant!" Canfield said loudly, pointing at the accused, "who knew the police would be there, took the time to plan very carefully, how he would pose as a policeman to gain entry to the house. To catch officer Farley off guard, and brutally murder him. He took the time to rent a policeman's uniform, plan how we would approach Agent Thornton, and kill her. Do you think a crazy man, a man totally out of his mind, a man incapable of telling right from wrong is capable of that kind of detailed preparation?"

"Objection!" Barbara interrupted sternly, "The counselor it grandstanding for the cameras. The witness nor the counselor, has any way of knowing what was in the defendant's mind."

"Sustained," Buckner said, looking at Canfield.

"Let me rephrase," Canfield scratched his ear as he thought, "as you understand it, the legal definition of premeditation, is where a person, plans, and takes deliberate steps to do harm to another person, is that correct?"

"Yes."

Canfield paced in front of the jury box continuing with his questions, "In the police report you said that you were able to locate the defendant's apartment, and obtain a search warrant. How did that come about?"

"Our response from the Houston Police Department."

"You mean the response to the profile you sent out through the FBI's database," Canfield interrupted.

"Yes, Houston identified an informant who knew the killer. A Gordon Delongpre was picked up on drug possession and plea bargained to help locate a Gaylord Harcourt who he said did the killings in Houston with the same M.O.. Mr. Delongpre was given 18 months, and probation. He disappeared and Houston has an outstanding warrant for parole violation. His probation file indicated that he lived in Charleston earlier. The Houston file indicated that he had an Aunt, Mrs. Alma Winslow. The information gathered from her statement was that Mr. Delongpre, that is his real name, he and his mother, lived, and worked for an Agnes Gladlow at 1624 Park Lane," Beau flipped to a new page in his pocket notebook.

"Go on," Canfield urged.

"Mrs. Winslow indicated that the Gladlows moved to Florida in June of 79. She died a few years ago of a heart attack. Henry Gladlow committed suicide a year before that. Our records show that she was buried here in Charleston."

"I see," Canfield said, returning to the witness stand, "So, the defendant, lived at this Park Lane address when he was younger."

"Yes."

"Tell the court what you found when you went to the Park Lane address."

"It was abandon, and in disrepair," Beau answered automatically.

"Anything else?" Canfield asked, turning his back to the jury.

"Yes, the property belonged to a Norma Pierce Agnes's sister."

"Other than being abandoned, what else did you notice?"

"We noted that the killer had a pattern. All the murders had taken place within a five mile radius of this address."

Canfield waited for the courtroom murmurs to subside, and allow time for this fact to germinate in the minds of the jurors. "So, you had a pretty good idea of where the killer was going to strike next."

"Yes. We now had a photo from the Houston Police, his M.O., and an idea of where he would hit."

"But that wasn't enough was it?" Canfield added.

"No, we had some luck come our way." Beau said, looking at Sally remembering that night in the park. "We had an unlawful assembly in a local park."

"You mean you had a riot," Canfield interrupted.

"You might call it that, anyway, at the station one of the rioters recognized our photo of the defendant. He remembers him posing as a Sears repairman."

"Please go on." Canfield ordered politely.

"Our team investigated all the Sears outlets in the area, and we got a positive ID on the defendant as having his car repaired. Subsequent investigation indicated that he had a drivers license, and a Charleston address. 1976 Brookside, Apartment 21. He had an auto insurance policy with Great Western. We searched his apartment, and the rest you know."

Canfield faced the jury again, "So you would say that the defendant took great pains to cover his identity?"

"Yes."

Canfield marched to his seat, and announced, "I have no further questions for this witness."

Judge Buckner looked at Barbara. Starkey rose, then studied her notes holding the courtroom in silence before she spoke. Barbara Starkey had strong feelings for Beau. She had a brief affair with him a few years ago. They both realized that she was going to put her career first, and personal commitment second, so they broke it off but still remained friends.

"You and your team should be congratulated. That was excellent police work." Barbara said, looking at her former lover. Beau knew that these platitudes were just a prelude to some hard questions.

"Lets see if I understand you? Gordon or David Delongpre worked with the Houston Police to find Gaylord Harcourt. Is that right?"

"Yes."

"When did you realize that Gaylord Harcourt was just another personality that existed inside the defendant?" That he was in fact helping the police look for himself?"

"We could not find a Gaylord anywhere. Later the thought did occur to us."

"Do you think he was in his right mind by helping the police look for his alter ego?"

"Oh, yes, that was very smart." Beau answered with a nod.

"So, up to that time you thought you were looking for two different people?"

"Yes, we did," Beau answered softly.

"Then it's evident that this duel personality, this alter ego, existed within the defendant as far back as Houston?"

"That appears to be the case."

Using every bit of her sensuality Barbara walked to the jury box. Again, the men were focused on her partially unbuttoned blouse, and her magnificent cleavage. "You had the opportunity to interview Norma Pierce, Agnes Gladlow's sister. Is that correct?"

"Yes I did."

"Didn't her written statement indicate that David Delongpre was sexually abused as a child by the Gladlows. Isn't it true, that he was beaten into submission until he performed every dirty little act that Mrs. Gladlow's perverted mind demanded?" Barbara raised her voice emphasizing every word. "Isn't it true, that Henry Gladlow sexually abused his sister to such an extent that at the age of 13 she ran away, knowing that it would be better to die on the streets than endure the torment under the Gladlows?"

"Objection, you honor," Canfield shouted, as he rose from his chair. "My worthy opponent is also grandstanding. The witness has no idea what was in the mind of Alice Delongpre when she ran away." Canfield sat back down

"Sustained. Rephrase counselor," Buckner demanded from the bench. Barbara nodded. "Did you interview the defendant's sister?"

"Yes."

"Did she state to you that she ran away to avoid further sexual abuse?"

"Yes."

"Thank you Lieutenant." Barbara walked back to her desk and scanned her notes again before continuing. "In your endeavor to arrest the defendant you had several altercation with him didn't you?"

"Yes," Beau answered, looking at the defendant who was fully awake staring coldly at him.

"Not just an altercation, but a fight to the death so to speak wasn't it?" Barbara asked, noticing the looks being exchanged with the defendant.

"Yes."

"Please explain," Starkey demanded, politely

"Our first violent altercation was at the Park Lane address when I hurt the defendant. He reacted like a child."

"You mean he cried, 'please don't hurt me'," Barbara demanded.

"yes."

"So, when the defendant was under severe pain. In danger of losing his life, he reverted to a little boy, and begged not to be hurt?" Barbara said, raising her voice to an emotional level.

"Yes, but that didn't last long. As soon as I stopped he came at me with a vengeance," Beau responded in anger.

"Yes he did," Barbara replied, "He growled, scratched, clawed, and spit on you. What you were looking at was the Beast. An ego that when all else fails, steps in to protect the little boy, who for so many years was brutalized by the Gladlows."

The courtroom sat in stunned silence. Starkey was an actress, and the courtroom was her stage.

"One final question Lieutenant," She paused, and walked to the witness stand, "that night, at the hospital, when you held him with one hand from the third floor, when you held his life in your hands, why didn't drop him?"

Beau remained silent. He looked past Barbara Starkey at Sally. She waited with intense interest. That was also the question she wanted answered. Judge Buckner looked at the witness. All eyes in the courtroom were focused on Beau waiting for his answer.

"You honor, I wish I could say something profound, something that might make sense to all this madness. All I can say is that we all deserve our day in court. At least I know that if my friend detective Sergeant Harry Mackland were alive that is what he would have told me. So, I guess I did it for Harry."

"One more question." Starkey said, breaking the courtroom silence, "did the defendant bring to the surface another personality named Gordon Delongpre?

"Yes he did?"

"And what did this Gordon personality ask you to do?"

"He told me to go ahead and drop him so he could end it all? Beau said, looking at the defendant who had put his forehead back on the table.

"So, the defendant asked you to kill him, he begged you to kill him. Is that right?"

"Yes."

"Lieutenant, if you were in his position. Holding on to the one man who controlled your destiny, who could say if you lived or died. Would you have asked him to kill you?" Barbara asked, then holding silent to let the intensity of the question build

"I don't know," Beau answered thoughtfully.

"Would anyone in his right mind ask such a question? Barbara asked sincerely.

"Objection, Speculation!" Canfield shouted from his chair.

"Withdraw your honor," Barbara replied before Buckner could speak, she continued, "That night, when the accused kidnapped Agent Thornton, you were in charge of the operation, how come you were not there?"

"I received a call that we had located the defendant's apartment. I left the scene in order to conduct a search of that apartment."

"If you knew that the accused might try again to attack Mrs. Wentworth did you think it was prudent to leave?"

"It was late. We had no movement of any kind, and we had four other men covering the area. I thought everything would be okay."

"You had no idea the killer would take the time to plan his attack by posing as a police officer?" Starkey stated firmly.

"No I didn't," Beau replied, giving an apologetic glance at Sally.

"Later, you were informed that Agent Thornton was missing, and officer Farley was also missing."

"Yes, I was."

"What did you do then?" Starkey asked, moving to the witness stand.

"I responded to the scene," He answered calmly.

"But you never arrived?" Starkey quickly interjected, "you went directly to the Park Lane address. How come?"

"Agent Thornton told me to." A cold silence filled the jury box as low murmurs echoed throughout the courtroom.

"Oh yes," Starkey agreed politely, "I've heard that Agent Thornton has telepathic capabilities."

"That may be true," Beau said quickly, "All I know is that Agent Thornton told me to get inside the killer's head. I knew that the Park Lane address had significance for him, and he would probably take his victim there if he was forced to."

"So you were playing a hunch." Starkey confirmed, 'not some telepathic message."

"Yes."

"I have no further questions for this witness." Barbara stated, then returned to her desk.

Canfield quickly rose, and announced, "The state calls Agent Sally Thornton to the stand."

Sally and Beau passed each other as she made her way to the witness stand. After being sworn in she seated herself comfortably on the stand. Sally had that unique quality of being both angelic in her facial features, and having a sexy appearance physically. Her rugged FBI physical training gave her a body that could have made the cover of Sports Illustrated any day of the year. Canfield moved to the witness stand as he began his questioning. "Agent Thornton, you are an FBI profiler. Is that correct?"

"Yes."

"Would you explain to the jury what it is you do?"

"I am a trained Clinical Psychologist in addition to my legal training. My masters thesis was based on 2 years of supportive counseling at the Atlanta Federal Penitentiary. The thrust of my work was extensive interviews with multiple killers. These studies were part of my training at the Behavioral Science Unit at Quantico. We cataloged the typical behavioral patterns of serial killers. In other words, although all killers had different stories to tell, the statistics revealed common patterns such as parental abuse, violence, neglect, childhood cognitive disabilities, alcohol, and drug abuse."

"How many cases has your profiling been successful?" Canfield question, as he casually walked to the jury box.

"First," Sally answered firmly, "criminal profiling is a tool. We don't solve crimes. Profiling cannot take the place of good foot pounding investigative work. The cases that we solve are not solved by profilers...they are solved by investigators like the Gray Lady Task Force, using all the resources available to them. So, to answer your question, I bring the investigators into the mind of the killer."

"And how do you do that?" Canfield questioned, leading the witness carefully.

"One of the first things we do is look at the victims. We compile a complete history of the victim. Family background, reputation, likes, and dislikes, drug or alcohol problems, financial troubles, routines that the victims had in common. Then we ask ourselves, 'why did the killer choose this person as his victim?' What this does for the investigator is to narrow down the field. Each question we can answer about the victim is a window into the killer's mind. It also answers another question about the killer. As you have learned from the testimony, from knowing the victims he chooses we had a pretty good idea where and when he would strike. We also used a victim's profile to draw him out into the open."

"Yes, your analysis of the killer's activities appeared to be very accurate. What other areas did you investigate concerning the defendant's mental state?" Canfield asked returning to his table so the jury could get a good look at Sally.

"Another important aspect of profiling the serial killer is, what is the single event that pushes him over the edge? What kind of stress did the killer experience when he was committing the crime? The other final question we had to solve was, what was the stress factor that made him kill? Did the killer act out of feelings he had years ago when this situation was happening to him as a child? Did he feel helpless to do anything about the situation? The killer may not even realize he is actually reacting to events that were once familiar to him?"

"Did you find this to be true about the defendant?" Canfield asked, trying to narrow down Sally's testimony.

"I did conclude that he was reenacting events that occurred to him as a child." Sally answered clearly.

"Did the defendant know right from wrong when he committed these acts?"

"Objection!" Starkey said loudly, "Speculation."

"Your honor," Canfield rebutted, "agent Thornton was beaten, kidnapped, and nearly raped by the defendant. If anyone should know what his intent was, she should."

"I am sympathetic to agent Thornton's point of view but in all fairness I have to sustain the objection," Buckner said, looking at Sally kindly. Canfield thought for a moment, then asked, "The night the defendant beat you senseless, smashed you face into a mirror, kidnapped you, stripped you naked, spread you out on the table helpless, did you fear for your life?"

"Yes I did," Sally answered nervously.

"Agent Thornton," Canfield asked, after a moment of silence, "How many serial killer cases have you successfully brought to a conclusion?

"Six, this will be my seventh," She said, looking at the defendant.

"In the FBI's database, the one that describes the serial killer, are there common characteristics that you can use in your investigation?" Canfield questioned, as he looked at the jurors, knowing full well what Sally's answer would be.

"Yes, he's usually a white male, between the ages of 25 and 35. Most of the time he will kill members of his own race. The ages of the victims will vary according to his desires. That's why understanding the victims is so important. His intelligence ranges from below average to above average. He won't really know his victims, or have any particular hatred for them personally. They will have some symbolic relationship to him. In our case the defendant was performing sexually for Agnes Gladlow as he had been programmed to do from an early age. That's was the one thing all the victims had in common. They looked like Agnes Gladlow. The serial killer will not come from any social class. They range from skid row to Beverly Hills. He will for all practical purposes appear normal. He might be married, have kids, work at a regular job, or, he may be a loner, not able to maintain a relationship for any length of time."

"I see," Canfield said, glancing at the jury box to assure himself that they were getting every word. "So, this mass murderer will at some point in the investigation display at least some of these characteristics?"

"Let me clarify something if I may?" Sally asked leaning forward in the witness stand, "There is a misconception in the media, and the public that a mass murderer, and a serial killer are one in the same. They are not. A mass murderer is someone,"… Sally paused, reaching for an example, "He's like someone who shoots everyone in the post office, and then he might commit suicide. A serial killer kills several people over a period of days, weeks, months, or even years for that matter. There is a cooling off period, the killer goes through phases or cycles."

"Did the defendant fit this type of killer?" Canfield questioned, carefully leading Sally through her expert testimony working slowly toward his ultimate objective.

"There is another misconception about serial killers I would like to clarify for the court," Sally said confidently, "There just isn't one type of serial killer. We have the visionary type, a psychotic who hears voices in his head, God is telling him to commit the crime. We have what I call the Missionary type. In his mind he has to rid the world of the immoral or unworthy victims. He usually kills prostitutes, or someone he considers of low moral character. Then there is the thrill killer. He's in it for the fun of killing. He's a sadist, a sociopath. Killing is just one big video game shoot up. He's into killing for the excitement. And finally, we come to the defendant. The lust killer. These are people who kill for the pure turn on. The amount of sexual pleasure they get has a direct correlation to the amount of torture they can inflict on their victims. Did you notice that all the victims were strangled, even the two police officers? We know that some mentally disturbed individuals experience what we call orgasmic asphyxia. They get a sexual high from being strangled or strangling their sexual partners. The more sexual perversion the more aroused he becomes. The killer is in touch with reality, and is able to have relationships."

The courtroom remained in stunned silence. Canfield walked to his desk, and looked at his notes again before speaking, "You said that our killer, the lust killer, was in touch with reality. In your opinion, did the defendant know right from wrong when he committed these crimes?"

"Objection!", Barbara responded loudly, "Speculation. She has no idea what was in the killer's mind."

"Sustained," was Buckner's answer from the bench.

"I'll rephrase your honor," Canfield quickly replied then asked his next question, "Did you or did you not classify the defendant as a lust killer?"

"Yes."

"Does the FBI, in it's database recognize that the lust killer as being in touch with reality when he commits the crime?"

"Yes it does." Sally answered, looking directly at the jury.

Canfield scratched the side of his head as he walked to the witness stand, "lets go back to the night of December 15th, 1998. The man who attacked you that night. The man who tried to rape you, is he in the courtroom today?"

"Yes, the defendant," Sally pointed at the defendant.

"Let the record show that the witness pointed at the accused." Canfield ordered coldly. "Now, as I understand your report, you were unconscious when he took you to the Park Lane address?"

"Yes."

"What do you remember next?"

"When I came to, I was laying on a table in the abandoned house." Sally stammered, she was becoming nervous, remembering the terror she experienced that night.

"Please, take you time," Canfield ordered calmly.

"I had been stripped naked. The defendant had lit several candles around the room."

"What kind of room was it?" Canfield questioned softly trying to make it as easy on her as he could.

"It was the dining room," Sally said gripping the side of the witness chair.

"What else did you notice about the room?" Canfield questioned cautiously.

"I saw a dead man impaled on the wall like some grotesque ornament. He had what I thought was a spear protruding from his chest." She answered in a trembling voice.

"That would be Joseph McGinney the local security guard," Canfield informed the court. "Please continue.

"I didn't move. I didn't want to anger him in any way. He began to touch me, to fondle me." She said cautiously.

"It was the defendant who told you he was going to rape you, was it not?" Canfield asked, getting quickly to the point.

"Yes."

"How did the defendant appear to you? I mean, was he excited, was he a frightened child, or some slobbering beast hovering over his victim?"

"He was acting alike a confident lover. He told me in great detail every thing he was going to do to me."

"So, you would say he was in complete control of his faculties?" Canfield asked pointedly, looking at the jury.

"Yes."

"What happened next?"

"I was able to free myself, immobilize the defendant for a short period, giving me time to hide." Sally answered nervously.

"As I understand it, other than the candle light, the house was completely dark?"

"Yes, I was able to crawl upstairs and hide.

"What did you discover in the upstairs hall closet?"

"I discovered officer Farley's body. He had been strangled and stuffed into the closet." She answered nervously.

"What did the defendant do after that?" Canfield questioned.

"He got mad, and swore he was going to kill me when he found me," Sally said. Her knuckles turned white from gripping the arm of her chair.

"So, the defendant's attitude changed from rape to murder," Canfield stated loudly.

"Yes,"

"He in fact screamed at you, shouted that he was going to kill you."

"Yes."

"He called you a cold bitch."

"Yes."

"Would an incoherent beast who could only slobber, call you a bitch? Or, would a rejected lover be more likely to say that?"

"A rejected lover," Sally answered automatically.

"The defendant found you in the upstairs hallway is that correct?"

"Yes."

"Did you sincerely believe that the defendant was trying to kill you?"

"Yes."

"You did not believe at that time he was going to rape you?" Canfield asked quickly.

"No, he was going to kill me," Sally answered emphatically, as she choked back her emotions.

"It was at this time officer Gasteneau confronted the defendant? Is that correct?" Canfield inquired.

"Yes. He saved my life. She answered, looking fondly at Beau.

"You mean after subduing the defendant, he carried you safely from the burning building?

"Yes."

"I have no further questions for this witness," Canfield stated, then calmly walked to his chair and sat down.

Without hesitation Barbara Starkey rose, and walked to the witness stand. There was an undercurrent of jealously in her questioning.

"Agent Thornton, when the defendant was yelling at you, did he use any other name other than Bitch when he was mad?"

"No."

"What about when he was about to have sex with you? What did he call you then?"

"Agnes," Sally answered softly.

"Excuse me? I didn't hear that." Barbara said, tilting her head slightly.

"He called me Agnes," Sally replied raising her voice again.

"So, in fact, the defendant thought he was performing sexually for the demands put on him by Agnes Gladlow, didn't he?"

"Objection! Your honor," She's leading the witness." Canfield barked.

"Sustained," Buckner ordered from the bench.

"Agent Thornton," Barbara asked, resuming in a normal tone of voice, "you testified, that you are a trained psychologist, did you not?"

"I did."

"You've had a chance to observe the defendant?"

"Yes I have."

"Have you observed a personality the defendant calls Gaylord Harcourt?"

"Yes I have."

"What was your impression of the Harcourt personality?"

"He enjoyed sex. He was that part of the defendant's personality that took pride in his sexual performance with Agnes Gladlow."

"Don't you think that the man that was about to rape you was Gaylord thinking he was performing for Agnes?"

"Objection!" Canfield challenged from his chair.

"Overruled," Buckner answered, "The witness is more than qualified to answer that question."

Sally thought for a moment. "Yes, however, that personality was articulate, knowledgeable, and would also know right from wrong. Counselor, let me make something clear. The serial killer is simply motivated to kill. You can apply as many factors as you want. He simply is motivated to kill just as you or I need a drink of water. His killing is fueled by fantasies that have been building for some time. The driving force behind these killings is control, power, dominance over his victims. This is why I was kidnapped, tormented, and threatened. It was the prelude to the ultimate act of killing."

Barbara Starkey remained silent as she walked to her desk and picked up one of her notes. "Thank you agent Thornton for that information. In your studies of mental disorders isn't it true that Ernest Hemingway suffered from suicidal depression?" Barbara answered her own question by quickly adding, "didn't Tennessee Williams, Edgar Allen Poe, even Winston Churchill all suffer from bipolar depression, paranoia, and alcoholism. In fact, Van Gough cut off his own ear. All of these famous people had some outside pressures that drove them to act the way they did. They acted outside of the norm. Outside of what we in society call 'free will'? They suffered alone from a mental disorder. They endured it in silence, because back then, they were shunned, ridiculed, called a dummy, the village idiot. I'd like to think we've come further than that. That we understand the seriousness of a mental illness. That society would seek to help the individual who cries out for help.. Apparently, in the defendant's case, no one heard him." Barbara had made her point. She waited for Sally's answer.

"Yes, but they didn't murder five people."

Barbara smiled, "Yes, as far as we know. And, they didn't live in the turbulent times we live in today."

The courtroom sat mesmerized as the two beautiful, intelligent women stared at each other in strained silence.

Judge Buckner broke the silence. "Ladies and gentlemen of the court. It is getting late and I think we've covered enough ground. This court is adjourned until ten o'clock tomorrow."

Chapter Twenty Three
The Damnation of David Delongpre

It was as if the whole courtroom had adjourned to the Stakeout Bar and Grill. Murphy pulled large cold beers from the white handled tap and carried eight large mugs to the table. Sally, Beau, Jack and the work a day cops of the Gray Lady Task Force sat around a long table in one corner of the room. "Here we go me buckaroos" Murph declared in an over accentuated Irish accent.

"You're laying it on a little thick tonight aren't you Murph?" Sally asked jokingly.

"Now, only a good Irish lass would be asking me that," he answered setting the frosty mugs of beer on the table. "I do it for the tourists, and of course those media folks over there," He nodded at the TV crew sitting at three small tables in the center of the room. "They are going to interview me tonight for the local news. You know, a man on the street sort of thing." He said, with a wink in his eye, and a grin on his face.

"So, what are you going to tell them?" Jack asked, wrapping his hand around a cold beer. Murphy looked at the group of his favorite cops, and answered firmly, "He's guilty as sin."

"There was never any doubt that he did it. Will he get away with it like Hinckley did?" Beau questioned, giving Sally a sly glance.

"Ah, now there's a good question. He has a good lawyer in that Starkey girl. She just might pull it off," Murphy replied, wiping his damp hands on his apron. Coates took a long gulp of her beer. Wiping off the foamed mustache she commented, "Probably, but you know something, people around here have a way of seeing that justice gets done, no matter what." Everyone remained silent thinking about the underlying truth in her statement.

"What does the press have to say about the trial so far? Sally asked, ignoring her beer.

"They're about fifty fifty on the insanity idea. I can tell you this, you, and Barbara Starkey are running neck and neck for who they'd like to see in the next issue of Playboy." Everyone at the table laughed at Murph's observation.

"So much for the news media," Sally replied sarcastically.

"Let me ask you something," Detective Brockman questioned, looking at Sally, as he grabbed a pretzel from the bowl in the center of the table. "I think this whole multiple personality disorder, what do you call it? M.P.D.?

This M.P.D. stuff is just a bunch of bull. You're a profiler, honestly, what do you think?"

Sally paused thinking about her answer. "It is, I believe, a legally recognized illness. Whether our guy truly has it, is another story. If the defense is able to prove according to the letter of the law, or even convince the jury he's insane we have a problem." She took a sip of her beer as everyone waited for her to continue. "Let me put it this way. Suppose a young woman walks into a room and shoots her father in front of twenty witnesses. She goes to trial and is convicted of murder in the first degree. She receives the death penalty but the death penalty is never carried out. In fact, she is set free. Can you think of a case where that could actually happen?" The table was silent, "The event where that could happen, is if she was a Siamese twin. She could not be executed without killing an innocent person. So, now we have to fall back on an old legal maxim, 'that it is better to let ten guilty people go free than to punish one innocent person'. So, today, some jurors have to consider the idea that it is possible that two totally different personalities, one good, and one evil, can exist inside one human being like Siamese twins."

"Personally, I think he's faking it," Mitchell interrupted.

"I think it's grandstanding for the media," Brockman added, "He's going to have these civil liberties types or anti death penalty tree huggers parading around the courthouse getting their mugs on TV, and not one of them has ever been on a crime scene, or had to tell a family that their loved one had been murdered, or their child has been raped by some sociopathic animal. You know what I'd like to do? I'd like to take all of them down to the morgue, and give them a good look," Brockman ended his speech with a long gulp of beer.

"Are you glad you got that off your chest?" Beau asked jokingly. Everyone laughed.

"Yeah!" He shouted with a grin.

The front door of the bar swung open. Father Marchello and Detective Sergeant Bradley made their way through the noisy crowd to the table. Murph and Father Marchello embraced. Murph automatically announced, "Two more beers coming up." Then quickly departed. Bradley handed Beau a note. "I just got this a few minutes ago," he said, as he eyed the cold beer on the table. Beau read the note then handed it to Sally.

"What is it?" Mitchell inquired.

"Well it seems as though Mr. Jo Jo Jones wants to see Father Marchello, Sally and myself," he answered. Sally handed back the note. Murph returned, and handed the beer to the new arrivals. Bradley beamed as he greedily grabbed his beer, "As they say, up to the lips, and over the gums," he swallowed half of the glass in a series of large gulps. "Aaah," was an echo of satisfaction emanating from Bradley's throat.

"Gentlemen, if you'll excuse us," Beau said, getting up from his chair. "We have to see what Mr. Jones has on his mind."

"Do you want some company?" Jack said, as he slipped on his jacket, and took a final sip of his beer.

Beau helped Sally on with her coat. The priest took one more gulp of his cold beer, and remarked, "God surely blessed the man who invented beer," then led the way to the door.

The police car made its way through the late evening Charleston traffic. The fog bank from the warm Atlantic was beginning to roll in. Beau slowed the car down to a crawl as he weaved his way through the narrow streets of the Charleston waterfront.

"Where are we headed?" Jack asked, as he read the note again.

"The alley," Beau responded thoughtfully.

"Never heard of it," Jack answered, looking out the window at the white mist that engulfed the car.

"It's been a long time since I've been there," Beau added, "It use to be on my rounds when I was a rookie," Beau commented thoughtfully, "It's down on the docks. The alley is not an address. It's a place," he paused, then continued knowingly, "It's a place for the lost to call home. Most of the street people hangout there. No one bothers them and they can get the damaged fruit from the ships when they off load. "It's a good source of information if you want to know what's going on at the docks."

The eerie fog horns grunted their low warbling sound through the darkened mist. Another fog horn some distance away would answer the first sound as if it was some mournful echo warning an unsuspecting sole that the edge of the world was just a few steps away. It seem to warn you not to step any further or you'll descend into oblivion.

The damp chill met the detectives head on as they stepped from the car. The alley descended slowly down to the water front. Large cardboard boxes with holes strategically cut provided shelter for some of the street people from the cold, damp night air. A few small fires illuminated the alley as Beau led the way. Sally saw the look of total despair on the faces of the street people as they continued to walk toward the waterfront. In their saddened eyes she saw hopelessness, despair, grief, loneliness, ravaged bodies and tormented lives. These derelicts who huddled by the fires eyed the intruders suspiciously. Sally noticed that this despair, this way of life, was not limited to men. She saw several women who squatted by the fire stirring some concoction of rotted vegetables that they hoped would provide them with enough nourishment to get them through just one more day. In her FBI training she had seen photos and videos of people who had no where to go, and no one who cared one way or the other if they lived or died. They were the unclean, the unwashed, and the unwanted of our modern society. They were the kind of people you just swept under the rug. Put them someplace so the rest of us didn't have to look at them. Sally glanced at Father Marchello. He had tears in his eyes. She knew he felt totally useless. He was a priest of a rich perish, and yet he had let this continue. It tested his faith. The question that ran through his mind she knew was, why? He knew he would feel like a bigot the next time he would preach from the pulpit about God's love when he is confronted with the way life really is. When he met the living truth head on.

Beau stopped at one brightly lit fire burning in a 50 gallon drum. Three raggedly dressed men squatted sharing a bottle of booze from a brown paper bag.

"I'm looking for JoJo Jones," He asked inquiringly.

The men looked at each other, then silently pointed to the far end of the alley.

The end of the alley joined a small ramp area which was adjacent to an abandoned warehouse. At one end of the open area was a tall wooden fence that closed off the area from the rest of the world. Another fire burned brightly as a tall shabbily dressed black man carved words onto the weather worn fence.

"Excuse me," Beau said politely, I'm looking for JoJo Jones. Have you seen him?"

The tall unshaven, tattered street bum turned to face the detectives. Beau saw strong penetrating eyes. It was if he could see into your very soul. Beau knew instinctively that this man had carried a hard burden for a long time. Immediately, he had a feeling of admiration for this man as well as an overwhelming sorrow.

"Step closer to the fire," He ordered. The detectives complied. The stranger took a long look at the detectives. Then his gaze fixed on Father Marchello. Satisfied, he spoke, "You are Lt. Gasteneau?" Beau nodded.

"I have a note to meet JoJo here," Beau responded, "Who are you?"

"I am Methusala, at least that's what they call me. My real name is Abe Livingston."

"Why do they call you Methusala?" Sally asked curiously.

"Because I'm the oldest one here. I don't know why the good Lord chose me to still be here but I am. The people don't last long down here so that's why the people call me that."

Father Marchello's attention was drawn to the names neatly carved onto the old wooden fence. "You're an artist," the priest commented, "those names, the lettering is perfect. You did all that with just a pocket knife?"

"Yes," the tall black man answered sadly. The stranger stepped back so the detectives could get a better view of his work. The priest quickly counted 150 names neatly carved. It reminded him of the Vietnam Wall. The newest name added to the list was JoJo Jones. Beau's gaze locked on to the name, he had a wave of overwhelming sadness cover him.

"Why?" Beau asked, as if he knew the answer.

"These are the names of my friends who have passed on to a better place. Lieutenant, JoJo is gone. They took him away an hour ago."

Beau didn't know why. He never really knew JoJo but a gripping sadness grabbed his stomach, clutched his throat. He needed to cry, he wanted to cry but couldn't. Sally felt Beau's emotions being held in check. She put her arm around him as if to say, "I'm here. I'll always be here for you." The stranger reached into a paper bag as he spoke, "JoJo told me you were a good man. He wanted to ask you himself but it was too late. He asked me to ask you if you would do him one last favor."

"Sure. I'd be glad to," Beau answered compassionately.

"He knew he'd be put in a pine box. He said that's okay." The tall blackman removed a piece of paper and a small leather box from the bag.

"What he wanted was a headstone. I mean it didn't have to be anything fancy. It didn't even have to be stone. Just something to let people who happen to pass by, know it's him."

"I understand," Beau responded softly.

The tall homeless man continued, "He knew it would be expensive. He didn't have any money so he hoped this might help pay for the marker. Methusala handed him the small leather box. Beau opened it. Still glowing in all its honor was the medal. The Silver Star. Beau was stunned. JoJo was a war hero. He had served his country with honor only to die in some cold waterfront alley. Where had this man gone wrong? Where had we gone wrong to allow a man like this end up here?

"It would be my honor sir," Beau answered, stifling his emotions.

"JoJo had one more request," The stranger added. He handed Beau a folded, tattered, worn piece of brown paper.

"I know it's a lot to ask. If it wouldn't be too much trouble he would like this to be put on his marker. It's a poem. Beau slowly unfolded the old paper. Tilting it to catch the light from the fire he began to read a loud.

To all who should pass by, This is my final inspection

The soldier stood and faced God
Which must always come to pass
He hoped his shoes were shining
Just as brightly as his brass.

"Step forward now, you soldier,
How shall I deal with you?
Have you always turned the other cheek?
To My Church have you been true?"

The soldier squared his shoulders and
said, "No, Lord, I guess I ain't
Because those of us who carry guns
Can't always be a saint.

I've had to work most Sundays
And at times my talk was tough,
And sometimes I've been violent,
Because the world is awfully rough.

But, I never took a penny
That wasn't mine to keep…
Though I worked a lot of overtime
When the bills got just too steep,

And I never passed a cry for help,
Though at times I shook with fear,
And sometimes, God forgive me,
I've wept unmanly tears.

I know I don't deserve a place
Among the people here,
They never wanted me around
Except to calm their fears.

If you've a place for me here, Lord,
It needn't be so grand,
I never expected or had too much,
But if you don't, I'll understand."

There was a silence all around the throne
Where the saints had often trod
As the soldier waited quietly,
For the judgment of his God,

"Step forward now, you soldier,

You've borne your burdens well,
Walk peacefully on Heaven's streets,
You've done your time in Hell.

May God have mercy on my sole."

There was a long silence. The group just stood in sad reverence, and looked at the fire. It was if an unsaid prayer for JoJo had just been given. Father Marchello wiped his eyes. "If you don't mind. I'd like to give a mass in his Honor next Sunday."

The carver of names answered softly, "He wasn't Catholic Father."

"That's okay. He was a good man. One of God's children."

"Thank you Father." The stranger replied, then took a worn piece of sandpaper, and began to clear the rough edges from around JoJo's name.

Beau tucked the paper bag under his arm as the saddened group turned to walk up the alley of despair.

"I have one more question?" Beau asked, turning quickly to address the tall homeless man. The group saw nothing. He was gone. Vanished in the cold night mist. It was eerie. There was no way he could have disappeared that quickly. There was no way out of the area except back up the alley. Father Marchello made the sign of the cross quickly upon himself, then kissed the gold cross he had on a chain around his neck.

"Now that's spooky," Jack remarked, trying to put some levity into the situation. Sally kept close to Beau. She had a cold shiver run through her body as she thought about what she had just witnessed. Was it a specter, a figment of her imagination, or was he the Angel of Death who waited to pass on JoJo's last request?

Jack drove the car as Beau sat thoughtfully looking out the window. He stared blankly into the mist still wondering. He fought with self guilt. He felt somehow responsible for allowing a man like that to end up in a pauper's grave. It wasn't right, and it wasn't fair.

Jack broke the silence, "That was a pretty heavy scene back there."

Father Marchello commented, "That poem said it all. It was quite moving. Did he write it?"

"No," Beau replied listlessly, "I believe it was written by a lonely G.I. in the Korean War who was afraid to die, and wondered how he would be judged by his God. I don't know if they ever found out his real name."

"You don't think?"... Beau cut Jack off in mid sentence, "Who knows?"

Beau and Jack spent most of the night, and the next morning on the phone. By the time court was ready to convene JoJo was going to have a funeral with full military honors. He would have a six horse drawn caisson, honor guard, and a rifle team salute. The American Legion was going to

397

attend. Beau had purchased the finest casket money could buy, and Jack had taken up a collection at Police Headquarters for the headstone. Father Marchello insisted he give the eulogy.

The Bailiff shouted, "All rise." Judge Buckner entered the courtroom, returned to the bench, and opened the court. Sitting back, adjusting his sleeves on his black robe, moving his glasses to the end of his nose, he turned his attention to the prosecuting attorney, then ordered, "You may call your next witness."

Homer Canfield rose from his chair and announced, "The state calls Dr. Thomas Crum."

Dr. Crum made his way carefully to the witness stand and was quickly sworn in. Crum had been in the witness chair many times providing expert testimony, and he knew what areas the prosecuting attorney would explore, but he was always surprised at the questioning the defense would present.

"Dr. Crum," Canfield asked, "What is your experience in Forensic Psychiatry?"

"I graduated from Harvard in 1975. Then Harvard Medical School. Interned in neurology, studied psychiatry as a resident. Then joined the faculty at Harvard. I've been a Forensic Psychiatrist for 10 years."

"Your Honor," Barbara interrupted, "The defense accepts Dr. Crum's credentials. We will also accept Dr. Hopper's credentials as an expert in the field of Forensic Psychiatry. Now, can we get on with it?"

"Let the record show that the court recognizes both Dr. Crum and D. Hopper as experts in this area," Judge Buckner ordered. Canfield picked up his question list, and approached the witness stand.

"Dr. Crum. Would you tell the court from your diagnosis, what the defendant is suffering from?"

"Right now he is suffering from a progressive illness I call Schizophrenia Spectrum disorder." Crum answered calmly.

"Dr. Crum, for the record could you define for the court, schizophrenia?"

Dr. Crum paused phrasing his words in non clinical terms. "Schizophrenia is characterized by distorted thoughts and perceptions, atypical communication, inappropriate emotion, abnormal motor behavior, and social withdrawal."

"With the exception of social withdrawal, that definition could fit most of the politicians in the state," Canfield remarked sarcastically. The courtroom responded with a low chuckle.

"Can you elaborate for us?" Canfield urged.

"Yes, we have catatonic schizophrenia. It is evidenced by excessive, sometimes violent activity, or by mute responsiveness, a stuporous condition in which a person may retain the same position for hours, or alternate between violent activity, and then remaining stiff, and immobile, totally unresponsive to outside stimuli."

"Does the defendant demonstrate any of these characteristics?" Canfield questioned.

"No."

"Please continue doctor."

"Then we have Paranoid Schizophrenia. This is characterized by prominent delusions, or auditory hallucinations in the context of relative preservation or cognitive functioning or effect." Crum explained, in a professional voice. Canfield looked at some of the confused expressions on the faces of the jurors.

"What you are telling this court is, that this type of person has delusions of persecution?" Canfield added, for clarification.

"Or, delusions of grandeur, or both. Crum said, glancing at the jury. "The Paranoid Schizophrenic trusts no one, and is constantly on guard because he is convinced that others are plotting against him. He may seek retaliation against some imagined enemy."

"Did the defendant display any of these traits?"

"Partly," Dr. Crum answered quickly, then paused before clarifying his diagnosis, "This is what I call Disorganized Schizophrenia which includes extreme delusions, and inappropriate patterns of speech, mood, and movement. These moods may be manifested by laughing, singing, or crying at unsuitable times."

"So you are saying that the defendant displayed all of these characteristics?" Canfield asked, as he calmly walked to the jury box.

"In a way, yes." Crum replied before continuing, "He experienced auditory delusions, by talking, and having sex with the dead women as through they were alive. He also had long discussions with the corpse of Dr. Michaels. He experienced delusions of persecution when the child personality came to the surface. This was brought on by being abused as a child, and forced to have sex with Agnes Gladlow. His pattern of speech would change from that of a 12 year old child in little David to a mature adult who craved sex in the Gaylord personality. Now, the little David personality displays extreme anger, and pain from forced sex, and physical abuse. Gaylord on the other hand, considers himself a lover."

"So, disorganized schizophrenia is what you consider the defendant is suffering from, as well as MPD?" Canfield asked pointedly.

"Yes, in the defendant's case these voices that the schizophrenic hears have taken on real personalities in the defendant." Crum explained.

"Now, it is my understanding that there are supposedly, two other personalities residing inside the defendant?"

"Yes, during our interviews we experienced Gordon who appears to be a normal, rational personality. He is the one David Delongpre would like to become. Then, there is the Beast, or Beastie, as little David calls it."

"How did the Beastie come about?" Canfield questioned, casually looking at the jury to see if they were absorbing this testimony.

"As far as we can determine, the Beastie is a mental reincarnation of his puppy, Snipper."

"Wait a minute," Canfield interrupted politely, "Are you saying the defendant actually acts like a dog?"

"Yes."

"Is it a male or female dog?" Canfield questioned lightly.

"I don't know?" Crum replied defensively.

"I mean, you observed the defendant. Does he raise his leg, and piss on the wall, or does he squat to relieve himself?"

"Objection! Your honor. This is getting a little gross," Barbara Starkey mocked.

"I'm sorry you honor. I'm trying to make a point," Canfield rebutted.

"Okay, I'll allow it. But keep it clean counselor," Buckner ordered.

"Dr. Crum, did you observe any physical anomalies where the defendant's conduct resembled a dog?"

"No I didn't."

"Then how do you know that this Beastie thing actually exists?" Canfield demanded.

"The defendant while under hypnosis told me about the beast, and the evidence recovered at the defendant's apartment indicated that, at times, his actions resembled that of some kind of beast." Crum elaborated confidently.

"Now doctor, if the defendant's interviews revealed that this beast was a reincarnation of his puppy, aah, Snipper was it? It isn't likely that a puppy would be prone to cold blooded murder, now would it?"

"No. A puppy figure wouldn't. However, little David needed a protector. So in his mind, the Beastie became a fierce flesh eating dinosaur. That's why you see the toy dinosaurs in his room. They were his images of the Beastie."

Canfield thought for a moment before asking his next question. "So, when David was in pain. When David was mad, when he was fed up with Gaylord, and his attempts to have sex with Agnes. I mean in this case, the Agnes image. He would use the Beastie to do the killing?"

"Yes, apparently," Crum answered softly.

"So, knowing that the Beast's primary function was to kill, wasn't that just like pointing a gun at the victim? Or stabbing her with a knife? Or pushing poison down her throat? The defendant knew exactly what would happen when he released the Beastie. He knew it was wrong, and would lead to death."

"Possibly," Crum responded. "The one problem I have, is that the method of killing is not consistent with that of a Beast. Especially, a flesh eating dinosaur."

"How do you mean doctor," Canfield asked, moving to the witness stand.

"The victims were strangled. If the Beast had killed them their bodies would have been mutilated."

"So, do you believe that this Beastie personality really exists?" Canfield asked pointedly.

"Oh yes," Crum replied emphatically, "He exists for our benefit?"

"Aah, yes," Canfield said, exhaling a sigh, "Our benefit," Canfield glanced at the jury before asking his next question. "Could the defendant be faking all this?"

Dr. Crum paused, gathering his thoughts carefully before answering. "When patients attempt to fake schizophrenia they fake positive signs, like seeing visions, or hearing voices. By repetitive questioning you can tell if the patient is lying. Time after time when addressing these alter egos his story was consistent, and accurate. The defendant never made up a story just to make himself look sicker."

"I see," Canfield said knowingly, "Do you consider the defendant to be a rational man?"

"That depends on what personality you are addressing at the time." Crum responded.

"Please clarify." Canfield urged politely.

"Gaylord, is articulate, smart, and intelligent. The same can be said for Gordon. David is a traumatized, yet normal 12 year old. The Beastie however, could not be evaluated. Communication could not be established with that personality."

"Well doctor, you didn't at any time communicate with any personality that wasn't normal in any sense of the word?

So, we can rationally say that either Gaylord, Gordon or David could have planned, and murdered the victims not the Beast. Is that correct?" Canfield asked bluntly.

"Yes. They are more than capable," Crum replied. Canfield glanced at the faces of the jurors. This was damaging testimony as to the mental state of defendant.

"As a result of your extensive interviews with the defendant did Gaylord, Gordon, or David, know right from wrong?"

"Yes."

"Does the Gaylord personality communicate with the other entities?" Canfield questioned cautiously.

"Yes. However, when Gordon protests to David about Gaylord's activities, he's put into the safe room," Crum added.

"But they have communicated with each other haven't they." Canfield emphasized.

"Yes."

"Now, David controlled the Beast, is that correct?"

"As I said before, yes."

Canfield paraded in front of the jury box as he framed his next question. "If these personalities knew right from wrong, and they communicated with each other, and David knew instinctively that if he called up the Beast it would kill, aren't they all guilty of premeditated murder?" Before Crum could comment Canfield continued, "Even Gordon, the normal personality, who could have prevented the murders was locked away. It makes no difference if you have two, or three, or a hundred and three personalities, if they know right from wrong they should pay the full price for murder."

"Objection!" Barbara shouted angrily, "The good doctor and the counselor should only comment on his medical diagnosis not the law. That will be up to you your honor, and the jury."

"Sustained," Buckner ordered.

"Withdraw your honor." Canfield answered, clearly knowing he had already made his point to the jury. Canfield walked to his desk and looked at his notes before continuing. "One more question," Canfield asked, scratching his head, as he walked slowly back to the witness stand.

"Dr. Crum, the testimony you gave about the defendant's mental state. I mean by that the multiple personalities that you were able to interview. How was that obtained?"

"Regression Analysis," Crum answered confidently.

"Please explain to the court exactly what Regression Analysis is." Canfield was carefully leading the witness to his next point of contention.

"In a clinical setting we hypnotize the subject then we take him back in time to his childhood. Through a series of questions we reconstruct events that led to the current trauma." Crum replied, glancing at the judge then at the jury.

"I see," Canfield responded, pacing slowly in front of the witness framing his next question. "Dr. Crum, how can you tell if your patient is truly hypnotized?"

Dr. Crum shifted uncomfortably in his chair before answering, "I've hypnotized more than 1500 patients I know when they are in a state of receptive thoughts."

"I didn't ask you that. What I would like to know, as a clinical Psychiatrist, is there any known method of knowing for sure when a patient is truly hypnotized? I mean, is there any kind of machine that confirms a true state of hypnosis?

Dr. Crum was becoming extremely nervous with this line of questioning. "No," Crum answered softly.

"I'm sorry, I didn't hear you," Canfield said, tilting his head slightly.

"No," Crum answered raising his voice slightly.

"Then, all the interviews, all the testimony obtained through hypnosis is hearsay, and should be stricken from the record, is that correct?"

"Objection, you honor. Counselor is impeaching his own witness," Starkey shouted quickly. Canfield shot back his rebuttal, "Your honor, statements of a hypnotized witness is inadmissible in the absence of clear and convincing evidence that the testimony being offered was based on facts recalled and related to events that existed before hypnosis. How can this court accurately determine if the defendant was actually under a state of hypnosis, and if he was, did the interviewer lead, or suggest facts to the subject?"

Barbara immediately replied to Canfield's challenge. "Your honor, I think the counselor is beating a dead horse. The learned counselor, and I, both know that the Supreme Court has already ruled on this issue. In a criminal case a state may not bar testimony, hypnotically obtained, or not. If you want an example, just read the transcripts of the Hinckley trial."

Judge Buckner peered over the top of his glasses at his two young lawyers and smiled. Looking at Canfield, he winked, "Nice try counselor, sustained."

Canfield smiled, and returned to his desk. "I have no further questions for this witness."

Judge Buckner nodded at Barbara Starkey who rose from her chair, and walked to the witness stand. "Dr. Crum please tell the court what other tests you, and Dr. Hopper performed on the defendant."

Dr. Crum glanced at his notes before answering, "We did the Stanford Binet Intelligence Test, the Wechler Scale Intelligence Test, the Rorschach Test,..." Starkey interrupted the doctor, "That is the inkblot test, correct?"

"Yes, then along with Regressive Analysis we administered the Minnesota Multiplistic Personalities Inventory. This was followed with and EEG or an electroencephalogram which is the clinical term. Finally, a CAT SCAN which is basically an X-ray of the brain."

Barbara Starkey stepped to one side of the witness stand so she could view the jurors as well as the courtroom, as the doctor continued, "The CAT SCAN is a tool that can be used in psychiatric diagnosis. Computerized Axial Tomography is a computer enhanced three dimensional X-ray of the brain. This is a new technique. We have found overwhelming evidence that the brains' physiology can be related to a person's emotions. We believe that an abnormal appearance of the brain can relate to schizophrenia. The CAT SCAN is a very powerful tool for viewing the brain. It can show whether or not an abnormal appearance exists."

"Objection!," Canfield shouted, then quickly approached the bench, "Your honor, I know where counselor is going with this line of questioning. The state will admit that the use of the CAT SCAN has made significant contributions to medicine in locating tumors, and other physiological problems in the brain. There are no grounds to allow it's use in diagnosing schizophrenia."

Barbara quickly challenged Canfield's contention, "Your honor, Dr. Crum's job is to provide expert opinion about the defendant's mental condition, before, and during the killings. He can't..." The judge cut Barbara off in mid sentence. "Hold it counselor," Buckner pushed his glasses back to their normal position then rapped his gavel, and ordered, "We will take a 30 minute recess. I'll see you two in my chambers."

A low murmur rippled through the courtroom as Buckner marched out followed by the two young lawyers.

Buckner casually plopped into his big leather chair that occupied one end of the judge's chambers. He put his elbows on his desk resting his chin in the palm of his hands and asked, "Okay let me have it."

"Your honor," Barbara said, "The court has accepted Dr. Crum as an expert. The jury has a right to hear the results of all diagnostic tests. To deny this would deprive the defendant of due process."

Canfield quickly presented his view, "Your honor, there is no clinical evidence that can substantiate that a picture of the brain can in any way illustrate a mental disorder of any kind. I will admit that a tumor on the brain could relate to a mental disorder. But no such condition exists. Your honor, we could go on and show that there are other theories out there that cannot be proved one way or the other. For example, there have been studies that have linked the double Y chromosomes in human cells to violent behavior, but it has not been proven scientifically."

Barbara Starkey gave Canfield a look of frustration.

"Well, young lady, what have you got to say?" Buckner asked.

"Your honor, the court solicited Dr. Crum and Dr. Hopper as expert witnesses. I believe federal statutes require him to testify as to his clinical assessment. We have to recognize, that his charter by this court, is to testify as to his clinical judgment, first, on the mental condition of the defendant not using legal terms, but in medical terms. He is required to present to the jury his findings using medical observations, and the medical tests that he would normally use when evaluating a patient. The doctor would routinely order a CAT SCAN, and use it in his overall evaluation. Both Dr. Crum and Dr. Hopper have stated to me that if they are not allowed to testify as to their medical opinion based on proven medical test procedures they can no longer fulfill their obligations as an expert witnesses to this court, and could not answer anymore questions."

Buckner was fuming, as he shouted, "That is God Damn contempt of court!"

"Your honor," Barbara said, trying to calm the irate judge, "You know they can contest that in court and win, meanwhile you've got a mistrial on your hands and the whole world is going to know about it."

Buckner's reddened face slowly returned to a normal color as he regained control of his temper. "I don't like the court being blackmailed. You see, that's why I don't like to have TV cameras in my court."

Buckner returned to the courtroom, assumed his position on the bench and called the court to order. He lowered his glasses to the end of his nose, and peered over them at the courtroom before he spoke, "The court recognizes that there is controversy over the use of the CAT SCAN as a tool for diagnosing a mental illness. The court has reviewed both sides of the issue. Due to the fact that the court appointed psychiatrists would use the CAT SCAN as a tool in their normal clinical evaluation, and in the interest of due process, the court will allow this testimony," Buckner nodded at Barbara Starkey.

The counsel for the defense walked to the witness stand before asking, "Dr. Crum, would you explain to the court your opinion of the CAT SCAN in diagnosing mental illness?"

Dr. Crum was relieved that his testimony concerning CAT SCAN was going to be admitted. He sat up confidently and began. "In my estimation the CAT SCAN as an instrument for viewing the brains is unquestioned. My colleagues agree that it is probably the greatest diagnostic advance in the past fifty years. We use it routinely in our evaluations.

Barbara moved slowly to the jury box as she spoke, "Most of us in the courtroom can understand its value physiologically, but how is it used psychologically? I mean, can the CAT SCAN tell us if the defendant was responsible for his acts or not?"

"Indirectly it can," Dr. Crum responded then folded his arms, and sat back in his chair. He was more comfortable with this line of questioning. "It is my view, and also the view of other psychiatrists I have worked with that widened sulci,..." Crum noticed a concerned look at Starkey's face.

"Excuse me," Crum said apologetically, before going on to explain, "Sulci are the folds, and ridges on the surface of the brain. These enlarged or widened folds tend to indicate that the subject is suffering from schizophrenia."

"Did the defendant's CAT SCAN reveal that he was suffering from this disease?" Barbara asked.

"Yes."

"Now, doctor, you mentioned the MMPI test earlier," Barbara queried glancing at her notes. "Could you explain to the court how your test results indicated that the defendant is actually suffering from schizophrenia?"

"Yes. This test is commonly used in forensic psychology. The test consists of five hundred and fifty statements requiring an answer of true of false. We have statements such as; I believe I am being followed; I believe I am being plotted against; I wish I could be as happy as others seem to be, and so on. The test was scored on a dozen different scales. Three of them screened for intentional distortion, and nine screened for various mental abnormalities, from hypochondriasis, to depression, hysteria and schizophrenia. The defendant's test scores indicated that he was far above the usual line indicating between normal and abnormal. In our scoring for depression the defendant's score rose almost to the top of the chart for abnormality."

"So doctor, what in your opinion is the bottom line as far as the defendant's mental state is concerned?" Barbara questioned cautiously.

"The chance of the defendant's score not indicating a serious mental problem is about one in a million."

"In other words you are positive that the defendant is suffering from a severe mental defect?" Barbara asked pointedly.

"Yes." Crum answered calmly.

"Did the defendant display any other symptoms that indicated a severe mental disorder?"

"Yes. He had several other symptoms. He experience acmesthesia. Acmesthesia is a pathological response to stimuli, normally painful, they are experienced as pressures, in other words, after the killings the defendant would have severe headaches. He demonstrated what I call bi-polar algolania. The Gaylord personality derived sexual pleasures from sadism, inflicting pain on his lovers. The child personality demonstrated the opposite, masochism. Also, the Gaylord ego was an exhibitionist. These were compulsions that were unique to each personality."

Did they share a common trait?" Starkey asked out of curiosity.

"Yes, ablutomania, or compulsive bathing. After each of the killings the defendant would bathe for hours as if he was trying to wash the guilt from his mind." Crum advised.

"Do you consider the defendant insane?" Starkey questioned bluntly.

"Do I think he has a mental disease? Yes. Do I think he needs to be institutionalized? Yes. Do I think he has a multiple personality disorder?" Yes. Do I think he's insane, no. Do I think he knew right from wrong when he committed these crimes? I don't know. I am sure the court will decide that issue."

"Thank you. I have no further questions for this witness," Starkey said glancing at the jury box to see if she had made her point.

"Redirect your honor," Canfield requested quickly. Buckner nodded, "Your witness."

Canfield approached the witness stand before asking, "The appearance of widened sulci as an indication of schizophrenia, is that a unanimous view of practicing psychiatrists?"

"No," Crum answered slowly.

"Isn't it true that research in this area indicate that most people who are schizophrenic don't have widened sulci?" Canfield questioned, placing emphasis on each word.

"Well counselor, lets define most. In our studies we've found that one third of the schizophrenics have widened sulci. It's true that isn't a simple majority. However, that is a powerful fact."

"Is that a fact and does that fact make it true?" Canfield asked sarcastically.

"It is a statistical fact." Crum replied defiantly. "Let me put it in perspective for you. Statistically, a male who smokes 20 packs of cigarettes a day is 20 times more likely to get lung cancer. That is a strong enough fact for the Surgeon General to put a warning on every package of cigarettes. Yet no one can say that anyone who takes the next cigarette will get lung cancer. I mentioned that one third of schizophrenics have widened sulci, and probably less than 2% of normal people have them. This is a significant statistical fact, and it bears on my opinion in this case."

Canfield revealed a sly smile before asking his next question. "Dr. Crum isn't true that the CAT SCAN test didn't occur until a clinical diagnosis by several qualified psychiatrists had already established the fact that he was suffering from schizophrenia? Isn't it true that these facts influenced your findings when it came to interpreting the CAT SCAN. How can the jury, or anyone in this courtroom, be sure of the validity of this information? Dr. Crum I can remember when there was a theory that you could identify the criminal mind by feeling the bumps on a man's head." Canfield quickly closed his questioning by saying, "I have no further questions for this witness your honor."

Dr. Crum returned to his seat when Canfield announced, "The state calls Dr. John Hopper to the stand."

In spite of all his prestige, Dr. Hopper was a humble man. He was not impressed with money, degrees, or status. He was extremely intelligent although you would never know it by just looking at the man. You could put this man in the finest clothes money could buy, and he would still look like he just got out of bed. Dr. Hopper, after taking the oath sat quietly in the witness chair.

Canfield approached the witness stand, and asked, "Dr. Hopper, your are the forensic psychiatrist petitioned by the defense?"

"Yes."

"In this case, you, and Dr. Crum both interviewed the accused?" Canfield questioned calmly.

"Yes."

"Your job basically was to interview the defendant, compile your diagnosis, and confirm that Dr. Crum's procedures were clinically correct?" Canfield asked pointedly.

"Yes."

"Do you honestly believe after observing the defendant, he is suffering from paranoid schizophrenia?"

"Yes, a severe case in my opinion."

"Is he also what Dr. Crum claims, a multiple personality?"

"Possibly. I observed those same personalities in my interviews with the defendant. When we compared our findings we found mistakes in the personality traits."

"In other words, the defendant may or may not be faking the MPD disorder?" Canfield declared.

"That is still a possibility. I have found some inconsistencies." Dr. Hopper stated, surprising the defense. "I've reviewed the Rorschack protocols of Gaylord, and Gordon with Dr. Crum. Gaylord in my opinion is a paranoid with a psychopathic overlay. I've only seen two cases like this. Gaylord is self centered, preoccupied with his own ideas. He is compulsive with marked incapacity to derive pleasure from interpersonal relationships. Believe it or not, he is intimidated by women, because of a love-hate relationship with the only mother figure he's really known, Agnes. Under conditions of stress, or fatigue he is capable of revenge type of rape and murder." Dr. Hopper paused, getting his thoughts together.

"Please continue," Canfield urged.

"One of the inconsistencies that bothers me is that the Rorschach tests for both Gordon, and Gaylord are similar. They reveal that both personalities have a certain amount of hostility, and sexual preoccupation. However, there is a perverse, and deliberate aspect about it that indicates a psychopathic intent not schizophrenic. The other thing that bothers me is that when I observed the hospital staff bringing him his food they were always met by Gordon or Gaylord. But when Dr. Crum entered the picture, he was always met by little David personality."

"So, what is it you're telling this court?" Canfield asked guardedly.

"From my experience the alter personality is usually a break off of the first personality, Gordon. In this case we have a merge. Gaylord appears to be a mirror image of Gordon, like Dr. Jekyll, and Mr. Hyde. He appears normal on the outside but the least little event could bring on Gaylord or Mr. Hyde in this case, and the whole process begins again."

"Now, your opinion, your diagnosis, and much of your data was obtained through hypnosis, and regression analysis. Is that correct?" Canfield questioned, as he moved closer to Dr. Hopper.

"Yes."

"And regression analysis depends largely on hypnosis, is that correct? Canfield added.

"Yes." Hopper answered quietly knowing exactly where he was going with this line of questioning.

"Was the defendant actually hypnotized by Dr. Crum? Or, yourself for that matter?" Canfield demanded.

Dr. Hopper thought silently for a moment before answering, "The issue you wish to raise before this court is, was the defendant actually hypnotized? For that matter, has anyone ever really been hypnotized?" Hopper paused again framing his words carefully. "There is no way to prove any person is in a state of hypnosis, since there is no universally accepted standard of behavior or measurable physiological process which is accepted as being a hypnotic state of mind."

"So you don't know if the defendant was telling the truth or not? Do you doctor." Canfield accused bluntly.

"My diagnosis was not solely based on hypnosis alone. I had cognizant interviews as well as test scores."

Canfield walked to the jury box then turned to ask his next question, "Lets get to the bottom line. Is the defendant a true multiple personality? Was he in his right mind when he committed these sex-murders?"

Dr. Hopper's answer was short and to the point, like a football coach giving pointers his players. "First, the defendant while under hypnosis followed my instructions too literally. I have never had a multiple personality patient do that before, even when I gave him the same instructions. I had a feeling the defendant was reading from a script, or, at least well thought out responses. The other thing that bothers me was that each personality blamed the Beastie for the murders. Multiple personality syndrome patients who have been arrested for some crime, know at some point, that they are guilty of some wrongdoing, but they are not sure what it is they did. They are usually willing to take their punishment, since they feel that they deserve it. They do not blame the other personality."

"So, he's faking," Canfield blurted out loudly.

"Yes," Hopper said, coldly looking at the defendant who was sitting upright glaring at the doctor.

"I have no further questions for this witness," Canfield said, and resumed his seat at his table.

Barbara Starkey stood, then moved to the witness stand before beginning her cross examination. "Dr. Hopper, isn't it true that the dissociative process begins in the multiple personality when some trauma occurs of a life threatening nature?"

"Yes."

"Isn't it true that a child when faced with a trauma too stressful to handle, he or she, would use a mental mechanism to survive?"

"Yes."

"Did the defendant reflect any of these traits?"

"Yes," Hopper answered dutifully.

Starkey continued her line of questioning in order to blunt Dr. Hopper's previous statements. It was surprising to her that Dr. Hopper's testimony, who was supposed to be on her side, was fast becoming the state's star witness.

"Dr. Hopper, isn't it true that an alter personality would most likely to have been created in the defendant's mind when his older sister ran away. When she left him alone to suffer the sexual abuse and torture from the Gladlows. When she abandoned him?" Starkey emphasized pointedly.

"Yes."

"Did you, and Dr. Crum confirm these facts?"

"Yes we did." Hopper answered firmly.

"Did you know that Dr. Michaels, a licensed psychiatrist, had been treating David Delongpre for a multiple personality disorder for over a year before his death?"

"No."

"That in his files he had a complete record of his sessions with David Delongpre?"

"No I didn't."

"How come two qualified psychiatrists have recognized that the defendant suffers from MPD, and you have not?"

"I have no idea. I can only render my opinion as I see it," Hopper answered defensively.

"Dr. Hopper, isn't it true that MPD patients tend to show different personalities to different hospital staff members? I mean don't they tend to polarize the hospital staff into camps of believers and nonbelievers?"

"Yes."

"So you really don't know for sure if he's a multiple or not? I mean, if you are not sure, then there is a possibility that he could be, isn't that true?"

"Objection, counsel is leading the witness. He has already given his opinion," Canfield snapped.

"Sustained," Buckner ordered.

Barbara Starkey moved to the jury box, leaned over and made strong eye contact with each juror as she continued her attack on Hopper's testimony. "Isn't it true that it is extremely hard, if not impossible to be sure if the defendant, who has not been in therapy for this disorder is in reality a multiple? Isn't it true, that neither you or Dr. Crum, have no firm criteria from which to measure him?" Before Hopper could answer, Starkey shot another rhetorical question, "Isn't it true that clinical patients have such different situations and motives, show such variations in behavior, mood swings, and thinking patterns, that there is not a typical multiple personality syndrome patient?"

"That's true," Hopper replied defensively, "That's why we only have general guidelines to determine who is, and who is not disturbed in this particular fashion."

Barbara Starkey returned to her desk, and faced the witness. "So it may be impossible to determine the state of mind of the defendant at the time he committed these crimes? The only thing the jury has to go on are these unverified statements, and opinions. The only real evidence we have is historical evidence that shows clearly he was repeatedly raped, and sexually abused as a child."

Before Hopper could reply Starkey announced, "I have no further questions for this witness." Starkey looked at the defendant who smugly popped a small Baby Ruth candy in his mouth, and began to chew slowly. Starkey rolled her eyes and shook her head slightly knowing that the defendant was doing absolutely nothing to create a positive image to the jury.

"The state calls Mrs. Sarah Smith to the stand." Canfield stated, trying to speed up the testimony. Buckner had warned both counsels not to produce repetitive testimony unless they were absolutely sure it was essential to their case. Sarah Smith emitted the aura of a purely sexual animal. Her body was in perfect shape. It filled a tight red mini-skirt with a revealing slit up the side. It was hardly the garment you'd ware to a trial unless you had a statement to make. The miniskirt revealed her fantastic legs, and most of her thighs when she sat in the witness chair, and crossed her legs. Most men in the courtroom stretched their necks to get a better view of this sexy lady. Even judge Buckner leaned forward to get a better look. Sarah in every since of the word was sexy, but hard looking. She wore too much makeup and cheap jewelry. Her hardness was evident in the way she justified her way of life. She did what she wanted, when she wanted, and to hell with everyone else.

411

Barbara Starkey smiled to herself as she took note of all the drooling, lecherous men in the courtroom. Canfield was no exception. He had to clear this throat before he could begin his questioning. The current rumor in the media was that Sarah had already agreed to pose nude for Hustler Magazine for a cool $250,000. Starkey had planned on buying that magazine just to see what she had to offer the world.

Canfield approached the sexy witness as he began his questioning. "Mrs. Smith, you knew the defendant in Seattle?"

"Yes."

"Would you tell the court your relationship with the defendant?"

"He was a patient of my late husband's."

"That would be Dr. Michael Smith, correct?"

"Correct," Sarah replied calmly.

"Do you know what Dr. Michaels' was treating him for?" Canfield asked.

"No, my husband didn't discuss his patient's histories with me."

Canfield nodded then continued, "Now, Mrs. Smith we know the defendant became more than a patient to you and Dr. Michaels, didn't he?"

"Yes, my husband and myself both became enamored with his sexual exploits," Sarah said casually.

"You became more that just enamored. You actually became financial partners, and active players in the Fetish Club, is that true?"

"Yes."

"Isn't it true that you and your husband used your patient list, and contacts in Seattle to recruit players in the Fetish Club?"

"No, it was a confidential service we offered to the customer who wanted sexual relief. They each signed consent forms. Dr. Michaels saw it as reality therapy. There are a lot of people out there with sexual hang-ups. The Fetish Club let them live out their fantasies in a controlled environment. That is a hell of a lot better than having a sexual predator running the streets." Sarah replied smugly.

"However, the good doctor didn't count on his murder being part of the defendant's fantasy." Canfield quickly countered glancing at the jury.

"Objection! Dr. Michael's death is not an issue. It's prejudicial, and there is no evidence that the defendant killed Dr. Michaels," Starkey countered loudly.

"Your honor," Canfield rebutted, "What are we suppose to think? I don't keep a dead body in my closet taped to a wheelchair."

"I understand where you're coming from counselor. But there is no evidence that supports that assumption. Let's stick to the issues. Sustained," Buckner ordered.

Canfield turned his attention back to the sexy witness.

"The Fetish Club was a successful business venture wasn't it?"

"Yes."

"How profitable?" Canfield asked pointedly.

"I'm not sure?" Sarah answered slowly.

"Just give us an estimate," Canfield demanded politely.

"Oh, I'd guess about $500,000 a year."

"What did the defendant do with the money?"

"He invested in stocks, bonds, real-estate," Sarah answered looking away as though she was bored with this line of questioning.

"So the defendant was a sharp businessman.?"

"Yes."

"Did you at any time observe in the defendant a sniveling beast or a little child named David?"

"No."

"Did you know a Gordon, or hear the name mentioned by the defendant?"

"No."

"Did the defendant sell drugs?" Canfield demanded.

"Yes."

"What kind of drugs?" He questioned cautiously.

"Uppers, downers, ecstasy, coke, marijuana."

"This was under the table money wasn't it?" Canfieled asked quickly.

"Yes."

"So, this drug money was under the table money and never reported to the IRS?" Canfield demanded glaringly.

"Yes."

"And you'd say that this money amounted to another $450,000?" He added.

"Yes, approximately." Sarah answered guardedly.

"Could a crazy man, a man totally insane, a man who would lose control of his senses be such a successful businessman?" Canfield demanded glaringly.

"No. Not likely," Sarah replied calmly.

"Do you consider this man insane?" Canfield asked loudly.

"No."

"Do you consider this man a good actor?" Canfield continued his questioning looking at the jury.

"Yes, he's good all right." Sarah said emphatically.

"I have no further questions for this witness." Canfield confidently walked to his chair and sat down.

Barbara Starkey rose quickly and approached the witness. "At the Fetish Club what kind of sex games did you play?" Starkey asked inquiringly.

"Objection!" Canfield blurted out strongly. "Hearsay."

"Your honor, the prosecution has already opened this line of questioning. It reflects state of mind your honor."

"Overruled," Buckner responded.

The sex questions didn't bother Sarah Smith in the least. She freely admitted her sexuality, and even took pride in it. She was, after all, a liberated woman.

"His favorite game was the sex slave bit," Sarah answered freely.

"You mean, you would be his sex slave?" Starkey confirmed noting that some people in the courtroom were keenly interested in this line of questioning.

"Not always." Sarah answered listlessly.

"How do you mean?" Starkey asked curiously.

"Sometimes he would be the sex slave," Sarah replied surprising Barbara Starkey as she asked, "Please explain."

"Well, these were times when he wanted to be tied up and whipped."

There was another low reaction in the courtroom. This time Buckner waited for the murmur to ebb on its own. He nodded at Barbara to continue.

"By whipped, you mean symbolically."

"No, he insisted on being whipped hard. There were times when he wouldn't be satisfied until we drew blood." Sarah stated dispassionately.

"Did he talk to you during these whippings?"

Sarah thought back, reaching deep into her memory before she answered.

"Yes, I believe once or twice he called me mommy, and begged me to stop. When I stopped he got pissed, and made me continue."

"Did he whip you?" Barbara asked taking a deep breath.

"Yes, and I'd call him 'master'" Sarah added.

"Did he draw blood when he whipped you?" Barbara questioned.

"Yes, I wouldn't have it any other way," Sarah said confidently then focused her gaze on Sally sitting in the front row. Somehow Sarah knew that she and Sally had connected sexually. She knew instinctively that these carnal thoughts lurked deep inside most women, and Sally or Barbara Starkey for that matter, were no different.

"What did you do after the whippings?" Barbara asked knowing deep inside she was becoming slightly aroused.

"We screwed our eyeballs off," Sarah uttered with a smile.

"Was the defendant a good lover?"

Not really. I faked it. You know, screaming, and told him how big he was. Actually, he was hung like a stud field mouse."

The courtroom broke into uncontrollable laughter at that remark. Buckner rapped his gavel to bring the court back to order before Barbara could continue.

"Why did you feel you had to lie to him?

"Because I've seen him with other women when they complained." Sarah said uneasily.

"What did he do?" Barbara questioned.

"I thought he was going to kill one of the women. He shouted, and called her 'Bitch'." We had to pull him off her or.."

"Or what?" Barbara quickly interrupted, "Or he'd kill her? Is that correct?" Barbara demanded loudly. "Can you possibly say that this man was in his right mind when he would submit to brutal whippings, go on a sex binge, then when rebuffed by a woman, would go into an uncontrollable rage?"

Sarah thought long, and hard at Barbara's observations before answering. "I don't know about that . I only know I wasn't about to piss him off."

"Of course you wouldn't," Barbara commented. "You were looking at a man who could totally change when his sexual advances were rebuffed. I have no further questions for this witness."

Judge Buckner glanced at the clock on the courtroom wall then announced, "It's getting late, and we all have other commitments. This court is adjourned until 9:00 Monday morning." Buckner rapped his gavel once then promptly exited the courtroom.

The media representatives made a hasty exit out the door. The defendant rose, then whispered something into Barbara Starkey's ear before he was led out of the room.

Sally's gaze followed the killer. As he grabbed several small candies from the dish, and stuffed them in his pocket. Sally noticed that there was something different about him. Outside of looking absolutely normal, something had changed. He was pale, gaunt, he'd lost weight. His eyes looked puffy red, set deep inside his head. Not at all like he was when she observed him from the other side of the looking glass. She wondered if he was finally realizing the evil he had brought into so many people's lives. Was it like some mental cancer that fed upon, and finally devoured its host?

Barbara Starkey toting her briefcase came along side Sally and Beau as they slowly made their way out of the crowded courtroom.

"How did you like Canfield's star witness? Barbara asked Sally.

"Which one?" She answered with a smile.

"Miss sex pot, or should I say, Miss Hustler Centerfold?"

"She sure sold me an issue," Beau added, with a slight chuckle.

"Men!," Barbara said with a sigh.

"What did David, or was it Gaylord, who just whispered to you say?" Sally asked out of curiosity.

"You know I can't tell you. I'm sure you've heard of client privilege," Barbara responded lightly.

Sally nodded as they moved slowly into the lobby of the courthouse. Barbara looked intently at Sally. For a split second they connected. Sally didn't know what it was, but something was exchanged between them without a word being spoken. It was as if they both shared a secret. Sally felt strange, maybe even slightly aroused. Barbara slipped her arm under Sally's then pulled her close, and whispered into her ear. "He said he wanted to do the three of us at the same time. Then he could die a happy man."

Before Sally could respond Barbara slipped away commenting, "I'll see you guys later." Within a second Barbara was lost in the crowd.

"What did she say to you?" Beau asked calmly.

"Oh, nothing."

"Barbara never says nothing," Beau remarked knowingly.

"How do you know," Sally inquired.

"Some time ago we had a thing going," He answered.

"My God! Have done every woman in this town?" She questioned sternly.

Beau took Sally by the arm, and gently led her to a quiet corner of the courthouse lobby.

"I am going to say it again. I love you with all my heart. I won't make excuses for myself. What you see is what you get. Remember, you said that. I want you to be my wife. Yes, I've had a few relationships, what the hell was I suppose to do? I was hurting I needed something. I needed someone who cared. Then you stepped into my life, and I knew you were the one. If you'll have me, I'll be the best husband, and father to Katie you'll ever see." Beau waited for a response. She stood silent looking at him.

"Was she as good as I was?" Sally asked with a pouting expression on her face.

"Oh my God! Am I going to have to compare you with all my social encounters?"

She secretly pinched his groin, "Social encounters? Is that what you call it?" She began to laugh. Sally couldn't keep a straight face any longer. "Believe me I know how men are. I won't ask about your social encounters if you won't ask me about mine." Sally walked briskly away.

"What sexual encounters?" He unconsciously shouted causing heads to turn. Beau pushed his way through the crowd trying to catch up with Sally.

Chapter Twenty Four
May God Have Mercy on His Soul

It was a cold, crisp, fall morning at the Charleston Memorial Cemetery. The new sun sat just beyond the eastern horizon illuminating orange red clouds that heralded the coming new day. For a morning service Beau was surprised at the early turnout. The black community was there dressed in their Sunday best. The local American Legion Post was in full attendance. For the first time since the killer came to town the white and black communities had finally come together to honor a blackman. It was ironic. Both the white and black communities were honoring a down and out homeless blackman. He was one of those dirty unshaven derelicts you see pushing a discarded market basket loaded with trash, bottles, and tin cans, hoping his foraging would allow him enough money to buy one more bottle of booze to get through one more miserable day. The sad part is that this whole insane routine would begin again, and again.

The caisson carried the flag draped coffin toward the gravesite. As the horse drawn caisson passed slowly down the street. A uniformed honor guard rendered a slow, final salute to the sad and lonely soldier who passed by. Six neatly dressed soldiers, in full uniform, from his old unit, lifted the coffin from the caisson and carried it to the gravesite as a lone bugler played Taps.

The mayor, and all the city dignitaries were present which surprised Beau. He thought most of them were self-centered assholes who cared more about their careers than they did about the street people of Charleston.

Father Marchello gave the eulogy. It was the standard Catholic diatribe honoring the man who so bravely served his country, and asking all of us to open our hearts to help these people with our charity. Beau knew Father Marchello's heart was in the right place but very little would be done. This would all be forgotten in a few days. It was a sad tribute to our life and times.

Gil Washington, the Mayor, stood up and proceeded to the podium. He revealed a letter from the Secretary of Defense. It was a letter of thank you to Staff Sergeant Jeremiah Joseph Jones for his long and faithful service to his country. The letter was meant to be a keepsake for the grieving family. JoJo had none. Beau wondered what Gil would do with the letter? He could tell it was a form letter with all the standard government platitudes. Nevertheless, someone had taken the time to have it ready to honor this man that no one really knew, yet many in the congregation felt close to at this time.

Beau turned to survey the crowd. There were no Klan protesters parading outside the cemetery. There were no Black Panthers raising their gloved fists in the air, there were only black and white everyday working people sitting together where a few weeks ago; they were fighting in the streets. Jack Bellamy nudged Beau as he gazed at the crowd, "What do you think of that?" he asked, pointing at his father in law, the Reverend Jesse Baxter. The reverend sat next to Obie and Willard Jackson, the two black gang leaders that had given the Mayor such a hard time. The good Reverend was making sure these boys behaved themselves.

"I see it but I don't believe it," Beau commented. Jack smiled. As they continued to survey the crowd Beau noticed District Attorney Blackstone sitting with Carl Hawthorne, the NAACP lawyer, in the seats reserved for the city counsel. Just about everyone involved in the trial was there. He was amazed.

When the mayor finished reading the official letter, he announced, "Detective Sergeant Jack Bellamy would like to say a few words." Gil Washington gestured to Jack. As Jack made his way to the podium Beau wondered what the hell was going on. Jack didn't say anything to him. He had no idea what Jack was going to say. It was appropriate for one blackman to stand up and talk personally about another. Jack didn't know JoJo. Like himself, he only had a few hours of conversation with him down at Headquarters. Beau smiled to himself thinking at least we're not going to have some preacher up their dancing around with a bible in his hand asking for a hundred amens from his brothers. Whatever Jack was going to say he knew he'd get to the point. Jack had made it clear along time ago he couldn't handle Bible thumping bullshit from the pulpit. He remembered Jack telling him about a child molestation case he worked on before coming to Charleston. They found out it was a black preacher who was molesting young girls in the church. It was all swept under the table and the preacher was assigned to another congregation in another state. Jack told him he knew that it would start all over again.

Sally, who was seated next to Beau, asked in a hushed voice, "What's going on?" Beau shrugged his shoulders.

Jack stood silently at the podium waiting for the murmurs among the crowd to subside before he spoke. "I'd like to thank all of you for coming here today to honor Mr. JoJo Jones," Jack paused, to get his emotions under control before he continued. "There is one truth that all soldiers know." He paused again forming his words. "There are no bigots in a foxhole. When men's lives are in doubt on a day to day, minute to minute basis, no one cares about the color of your skin or the shape of your eyes, or anything else for that matter. Mr. Jones knew that. He lived that in the hell we call war. I feel honored, and sad, to talk today about Staff Sergeant Jones. Look around you. Look at the person sitting next to you. You have come together not as black or white, but as one, to recognize what this man already knew. That we are one nation indivisible. In spite of all the controversy, all the hidden agendas, all the perceived, or ill-perceived inequities, we are just simple people who love our country. This old soldier knew deep down, what we are, and what we could be. So in that sense I am honored to talk about this man I hardly knew. I am sad to think that a man who made these sacrifices for his country had to end up homeless, living in the streets and back alleys of our city."

Jack noticed that the media was taking it all in. TV cameras cranked away as flash bulbs randomly sparkled through the audience. Jack continued with conviction. "I'd like everyone to know since the birth of this nation it was the soldier, not the reporter, who has given us freedom of the press. For the artist among you, it was the soldier, not the poet, that gave you freedom of speech. It is not the campus hothead, but the soldier that gave you the freedom to demonstrate. It is the soldier that honors, and salutes the flag. He serves, and fights under the flag, and that flag today drapes his coffin. Yes, and it is his ultimate sacrifice that allows the protester to burn that flag. This is what Sergeant Jones has given each of you sitting here today. Honor him, thank him, and all men who have given of themselves to bestow these freedoms upon our country." Jack nodded at the rifle team who rendered a volley of rifle fire into the air. A lone bagpiper played Amazing Grace as JoJo's coffin was quietly lowered into its final resting place. Everyone stood with bowed heads, and the American Legion rendered a final salute to Charleston's Unknown Soldier.

The trial had drug on for six more days as Canfield paraded witness after witness building his contention that the defendant, no matter how many personalities he had, they all knew right from wrong. Barbara Starkey pulled every trick out of the hat to blunt the testimony of the prosecutor's witnesses, by casting doubt as to the value of the testimony. The media laid odds of 4 to 1 for a guilty verdict. It was rumored that even Las Vegas was laying odds in Canfield's favor. Now it was time for the defense to present its case. Meanwhile, the sexy Sarah Smith was on just about every local TV in the area. She was flown to New York, and was on national TV. Men from all over the country were falling all over themselves trying to score with this sexy lady.

The courtroom was again jammed with spectators, and the media. The defendant was escorted into the courtroom. Sally followed his every step observing the changes that had overtaken him. Gaylord Delongpre had changed from a bragging, self indulging ego, who ejaculated in front of her, to a gaunt, sickly, young man who shuffled slowly as he walked to his chair at the defense counsel's table. His skin was a yellow white jaundice texture.

His eyes were bloodshot, set deep into his face with dark rings surrounding them. Something was tragically wrong with this pathetic man. Sally wondered if the trial had brought all this evil to the surface. Was it like the picture of Dorian Gray who was a man who could never grow old? She quickly remembered the story. All the evil that Dorian Gray had brought into this world appeared in his portrait while he stayed young. When he destroyed his picture in a fit of rage all the evil that he had done suddenly disappeared in the painting and was given to the human form of Dorian Gray. He became grotesque, ugly, and an evil demon, and died consumed by the evil in his soul. Was this madman, this killer, and ravager of women, reaping the curse of Dorian Gray? Was the trial bringing out the evil in this man's twisted mind, and destroying him slowly, bit by bit?

"All rise," the Bailiff announced loudly as judge Buckner entered, and opened the court.

"Is the defense ready?" Buckner asked, looking at Barbara Starkey.

"The defense is ready you honor," She replied.

"You may call your first witness," Buckner ordered.

Barbara stood up and looked at her list, "The defense calls Norma Pierce."

Norma Pierce rose quietly from her seat, and made her way to the witness stand, and was sworn in. Norma was a handsome woman. Tall, thin, with slightly graying hair. She held her head high, and had a graceful air about her. She could have easily been mistaken for a banker's wife or a principle of a local high school. She was a pillar of the community, or at least gave that impression.

Barbara Starkey knew all that was about to change as she approached the witness stand.

"Mrs. Pierce. You are Agnes Gladlow's sister?" Barbara asked politely.

"Yes."

"You lived with the Gladlows for some time didn't you?"

"Yes. Three years. Then I met my husband," Norma answered with a calmness in her voice.

"Did you know the defendant during that time?" Barbara asked nodding at the defendant who remained with his forehead resting on the edge of the table gazing at the floor. It was as if he didn't want to hear any more words from anyone. David Delongpre seemed to be the dominant personality in the courtroom at that time when he raised his head momentarily and looked kindly at Norma. Their eyes locked in a moment of understanding, remembering what they had both endured.

"Yes, I knew David." She answered softly ignoring Barbara, looking compassionately at the defendant.

"From your personal observation, was the defendant sexually abused by the Gladlows?"

"Oh Yes. For over three years that poor child was whipped, and sexually abused by the Gladlows," Norma answered remorsefully.

"Who was responsible for the sexual abuse of the defendant?"

"As far as little David was concerned, Agnes was the one who enjoyed beating the boy," Norma replied sadly.

"Please go on," Barbara urged.

"Agnes enjoyed sex with the little boy, while Henry had sex with his sister."

"Where was Leah Delongpre, the mother, at all this time?" Barbara questioned angrily.

"She was high on drugs. In fact, to get her next fix the Gladlows had her participate in the sex games."

"Are you telling this court that their mother had sex with her own children?"

"Yes." Norma affirmed with emotion welling up in her throat.

"During the three years you were at the Gladlow's did you notice a change in the defendant?" Barbara asked turning to glance at the defendant.

"Yes, after his sister ran away David's attitude changed." Norma commented.

"How?" Barbara asked quickly.

"Well, he became more submissive, then he would be arrogant, bragging about how he could screw Agnes into the ground, and anyone else she brought around."

"So, with his sister gone. The defendant's only choice was to accept the sexual abuse in order to reduce the beatings." Barbara stated loudly so the jury would catch every word.

"No, it was more than that. At that time he actually enjoyed his sexual encounters with Agnes, and she praised him every time he had sex with her." Norma explained promptly. "He was now enjoying sex. The kinkier the better. Agnes was thrilled, bought him presents, new clothes, took him on trips."

"Did you have sex with the defendant when you were at the Gladlows?" Barbara asked bluntly.

The courtroom was hushed waiting for her answer

"Yes," Norma answered with tears welling up.

"So for some reason the Gladlows forced you to have sex with this child. Or did you just enjoy raping a little boy?" Barbara asked sarcastically.

"Yes. I'm sorry to say. I did not want to do it but I was forced into it." Norma replied sadly.

"Now you've observed the defendant during this time, lets see," Barbara glanced at her notes, "For about three years, correct?"

"Correct."

"Are you surprised at all that the defendant is in this courtroom today charged with these murders?"

"Not in the least." Norma answered wiping a tear from her eye with a small white handkerchief.

"I have no further questions for this witness," Starkey said then sat quietly down.

Canfield rose immediately to begin his cross-examination. "Mrs. Pierce am I to understand you sat around for 3 years watching a child being sexually abused, and you did nothing about it?" Before Norma could answer Canfield interrupted, "Isn't it true you enjoyed the sex with these children?"

"Objection!" Barbara shouted angrily standing up.

"Your honor he's badgering the witness. It's cruel, and totally uncalled for."

Before the judge could rule on the objection Canfield replied, "I withdraw the question your honor."

Buckner nodded, and motioned for Canfield to continue his examination.

"Mrs. Pierce," Canfield said politely, "Why didn't you inform the police about what was going on at the Gladlow's?"

Norma Pierce became nervous, she hesitated looking at the judge as if asking him to please not to allow her to answer the question. The courtroom waited in silence for her answer. Judge Buckner spoke calmly to Norma. "Please Mrs. Pierce, you have to answer the question."

All the pride seemed to fade from her face. Her shoulders sagged in resignation as she said with a sigh, "I was blackmailed."

"By whom?" Canfield asked quickly.

"By my sister, and her husband," She replied with an undertone of anger in her voice.

"Please explain." Canfield demanded calmly.

"When we were growing up my sister and I played sexual games together."

"You mean you had a lesbian relationship with your sister," Canfield interrupted.

"Yes," Norma affirmed with a sad sigh, "Then when she got married she carried our relationship into her marriage. Henry Gladlow loved the idea of having sex with the both of us. What I didn't know at that time, he was secretly video taping our having sex together. When they brought the Delongpres into the household for their sexual perversions, I wanted no part of it."

"Why didn't you quit or leave? You could live with that. The Gladlows had more to lose than you did?" Canfield remarked sternly.

"No, they didn't. I was dating my future husband at that time, and they threatened to expose me if I did anything about it. If I'd keep quiet, they'd keep quiet."

Canfield paused, and looked at the jury before asking his next question. "Do you think the defendant is insane?"

"Objection, hearsay, she's not qualified to testify as to the mental state of the defendant." Barbara rebutted loudly.

"Sustained," Buckner ordered.

Canfield looked at the witness thoughtfully before asking his next question. "Why do you think your sister, and her husband suddenly packed up, and moved out of Charleston? I mean, Charleston was her home. She grew up here. Then for no reason, they just up and leave. Not even taking the time to sell their home. Why was that?"

Norma Pierce answered thoughtfully, "I believe someone got hold of one of those sex tapes, and I think there might have been a little blackmail going on. Later, I found out that both my sister, and her husband had AIDs." Norma paused, "It was as if God had punished them or had played some cruel joke on them."

The courtroom sat in silence as Canfield carefully phrased his last question, "At any time, during the time you had intimate encounters with the defendant did you notice anything unusual? I mean, did you encounter the Gaylord personality, or Gordon, or a slobbering grunting beast?"

"No, just little David. We were close. We both felt like we were being used, and there was nothing we could do about it. We kind a consoled each other."

"I see, so if you consoled each other you must have rational conversations with him." Canfield responded, then quickly dismissed the witness before she could answer. "I have no further question for this witness."

Barbara Starkey quickly rose from her chair and said, "The defense calls agent Sally Thornton to the stand."

Beau gave her hand a little squeeze of support as she rose and walked to the stand. The judge reminded her that she was still under oath. Sally nodded as Barbara asked her first question.

"Agent Thornton, we've covered a lot of ground in the cross-examination, but there is one area we haven't discussed," Barbara paused, framing her next question. "The night you and detective Gasteneau engaged the defendant at Henrietta's house you stated that you were able to free yourself from his attack. Now, I know you are in good physical shape, and you've been trained in self defense, but to overpower the defendant when he has the advantage over you, now that is some feat. How did you accomplish that?"

Sally sat upright as she responded to the defense counsel's question. "I told Gaylord to stop it. I shouted those words."

"And did the attack cease?" Barbara asked pointedly.

"Yes, It gave me time to counter his attack by rolling him over my shoulder, and we both fell down the stairs."

"How did you know to say, 'Gaylord' when he was attacking you? Barbara asked out of curiosity.

"We had a telephone call to the Houston police in response to our query on the killer's MO. Houston told us that their investigation on three unsolved murders with the same M.O. revealed a suspect named Gaylord Harcourt who bragged to a friend about the killings. The friend's name was Delongpre. He was picked up on a minor drug charge and opted to help the police look for Harcourt in exchange for a reduced sentence. Nothing turned up. So, when the defendant had me by the throat I was running out of options fast, the name just popped into my head, and I shouted his name. It worked. Houston Police, and us for that matter, didn't know at time that Harcourt and Delongpre were the same person."

Barbara had taken Sally to the very point she wanted her. "So, before capture, before any court appointed psychiatrist ever examined the defendant, you met the Gaylord personality first hand. Is there any reason in your mind that the defendant is not a multiple?"

"No, he responded to the name by relaxing his grip on me, and that probably saved my life."

There were low murmurs in the court as heads turned and whispers were exchanged.

"I have no further questions for this witness."

Canfield stood quickly for his cross-examination. Then questioned Sally from his table.

"Agent Thornton, when you called out one of the aliases used by the defendant when he stalked, and carefully planned the murders of his victims, couldn't he have been surprised that the police were on to him? Could that have been enough of a shock to him to ease his grip on you?"

"I suppose so," she responded

"I mean, in this struggle you didn't encounter a slobbering beast. You didn't encounter a flesh eating dinosaur did you?" Canfield asked sarcastically.

"No I didn't," Sally replied.

"Thank you Agent Thornton. I have no further questions. Canfield announced smugly.

"The defense calls Lieutenant Gasteneau to the stand," Barbara promptly stated, as she stood, then removed some papers from her briefcase.

Sally and Beau gave each other a nod as they passed. Beau took his seat on the stand and was reminded again that he was still under oath.

Barbara Starkey moved toward the witness stand as she said, "The defense would like to enter into evidence defense exhibit A., a deposition taken by Lt. Gasteneau from an eye witness Mr. JoJo Jones. Unfortunately, Mr. Jones is no longer with us." Barbara handed the deposition to the Bailiff. "Lt. Gasteneau, you took this deposition from Mr. Jones, did you not?"

"Yes I did," Beau replied quickly.

"I mean you had a one hour face to face interview with Mr. Jones, did you not?" Barbara asked making eye contact with her old friend and lover.

"Yes," he answered knowing that the sexual aura that she emitted said, "take me whenever you want."

"Please explain to the jury what he described to you."

"He said he saw a man-like beast moving through one of the cities sewers," Beau replied, glancing at the jurors.

"You mean a grunting, slobbering, man-like beast as the prosecution has belittled, made fun of, and tried to prove didn't exist?"

"Essentially, yes," Beau replied assuredly.

"Did you believe Mr. Jones?" Barbara asked pointedly.

"Yes, he had no reason to lie," Beau replied.

"Thank you. I have no further questions," Barbara said, quickly returning to her seat.

"Lieutenant," Canfield said, raising his voice, then quickly approaching the stand. "You said Mr. Jones observed this man-like beast in the sewer, is that correct?"

"Yes."

"That was also at night wasn't it?" Canfield questioned in a nonchalant manner.

"Yes."

"Did he have a flashlight? A candle?" Canfield asked smugly.

"No."

"So, what you have is a drunk sleeping off a binge, in a sewer, at night, when it is pitch black, no light, tells you he saw a man beast, and you believe him?" Canfield added, shaking his head in disbelief mocking Beau's statement.

"Yes I do," Beau answered sternly.

"Come on Lieutenant," Canfield replied, challenging the witness sarcastically, "I'm surprised he didn't report pink elephants. Is that what you call good police investigation?"

"Yes," Beau answered, leveling a cold stare at Canfield causing him to back off his sarcasm. "When a man comes to you scared out of his wits, a man who has seen death first hand, and there isn't much in this world he hasn't seen, you believe him."

Beau's eyes locked on to Canfield's. His expression caused Canfield to realize he was going no where with this line of questioning. He had already made his point. "I have no further questions for this witness."

Barbara Starkey quickly announced to the court, "The defense calls Dora Philburn to the stand."

Dora Philburn was a big portly woman, in her middle forties, overweight, and immediately you could tell she had a low self image. She had dirty blonde hair cut short and permed too tight. The short hair, the double chin and the rotund figure gave a lopsided, ill-proportioned image to the woman. She looked like some South Borneo native had shrunk her head while she was still alive. Dora was quickly sworn in and it took several clumsy attempts before she could comfortably fit into the witness chair.

Barbara Starkey approached the witness stand trying make eye contact with Dora. She avoided every attempt until finally she ran out of places to look. She had no recourse but to finally look at the beautiful, and intelligent lady who was about to question her.

"Miss Philburn, you were part of Dr. Smith's encounter group in Seattle, were you not?" Barbara asked calmly.

"Yes." Dora answered with a demurred tone in her voice.

"Was the defendant part of that group?"

"Yes."

"What name did the defendant use during these sessions," Barbara questioned, glancing at the jury box to insure they caught the name.

"Gaylord Harcourt." Dora answered quickly.

"Did Dr. Smith control these sessions?"

"Yes, at first. Then when Gaylord got started we all just listened."

"So Gaylord for the most part dominated the conversation?" Barbara continued slowly.

"Yes, sometimes," Dora said, looking down at the palms of her hands which she was constantly rubbing.

"What did you think of the defendant at that time?" Barbara questioned casually.

Dora waited. She gazed at the sickly defendant who kept his forehead on the edge of the table looking at the floor.

"I loved him. He never knew it. I never told him, but I loved him." Dora replied, with a quiver in her lip then wiping a tear from her eye.

"Why didn't you tell him how you felt?" Barbara asked curiously.

The anger and self guilt began to rise within Dora. She lifted her head and said loudly, "Look at me! Take a good look! Then look at Miss Carla Dawn or Sarah Smith. Do you think Gaylord would give me the slightest look? I'm fat, I'm ugly. It's the anorexic Barbie Dolls that gets the guy or haven't you heard." Dora said scornfully.

"I'm sorry," Barbara said softly, trying to ease Dora's anger. "So what did you do?" Barbara questioned slowly.

"It was the encounter group. That was when he would talk to me. He would tell me that true beauty came from within, not just someone who looks sexy. It comes from a woman who totally gives herself to her man."

"Did Gaylord recruit you for the Fetish Club?"

Dora waited in silence, she moved nervously in the chair mustering the courage to let it all out. "Yes, he did. I loved every minute of it. I know you can't understand that can you." Dora shook her head in contempt. "No, you wouldn't. Look at you. You could have any man you wanted. For the first time in my miserable life I had relationships with men. They didn't see this bulging hulk of fat. They saw a woman with sexual appetites just like anyone else, and in that, they saw me as being beautiful." Dora's lower lip quivered as she held back an ocean of tears.

"So what did you do?" Barbara asked. The tone in Barbara's voice gave a small indication that she might be slightly aroused by this line of questioning.

Dora had let it all out. She suddenly felt free of guilt. The whole world was going to know. Fat people have a life. Fat people have desires, they needed to be loved, she needed to be loved, and she'd do whatever it took to get the attention of men. Men who really saw her as a woman. At the Fetish Club she knew she could be absolutely free sexually. No one cared what she looked like, only how well she performed sexually.

"I did anything they wanted." Dora said proudly, "I could do twice the men Carla could do, and my men would walk away satisfied."

With all the testimony about the Fetish Club the courtroom shouldn't have been shocked, but they were. They sat in stunned silence. Barbara had to get to the point, this was beginning to drag out. "Did you ever encounter a personality named David, a child personality in the defendant?"

Dora thought back to the early days of the Fetish Club, "Well, during the whippings maybe."

"What do you mean, whippings?" Barbara asked, moving closer to the witness.

"When Gaylord made love to me, he'd tie me to a post, you know with my hands tied over my head," Dora raised both her hands demonstrating how she was tied, "Then he'd use his leather strap and whip me." Dora leveled her eyes at Barbara and said, "If you haven't tried it you're really missing it. It really turns you on. Then he'd want me to whip him the same way. When it was my turn he'd call me mommy, and beg me to stop. It was all just acting to get us in the mood."

"Did he ever call you Agnes during these whippings?" Barbara quickly asked. Dora thought for a moment, tilting her head slightly thinking back, remembering, "Yes I believe he did."

"So, from what you've heard in this courtroom, is it possible that the defendant was reliving the sexual encounters with Agnes through you or Carla or anyone else in the Club for that matter?" Barbara demanded.

Objection!, the witness has no idea what was in the defendant's mind," Canfield shouted. Buckner scratched his head mulling over the prosecution's objection. "No, I will allow it. The witness should have a good idea of what kind of sexual game the defendant had in mind."

"Go on Miss Philburn," Barbara said, in an even tone.

"Yes, after what I've heard, he probably was seeing me as this Agnes person."

"So in fact, at this point, you saw both Gaylord Harcourt, and the abused little child David in the defendant's actions." Barbara demanded sternly, choosing her words slowly so the jury would catch every syllable.

"That appears to be the case." Dora answered casually.

Before Barbara could call her next witness the courtroom doors bumped open, and the Chief of Security strode quickly through the courtroom bringing the proceedings to a momentary halt. The interruption perturbed judge Buckner. However, he waited patiently for some explanation. The Chief whispered a few words into the Bailiff's ear. He nodded, then approached the judge and also whispered, relaying the Chief's message. There was an unheard exchange of information and an expression of frustration appeared on Buckner's face. The judge stood and waited for several more guards to position themselves at the doors before announcing, "ladies and gentlemen, I want everyone to quietly, and in an orderly fashion, exit the courthouse. It appears we have had an anonymous bomb threat. The court will be adjourned until ten o'clock tomorrow morning." Buckner rapped his gavel, and made a hasty exit to his chambers. The guards at the courtroom door saw to it that there was no panic by consoling the departing spectators. Surprisingly, everyone was calm. Homer Canfield, and Barbara Starkey gathered their papers and joined Beau and Sally at the end of the parade of departing spectators. Barbara Starkey looked at Beau and remarked lightly, "Chaos, panic, and disorder, looks like my work here is done." Everyone chuckled at Barbara's quip. Canfield commented, "Are we going to see you at Murph's? It's Miller Time."

"It's not the beer you're after, our Miss Sarah Smith is headed over there isn't she." Barbara chided, then nodded at the sexy centerfold in front of them, just out of earshot.

Sally sniffed the air mockingly, "Nice perfume, she must marinate in it."

Barbara laughed then tugged at Sally's arm, "You've got that right."

"My, my, aren't me catty today," Beau quipped, glancing at Barbara then at Sally.

"Sarcasm is just one more service she offers," Canfield said, nodding casually at Barbara.

Barbara playfully bumped Canfield then remarked, "How many times do I have to flush you before you go away?"

"See, she really wants me. She's warm for my form," Canfield said jokingly.

"In your dreams buddy," Barbara said raising her voice slightly, causing heads to turn. Beau and Sally laughed out loud.

"You see, everything with her is the battle of the sexes," Canfield rebutted. "She knows her client isn't crazy. He's just been in a bad mood for forty one years."

As the departing crowd thinned out, and descended the front steps of the courthouse Barbara stood in front of Canfield defiantly, stopping his descent, "That may be your crybaby, whiny-assed opinion but it's not mine," She turned quickly and marched away.

Canfield shouted after her, "I'll see you at Murph's in one hour." Barbara without looking back, held up her hand and gave Canfield the finger. Beau laughed, "That's some relationship you've got going there."

Homer Canfield stood quietly watching his beautiful adversary walk away, "Yeah, she's really something isn't she."

Sally realized that all these insults between these two was just foreplay. Canfield really cared for Barbara.

"You really like her," Sally observed out loud.

"It's sad, but this is the only relationship she wants at this point in time," Canfield said sadly.

"And you'll take it. This kind of relationship is better than no relationship," Sally commented looking deep into Canfield's mind as though she could see his inner most thoughts. Canfield looked sadly at Sally, "See you later," then turned and walked slowly toward his parked car.

"He's got it bad," She remarked, taking Beau's arm.

"Lets go for a walk," Beau suggested, as they turned and walked down Meeting Street. The two lovers walked slowly down the side streets and narrow alleys of old town Charleston. For a fall day the sky was clear, and the sun had a warmth that settled quietly on their shoulders as they walked. Beau stopped and pointed at an old church across the street.

"That is St. Philips Episcopal Church. We call this the lighthouse church. See the tall steeple?" Beau pointed up. Sally nodded. "They use to hang lanterns up there to warn ships of shallow waters." Sally gave Beau a warm hug. It was nice of him to share this beautiful old city with her. Their walk continued down to the Battery past old mansions that overlooked the waterfront. He pointed at the Porcher-Simonds House and noted that JFK had an office there for a while during World War II. He pointed out Fort Sumpter where the Civil War began. They meandered up Church Street in the oldest part of the city that Beau said predated the revolutionary war. Arm in arm, they window shopped at the small antique shops along the narrow street. He could see she had fallen in love with the city. She enjoyed the friendliness and outgoing nature of the people, and the history that still lived here.

As the couple rounded the corner, Beau opened an ornate wrought iron gate. He said it was made sometime in the 18th century. The pathway gracefully twisted through four blocks of the old city passing luscious church gardens, bristling with the color of fall flowers, and old tombstones. The sweet aroma of the flowers provided a magic with an invisible mist that floated in the air. Large palms, and tropical ferns provided shade from the sun. Sally laid her head quietly on Beau's shoulders as they strolled side by side.

"I wish this trial would hurry up and get over," She said, looking lovingly at Beau.

"Me too," He replied, putting his arm around her waist moving her closer to him.

"I want to make babies with you." She quipped wrinkling her nose before she kissed him on the neck. "I am going to make you a promise," She declared lifting her head from his shoulder looking into his searching eyes. "I am going to give you a son. I had a dream. Mark came to me in my dream and said he was coming back to you. I didn't know what it meant at the time, but he meant I was going to give you a son."

Beau stopped under the shade of a large Elephant Fern, faced Sally momentarily, then kissed her passionately. She opened her mouth and took his probing tongue into her parted lips in excited hunger. When the kiss broke she was totally aroused. With one touch, one kiss, one look, this man of hers could instantly get her sexually excited. She had never felt this way about any man in her life. Even Katie's father was an accident of youth.

Beau took her by the hand and walked briskly out of another old wrought iron gate then gave a loud whistle using his fingers between his lips. It was as if he knew that the horse drawn hansom cab would be there. Moses Miller, the old black cab driver knew Beau instantly. Moses beamed with delight upon recognizing Beau.

"Hi Moses, how goes it?" Beau asked lightly as they hopped into the one horse hansom cab.

"Real fine, just real fine," Moses answered, in a long southern drawl, "Where to Mr. Beau?" Moses asked, slapping the reins against the hind quarters of the horse bringing the old nag to a slow trot.

"I want to take my future wife to see the Angel," He ordered politely.

"The Angel it is," Moses replied, knowing exactly what Beau meant. The old man guided the carriage through the narrow streets of old Charleston. On the edge of the city the landscape leveled out, and a scrub oak and pine forest became the resting place for the Spanish moss that swung in the afternoon breeze. Moses pulled the carriage to a gentle stop.

"Moses, would you wait for us?"

"You've got it Mr. Beau," Moses replied, securing the reins, then lighting up his old corn cob pipe while smiling at the young lovers. They strolled into the old grove of oak.

The Angel Oak stood in a clearing of young oak and pine. It was majestic tree spreading its twisted arms upward capturing the warm life giving rays of the sun. It was over 65 feet high, spreading it's gnarled arms 25 feet in width. It's massive roots looked like some giant fist grabbing at the earth. Some of the sagging twisted arms of the tree hung low over the ground supported by wooden planks to give it strength. It was cool under the old oak. Sally felt an air of reverence as the entered the shade of the old tree. It was as if they had entered sacred ground, a church of God that Mother Nature had given the people of Charleston. Sally couldn't take her eyes from the old tree. It seem to cast a spell over her. She felt like praying, or crying, or both.

"The tree is over 1,400 years old," Beau remarked in a hushed tone as if God was listening. He felt the same as Sally. They had entered a holy place, blessed in some way by God. "I believe it is the oldest living thing east of the Mississippi," Beau added reverently.

Beau held Sally closely as they both stared upward at the spreading arms of Angel Oak.

"It's beautiful," She said softly, leaning her head back so it rested just under Beau's chin.

"You know something?" It was a rhetorical question Beau offered, still looking at the tree, Sally gave a small nod, "What?"

"It makes you think about the time we have in this life. I want whatever time we have left, I want it to be with you." She kissed his hand gently. He gave her another kiss on the side of the head, then said, "An old friend told me this. If you live to be a hundred, I want to live to be a hundred minus one day, so I never have to live a day without you."

431

"That's sweet," She answered, turning to see her lover she kissed him passionately again. "Whose your friend?" Sally asked lovingly, as she broke the embrace.

"What friend"?"

"The friend that told you that," She asked, giving him another quick kiss on the cheek.

"Oh, Winnie the Pooh," He said, with a small chuckle.

"You rat," She said poking him playfully.

"No it's true, I remember reading it. I just never forgot. It was one of those things that just seem to stick in your mind." He replied, putting his arm around her as they walked slowly away from the angel oak.

The hansom cab moved easily down the narrow streets of old town. Sally laid her head back against the soft leather seat and let the shadows from the oaks dance across her face. The hoofs of the old nag made a steady clip-clop noise that echoed between the old buildings on the narrow street. The cab moved slowly across the old cobble stones continuing a rhythm that sat peacefully in Sally's mind. She was happy. She was content. The stress of the investigation, the reports, the press briefings, most of that was behind her. She felt as though a ton of weight had been lifted from her shoulders. She had finally met the man she wanted to spend the rest of her life with. She knew that the tough exterior Beau displayed was just a front. He was a kind, gentle, loving man who so desperately wanted a family and was totally in love with her. She smiled thinking about her first night in Charleston, at the airport, falling in the mud, getting wet at the crime scene, and having to stay at Beau's apartment. They didn't hit if off very well in the beginning.

"What are you smiling about?" Beau interrupted her day dreaming.

"Oh, about our first meeting. How I thought you were a smart ass." She touched Beau's hand gently.

"I was. I didn't want the FBI involved. I'm sure glad they talked me out of it." He said, smiling at Sally.

Moses maneuvered the cab to a small parking spot in front of the Stake Out Bar and Grill. Beau handed Moses a ten dollar bill, then remarked, "Let me know when you want to put her out to pasture," Beau nodded toward the old nag whose head was bent down as though it took every ounce of energy just to pull the cab here. Beau hated to see any animal suffer. Although Moses loved his horse, and it had been his friend for some years he knew he wasn't being kind to the animal by allowing him to work all this time.

"I've got some nice stock out on the farm. You can take your pick," Beau added.

"Thank you Mr. Beau. I just might take you up on that." Moses took a long puff on his corn cob pipe. "I think I'll hang around here and pick up a few drunks as they carry em out,"

"It's going to be a good night," Beau acknowledged.

Opening the bar door Beau and Sally entered the noisy room. It was packed as usual. Country, shit kicking music was echoing throughout the bar. Murph waved at Beau and Sally then pointed to the long table in the corner of the bar. The Gray Lady Task Force were all comfortably seated each with a cold beer and a bowl of pretzels in the center of the table. As expected, Barbara Starkey and Homer Canfield were also seated at the table. Canfield pointed at two empty chairs. Beau and Sally quickly navigated through the crowded room. They seated themselves between Barbara and Homer. Murph sat two cold beers in front of them. "There you go. Where've you been? The troops have been waiting for you," Murph commented happily.

"Since when do they wait when they're drinking beer?" Beau joked.

"It's stress relief," Coates remarked, taking a big gulp of the cold brew.

"Speaking of stress relief, what are you two going to do to take the load off?" Brockman asked looking at the two lawyers, "I mean you guys have been going at it hot and heavy out there."

"Oh, I guess there might be a hundred different ways to keep a healthy level of sanity. When I've got the time I'll pick one." Homer commented.

"I know what I do," Singletary interjected loudly. Singletary was a good cop, but normally, she didn't have much to say. Her eager interruption caught everyone by surprise.

"What do you do?" Coates asked, knowing that her statements usually weren't too impressive and a little on the boring side.

"Well, you guys know the public school my kids go to." Singletary said, assuming everyone cared where her kids went to school. They really didn't but they listened.

"Anyway," Singletary continued, "On my day off, sometimes I sit in my car with dark glasses on and point my hair dryer at speeding cars, and watch them slow down."

Sally erupted in the middle of her beer laughing. The laughter was contagious. Everyone could picture her in a car pointing her hair dryer.

Getting into the spirit of saving sanity, Coates chimed in by adding, "You know that memo line on your checks. I like to write in, 'for sexual favors' and see what kind of reaction I get." Chuckles were heard from around the table.

"Now that might be closer to the truth," Brockman chided, as he took a long gulp of beer.

"You know what I'd like to do?" Barbara added.

"What?" Canfield asked, sarcastically.

"Something devious. Let's see, at the office I'd put DECAF in the office coffee maker for about 3 weeks. Once our Clarence Darrow here," she nodded at Homer Canfield, "got over his caffeine addiction, I'd switch to espresso and watch him climb the walls."

"Now that's cruel," Jack Bellamy quipped. Canfield gave Barbara a sly look, "She'd do it too."

"While we're confessing as to dumb things we do, or like to do, I have a confession." Brockman interjected.

"What?" Coates replied, giving Brockman a doubting glance.

"Once, when I was a kid, my church group went to the zoo. On the way out, a couple of my buddies and I ran out into the parking lot shouting, 'They're loose, run for you life.' Boy, you should have seen the movement. That's when I decided I wanted to become a cop."

"Why did that make you want to be a cop?" Jack inquired with a big smile.

"When my folks came to the station to pick me up I realized I'd had a good time talking to the cops. I knew that's what I wanted to be."

"How about that, we've got a felon in our midst," Coates remarked with a snicker.

Sally was still laughing, unable to finish her drink when she said, "You'll have to excuse me. I have to use the ladies room." As Sally stood up Barbara declared quickly, "Just a minute, I'll go with you."

The ladies room was not what you'd expect to find in a down town bar. There were two, clean, well decorated large rooms, one with toilet facilities, and the other specifically dedicated to putting on makeup. Barbara was the last to enter the room. Before closing the door she hung a sign on the door handle that read, "Close for Cleaning," then locked the door from the inside. Barbara Starkey was still dressed in a tight pen-stripe skirt with a white button down silk blouse. She quietly unbuttoned one more button to ensure that her cleavage would catch Sally's attention.

Sally dried her hands, tossing the paper towel quickly into the trash, then began applying lipstick and fresh makeup. Barbara, who stood next to Sally, leaned over the sink checking her makeup in the large mirror. She immediately noticed that Sally could not take her eyes from her overly exposed cleavage.

"Well, what do you think?" Barbara asked softly, with a tone of sensuality in her voice. Sally's eyes darted quickly away from Barbara's bust line.

"What?" Sally replied to Barbara's image in the looking glass.

"The trial. I was watching you. All that talk about sex, the Fetish Club, it turned you on didn't it."

"No, not really." The tone of Sally's reply told Barbara she was probably lying.

"Well, I don't know about you. I sure the hell was." Barbara took a lipstick from her purse and began applying the gloss to her luscious lips. "Did Beau tell you about us?" Barbara asked nonchalantly. Sally glanced at the sexy lawyer.

"Yes he did."

"Have you slept with him,?" Barbara questioned, glancing at Sally then moving her lips in and out to insure the lipstick was evenly applied. "Why do I ask? of course you have," She added.

"It's none of your business," Sally answered curtly.

"When you get him started, he's an animal," Barbara commented casually. "Believe it or not I'm your friend. Beau and I both knew a long time ago it wasn't going to work out. We're still good friends and I wish you two all the happiness in the world." Barbara patted Sally's arm in friendship.

Barbara pulled her blouse out from her tight skirt, reached up under the white silk garment and began adjusting her bra. "This damn thing is too tight. It's cutting off my circulation," Barbara continued to fiddle with the back bra strap. "I must be putting on a little weight. When this is all over I'm going to hit the gym big time." She bent over again as she struggled with her bra. Sally's gaze seem to be locked on to her firm breasts which were now about to spill over the top of her push-up bra.

"Could you be a sweetheart and move my bra hook out just one more notch?" Barbara turned her back to Sally and raised the back of her blouse. Sally reached up slowly, her hand touched the firm, smooth skin of the sexy lawyer. She felt an immediate shock, a warmth of hidden desire. Barbara watched Sally's expression in the mirror. She could read people pretty well. Just as she thought. Inside the professional FBI exterior was a woman capable of deep passion. A woman that for some reason kept her sexual fantasies repressed. As Sally unhooked the bra Barbara turned quickly around to face Sally with her hands coming to rest on Barbara's firm breasts. Barbara silently guided Sally's hands from the top of the bra to her bare breasts. Sally for some unknown reason, did not, or could not, remove her hands from Barbara's breasts.

"You were turned on weren't you. So was I," Barbara said, looking directly into Sally's eyes. Sally was lightheaded, with forbidden excitement. She had never done this with another woman before in her life although she'd thought about it enough times.

"Tell me you're not a dike." Sally asked in a quivering voice.

"No, but if the mood hits me I can go both ways," Barbara answered, then leaned back against the sink and pulled Sally into her so their stomachs pressed against each other.

"I was envious of those girls, you know, Sarah, and that Philburn woman. Even a fat woman can find sexual freedom." Barbara moved Sally's hand around her breasts as she rotated her hips slightly imitating sexual penetration. Sally was still locked into the sexual moment as if hypnotized by desire. Barbara's hands reached for Sally's crotch and she began a slow motion causing Sally to automatically open her legs to allow easier access. Sally closed her eyes and gave a soft sigh of surrender.

By now, both women were breathing hard, caught in a moment of pure passion, and sexual lust. Barbara slowly pulled Sally's face to hers and they kissed as two totally engrossed lovers. Barbara's aggressive tongue met Sally's, eagerly searching for the depths of her throat. Suddenly, Sally shouted, "No! this is wrong," and pushed away from Barbara who had spread herself against the sink. In the heat of the moment Barbara had managed to slip her bra up exposing her firm breasts. She displayed them proudly.

"You want me and you know it. There is nothing wrong in the way you feel." Barbara replied sensually. "If you're going to have a real relationship with Beau you've got to let it all hang out. Let him know how you feel about everything."

"You may be right. This God damn trial, all this sex talk has got me all mixed up. I know one thing. I love Beau. I have a daughter and I want a family and I'm not going to blow it." Sally stepped back and fixed her skirt. Barbara Starkey had made her point. She knew Sally had the same fire burning in her stomach as she did.

Barbara quickly refastened her bra, tucked in her blouse, adjusted her skirt then looked at Sally. "Do you want to keep your marriage going? Don't loose touch with your sexuality. Beau will do anything to see that you're satisfied, mentally, and sexually. Still friends?" Barbara asked, holding out her hand.

"Friends," Sally replied, shaking her hand cautiously.

"Oh, if you ever want to do a threesome, give me a call," Barbara said, as she patted Sally on the butt.

"Let's get back to the party."

When Sally and Barbara returned to the table Beau sensed that some exchange had taken place between Barbara and Sally. Sally seated herself closer to Beau then whispered into his ear. "Are you really an animal?"

Beau glanced at Barbara who smiled ever so slightly. He whispered back to Sally, "Try me."

Chapter Twenty Five

Summation

It took another five days for Barbara Starkey to present the case for the defense. She had pulled every trick out of the hat to present her contention that the defendant was only acting as he was programmed to do as a child, that is, to have sex with Agnes. She pointed out that each victim had the same physical characteristics as Agnes Gladlow. Starkey argued that the defendant was actually in a dreamlike state while he was committing these sex crimes.

Beau was surprised. Starkey was able to convince Alice Delongpre to testify for the defense. As the wife of a respected judge in Seattle she had everything to loose and nothing to gain, yet she decided to testify. She was able to verify the sexual abuse in great detail and validated the defense's contention that the defendant had resorted to acting the part of any sexual demands Agnes required of the little boy David. Alice added by saying that these roles had taken on a reality of their own. That David was compelled to seek out Agnes for the purposes of sex. That he could never have a normal sexual relationship with anyone.

Canfield, on cross examination, countered with the argument that it made no difference whether he was sexually abused or not. The burden of proof still lies on, did he or did he not know right from wrong at the time he committed these crimes?

Starkey called all the members of the Seattle encounter group to the stand. During testimony it was learned that Bruce Hickman was a Baptist minister who had been an accused child molester. The church hushed the whole episode by paying money to the family, then assigned him to Seattle, and demanded that he participate in therapy. Gaylord, armed with this information provided by Dr. Smith, recruited him into the Fetish Club. This gave him access to Carla's daughter. It was Bruce Hickman that turned Gaylord on to the charity scam which he used from time to time in Seattle. Hickman kept silent about the club because he was being blackmailed by Gaylord.

When Kieth Blackburn, the one armed retired railroad worker, took the stand it was another sordid story. It was learned that his anti-social behavior was not because of the loss of his arm. It was because he was impotent. His only sexual satisfaction came from inflicting pain. He was the enforcer for the Fetish Club. He enjoyed whipping the women.

Starkey pointed out that the defendant had sought medical attention through Dr. Smith while he lived in Seattle. The problem arose when Dr.

Smith broke his code of ethics by getting socially involved with his patient. The courtroom debate was getting down to the nitty gritty. The Las Vegas odds on the outcome of the trial of the decade was now even.

The media continued to run front page stories describing the day to day details of the trial. National television solicited law professors to discuss the legal aspects of a plea of not guilty by reason of insanity. The TV show 48 Hours ran a news special on every aspect of the trial paying particular attention to the sexual descriptions provided by the testimony of the witnesses. Witnesses from the killer's encounter group who participated in the Fetish Club were instant celebrities. Carla Dawn received offers to do porno movies, and was on her way to Hollywood. Sarah Smith on the other hand, maintained a low profile, however, it was revealed that she had received a substantial advance to do a tell all book.

Beau, Sally and Jack moved slowly into the courtroom and assumed their assigned seats. The room was again packed with news hungry media.

The legal ritual began as it had for the past several weeks. The defendant was led in, and seated next to Barbara Starkey. A bowl of candy bars was conveniently set on the table. An armed guard was positioned just behind the defendant to restrain him should the need arise.

Other people may have been blind to it, but Sally could see it. There was something terribly wrong with the defendant. He was even more gaunt and pale than before. His skin had blotches as though he had a sudden case of acne. The dark rings around his eyes had deepened. This was not the man she had seen from beyond the looking glass.

"All rise," the Bailiff announced in a formal tone.

Buckner entered the room, took his normal seat. The Bailiff announced that the court was now in session.

Judge Buckner lowered his glasses to their normal position at the end of his nose, and looked at both counselors. Folding his hands, he leaned back, and nodded at Homer Canfield, then ordered, "Counselor, you may present your closing arguments."

Canfield rose slowly and walked to the jury box clasping both hands behind his back as if in deep thought. The judge smiled to himself. He knew this was just acting on Canfield's part. Homer knew exactly what he was going to say and had probably rehearsed it over, and over, in his mind.

"Your honor, ladies and gentlemen of the jury. The issue here is not if the defendant committed these acts of rape and murder; acts so horrific that you'd say to yourself, he has to be crazy to have destroyed so many lives." Canfield paced up and down in front of the jury making strong eye contact with each member, driving home his words with maximum impact.

"Some of you harbor the idea that a mental illness in itself makes the defendant incompetent. That all his actions are the result of his illness. It makes you feel comfortable with the idea that his actions are the product of some quantifiable mental illness. That he was some slobbering, delusional psychotic, or in some catatonic state when he killed his innocent victims," Homer gazed at the floor thinking, scratching he side of his head lightly before continuing, "In your father's time, or even your grandfather's time we lived in a simpler environment. We were more accustomed to a wide range of human behavior. At the far end of that spectrum we saw insanity. However, the homogenization of our society in this century created by TV, and other mass media, has resulted in people living far more similar lives than they previously did. They experience a much narrower range of human behavior. This has resulted in narrowing what is acceptable human behavior. When we try to relate to the term 'insane' in its legal context today we have a broader range of human experience such as anger, frustration, longing desire, and fearfulness. There are some people in this world that think if I lose control I will not have to be held accountable for my actions." Canfield walked slowly back to his desk, and took a drink of water before continuing, "As you begin your deliberations I want you to take some ideas with you. There are many psychiatrist and health professionals who have gone on record stating that psychiatrists have no special knowledge to contribute to the guilt phase of a criminal trial. Some psychiatrists have gone so far as to say that they should never be allowed in the courtroom," Canfield turned quickly and nodded at the two forensic psychiatrists sitting in the front row, then moved slowly back to the jury box and leaned on the oak rail as he spoke. "There have been book after book written that concedes that the origins and categories of mental illness have not been scientifically validated. All the testimony by the court's psychiatrists are mere speculation which may or may not be true. So let me put this question to you." Canfield paused, framing his words to provide maximum impact on the jury, "Why should we even listen to such testimony when at its best, it's only a little better than guessing? If we cannot have better than second guessing why should we have it at all?" Canfield slowly walked to the empty witness stand forming his next statement. He smiled before continuing. "This whole legal set up seems like some big cop-out. If the defendant successfully maintains an insanity defense, the psychiatrists can walk away and not consider himself responsible for the outcome because it's the jury that makes the decision about the verdict, and the psychiatrist has only entered an opinion. And you, the members of the jury, shed your responsibility because you have taken into account scientific opinion of the doctors. So, quid pro quo, no one has to feel responsible for the crime. Everyone can point to someone else as being responsible for what ever happens." Canfield gestured with his hands as he raised his voice in a sarcastic tone. "See, every one is happy. It's an ideal arrangement. You can justify letting a mass murderer go free, when you are blind to your own hidden and hostile nature. Too sympathetic to a defendant's sordid past. Too frightened of madness to face up to it. Too quick to be compassionate to some one you can identify with, and too irresponsible to make your own decisions."

The courtroom remained in hushed silence. Canfield was on a dangerous path in his summation by attacking the jury. However, it might pay off by having them disregard much of the psychiatric testimony that tended to validate the multiple personality syndrome. Canfield walked back to his desk, then nodded at Barbara Starkey before speaking, "Maybe, just maybe, this adversarial system that you've seen over the past few weeks is the best method for ferreting out the truth. But it doesn't work too well for trying to understand, and evaluate the complex workings of the human mind." Canfield sighed, and gazed momentarily at his notes. "So what is the truth?" He asked, putting his hand casually behind his back, walking toward the jury box. "The truth in this case are the simple proven facts. Fact!" Canfield stated emphatically, "The knife found in officer Mackland's chest belonged to the defendant. Fact! The piece of wood attached to the wire that strangled officer Mackland had blood on it that belonged to the defendant. Fact! The DNA of the semen taken from the bodies of the murder victims matched the defendant's DNA. Fact! Signed checks from each of the murder victims were found in the defendant's apartment. Fact! The defendant stole a vehicle after murdering officer Farley, and kidnapping Agent Thornton. Fact! Fibers taken from his police officer's uniform were found in the car and on the remains of officer Farley. Fact! Agent Thornton is an eye witness to the defendant's behavior. She was brutally beaten, and taken by the defendant to the Gladlow estate for the purpose of rape and murder. Fact! Semen taken from the rape victim Judy Hampton, its DNA also matches the defendant's. Fact! The defendant kept the decomposed body of Dr. Michael Smith in his apartment for some sadistic ritual which we cannot begin to imagine. So, what does all this tell us?" Canfield paused waiting for these rapid fire facts to sink into the minds of the jurors.

"What it tells us, is that the defendant with malice of forethought, with premeditation, did stalk his victims, picking only those older, and lonely victims for his prey who were the most vulnerable. He went so far as to disguise his appearance, posing as a priest, or an officer of the law in order to gain easy access to his chosen victim. I ask you does that sound like the mind of a madman who kills in a sudden rage? I believe that this animal sitting in this courtroom today got his kicks not from sex, or rape, but from the act of killing. That was his ultimate high, the simple act of strangling helpless women slowly, deliberately."

Canfield pointed dramatically at the defendant who still sat with his forehead on the edge of the table, not wanting to hear the truth presented in blunt, factual, heart rendering terms. It was as if he could close his eyes, close him mind, and all this would go away. That this never happened. That it was some nightmare, he would wake up and everything would be okay. Canfield walked to his desk and nodded at Barbara Starkey before he spoke. "Now, the defense will argue that the defendant is suffering from a multiple personality disorder. You the jury have to determine if he is telling the truth, or is he lying?" Canfield walked casually to the jury box and resumed his pacing. "Lets say for argument sake that he is a multiple. If you accept this premise you have to ask yourself, did each of these alter egos know right from wrong at the time he committed these murders? The defense keeps talking about a Beastie personality who kills on command yet no one has ever seen this personality. Our learned doctors have not been able to call up this personality even under hypnosis. We only have a written statement from a known drunk who says he saw something in the middle of the night in a dark sewer. This is hardly reliable. The psychiatrists have all testified that these supposed personalities all knew right from wrong. Therefore, even if this Beastie personality did the killing, they are all guilty of murder in the first degree because they all knew that the ultimate result of the Beast's actions would be death. In criminal law if a party to a crime has suspicions that a crime has been committed but elects to remain silent because he wishes to remain ignorant of the crime he is deemed to have knowledge. This is called 'willful blindness.' That puts culpability on all the personalities just as if they all had pointed a gun and pulled the trigger. The criminal statutes of the State of South Carolina state that all murder which is perpetuated by means of poison, laying in wait, or by any other willful, deliberate or premeditated killing, or when such a killing is perpetrated during the attempt to commit rape, arson, robbery, or burglary shall be deemed murder in the first degree. The state has proven this far beyond a reasonable doubt. That the defendant with rape and murder as his primary motivation is guilty of murder in the first degree."

Canfield's words echoed through the walls of the oak paneled courtroom and held the audience in stilled silence. All eyes followed Canfield as he returned to his desk. "Ladies and gentlemen of the jury. We cannot, and should not, let wanton, and deliberate murder on such a scale go unpunished. For that reason I ask you to return a verdict of murder in the first degree," Canfield quietly sat down. The courtroom remained in a tense silence absorbing the summation of the prosecution.

Barbara Starkey rose slowly from her chair. She wore a gray silk business suit with a scoop neck blouse that took advantage of her fantastic figure. The two button suit top gave the impression that she wore nothing under the coat. Her cleavage was even more prevalent than it had been in the previous days of the trial. Judge Buckner nodded at the defense counsel to

J. A. Smith

begin her summation. Barbara walked slowly toward the jury box insuring that the men seated in the front row would get a good look at her.

"Your honor, ladies and gentlemen of the jury. What you've witnessed over the past few weeks, the testimony, the evidence, the expert medical opinion, the money spent on the trial have all been for the purpose of establishing blame, insuring that the criminal statutes of the state are upheld, and in some part meting out retribution. There is one other purpose that we tend to overlook, and this is providing some measure of justice and compassion to the accused. We do not deny that the defendant committed these crimes. The prosecution aptly stated that the defendant must have been crazy to commit such horrific crimes." Barbara walked to the far end of the jury box and placed both hands on the oak rail revealing just a little bit more of her cleavage. All eyes followed her every movement. "The verdict of not guilty by reason of insanity establishes two facts. One, the defendant committed the act that constitutes the crime of murder and two, he committed the act because of a mental illness. If you render a verdict of not guilty by reason of insanity he may be committed for as long as he is deemed mentally ill, and or dangerous to the community. This could be for the rest of his natural life." Barbara turned casually away from the jury box and walked to the empty witness stand then turned to face the jury. "As we discussed at the beginning of this trial, criminal law is an expression of the moral sense of the community. You the jury will decide what that moral sense is. Our law for centuries have regarded the insane as improper subjects for punishment. The three assertive purposes of criminal law are, rehabilitation, deterrence, and retribution, non of which applies to an insane person. To punish a man who lacks the power to reason is undignified, and is unworthy as punishing an inanimate object or an animal. Your conscience will not allow you to punish where you cannot impose blame." Barbara paused, sighed lightly, tugged softly at her earring and resumed her pacing. "In any statutory definition of a crime, malice must be taken not in the vague sense of wickedness, but requiring two things. One, an actual intent to do a particular kind of harm, that was actually done. Or, two, reckless abandon, with knowledge that his conduct would possibly result in harm. So in our law we have something called, 'mens rea', which means guilty mind, or vicious will, immorality of motive. To put it in simpler terms, a morally culpable state of mind. In this sense, the defendant is guilty of a crime if he commits the offense with a morally blameworthy state of mind. What this means is, that the defendant is guilty of murder in the first degree only if he specifically set out to murder his victims. We have proven far beyond a reasonable doubt that the defendant was merely doing what he was programmed to do as a child. To seek out Agnes Gladlow for the purpose of sex. The murder was a result of a jealous rage when he was rebuffed by who he thought to be Agnes Gladlow."

Barbara stopped her pacing and looked at the judge as she continued. "Are we here today going to accept an old rule of insanity over a hundred years old that relies on a single test of mental capacity to distinguish right from wrong? Can the court today say that the only test or rule of responsibility in criminal cases is the power to distinguish right from wrong, whether in the abstract or applied to the defendant?" Barbara put her finger on her lips as she posed a rhetorical question, "maybe there are insane people who while capable of perceiving right from wrong are so far under the duress of such a mental disorder as to be unable to muster the power of will to choose between right and wrong."

This was a new area she was exploring. Putting into the minds of the jurors the idea that you could be in a rational state of mind but lack the free will to choose the right course of accepted behavior.

"My worthy opponent has pointed out that there must be two constituent elements in determining legal responsibility in the commission of any crime. That is the capacity of intellectual discrimination, and free will."

Barbara returned to the jury box, leaned over to face each member of the jury in close eye contact before continuing. "Intellectual discrimination. Hold on to that thought for just a minute. I believe we all know that it's possible that the disease of insanity can so affect the mind as to subvert the freedom of will, and thereby destroy the power to choose right from wrong even though we can perceive it. Can we say that the defendant, who is suffering from such a debilitating mental disease, be held criminally responsible for an act done under the influence of such a controlling disease?"

Barbara waited for this concept to germinate in the minds of the jurors. "The next question that you have to consider is sanity itself. Is the defendant really suffering from a mental disease or is he faking it in order to escape punishment for his crimes? The medical experts all agree that he has a mental disorder. That he suffers from a multiple personality syndrome" Barbara paced slowly in front of the jury box, "If you are skeptical, you don't have to take the doctor's words for it. Just look at the facts that the prosecution has so eloquently identified. Fact, the coroner testified that the defendant has sex with the victims after death. That leads me to believe that he was not in a rational state of mind. He thought the victim was alive and enjoying the sex that he was programmed to provide. Fact, the defendant sat a full tea service in front of the corpse, served tea and scones, then had a friendly conversation with a corpse. Does that, in any sense of the word, sound like a man with a rational mind? A man that had any sense of reality? Fact, the defendant completed this same ritual with each victim right down to providing cut flowers. These flowers were Forget-me-nots, Agnes's favorite flower. His apartment reflected that two different personalities, with two different life styles, occupied these facilities and there was even an indication that an animal had been present. Can you honestly say that the defendant is sane? He may have long periods of sanity. He may even appear rational, but the facts indicate that at the time of the murders he was anything but rational."

Barbara stopped her pacing and stood facing the jury. She scanned each member of the jury wondering if what she was saying got though. The expression on one woman's face was total confusion. Did she comprehend these arguments? Maybe confusion was better than nothing. One of the men in the back row, Barbara determined, had already made up his mind, while another was totally bored. Nevertheless, this was her last chance to get her point to the jury and she was going to give it her best shot. She continued her summation in an even tone. "Our law assumes a person, regardless of his earlier experiences, when he reaches the age of discretion, he sees the wisdom of being discreet, of exercising necessary control of his behavior, except when overcome by passion or temptation. The defendant, like all men, are equal in the eyes of the law. But modern psychiatry has proven that they are extremely unequal with regards to the endowment of discretion, equilibrium, self control, and intelligence. These differences depend not only on inherited genes, and brain cell configuration, but to a great extent childhood conditioning. We have proven far beyond a reasonable doubt that the defendant was sexually abused. Who repeatedly, was asked to perform sexually for Agnes Gladlow. Who was brutally beaten, and deprived of normal sensibilities when he failed to perform." Barbara looked at Homer Canfield, then at judge Buckner before turning her attention back to the jury and resuming her summation. "In your deliberations your attention will be drawn to the testimony of the examining psychiatrists. There are two things you have to understand when evaluating their testimony. First, we lawyers are primarily concerned with placing or rebutting blame for a specific crime. Two, the psychiatrist on the other hand, are interested in correcting patterns of behavior. They do not seek to identify blame. They seek the underlying motives to the commission of the crime. So, lawyers and psychiatrists speak two different languages with regard to the law and mental disorder. For example, the word 'justice' is a word we lawyers hold dear. This is what we seek in this courtroom today. This is a word the doctors can't readily grasp. There is no justice in a chemical reaction in the brain, or in the illness that affects behavior. A surgeon never expects to be asked if an operation to remove a malignant tumor is just or not. The psychiatrist cannot answer your final question. Was the defendant's criminal act the product of his mental illness. Only you the jury can answer that." Barbara gazed intently at the jurors. "The prosecution has asked you to take an ostrich approach with regard to the psychiatric testimony. To throw it out as hearsay. If we are to find justice in this courtroom today. It is the responsibility of all of us, the psychiatric experts, the counsel, and the judge to see to it that all underlying reasons for the defendant's conduct is presented fairly, and is not confronted with a take-it-or-leave-it ultimatum. Instead, in these cases we allow the jury to hear all relevant testimony, and ask it to decide whether, by prevailing moral standards, was the defendant at fault? As you go into your deliberations there are three issues you will have to address. One, that the defendant behaved in a certain manner. Two, that his mental condition was of a certain character, and three, you must determine the legal norm against which the mental condition, and it's relationship to his behavior is measured."

Barbara knew she had opened the door for the jury to consider the psychiatric testimony. She felt she had been successful in blunting Canfield's attempts to have the juror's disregard this type of testimony. She walked slowly to her desk. Took a drink of water. Every eye in the courtroom followed her. Having cooled her throat, she moved back to the jury box and confronted the jury.

"Ladies and gentlemen of the jury. Over these past few weeks we've all learned a lot about the defendant. I know that when a person is suffering from a mental abnormality commits a crime, there is always a likelihood that the abnormality has played some part in the crime. Normally, the graver the abnormality, the more severe the crime, and the more severe the crime, the more probable there is a causal relationship between them." Barbara hit the jury box rail lightly with her fists as she spoke emphatically. "We have proven again, and again, the connection through the repeated sexual abuse of the defendant," Barbara paused. Put her hands casually behind her back and continued. "A psychotic person, such as the defendant," Barbara gestured to the defendant who remained as he had when he entered the courtroom, face down with his forehead perched on the edge of the table. "Finds it difficult or impossible to differentiate between fantasies, and actual experience. His wishes tend to be confused with facts, imagined dangers, slights, and imagined misdeeds are accepted as real, and the real ones are grossly exaggerated or misinterpreted. Now the prosecution argues, so what? There are a lot of psychotics out there that don't go around killing people. What distinguishes the defendant from the rest of the world is, not the presence of delusions and hallucinations, but rather the extent to which they dominate, and distort his perceptions, feelings, decisions and actions."

Barbara Starkey held the courtroom in concerned silence. The TV camera zoomed in on the slim attractive defense attorney.

"We have over the course of this trial proven repeatedly, that through no fault of his own the defendant, after repeated torture, and brain washing, was programmed to respond in the only way he knew how. There was no premeditation, no malice, only what he had been taught as a little boy. I ask you to look beyond the physical facts to the underlying reasons behind these crimes, and find him not guilty by reason of insanity. In doing this he may be committed to a mental hospital where he will be treated until such time the court determines he is fit to return to society. Thank you." Barbara returned to her chair and sat down.

Judge Buckner pushed his glasses back up to their normal position, and rapped his gavel, "There will be a ten minute recess," He said tonelessly then entered his chambers.

Most of the courtroom made an orderly exit to the lobby. The defendant remained in his normal position, face down, with his forehead resting on the edge of the table.

Media reporters punched their cell phones relaying the latest trial developments to their editors. The witnesses in their reserved seats chose to remain seated. Jack Bellamy leaned forward and asked, "What do you think? guilty or acquittal?"

Sally shrugged her shoulder, "Don't know. It's hard to say right now." She looked at Beau for his answer.

"Don't know," he said nonchalantly.

"I've got five bucks on acquittal," Nancy Coates interrupted from the row just behind Beau and Sally.

"You're covered," Jack replied, with a smile.

Singletary tapped Sally on the shoulder, "We've got more important things to talk about than the outcome of this trial."

"What's that?" Coates asked, giving her partner a questioning look.

"The wedding date. When are you two going to get hitched?" Singletary questioned lightly

"Yeah, I've got plans and I'm not gong to miss this historic event. Mr. Hard Ass here is getting hitched." Coates nudged Beau with a smirk.

Beau smiled at Sally, then nodded at the two inquisitive cops sitting behind them.

"I'll bet you five bucks your mom and mine have already decided when that's going to be." He said, looking at Sally.

"You better have a lot of booze, and food or old Jack here won't come." Singletary added with a chuckle.

The light conversation was interrupted when the Bailiff announced, "All rise."

Judge Buckner entered the courtroom. The Bailiff quickly brought the court back into session. Everyone scurried back to their seats and waited for Buckner's instructions to the jury.

Judge Buckner carried several pieces of paper to the bench. He seated himself firmly in his leather chair, pushed up the sleeves of his black judicial robe and leaned forward on the judge's ornate podium. He scanned the courtroom noticing that the TV camera was clearly focusing on him. He turned his attention to the jury box before speaking. The jury listened intently on what the judge was about to say.

"I have allowed the broadest latitude in testimony and taken great care over the past few weeks to provide you the jury with access to every aspect of this case. Your task of delivering a fair and impartial decision will not be easy. We have all been bombarded with media speculation, and misinformation. As you retire to your deliberations I want you to take with you these considerations and instructions. First, under the law, every man is to be presumed to be sane, and possesses a sufficient degree of reason to be responsible for his crimes, until the contrary can be proven to your satisfaction. To establish a defense on the grounds of insanity, it must be clearly proven that at the time of committing the act, the accused was laboring under such a defect of reason, from a disease of the mind, as not to know the nature, and quality of his act, or, if he did know, he did not know what he was doing was wrong." Judge Buckner paused, flipped to a new note page, adjusted his glasses, and turned his attention to the foreman of the jury.

"Having said that, let me add that the simple fact that a person who has a mental disease, or defect, is not enough to relieve him of responsibility for the crime. There must be a relationship between the disease, and the criminal act. That relationship must be such as to justify a reasonable inference that the act would not have been committed if the person had not been suffering from the disease."

Buckner turned his attention to the courtroom at large before continuing. "A free society requires mutual respect and regard, aided by mutually reinforced relationships by it's citizens. It's ideals of justice must safeguard the vast majority of citizens whose responsibility shoulders the burdens defined in it's ordered liberty. Another aspect of our judicial system is the requirement for rules of conduct that establish reasonable consistency, and neutrality. This concept is not absolute, or static. It would be weakened if we had only one law decided by some AD HOC committee. There is a redefinition that is decided on a case by case basis by you the jurors. Unfortunately, in cases such as this, when the defendant's sanity is in question there is only generalization. It places a great burden on you the jury. You may find the defendant innocent or guilty for no other reason than your personal feelings about him. The law today is our only means to justice, and you, the jury, are the only appropriate tribunal to ascertain that justice. You are to weigh the evidence on the impairment of the defendant's capacity to know right from wrong, his ability to control his actions, then focus on what seems to be just for this individual. Do you have any questions?"

The members of the jury remained quiet. The courtroom echoed that silence. Buckner scanned the courtroom one more time. "The jury will retire to determine the verdict. The court will recess until three o'clock this afternoon." Buckner rapped his gavel. The Bailiff ordered, "All rise."

The courtroom rose immediately like some army battalion coming to attention for the departing commanding general. Buckner had taken only one step when he stopped and noticed that the defendant was still sitting with his forehead resting on the edge of the table gazing at the floor. Buckner had no patience for people who were unruly, and displayed no respect for his court. He was quick to put a contempt of court citation on such individuals.

"Counselor, will you kindly ask the defendant to respect the protocols of this court." Buckner ordered with a tone of harshness in his voice.

"Yes your honor," Barbara answered, embarrassed by the defendant's lack of respect. Barbara nudged the defendant.

"You have to stand now."

There was no response. She nudged him again.

"Please, you're not making it easier on yourself," Barbara shook his shoulder gently. Suddenly, she felt cold as though she had just touched death. Her face turned pale. The self confidence she displayed in court was gone.

"Your honor," She covered her mouth with her hand unable to say what she was thinking. The security guard immediately shook the defendant again causing him to slump over to one side of his chair, then roll off onto the floor.

Someone in the courtroom screamed knowing that something terrible had just taken place, but not sure what. The guard felt for the defendant's pulse. There was absolute silence in the courtroom. It reminded Beau of some biblical story where everyone turned into a pillar of salt.

The guard announced, "He's dead your honor."

There was an immediate stampede for the door. Not out of fear, or panic, but rather to see who would be first to get the story on the wire. The guards automatically closed the doors and held everyone at bay.

Buckner shouted above the noise, "Please, no one leave this room." He motioned at Beau.

Beau, Jack, Sally and Dr. Mudd moved into action. The coroner began to examine the dead defendant. He turned the body over. Sally saw his face for the first time. She was shocked. The grotesque expression on the dead man's face looked as if some force had pulled his soul, his very life, downward through his shoes, into some deep abyss, some dark domain, in some forbidden place we call hell. His lips were dark purple. Blood ran from his nose. His eyes had filled with blood and bulged outward as if his head had imploded. The face of evil she remembered so vividly was now wrinkled and gray. Sally had seen death before. It was nothing new to her. But this, this was the most horrific sight she had ever witnessed. She turned away and covered her mouth fighting the need to throw up.

Beau moved her away from the mass of dead flesh laying on the floor, then gave orders to the Gray Lady Task Force officers to bring the crowd under control. Buckner came down to observe the coroner as he attempted to find some sort of pulse.

"In all my days in court I've never had anything happen like this." Buckner commented. Beau asked, "May I?" then gestured at the courtroom panic, and gawkers who leaned forward to get a better look.

"By all means." Buckner replied, relieved to have someone take over the chaos.

"Please," Beau shouted over the commotion, "No one will be allowed to leave this room until we have an official statement."

Moans were heard from the media reporters. Coates and Singletary had swung into action, getting a tape recorder, paper, and a table to take statements from the people.

It had taken just over four hours before they had a list and a statement from everyone. Close attention was paid to the whereabouts, and location of all the spectators in the room. The Courtroom TV tape was impounded and taken to police headquarters for review. The tapes from the building security cameras where also impounded.

It was 11:00 p.m. The crowd at the Stake Out Bar and Grill had thinned out. The District Attorney, Homer Canfield, Barbara Starkey and the Gray lady Task Force were all seated at the big horseshoe shaped bar at the back of the big dining room.

Murph leaned his back against the bar and gazed up at the colored TV above the bar. Everyone sat resting their chin in the palm of their hands. Their eyes were fixed on the TV. They lifted their drinks mechanically to their lips as if on some hidden command. They looked with disinterest at the eleven o'clock news. Apparently the old hatred just wouldn't go away. In order to maintain their ratings the news casters were interviewing the professional racists. One Klan member blamed the blacks for a cruel assassination of some poor white guy who was just two steps away from the

449

funny farm. A member of the black coalition suggested it was a Klan assassination to cover up a conspiracy against the blacks.

Barbara Starkey downed her fifth gin on the rocks, then ordered in a slightly slurred voice, "do me again Murph."

Murph smiled to himself, then filled her order. As he put the drink in front of the attractive lawyer he said,

"You're not driving home young lady."

"You're a drag, you know that?" She answered, scratching an itch at the end of her attractive nose.

"What do you do with someone who has no regard for the law?" Homer Canfield chided jokingly.

Barbara took another long jolt from her new drink, "There's a train leaving at four o'clock, be under it,' then laughed at herself for the poor attempt at humor.

"You know what I do?" Murph asked, reaching quickly for Barbara's purse on the bar. "I take their keys," Murph searched the purse then held up Barbara's keys for everyone to see.

"Sweetheart," Murph said, gently touching her head moving a` wandering curl back into it's proper place. "You are a sweet, wonderful young lady. You did a wonderful job out there and I am not going to let anything happen to you. Someone else is going to drive you home."

"I love you," Barbara said, in a sensual tone that had sexual implications hidden under the slurred speech, "but you suck!" She exclaimed, then laughed out loud.

"What makes you so sweet?" Starkey asked gently. Barbara was drunk. She was completely bombed. Sally and Beau had never seen Barbara out of control. She always had her emotion firmly under lock and key. It was though the trial had eaten away her reserve. She needed to let it all hang out. It took a large amount of gin to finally let the damn break.

Murph looked at her with a father's love. Ready to take her in his arms and let her cry away her fear, her disappointment. "Don't knock yourself. You were brilliant in that courtroom. You would have won hands down," Murph said, holding her hands.

Barbara smiled, "Thank you. But you haven't answered my question."

"What?"

"Why are you so sweet?" Barbara questioned, taking a small sip of her gin.

"See, once a lawyer always a lawyer," Canfield interrupted.

"Overruled," Beau uttered, "go on, tell us why are you so nice."

"Yeah," Coates added, "You've seen it all. You've been around longer than any of us, and you're still a nice guy. How did you manage that?"

Murph replied with a smile, "It's good for business."

"Come on Murph, cut the blarney. What's with the sweetness?" Brockman asked, in a brusque manner, then held his hand over his mouth as he burped, "excuse me."

Murph wiped his hands on his apron then fiddled with the clean glasses aligned neatly on a bar towel behind the bar. Everyone waited for Murph's answer.

"I guess it's because I'm older. You see, I have more to remember than you guys." Murph rested his elbows on the bar. "It's like this, I've had the time to think about all the good things in my life. As I get older all the good memories, drown out the bad ones. Now, you young pups are so busy getting things done you don't have time to stop and think."

"Like what?" Sally asked, putting her drink down listening intently.

Murph's face displayed a big lovable grin as he spoke, "Okay, here's what I want you all to do." He had complete attention of the bar. "I want you all to close our eyes and think back as far as you can. Think back to before there was an Internet, before your PC, before automatic weapons, and crack cocaine. Back before they had those video games. What did you call them? Yeah, Super Nintendo, Tomb Raider or whatever. Go way back. You see when I go back, way back, I remember sitting on the porch, or playing kick the can. I remember laying on my back in the grass with friends staring at the clouds, saying 'that one looks like superman, or that one looks like a butterfly'."

"I remember running through the sprinkler," Coates interrupted with her eyes still closed, remembering for the first time all the things she'd forgotten. Everyone at the bar sat with their eyes closed as if at some nostalgic seance, thinking of those wonderful things that had sadly slipped from their minds.

"I remember making forts," Canfield said before Murph could continue.

"I remember playing cops and robbers," Jack added, smiling.

"You would," Singletary jibed, and everyone laughed still holding their eyes closed, not wanting to let go of the moment.

"Beau? What do you remember?" Murph asked.

Beau tilted his head slightly thinking as far back as he could. "I remember climbing trees, and when going to town was like going somewhere. Then there were the pillow fights at bedtime."

Sally touched Beau's hand under the bar then added, "I remember angel hair on the Christmas tree, the paper chains we made at Christmas. And I remember the taste of paste.

"You ate paste? Yuck!" Singletary interrupted.

"I remember playing Simon Says, and hopscotch." Sally continued, "I also remember those funny wax lips and the mustaches."

"I remember butterscotch," Coates chimed in.

"I remember 20 year old Scotch," Homer jested, laughing with everyone at the bar.

It was like magic. Here were these everyday working people, sitting at the bar, talking with their eyes closed to themselves in a normal conversation. They looked like escapees from the Braille Institute.

Barbara Starkey seemed to take on a sad demeanor listening to everyone's memories.

"I remember bedtime. My dad telling me stories. I remember walking to church, and not stepping on a crack or you'll break your mother's back," Barbara said softly, "and I remember how nice it was just being tired from playing and having fun."

Everyone sat in silence with their eyes still closed savoring every memory, holding each moment, no matter how fleeting, in their mind.

"You see," Murph said, breaking the trance, "If you take the time to remember the good things, it makes you a nicer, kinder person." Murph made a few swipes with his towel across the top of the bar and announced, "Okay, last drink is on the house," Nodding at Barbara Starkey, he remarked, "and you young lady are going to get driven home."

Barbara smiled lovingly at Murph, "You still suck."

Beau and Sally lifted a staggering Barbara Starkey into their car. They had volunteered to deposit Barbara safely in her apartment which was only a few miles from Beau's townhouse. During the short ride from the Stakeout Bar and Grill to Barbara's apartment they were serenaded with old college songs, and football cheers, from an inebriated Barbara Starkey who had assumed a horizontal position in the back seat. It was as if Barbara had finally let it all go. Tonight, like, some pressure relief valve letting go, she said what she wanted, and did what she wanted. The trial, the debate, the TV and media blitz as far as she was concerned was mute. The defendant was dead and she was off the hook. So tonight was her night to party, and like Scarlet O'Hara said, "Tomorrow's another day."

Beau brought the car to a slow stop and looked at Sally.

"I'll take her up," She said, turning to look at a happy Barbara who winked back.

"Thank you ladies and gentlemen," Barbara slurred as she pulled herself up and fumbled with the door handle. "Well, lady anyway. The gentlemen part is still open to debate." Barbara added, stepping out of the car, slipping and falling to one knee. "Oops," she remarked.

Sally was at her side, picking up one arm and putting it over her shoulder to keep her from falling flat on her face. The wobbling Barbara pulled Sally to the front window of the car and slurred, "Isn't she sweet?" Then nodded at Sally, "You better take damn good care of her or I'll put one of my Cajun curses on you."

"I promise counselor," Beau responded with a chuckle.

Beau couldn't help but smile to himself as he watched the two women stumble their way up the front steps, fumble with the keys and enter the old brownstone. In all the time Beau had known Barbara Starkey he had never seen her let go emotionally. She was always in control. He wondered if Barbara wasn't having second thoughts on the course she had chosen for her life. Maybe she was wondering if there wasn't something missing in her life. Some great void that had gone unfulfilled, and that maybe, it was too late, time had passed her by. Beau felt a tinge of sadness come over him.

Sally unlocked the apartment door and fumbled for the light switch. Suddenly, Barbara grabbed Sally and pinned her against the wall. Barbara pressed her lips against Sally's. Her tongue search the depths of her mouth with a sexual penetration. She was caught off guard. She automatically opened her mouth to receive Barbara's searching tongue. Barbara pushed her hips hard against Sally's body. She took Sally's free hands and placed on her breasts. It was as if she was in an erotic trance. Barbara had managed to completely unbutton her blouse. Sally felt the soft, smooth skin of her firm breasts. Barbara was fully aroused, breathing hard.

Still numb from what Sally had just let happen to her, she was led into Barbara's bedroom. Sally stood transfixed, hypnotized and aroused by the seductive antics of this sexual animal that had been held hidden just below the surface of this attractive young woman.

Barbara stripped to the waist leaving only a tight fitting mini-skirt. Her breasts were fully erect. Her voice was not inhibited in any way by alcohol. She was totally aroused by Sally's reluctance to say no. She wanted desperately to have sex with Sally. Barbara seductively laid back on the bed, raised her arms over her head, and spread her legs invitingly.

"Come on. I know you want me." Barbara pleaded like a whore in heat.

Sally, as if responding to a hypnotic command, moved to the side of the bed and stood between Barbara's open legs. She was undulating her body. Moving her hips in a sexual invitation. All the dreams, all the sexual fantasies that had nagged her for all these days was there for the taking. Barbara, was begging for sex. After all this time, after all these forbidden dreams all she had to do was act. "Do it," A voice from deep inside her passion shouted at her inner most thoughts, yet she didn't move. She didn't act. Something held her back. Something said that it wasn't right. This wasn't what she wanted. She'd have to come to grips with her own desires, but there was something more important to her than just carnal desire.

"Barbara," Sally responded quietly, "I respect you. I want to be your friend. If I did what you wanted me to do all that would change. I have a life downstairs waiting for me in the car. I will not do anything to jeopardize that. So, right now I suggest you go in and take a cold shower," Sally walked to the door, opened it, then turned to face Barbara, "Barbara, I know all the intimate details about you and Beau. That's okay. I love him, and we are going to get married. So please don't do anything to stop it."

There was a hidden threat in Sally's voice.

Barbara Starkey raised her naked body up on one elbow as she spoke seductively, "I won't have to. You'll come to me. After the honeymoon is over. When you get back to the mundane tasks of everyday living. When Beau is off slurping beer with his buddies and your are bored out of your ever loving mind, you'll come to me." Barbara laid back, pulling up her mini-skirt revealing more of her voluptuous body and began to manipulate herself. Sally stood by the open door and watched Barbara turn herself on.

"Don't hold your breathe," She replied and gently closed the door.

It was a twenty minute drive from Barbara's apartment to Beau's townhouse. Sally sat pensively looking out the window at nothing. She hadn't spoken a word since they had dropped Barbara off. Beau knew instinctively that Barbara and Sally had exchanged words.

"She came on to you didn't she." Beau remarked as he drove slowly through the streets of Charleston. Sally didn't answer confirming Beau's suspicions.

"Don't let it bother you," Beau said. "She likes her sex. It's like a tonic for her. She usually gets what she wants," he added.

"Did she get you?" Sally asked avoiding eye contact with Beau.

"We had sex, but no, she didn't get me," he replied emphatically, "and she didn't get you did she?" he added knowingly.

"No," She said, putting her head softly on his shoulder. "Lets get married. I don't want to wait. Lets run off tonight like some teenagers and just do it."

Beau put one arm around Sally as he drove, "Don't worry. You won't loose me. I love you and I've made a commitment to you. I love the future Mrs. Gasteneau, and that will never change."

Chapter Twenty Six
The Wedding

The Gasteneau dynasty began with the birth of this nation. The first Gasteneau came to this country with Lafayette to fight along side Washington for America's independence. He was a staff officer for Lafayette and led numerous attacks against the British. A thankful nation gave Jean Paul Gasteneau five thousand acres of prime land that is now Falconbriar. Falconbriar was mainly wooded with one small secluded valley that was perfect for starting an orchard.

The Gasteneaus' were not for wasting resources. They took the lumber from clearing the land for farming and built trading ships in the port of Charleston. Over the years the Gasteneau Trading Company grew to over 23 ships that brought trading goods from all over the world to New York and Charleston. The Gasteneaus did not believe in slavery but respected other land owner's right to hold slaves. The second generation, Horace Gasteneau bought slaves then set them free with the option of an indentured contract for ten years, after which, they would own 100 acres of land, free and clear, with a cabin. Most slaves chose to stay and work for wages and tend their land. As a result many of the old black families of Charleston honor the Gasteneau name. Most of the state's politicians breathed a sigh of relief when Beau Gasteneau shied away from politics and opted to be a police detective instead. It was common knowledge that a Gasteneau could have any elective post in the state if he wanted it.

During the Civil War the Gasteneaus became rich beyond their wildest dreams. Horace Gasteneau became a privateer, running the northern blockade to deliver arms, medicine and supplies to the south. The Gasteneaus were considered southern heroes. What they didn't know, was that he also delivered supplies to the north. This gave him access to the location of the north's blockading ships.

As his wealth grew so did the Gasteneau shipping empire. After the war Horace Gasteneau wisely invested in railroads, banking, shipping and steel. Today, Beau has no idea of his total wealth. Money, and power have never been a big issue with him. He leaves the money management to a host of accountants and lawyers in New York and Switzerland. The last time he talked to his lawyers, he had accounts in Charleston, New York and Switzerland each totaling in the millions of dollars.

The work of Horace Gasteneau during the Civil War, his position of not supporting either side of the conflict paid off. Falconbriar was spared the ravages of war. When the north occupied this area Falconbriar was spared while other estates were burned to the ground. It was said that Lincoln himself issued an executive order that Falconbriar was not to be touched. Horace Gasteneau was not just a profiteer, acquiring wealth from the sufferings of others. After the war he loaned destitute landowners money to rebuild, and to start over. These loans were interest free. For everyone in the state the Gasteneau name still brings to mind, God, honor, country, and fair play.

When it was formally announced that Beau Gasteneau was getting married, everyone knew it would be a special event. They knew that Josey Gasteneau would spare no expense to provide the biggest, most lavish wedding that Charleston had seen in the past ten years.

St. Michaels sparkled with festive decorations. Josey had paid $25,000 to the church to have the stained glass windows cleaned by an international company that provided restoration services. Another $20,000 dollars was spent on flowers for the church. Over 500 friends of the family and guests packed the church.

The light beamed through the colored glass windows spreading red, greens, and blues over the audience. The happy couple knelt at the altar, took communion, and repeated their vows. Sally wore a white wedding gown decorated with white pearls, lace, and white on white silk embroidery. She looked angelic. The small scar on her cheek was barely visible, nevertheless was a reminder of what these two lovers had been through together. This was a bond of true friendship, respect, and love. Sally's scar will always remind Beau of the pure will, and fortitude of the woman he was marrying. He was thankful that she loved him. For the first time in his life he felt fulfilled, happy, and content.

Jack Bellamy was his Best Man and his wife Emma Joe was Maid of Honor. Barbara Starkey gazed intently at Beau. He was a ruggedly handsome man even when he was dressed in his formal tux. She wondered if she hadn't made a mistake in letting him go when she had him. Was her life style, her sexual appetites going to make her an old maid? Was she incapable of accepting any man in her life? She looked at Homer Canfield. Outside of Beau, he was the only man she had any respect for.

Little Katie Thornton was the Flower Girl. She wore a white lace dress and preceded her mother, tossing petals of white roses on the floor, while the choir sang Ave Maria. It was a beautiful sight. It reminded you of a royal wedding with the handsome prince walking down the isle with the pretty maiden.

Even the Gray Lady task force was dressed in their Sunday best. Detective Coates, who was normally outspoken, dressed a little on the wild side, had on a simple blue dress with a single strand of pearls. She had a tear in her eye. Brockman put his arm around Coates as Sally walked arm in arm with Beau down the isle bringing the long ceremony to a dramatic close.

Murph was the first one outside St. Michaels. He handed out bags of rice, for the final send off. There wasn't going to be much of a send off. In three hours everyone would be at Falconbriar raising hell. Josey Gasteneau, wouldn't have it any other way.

It was as if the cloud of dispair and discontent that had hovered over Charleston for the past few months was suddenly lifted. The sun was bright and warm. This was unusual weather for so late in the year. A warm tropical front had moved up from the south and gave an air of freshness to the city. The flowers still held their summer blossoms and the birds warbled their song as though winter was a long time away.

Josey and Casey were like two field generals, ordering, and directing caterers in preparation for the wedding reception. The day was finally here. The old antebellum mansion was open front and back with lawn tents, food buffets, an outdoor dance pavilion with a full orchestra and a play yard that had been set up especially for the children. Cut flowers adorned every room in the old house. Even the old Magnolia tree had honored the occasion by putting out extra blossoms.

Normally, the wedding reception is a ordered, concise, well planned occasion with official invitations and RSVPs. Their were 500 invitations mailed, but Josey, with her big heart, and outward demeanor with everyone she met, issued who knows, how many vocal invitations to the reception. Beau estimated that they had about 900 people at the party.

Judge Buckner arrived with Barbara Starkey and Homer Canfield at his side. He made it perfectly clear that he planned to get plastered and he wanted Homer to make sure he got home safely.

Josey, Casey, Sally and Beau stood in the reception line and shook every hand of the nine hundred guest who showed up for one of the major events to come to the city in over a year. The state's Lt. Governor, Attorney General, the mayor, and everyone else in between was there. Carl Hawthorne, the NAACP lawyer, Jack's father-in-law, the Reverend Jesse Baxter was there. He even had Obbie and Willard Jackson, the two black gang leaders with him. They had been washed, cleaned, shoes shined, and in their Sunday best. The reverend said that he wanted to show them how civil people acted, and how important good manners were. Even Moses Miller with his one horse cab showed up sporting a white tux and a formal white stovepipe hat. Sally didn't shake hands with Moses. She gave him a warm hug and said, "I want you to take us for a ride later. Is that okay?"

"It would be my honor, Mrs. Gasteneau," the gentle man replied.

Moses had cleaned up his hansom cab. It was decorated with garlands of white roses. As the celebration wore on you could see Moses and his old nag taking laughing children and young lovers for buggy rides around the farm.

Studs had been washed, shampooed, and given a small bucket of beer which resulted in a wobbling dog curling up under the old Magnolia to sleep off his binge. The party was in full swing. Beau and Sally had just finished the traditional wedding dance when he took Sally's hand, then Katie's and walked outside. Beau gave a whistle at Moses who was unloading a group of laughing children. Moses motioned the new family to step up for a nice easy ride.

It was a chance to get away as a family for a few minutes of quietness. Tapping the flanks of his old nag, the buggy meandered slowly down the small country lane toward the orchard. The fall colors of the trees seem to beam in the sun that hid occasionally behind billowing clouds that were sitting on the western horizon.

"Moses?" Beau asked, tapping him on the shoulders, "Take us to the barn will you?" Moses nodded, then steered the buggy down a small path leading to the barn. Moses pulled the carriage to a slow stop in front of the barn.

"Come on, I've got something to show you," Beau said, getting out to the cab, then helping Sally and Katie down. "You too Moses." The old man smiled, then complied.

"Can we tell him now? Katie asked excitedly, tugging at Beau's sleeve.

"What are you two up to?" Sally questioned, with a suspicious smile.

"You'll see, you'll see, come on Moses," Katie said taking Moses by the hand, pulling him ahead, then opening the barn door.

"Close your eyes," Katie commanded, showing Moses how to put his hands over his eyes. Moses complied. Katie led him inside the barn. "Okay, you can open them," Katie said in a happy tone.

Moses looked around the barn. Each of the six stalls displayed a beautiful horse. The old man saw everything from a quarter horse to a huge Clydesdale staring back at him.

"Take your pick." Beau said happily.

"What?" Moses answered. He was awestruck. The animals were beautiful. Far more than he could afford. "I don't know what to say?"

"You don't have to say anything," Beau said, putting his arm around the old man.

"You know Miss. Priss out there and I have been through a lot. I mean she's the only family I've got. I just can't throw her away. I wouldn't do that," Moses replied sadly.

"I know. It's hard to let go of someone you love. But she's getting old, and she deserves her time in the sun. I'll tell you what. We'll put her out to pasture right here on Falconbriar," Beau pointed to the beautiful pasture that laid behind the barn. "You come and visit her anytime you want. She'll have other horses to be with while you are gone."

Moses scratched his chin as he thought. He knew it was the right thing to do for his long time friend. "I can't afford to pay you for a new horse, especially these. These are the best I've seen. No, I can't afford it and I won't take your charity."

Beau winked slyly at Sally and Katie as though he was haggling which was a tradition in this part of the state.

"I'll tell you what. I'll sell you the horse, any horse. Take your pick. You can pay me back in trade. You can give Mrs. Gasteneau, my daughter, and myself, free rides for as long as you own the horse."

Moses's ego was satisfied. He took off his glove, spit in his hand then shook Beau's firmly. In these parts that was as good as a written contract.

Moses selected a white appaloosa with spotted flanks. It was instant bonding between them when Moses handed him a sugar cube. The horse had been trained to bridle. It had three distinctive gates which he would happily display by just tapping his flanks lightly.

Moses led his old friend Miss Priss to the pasture gate. The old nag nuzzled her friend lovingly. Moses held out his hand with one last cube of sugar.

"I'm gonna miss you sweetheart. I know you're gonna miss me," The horse nodded as though she understood every word. "Don't worry, I'll come to see you. I want you to go out there, eat a lot of grass, lay in the sun, and have fun. Will you do that for me?" The old horse nudged him gently. Moses opened the gate then slapped Miss Priss gently on the hind quarters. The horse trotted into the pasture then stopped and looked one last time at her old friend.

"Go on," he ordered. The old man was on the verge of crying. His lip quivered slightly as he turned away, not wanting to look back at the horse that just stood alone in the pasture and watched her friend disappear into the barn.

Moses Miller with his hansom cab was a sight to behold as the high stepping appaloosa pranced back to the old house. Katie sat along side Moses and gave him a big kiss before jumping down.

The wedding reception went on most of the day and into the night. It was eleven o'clock. Beau and Sally danced alone to the last set before the orchestra would pack up and depart. Most of the guests had said their good-byes and left. Gil Washington, standing with the city fathers, which included the District Attorney, and the Chief of Police motioned for Beau and Sally to join them. Beau was a little perturbed at the intrusion into his private moment with his new bride. The lovers continued to dance ignoring their efforts to get the happy couple to join them. Sally kissed Beau on the cheek, "Maybe if we see what they want they'll go away?"

Beau kissed her back, "Okay, lets get them on their way."

The newly weds joined the group reluctantly.

"Can we talk to you two in private?" The mayor asked.

Beau looked at the nearly empty room. The only people around were the caterers who were scurrying around to close things up before the thunderstorm hit.

"What have you got on your mind?" Beau asked cautiously.

David Blackstone the District Attorney spoke first, "I know it's a lot to ask. The city owes you two a great deal,"

"Ouch!, this is going to hurt," Beau interrupted.

"Please, hear me out," Blackstone asked politely. Beau folded his arms and waited impatiently.

"You know we've got a murder on our hands."

"That's your problem," Beau chided. The mayor stepped closer to Beau, "Look, this fiasco isn't over. The media is having a field day with this. It's going to be another Ramsey case if we don't get to the bottom of it."

"Christ!, we've got the Klan still saying that we've killed a token white before the truth really came out just to make the blacks happy," Wexford exclaimed.

"This isn't going away anytime soon," Carl Hawthorne, the NAACP lawyer added.

"Now look," Beau replied, knowing what they were about to ask. "We've put in a hell of a lot of overtime," Beau put his arm around Sally, "You've got Jack, he's a hell of a good cop, and you've got the rest of the team. You don't need us."

"Yeah, but we've got the Millie Fergerson and Gale Brisby investigation to contend with," Chief Wexford added.

"Why us?" Sally asked in frustration.

"Because you guys have first hand information about the killer. You've interviewed almost everyone involved in this case." The District Attorney commented strongly.

"No dammit!" Beau shouted angrily, "We've got pre-paid tickets for two weeks in Bora Bora. I've got a ton of leave coming and so does Sally. Dammit we've earned it so go screw yourself. You can wait two weeks."

Blackstone looked at the other politicians before he spoke, "I'll tell you what we'll do. If you'll put off your honeymoon, and give us two months of hard investigation. I'm pretty sure we can talk to the FBI and get Sally assigned permanently to the district office here in Charleston. The governor is in Washington right now. We'll call him. He knows how to push the right buttons."

Sally tugged at Beau's arm. She nodded confirming that she'd delay the honeymoon if it meant being assigned to Charleston.

Beau shook his head in frustration but had no choice but to give in to their demands. "Okay, two months and you pay for the new tickets to Bora Bora. First class!"

"Done!," Blackstone acknowledged with a smile.

Beau and Sally were finally alone. They sat on the front porch in the white wicker swing that creaked from the heavy rusted chain that secured it to the ceiling. The approaching thunderstorm was almost on them. Black clouds made the night even darker. The darkness erupted with great flashes of light as the lightening danced across the tree tops bringing seconds of blinding light to the front porch. The approaching storm announced itself by providing a cool breeze across the porch. It was the perfect ending to a perfect day.

"Daddy," Katie stood in the open front door in her jammies, clutching a tattered Teddy Bear. "I'm afraid," Another bolt flashed across the sky followed by clapping thunder. Katie ran and jumped into Beau's lap and hid her face clutching him as though he could make everything go away. The crying little girl melted Beau's heart. He now had a sweet little girl he could call his own. One he could spoil, and love, and watch her grow into a beautiful woman like her mother. Sally put her arms around both of them as if to give them another layer of protection and love.

The storm subsided momentarily. Beau sat Katie up on his knee and looked seriously at her. "Why are you afraid?" He asked calmly. The frightened little girl said, "I don't know." Then hugged her Teddy Bear a little closer.

Another loud bolt of lightening flashed its fiery fingers across the sky with a thundering bang. Katie buried her face in Beau's arms.

"You shouldn't be afraid," Beau said calmly. Katie lifted her head up slowly and looked at Beau waiting for an answer. Beau cradled the little girl closer to him. "Remember a long time ago I told you that God always meant for me to be your father.?"

"Uh huh," Katie acknowledged shyly.

"You remember it took a long time for me to find you and your mommy?"

"Uh huh,"

"Well today is the happiest day in my life, and God is happy too. So, God is taking photographs with his camera of the wedding. He's taking pictures of you, your mommy, and me. Now, he's going to keep these pictures in his Happy Book, and he doesn't want to see you crying. He wants to see a happy face. You see the lightening are his flash bulbs. I mean God has to have really big flash bulbs," Beau gestured with his arms. "Now, come on sit up. The next time we see lightening lets make a funny face so God will know we're having fun." Beau and Katie waited intently for the next bolt. When it came, Beau stuck out his tongue. On the next bolt, he looked cross eyed. On the third bolt, he put both fingers in his mouth, stretched his lips apart and wagged his tongue. By the fourth bolt Katie, Beau, and Sally were all making funny face at each bolt of lightening and laughing themselves silly.

When the storm had passed, Beau put Katie to bed then joined Sally on the porch. Sally sat in her Levi's with Beau's plaid shirt casually buttoned half way up.

"Come on," Beau said, as he took Sally's hand.

"Where are we going?" She asked happily, following Beau down the steps.

"We're going on a quick honeymoon," He replied opening the pickup truck's door. A light rain was just beginning to fall as he drove through the orchard. The truck lights flashed over rabbits and other night animals scurrying out of harms way. It was a ten minute drive down a narrow mountain road to a clearing next to a small stream with a bubbling waterfall. It was a magnificent Swiss chalet nestled quietly in the forest.

"Five bedrooms, five bathrooms and four fireplaces," Beau announced proudly. Sally was amazed. This was another rustic mansion that was a hidden part of Falconbriar she never knew existed. Beau put the truck in the garage.

Walking together in the light mist, they admired the scene.

"I call this the Lodge. I come here when I want to get away from things. Now, it's ours to enjoy." Sally gave him a quick hug. Beau unlocked the front door revealing a fantastic family room with a massive stone fireplace.

"Just a minute," Beau said, then picked up his bride and carried her over the threshold. "Welcome home sweetheart."

Sally kissed her husband hungrily. Her tongue searched his open mouth. They both stood just inside the open door locked in a passionate embrace. Sally was immediately excited. She hungered for his body, his passion, his love. She was going to let everything go tonight. There would be no holding back. Just total abandonment for her lover and husband.

"I'll light the fire," He announced,

"You already have," Sally quipped. Beau laughed.

It only took a few minutes when a warm, toasty fire flickered across the big room. Sally sat on the couch with her knees tucked under her chin gazing at the glowing embers. Beau carried in a chilled bottle of champagne and two frosted glasses. He quickly popped the cork and poured two bubbly glasses.

"What shall we toast to?" He asked lightly. Sally raised her glass, "I give you my love, my life, all that I can be, and all that you want me to be." Beau thought about Sally's sincerity, "I give you all my love, all I have. I will never hold anything back from you. I will always love you, take care of you and Katie," they both downed their champagne.

"OooH! That was good. Fill her up," Sally asked with a smile. In a matter of minutes the champagne was gone and the lovers laid in each others arms and watched the fire.

It was a night she never wanted to end. They finished two more bottles of champagne in less that two hours. Sally felt warm and comfortable in Beau's arms. The champagne had relaxed her totally. She snuggled closer to her husband. Beau lifted her chin. She could see the hunger in his eyes. He wanted her.

Beau thought to himself, how lucky he was. He was her husband. This wonderful, kind, beautiful, sexy woman was his. Tonight he was going to give her everything she wanted. Whatever hidden desire, whatever fantasy she desired he would perform. It was going to be four days of unbridled passion, love and sex.

Beau prided himself on his self control. Since the beginning of this trial, with all the testimony about sex, the Fetish Club, he'd been able to keep his desires, his fantasies, under control, but not now, not tonight.

"I want to show you the rest of the house," Beau said, standing up taking Sally's hand gently. Sally was a little tipsy. Arm in arm the two mellowed lovers ascended the staircase to the second floor of the Swiss Chalet.

Beau flicked on the light revealing the master bedroom. It was another large room dominated by a big oak canopy king size bed. Four large ornate oak posts supported large canopy rails. On the other side of the room were mirrored sliding doors that led into the walk-in closet. The window opened to the stream side of the house so one could listen to the bubbling waterfall. Inside the walk-in closet was a large armoire and an array of hanging clothes.

Sally kissed Beau lightly, "It's beautiful. I want to spend all my time here. We've got three more days. I want to spend it right here with you, and no interruptions."

Beau led Sally to the foot of the big four poster canopy bed. She looked lovingly into his eyes. She saw an intensity there she hadn't seen before. She knew instinctively that he was sexually aroused, yet kept it under control. He unbuttoned her shirt and let it drop to the floor. The mere touch of his hand sent Sally into erotic ecstasy. Beau just looked at his beautiful bride. Automatically, she unbuttoned and stepped out of her Levi's. She stood before him totally naked. He gently kissed her with his tongue penetrating her open mouth. Sally, while still lock in a passionate kiss, unbuttoned Beau's shirt tossing it to the floor. He unzipped his Levi's and stood naked in front of Sally with his erection touching her soft stomach. She stroked his erection slowly, feeling it getting larger and firmer in her hand. Beau fondled her breasts, making her nipples stand erect. She was totally and uncontrollably aroused. She moaned in absolute surrender to her man.

"I want to give myself to you totally," she panted.

Beau kissed her passionately again, "You will give yourself to me totally," Beau reaffirmed in a commanding voice.

"Yes, Take me. I'm yours. I'll do anything you want," Sally responded gasping with desire.

"You will be my sex slave," He ordered.

"Oh yes," She had totally and unconditionally surrendered to him.

"Do you want me to rape you?" he asked softly.

Sally nodded affirmatively,

"Say it," Beau commanded, applying pressure to her breasts that excited her even more.

"Yes, rape me. Rape me now. Rape me all night. Do whatever you want to me. I am your slave,"

This was fantastic she thought. Beau knew all her fantasies and would be her partner in whatever she desired. Beau stepped back, went to the armoire in the closet and returned with a small gym bag. He took some soft silk rope then tied Sally's wrists to the upper canopy rails, then tied her ankles to each foot of the bed. She stood spread open, naked, and totally helpless to his whims. She could see her image in the mirrored doors. Beau moved close to her and asked, "Am I your master?"

"Yes master," Sally answered automatically. Beau placed two gold clips connected by a gold chain on Sally's nipples. This new pressure excited her even more. She arched her back giving Beau full access to her beautiful breasts. He then placed around her neck a leather dog collar, a symbol of her sexual submission. "Slave, I am going to rape you like you've never been raped before," She nearly fainted with anticipation. He knelt before her and with an oily finger began to manipulate her clitoris. Sally hung limp by her wrists trying desperately to lower herself onto his hand so he could penetrate deeper into her quivering body.

Beau poured mineral oil on his hands and began to slowly message her firm body, then taking his oily fingers and penetrating her, simulating sex. Sally responded by moving her hips down hard on his oily hand. Beau finished his torture by kneeling in front of his spread eageled slave and inserting his tongue inside her sex as deep as he could. Sally groaned with pleasure on each thrust of his tongue. She climaxed then went limp, hanging from her wrists. Beau untied her, then held his bride in his arms. She kissed him hard then dropped to her knees and swallowed his manhood. Putting her hands on his buttocks she crammed his erection down her throat, sucking and fondling his anus with her fingers. Sally knew he was about to climax she stopped then stood facing him.

Beau took her to the big bed and laid her back crosswise so her head hung over the edge. Her hair touched the floor in front of Beau's erection. He tied one wrist to the foot of the bed, and the other to the head of the bed. Walking to the other side of the bed he lifted Sally's firm legs, spread them far apart tying them to the top of the canopy rail. She was totally helpless, with her head bent back over the edge of the bed and her legs spread out, and upright, tied to the top canopy rail. He began slowly to pour oil over her body, rubbing the tense muscles of her firm body. Sally moaned with satisfaction and opened her legs wider anticipating penetration.

"Rape me, please rape me," The sex slave begged. This was pure torture, teasing, touching but no penetration. Beau stood over Sally's head, inserted his erection in her mouth and ravished her with deep hard and fast thrusts. She took it all. She swallowed everything he had. Before he climaxed he stopped, then stood between her open legs and inserted his manhood. With each downward thrust Sally moved her hips upward to get maximum penetration. She groaned with pleasure. He began slowly with wet, easy thrusts, then pushed deeper, harder, faster, bringing his erection to full penetration. Beau screamed with satisfaction as he unloaded all his sperm inside her. Sally flexed her vaginal muscles hold him tight inside her. It was as if she would not let him remove himself until she had sucked every ounce of sperm out of him.

He untied his lover and they both collapsed in exhausted sleep, laying naked in each others arms.

A little more than an hour had passed when Beau felt a tongue in his ear. Sally whispered softly, "Now it's my turn."

"What do you mean?" Beau said, still trying to wake himself. Sally was fully awake and excited. She took the silk ropes from her wrists and tied Beau's hands to each of the head posts. Then secured his feet in the same manner. Beau was now spread open on the bed. She ran her fingers lightly over his body admiring all his muscles. She began to fondle his maleness. Playing with it, trying to foster another erection. Sally was an animal and she was in charge.

Sally put an oily finger in Beau's anus as she began oral sex moving her head up and down. It took only a few penetrations with her finger and a few minutes of oral copulation when she had the erection she was after. She mounted Beau sending his manhood deep inside her. She groaned and manipulated her own breasts as she impaled herself on his erection.

Beau climaxed again. Sally kept him fully inside her, using her vaginal muscles to suck every ounce of sperm out of him. She rubbed her stomach, then collapsed on top of him. After untying him she cuddled in his arms once again.

"I hope, no, I know it's going to be a boy. The two lovers finally fell asleep as the new dawn broke on the eastern horizon.

Chapter Twenty Seven
Who Done It?

It had been four wonderful days at the Lodge. Early morning breakfasts in the kitchen. Quiet walks in the woods. Sitting in front of the fire, talking about their future together and at night unrestrained sex. It had been so long since she had a man that totally understood her. She was completely free. She didn't have to hold back. She could be completely honest with Beau. And she knew he loved her for it. She could hardly wait for the sun to go down before she had Beau up in the bedroom, and it would be wonderful, exciting sex until the early hours of the new day. She eagerly shared all her sexual fantasies with him. Beau complied with all her demands. Sally admitted that she wanted to get pregnant as soon as she could. She told him in explicit detail about her dream when Mark came to her, and said that he'd come back through her womb.

Beau had called the Gray Lady Task Force together for a status meeting. When Beau and Sally returned to police headquarters it was easy to see the glow on her face. She was so much in love with Beau it was hard for her not to touch him. However, they both knew that, when at work, they had to put their personal feelings away and keep their distance from each other and focus on their jobs.

The Gray Lady Task Force Conference Room was small and slightly cramped but it had everything the team needed and offered them the privacy they wanted away from the media's prying eyes and ears. There was a large conference table in the center of the room littered with papers, folders, coffee cups, and a plate of brick hard doughnuts. At one end of the room was a TV with a video cassette player and a computer. The computer was attached to the TV through an array of cables.

Beau seated himself at the head of the table. Sally seated herself next to Beau. Coates whispered in Singletary's ear, "There's the look of a woman who has just been laid."

"How would you know? You haven't been laid in months," Singletary quipped sarcastically.

"I heard that," Sally said jokingly, then tossed a paper wad at both of them.

"Okay troops," Beau interrupted, "Lets get down to business." Before he could continue Roger Mudd, the coroner, entered the conference room.

"Good morning everyone. Good morning Mr. and Mrs. Gasteneau," He said with a chuckle in his voice. Beau had resigned himself to the fact that he would have to endure these little innuendoes for a few more weeks, and then it would be business as usual.

"I suppose everyone is ready for the autopsy report?" Dr. Mudd asked, as he passed out copies of the report to the team.

"That would be nice," Jack Bellamy answered snidely.

"Don't tell me? Let me guess. He was poisoned," Brockman joked.

"My friend you have a tremendous grasp of the obvious," Dr. Mudd replied with a smile, seating himself next to Sally.

"Okay, lets start with that," Beau announced sitting back casually in his chair, taking the autopsy report and giving it a quick scan.

"All right, let me draw you attention to page one paragraph three. Yep, we all had a pretty good idea from the first day that it was poison. Ah, but what kind?" Dr. Mudd asked rhetorically, tapping the side of his temple as though in deep thought. "The poison was Thevetia Peruviana."

"Oh that's nice," Singletary interrupted with a low sarcastic chuckle.

"Ah yes," Mudd continued tolerantly, "for you uneducated peasants, that's Yellow Oleander. This is a shrub or a small tree in the Dogbane family. It has a milky sap. Their leaves are linear, pointed, they can be dark green or glossy. Their flowers are tubular, fragrant, yellow, white, or orange and hang in loose clusters. They have small fruits that are triangular, red or yellow, which turn black when they are mature. These plants were introduced into the U.S. some time ago and are grown throughout the south. In fact, I have several of them in my back yard,"

"Roger, that's really more than I ever wanted to know about oleander," Coates chided smartly.

Dr. Mudd ignored her little joke and turned to another page in the report and smiled at detective Coates before continuing, "For Coates's benefit, here's a little more background for the troops," He paused, and looked at the detectives gathered around the table. Their attention was focused on the report. "This plant is the leading cause of human poisoning in the state of Hawaii. From what I can find out, most of the deaths in Hawaii come from the native population that use this plant in their native medicine. Many of these people believe that the stone of the fruit brings good luck," Dr. Mudd adjusted his glasses, turned to the next page in his report before continuing, "All parts of the plant are poisonous. In Hawaii the natives have used the nut of the Oleander to poison fish. The plant contains very toxic cardiac glycosides thevetin and peruvosides which is similar to digitalis. One nut or a combination of leaves, sap and other fiber can easily cause death of an adult. The symptoms are nausea, vomiting, diarrhea, high blood pressure, altered state of awareness, irregular pulse, dilated pupils, convulsions, and death due to heart failure." Dr. Mudd sat back and folded his arms with a smug expression. "Now, the autopsy shows that he had a mixture of Karo

Syrup, and the poison in his blood and body chemistry. The syrup was used to sweeten the poison which is bitter. The poison itself is easy to process into a liquid form. Anyone can do it in their own kitchen." Dr. Mudd reached into his pocket and revealed a small Baby Ruth candy bar.

"This is one of the candy bars that the defendant munched on during the course of the trial. If you will notice on the back of the wrapper is a small puncture hole. The poison was administered to the candy via a hypodermic syringe. Our analysis of the candy bowl resulted in over 85% of the candies contain the same poison. All right folks, there you have it. The Oleander toxin in its diluted form did not kill him right away. However, over the weeks of the trial, his sweet tooth did him in. Any questions? Miss Coates do you have any questions?" Coates and Mudd exchanged sly smiles.

Everyone sat in stone silence gazing at the coroner's report.

"Well, we knew it was poison, but we didn't know how. That's a start," Beau remarked with a sigh. "Okay, what else do we have?"

Everyone remained silent not offering one comment or idea. "Okay, let's start with motive," Beau offered up for discussion.

"Oh my God!" Coates blurted out, looking at the ceiling, "Pick anyone," she scowled, "everyone had a motive. I wouldn't even omit the mayor for that matter."

"Agreed," Beau nodded, "you've all had a chance to go over the folders. You've read the transcripts of the trial. Pick one, anyone and give me a motive," Beau nodded at Coates.

"My guess would be Mildred Potts," She answered. "First, she was a close friend of Molly Philburn. They grew up together. She was her maid of honor. She was a retired nurse. I did a little digging into her past. She was an army nurse in Korea. She was involved in some kind of medical research for the army after the war. It was classified. I couldn't get any more information."

Everyone nodded. Beau put a question mark by her name. "Anyone else?" He asked. Brockman raised his hand as he spoke. "Yeah, we all tend to go for the obvious and over look the not so obvious. You remember Joseph McGinney, the security guard murdered at the old house?" Everyone nodded, "Well, I interviewed Mrs. McGinney. She happens to be a pharmacist. And, if my memory serves me correct, she has oleander growing in her yard. Now, if anyone would have first hand knowledge of poisons, and how to process oleander, she would." The task force looked stunned. Jack Bellamy buried his face in his hands and said nothing.

"We're forgetting something," Singletary interjected. "Remember we have those nice folks from Seattle that Delongpre was blackmailing. Any one of them might want to get even. I believe Sarah Smith was the wife of a doctor, right?" She paused, looking up and down the table for a reaction,

"Then there is Miss Boobs, Carla Dawn who lost her daughter then got left high and dry, not to mention the priest who will probably be out on the street in a few days for his Fetish Club membership. I think any one of these people could have a strong enough motive to put that poor bastard out of his misery." Everyone was surprised. Usually Singletary didn't have much to say, but here she was barking out her ideas. Beau smiled. He was proud of her. Beau looked at Dr. Mudd. "Is there any likelihood that he could have been poisoned while he was in jail?"

"That's not likely," Mudd answered assuredly.

"If they were going to poison his food there would be no reason to sweeten the poison. They would have diluted it with something else. No, the poison was meant to go into the candy. In fact, we found candies that had been injected two or three times."

"It was lucky no one else ate any candy," Jack added shaking his head.

"One candy would have made you sick as hell but probably wouldn't have killed you. But over the weeks that's a different story," Mudd commented.

"Our killer, or killers, knew that," Sally added, looking away as if in deep thought.

"You think there was more that one person involved in his death?" Beau asked, looking at Sally who seemed almost trance-like.

"Okay, we have motive. Now lets look at opportunity. Has anyone looked at the courtroom security tapes?"

"Just a minute," Bradley snapped, then retrieved a large cardboard box from the adjacent table full of video tapes. "If you've got a few days we can probably get through all of them." He assured Beau with a stifling laugh.

"How about the bomb scare? That could have been a distraction to put the poison in the bowl?" Mitchell chimed in quickly.

"I thought of that," Jack answered. "The courtroom tapes continued to run while the room was empty. I took a look at them. No one came near the bowl."

"Could the tape have been altered?" Coates asked.

"No, we've had this tape in the lab to see if there were any alterations, erasures, or record overs'. They are all clean," Jack assured.

Beau rubbed his eyebrows in deep thought. He continued to rub his eyes as he spoke, "That leaves us with one other option. Where was the candy bowl before the court convened?"

There was silence around the table. Heads turned waiting for some one to speak.

"As I remember," Coates muttered, taking a deep breath, "I think the Bailiff brought it in when the prisoner was seated."

Beau leaned forward in his chair, "I believe it's time we had a conversation with the Bailiff."

It took over two hours before the Court Bailiff and the Chief of Courthouse Security could be summoned and respond to the request of the investigation team. The Bailiff, Jim Butterfield was a twenty year veteran of the force. He was a big black man six foot six inches tall, 285 pounds. He was a formidable looking man with a barrel chest, massive arms with meat hook hands. Yet with all his outward appearance he was a kind, gentle man. Kevin Johnson, on the other hand was small, lean, nervous, and gave the impression of a used car salesman. Standing next to Big Jim he looked like one of the seven dwarfs.

Beau offered them coffee, then sat them at one end of the conference table. Everyone sat in silence waiting for Beau to start the questioning. Kevin twitched nervously, patting his coffee cup with his index finger. Before Beau could ask his first question, Kevin snapped bluntly, "Look, we went by the book. You guys have to remember this is the first time we've every had a situation like this. Beau, you know the problems we've had with the media, and all the other crap. We worked all this out with Wexford. He approved the ops plan."

"Hold it!" Beau exclaimed knowingly, "No one here is pointing fingers. That's not what this is all about."

"Kevin sat back relieved as he sipped his coffee. Big Jim remained calm waiting for what Beau had to say.

"Right now we have about about a half a dozen suspects that all had motives to put this guy out of his misery. We also know that he was poisoned. We know what kind of poison was used," Beau paused, making sure his words were getting through especially to Kevin who was constantly fidgeting with his coffee cup.

"We also know that the poison was in the bowl of candy that the defendant was eating in the courtroom"

Kevin and Jim looked at each other surprised.

"What we don't know," Beau speculated, "Is how the poison got into the candy."

Jim interrupted defensively, "Look, I checked that bowl every day. I even counted the candy bars to sure that no new candy was put in unless I put it there."

Beau tossed Jim the candy bar given to him by Dr. Mudd.

"Take a look at the back of the candy wrapper," Beau commanded. Jim and Kevin both examined the candy bar and saw nothing.

"What?" Kevin inquired quickly. "What are we looking for?"

"Look again." Beau demanded.

Big Jim held the candy up to the light, turning it left and right.

"Shit!" He shouted, then handed the bar to Kevin who also held it up taking a closer look.

"Yeah, the poison was injected into the candy through the wrapper using a syringe." Beau prompted glaringly.

"Fuck!" Kevin shouted contemptuously. "How in the hell are we going to catch something like that?" Kevin asked defensively. "Look, we took every conceivable precaution. Hell, we were geared for someone to come in there and blow him away. We weren't ready for this kind of shit. If you ask me, the judge should have never let him have the candy in the first place."

"That's not what this talk is all about," Jack injected, "What we need to find out is how the poison got in there in the first place?"

Big Jim who was usually quiet, spoke, "Well you've got about 300 people in that room who had access to that bowl."

"No, that's not true," Beau stated emphatically, exhaling a sigh. "We've looked at all the courtroom tapes. No one came close to that bowl except Barbara Starkey, and she had no motive. Even when the court was cleared for the bomb threat, no one came close to that bowl. The only people that handled that bowl were you two, and possible one of your staff." The two men looked at each other searching for an answer.

"Hey, don't look at us," Kevin objected angrily. "Like the pretty counselor, we have no motive. I didn't give a shit one way or the other about this guy."

"We know that," Beau responded assuringly, "What we don't know is, what you did with that bowl, and who other than yourselves, had access to it?"

Kevin's twitching stopped as he and Big Jim thought back over each day of the trial. Big Jim spoke first, "Let's see, two guards from the transportation unit were on standby. When the judge adjourns, they enter and escort the prisoner out, and he returns to the hospital. Lets see, then I do a scan of the room. I look for bugs."

"Bugs?" Coates questioned.

"Yeah, bugs. I believe some time ago one of the networks tried to bug a courtroom, even the judge's chambers. They wanted in on his sidebars, and anything else that went on outside the court. They put a bug on the witness stand." The Bailiff paused, "Then I check to make sure no suspicious packages are left in the room. After that, the room is secured, and a security guard is on duty all night. No one is allowed in without written authority or is on the access list."

"What happens to the candy bowl?" Sally asked quickly.

"Then I take it personally to the courthouse Security Ops Room," Big Jim answered, recalling his daily activities.

"The Ops Room is open 24 hours a day, and the bowl is never out of the sight of the duty officer." Kevin assured defensively.

"That's it," Sally muttered thoughtfully, "That's the weak link. Whatever happened to the candy happened while it was in the Ops Room. It happened right under your nose while everyone was watching."

"Bullshit!" Kevin responded defensively.

"There is one way to find out," Big Jim announced taking a deep breath. Everyone focused on the Bailiff as he continued. "All we have to do is look at the Security tape. It will tell us if anyone came near that bowl. It sat right on the duty officer's desk."

"You wouldn't happen to know which one of these tapes happens to be the one of the security room would you?" Brockman asked, as he fumbled his way through the cardboard box full of tapes.

"Yeah, I believe it's number 114 or 115," Kevin replied knowingly.

"Here it is," Brockman held up the tape marked 114. He loaded the tape into the VCR, then booted the computer. The computer program software was specially designed for the police. It was called "Image Express". This software could capture any image on the TV and make a digital image copy of it immediately. It was only a matter of minutes before the tape was up and running. As luck would have it the bowl was clearly visible on the duty officers desk. The team moved their chairs around the TV and watched. The tape displayed the local time in the upper right corner of the picture. The duty officer sat alone reading a magazine. The time read 10:00 p.m. No one had entered the room in the past thirty minutes.

"Lets fast forward," Beau ordered listlessly. Brockman pressed the fast forward button and the taped jumped. Everything moved in quick time until the ops room opened and several people entered.

"Stop!" Beau demanded. The tape resumed its normal speed. "Back up," He commanded. Brockman backed the tape to the point where the front door first opened, then resumed at normal speed. Four elderly ladies entered the ops room carrying trays of coffee, sweet rolls, paper plates, paper cups, small breakfast sandwiches, fresh fruit, and began setting up a table in the ops room.

"What's that?" Beau asked glaringly, "Stop the tape," he ordered angrily, "Back it up." Brockman backed the tape up then let it run forward one frame at a time.

"What the hell is that?" he questioned bluntly.

"Well, we had the ladies come in, in the morning just before shift change. It was a breakfast snack. These guys had been putting in 12 hour shifts and hadn't time to grab a bite. I thought it was nice of the ladies to think of us," Kevin said defensively, "But no one touched the candy," Kevin added guardedly.

"We'll see," Beau commented as Brockman ran the footage one frame at a time. Each frame saw the women layout the table carefully. "Hold it," Beau demanded. "Take a look," Everyone squinted noting carefully the position of everyone in the room. They could see one lady giving the duty officer a cup of coffee, distracting him from the bowl while another lady, with her back to the camera, hid the bowl from plain view. "That's it," Beau exclaimed, "The duty officer doesn't know jack shit about what's going on. That's when they did it."

As the lady in front of the bowl turned around, Beau shouted, "Freeze it. Copy it," Everyone waited for the digital image to appear on the computer screen. There she was, a kindly old lady in her 70's with white hair, granny glasses and a flowered straw hat."

"Expand it," Beau ordered softly.

The picture was expanded. With a few more manipulations the team had a clear picture.

"Print it," Beau ordered.

Jack grabbed the photo from the inkjet printer. In the upper right hand corner of the photo was the date and time.

"That was the first day of the trial," Jack advised.

"Okay, lets forward to the next day, same time." Brockman complied. It took about 30 seconds when the same scene was played again. This time the same ladies entered the room and began to set up the breakfast table, however, this time another lady stood with her back to the camera obscuring the bowl. As the lady turned around they froze the frame only to see a totally different face. This lady wore a flowered print dress. She was in her late 60's and had white hair with a blue tint to it. Again, the enhanced photo revealed a kindly face with a happy smile. She looked like anyone's grandmother.

On the tape for the third day the same scene was played again, at the same time, with the same scenario. However, the lady that turned away from the bowl, Beau and Sally recognized as Henrietta Wentworth. On the fourth day the woman in front of the bowl was Mildred Potts. That same scenario was repeated for eight days with a different lady standing in front of the bowl before it started all over again with the lady they had seen on the first day.

The Gray Lady Task Force had eight enlarged photos of little old ladies that had access to the candy bowl while the Ops Duty Officer was distracted. The question was, which one put in the poison in the candy?

"I think if you'll look at the whole tape you'll see we also had media folks in there asking stupid questions. Most of the time they were just in complaining," Kevin added.

"I understand," Beau replied, "However, the poison had to be applied to the candy over a long period of time. The syringe was mainly plastic, small, could be carried in someone's purse, or under a plate of doughnuts. This group of ladies were the only ones who were regular visitors to the ops room."

"Come on," Coates said shaking her head, "You don't believe these little old ladies could kill anyone do you?"

"Hey, Lizzy Borden, chopped her poppa up when she was a little old lady," Brockman quipped, winking at Singletary.

Sally spread eight enlarged, digitally enhanced photos on the table. The team hovered over the photos as Sally spoke, "We have eight old ladies who blocked the view of the bowl while the duty officer was distracted. Now, we know who three of them are," Sally pointed with her finger to each photo as she spoke, "We have Norma Pierce who may or may not have a motive. At this point I'm not sure. Then we have Henrietta Wentworth, who was one of the intended victims. But she doesn't seem like the type to take revenge. Then we have Mildred Potts who does have a motive. The rest of the ladies I have no idea who they are."

The team gazed in silence at the enlarged photos laying in front of them.

"I don't know," Singletary commented casually, "But one of them looks familiar to me."

"Me too," Sally added, "Was she in court?"

"No," Singletary said thoughtfully, "No, it was someplace else."

"Was it this one?" Beau asked pointing to a photo of a slightly younger woman with salt and pepper gray hair and a mole on her left cheek.

"Yeah," Sally replied.

"Me too," Singletary confirmed.

"I know. We met her at our reception," Beau confirmed.

"Of course," Sally exclaimed, "I shook hands with her."

"Oh ho," Kevin gasped, taking a deep breath as he resumed tapping his coffee cup. "The press is going to have a field day with this. I can see the headlines now, 'Police Lieutenant in murder plot of defendant.'"

"Knock it off," Jack sneered.

"Well, I think it might be time to have a long talk with Josey," Beau nodded, looking at Sally. "Now, I want everyone to get copies of these photos. I want you to run IDs on the rest of these photos. Jack, I want you and Coates to call in Potts, Wentworth and Pierce for questioning. I want you to work in teams. No hard balling these ladies. Go by the book, Okay? Now you two," Beau pointed his pencil at Kevin and Big Jim. "If any of this gets to the press I'm holding the both of you responsible. You got that?" The two men nodded.

"Okay, lets' get with it," Beau ordered, and the meeting was abruptly adjourned.

After calling Josey, Beau and Sally made a fast trip to Falconbriar. The tone of Beau's voice had Josey concerned as she busied herself in the kitchen. Josey wiped her hands on her apron, quickly untied the garment, folding it over the kitchen chair as she heard Beau bring the car to quick stop in front of the old house.

Beau and Sally were already on the porch before she could exit the kitchen.

"Mom," Beau called out.

"I'm in here," Josey answered.

The kitchen swinging door almost knocked Josey down as Beau and Sally pushed their way in.

"What do you know about this?" Beau demanded harshly throwing the enlarged photos on the kitchen table.

"What?" Josey replied surprised by Beau's blunt demeanor.

"Do you know any of these ladies?" Beau demanded.

Josey examined the photos, "Just a minute I need my glasses." Josey removed her glasses from her pocket, then bent over the photos and examined them closely. "I sure do, and so do you." Josey said knowingly.

"What do you mean?" He asked, slightly confused.

"They were at your baptism, and they were there when you were confirmed," Josey answered softly with a smile, "Except this one," Josey pointed and Norma Pierce, "She's new."

Beau and Sally looked at Josey totally confused.

"What do you mean, new?" Sally asked tenderly not wanting to alarm Josey.

"Beau, don't you remember?" Josey asked casually.

"No," He answered, shrugging his shoulders.

"This is the Charleston Garden Club." Josey announced as though she was looking through an old family photo album.

"You know I sponsor their annual flower show. This lady," Josey pointed to Norma Pierce, "She's a new member."

Beau was dumbfounded. He shook his head in disbelief as he sat down. "I'm sorry, I forgot." He laid the photos in a single line. "Now, refresh my memory. Who is this?" He asked pointing at one of the photos.

"That is Grace Billingsley," Josey answered happily.

"And this?"

"That is Mildred Dunbar, you know the Dunbars. You and Spoony went to school together."

"And this?"

That is Courtney Calhoun, she provided all the flowers for your wedding. Remember?"

"And this?"

That is Martha McGrady. Her husband, God rest his soul, was Mayor a long time ago."

"And this?"

That's Celia McGowan, she's the city's Chief Librarian.

Beau folded his arms on the table and buried his head. Sally started to laugh. Beau just laid there shaking his head in disbelief.

"What's wrong?" Josey asked, totally confused. Not knowing whether to laugh or not. Sally sat down next to Beau. "We believe that these ladies killed the man on trial," Sally said compassionately.

"Oh no. That's impossible. These ladies are primarily responsible for all the beautiful flowers that you see around our town. I know Mildred, she doesn't even use bug spray in her garden. She couldn't kill a bug. She actually buys Lady Bugs to eat her white flies," Josey shook her head in disbelief, "No, these ladies are not capable of this sort of thing."

"Let me ask you something," Sally said softly, "Were Molly Philburn and Amanda Hollingsworth members of the Garden Club?"

Josey's face turned white. She put her hand over her mouth. Sally waited for her answer. She knew from her reaction what the answer would be. She waited patiently.

"Yes," Josey muttered gravely.

"So, that's the connection," Beau responded sadly.

"I can't believe that the Garden Club of Charleston, these nice old ladies. I mean, they come from the old families. Here they are, dropping poison into candy bars? These people have been a part of my life. I grew up with their kids. They've been in our house. They're friends of my mom's, Beau said shaking his head.

"Well, we only know they've had opportunity," Sally acknowledged thoughtfully. "The tapes only show them in front of the bowl. It doesn't show any of them actually putting the poison in the candy. We don't have the poison, we don't have the syringe, we don't have finger prints on the bowl." Sally summarized trying to comfort Josey and Beau.

"I think it's time we got these ladies together." Beau announced sadly.

"What can you tell us about these ladies?" Sally asked curiously, "Could any of them have knowledge about poison?"

Josey replied thoughtfully, "They all could. We have plenty of rat poison around the club house. So any of us could have access to that sort of stuff. We all have keys. My keys are up there on the wall," Josey pointed to a large brass ring containing a collection of keys of every description.

"Lets see," Josey continued, "Courtney is married to a doctor. However, he's retired now. But he did write a book. I think I have a copy in the library. She could have knowledge of poison. Then I believe Mildred Potts was a nurse. The Dunbars, I believe they own a cosmetic company, or they did own one. I think they made soap or something. Then there is Celia McGowan, she still works at the library. She would have access to any amount of books in the library. There are plenty of books on poisons I would imagine. I don't know about Martha. She's our leading expert on gardening."

"How do you mean?" Sally asked.

"I believe she is a botanist. If you want to know anything about plants just ask Martha."

"Would she know anything about poisonous plants?" Sally inquired.

"Oh my yes. She has this lecture she gives every year about poison ivy, and other dangerous plants to keep your kids away from. She goes around to the schools and gives her talks."

"Does she know anything about oleander?" Beau asked pointedly.

"Oh my, we all do. I even caught you with a handful of that stuff when you were a little tike."

"I bet he was a handful," Sally quipped with a chuckle.

"Oh he was hell on wheels," Josey said laughing, "I remember the time…"

"Okay you two," Beau interrupted, "can we get on with it? What about oleander?" He inquired not knowing where any of this would take him.

"We've got oleander all over this city. Even the state for that matter. I believe about ten years ago the club sponsored the planting of about 1,500 oleanders around the city,'" Josey answered proudly.

"Oh that's nice, just about everyone has oleander in their back yard," Beau scowled.

"What's wrong with him?" Josey asked. Sally laughed softly, "Oleander was the poison used to kill the defendant." Sally patted Beau on the shoulders.

"Oh I see," Josey acknowledged sadly, "Well, you have a lot of people to pick from," Josey remarked trying to cheer him up.

"Poor Baby," Sally mocked, kissing him on the forehead.

"Have I covered everyone?" Beau inquired tonelessly.

Josey thought for a minute before answering, "Then there's Grace Billingsley. I forgot what she did," Josey tapped the side of her cheek remembering, "Oh yes, I believe in her younger days she was a chemist. Something else, you know that book that Courtney's husband wrote? I believe Grace helped him. She got a mention in his book. Wait a minute, I'll get it for you," Josey pushed through the kitchen door and was gone.

"What are we going to do?" Beau asked, throwing up his hands in surrender. "We have some Garden Club, with little old ladies going around poisoning people. It reminds me of that movie, 'Arsenic and Old Lace'. You know, where these nice little old ladies go around poisoning everyone."

"Not people," Sally answered softly, "A killer. Don't you think it's ironic. Here was a killer, raping and murdering little old ladies and it's little old ladies that did him in. I believe in the law, due process, and all that sort of stuff, but I wonder if someone upstairs may have ordained his demise?"

"Are you telling me they may have committed the perfect crime?" Beau questioned with small chuckle.

"No, but they may have figured out a way to get around the law." She answered with a sly smile.

Josey returned with a frown on her face.

"What?" Beau asked curiously.

"You're not going to like this," Josey answered holding the book behind her back.

"Try me." He replied taking a deep breath.

"'The AMA Handbook of Poisonous Plants' and Grace was one of the researchers. She ran some of the lab experiments," Josey said shyly, handing him the book. Beau leafed through the book quickly, stopping on one particular page. He looked up at Sally, then handed her the book. The chapter on Common Toxic Plants of the South had been high lighted with yellow marker. Photos, and paragraphs on yellow oleander had been marked.

"Don't look at me," Josey demanded, "We had over 500 people here the other day. Any one of them could have marked the book."

"Over 900," Beau corrected. "Well, it's back to the old drawing board," He quipped.

"Not quite," Sally replied thoughtfully, "Let's see what the ladies have to say."

Beau and Sally briefed the team on the Garden Club connection and provided names and addresses of all the women involved. The ladies were politely invited to come down to Police Headquarters in order to assist the police in their investigation. Beau had isolated one second floor wing of Police Headquarters. He wanted no prying eyes or ears. A long table had been set up in the center of the line up room. Sally had Murph provided a complete tea service with scones and an assortment of delicious pastries. The ladies of the Garden Club were more than happy to help the police in any way they could. They felt it was their civic duty. There wasn't one dissenting vote or objection to coming down to police headquarters. That was hardly the actions of a guilty mind, Beau thought to himself.

The team sat behind the two-way mirror and observed the ladies at the table. Mildred Potts and Grace Billingsley rummaged through their purses and compared lipsticks, while Mrs. Dunbar, continued to knit. Mildred made the point that most cosmetics sold today women don't need. It's just for their vanity. Henrietta casually read a magazine, while Martha McGrady displayed photos of her new grandchild to Courtney Calhoun, Norma Pierce and Celia McGowan.

Not one of these ladies seem to have a care in the world. It was as if this was just another ordinary day in their ordinary lives.

"What do you think?" Beau asked the team as they observed the Garden Club from behind the looking glass.

"Either they are all very good actors, or we are witnessing the first documented case of group Alzheimer's disease," Jack said jokingly.

"Is senility a communicable disease?" Coates inquired stifling a laugh.

"If you were looking for stress, I don't see any." Mitchell commented thoughtfully.

"Stress? Coates asked rhetorically, "Stress is when you wake up screaming and you realized that you weren't asleep. I don't think any of these ladies has lost a wink of sleep in the past twenty years." Coates said with a low chuckle.

"What do you think Miss psychologist?" Brockman inquired looking at Sally.

"It's not Miss," Coates corrected quickly.

"Excuse me. Mrs. Gasteneau, What do you think?" Brockman asked again.

Sally sat quietly resting her chin in the palm of her hand. "It's a matter of degree," She remarked calmly. "Can you remember the last time you squashed a bug?"

Brockman shrugged his shoulders, "No."

"That's it. If the killer had no more significance to them than a bug, you'd have no guilt. It's just a fact of life. You squash bugs because they eat flowers."

"So, you're saying they regard the defendant as a bug?" Singletary questioned.

"Something like that," Sally responded calmly.

"All right folks," Beau announced, turning in his seat to face the team. "Lets see what happens when we separate them. We'll work in separate rooms. Sally and I will take Mildred Dunbar. Jack, you take Celia McGowan, Coates has Courtney Calhoun, Singletary, you take Martha McGrady, Brockman, you've got Grace Billingsley, Mitchell, take Mildred Potts, and we'll save Norma Pierce for later, and Bradley, you take Henrietta Wentworth. I want you one on one in separate rooms. Treat them like your long lost mom. I want recordings. Make sure you get consent. Now, don't go and scare the hell out of them. They are not suspects. They are assisting in an investigation. Be kind, don't push and don't be in a hurry.

"I hated my mother," Bradley muttered with a chuckle. Everyone tossed the paper cups at him as they left the observation room.

Mildred Dunbar sat alone in the interrogation room. A small table with four chairs was centered in the small room.

Mildred hummed to herself as she busily knitted away at a pair of wool socks. Her face lit up with a broad smile when Beau and Sally entered. She stood, and held out her arms waiting for a hug from Beau as if he was some long lost child. Beau kissed her on the forehead, "How are you, sweetheart? He asked lovingly.

"I'm fine. How are you two lovers?" Mildred questioned, holding open her arms embracing Sally. "I must say you looked like an angel at the wedding, and you've got the sweetest child.

"Did you talk to Katie?" Sally inquired politely.

"Oh yes. We had a wonderful talk. She told me all about her pony, and the animals she gets to play with. But Best of all, she talked about her new dad. That child loves you," Mildred acknowledged, pushing her finger against Beau's chest. "So you be good to her," She ordered.

"I will. She's a wonderful little girl. I am very proud of her," Beau replied as he seated Mildred in her chair. The kindly old lady sat quietly for a few seconds as Beau thought about how he could tactfully approach her involvement in the murder of the defendant.

"Mildred," Beau said softly, "You know we are trying to solve the murder of the defendant." Beau wasn't sure if he was getting through to Mildred, "You know, the man on trial? The one who murdered those old ladies?"

"Oh, wasn't that terrible. I guess things have a way of working themselves out." The old lady resumed her knitting.

"Mildred. You wouldn't happen to know anything about that would you? I mean, anything that maybe someone said, or told you?"

The old lady nodded, "No, I don't think so," She answered, flipping the needles faster, as she resumed her knitting. "Do you mind if we record this interview? We are trying to get all the facts together so we can make a report." Mildred nodded approval before Sally resumed her questioning.

"Mildred?" Sally asked politely, "did you know Molly Philburn or Amanda Hollingsworth?"

"Oh my yes. It was a shame what that man did to them," Mildred knitted faster as the questions became more pointed.

"Mildred," Sally continued slowly, "We've found out that his candy was poisoned."

Although Mildred remained calm her body language told Sally that she was becoming nervous.

"Mildred, we've also found out that the candy was poisoned using a syringe. They used it to inject the poison into the candy," Beau stated casually. Mildred's knitting increased in speed, and she would not make eye contact. It reminded Sally of a little child being called to the principle's office having been caught in a lie.

"You wouldn't know anything about that would you?" Sally asked, bending forward trying to get Mildred to look her in the face. The old lady continued to avoid eye contact choosing to concentrate on the knitting which had increased in speed again.

"Mildred?" Beau asked softly as he turned on the TV. He had pre-loaded the tape and ran it to the point where Mildred enters the Operations room and moves to the candy bowl with her back to the camera. "I want you to help us. Would you watch this tape with us?"

The nervous old lady nodded affirmatively. Beau ran the tape in slow motion displaying Mildred entering the Ops room with the other ladies, then proceeding to the bowl of candy while they distracted the duty officer. Her face turned cold white. Her busy knitting stopped in mid stitch. Her expression changed to one of despair as she watched.

Beau stopped the tape. He held Mildred's hands tenderly, and looked into her teary eyes.

"Did you poison the defendant?"

The little old lady dropped her knitting, and sat back sadly in her chair. She sat with a bowed head as if in prayer. Then she looked squarely at the two detectives who she loved dearly. Then looking at Beau, she asked, "You two made a vow to God to love honor and cherish each other for the rest of your life. All that means nothing unless you believe in God. Do you believe in God? I mean really believe. Do you believe in the hereafter? Do you believe that we will all be judged in time by the all mighty?" Do you truly believe in God?" She emphasized her last question with a soft inflection in her voice.

Beau was startled by the question. "Yes I do, we both do," He replied. Sally acknowledged Beau's statement by nodding approval.

"If God is good, by his very nature there must be evil."

Beau wondered where she was going with this logic. "Yes," He acknowledged.

"That's right," the old lady said, "Goodness is a choice between good and evil. Without evil goodness cannot exist. God cannot exist." Both detectives nodded in agreement.

"We know our Lord Jesus Christ embodies goodness and we also know that Satan, the Devil embodies evil or badness," The old lady happily continued, "I believe that God has, from time to time, given us angels to guide and help us. Molly Philburn and Amanda Hollingsworth were in every sense of the word angels. They gave only love and understanding to whomever they met. Myself included. Only God or Satan can take an angel while she's in mortal form."

Beau and Sally sat motionless listening to this kind old lady's explanation of why she killed the defendant.

"God guided you," Mildred touched Beau's hand tenderly, then she touched Sally's, "God gave you two the strength, the courage to fight Satan. He protected you in your hour of need. God sent both of you to do battle with Satan. That's why your love is so strong. That's why your little girl loves Beau so much. God meant for you both to do battle with Satan and win."

Beau touched Mildred's shoulder lovingly. "What are you trying to tell us sweetheart?"

Mildred paused, then said bluntly, "That's not a human being you had on trial. That was Satan himself. That poor miserable man that sat in the courtroom was possessed. Satan had taken his sole. He was already dead. Only some evil thing was in that courtroom."

The two detectives sat quietly and looked at the old lady.

"I'm not crazy," She said angrily, "There is no court in this world who can pass judgment on the Devil. Only the highest court. God's court. He will stand in judgment of the all mighty himself. If you truly believe in the hereafter you know I didn't kill him. I just sent him on his way."

"So you did put the poison in the candy?" Sally asked sadly.

"Yes. I did. It was my duty before he had a chance to destroy us." Mildred Dunbar put up her knitting and folded her hands. "I am not crazy. God didn't speak to me, or an angel in blasting light didn't order me, so there." Mildred sat back in her chair defiantly.

"We understand," Beau replied compassionately.

"What kind of poison did you use?" Sally asked calmly. Mildred displayed a blank expression as she thought. "Rat Poison!" She exclaimed, "We have plenty around the clubhouse. Just a little and a little water and you're in business." Mildred was relieved, almost happy about finally revealing her secret.

Beau sat back in his chair and smiled at Sally. She could tell that he was relieved to find out that Mildred didn't do it.

"You're not off the hook yet," Sally said, looking at Beau.

"What?" He responded.

"Would you excuse us?" Sally asked Mildred then nodding at Beau to follow her.

The two detectives sat in the observation room and watched Mildred resume her knitting.

"What did you have on your mind?" He questioned curiously.

"We know she injected poison into the candy. She's admitted that." Sally took a deep breath before continuing. "But she didn't know what the poison was. That means someone else was involved. Someone gave her the syringe and a vile of poison."

"I agree. You don't think she's confessing just to protect someone else do you?" Beau asked, as they both gazed at the kindly old lady knitting in the two-way mirror.

"No." Sally shook her head gently, "she knew too much. Also, her statement wasn't rehearsed. The other thing, was, that she believed what she was doing was right."

"Back to the bug theory, right?" He responded. Sally nodded.

"Okay," Beau said standing up. "Lets see what else we can find out."

Sally touched his hand, then looked into his eyes for some sort of answer. She knew that these women had always been a part of his life and now he was faced with the possibility of having to put them in jail for murder.

"What are your going to do," she asked?

Beau stood stoically, as Sally continued, "I mean you care for this woman. So do I. She's been a part of your life, part of your family for as long as you can remember."

He gave Sally a reassuring hug. "God, I wish I knew. Let's get to the bottom of this, then we can decide."

The two detective re-entered the small room. That same broad smile was there again as Sally and Beau sat down. Beau rested his chin in the palm of his hand and jotted notes on his legal pad as he thought.

"Mildred?" Beau looked sadly at Mildred. He hated what he was about to say but it had to be said. "You know what you did was a crime."

"Not in the eyes of the Lord." She replied happily.

"I know, but I'm going to have to have this confession typed and entered into the record. Will you sign it?"

"Of course," Mildred answered touching Beau's arm lightly. "I know you're only doing your job."

The two detectives shook their heads sadly. Sally interrupted Beau before he could speak.

"Mildred, before we can type the report we have to clear up a few items."

The old lady smiled politely, "Of course."

"Now, you said that the poison used was rat poison. Right? Mildred nodded affirmatively.

"Mildred," Sally said with a slight firmness in her voice. "It wasn't rat poison that killed the defendant. You lied to us. I know you don't lie except for a good reason. Why did you lie to us? Are you protecting someone?"

Mildred froze. She couldn't answer. A look of confusion covered her face. She stuttered, but no answer was forthcoming.

"We know someone gave you the poison and the syringe. Please, tell us who gave those items to you." Sally pleaded gently, touching her hand giving her reassurance. Tears welled up on the old lady's face.

"I don't know. Believe me, I don't know." She answered sadly.

The two detectives sat quietly in their chairs waiting patiently for Mildred to calm herself.

"Let's take it from the beginning," Beau said reassuringly. "Just tell us how all this came about."

Mildred regained her composure. "I guess it might have started with the nice man from KXFC. Ah, what's his name? You know, that newsman?"

"Stan Rush," Beau interrupted.

"Yes, Mr. Rush. Well, you see he interviewed the ladies of the Garden Club. We were all on TV. Everyone called and said they enjoyed the interview.

"Did you tell Mr. Rush that you thought the defendant was Satan?" Sally queried quickly.

"No, Martha McGrady said that. But we all agreed with her."

"I see," Beau replied in acknowledgment. "So what happened after that?"

"I guess it was about three days before the trial was about to start. We all got a message that said that it was God's will he stand trial before the highest court. It said that we should step in and do the Lord's work and send him to stand trial before the all mighty."

"Then what did you do?" Sally inquired, intrigued by her story.

"Martha called a meeting of the Garden Club to discuss our messages. We voted, and all agreed to follow the instructions."

"What kind of instructions?" Sally asked.

"The message told us that a syringe, and a vile of poison would be placed inside our car on the day it was our turn. The selected lady would wear a flowered dress or hat. It told us to distract the officer to allow the other one to inject the candy."

"What kind of message was it?" Beau asked casually trying to keep Mildred's train of thought continuing until the whole story came out.

"It was on a brown paper shopping bag. The words were clipped out of the news paper, and pasted, you know, like in the movies." The detectives nodded.

"Do you have one of these messages?" Sally inquired.

"No, the message said I was suppose to burn it after I was done." Mildred replied as though she was relaying a piece of gossip.

"How about the vile, or syringe?" Beau inquired eagerly.

"No, the note told us to put them in the trash behind the courthouse," Mildred sat back relieved that all the truth had finally came out. Beau buried his face in the palm of his hands, closed his eyes as he spoke, "Sweetheart, let's see if I understand everything. After your interview on TV. Someone, you don't know, sent you an untraceable message on a brown paper bag. The note told you that on a certain day, you would inject the candy with poison that magically appeared in your car. Am I right so far?"

Mildred nodded happily oblivious to the consequences of what she had said.

"Now, you had no idea if what you injected into the candy was poison or not? You just assumed it was. Right?"

Mildred nodded again.

"Then you were told to throw the vile and the syringe in the trash bin behind the courthouse, right?"

"Right," Mildred replied softly.

"Did all you ladies follow the same procedure?" He asked?

"Of course, we voted on it." Mildred affirmed casually.

Sally interrupted Beau's questioning, "A single dose would not of killed the defendant, so we don't know for sure who provided the lethal dose. In fact, we don't even know if the vile she used even had poison in it?"

"And we have no way of proving it," Beau added.

"The trash bin would not contain the needle either. Who ever planned this would be waiting to retrieve the evidence," Sally commented.

The two detectives stood up. Beau kissed Mildred on the forehead, "Would you wait here while we get all this typed for your signature?"

Mildred nodded politely and without a care in the world resumed her knitting. Sally gave the kindly old lady one more glance as she shut the door.

It was 11:30 p.m. The Gray Lady Task Force sat quietly in the conference room and listened to the final interview tape. Jack pushed the stop button on the tape player as they pondered what they had just heard. Beau buried in face in the palms of his hands and propped his elbows on the table. The detectives eyed each other in silence waiting for some comment that made sense. Sally laid her arms on the table as she lazily thumbed through eight typed and signed confessions by the entire Charleston Garden Club's presiding Community Citizens Committee.

"This reminds me of something right out of Agatha Christy. It would make a great movie," Coates commented, stretching back in her chair with a big gaping yawn.

Singletary sat erect, eyes closed, as if in prayer asking for divine guidance. "I can't believe any of this," She exclaimed, shaking her head. Martha McGrady was my Sunday School teacher and she took care of my baby brother for God's sake. Here I am looking at a confession of murder?"

"The confessions, the tapes, they all tell the same story. So, who are you going to believe?" Brockman inquired.

"No they don't." Jack Bellamy added. "If they did, I'd be suspicious. They all tell similar stories but not identical."

"If they did I'd be suspect too," Sally confirmed. "What they were telling was the truth."

"I have a question," Beau asked, lifting his head from the palm of his hands. "They all believed they were doing God's work, right?" Everyone nodded in agreement.

"Could one of them been responsible for the master minding the whole thing? I mean, writing the letter, knowing how the ladies would react. It had to be someone personally familiar with the Garden Club in some way. The letter had to push the right buttons to set them off. Did anyone give you the impression that they might be in charge of the whole operation?"

The detectives pondered Beau's question. Singletary rapped her fingernails on the table creating a rhythmic chatter. Coates made notes to herself on a note pad then erased them while Jack tapped his pencil on the long table. No statements were immediately forthcoming. Beau waited for an answer. "Anything? Anything that might be indicative of motive or opportunity."

Brockman held his coffee cup in mid air as he remembered, "Grace said something. Lets see, oh yes, when we got on this Devil thing, I asked her if she really believed in the Devil. She said, yes for three obvious reasons. One, the Bible plainly says he exist. I see evil work everywhere, and because great scholars have all recognized his existence."

"What's that got to do with anything?" Coates quipped sarcastically.

"It's not what she said, it was how she said it. She sounded fanatical. That could be the mind of an avenging angel? Or, at least someone who thinks she's on a mission from God."

"God! Is everyone going crazy around here?" Singletary questioned.

Jack Bellamy picked up the transcript of his interview with Martha McGrady and quickly scanned to page four. "If we are discussing motives or religious fanaticism, here is something in McGrady's transcript. I asked her how did she know for sure that the defendant was the Devil? She began to recite some text from someplace. I don't know from where." Jack began to read her statement a loud. "I called the Devil and he came. And with wonder his form I did closely scan. He is not ugly, and is not lame, but really a handsome and charming man. A man in the prime of life is the Devil;

obliging, a man of the world and civil; a diplomat too, well skilled in debate. He talks quite glibly of church and state. Again, I don't know where she got that quote but I am convinced she totally believed in what she was doing."

Beau put a question mark by Martha's McGrady's name.

"Well, why we are at it," Coates injected lightly, "Courtney Calhoun wasn't quite so eloquent. But, I remember her saying, 'Man is unjust, but God is just, and finally justice triumphs.' And she said it with conviction. They all seem to have the same theme. Sending him on his merry way so he can be judged." Coates turned to another page in her interview transcript. "These ladies seem to have a lot of religious hang ups. I mean they are really into this God stuff. She also said, 'the path of the just is the shining light, that shineth more and more unto the perfect day.' I looked that up. It's from the Old Testament, Proverbs 4:18."

"These gals should hook up with Billy Graham's Crusade," Brockman quipped with a chuckle.

During the discussion Sally had been scanning the transcripts of the remaining interviews. She laid several pages in front of her as she spoke. "Gentlemen, we may be barking at the moon with this kind of logic. For example, all of these ladies have quoted scriptures, or some sort of metaphysical literature for moral support. Here's one that says, 'Evil enters through the eye of the needle and spreads like an oak tree. Then there is a poem from Henrietta, 'For every evil under the sun, there is a remedy or there's none. If there is none, never mind it. If there's one try to find it.'"

"They found one didn't they." Coates joked.

Sally continued, "And here is one from Norma Pierce, 'It was handy for Satan to mislead the world, so he appointed deciples in different locations.' Norma had sympathetic feelings for little David Delongpre. Now however, she's going along with the Devil idea. I wonder what or who changed her mind? Or, could she be behind it all?"

Singletary started to speak, then changed her mind.

"What is it?" Beau asked, nodding at Singletary.

"Nothing," she responded.

"No, we need to hit every aspect of this case no matter how outlandish." Beau said glaring around the table. Singletary looked at Beau then reluctantly said, "What if they are right?"

"What do you mean, right?" Coates replied curiously.

"I mean, what if the old ladies were right. He was the Devil?"

"Ah come on!" Brockman chided sarcastically.

"Look, we all go to church," Singletary gave a caustic glare at Brockman. "Well, at least some of us do."

Brockman rolled his eyes upward and glanced at the ceiling in disgust. Brockman's antics didn't deter Singletary from telling her story.

"Some people have an unshakable, pure, and simple belief in God. If you believe in God you have to believe in the Devil. I think the old ladies have already made that perfectly clear. So I have to wonder if they have a point. Martha McGrady, God bless her soul, use to baby sit my baby brother Billy." Singletary hesitated before continuing. "What I haven't told you is that Billy is retarded. He's been that way since birth. When mom and dad passed on Martha stepped in and took care of Billy. Now, Billy thinks, no he believes, that God lives in his closet."

Brockman and Coates both snickered at Singletary's statement.

"Go ahead, snicker. He actually believes it. Billy is now thirty years old, six foot four, and weighs 230 pounds. Outward, he is an adult. He has the mental capacity of a seven year old, and that will never change. I use to listen outside his bedroom as he talked to God in his closet. He still believes that Santa fills his stockings, and that balloons are toys that angels play with, that's why they float in the air so gracefully. Now Billy has a monotonous life. He's up every morning to take the bus to work. He has a simple job at the workshop for the disabled. He puts those brass erasers on pencils. He comes home, walks the dog, then likes to have hot dogs for dinner, then off to bed where he talks to God in the closet. He gets excited and hovers over the stove waiting for the water to boil. He waits excitedly for the microwave to ding. He does the wash without complaint and on Saturday, we go to the park and have a coke. Then we watch all the people go by. We make up funny names for the people we see. We laugh, we play tag. Billy really doesn't know anything exists outside of his little world except God. He doesn't know what it means to be unhappy. He will never experience any of the problems of money or power. He doesn't care about designer jeans, or dining at the best restaurants. He recognizes everyone in the same way, as a friend. No one has ever been unkind to him. His needs have always been met. He doesn't worry from day to day that he won't have a home, won't have me, or a friend like Martha. He loves to work. He tells the truth. He believes that promises are sacred. That if you are wrong you should say so and apologize instead of arguing. He doesn't have an ego and he's not afraid to cry when he's been hurt, sorry, or angry. Most of all, he trusts God. This trust is not the result of intellectual reasoning or Biblical study. Before the eyes of the Lord, he is a child. You know something else, he sees God as his friend. God is someone he can reveal his inner most secrets." Singletary looked around the table. The detectives were captivated by Singletary's revelation.

"Now I know it's hard for you sudo-educated people to grasp my point. God to Billy is real. He is his closest friend. You know something else? When I see the scum, the depravity, the senseless killings, the mayhem, people do to each other, I begin to doubt my own faith. That's when I envy

Billy, and his simple faith in God. I often wonder if he has some divine guidance that sees beyond what I see? That's when I realize that maybe I am the one that's handicapped."

Singletary sat back in her chair in saddened thought before she continued, "Our obligations to the law, our fears, our egos, even the circumstances of this trial, this investigation, are in the real sense, our disabilities, because we all, deep down inside, reject the idea of God. Maybe, these nice old ladies like my little brother comprehend things that we can never understand. Maybe they've lived long enough to renew their belief in God. There was no malice in these ladies, only blind faith in what they were doing was right."

Everyone sat quietly around the table. Beau noticed that Singletary, who by nature was shy, was trembling, afraid that her story might have offended someone. Beau walked around the table and gave Singletary a brotherly kiss on the forehead before announcing. "Okay, lets call it a night. Now, nothing leaves this room. Not one word, not one syllable. As far as anyone is concerned these confessions do not exist. That goes for the Police Chief as well. If anyone asks you about the investigation tell them it's ongoing. Do not give them any specifics. Understood?"

Everyone nodded as Beau brought the meeting to a close.

Chapter Twenty Eight

Closure

It had taken Beau and Sally thirty minutes to get from Police Headquarters to their city apartment. They were dog tired, talked out, and confused as to what was the next step in the investigation.

Turning on the apartment light, Beau put his briefcase next to the phone desk in the short hallway leading to the living room. Sally gave her husband a small kiss on the cheek and remarked, "I remember when you first tried to get in my knickers here."

He smiled, then patted her on the butt as she walked to the bedroom. "I didn't know I was that obvious."

"Yeah, you were about as subtle as a train wreck." She quipped from the bedroom. The newlyweds laughed at how they had played games with each other in the beginning.

Beau's eye caught a glimpse at an official letter laying on the phone desk. The letterhead revealed it was from FBI Quantico.

"Agent Thornton," Beau announced lightly, waiting for a response from the bedroom, "You have an official letter from Quantico. You know, you're going to have to change you name from Thornton to Gasteneau. Wow, I wonder what it's going to be like to have an FBI agent in the family?"

Sally returned to the phone desk. She had already undressed, and stood there in her bra and bikini size panties. She was not in the least bit shy about her nudity. She opened the letter and quickly scanned its contents. Beau smiled knowing that this beautiful, loving, smart and sexy woman was his. He loved just looking at her, the way she walked, the way she smiled, the way she curled her lip when she pouted at some minor disappointment. This time she smiled and handed Beau the letter.

"It's my orders. I've been promoted. I am the Southeast District Director of Forensic Psychology for the Bureau. I am officially assigned to the Charleston office." She jumped up and straddled Beau locking her legs around his waist, putting her arms around his neck. "How about that Mr. Stud?" She joked, covering his face with quick kisses. With Sally firmly attached to his waist, Beau walked her into the bedroom and tossed her on the big bed. Sally sat up and held out the letter for him to read.

Beau sat casually on the edge of the bed, took off his shoes and socks, then took the official letter and began to read. Sally sat quietly with eager anticipation waiting for Beau to finish the final sentence. She noticed that he wasn't as excited as she was. Something was wrong.

"What?" Sally asked, holding her hand out to retrieve the letter.

"Notice, these orders were dated before we were married." He said, shaking his head in disbelief.

Sally snatched the letter away from Beau and began to reread the letter carefully.

"They lied to us," Beau reaffirmed, "The Governor didn't talk to anyone. We've been had by the D.A. and all those assholes at City Hall."

"That sonofabitch!" Sally cursed loudly. "Just a minute. I'll find out." She quickly dialed a Quantico number from the bedside phone.

A sleepy Bill Bixby, Chief of Academics and Training at Quantico, grappled for the phone in his darkened bedroom. Clicking on his bedroom light, Bixby mumbled, "Bixby here."

"Bill, wake up. It's Sally." The phone barked into his ear.

"Sally? Do you have any idea what time it is?"

"Think about it Bill. I'm in the same time zone you are. You're God Damn right I know what time it is," she shouted angrily.

"Oh no, you're pissed. I can tell," Bill responded defensively.

"No shit!" Sally yelled back.

"What's the problem? I'd really like to get back to sleep." He replied with a deep, uncaring yawn.

"Did anyone talk to you about getting me assigned down here?"

"No. Hey, I thought I was doing you a favor. I got your wedding invitation. Sorry I couldn't make it. Look, you were up for reassignment, and I thought that was what you wanted." Bill replied clarifying his actions.

"I did," her voice echoed over the phone.

"So what's the problem?" Bill challenged tersely.

"No problem. I just wanted to confirm that no one from down here talked to you, or anyone else, about my assignment."

"No, you know how it is up here. We've got a bunch of Fordham graduates in the bureau keeping our eyes on these Harvard guys in politics. I usually tell them to fuck off. So much for my education, right?" Bill laughed at himself.

"Thanks Bill. I just wanted to check."

"That's okay. By the way, you did a great job down there, and you look great on TV." Bill replied sleepily.

"Go back to sleep." Sally ordered, then hung up the phone.

The two detective sat quietly in bed. Sally could see the wheels turning inside Beau's head.

"What are you going to do?" She questioned.

"You'll see tomorrow," He answered then quickly turned out the light.

Josey Gasteneau was the Queen Mother of the Gasteneau empire which now was a multibillion dollar conglomerate that stretched around the world. Beau's grandfather made it big during World War I in the industrial manufacturing arena. He also foresaw the coming of World War II. This time, tutoring Beau's father, they expanded their investments into arms, automotive, and petroleum production. Although the objective was to make a profit, the main objective was to keep America strong by using Gasteneau money to build a strong military industrial complex. When Beau's father married Josey it was not only love but a partnership. Josey was in on every deal and was a tough negotiator.

When Beau's father died, the company looked to Josey for leadership and they were not disappointed. Josey forecast the slow down of the US post war industrial complex and before the stock market felt the change Josey had already moved the Gasteneau money into investment banking, knowing that she would invest in the expanding industrial economy of Europe, Asia and Japan. This strategy proved to be the biggest money maker for the Gasteneau empire.

In Europe the Gasteneau empire invested in everything from wine to shipbuilding. By the time the Korean War was over investing in post war economies was standard practice. The corporation had even more profitable investments in Korean and Chinese textiles.

Although Josey had retired from active management of her empire she kept close tabs on its day to day operations. Next to her bedroom at Falconbriar, Josey had her computer room. To call it a computer room was a gross understatement. It was an operations room with banks of phones programmed to reach her executives and money managers through out the world. An array of color monitors covered stock markets in every major county of the world. A large computer kept minute to minute calculations of the net worth for the total Gasteneau empire at her fingertips.

An old adage equates money with power. Josey was fast to use her power when needed, but never abused it. She was a modest unassuming woman. However, she also new that it was good for business to have the right people in the right place at the right time. She was a powerful influence in state politics. She knew monied, influential people. She could get things done, get big donations for national political campaigns. The state senators and governors all admit they wouldn't be where today were if it wasn't for Josey Gasteneau.

When Beau called her and said he wanted a meeting with the state's attorney general, the mayor, District Attorney and the Chief of Police, all Josey had to do was pick up the phone and it was done. Beau had also asked if Josey herself would attend this ten o'clock meeting. When Josey asked why, Beau said he would tell her when he got there.

It was five thirty in the morning. The new day was just beginning to announce its arrival on the eastern horizon. Sally nudged Beau awake.

"What?" He murmured, then rolling away from Sally who punched him again.

"Wake up," She demanded quietly.

"What?"

"Come on, I want you to take me for a ride."

"Now?" He asked, turning on the bedroom light.

"Now," She replied, "Lets take a shower then we have to take a trip."

Beau sat up and looked intently at her and asked, "What's on your mind?"

She stepped out of bed and stood naked in front of Beau displaying a seductive pout. "Are you coming or not?" With sensuality in every step, she walked to the bathroom and turned on the shower. The steam surrounded Sally's body giving her a warm relaxing feeling. She held her face up to the warm water letting the droplets caress her forehead. She leaned forward and put her head against the cold shower tile. She couldn't shake this feeling that had wakened her from am uneasy sleep. She had everything she'd ever wanted. She had a man she respected who loved her. Who had committed to her. A man who loved Katie. A man who would take care of her and grow old with her, and yet, she had this feeling of despair. She felt as though she had lost something precious, something she loved. She didn't know for sure what was making her think like this. Something deep inside her said that she needed closure. The killer, the demon inside her, the Devil's deciple, or whoever he was, had to be put to rest. He had to be banished from her mind. She had to cleanse herself once and for all.

The steamy shower door opened and Beau stepped in. Sally remained with her head against the tiled wall. Beau's soapy hands began to apply soap to her firm back. The mere touch of his hands on her naked body aroused her immediately. She turned quickly to her lover and kissed him passionately, again and again. They made love in the shower. This time the sex wasn't fantasy, or unbridled passion. She opened herself and gave herself to him as though it would be the last time she would ever see him again. She wanted to feel him inside her for as long as she could. Without any idea of why, she began to cry, sobbing uncontrollably, kissing Beau relentlessly.

"I love you so much. If I should loose you my life would be over." She said looking tearfully into his eyes.

"You'll never loose me," he replied softly returning her kisses. Sally with her back against the cold tiles and her legs firmly wrapped around his waist, kept his manhood deep inside her as the shower continued to rain down on the two lovers.

Beau and Sally had dressed silently, left the apartment and drove slowly in the predawn traffic.

"Where are we going?" He asked, glancing at her. Wondering what had turned her on.

"I need to get some closure," She answered looking out the window at the dark, empty streets of Charleston.

"Is that what this was all about?" He asked, not looking at her, keeping his eyes on the road. Beau knew she had this gift of second sight. In her dream she had probably seen something that troubled her. She had to get to the bottom of it. She had to face it, whatever it was.

"You saw something didn't you," He said, concentrating on his driving.

"Yeah, I did," She replied automatically, still looking into the blackness of the night.

"I want to go to Amanda Hollingsworth's house."

The words came from her mouth, but she had no idea why she had asked to return to the murder scene. Beau was well aware that when she had one of these visions, or maybe it wasn't a vision but a feeling, there was no room for discussion. He complied quickly by turning the car sharply, and headed for the old deserted mansion.

The old house stood majestically in the predawn light like a monument to the murder that had occurred many months ago. The windows had been boarded over and the flowers that adorned the once beautiful landscape had died due to neglect. The old magnolia tree that stood guard over the front of the house seemed to be the only living thing that had survived the months of neglect. It's deep roots had somehow found the water it needed to survive. The morning dew laid a carpet of tears on the brown grass in the front yard.

The estate was still closed while the house was in litigation. Beau had no trouble in picking the lock. The large foyer was dark with only a slight glow from the new dawn peeking through the windows. Beau retrieved a candle from the kitchen. He returned walking slowly to insure that the flame would remain lit. He gave the candle to Sally and watched her carefully, observing the slightest change in her expression. A thin layer of dust covered the cherry wood floors of the foyer. Cock roaches scrambled madly for the cover of darkness as these intruders interrupted their midnight meal. The large ornate cut crystal chandelier in the center of the room had become home to a host of cobwebs. Sally felt an air of sadness at the sight of all this beauty being left to rot away from the love that once cared for it.

"Do you smell it?" She asked, in a trance-like voice.

"Smell what?" He replied, concerned with Sally's behavior.

"He's been here," She said, as she walked slowly around the room holding the candle high as though looking for some lost soul.

"Whose been here?" Beau answered, moving closer to Sally.

"You can smell him. Some people say it's fire and brimstone, or the smell of evil. No, that's not it. It's the smell of death. The coldness? Do you feel it? I can. It's all around us."

Holding the candle higher the two detectives ascended the staircase to the first landing where Sally turned, and faced the large mirror on the wall. The large baroque gilded frame held the looking glass firmly in place even though it had been smashed into hundreds of pieces. She remembered it was the killer who had broken the mirror on the night of the murder.

The flickering candlelight danced on the face of the broken mirror revealing hundreds of smaller distorted images. Beau stood quietly behind Sally as she stared transfixed into the looking glass. Beau was getting concerned. She seemed almost hypnotized by the hundreds of small images in the broken mirror. It was as if the mirror could talk to her. That she was seeking the answer to her dream from the broken mirror.

"He's here. He's in this house. He's with us right now," she said, reaching out toward the mirror.

"Who?" Beau asked carefully, not wanting to break Sally's trance.

"You know him. You've met him," She replied knowingly.

"What's his name?" Beau asked, leading Sally for the answer.

"The angel of death," She said calmly.

"You mean the guy with the big scythe and the black hood?" He said, trying to keep the conversation on a lighter side.

"No, the angel of death is the writer of names on the wall," Sally replied, in a low tone as if seeing images from beyond the looking glass.

"You mean the guy we saw."...

"Yes," She said, interrupting Beau before he had a chance to finish his comment.

"Look into the mirror. Look at each of the images, then look beyond the mirror." Sally commented softly, not taking her gaze from the broken mirror.

Beau concentrated on Sally's demands hoping that he might glimpse at what she was seeing. All of the images seemed to blur, then magically cleared in his vision. Standing behind their reflection, he saw the tall blackman Matheszula. Beau turned sharply waiting to see the image behind him but there was nothing but blackness. He returned his gaze to the mirror and the angel of death was gone.

"I wonder," She said softly, "I wonder if there is a realm beyond the looking glass that could be the doorway to heaven or hell, whatever the case may be? Just maybe our friend knows which way to take the departed soul."

"I saw him," Beau confided solemnly.

"I know you did," Sally replied confidently.

"What else did you see?" Beau asked, putting his hands gently on her shoulders.

"You know something?" She asked, posing a rhetorical question while moving closer to Beau for comfort.

"What?"

"The ladies of the garden club were probably right. Something besides death was in this house. Something I can't explain something evil was also here."

"What are your saying? Beau asked gently.

"That's why we were summoned here," She replied knowingly.

"I don't understand?" He said, shaking his head slightly.

"Mathuszala wanted us to know that there was something else. Something dark in the soul of Delongpre. His madness was his avenue to whatever evil he was called on to do."

"Are you saying he was possessed?" Beau questioned in disbelief.

"Look into the mirror," Sally commanded gently.

Beau complied automatically.

"Look, look again. Look beyond. Take your mind behind the looking glass. Open the door to your mind." Sally ordered hypnotically.

Beau focused his concentration onto the broken mirror. Mystically, he saw Harry Mackland's image. Harry was happy. He smiled at Beau and gave him a gesture that everything was okay. It was a sign that Harry always used when he was satisfied with Beau's actions. Harry's dark imaged waved goodbye and was gone.

The two detectives sat quietly in the car and stared blankly at the predawn light.

"This thing you have?" Beau questioned calmly.

"You mean second sight," Sally added.

"Yeah."

"That's what the Irish call it. It's like seeing beyond the surface of things," She commented.

"Is it like what I just saw?" Beau asked, turning to look at her.

"No, not always. Sometimes its just a feeling I get about someone,' She answered.

Before Beau could ask, Sally continued to explain this phenomenon she'd been blessed with. "Sometimes I see people's auras."

"Auras?" He asked quickly.

"Yeah. You know, it's a glowing light that surrounds a person. From someone's aura I can tell what kind of person he or she might be. For example, Josey." She paused, and smiled, "she's got an aura that lights up every room. She's truly blessed. You know something else?"

Beau nodded, waiting for her to continue.

"Falconbriar is blessed. I can feel it every time I come home. God has touched it. Smiled on it. Made it clean. A little spot of heaven on earth. I also know that Josey and Casey are soul mates. It was as if.".…Sally stopped herself in mid sentence, then smiled at Beau. "Remember the story you told Katie about God always meant for you to be her father?"

Beau smiled, "Yeah."

"There is a little bit of truth in that story. I've been to Falconbriar before. I've seen the house, the barn, the trees. I knew you. Not right away of course. But I knew that all this, you and I, It was all set in motion by something or someone." She kissed him gently on the cheek. "Now, you've had a glimpse at what I see."

Beau kissed her lovingly, "You know something?" He inquired lightly. Sally shook her head.

"I love you, but you are one spooky lady." He said. They both began to laugh.

The mayor's oak paneled conference room had all the modern conveniences yet kept it's old world charm by a display of antique furniture and a gallery of paintings depicting historic Civil War battle scenes and portraits of southern heroes.

Josey Gasteneau sat erect at the head of the big table like the chairman of the board. Although confused by Beau's request, she had done her part. The state's Attorney General, Gil Washington, Charleston's Mayor, sat on either side of Josey. Chief Wexford and District Attorney Blackstone sat facing each other.

Chief Wexford waited on Josey like she was the Queen Mother, bringing coffee, a sweet roll and a napkin before she could be seated. Blackstone smirked at Wexford's efforts to kiss her ass. Blackstone rapped his fingernails nervously on the big oak table. He was impatient and resented being called away from his office because some biddy demanded it.

"How long are we going to have to wait?" Blackstone complained.

"Until I dismiss you." Josey answered, leveling a cold stare at Blackstone that made him nervous. He looked at the mayor with concern.

"You heard the lady," The mayor said, in a threatening voice. Everyone at the table shot angry looks at Blackstone who cowered back into his seat and folded his hands.

The conference room door swung open. Beau and Sally marched quickly into the room and faced the waiting audience. Beau dropped his briefcase defiantly on the big table, glaring at Blackstone, then at the mayor.

Josey knew that look. Her son reminded her so much of his father. He was pissed and she knew it. He had to get his emotions out before he could calm down. For some reason, this panel had done something wrong. Josey knew instinctively that they had dishonored him in some way.

Beau walked to the sideboard and ripped the intercom box plug from the wall. "There will be no recording of this conversation." He ordered angrily. The panel nodded. Everyone was surprised, they had never seen Beau this angry. He usually kept his emotions under control. But now, this was too much for him to hold back, and he was about to let everyone know it. Beau removed the FBI letter from his briefcase and marched angrily to Blackstone then threw the letter in front of him and shouted, "You lied to us. This letter is dated before our wedding. You knew all along that Sally was going to be assigned here."

Blackstone answered nervously, "Look, what other choice did I have? I needed the both of you to bring this case to a close."

"I don't like being lied to," Beau replied raising his voice in an angered reply.

"Sorry about that. So sue me," Blackstone answered with an air of bravado.

Beau quickly grabbed Blackstone in an arm lock bending his fingers back upon his wrist. The District Attorney screamed in pain then slipped from his seat to his knees in front of Beau. Blackstone grimaced in pain as the angered detective applied more pressure. Beau moved his face to within inches of the crying District Attorney. With a calm, cool, leveling voice, he said, "If you ever lie to me again. If you ever pull a stunt like that again, I will use every penny I own to ruin you. When I'm finished with you, you won't be able to run for dog catcher."

Beau released his grip on the District Attorney who laid on the floor cradling his aching hand. Beau looked coldly at the rest of the shocked table. "That goes for the rest of you," He paused. Looked at Josey, then at Sally before continuing. "That's not a threat, that's a promise."

The mayor sat calmly, knowing what they did to Beau and Sally was wrong.

"It seemed as the only way to expedite the investigation at the time," The mayor said, in a sincere voice. "I should have never let this happen, and I promise you I won't let it happen again."

Beau had said what he had to say, and calmed himself. He also knew that Gil Washington was a man of his word and meant what he said so it was time to put an end to this case once and for all.

"Okay gentlemen, we know how he was poisoned, when he was poisoned, and who poisoned him."

Blackstone struggled back into his chair still holding his sore hand. Everyone leaned forward in their chairs hanging on his every word. Beau removed the coroner's report form his briefcase and tossed it on the table.

"The poison was extracted from Yellow Oleander. This is a common plant around the city. So anyone and everyone had access to the poison. The poison was a mixture of Karo syrup and Oleander extract. It was injected into the candy that the defendant ate during the course of the trial." The mayor quickly scanned the report as Beau continued, "Review of the courthouse security tapes revealed that the only people to have had access to the candy were these ladies," Beau threw eight typed and signed confessions on the conference table.

Each of the panel members gathered up the confessions and began to read. Beau stood calmly watching the expressions on their faces change from one of anticipation to one of astonishment. Josey shook her head in disbelief,

"This can't be true?"

"What the hell are you trying to pull off with this kind of stunt?" Blackstone asked sarcastically.

"Do you know who these people are?" The mayor questioned sternly.

"This has got to be some sort of a joke?' Chief Wexford exclaimed loudly.

Sally stood next to Beau and explained, "Gentlemen, look at these confession carefully. They all say the same thing. Someone, somehow, convinced these nice ladies that the defendant was possessed. That he was Satan incarnate. Now the problem we have is that this someone conveniently supplied them with the poison, a syringe, and convinced them to send him on to a higher court."

"What do you mean a higher court?" The mayor asked concentrating on Sally's statement.

"They were convinced that he was in fact Satan or the Devil whichever you want. They all felt that he would defeat a mortal court. That only true justice would be served by God's court."

"That's idiotic," Chief Wexford blurted out.

"That may well be," Sally retorted, then continued. "The other problem is that anyone could have made the poison in their own kitchen. The security tapes show each of these ladies standing in front of the candy bowl in the security operations room. It does not show them actually putting the poison in the candy. Even if it did, any one dose would not have killed him. Only repeated doses over a long period of time did him in. So we have no way of knowing who actually administered the lethal dose." Sally paused, looking at the astonished expressions on the faces of the panel.

"Then there is also the possibility that additional poison was administered at the hospital," She added.

Josey had quickly scanned the last confession before looking up. "You have any idea who these ladies are?" Josey asked knowingly. "This is the elite of the Charleston Garden Club. Gil, Mildred worked on your campaign committee. They are good people and they've been apart of this city for generations. They only thought what they were doing was the right thing."

"But they broke the law," Blackstone exclaimed moving his gaze around the table for support.

"What law?" Sally retorted quickly.

"Attempted murder," Blackstone replied.

"Prove it," Josey said with a cold stare directed at Blackstone, then at the state's attorney general.

"We have their confessions." Blackstone answered reaching for the confessions. Josey had managed to collect all the confessions and calmly handed them to Beau while Blackstone's hand remained extended and empty.

"You have nothing. And you will have nothing." Josey replied with a hint of threat in her voice.

"What do you plan to do?" Josey asked, looking at Beau and Sally. The two detectives looked at each other intently. As if on cue they both smiled as though they had reached an unsaid agreement. Beau took the confession from Josey and locked them in his briefcase, then replied, "Nothing. We are going to do absolutely nothing. All this will get locked into a safe and forgotten. The security tapes will get accidentally erased, the interviews will get lost, and my people are sworn to silence. I could have stonewalled you but I don't work that way. It's up to you. I can say this, you don't have a case. But you can bring the city a lot of embarrassment. Let me put it this way. If any of this gets out I am coming after you with both barrels." Beau paused and locked in on the expression from each of the members looking for some recognition or acknowledgment. He picked up his briefcase and asked, "Are you coming mother?"

"Just a minute son," Josey folded her hands on the table as though she was the CEO talking to her staff. "Let me make my position perfectly clear." She leveled cold stares at the city fathers.

"As you know I own the Charleston Ledger. I also own the local TV station. In fact I own TV stations in three states. I have a standing policy that articles that involve people I am connected with will be cleared through me for my personal approval. I have little regard for a city official who fathers a bastard child of an underage teeniebopper. Or, a member of the legal establishment who takes political payoffs to minimize the investigation into corporate greed. Or for that matter, a man in law enforcement who is so incompetent that he couldn't run a boy scout troop if his life depended on it." Josey looked sternly at the state attorney general before continuing. "How does the governor feel about all this?"

The attorney general cleared his throat and replied,

"I think I can speak for the governor when I say that this issue is nonexistent."

"Have I made myself clear gentlemen?" Josey asked as she rose from the table and joined Beau and Sally.

The men at the table all knew that Josey had the power and the means to ruin their careers in this state or anyplace else if she has a mind to. They all nodded in agreement.

The Gasteneau family walked calmly to the conference room door. Josey turned one more time to address the astonished panel. "Now gentlemen, remember, just one word, one mistake, and you will all go down. Now, you all have a nice day." She said in a easy southern drawl then left the conference room.

The weakest link in this chain of secrecy was Kevin Johnson the ambitious Chief of Courthouse Security. To cover this Josey offered Kevin a lucrative job as Chief of Plant Security and shipped him off to Germany with the promise that he would never reveal any details of this case to the media or any other source. Kevin eagerly accepted and was out of the picture. Beau knew that Jim Butterfield, the court Bailiff was a man of his word, and would keep quiet about the actions of the Charleston Garden Club. Unlike Kevin, Big Jim didn't ask or imply for any compensation for his silence. However, Beau saw to it he got Kevin's job as Chief Of Security and a healthy raise in pay.

The final meeting with the Gray Lady Task Force inner circle ended with the solemn pledge to keep details of the investigation into the defendant's death a secret. They would stonewall all queries about the investigation. They were going to let nature take it's course. They would wait until it was ancient history. Until it would be just another unsolved case on the books.

In less than two weeks the media had packed up and left town. The skinheads had lost their cause, the Klan had been told to lay off the issue and life in the city had resumed its normal easy pace.

The night had settled quietly on Falconbriar. A full harvest moon rested on the treetops of the colorful fall forest. The old lodge tucked away in the deep virgin forest stood silently waiting for the early dawn to break. A small candle flickered faintly in the window.

Sitting neatly in the large family room near the front door were two large suitcases. The bags were fully packed, zipped and tagged. The tags read Mr. and Mrs. Gasteneau. Folded on top of these bags were two jackets and two tickets to Bora Bora.

The fire in the lodge's big fireplace had run its course. Only glowing embers remained. The two lovers laid naked on a lambskin rug in front of the fire, covered only by a thin flannel sheet. The newly weds had made love in front of the fire. It was a soft love. A fulfilling love filled with tenderness and understanding.

Although it was 4 o'clock in the morning they both were still awake, thinking finally about getting closure on the events that rocked the very fabric of the Charleston Community. Recalling events that had brought two people together. Events that had brought two families together. Sally smiled contentedly, kissed Beau on the neck and smuggled closer to her man.

"What are you thinking?" She asked lovingly.

"I don't know. I guess about everything. I wonder if we've covered all our bases?" He replied, giving Sally a warm hug.

"I think you have. And, if its bothering you, I think you did the right thing. I think its time to put it all behind us. Get some closure." She said, moving closer to him. Letting him feel the warmth of her body comforting him.

"You never really get closure," He commented sadly. "Closure never really comes. In time you may forget some of the dirty details, but he will never be completely out of my mind."

"What about me?" Sally replied jokingly with a small pout on her lips.

"That's the good part. I've got you and we've got a home and I'm a father. That's my joy," Beau replied, then gave Sally a long tender kiss. Still cradled in each others arms the two lovers fell fast asleep.

The flickering light from the candle in the window had turned from orange to blue then silently went out. In the old stone fireplace the embers from the dying fire glowed as the last remnants of their energy was consumed. Softly, a glowing ember popped and a spark floated freely in the fireplace, swirling, darting back and forth on the whim of the wind which played above the embers. Without warning, the little spark of light was sucked up through the chimney and rose, gaining speed, into the quiet night. The harvest moon lit up the night sky. The stars vividly displayed their splendor. The Milkyway splashed across the night sky giving a new light to the quiet forest and spinning the web of thought upon which lover's dreams are made. Calm once again had settled on the beautiful city of Charleston.

The little spark streaked ever upward towards the cosmos, upward until at some distant point, it too disappeared into nothingness.

The end.

About the Author:

James A. Smith LTC- USAF- R
Entered the USAF and became a Command Fighter Pilot. After 23 years, retired as a Lieutenant Colonel. Completed three combat tours in Southeast Asia.

Was lead test pilot Director of Flight Test and Training, for project Tropic Moon (classified project) at the Tactical Air Warfare Center, Eglin AFB Florida.

Attended the Squadron Officer's School, Air War College and the British War College at Old Sarum England, Bailbrook College, Bath England. Fighter Weapons School, Nellis AFB. BA Pepperdine University, Completed my MBAA at Embry-Riddle Aeronautical University, was a member of the adjunct faculty.

Flying awards and combat decorations include: Distinguished Flying Cross(DFC),Bronze Star with V (Valor Device), Air Medal with 8 OLC (Oak Leaf Clusters),Vietnam Service Medal with 2 OLC, Joint Service Commendation Medal, Air Force Commendation Medal with Cluster, Valorous Unit Award, Vietnam Cross of Gallantry with Palm, Presidential Unit Citation, Air Force Outstanding Unit Award, Vietnam Presidential Unit Citation, Combat Readiness Medal.

Upon retiring was a system design engineer and consultant for Lockheed Aircraft International where I spent 9½ years as a special advisor to the Royal Saudi Air Force. During the Iraq - Iran War was special advisor to RSAF Sector Operations Center (SOC) Dhahran AFB for air defense of the Arabian oil fields.

In the post Desert Storm era, working for Hughes Aircraft Company, was special advisor to the RSAF General Staff at the Command Operations Center (COC) in Riyadh Saudi Arabia. The COC is a classified command center which is underground, hardened, bio-chemically safe war room that houses an array of computers for the sole purpose of tactical air operations in the defense of Saudi Arabia. From this facility we tasked and monitored air operations over Iraq.

Currently a Senior System's Engineer with Hughes/Raytheon Technical Services. More recently, spent another 2 ½ years in the Kingdom of Saudi Arabia on test and validation of advanced air defense systems. Have developed and written numerous technical publications for these companies.

For the past eight years was an adjunct writer and researcher for MDR Productions Hollywood. The late Marty Roth, a writer for 40 years in Hollywood, was my mentor and good friend. Have completed three screen plays and wish to dedicate the publication of this work in his honor.

Printed in the United States
1192400002B/274-276